THE LION'S DEN

A Story of American Renewal

Frank B. Atkinson

UNIVERSITY *of* VIRGINIA
CENTER *for* POLITICS

DORRANCE
PUBLISHING CO
EST. 1920
PITTSBURGH, PENNSYLVANIA 15238

The contents of this work, including, but not limited to, the accuracy of events, people, and places depicted; opinions expressed; permission to use previously published materials included; and any advice given or actions advocated are solely the responsibility of the author, who assumes all liability for said work and indemnifies the publisher against any claims stemming from publication of the work.

UNIVERSITY *of* VIRGINIA
CENTER *for* POLITICS

Dorrance Publishing Co
585 Alpha Drive
Suite 103
Pittsburgh, PA 15238
Visit our website at *www.dorrancebookstore.com*

Cover photo by Jennifer D. James and courtesy of James Madison's Montpelier and The Montpelier Foundation.

ISBN: 978-1-6442-6664-9
eISBN: 978-1-6442-6683-0

That no free government, nor the blessings of liberty, can be preserved to any people, but by a firm adherence to justice, moderation, temperance, frugality, and virtue [and] by frequent recurrence to fundamental principles….

Virginia Declaration of Rights, June 1776
Constitution of Virginia, Art. 1, §15

Ambition must be made to counteract ambition. The interest of the man must be connected with the constitutional rights of the place. It may be a reflection on human nature, that such devices should be necessary to control the abuses of government. But what is government itself, but the greatest of all reflections on human nature? If men were angels, no government would be necessary. If angels were to govern men, no external nor internal controls on government would be necessary. In framing a government which is to be administered by men over men, the great difficulty lies in this: you must first enable the government to control the governed and in the next place oblige it to control itself.

James Madison, *The Federalist No. 51*

Shadrach, Meshach, and Abednego answered and said to the king, "O Nebuchadnezzar, we have no need to answer you in this matter. If this be so, our God whom we serve is able to deliver us from the burning fiery furnace, and he will deliver us out of your hand, O king. But if not, be it known to you, O king, that we will not serve your gods or worship the golden image that you have set up."

Daniel 3:16-18 (ESV)

Have faith in reason,
And reason on to faith,
Ever ready for His revelation,
Ever grateful for His grace.

Rev. Samuel Davies Thomas, "Therefore"

For Diane, Robert and Paul,
Tommy, Corey, Larry, and Ken

————————————————

In Memoriam
Margaret Whittle Atkinson "Peggy" Rosen

CONTENTS

THE STORY

AUTHOR'S NOTE (PART I)

Everyone who read the manuscript said this book would be too long. I have learned from my work with museums, however, that there are three types of visitors: the streakers, the strollers, and the students. A good museum will be designed to accommodate all three of these variations in time, taste, and tendency, with alternate entry points and pathways to suit each group.

So if you are a streaker encountering this book for the first time, and you want just the gist of the message, I suggest you read the Prologue and then go to Chapter 10 and read Danny McGuire's 400th anniversary speech at Cape Henry. If that chapter and speech still seem too long, skip to page 559, the part of the speech where Danny mentions the lions in Madison's garden, and read from there to the end of the chapter. Then read the Epilogue, and streak away with what I hope is a useful message about how we can preserve and improve the republic Madison helped craft for us.

If you are a stroller, and you want the main story without the deep background on the characters and their journey, I suggest you read the Prologue, bypass Part I (Chapters 1-4) entirely, and start at the beginning of Part II, which is Chapter 5. There you will encounter the gubernatorial campaign that sets the main story in motion, and you can get that full story by reading from there to the end of the book. That will reduce your investment of time by about 40 percent.

If you are a student, then begin at the beginning and end at the end. With due respect to the astute advisors who counseled abbreviation, I offer this explanation for my contrary choice: Fixing our broken politics is like fixing our broken lives; it is complicated and difficult, and there are few reliable shortcuts. Understanding how we have gotten here is a crucial part of the self-examination and surrender necessary to

ix

seek and find a better way. To paraphrase Dickens, it is about how we <u>wander and struggle and get lost but at length strike into our road and see its end</u>. Perhaps, by retaining the long form, I will help at least one searching student strike into his or her road and see its end.

In the meantime, I encourage you to take the path best suited to your situation. And if that means taking a shortcut, by all means do so without the least hesitation. You can always come back for more.

Before you begin the story, though, I need to dispel a couple of errant notions that the fictional genre and my choice of the storyteller's voice might otherwise encourage.

Although this story is presented as a first-person narrative—a choice inspired by Larry Sabato, who urged me to begin the project by reexamining the great American political novel <u>All the King's Men</u>—this book is most certainly not autobiographical. For anyone familiar with my limitations and shortcomings, that fact will be self-evident. The Daniel of this novel, like his biblical namesake, is a model to emulate. Though I can claim frustratingly few of the protagonist's exemplary attributes, I certainly aspire to a good many of them and trust we all do. Indeed, that is the point of this project. As challenging as I have found this book to write, it is far easier to describe a Daniel than to be one. Fortunately for us all, the virtue lies in trying.

The second point is that none of the characters in this novel bears any intended resemblance to the real Virginia political characters of the period in which it is set. We are all so accustomed to this formulaic disclaimer that we tend to disregard it, but in this case it is true. Beginning in 1980, with a few explicit exceptions (Reagan, Thatcher, 9/11, Iraq's invasion of Kuwait), the people and events of the story you are about to read are fully fictional. Some readers may have come to the book anticipating real-life revelations scantily clad as fiction, and if so they will be disappointed. What I have to say about the real people and politics of the final quarter of Virginia's fourth century, I said in my nonfiction work, <u>Virginia in the Vanguard,</u> or will say in the future—on the record. This story I made up.

There is more to say about this project, especially the contributions of many to acknowledge. Rather than keep you from entering the museum any longer, however, I will resume this Author's Note at the end of the book. I hope everyone—streakers, strollers, and students—will meet me back there after the story for some important thank-yous and a concluding suggestion.

(continued at page 633)

THE STORY

PREFACE

The ghastly image had been my dreaded companion since that calamitous Independence Day weekend in 2003. It diverted me in the daytime and forced its way into my dreams at night.

Under an exquisitely cloudless, cobalt-blue sky, the boat was bobbing serenely on an unusually calm Chesapeake Bay. The soundwaves were as placid as the watery ones, with only the gulls' plaintive cries occasionally drowning out the joy-filled banter of the fishing party. In the next instant it struck like a bolt of lightning colliding with the earth: a massive, all-consuming, all-destroying blast that sent parts of the boat—and, inescapably, parts of the 68th governor of Virginia—flying six stories high and in every direction. In my tortured mind's eye, there was scarcely time to blink before the idyllic picture became a grisly portrait of horrific death, a debris field and crime scene, a source of sorrow and terror, and the cause of everything—good and bad—that had followed.

That explosion had seemed to take everything from me—my friend and mentor, my purpose and predecessor, my innocence and excuses—but it had taken infinitely more from Virginia and the nation. Less apparent, except in hindsight, is how much addition would be accomplished through the subtraction.

Whenever the searing image came, by night or day, it mercifully would not linger. Instead, my old friend Longfellow would weigh in, right on cue, and I would drift off again … or get back to work:

Tell me not, in mournful numbers,
Life is but an empty dream!—
For the soul is dead that slumbers,
And things are not what they seem.
Life is real! Life is earnest!
And the grave is not its goal;
Dust thou art, to dust returnest,
Was not spoken of the soul.

PROLOGUE

My name is Daniel Madison McGuire, and this is my story. I start, however, not with the violent blast that ended the life of Governor Ned Nevers in 2003, nor with my own reluctant entry into the political world two decades earlier. I begin instead on the shore where Virginia, and so America, began....

It was a crisp spring morning—the morning of April 26, 2007—and I was strolling, anxiously at first, along the beach at Cape Henry just before sunrise. It is there the relentless Atlantic, bountiful Chesapeake, and terra Virginia first meet and make their portentous peace—a place where history casts a shadow now 400 years long.

I meandered up and down the sloping surface, avoiding the encroaching and receding waves, considering the task ahead. The air was chilly and damp, and the water, asserting its superiority in a single determined surge, already had pricked my ankle like a thousand cold needles. The impact, though, had been only superficial. Anticipation of the morning's activities had my heart pumping faster than normal, supplying inner warmth.

My role in the ceremonies marking this singular anniversary would have surprised most Virginians, including me, just a few months earlier. The intense political and legal storms that buffeted Virginia had threatened to dash me on the rocks. Yet I had come through them, and I was still pondering how and why.

The voyagers to this place four centuries earlier were brought through tempests for a purpose greater than they could comprehend or imagine. The ensuing struggles tested them and refined their character, giving value to lives

xiii

and labors whose importance would appear only in the fullness of time. Yet, each had lived in the moment—daring and difficult moments—striving for something that Providence had set before them as an object of endeavor.

Striving ... *and persevering* ... as we all must.

Was there a message in this history? Could it be that my own improbable journey at last had deposited me on the shores of a purpose—the place where freedom and faith converge, where the living mass of all creation breathes with the rhythm of the ebbing and flowing tide, and the exile (because we are all exiles) sees the part he should play and heeds his calling?

I wondered.

My task on this day was a relatively simple one—just another in a long line of speeches, I tried to convince myself. Yet, this was a moment that mattered. The great and powerful, republicans and royals, would have their say over the course of the ensuing fortnight. The Governor of Virginia, President of the United States, Queen of England, and sundry other commentators of high station would hold forth at the coming observances in Jamestown, Williamsburg, Richmond, and Washington, their pronouncements registering much farther and wider than mine. But this was the opening event of the *America's 400th Birthday* commemoration—an early-morning prayer service and monument re-dedication at the site of the settlers' first landing in 1607. It was the place where, 400 years earlier to the day, hearty travelers debarked their three small ships, knelt in thanksgiving, and launched a new nation. It was also the place where everything changed for the native peoples, and just a few miles from where Africans first arrived in bondage. Perhaps the greatest advance in human freedom and the greatest affront to human freedom—good and evil—planted together on the same fertile Virginia shore. I could imagine no more appropriate setting in which to address the fraught subject that these secular-ized times conditioned people to avoid: the interconnectedness of God and man and the state—*the essential truth about freedom, faith, and purpose in politics.*

It was odd, in a sense, that this responsibility had fallen to me. Unlike so many I had encountered over the years, I had never coveted center-stage. The pen, not the pulpit or podium, was my preferred medium. My distaste for the limelight could have been a reflection of timidity, indifference, or even selfish-ness, I supposed. But in my best moments I was sure it was something else. My parents instilled in me the conviction that there is greater good in doing useful things without applause or accolades, because then you can be sure you are doing them for others and not for yourself. From that early programming came a genuine yearning for consequence rather than credit. But it carried with it a corollary principle that often proved quite inconvenient: when duty called, you had to step up and do it even if it took you far outside your comfort zone.

In such circumstances I was reminded how much I needed help.

Arriving at Fort Story before dawn by special arrangement with the base commander, I strolled in solitude on the shore that wraps around the Cape, marveling in the cool breeze and lingering moonlight at the power and permanence of the pounding sea. As dawn approached and the advance and security people began to swarm around intrusively, I walked a ways down the breezy beach to preserve the solitude, take in the magnificent pre-sunrise vista, reflect on the meaning of the occasion, and commune with God.

I considered the extraordinary chain of events that had preceded this day— the explosion that had occurred just a few miles across the waves from this spot and all that had flowed from it—and for the first time it occurred to me that those misadventures not only had thrust Virginia into crisis. They also had brought the once-placid Old Dominion to the forefront of national and even international notice just as its 400th anniversary approached. It was not the kind of attention anyone would seek, but, even so, perhaps a good purpose was being served. Like those storms that nearly wrecked the first voyagers, perhaps the recent trials had brought us to this crucial junction with humble, grateful hearts, ready again to strive and serve, our renewed spirit supplying a glimmer of hope for the watching world.

The need for renewal, I understood by now, was acute. Politics—that system of ordered liberty supposed to be of, by, and for the people—now had broadly alienated, confounded, and disillusioned the people. Instead of gaining ground through principled collaboration and creative compromise as the founders envisioned when they erected our constitutional checks and balances, the people (many of them) and their politicians (most of them) had retreated to the safety of their insular base camps where they heard more of what they already knew, or thought they knew, while hurling insults at their fellow countrymen. To explain this broken politics, the people and politicians routinely pointed to some faulty feature of "the system"—the finance laws, the ethics rules, the district lines, the election procedures—or to the man who was holding them down. Rather than gratitude, all seemed to have a grievance and an excuse. Rarely did any of them—which is to say, *any of us*—pause to look in the mirror and acknowledge: "The fault, dear Brutus, is not in our stars, but in ourselves."

The situation had degenerated to the point where one could be forgiven for wondering whether we contemporary Americans still were capable of governing ourselves. Madison, the system's chief architect, had emphasized the deployment of self-interest in defense of liberty, but in bowing to the inevitability of vice he had never doubted the necessity of virtue. A basic decency and empathy for others inhered in the very notion of a community founded on the Golden Rule, and a self-governing republic depended on members of that community having the clarity and character to adhere to that rule and other core precepts, no matter how inexpedient in the moment, because of their inherent rightness and transcendent importance for the common good. Without the habitual practice of this principled self-restraint, the whole house was in danger of collapse. As Virginia's visionary Declaration of Rights counseled, "[N]o free government, nor the blessings of liberty, can be preserved to any people, but by a firm adherence to justice, moderation, temperance, frugality, and virtue [and] by frequent recurrence to fundamental principles...."

Those last two words were the ones that resonated as I strode the sands traversed four centuries earlier by hungering souls who risked all for a chance at a freer, better life. "Fundamental principles"—timeless values derived from reason, experience, tradition, revelation—essential tenets of belief and behavior grounded in the foundational ideals of Freedom and Love. They are the secret sauce in the republican recipe, enabling a diverse and democratic community to be cohesive and constructive. They supply the *order* in ordered liberty—the only real brakes on the great modern centrifuge that, left to its own devices, can spin individualism into narcissism, and diversity into relativism, and populism into authoritarianism. But do we "recur" to these principles "frequently"? Do we articulate them ... reflect on them ... teach them to our children ... impress them on those who journey to join us ... measure our politicians by them ... practice them ourselves?

The truth, of course, is that we seldom bother, and that is mainly because our modern minds have been conditioned to think that little matters except what we can perceive, possess, and consume in the present. In effect, we are gambling everything on the hope that our founding visionaries got this central point about freedom's survival *wrong*.

How absurd, I thought. *How can we expect the people and their politicians to be able to draw the line when all we hand them is an eraser?*

That jarring thought brought back to mind the morning's mission, which was now close at hand. The sun was about to rise out of the Atlantic. The predawn pastels soon would turn to brilliant orange rays that would overwhelm the man-made light slicing through the air from the newer lighthouse just beyond the bushy, windswept dunes of the Cape. Not long thereafter I would stand before the assembled worthies—in the shadow of a stone cross erected by earlier generations as a monument to those first faithful settlers—and say what I had come to believe about the lion's den of politics and life....

———————

The morning's big moment (actually, it was many moments, because "the speech" covered quite a lot of historical terrain) came and went, taking with it all the excitement, anxiety, and adrenalin that such events ordinarily produced within me times a factor of seven ... or seventy. Wading into the treacherous waters of politics and religion had been perilous enough, but I had chosen to comment on the acutely divisive and increasingly dysfunctional character of contemporary self-government in America and had dared even to offer some recommended remedies. The esteemed audience on-site seemed attentive and appreciative, if a bit bemused, but the more far-flung impact was then unfathomable. You never can tell who in a crowd actually may be listening and what they may be hearing. It is like throwing a rock in a river—you never know what the ripples will shake loose downstream.

One consequence of the speech is clearly discernible in hindsight, however. It is central to my story, and I will share it, along with the full text, in due course. For now, this brief passage will suffice:

> As I reflect on the hardships suffered to plant freedom in this good earth, I am reminded of the trials and triumphs experienced by the prophet Daniel—a hero, saint, statesman, and, yes, a politician.
>
> If you have not studied the life and times of Daniel, a Jewish captive who became a senior official in the government of ancient Babylon, then it is worth your while to do

so. Because you will learn timeless lessons and discover that things really have not changed much in the more than two dozen centuries since Daniel's day.

We, like Daniel, are exiles in a foreign land, and sooner or later we will find ourselves in a lion's den.

Daniel was an extraordinarily capable man, a gifted leader. Though of noble birth, he was a humble and caring person who lived a life of integrity rooted in his faith. Ripped from his home and family as a young man, cast into servitude and powerlessness in a far-off land, he did not conform to the dominant culture but engaged intensively within it. In the process he came to wield great power. Yet, even with all his gifts and all the influence he acquired, he found himself cast into the lion's den, requiring the saving intervention of Providence.

Daniel's story is a universal story. He was from Jerusalem, born into the Judean ruling class, brought up in the Jewish faith, and cast into Babylonian politics. I am from a little town called Orange, brought up as a Presbyterian and a Republican (not necessarily in that order), and caught up in the political affairs of Virginia. Each of you has your own origin, identity, faith, creed, and forum. Yet here we and our fellow travelers are, more than two millennia after Daniel, still engaged in the same great struggles—the external ones over liberty and power, religion and politics, and the internal ones over how to overcome ourselves, set our sights on the loftier things, and step out in faith to love and serve.

Daniel trusted God in these struggles, and God intervened to save him from the lions. So has miracle followed miracle in the 400 years since settlers first came to these shores—and all, we trust, for a good purpose....

When a big moment in your life looms, your mind is apt to wander in search of meaning as well as relief. Mine that morning had ranged back to the people whose love and counsel had helped direct the course of my life. I had thought of my wife and children, my parents, and my three very close friends. I had thought of mentors and pastors and role models, standouts from history and life whose examples had been impressed upon my character. I had thought of the choices I had made—the good ones and the bad ones and, most of all, the fateful one that everyone (myself included) was still second-guessing.

And then my recollections had run back, as they often did, to the good times out on the campaign trail across Virginia, to the people I had met there, and to one in particular.

An aged craftsman from the hardscrabble foothills of the Blue Ridge where Virginia's "Southside" and "Southwest" converge had greeted my traveling partner and me, both cast improbably now as city slickers, with an impatient, why-are-you-bothering-me expression and a handshake that managed to convey both strength and indifference. We were crossing his path, which put us in the way of his work, and he did not have much interest in why. But that was before he realized that one of the men in his presence might become the state's next governor. The dour expression immediately gave way to a broad smile, an unexpected portal into a generous soul, as he proudly declared, "Well, I reckon you'll be right comfortable in that chair I made if you get the votes."

The man we met that day, Otis Lloyd "O. L." Founder, indeed had built the governor's chair—the one that enjoyed the honored position at the head of the long mahogany table in the governor's conference room on the Virginia Capitol's rarefied third floor. He was the one who had framed its sturdy hardwood structure, attached its four steel casters, dyed and fastened its light blue leather, and embossed in gold the obverse seal of the Commonwealth of Virginia. His passion for his work was evident as he described the process for me, step by step, well past the time allotted on the campaign schedule.

Thinking back on that encounter from the water's edge, I knew that O. L. Founder would be disheartened to see his chair now, so badly did it show the effects of daily wear and tear. The wood was scuffed, the leather was torn, and the once brilliant gold seal was now barely visible. Mr. Founder had not known, when he sent his handiwork to Richmond, whether good or bad people would occupy his chair. He was probably a practical man who, if he had paused to consider the matter, would have expected some of both. But that had not been his responsibility. He had done his part and done it well: he had built the chair and affixed its official emblem.

He had done his duty, and, like all the others who served, he had counted on those down the line to do theirs. That meant he had counted on me, because I would be one of the men to occupy his chair. How he and others might judge my time in that seat, I had paused little to ponder before now, so fully had I been consumed with judging myself. But the day's distinctive duties had forced me from my self-imposed banishment, and there by the sea my mind was pondering possibilities again.

As I contemplated the state of things beside the water, the life-giving substance and sacramental symbol began once again to impart its counsel. It yielded three noteworthy insights, reminding me of lessons I had learned in the course of the story I am about to tell.

The first lesson was that people, like water, can get to the same place by a lot of different routes, and they are apt to understand, or at least come to believe, a lot of different things in the process of getting there. In fact, they can get to the very same place by different paths, discover they have arrived, and still disagree on where they are and where they are going and what, if any, purpose is being served by the journey. Things would be simpler if everyone took the same route. Yet, these differences in experience and perspective can be endlessly interesting and enriching if you let them.

The second lesson was that people, like water, are going to run to the lowest point. And when water and people arrive at that point, what you have is a lot of suffering, confused, even desperate folks waist deep in mud and muck and mire, needing help. Whether you decide to render aid then and there is a crucial choice.

And the third lesson was that life, like water, runs away in an endless stream, or almost endless, and it carries us away with it in a singular symphony of energy and grace. Yet, the stream is full of rocks, and though the water is bound to resent and even fear the rocks, it needs them. It needs them because, in answering the rocks—in confronting them, in overcoming them, in navigating around them, in chiseling away at them—the water carves a new path and defines a new stream, which means it defines itself.

As I look back on it, I am struck by how long it took for me to learn these lessons. They seem rather obvious now, and it all might have been easier if I had paid attention to the water's example from the beginning. But that is why you tell a story—so people can learn something from it without having to live through it themselves. And maybe so you can learn something about yourself....

The mind does funny things when you go inside it to pull out a story. People remember things differently, and they can get to the same present reality by very different paths and see very different things along the way.

There are places in Montgomery County, including on the Virginia Tech campus, where, when a bank of clouds moves across and the rain falls on one side of the hill, it flows into the New River Valley and begins a journey that will take it west, then south, down the Mississippi and into the Gulf of Mexico. But if it falls on the other side of that same hill, it runs down into the Roanoke River basin and makes it way out to the Albemarle and Pamlico Sounds, past the Outer Banks of North Carolina, and into the Atlantic. And if it falls just a short ways to the northeast, it flows into the headwaters of the James, and then east and eventually into the Chesapeake Bay, on its way to the same great ocean.

But, regardless of the path chosen from this common point of origin at the Eastern Continental Divide, the water all flows down to where I stood that morning—to the same great sea. And the sea will give up its moisture to the clouds. And the clouds will water the land again.

Like the students and ideas that proceed perennially from Virginia Tech and other great universities, the water will shape and nourish the landscape in myriad ways as it takes its distinctive paths to the sea.

If you could hitch a ride on each of those raindrops that come out of the same cloud but join separate rivers on their way to the sea, you would take a very different path, see very different things, and have a very different version of events. You would end up at the same place, but your perspective at that important junction would be the product of a distinctive journey and set of sights along the way.

That is the way the natural world works, and it is the way human experience works, too.

My story began when the cloud deposited me on the side of the hill where people do not want anything to do with politics. They do not care about Mr. Founder's chair or whose back rubs against its seal.

Maybe it is because they think they are above politics and are afraid to find out they are not. Maybe it is because they feel left out, or because life has not treated them well or has hurt someone they love, and politics is where they can find someone to blame. Maybe their religion has taught them that the wisdom of the world is foolishness, and they think politics just conforms to the world, even panders to it, and is not able to change anything for the better.

Or, maybe they think politics might have been good at one point but somebody or something long ago wrung all the good out of it—that history already milked it for all the virtue it was allotted—and so there is nothing there now but the cow's rotting carcass, with flies buzzing around and maggots doing their dirty business, and it all stinking to high heaven.

Whatever the reason or combination of reasons, politics turns off a lot of people like me—or, at least, like I used to be. The ironic thing, though, is that most of the folks on that turned-off hillside have a decent appreciation for the heroic deeds of man *in the past*. Depending on their faith or lack of it, they are apt to appreciate the beneficent interventions of Providence or the random dispensations of fate, or both, because in some past age Providence or fate collaborated with mortal deeds to bring them to this happy "Here and Now" crossroads. And the things they like about the Here and Now invariably trace their roots—for those who pause to reflect on such things—to those heroic deeds.

So, even on that hillside where politics engenders disdain there are monuments to the grand icons of American history—Washington, Madison, Henry, Mason, Adams, Jefferson, Hamilton, Marshall, and the rest—who were the founding era's great achievers. Those monuments foster a perception that today's rights and privileges—things like freedom, justice, the rule of law, religious liberty, personal autonomy, economic opportunity, national security, and so on—are all the salutary legacy of the great minds and great deeds of our glorious *past*.

On that side of the hill one is likely to romanticize that past, as I did, and to distinguish the high-minded statesmanship that supposedly characterized our noble history from the seedy politics that pervades our ignoble present. And, one is likely to distinguish contemporary political practice from that historic statesmanship not merely in degree, frequency, or form of expression, but in its essential character and intrinsic value.

My hill, of course, was in a place called Virginia. It was the place where the convergence that we call "American history" got its running start 400 years ago—home to the most influential founders and framers, the visionary patriots who laid the foundation and constructed the sturdy edifice that is the American Republic, the longest surviving and most influential such contrivance in human history.

I grew up in Orange County, just a few miles up the road from Montpelier, the stately home where James Madison, one of the greatest of those builders, was raised, lived, learned, cultivated and shared his knowledge, greeted other giants of his era, died, and is buried. I share his birthday, and my parents even gave me his name. When I was a boy, my dad would take me on hikes all around the Montpelier grounds and adjacent forest—moments that, even today, are among my happiest memories. My mom taught fourth-grade Virginia history, so I had the perfect tour guide as we made family excursions during my youth to all the other hallowed places—to Mount Vernon and Monticello, Jamestown and Williamsburg, the State Capitol and St. John's Church, and many others. Often on these trips she would mention, matter-of-factly so as not to swell my head, that this or that preeminent Virginian was my ancestor.

So, I emerged, if not from the womb then at least from the cradle, enthralled with past glories. I grew up in the land where great men once trod, and I dwelled in the lengthening shadow of their extraordinary achievements, and I loved it.

I loved history, and when you love something you resist anything that threatens to take it away from you or diminish it in any way. Politics, the kind practiced today, posed that kind of clear and present danger. In its attenuated and even corrupt claim to succession, in the stunning presumptuousness of its ambition to imitate, politics threatened to pull down true history from its pedestal. And that aspiration seemed as vain and contemptible as any I could imagine.

In the course of my journey, however, I came to realize that there is a flawed humanity that inevitably belies and punctures all our romantic notions about history's icons. The men and women who did great things still belong on pedestals, for their examples can illumine our condition and supply inspiration. But it is the real people who belong on the pedestals, not the romantic reproductions.

I learned that even the founders, as great as they were, could not live up to the ideals they espoused. Their applications of liberty, justice, and equality left many people out. They embraced a classical conception of republican virtue, and most genuinely aspired to be models of disinterested statesmanship. But they quickly found that the real business of representative democracy would permit no such aloofness. Almost against their will, yet with an intensity rarely matched in the centuries since, they became seekers of office and champions of faction and catalysts for partisanship. Their nobility resided not in the purity of their methods but in the ferocity with which they pursued the wellbeing of their fledgling nation.

They were politicians before—and while—they were statesmen.

I had discovered those things about the founders, and I also had learned the timeless truth that a flicker of virtue resides in every human breast, a divine spark out of which much good can come through the collaboration of God's grace and our enterprise.

In fact, the deeper I had dug over time, the clearer it had become that history and politics are one and the same. They cannot be distinguished on any basis other than temporal position, which by definition cannot remain constant. They are on the same plane; their business is motion; and the forces that move them have been the same since the beginning of time and will be the same until the end of time.

They are human enterprise, animated often by high ideals but beset always with natural frailties, and in need of help.

That part about needing help, of course, is the key to the whole business. It is the source of every republic's saving substance—*humility*. And, when you realize that truth, it moves you from the illusory tension between history and politics to the far more real and relevant tension between religion and politics—or, more aptly, between faith and freedom. And that brings you to the center of things where resides the whole matter of the relationship between church and state in all its wonderful majesty and divisive madness: the great contentious conundrum of our country, the defining genius of our republic, the divine mystery of our national purpose.

What happens when the cloud deposits you on that holier-than-thou hill above politics is a lot like what happened to the awkward apostle Peter when he suddenly found himself up there in the clouds with the giants of his faith, Moses, Elijah, and the transfigured Savior. What you want to do when you find yourself in the presence of the giants of your faith, or the giants of your republic, or both, is set up a tent and take up residence there. You want to stay and bask in the reflected glory of Moses and Elijah, or of Washington and Madison, because who would not want to do that? Their great deeds become your passion, and there is no risk because you are passionate about something that has already happened, and so there is no burden on you to make something else or something more happen. You are in the clouds with these icons of your imagination, and so you do not have to worry about the world of pain and struggle and disappointment below. You are there where the ideal and the real, the theoretical and the practical, the divine and the human, have already made their peace and made it quite well, it would seem. And so you can just bypass the whole untidy business called Existence, and the risky, goal-oriented quarter of it called Striving, and the other-directed venues known as Helping and Serving and Improving. You especially can avoid the vexing zone of quandary and conscience that the still, small voice calls Sticking By Your Principles but the world calls Unrealistic, Idealistic, Ideological, Impractical, or any of the other disparaging terms it uses to try to convince you that everything is relative and random.

On the hillside you are covered by the cloud, and the cloud, like an artist painting in fog on a once-brilliant scene, brushes out all the earthly complications posed by the interplay of principle and practicality. But it cannot avoid brushing out the beauty and joy at the same time. Those things reappear when you come out of the cloud and into the light and make your way down the rocky slope.

So the hillside above politics is indeed an alluring place. It is alluring because there you can indulge in indifference about all the defects and difficulties, like the dimming seal on the fraying seat of power. But you cannot stay on that hillside any more than the raindrops that fall there can resist gravity. The raindrops must run to the stream and into the river and on down to the sea because nature, like man, has a whole lot of work to do before its earthly business is done.

The drops of life-giving water arrive on their mission of mercy from diverse hills and valleys, from meandering streams and mighty rivers, to a common place and identity and purpose: *E Pluribus Unum*—out of many, one.

That is the first lesson I had learned from the water. And for a time it had made me cheerful and eager.

The second lesson had made me sad, even distraught, for a while.

The water is compelled by its essential character, and by the forces of nature that act upon it, to head downward. Its nature is like human nature. And that means eventually it is going to reach the mud and muck and mire.

It reaches the low point in life.

You may be the fair-haired boy, heir to nobility, living an idyllic existence in the heart of the promised land. But one day a great army is going to swoop in and sack your city and steal the holy vessels from your temple and carry you off to Babylon where proud people not only worship themselves but trick others into thinking they can be god, too. In that far country you will be a slave, or at least an alien, and you will have to decide what you believe.

As startling and unreal as it seems, this strange Babylon is the real world. And that world is going to own you or keep trying to, and it is going to make you answer the question it always asks. It asks it with a sneer and a threat, like the neighborhood bully who pins you on the ground and snarls, "So what are you going to do now?"

The water runs to the lowest point, and it takes you there with it. It runs down and detours into a stagnant place where it does dirty duty. There is mud and muck, and people are sinking in it, stuck in it, wallowing and fighting and even laughing in it ... and all in their own ways are suffering in it. But they are also there trying to help each other in it. And you go there not only because it is where the water runs, but because it is where the water finds the people, and so it is where you find them.

You find them there, and you may not like all of them. They may disappoint and depress you, disillusion and even disgust you at times—and a lot of them probably are not all that crazy about you, either. But you are part of them. In fact, if you are honest, you will admit that you are more alike than different from them because you are suffering, too, or you have been, and the grace you need to receive is the same grace you need to give. This is where your own depths of misery give you empathy for the pain of others. And if you are fortunate, you have been taught that what you do for and to and with the people there in that pit with you, you also do for the one who put you there—and ultimately for your soul.

It is where, if you have love in your heart, you have the opportunity to express it. It is also the place where you can find all sorts of excuses not to express it, or just not get around to it, and miss the opportunity forever.

The irony is that, almost as soon as you arrive and get engaged at that place, you discover that this low point in life, this inevitable place of suffering in a broken world, is really not the end of the journey after all. The place where the water runs and where the people suffer and struggle is a detour, a stopover. Like all our modest attempts at virtue and service, it is necessary but not sufficient—a place you must consent to go but cannot be content to stay.

You must leave the pit, with God's help, because the mainstream is still flowing downstream, moving from suffering on to joy.

And then you come upon the third and most important of the water-borne truths.

The raindrops that find their way from hillsides into streams and from streams into rivers and on to the sea do not flow evenly or straight like rains that land obligingly on well-sculpted rooftops, run to securely fastened downspouts and drains, and are channeled efficiently and obediently out of harm's way.

The real raindrops, instead, are on an *adventure*.

But how can that be, you ask, when there is nothing new under the sun? "All streams flow into the sea, but the sea is never full…, to the place the streams come from, there they return again…," and "all is vanity and a chasing after the wind."

This is true, of course. But the Teacher of Ecclesiastes tells us this truth not to numb us but to challenge us. The challenge is to look between the re-dundant points of departure and destination and appreciate the beauty and drama of the journey and the opportunities to express love along the way. For God created time to make the journey possible, and he created the journey to make the time meaningful, and the history that holds that meaning is not van-ity if it teaches us to love and serve while waiting in hope for what lies, not under the sun, but beyond it.

Like exiles in a strange country, the raindrops are on an adventure that is not of their making, and the streams they fill, like Robert Frost's west-running brook, are full of "contraries." The water flows busily, frenetically, inexorably toward the sea. It flows like life—it "seriously, sadly, runs away," as Frost put it.

Yet, it is not sad, not ultimately, because the journey and the encounters with the rocks in the stream bed shape and reveal the truth about us. The stream supplies the motion that fulfills our purpose, and the rocks provide the obstacles that forge our character. Together they inspire the fear without which we would never learn to trust.

The water that is flowing over us and between us and with us suddenly encounters those rocks—hard, immoveable, *principled* objects, unimpressed by the flow, deriving their very relevance from sitting contemptuously in its path. And if you have ever paused to contemplate the business of a stream, you know that when the flowing water hits the rocks, it does a most dramatic thing: it flares upward and arcs backwards.

Yes, the water runs away and takes life with it, but in the process it does some-thing quite vital, if easy to overlook. It has "this throwing backward on itself…," observed Frost. "It is this backward motion toward the source, against the stream, that we most see ourselves in … the tribute of the current to the source."

This, I had come to believe, is the ultimate purpose of the journey: *the tribute of the current to the Source.*

We know not where the journey will take us or by what means we will come to its end: "Time, like an ever rolling stream, bears all its sons away; they fly, forgotten, as a dream dies at the opening day." But we know what we have been taught about the good river: that "justice rolls down as waters and righteousness as a mighty stream" … that its "streams of mercy [are] never ceasing" … and that those "streams make glad the city of God."

Our purpose, then, is tribute. Our tribute is to the source. And the source is Love.

It is an apt metaphor for my story, this adventure of the raindrops finding their varied ways back to the sea, leaving their marks on the landscape, paying tribute to the source. But, then again, I do not need a metaphor for my story. My story is a metaphor in itself.

PART ONE

FREEDOM

1980-1996

CHAPTER ONE

UPROOTED

More damn politics.

That is what I remember thinking as I returned to the gym and the throng of people there to pay their respects.

A lot of it is a blur now, faded by time and the relentless, mind-numbing pace and proliferation of events. Crowded out the way the mind does when there is just too much in there to keep straight ... and maybe too many places where things can hide.

At night while you are asleep, a hatch opens, and the custodian tosses out some unneeded or unwanted memories. Maybe they are not really unneeded or unwanted, but he throws them out anyway because one man's treasure is another man's trash, and the custodian knows which is which because he is in charge and gets to decide. And so, while you are asleep, he comes and collects all the discarded memories and hauls them off to the landfill. And they are buried there, and others are dropped off and buried with them, and then the whole area is covered up with dirt, and grass is planted on it, and a green hill appears where nature had not put one, and then in the winter it is a bleak beige hill, and the memories are all gone. Returned to the ground—ashes to ashes, dust to dust—and that is the end of it.

Except that is not always the end of it.

Maybe some engineer missed something, or maybe somebody took a shortcut to save money, or maybe despite everyone's best efforts the thing just happened. But, one way or another, the landfill lining is breached, and the memories leach out into an aquifer, and the aquifer is connected to a spring, and the spring bubbles up to form a stream, and the stream flows back to your house, into your bedroom, and re-deposits those memories in that delta between your ears as you sleep some other night.

Maybe you dream about it, or maybe you think about it in the shower the next morning, or maybe something catches your eye the next day that reminds you. Or maybe it is a week or a year or a lifetime later. But there it is—a memory you thought was gone, or maybe it is a notion you never thought about at all. But now it is right up front in there, commanding your mind's attention, so you have to deal with it.

I remember some things from that time just like it was yesterday. Other things I do not remember at all.

What I do remember is a carefree kid who was asleep in his room on the third floor in Venable on a normal night in early September during his sophomore year, which made it 1980. He was sleeping the really deep kind of sleep that a college kid sleeps when he has spent the day overdoing it, as youth obliges him to do, studying, partying, playing touch or hoops or cards, or just hanging out—always the same things in varying combinations—until he is bone-tired and finally crashes. His head hits the pillow, and his next conscious thought is going to be how much he hates the buzzer on the alarm clock and wishes he had 30 more minutes to sleep. But then a vivid image cuts through the fog of his mind: the terrible gaze of the presiding gray eminence as he pronounces silent judgment upon late arrivals to class. So the kid hauls himself out of bed and stumbles down the hall to the shower that will bring him back to life.

Except that night it was not the buzzer that awakened him. Instead, he had been shaken, gently, the way his mom used to wake him when he was a kid growing up in that comfortable house on the hill above Caroline Street in Orange and it was time to get up and go off to school so he could make something of his life.

"Rise and shine!" she would always say.

But then he realized that this time it was not morning, and he was not at home, and the person shaking him definitely was not his mom. Bending over him this time were the courtly president of Hampden-Sydney College, V. Algernon Small, and "Dr. S. D.," the kind pastor of College Church. And it

4

struck the kid right away that their usually smiling, confident countenances bore very grim, uncertain expressions. But the expressions were not nearly as grim as the situation warranted, because people who do not want to scare a vulnerable college kid try hard not to look that grim.

Anyhow, they told me what had happened, and one of them told my roommate Chad, and then Chad and Dr. S. D. rode with me to Charlottesville to the hospital. But we got there too late. And I guess the memories of the rest of that evening got thrown out by the custodian because it is all a blur now, even though I have tried to remember it.

What I do recall clearly—besides the funeral itself—is the large crowd that gathered in the high school gym after the service was over.

The ladies at our church laid out quite a spread of food, which covered the folding tables that ran all the way across the baseline at one end of the gym. There was lemonade and sweet tea and hot coffee over where the home team's bench normally is, and there was a guest book over by the door where the booster club normally sells raffle tickets. The scorer's table was in its usual position, but covered by a big basket of flowers that looked very out of place. And the rest of the gym was just full of people, talking and eating. Some were sitting at the long tables at the opposite end of the gym, but most of them were standing and talking and eating in the large open area in-between. It created such a cacophony that it made my head hurt, and the noise combined with all the emotional pain wracking my body so that, for a moment, I imagined it might be fatal and afford a means of escape. But then something reminded me I was 19 years old and indestructible.

This place had been a lot of fun when there was a round ball game going on—like when Mitch and the guys upset Goochland on their way to the 1977 regional championship. They did not go as far as we went in our Great Football Season, but it was still a big accomplishment for our small high school, and we had a blast in that deafening gym, cheering them on.

Now this place was never going to be fun again—not for me, anyway—not after today. The memories of this sad time would smother all those good ones. And that seemed like a shame.

I was glad to see many of my old friends and teammates from Orange County High in the gym that day. You never really get over your glory days in high school. Even if all those days were not glorious—in fact, far from it—the mind is all about regeneration, and so it focuses on the moments that were glorious, and your high school friends stay forever young in that photo album that doubles for your brain.

In my high school days, as I reflect on it now, there was Danny McGuire the Image and Danny McGuire the Idiot.

The Idiot had a lot on his mind. He was right much of a know-it-all, as kids tend to be at that age, readying to wrest themselves from parental clutches. Yet he was full of self-doubt. And he was more thoroughly dependent on his parents for everything—from his material needs to his most basic beliefs and goals—than he would have admitted or even imagined at the time.

That was the *real* Danny McGuire.

But in everyone else's photo album there was only The Image. The nonchalant and quietly confident scholar-athlete. The tall, sturdy "heartbreaker with the gleaming smile radiating from beneath dreamy blue eyes and sandy blonde locks," as my persecutors on the yearbook staff had described me, to my mortal embarrassment. From then on, I was not "Danny" to my teammates; I was "Dreamer"—and occasionally even "Goldilocks," though I pretty much nipped the latter nickname in the bud by flattening one of the wisecrackers in practice.

The Image forever would be defined by the Great Football Season, when he hauled in 17 touchdown passes from QB Mitch Jackson, including several that were truly amazing acrobatic feats, and rolled up 1,421 receiving yards on the way to the Fighting Hornets' shocking Group AA state championship.

But The Image had a controversial side, too, because he and Mitch and their small coterie of friends were inseparable, and Mitch was black, and The Image was white, and so were their friends, which included males and females, and in rural Virginia in the 1970s that was a problem. Officially speaking, the schools had been integrated for a few years, but some things—even simple things like hanging out—you just did not do back then.

Mitch was at the funeral and at the gym afterwards, as he was bound to be by the unbreakable bond of true friendship. So were several other friends who stood out in the largely lily-white crowd. At first I worried about how they would feel, but then I decided it was not a problem. Even with those times' rigid taboo against social interaction across racial lines, I figured a funeral was a special case. Death has a way of equalizing things, and even the most unreconstructed rebel would have to acknowledge the practical obstacle to holding separate-but-equal burials.

Of course, neither practicality nor any other form of rational thought tempered racial reactions in those days. And it was not rationality or enlightened goodwill that had gotten Mitch and me cut some slack—it was *football*.

"That Jackson boy is a good kid," they would say to themselves and each other, justifying a suspension of the rules when it came to Mitch. "His father's a preacher, and his preachin' sure 'nough must meet with the Good Lord's satisfaction 'cause he gave his boy one helluva passing arm...."

Football, it seemed, covered a multitude of sins and shortcomings—even racial ones—so long as you won on Friday night.

It all seems very strange to me now, and it made no sense to me back then, either. Good and normal people just had very screwed-up ways of looking at other people. But it was the way things were, and you just learned to look past it somehow. In fact, I am careful now not to pass judgment on anyone else, because I do not really know how I myself would have turned out if our public school, and especially football, had not thrown Mitch and me and our friends together.

Football is an arena where you have to depend on your teammates, and so you learn to respect them as individuals, regardless of where they come from, or what they look like, or what you or they have been convinced to think. Every arena should be that way, but that was not the place where you usually found folks back then. The usual place was the one burdened with generations of separation and resentment, feelings of inadequacy, superiority, victimhood, and guilt—layer upon layer of society's hang-ups and someone else's problems.

And so it cheered me a little on this sad day that none of those things had mattered in the slightest to Mitch and my other black friends. They were there because they cared about me.

Also at the gym that day were my new pals, my college friends, their presence bearing witness that I had moved on from my small town, grown up, and become exceedingly worldly and erudite since those OCHS days a lifetime— about a year and a half—earlier. The close-knit Hampden-Sydney community had turned out in force, with Chad and dozens of fraternity brothers, classmates, and faculty members making the sun-drenched, 80-mile pilgrimage up Route 15—"James Madison Highway"—from Kingsville to Orange.

By far the most important to me at the time was Dr. S. D. Our home church was between pastors, and he had come to the rescue by offering to officiate at the funeral service. I had known Dr. S. D. only casually before this, and more by reputation than personal experience. People said he was a normal, decent fellow and a very dynamic speaker—someone who related well to college men. But I had been forced to admit, upon regular inquisition by my parents, that my record of attendance at College Church had not been what it could have (meaning, I practically never went). I had not required Dr. S. D.'s pastoral attention nor had any reason to expect I would require it. Yet, he had dropped everything and had been a constant presence and fatherly counselor during the three days since his gentle shake roused me that awful night and I opened my eyes to observe his kindly face and furrowed brow.

I mentioned that Mitch and Chad were present that day, and so was the third in the trio that would become my tightly knit circle of trusted friends. I had met Abby Wingo only recently during one of my trips to Charlottesville to hang out with Mitch. She and her second-year roommates occupied the apartment next door to Mitch's in one of the aging three-stories on Jefferson Park Avenue, or "JPA," as the students all called it. Effervescent and stunningly attractive, possessed of such a quick wit you always seemed a step behind, Abby was someone with whom, in another lifetime, I might have fallen head over heels in love. But in this particular lifetime she happened along at a moment of consuming tragedy in my life, and she immediately, if unconsciously, embraced me as an object of her sympathy and maternal affections. She had no reason other than unalloyed compassion to drop what she was doing and come up to Orange to nurture a virtual stranger. But she was there that day, and it sealed a lifelong friendship.

Of course, the throng that filled and overflowed the gym that day was made up mainly of the legions who had called Martin and Mary-Virginia McGuire their friends. There were literally hundreds of them. Mom and Dad had their church friends. They had political friends from all over the state. They had friends from the bank and the post office, the beauty parlor and the hardware store, and all the other places they frequented, because they were the kind of folks who spoke and greeted you with a smile, even a chat if you would indulge them, though you barely knew them. Mom had friends among her fellow teachers at the elementary school, and Dad had his employees at the plant and his customers. He had hunting and fishing buddies, and she had the ladies from the bridge club. They had their separate friends from the Ruritan Club and the Garden Club, respectively. And, of course, all the neighbors were their friends, too. I am sure they had people who were not their friends—

in fact, there must have been some people they simply could not abide, and the feeling presumably was mutual, because you have that in every community. But today *everyone* was their friend, or at least everyone wanted to assume that posture as the goodly McGuires cast off for their heavenly reward. And so they all had very nice things to say … and say … and say.

As I reflect on it now, this remarkable show of respect and affection, this rallying-around by the community, said something profoundly positive about the character of small-town life. A couple of selfless saints, pillars of the local Presbyterian church and the tranquil community of Orange, had suddenly and tragically lost their lives. Their friends and fellow citizens—some close confidants, others casual acquaintances, and the rest respectful strangers—gathered to express a collective sorrow, to console the family (that is, to console me because I was about it except for some stray aunts, uncles, and cousins), and to turn their personal grief into mutual support. Together they told their stories and shared their memories of Dad and Mom; they celebrated the positive impact my parents had on others; and, above all, they reaffirmed their faith in the resurrection, for it gave them hope.

It was a healthy ritual—an affirmation of community and faith and a moving expression of gratitude for a pair of lives exceedingly well lived. But that is how it looks in the rearview mirror. Time has healed things, as it always does.

Back then, I was hardly in such a reflective mood. In a single night my life had been ripped to shreds. It seemed like it had been transformed horrifically … and permanently. And my overwhelming feeling was one of anger.

But there was a problem with that.

I could not be angry at my parents because I loved them too much.

And I could not be angry at God because my parents had always taught me to trust his "sovereign will and perfect purpose." Plus, I remember thinking, somewhat irreverently, that since God had the keys to heaven and my folks were suddenly at the gate seeking entry, it would not be a great time to tick him off.

So I decided to be mad at Politics instead.

In truth, I had a head-start on that even before the accident because of my Mom's father, Everett Daniel.

As a young boy, I did not understand much about politics. I was told that Grandpappy, who had a big dairy farm, also had another important job: he was a leader in the Virginia Senate, and had been for many years. Of course, I was more interested in the farm, and I remember wondering why a person needed two jobs anyway, especially when one of them was as cool as a dairy farm. But then, when I was in the third grade, Grandpappy unexpectedly lost an election to some Young Upstart who accused him of some awful thing. The thing really was not all that awful, I suppose, but it sounded bad at the time. And the people, who had always loved my Grandpappy, or so I figured, decided all of a sudden that they did not love him anymore. They decided instead to believe some unpleasant thing the Young Upstart had said about him. At least some of them decided to believe it, and that was enough, and so it brought an abrupt and unhappy end to Grandpappy's time in politics.

At that point, politics moved right on ahead and left the wreckage that was Senator Daniel's political career along the roadside. But the problem was that Senator Daniel was still my Grandpappy, and I loved him, and all I knew was that those people in politics had hurt him, that they had made him very sad, and that he never seemed quite the same after that.

A young boy can become a young man and even an old man, but he will never forget those angry feelings from his youth, when politics hurt someone he loved.

The thing with Grandpappy was bad enough. But then I grew up and went off to college, and politics decided to kill my parents.

If it had not been for politics, Mom and Dad would not have gone to Richmond that weekend and would not have been traveling home during that freak late-night storm. They would not have been anywhere near that dark dip in the road where the large, dead oak limb landed, and they would not have had their lives suddenly and brutally extinguished in a blazing roadside inferno.

If it had not been for some stupid political event with some useless bigshot, the contented couple that was Martin and Mary-Virginia McGuire would have been at home that evening doing what ordinary parents do, which would have been knitting or sewing or reading a book or tying fishing flies or watching TV, or maybe even writing a letter to their son down the road in college asking when he is coming home to visit because they sure are missing him.

They would have been at home, and at home they would have been safe. Instead, they were on the road coming home late at night ... because politics had insisted on it.

Well, what damn good did that do for anyone?

10

I mean, what in God's name did they have to show for it? Politics had not built a straighter road between Cuckoo and Louisa. It had not gotten some conscientious public employee there ahead of my parents to clear the road or made somebody manufacture a car safe enough to withstand the crash. Politics had not allowed my folks the satisfaction of seeing the fruits of their good labors before it yanked them from the world. And it was not going to fill the empty seats at my graduation, or give me a hug and kiss at my wedding, or be there when I desperately needed to talk to someone, or patch the gigantic, gaping hole that had suddenly been ripped in my heart....

Politics just took; it never gave back. It was a cancer eating away at my life, and it had just eaten away at my heart.

Even the death ritual itself struck me as a ridiculous sort of political exercise—the visits, the calls, the funeral, this Big Event at the high school gym. And for what purpose? To make everyone else happy? To make some grand statement? To satisfy some social standard? To send Mom and Dad off like a ship leaving port with everyone on the dock waving and shouting, "Bon voyage"?

It just seemed absurd to me—like everything else about politics.

It was not that my mind could not grasp on a logical level why things were as they were. People were shocked and sad, and there are only so many things people can do when that happens and you live in a small town—or anywhere, for that matter. They can send some flowers and cook some food and put on their Sunday-best and go to the funeral home and the service and the cemetery, and then come to the high school gym to say they are sorry because that is the only place in town big enough to hold everyone who wants to come and say they are sorry. People were doing what people are supposed to do in this situation. And I knew I had to be there to speak kindly to all of them and thank all of them, because that is what my father and mother would have done.

I would do my duty the way my parents taught me, the way they would have expected, the way that would have made them proud of me. But I did not have to like it.

Fortunately, Mrs. Denton, the tough old bird who ruled the place as principal, had a compassionate side even though she worked hard at concealing it and succeeded impressively. She had the presence of mind to offer up her office as a place of occasional refuge for me during the long afternoon ordeal in the gym. And so I went in there a couple of times just to wipe off some sweat from my face, swill some mouthwash, and clear my head before plunging back into the crowd of well-wishers.

As I returned to the gym modestly refreshed after one of those breaks, I remember thinking that this must be what it is like for those politicians who are always pressing the flesh. People keep coming up to you, so you act like you remember the names or at least the faces, whether you really do or not. You feign interest in the comments, no matter how awkward, inaudible, or inane. You ignore the smokers' bad breath and the alcoholics' tell-tale body odor and the ladies' nose-numbing perfume. You hug or kiss the older women, but you just offer your outstretched hand to the young, good-looking ones so you do not set people talking. You clasp the male hands assertively—sometimes you even clasp the elbow with one hand while shaking hands with the other— as you wait to discover whether the return shake is a limp dishrag, a death clamp, or something comfortably in-between. You nod appreciatively and thank them for coming. If they linger, you ask about their family. You give them a reassuring smile or tap on the shoulder or pat on the back. You press on, person after person—poised, steady, unflappable. You are doing-just-fine-thanks-for-asking. You are acting, always acting, like you are completely in control and there is nothing abnormal about any of this.

Of course, you are really not in control at all, and there is nothing normal about any of it. And inside, if you have half a brain, you are saying to yourself, "Scotty, beam me aboard…. Mr. Scott, beam me up *now*…. Mr. Scott!"

Unlike my situation that day, the politicians and their adoring crowds engage in this bizarre practice because they *want* to. They actually *choose* this life. I had not chosen any of it—not by a long shot. But things were as they were, and self-pity was not going to change it. So I put on my best brave and reassuring countenance and returned to the gym, resuming the genteel Southern scene where good social graces take you perilously close to abject phoniness, all in the name of making everyone feel comfortable.

I was barely through the doorway when I came face-to-face with a thirtysomething woman I am sure I had never seen before.

"I am very, very sorry for your loss," she stammered. "Your father was like a mother to me—I mean, he was like a father to my mother—er, I mean, you know, he was very special … like a family member … and …."

"Thank you so much for that," I said, applying a tourniquet. "And thank you for being here. How are all your folks doing these days?"

The question plainly suggested I knew this woman and her family and had an interest in their wellbeing when, in truth, I had no clue. She was actually starting to explain how "all her folks" were doing when a large man grabbed me by the shoulder and spun me around. I recognized him from our church but could not recall his name.

"Daniel, this is a tough time for you. I know that. You know that. We all know that. But it is just part of life, and you have to accept it."

The man said this with authority, as if he himself had lost both parents in a flaming auto crash seven or eight times now and was really expert at it. "So, you are gonna do just fine—you're gonna do that for sure. And if you need anything, anything at all, just call me and Mabel. She will cook up a good meal for you, and I'll take you down to the pond and we'll haul us in a big catfish from that deep spot at the end of the dock. Now, we mean it...."

"Sounds like a plan—I really appreciate it," I replied submissively, with a measure of gratitude but mostly diplomacy as I dipped slightly in a bid to free my shoulder from the burly man's grip.

I was just beginning to feel good about my adroit escape when a sudden impact from behind nearly knocked me off my feet. I caught myself, using the balance honed during nearly four years at wide receiver (or so I flattered myself), and I looked around to see a pudgy kid in a seersucker suit with a clipboard under his arm backing through the crowd. He was looking the other way and paying little heed to those in the path he was unceremoniously clearing, giving his whole attention to the well-starched politician who was gripping and grinning forward in his wake.

"Uh, sorry about that, but could you please get out of the way," the kid said to me. "Congressman Nevers only had 30 minutes on the book for this event, and he is already late for the Lions Club fish fry over in Madison."

I was happy just to have avoided the indignity of falling flat on my face, and I moved aside obligingly. Then his comment sank in and I started to tell the clueless cherub what I thought of his congressman and his fish fry. Before I could act on the impulse, I spotted Bart Bell and he spotted me.

Now, the saga of Bart Bell is a deeply troubling and tragic story. But at that time he was a political phenom, the dashing student body president at H-SC and president of the College Republicans, a kid on the move who was already playing in the political big leagues beyond campus, helping Nevers in his campaign and interacting importantly with Republican luminaries two or three times his age. He had the looks, money, ambition, and political savvy to go far. And if that was not evident to you, he would be happy to fill you in.

Once our eyes met, Bart stepped in quickly, elbowed the hapless staffer out of the way, and pulled me forward.

"Congressman Nevers, this is my friend Danny McGuire. You asked me to introduce you," he said, instantly commanding the skillful politician's full attention.

"Oh, Mr. McGuire, there you are. I cannot begin to imagine what you are feeling right now, and I want you to know how very sorry I am," Nevers said, clasping my right hand with his right, squeezing my elbow with his left, and earnestly peering deep into my eyes. "Your parents were wonderful people. They were outstanding and valued leaders in this community and in this Commonwealth. They stood up for what they believed in. They were the kind of unselfish, patriotic, freedom-loving folks who make you proud to be a Virginian and an American. And, on a personal note, I am pleased to say that Martin and Mary McGuire were two of my most active and dedicated supporters. We will all miss them terribly, as I know your family will...."

I was listening politely, looking as grateful as I could, and I stole a glance over at Bart, who was smiling with evident satisfaction. The Congressman's presence at this gathering was a tribute to my late parents, no doubt. But it also was proof of Bart's political connections, and that was something our small college community, attuned as it was to my personal tragedy, would find impressive—or so Bart figured.

Bart's smug smile quickly disappeared, though, as Nevers completed his canned soliloquy: "... and please know, Mr. McGuire, that we will keep you and your precious little sister in our most heartfelt prayers."

"Well, that is very kind of you, sir," I replied evenly, struggling unsuccessfully to suppress the sarcastic juices that immediately formed in my mouth. "This indeed has been a great trauma for my *precious little sister*."

I should have stopped there, but it was not in the genes.

"We are all hopeful that she will rebound quickly so she, too, can dedicate her every waking moment to advancing your stellar political career—as soon, of course, as she is old enough to vote."

The Congressman cocked his head like a dog that hears a curious sound. His quizzical look confirmed that I had momentarily nudged him off his script, and I thought he even seemed intrigued by it. But then he quickly reverted to form. "Ah, yes, wonderful—well, you take care now," he said with a self-satisfied smile before departing for the gymnasium door in the widening wake of the freckle-faced seersucker man-boy whose elbows, clipboard, and buttocks were quickly back at work parting the crowd.

"Of course," I said, turning smartly to Bart, "my *precious little sister* will have to be born first, and that will be rather difficult in light of recent events."

"Uh, yeah—real difficult," he acknowledged with a shrug. "The Congressman had two funerals today," Bart mused aloud, "so he must have gotten the two sets of talkers mixed up. No excuse for that, really. Can you imagine what the press would do to him if he ever screwed up like that at the funeral of someone important?"

Ouch—did he really say that?

Of course he did. It was not that Bart meant to be mean. He just lacked the bandwidth to factor in the feelings of others when his whole focus was the all-important politics that one day, he was quite certain, would make him lord of all he surveyed. His callous words did not particularly surprise or bother me because I already had a pretty good idea what I was dealing with.

"Bart, you and those plastic politicians are all alike," I said, as I shook my head and turned away.

Then I remembered my father and my mother, my manners and my duty, and so I turned back. "But, hey, Bart, thanks for getting the Big Man over here for this. Mom and Dad would have thought it was cool."

My words did not reach Bart's ears, of course. He already was racing toward the door, eager to stay in the influential politician's orbit. They belonged together, Bart and his Congressman, in their own charged universe, and I was more than happy to leave them to it. Never in my wildest dreams could I have imagined how interwoven our courses would become. Bart and Nevers seemed alike, and they may have started that way. But over time I would discover they actually were like the moon and sun—propelled by powerful, unseen forces and as different as night and day.

LIFE OF CONSEQUENCE

A week or two after the funeral, I figured it was time to go by and see Dr. S. D. I had not crossed his path since the time in the gym after the service, and I did not see much of him there. I had thanked him then for conducting the funeral and for all the other kindnesses, but I really had nothing else much to say to him. I was not a member of his congregation or a regular at College Church, and I did not think I deserved to lean on him now, after things had gone south for me, when I had given him no time when things were rolling along well.

But at the gym he had come over to me, patted me once on the shoulder, and told me that when things settled down he needed me to stop by so he could "go over some details." I could not for the life of me figure what additional details could be awaiting my attention, and so I set the request aside. But as the funeral-related chaos receded, I recalled his words, and my curiousness about the matter grew.

So one afternoon I went by his office.

It was not a long conversation, and I do not remember much of it. I just remember one thing he said: "Daniel, when things like this happen to people, especially sudden and horrible and inexplicable things like this, they have a choice to make. They can turn *toward* God, or they can turn *away* from him. They can reach out in faith for help, or they can let their anger and sadness consume them. Either way, it's a turning point."

He went on to say that he had not been through an ordeal like mine, and so he would not presume to tell me what I should do. "What I can tell you is this. The choice you make may very well decide the course of your life. You don't have the option of staying the same, somewhere in-between. You have reached a fork in the road, and, as Yogi Berra says, you have to take it. If I can help you as you work through it, I want to do that. But, no matter what, I'll be praying for you."

I thanked him and muttered something about having too much on my mind and being too far behind in my classes to worry right now about things like forks in the road and Yogi Berra's tiresome inanities and the future course of my life. Or at least that is what I thought, being too well-mannered, thankfully, to express any of that to this generous man.

But there are some things you cannot get out of your head. You are in the library studying about Leonidas at Thermopylae Pass and your Mom's face pops into your head again. Or, you are trying to write a paper for your Greco-Roman Thought class and you recall a ten-year-old conversation with your Dad. Or you are in line for lunch and the picture that appears in your mind is a battered young mother and her two little children, who had relied on Mom and Dad's help to put food on the table and clothes on their backs, and who now had lost that lifeline, just as I had.

16

The thoughts just keep bubbling up. The custodian of your memories is working overtime, dredging them up. You cannot concentrate on anything or enjoy anything. And it is just awful—and sad, very sad.

After a while of that, I walked over to the church one day after lunch and dropped in to see Dr. S. D. again. That fork in the road was the main thing on my mind. I was curious about what he meant, and I figured listening to Dr. S. D. might at least change my focus and take my mind off all the other stuff that was rattling around in there and making me so bummed out.

The conversation that day ended up not having anything to do with forks and roads—at least, not overtly so.

I had come over on an impulse and had failed to think ahead about what happy-go-lucky line I might use to maintain my facade of easy, confident coping. So I fumbled for something nonchalant to say, producing a momentary awkwardness that Dr. S. D. quickly remedied with a question.

It was about my name, of all things.

"I noticed that your middle name is 'Madison,'" he said, "and since you are from Orange, I wondered if that was a family name. You may know that Madison was one of the founding trustees of the College."

"Yes, I do know that. Both James Madison and Patrick Henry were founding trustees," I answered knowledgeably, surprised that anyone might imagine the fact could have escaped my notice. "I am a history major—although, to be honest, I first learned that fact when I was pledging my fraternity and they made us memorize the historical marker in front of Atkinson Hall."

"Well, at least they're good for that, aren't they," he nodded.

"Historical markers?" I asked.

"No, fraternities," he answered.

"Well, sure," I concurred warily, fretting that the chat now might meander toward the fraternity lifestyle and its impact on nearby College Church, where the frequent revelry no doubt disturbed the tranquility of the pastor's family in the manse and the peace of the dead in the cemetery.

"I was born on Madison's birthday—March 16, 1961—and I assume that's the reason my folks named me for Madison. My mother was a 'Daniel' before she was married, and her family goes back in Virginia to Powhatan and Pocahontas, John Rolfe, and the so-called 'First Families,' and all that stuff, so I guess my first name was an easy call for them. But if my arrival had been postponed by a day I bet my father would have insisted on 'Patrick' as my middle name—you know, in deference to the patron saint of his forebears—and then we wouldn't be having this conversation."

"But," I mused on as Dr. S. D. listened, "my folks never really said much about why they gave me that middle name. James Madison obviously is Orange County's most famous son, so I always figured Mom and Dad probably wanted to highlight their roots and their affection for the place. Or maybe they wanted to get me interested in history and had a notion their little boy might follow the family tradition of messing around in politics, even grow up one day to be governor or president. I don't know. It's a good question, and I guess I should have asked them about it when I had the chance. But it was something like that, maybe all of the above."

"Well, I was interested in it because names can matter, and, like you, I am named for an historical figure," the pastor continued. "I really think having that name shaped my life."

I thought about it for a moment and came up with nothing, so I inquired sheepishly, "What is your full name?"

"*Samuel Davies* Thomas," he answered, looking for a reaction but seeming unsurprised by my blank visage. "Have you heard of Samuel Davies?"

"I'm sure I should have, but apparently my education here has been woefully deficient," I replied with a wry smile, attempting to deflect the slight. "I probably should have gone to U.Va. with Mitch after all…."

"With whom?" he asked.

"Mitch Jackson, my buddy from Orange. You may have seen him at the funeral," I said.

"Oh, yes, I did meet him—a very impressive young man. In fact, he engaged me in quite a chat about you there at the high school."

"He did? What did y'all talk about?"

"Well, let's see. I'm sure you're aware he has a pretty high opinion of you, which is unsurprising given your friendship. He said you are the toughest kid he's ever known. He told me about the game when you came down on your arm and broke it and a couple of ribs, but held onto the ball anyway for a 43-yard completion. Impressive story there, Daniel."

I could not suppress the self-laudatory grin that formed on my lips as I acknowledged the compliment with a nod.

"He also told me about the late-season injury that killed your chances of playing college ball. He said you bounced back from that setback amazingly well—that you sucked it up and accepted it and refused to let it get you down."

I winced at the reference, but covered it quickly with a shrug. "Well, that's the breaks, right? I mean, what can you do? At least it gave me time to focus on something really valuable to society ... like *golf*," I joshed awkwardly. "What's that saying—'When God closes a door he opens a window.' That's what the Good Book says, right?"

That last comment came from somewhere in the recesses of my mind and popped out involuntarily. It must have sounded quite pretentious because I certainly was no expert on the "Good Book" at the time. Before Dr. S. D. could respond that, yes, the saying was quite true though not actually found in the Bible, I recalled where I had heard it. It had come from my mother as she consoled me after the doctor's news about my injury. How she happened to be ready with that nugget of encouragement at that particular moment, I do not know. Maybe she got it from her mother or her pastor or even from *The Sound of Music*—I have since noticed it in there. But I had not really paid much attention to it until this point, when the custodian shoved it up unexpectedly into this conversation.

"Yes, God has a way of turning obstacles into opportunities," Dr. S. D. confirmed. "Mitch said he admired the way you handled that life-changing setback. But he said this one would be far different. He doubted that you would be able to bounce back at all well from your folks' death. He told me that you and your parents were very close, remarkably close, and that losing them would really knock you back on your heels. He said you would try to keep it all bottled up inside and not talk about it...."

"Yeah, well," I interjected, cutting off the suddenly intrusive foray into my bleak situation, "Mitch is quick to form conclusions about everything. 'Often in error but never in doubt,' as the saying goes. If he knew half as much about everything as he thinks he does, he'd make Albert Einstein seem like a dullard."

My defensive overreaction thus confirming the accuracy of Mitch's prediction, Dr. S. D. nevertheless heeded my wave-off and changed the subject obligingly. "I was interested to learn his dad is a pastor. Do you think Mitch will follow in his father's footsteps?"

"No, Mitch is into politics," I answered. "He's a preacher, for sure, but not the religious kind. That's obviously a big disappointment to his dad, and it's a source of real tension between them, I think. Plus, Mitch is the kind of person who knows what's wrong with everything, and he wants to tell you and everyone else how to fix it, and you had better agree with him, or else.... I mean, he's a true believer. And since his political ideas don't much resemble his dad's, that has always been an issue between them."

As Dr. S. D. practiced his fine art of listening, I unconsciously turned the discussion back to my own parents.

"We never had any big disagreements like that in my house; we never argued about politics or anything much, really. About the biggest argument I can recall was over how long I could go between haircuts. It always has bothered me how much conflict there is between Mitch and his dad. If something happened to his parents, I think he would be stuck with a lot of regret...."

Dr. S. D. studied my reaction to my own words, as if to discern whether I bore such a burden. Apparently satisfied that I did not, he turned the conversation in a different direction.

"Well, religion and politics do tend to cause conflict," the pastor said. "And my namesake, Samuel Davies, is a good example of that. He was a preacher, and as a good Presbyterian you should know about him. In fact, as a Virginian, indeed as an American, you should know about him. They tell me you like history; well, he's an unsung hero who changed the course of history."

I sensed I was in for a good story, but I did not know how good. "Okay, I'm all ears," I said.

Dr. S. D. then proceeded to tell me—in an animated discourse that carried him away and took me with him—about the life and times of his ancestor, Samuel Davies.

Davies, he recounted, was a leader of the 18th-century Great Awakening unsurpassed even by the renowned Jonathan Edwards in the eyes of their contemporaries and several ensuing generations of historians. Centuries on, Americans' collective memory had narrowed and fixed on Edwards as the personification of that pivotal period's revivalism, but the evidence of Davies' influence was palpable nevertheless. A treasure trove of sermons, letters, hymns, and historical tracts bears witness that he was among the most acclaimed ecclesiastical figures of his time. His travels in England and Scotland, raising funds and awareness of the American religious awakening, brought him into close contact with the leading Protestant thinkers of his day. After tending his Virginia flock, he went "home" to the region of his youth and became the fourth president of the College of New Jersey, now Princeton, succeeding Edwards.

A New Light, or "New Side," Presbyterian minister bent on evangelism, the young Davies had come south to Virginia on a mission, responding to an earnest invitation signed by the heads of more than a hundred families in Hanover County. "Dissenters" from the established Anglican Church, the petitioners were among a disfavored but growing minority in the colony. When the 23-year-old Davies arrived in Hanover in April 1747—at Samuel Morris's meetinghouse, later called Polegreen Church—he brought the dissenting faithful some unexpected good news. During a time when Anglican clergy were insisting on vigorous enforcement of colonial strictures against competing sects, and when itinerant preachers were routinely prosecuted, Davies had come by way of Williamsburg and had obtained a coveted preaching license from the General Court, comprised of Governor William Gooch and the Council. Davies's erudition, diplomacy, and quiet, dignified manner—so contrary to the ways of the itinerants—had especially impressed the Governor. It enabled the inspiring young preacher to launch a ministry that would range across a significant swath of Virginia's central Piedmont, tilling the soil in which, a quarter century later, dissenters with a passion for liberty and learning would plant the very college where Davies' descendant now enlightened me.

Displaying not only his pastoral gifts but the insights of an accomplished scholar in late colonial American history, Dr. S. D. went on at length about the connection between Davies' work and the eventual casting off of Anglican establishment, leading ultimately to the emergence of religious freedom in Virginia and America. The dynamic Davies had been prominent among those dissenters who, contending for the right of conscience unfettered and unfavored by the state, had propelled Virginia on a course that would take it beyond tolerance, beyond disestablishment, to actual religious liberty embodied, first, in the Virginia Statute for Religious Freedom and, finally, in the First Amendment to the United States Constitution. This I found somewhat interesting, and it would become much more so as my passion for the subject awakened later. But what then struck me as really fascinating was the tale Dr. S. D. told about his namesake's impact on one of the weekly visitors to the Morris meetinghouse—young Patrick Henry.

It was Patrick Henry's mother, an exuberant dissenter, who brought her son within Davies' powerful orbit. This was no small feat, as Dr. S. D. explained, since young Patrick's father was a practicing Anglican and his uncle, also named "Patrick Henry," was the parish priest, and a jealous one at that. Davies' sermons enthralled young Patrick. Small in stature, his pallor a sickly pale, Davies spoke with incomparable clarity and force, uniting reason and emotion in tones alternately soft and lyrical then soaring, booming, even terrifying, with transformational effect. On the carriage ride home, Sarah Henry would have her son repeat the substance of the sermon, making it inevitable that he would mimic the style as well. Later, when Henry's reputation as the foremost political speechmaker in Virginia was well established—"the greatest orator that ever lived," Jefferson said of him—the *Son of Thunder* himself would credit the passionate preacher. Samuel Davies, said Patrick Henry, taught me "what an orator should be."

Dr. S. D.'s discourse had fascinated me, and I was not about to interrupt it. But now the pastor was pausing as if finished, and it occurred to me that he never really explained how being named for Samuel Davies had changed his life. So I asked about that.

"I don't know whether it affected my choices directly," he responded. "But I presumably would not have learned so much about Davies if I had not been named for him—like you and Madison, I bet. It probably was the thing that first got me interested in colonial history. Davies' life of consequential service became a real inspiration, especially since he accomplished all that while living only to the age of 37."

This last fact surprised me. I had just assumed that such an important historical figure had spent decades amassing the resume that Dr. S. D. had just reviewed. But not so—he had done it all as a young man.

"We all learn about Patrick Henry, the great orator of our liberty," Dr. S. D. continued, "but not many of us know about Davies. Yet, if it had not been for Davies, there would have been no Henry. At least, there would have been no Henry able to frame the choice as liberty or death and arouse people from their lethargy to join a great cause," he said.

"Some people labor in obscurity, Daniel. Some are heralded in their time because of the ways of the world, and some are even heralded in their time for the right reasons. Yet, the memory of nearly all is lost to history. And for the select few that history chooses to remember, what typically survives is a dumbed-down, sanitized version. The human complications are glossed over in the telling. Then, after a while, some 'critical' historian, most likely suffering from low self-esteem and a desperate desire for attention from the academy, comes along and rips a hole in the poor fellow's reputation by offering a viciously negative perspective that is even more one-dimensional than the one offered by the icon's apologists. So, what's the lesson? It is this. If you want history to remember you and tell your life's story ages hence, you have a 99-percent chance of being disappointed. The odds are hopeless. *But if you make it your quest to live a life of consequential service and you really don't worry about who gets the credit, then you might just be able to have an impact that matters."*

I was pondering the message when the pastor added the analogy that would stick with me. "God wants mankind to write poetry, Daniel. He has a purpose for each of us, and he honors the person who sharpens the poet's pencil as much as the person who conceives the verse. Men remember only the poet's name, but God remembers the labors of both, because both are indispensable parts of his plan."

"That's what I learned from Samuel Davies," the gentle pastor said, "and it makes me proud to bear his name. He showed me the extraordinary power of faith in action. Seeing his example of selfless service made me want to accomplish something with my own life."

Then he came in for the kill.

"Of course, Daniel, neither Samuel Davies nor Patrick Henry had it easy. They both had loving parents who taught them well and other angels who helped light their paths—they had a lot going for them. But they also knew great tragedy and hardship in their lives. They both lost their dearly loved wives—Davies, just before his most energetic work spreading the gospel in Virginia, and Henry, just before his immortal speech at St. John's Church. The profound loss could have sent each into a tailspin of grief and doubt, even turned them against God, but instead it drew them closer to him and propelled them on to even greater deeds."

"You go reflect on that," he concluded after a pause. "I have to get back to work or I won't have a sermon to preach on Sunday."

I left, but on Sunday I was there to hear the sermon. At least, I heard the one he gave, but it was probably not the one he had originally planned.

He began it with an *a capela* rendition of an old African-American spiritual, "Lord, I Want to Be a Christian." Then he went on to explain, with the same animation I had seen a few days earlier, how that simple, soulful hymn had been sung by the slaves that Samuel Davies taught in Hanover County. He taught the slaves to read so they could be saved. He wanted them to be able to read and understand the Good News for themselves.

In this, as in so many other things, Davies had been ahead of his peers and ahead of his time. Soliciting support from the Society in London for Promoting Religious Knowledge among the Poor, he wrote, "[T]he poor neglected negroes, who are so far from having money to purchase books, that they themselves are the property of others; who were originally African savages, and never heard of Jesus or his gospel, till they arrived at the land of their slavery in America, whom their masters generally neglect, and whose souls none care for, as though immortality were not a privilege common to them with their masters—these poor unhappy Africans are objects of my compassion, and I think the most proper objects of the Society's charity."

And here, after all these years, was Samuel Davies Thomas, singing that song of the slaves to a nearly all-white congregation in rural Southside Virginia. He was telling them, as he had told me, the story of a now-obscure figure, a consequential man that history had nearly forgotten—a man who *changed the world.*

That was my introduction to the Song of the Slaves. Not just a hymn, but the whole mournful, painful, powerful, hopeful song of those yearning to be free—the universal song of mankind.

And not just, "Lord, I want to be a Christian," but also, "Give me liberty or give me death!"

MARKETS MATTER MOST

Those conversations with Dr. S. D. took place during what would be, for many years, my lowest of low points, and they supplied comfort, diversion, and ultimately inspiration. After each, I would return to my dorm room and enthusiastically relate what I had learned. Chad was utterly uninterested and ill-equipped to pretend otherwise. But I carried on anyway, and in his marginally well-meaning and distracted way Chad sort of listened.

Looking back, it still amazes me how Chad and I became such good friends.

United randomly as roommates upon our arrival at Hampden-Sydney a year earlier, we quickly realized we had virtually nothing in common. The embodiment of stereotypical Old Virginia, Reginald Chadwick Braxton IV was the proud scion of lowland blue bloods whose lithe fingers traced their multiple lines to merry old England. I was the grandson of a tough old Irish immigrant and a Piedmont dairy farmer, unpreoccupied with my pedigree.

Chad was the consummate preppy, having emerged from the womb, as I saw clearly in my mind's eye, fully clad in a pink Oxford shirt and bow tie, khakis, blue blazer, and penny loafers. I was inclined toward indifference in such matters but developed an earthy predisposition toward jeans.

I had attended public schools, the great American melting pot, and unselfconsciously had befriended folks who happened to look different. Chad had never set foot in a public school and apparently regarded "separate but equal" as an unremarkable expression of the natural order of things.

I got along well with most people but was an introvert at heart, rarely stepping out of my comfort zone to make new friends. Chad was the socialite par excellence, the center of attention at every opportunity, a fount of wit and wisdom in every conversation.

While I was prone to retreat into the annals of history and take refuge in the shadows of heroes, Chad was always in the moment and out in the crowd, reveling in the marketplace, selling his wares.

Selling, in fact, was Chad's organizing principle, his *raison d'etre*.

If he was not selling his products, and he sold many products, then he was selling himself: his cleverness and creativity; his ability to recall every joke he ever heard and summon it at just the right moment for optimal effect; his gimmicks and plots and penchant for the outlandish; his intrepid spirit and utter fearlessness.

He was the portrait of the brash and gregarious American—an entrepreneur and entertainer—the kind of person who makes things happen.

Unfortunately for Chad, he sometimes made things happen without thinking them through.

During our first year at Hampden-Sydney, inspired by a local tale of glory, he had the bright idea to steal (he would say, "borrow") old Esmeralda, the aging Holstein that supplied milk to the friendly Armitage family down the road past Worsham, and put her in the classroom of the legendarily taciturn Professor J. Noakes Kaine. Chad had suffered through Dr. Kaine's 8:30 A.M. "Western Civilization" class for almost half the semester, and "Nova" (as earlier students aptly had dubbed him) had done nothing to diminish his reputation for an anesthetizing lecture style that made early morning sessions especially excruciating.

Chad's clever way of livening it up was to have the august professor and his two dozen long-suffering students arrive to the indubitably hysterical site of a cow unexpectedly resident in their ground-floor classroom in Morton Hall. Sensing an opportunity to make money as well as fun, he solicited sizeable dare wagers from several of his fraternity brothers and embarked upon the enterprise with the aid of persons who to this day have remained nameless.

What Chad did not know—due to a failure of due diligence that would have been unthinkable in his later years—was the unassuming Esmeralda's apparent distinction as one of Prince Edward County's biological wonders. Though middling as a milk maker, she was a peerless flatulent and no piker when it came to producing the sterner stuff. Several disconcerting hours in that strange, stress-inducing hall of human discernment apparently had tightened her bowels for an extended time, heightening the internal effects so that when the dam finally burst, presumably not long before daybreak, a muddy river of half-digested grass, grain, or whatever the poor creature had ingested ran wide across the classroom. An evidently crazed Esmeralda then appeared to have run circles around the room, overturning desks and flinging feces as high as the chalkboard and chair railing in a frantic but vain effort to free herself from the stench and squalor she had supplied. Maybe freedom was her aim, or maybe she just wanted to assist Chad in achieving the maximum effect for his prank. Whatever her motivation, her achievement was unimaginable. And so when Nova Kaine and his students arrived a short while later, the sight and smells were ones no one would ever forget.

As I say, Chad did not always think through all the potential consequences. An optimist by nature, he had assumed the harmless stunt would produce good laughs all around. Esmerelda would be hitched outside until the end of class and then would be returned to the easy-going Armitages with due apologies. With feigned reluctance, Chad would own up to the clever deed, endure the modest punishment the professor dished out for the good-natured prank, collect on all the bets, and then bask in the accolades of students and faculty alike, for surely such a bold and creative gambit would produce kudos galore. He would, Chad no doubt imagined, be a legend overnight.

He was right about that.

Not only did Chad, a student of social rather than natural science, fail to fully grasp all of the biological implications of his plan. He also badly misgauged the reaction of unflappable old Nova. As recounted by Chad's traumatized classmates, the distinguished professor arrived a few minutes ahead of the students, as usual. After surveying the scene for the briefest of moments, he closed the classroom door and waited outside until the ringer in the iconic Bell Tower commenced his task, signaling to the campus community that the class session was about to begin. Then he entered the room, righted the lectern, and stood erect behind it in the customary manner. "Get in here, boys," he intoned impassively to the incredulous students, "so we can get started."

After designating two lucky students to rid the room of the bovine visitor, Professor Kaine began his lecture. Seventy-five minutes of pure, unadulterated hell ensued. Nova appeared impervious to the effects of the pungent setting, but the students were dying. With the morning sun shining brightly through the massive windows on the unseasonably warm and humid spring day, one desperate young man rose to open a window in a bid for a modicum of relief. "That won't be necessary," Nova advised in a stern tone with a peremptory glare before resuming his lecture without missing a beat. No one else dared rise for the remainder of the session except Chad, who after ten minutes in silent horror suddenly sprang from his seat and reached the doorway just as vomit burst from his chest.

Chad indeed was a legend overnight. In fact, he was famous the whole campus wide by lunchtime. By that evening, it is safe to assume, students, professors, parents, and friends had heard the news and were eagerly repeating the tale. Fortunately for Chad, iPhones and social media were things of the future, or his feat would have gone viral and made him a global laughingstock by sundown.

A person of lesser self-confidence might have been unsettled by the widespread ridicule and stiff discipline that ensued, but Chad collected on his bets and moved on. "The hardest money I ever earned," he said years later.

While the incident was much discussed by everyone else, I do not recall ever hearing Chad say another word about it, and I chose not to bring it up until long after we had said our goodbyes to Prince Edward County. But when I caught up with Chad that morning, the magnitude of the deed and its more serious implications had not dawned on me. I just thought the whole thing was hysterical. "Geez, Reg-ee-nawld, that was amazing!" I crowed. "But for someone so smart, you sure were stupid to have the cow crap all over your own classroom rather than someone else's."

Chad uttered a familiar epithet unworthy of this account, swung fecklessly for my jaw, and then left with a slam of the door. The next time I saw him he was accompanied by his parents, and there were no wisecracks since the purpose of their visit was to gather their son and his belongings for an involuntary off-campus vacation spanning the rest of the semester.

It is interesting, though, how people are shaped by events. It is fair to say that Chad's reputation among his peers was enhanced by the episode. From then on, all understood him to be a daring and consequential man of action, and I suppose that was a good thing for Chad and his entrepreneurial pursuits. He did, however, have to endure a nickname change—he was "Cud" rather than "Chad" thereafter—and all manner of redundant bovine humor as the price for his notoriety.

When he returned in the fall—I had re-upped as his roommate more out of sympathy than anything else—Chad evinced a notable change of attitude. I doubt that he was fully conscious of the lessons learned, but after his freshman disaster Chad was much more focused on his studies, more thorough in his preparations, and, above all, more careful in his choices. There was no perceptible change in the carefree visage and plucky banter that were his hallmark, but beneath the nonchalant exterior I think there was a new seriousness to Chad. Actions, he had discovered more abruptly than most, have consequences—and sometimes quite *unintended* consequences.

The Esmeralda episode probably supplied a strangely constructive stimulus; at least it got his attention. But what really transformed Chad was the tutelage of a free-market economist, a self-described adherent of the "Austrian school" named Hans Hayden. Dr. Hayden was Chad's Intro Economics professor, attentive faculty advisor, and scholarly mentor. He literally changed Chad's life.

Chad had grown up in an old-money Virginia family where one was almost congenitally obliged to strike a benevolently snobbish pose, engage blithely in country-club conversations on a wide range of inconsequential topics, and take neither politics nor religion (nor much of anything else, for that matter) too seriously. He wore this mantle quite well and arrived at Hampden-Sydney with it fully intact.

The problem for Chad was that his branch of the Braxtons had suffered some reverses, presumably during the War Between the States or its aftermath, that had depleted the lion's share of their resources. So, while the Braxtons maintained all the outward indicia of their historic rank and privilege in the Old Dominion, Chad learned early on that making money was important. It was *new* money, to be sure, but it came with the satisfaction of earning it, and from Chad's perspective it had another distinct advantage over old money in that you actually could spend it.

His family's problematic if well-concealed circumstances thus had accelerated Chad's escape from the stupor of privilege and entitlement that hobbles many young people who proceed from elegant homes to elite prep schools to exclusive-seeming colleges. Inherited wealth and opportunity being the least appreciated and most easily dissipated, many to the manor born discover only too late that, in the real world, competition is ferocious and rank no longer has its privileges. Chad had the advantage of discovering this useful truth before he set foot in the real world.

In fact, Chad discovered as a young boy that making money was his unusual gift. Instinctively entrepreneurial, he was forever coming up with new and creative ways to cause others to part with their funds. By the time he neared graduation from high school, his classmates proclaimed him "Most Likely to Succeed," and the Southside Virginia Academy yearbook predicted he would be the cause of some great invention or breakthrough, make millions in a hurry, and appear on the cover of *Money* magazine by the age of 40.

With all the emphasis on financial success, one might jump to the conclusion that Chad was materialistic, but I found this not to be the case at all. Chad was a saver, not a spender, and he indulged himself little. Making money was a competitive challenge, almost a sport, for Chad. And in that sense, if none other, he was an especially talented sportsman.

Unlike hucksters who sought to make money at the expense of others, Chad relished delivering things of real value in exchange for the cash. He wanted to be loved, or at least appreciated, and that meant he had to find ways to give people what they wanted, or needed, or at least thought they wanted or needed. So while in junior high he designed an underground drain system for a house-bound old lady down the street that channeled water from her gutters to several nearby flower beds. He tended the flowers daily until they were in full bloom, whereupon he photographed the beaming customer and her flowers for a local newspaper ad suggesting that folks needed only to buy one of Chad's custom drain systems and they, too, could have a flora-festooned yard that was the envy of their neighbors.

The drain system business did fine, but Chad soon found the work too time-consuming to be lucrative, plus the labor supply was short because most of his classmates with strong backs had superseding farm obligations or sports interests. So he canvassed the landscape for other unmet needs and soon started a disc-jockey business. He recruited his more hip, attractive-looking friends and sent them to nearby rural communities where they provided musical entertainment for dances, weddings, and all sorts of functions. He was better at managing the enterprise than spinning discs himself, however, so while his employees raked in the dough from dances, Chad looked around for an outlet for his personal talents.

Chad found his niche when his mother returned from the beauty parlor one day and reported that Betty Lou Hardin was distressed because her young Johnny was having trouble mastering his reading lessons. By the time Chad had been at it for a few months, no fewer than a dozen kids, including the precocious Master Hardin, were showing up in the Braxton family living room twice a week for what proved to be highly beneficial remedial reading sessions. It taxed his parents' patience, but the valuable instruction made the Braxtons one of the most popular families in town.

Chad related these stories with pride, and he acknowledged, with uncharacteristic self-awareness, that until college he not reflected on the *process* by which these good things happened. He had not studied the science of human behavior or the conditions in which commerce thrived, nor had he considered how innovation and entrepreneurship might fit into a larger picture of societal improvement. Chad simply had come up with innovative ways of doing things for and with people that made people like him and pay him money. He had done what any enterprising young American boy could do. And if most of his contemporaries were otherwise preoccupied— "ordinary" kids, for example, were more interested in football, baseball, and partying—well, that was just fine with Chad. They might think him a bit weird, but it also meant he had fewer competitors.

When Dr. Hayden introduced Chad to economic theory, however, it all clicked. It was as if someone had opened a wide curtain and in one brilliant panoramic burst revealed to Chad how the world really works. I watched his transformation happen. I had no choice, really, since he talked about it incessantly, and it was truly amazing to behold his metamorphosis. Within little more than a year or so, this faux aristocrat, money-making marvel, and gratingly ingratiating super-salesman had been converted into an ardent advocate of reason, meritocracy, and free markets. He came to appreciate intellectually what many—even we who sing the praises of free enterprise—know only superficially.

Ironically, the thing that made all this possible was the extended opportunity for reading that Chad's suspension from school afforded. With Dr. Hayden's guidance, he used the remainder of the spring and then the summer to delve deeply, almost voraciously, into the literature on economic liberty. He studied the classical economists, spending time on Smith, Petty, Ricardo, and Mill, and read Marx and Keynes for further context. Reflecting Dr. Hayden's influence, he was most enthralled with the work of 20th-century thinkers like Friedman, Hayek, Mises, Rothbard, Hazlitt, Schumpeter, Strauss, Voegelin, Kirzner, and Sowell. The more he read, the more he wanted to read. Thus began Chad's practice, which continued long after, of phoning Dr. Hayden to test his understanding of the works he had read, propound his own theories, and get recommendations for additional resources. Chad often would say he got more out of the time he was kicked out of school than during all the semesters he spent on campus put together. Not even Chad really believed that hyperbole, but if ever there was someone who made the most of his time in the penalty box, it was my odd roommate.

Only many years later would I come to appreciate fully how the disparate threads of personal experience, doctrinal instruction, and competitive ambition had been woven together in Chad. Much later still would it occur to me how much of Chad had been woven into me. During this time, my roommate simply struck me as weird—a source of annoyance and awe in equal measure. I responded to his weirdness mostly with sympathy until one night in the fall of 1980 when my parental tragedy suddenly reversed our roles.

Somewhere along in there Chad and I became close friends. And something else important happened, too. "Mr. Republican" on campus, Bart Bell, got wind of Chad's fascination with conservative economic theory and recruited him for the Hampden-Sydney College Republican Club. It was not a hard sell. Once enthralled with the brilliance of the free market and alert to the ways that hapless governmental meddling and cronyism could erode its benefits, Chad's turn to politics was natural. Bart could have cared less about economics, but he understood the value of channeling zeal like Chad's into political activism, especially when he could bend that activism to serve his own political ends.

And so the hook was set—for Chad ... and, in time, for me as well.

GOD DOES SPEAK

A variety of things helped me through those rough times after my folks' death. Chad's entertaining antics took my mind off my problems. Mitch and I were back and forth between Charlottesville and Sydney playing golf, going to ball games and concerts, and generally hanging out, often with Chad and Abby in tow. Adhering to Tiger tradition, there were frequent road trips to Sweet Briar and Hollins for parties and female companionship—an agreeable necessity due to our school's conviction about the advantages of single-gender education. And there was even some actual studying mixed in, too. The guys in my dorm, my fraternity brothers, even several of my professors went out of their way to look out for me. Perhaps most important, I started showing up for Dr. S. D.'s sermons on Sundays. I discovered that they were not mind-numbing, as my youthful observations in Orange had led me to presume all sermons must be, but instead were stimulating and entertaining. Like my occasional chats with Dr. S. D., things always seemed to make more sense after I listened to him preach.

But I did not really turn the corner until I finally cried.

Chad and I were in Charlottesville crashing at Mitch's after a Dave Mason concert, and I was taking a shower the next morning. I remembered a time with my father early during my high school years, and as I replayed the conversation in my mind the floodgates opened.

Thank you, Mr. Custodian. You have an impeccable sense of timing. All I wanted to do was get up, shower, get some coffee, and head over to Foxfield with my friends for the races.

My teenage disdain for politics was already well entrenched when I heard some political preacher, one of those conservative televangelists, make the outrageous claim that God had told him in a vision to support a particular candidate. The divine endorsement went to the Republican nominee in this instance, something that would become a lot more common a few years hence with the advent of the so-called "Christian Right." The apparent idea was that, unless all God-fearing people voted for this character, we and our country would face some sort of plague, pit, cataclysm, or worse. I do not recall all of the promised punishment or even the identity of the candidate for whom the appeal was made. All I recall is being supremely annoyed that someone purporting to be a religious leader would exploit his followers' trust, faith, and ultimately their fears as a tawdry tactic to grab their votes.

School had just given me my first exposure to world history, and I had been shocked to learn how much conflict religion had caused, how men had manipulated religion for their own gain down through the centuries. So much evil, it seemed, done in the name of godliness. When one considered this history, religion hardly seemed like the source of comfort and counsel it had been portrayed throughout my youth. It seemed more like a joke—a really sick joke—that kept making a fool of humanity.

And here, now, was a real-world, contemporary example of it. Nothing seemed more disgusting to me than these plastic, plug-in preachers exploiting their gullible flocks, implying that God comes down and votes in elections and presumably strikes down anyone who dares to cancel out his ballot. Everyone, it seemed, was in it to game the system and deceive someone else. The politicians and the preachers were all selling the same snake oil.

So one Sunday afternoon while we were canoeing and fishing on the Rapidan River, I asked my father whether he thought God gave voting instructions to the rest of us through his priestly messengers and whether Dad approved of that kind of cynical exploitation. I do not recall exactly how I posed the question, but I am sure I asked it in the characteristically contemptuous manner of my teenage years, dripping with sarcasm, designed to arouse the maximum reaction.

"No, I don't believe that God tells people how to vote," he answered, responding more patiently than my derisive tone deserved. "In fact, I don't think he speaks to people on any subject in the way you mean—not usually. Moses got the burning bush treatment, but I don't think it works that way for most folks."

"Well, that's a relief," I mocked. "Because if this supposed separation of church and state means anything, it's gotta mean you use your own brain for the purpose of self-government rather than letting someone else lead you around by the nose claiming that God gave them the word."

I was relishing this opportunity to display my superior teenage insight and perspective, and Dad apparently was going to let me continue until I had spent myself, or until I wandered too closely to the DMZ that separates youthful skepticism from sacrilege.

"I mean, I don't see much point to voting anyway. But if God is going to tell me how to vote when I get to be 18, I hope he just comes out and gives me the word directly," I exclaimed. "That would impress me a lot more than having him slip the instructions to Pastor Joe-Bob Throckmorton and making me call the 1-800-GOD-SAYS line to get my marching orders!"

I was finished, at least for the moment, and was very pleased with myself.

"I take your point," Dad said evenly, ignoring my puffing. "But if you mean to say that God doesn't ever speak to us, Danny, then you are missing something important." I thought I was in for a lecture, but it was soon apparent that this was something different. My father was generally private about his personal faith, but something I had said caused him to open up.

"No, I don't believe you can dial up 1-800-GOD-SAYS and get the latest heavenly edict like the weather forecast. But I do believe that God writes things on people's hearts...."

I released a sigh, signaling my resistance to what I supposed was coming, but Dad ignored the interruption.

"God speaks with a still, small voice inside of you—and he speaks every day in ways big and small. But you have to be listening, Danny; you can't always be *talking*."

He let that last phrase hang before continuing, its point obvious.

"He speaks through the miracle of your mind. Through a movie or a book that inspires you. Through a poem or a song that touches your soul. Through the beauty of nature ... like this lazy, rolling river and the sunlight that peeks through the trees and ignites the brilliant colors of the sweetgum and maple and beech trees. You can almost hear God saying, 'Look at this scene. This is the kind of thing I can do. Do you really believe beauty like this happens by accident?'"

I scanned the vista and had to concede it was a remarkable sight.

"Now, about church and state," Dad continued. "I agree with you—it's a basic freedom we enjoy as Americans. And, by the way, it's at least as important for those who believe in God as it is for those who don't. An individual's free choice to believe is an essential condition for acceptance of God's grace."

In the shower it occurred to me that I had heard this same idea expressed recently by someone else. It took several moments of retracing my steps to recall that Dr. S. D. was the source. *Interesting*, I thought, before resuming my journey with Dad.

"But to say that church and state should be independent from each other does not mean that God doesn't watch over our political affairs, or that faith does not inspire free men and women to serve and govern well. When I see our flag fluttering, that's a scene of beauty to me just like this river. It reminds me of what our country stands for and how much good has been accomplished in the world because of it—how human potential and faith and hope have been unleashed for millions around the world because our country has taken stands for freedom again and again. And it didn't just happen. People were inspired to sacrifice for it, some with their lives."

He was talking about America now ... and *history*—speaking my language.

"Sure, there has been evil done in this country's name. There have been false promises and betrayals of our ideals, sins against our own citizens as well as others. I see our country as a good but imperfect work that God is still re-fining. But no country has been a greater force for good in the world than ours, Danny, and I firmly believe that faith is a *crucial* part of it."

This my quiet father said with passion, revealing an intensity within that was rarely on display.

"I know you have your doubts, Danny, and that's okay. At least it means you are tuned in and asking the questions. At one time I had doubts like yours, but no more."

"But the political preachers, Dad—*what about the political preachers?*" I pressed.

"Do I approve when a televangelist or a politician or anyone exploits religion for political purposes? Of course not. Some are prophets in their own minds and some are just scam artists," Dad acknowledged. "But that is nothing new, Danny—the Bible is full of warnings about false prophets. And the fact that there are people who will mislead others about religion and bend it to their own ends doesn't mean that faith is false. It means that faith is *needed*."

Huh? This was not computing for me.

"Okay, I have an example for you. Take Patrick Henry's speech ... 'Gen-tlemen may cry, Peace, Peace, but there is no peace.'"

This, Dad knew, was sure to get my attention. As a four-year-old, I duti-fully had memorized and recited for my mother's class the most familiar lines of the patriot's famous oration at St. John's Church. Sometime later, after my run as the orating toddler freak ended, I had come to appreciate Henry's piv-otal role in arousing the revolutionary spirit in Virginia. The lines of his pow-erful speech had remained part of my repertoire, and I seized upon any excuse to reel them off.

"Do you know where Patrick Henry got that famous 'Peace, Peace, but there is no peace' line? It's in the Bible—in Jeremiah—not once but twice. Jeremiah was quoting an exasperated God who was saying something like this: 'Prophets and priests tell lies. They tell my people their wounds are not serious. They say, "Peace, peace," when there is no peace.'"

This tidbit, a totally new take on an old story, had come to my father's attention during a recent meeting of his men's Bible study group, and he seemed eager to share the context with me. I was intrigued by Henry's apparent plagiarism, but Dad had a bigger message in mind.

"So you go back centuries before Jesus's birth, to the time before the Jews were carried off into exile by the Babylonians, and what do you find? False prophets and corrupt priests telling the people not to worry—no need to mend their ways, no need to reform, because everything is going to be just fine. Comfortable religious leaders and princes and politicians, all doing quite well for themselves and not wanting anything to rock their boat of prosperity and power. So they all say, 'Everything's fine; peace, peace is here to stay. Ignore Jeremiah's ravings; just keep on doing like you're doing; don't fret about anything at all…' But they were wrong; Jeremiah was right. And after Jeremiah had witnessed the total destruction of Jerusalem, he actually blamed the corrupt prophets and priests for the calamity, not the Babylonian invaders."

The notion that people have been battling religious exploiters for centuries was a revelation for me, and now I was listening intently.

"Patrick Henry obviously knew that Bible story and was struck by the similarities between those comfortable political and religious leaders of Jeremiah's day and the complacent folks who wanted to wish away the crisis with England. If you go back and read the whole speech, like I did after this came up in my Bible study, what you find is that Henry was laying out a forceful case that God would bring allies to the colonists' aid and uphold their cause if only they would trust God and step out courageously to defend their rights."

Pausing to make sure I had stayed with him—*how could I not?*—Dad continued, "You should read and reflect on Henry's whole speech sometime, Danny, especially in these moments when you suppose that religious people and values have no place in politics. If Henry had been agnostic … if he had not been raised in the faith … if he had not had confidence that a just God existed who was able to sustain the American cause … would he have said and done the things on which human history may well have pivoted? I wonder."

36

It was a fair point, and I was pondering it as my father drove on toward his bottom line.

"You're absolutely right that religion has been used and abused down through history. But it is also true that people of faith are the reason for many of the great advances and reforms throughout history. The abolition of slavery and the civil rights movement are two obvious examples in our country. And one day, when the preciousness of all life is finally accepted, people will say the same of the pro-life movement. So when you hear someone invoking religion for some political cause, be careful and even skeptical, Daniel, but try not to be judgmental. Not everyone who thinks God has a hand in human events is an exploiter or a nutcase. Many are sincere, and whether they're exactly right or not is beside the point. A lot of them have foregone the easy life and are giving voice to their faith out of a genuine desire to help and serve others. *Those well-meaning people really deserve more than a young man's hasty judgments and superficial sarcasm.*"

A pause followed this last statement, too, with the obvious aim of allowing some embarrassment to creep in. The tactic may have worked, at least a little.

"God may not tell us how to vote, Danny, but he does speak, and often in a gentle whisper, when we are asleep or when we are awake, in our dreams and in our thoughts. His Spirit speaks to us in our quiet times, in our private prayers, in Scripture readings and our discussions of them, in an inspired sermon or a bedtime story or a kind word from a friend. He'll speak through those who share our faith, and he'll speak through those of different faiths, and he'll even speak through those who have no faith at all. He speaks in all the ways that normal people speak—in books and movies, poems and songs. He speaks *in* the popular culture and *through* the popular culture and often *against* the popular culture, because a lot of times he wants to help us lift our sights to something better than what everyone else is saying and doing. He speaks to us in our suffering and our overcoming. He speaks through what Lincoln called 'the better angels of our nature.' And I believe that sometimes he speaks through angels we mistake for ordinary people."

"One day, Daniel, he may speak to you through someone you love ... *or someone you lose.*"

I gasped as that last message hit me like a roundhouse punch. Suddenly, as the water kept flowing over me, I knew what this memory was about.

37

My father had stopped there, and for a moment it seemed the mental movie might be over. But I watched on that river of recollection as Dad cast and reeled his beetle-spin in silence a few more times. Then he continued, as if he had opened up this far and now felt he had to complete the message while he had the chance.

"Keep this in mind, though, Danny: God rarely speaks to us in our pride or strength. If we are sure we can have 'peace, peace' through our own effort and ingenuity, we probably are not listening for what he has to say. If we think we have a pretty good handle on God—you know, like we are good and decent folks who generally do the right thing and are behaving our way into heaven—then there's no urgency or mystery in any of it, which means there's no joy, either, and no room for any of his miracles. It's a sad reality of human nature that we tend to take God for granted when things are going well even though that's when we have the most to be thankful for—and the most to *lose*."

There was that word again—*lose, losing, lost!* The pain of my recent tragedies invaded my space again as the relevance of this fatherly wisdom hit home hard.

"It seems totally contrary to reason and to everything the culture teaches," Dad was saying, "but you will eventually discover that true strength comes when we acknowledge our weakness. That is when we are moved to trust God and nurture the Spirit he has given to us. Nourish that Spirit, Danny. Feed it with prayer; mine the Bible for the wisdom and comfort and counsel it can give you. Pause to savor the beauty of nature, the miracle of science, the joy in music, the gift of friendship, and remember the source of all of these gifts. Trust God to help you when you are hurting—in times of adversity, in times of sorrow, in times of confusion. But seek him all the time, not to ward off adversity, because adversity will inevitably come, but to gain the peace that will enable you to overcome the trials you will face on your journey."

This, I realized, was my good father's psalm of life.

"Remember this, too, son. Your mother and I love you more than we could ever say. You have been God's great gift to us. You ask me whether God speaks to us. Well, I know he does, because he has spoken most clearly to me through you. I have never felt more completely dependent on God than when I have gone to him in prayer every night and every morning asking him to watch over you, to keep you safe, happy, and well, and to guide you along your journey. That's what love does, Daniel. It teaches us to trust him because we care desperately about people who are *beyond* our protection. So, you see, God does speak to us through other people, because he is speaking to your mother and me through you. *Use your gifts to let him speak through you to others....*"

As soon as my mind finished replaying that conversation, I believed—for the first time in my life—that God actually does speak to people, because right then he was speaking to me through my father's words, through the echoes of the man who was dead to the world but more alive in my memory and in my imagination than he ever had been in the flesh. God was speaking to me through my father from beyond the grave, from down on the river, from deep in the recesses of my memory.

And so I cried for the first time since that awful accident. I cried a flood that mingled with the water from the shower head and washed over my body. Like the exiles before me, ripped from home and family, I wept as I remembered my Jerusalem. But mine were not long tears of sorrow; the memories and the message they carried quickly turned them to tears of joy.

I dressed and emerged to find Mitch waiting for me in the living room while Chad sat impatiently in the car outside. Mitch had been devouring a new book about Satchel Paige, one of his childhood heroes, and he was excited by a quote there that seemed to speak to my situation.

"My man Satchel is righteous!" Mitch exclaimed in that trademark tone that merged the Godfather of Soul's good feeling with his preacher-dad's soaring exhortation. "Listen to this thing Satchel says. He says: 'Never let your head hang down. Never give up and sit down and grieve. Find another way. *And don't pray when it rains if you don't pray when the sun shines.*'"

"He's preachin' to you, Dreamer—can you give me an 'Amen'?"

Another blast from the car horn outside drowned out Mitch's "Amen," giving me the excuse to head straight out the door, leaving him and his high-five hanging. But the coincidence made me shake my head and smile. After weeks of anguish, I had gotten the message that mattered most ... and twice in the span of 30 minutes.

So we went to Foxfield, the big party that has some horses occasionally running through it, and I had fun for the first time in what seemed like a lifetime. I had a mint julep because it was tradition, and I had a few bourbon and gingers because I liked them, and I placed some bets, and I enjoyed the company of Mitch, Chad, Abby, and our other friends during the long afternoon while the sun shined again. And I watched the thundering gallop of the horses and the excited, happy faces they raced past, and I gazed out over the sloping Albemarle hills at the hazy blue mountains to the west, and I realized that life is a gift and an adventure, and I smiled at the amazing beauty and mystery of it all.

CHAPTER TWO

PALACE

Standing on the floor of the packed Richmond Coliseum for the first time since the balloting began, I was at once fascinated and bewildered. It was the loudest, most colorful, most chaotic assemblage of humanity I ever had witnessed. Much about the convention proceedings puzzled me, but I had no difficulty reaching a firm conclusion on one matter: the large woman with the fire-engine-red lipstick, colossal elephant hat, and sticker-laden green corduroy vest—the one whose bearish hand now clutched my arm—was not to be trifled with. Grunting, "I'll show the bastards!" or something along those lines, she ripped at least two dozen oversized "Nevers NOW!" lapel stickers off the spool in my right hand and then plunged her frantic force back into the crowd, vanishing as fast as she had appeared.

I thought I had experienced my first authentic encounter with a clinically insane person, but now I realize she was just another zealous convention delegate.

Moments earlier I had been released from the Nevers for Senate "count room"—my assigned place deep in the bowels of the Coliseum and my post for the past seven hours—because the impending fifth ballot was expected to be the last. Now I scanned the remarkable scene in an effort to make sense of it. Over here people were furiously waving campaign signs and blowing on whistles and kazoos as they marched about in mini-demonstrations. Over there the media was huddled around one of the candidates as conventioneers variously gawked and jeered. In multiple places impassioned advocates for this or that candidate were desperately trying to be heard over the din, making their cases to rows of weary delegates who seemed frustrated by the exhortations, the noise, or both. Everywhere people were in motion, some racing about officiously while others wandered aimlessly. Some were artfully, or ludicrously, covered in political regalia and signage while others donned conservative business suits and blazers. The beer was flowing in the concourse outside the arena while a blanket of cigarette smoke hung menacingly inside.

A crazier circus, a more nonsensical scene, one could hardly imagine. But then I noticed some things and began to detect a pattern. All around the hall, people in pairs and clusters were engaged in animated, apparently heated, exchanges. And the focal point of their discord—evident from what they were waving and where they were pointing—was a certain neon orange flyer.

The pattern might not have been apparent to me if I had not immediately recognized the bright-colored missives. A couple of hours earlier, after receiving what I took to be a valid instruction, I had helped distribute boxes of them to a crew of fresh volunteers downstairs.

The dirty trick eventually would play a significant, probably even decisive, role in the outcome of the 1982 Virginia GOP state convention. But I was clueless.

"Danny, I'm glad they let you out of that dungeon and up here where the action is!" Mitch shouted, startling me from behind. "Isn't this the wildest thing you've ever seen?"

"Yes, it's absolutely crazy!" I yelled. "What's going to happen?"

"We're going to win, man—the tide is running our way big time!" he declared ecstatically. "They said it was impossible, but Nevers is going to pull off the upset!"

The growing enthusiasm in the Nevers count room had been palpable, and the robust demand for the lapel stickers I was distributing on the convention floor confirmed the favorable momentum, but Mitch's statement still was a stunner. For Nevers to come from so far back was possible, I supposed. But surging all the way to a win?

I wanted to pull my friend out into the concourse and probe the reason for his confidence. But before I could do so a well-dressed man and woman— evidently husband and wife—immediately approached from the other direction, and the woman tapped Mitch on his shoulder.

"Young man, that was one of the best speeches we have ever heard!" the woman declared directly into Mitch's ear. "Really, the very best—you have quite a gift ... *quite a gift!*"

"Yes, you do, son. You need to run for office yourself one day!" the husband chimed in emphatically. As they turned to leave, the man shouted over his shoulder, "By the way, we're voting for your man on the next ballot!"

These, too, were delegates, though of a decidedly more conventional stripe than the woman I had encountered a few minutes before. And they obviously were smitten with Mitch.

He nodded to them appreciatively, and turned to me with a broad smile as the couple ambled away. "It's unbelievable, Danny. This has been going on all afternoon—people just keep coming up. I guess I really nailed it with that speech."

"Hey, we don't call you 'Preacher' for nothing," I shrugged, bypassing the chance to feed his ego by offering my own redundant verdict on his tour de force.

Not given naturally to modesty or understatement, Mitch now was displaying both and doing his best to temper his euphoria. But I knew he knew exactly how well his speech had gone. Much more was at work in this convention hall than Mitch's well-chosen words, but apparently ... *amazingly* ... the object of his elocution was on the verge of an upset victory.

It would have been most unusual, of course, for a 21-year-old college student to be tapped to give the nominating speech for a U.S. Senate candidate at any political convention. That Mitch was an African American and this was a Republican convention in the erstwhile Capital of the Confederacy produced cognitive dissonance on a scale heretofore unimagined. Yet, the even stranger story is the chain of events that brought Mitch to that stage.

PREACHER AND PROVOCATEUR

In the "Peanuts" comic strip that was popular when I was growing up, there was a character named "Pig Pen" who was always surrounded by a cloud of dust and dirt. That image is the one that comes to mind whenever I think of Mitch, only with him the enveloping cloud was not dust and dirt—it was controversy and chaos.

His driver's license reads "Jonathan Mitchell Jackson," and family and friends address him variously as "Mitchell," "Mitch," "JJ," and "MJ." I supplied the nickname "Preacher," which stuck. But by early in his second year at U.Va., Mitch had earned a variety of other monikers, and none was designed to flatter.

If you could have Googled him in those days, you would have found a number of articles in the *Cavalier Times* in which his overwrought peers and occasionally even an injudicious faculty member excoriated him with epithets calculated to open the most jagged of wounds. He was a "right-wing nut case," "a traitor to his race," "the ultimate Uncle Tom," "a self-hating apologist for the dominant white racist culture," "the overseer's boy," and—my all-time favorite—"a sophomoric iconoclast whose reckless blather gives aid and comfort to the KKK, skinheads, flat-earthers, and all the other evil forces of intolerance that plague the civilized world." Some of the rhetoric was pedestrian and brazenly vicious, but a good deal of it was wrapped in elegant prose and vivid imagery, the better to impress the erudite in Mr. Jefferson's academical village while eviscerating the outspoken young man.

There was only one reason for this cascading calumny—one thing that unhinged the left-wing elements of the University community and sent those self-appointed guardians of truth scurrying to strap on their righteous armor and man the ideological ramparts.

It was not that Preacher had the temerity to be black and conservative at the same time. As disagreeable as that phenomenon was to the guardians, it was a circumstance then so unusual, so downright strange, as to be readily dismissible as a sort of quirk or mutation. It was the kind of oddity one could stroll past while pretending to focus on some distant object of interest, much as one might do when avoiding eye contact with a panhandler or a pitying glance at a person of severe disability.

No, the dissonance caused by the improbable merger of young Mitch Jackson's race and political beliefs, though quite problematic, was insufficient by itself to cause such a stir. The firestorm came when Mitch had the effrontery to suggest that, since his own admission to the University of Virginia was not the least bit a product of preferential treatment based on race, perhaps the school's affirmative action policy was counter-productive for people like him. It had the effect, Mitch observed, of causing students, professors, teaching assistants, and prospective employers, whether white, black, or whatever, to engage in a fallacious assumption about him and about others like him. Mitch wanted only one thing—to be fairly judged on his merits, by the "content of his character" rather than the color of his skin, as Dr. King had so forcefully urged. And yet, as he saw it, this perverse assumption meant that often he would not be judged on his merits; instead, he would be prejudged based on his race and found wanting.

Of course, Mitch being not just Mitch but by nature and necessity Preacher, it was not in the realm of possibility for these profound and even poignant thoughts to issue from his lips in a cool, calm, "come, let us reason together" manner. Instead, he verily screamed them from atop the Rotunda, fingers pointing, voice raising, righteous indignation flowing in convulsive wave after wave like lava issuing from a volcanic eruption.

It was soon apparent to everyone that Mitch not only relished being an agent of provocation. He also was really good at it. He proved as adept at finding the flaws in his opponents' arguments as he had been at picking apart pass defenses. And just when it seemed certain that the avalanche of opprobrium would smother him, he would scramble out of the pocket and throw the ball downfield again.

In his most memorable moment during the fracas, my friend sat stoically in the midst of several hundred fellow Intro Philosophy students in Old Cabell Hall as an indignant young graduate student serving as teaching assistant seized the chance to launch a personal diatribe against Mitch and his heresies. In so doing, the bearded zealot so abused the educational forum and exploited the imbalance of power that even the most kindred spirit—and probably 99 percent of the faculty—would have viewed the action as highly inappropriate. Yet, it occasioned enough sarcasm-induced laughter at Mitch's expense that the caustic academic wannabe no doubt felt he had accomplished the put-down in fine fashion.

When the alternately snarling and smirking presence in front of the class appeared ready at last to change the subject, Mitch rose with calm dignity and headed toward the stage. Misjudging the movement at first, the instructor soon realized that Mitch was not retreating ignominiously to the exit but instead was coming his way.

"I gather you have something to say," the T.A. observed tentatively as the class watched in stunned silence. "Very well, then," he said, shrinking stage-left for safety, "Take the podium, there, and say whatever you wish."

Preacher nodded, and approached the lectern. But once there, he turned and paused, his back to the audience, and gazed upward at the giant copy of Raphael's masterpiece, *The School of Athens*, which spanned the front of the hall.

"I would have thought," he said slowly as he turned to face his fellow students, "that there would be room in this great university for people to exchange

45

serious ideas with mutual respect. In fact, I came here because I was sure it was so. But, sometimes, I wonder … I wonder."

He paused, allowing the words to hang while he appeared to reflect on the moment. Not a sound was audible in the massive hall until he continued.

"I wonder how a man can stand in the shadow of great teachers like Socrates and Plato and Aristotle and deliver a tirade like we just heard—not teaching us to think for ourselves, but bullying us into thinking just like he does. I wonder about that…. Yes, I do wonder."

With each sentence more pronounced than the last, Mitch's voice rose and fell with a melodious, resonating quality that he had acquired through countless hours in the pew listening to his father's sermons and in our high school library watching reels of Dr. King's speeches.

"Sometimes I wonder how we'll ever learn to think for ourselves when the supposed champions of free expression on college campuses go to such lengths to suffocate us with their monolithic ideology. I wonder why they are so afraid of our ideas, why they are so appalled when one of us challenges their code. I wonder why they don't just disagree; they *demean*—why they can't just debate and illuminate; they have to *dominate* and *intimidate*. Don't you wonder about that? I know I do."

Some heads were nodding now. "Damn right," one student said loud enough for all to hear.

"I wonder why they talk about us as 'eager young students,' saying that we are 'the brightest ever,' that we are 'alive with energy and imagination,' with 'freedom of the mind' and 'the whole horizon of knowledge open wide before us'…" He was exclaiming now with his arms outstretched widely in front of him, then he suddenly pulled them in until his wrists were raised together as if bound. "Yet every day they try to *shackle* us to a deadening conformity!"

"Yes, I wonder about that," he said, as he lowered his voice again ponderously. "And, I have to tell you, I wonder about something else, too. *I spend a whole lot of time wondering about the future of people who look like me when so many of us have surrendered our ideas and independence*" —now he paused and tilted his head unmistakably toward the figure lurking stage-left—"*to people who look and think like him.*"

"I adore Thomas Jefferson," he continued after a moment, "because he gave voice to timeless ideals of freedom and equality. He set the liberating course for this country and the illuminating course for this university. But he was also a slave owner. In his own life he failed to live the ideals he espoused. And though we may want to excuse or forgive him because we know he accomplished so much and because we know no one is perfect—not back then, and not now—still we cannot forgive him, we cannot excuse him, not really, not fully, because we can't escape the knowledge that he got it wrong on the one thing that was totally within his control, and that was *the freedom of the people he owned.*"

He was preaching now, and the audience was mesmerized.

"And so I wonder: If we cannot excuse even Thomas Jefferson, whom we all adore, then must we excuse these latter-day Jeffersons, these benevolent white masters who speak of our freedom but never set us truly free, these kindly hypocrites who pose as our saviors but never accept us as equals? Must we excuse the 20th-century slave masters who say they have our interests at heart, but who would have us remain perpetual victims they can pity, sad souls they can exploit, rather than let us become the strong and proud and self-sufficient people God created us to be!"

His voice was booming now, and, as the shocked audience gaped, he cast his eyes upward and exclaimed, *"God Almighty, if there is one thing I ask today, it is that you save my people from these white liberals, because they are going to love us to death!"*

There were gasps and murmurs, a few uneasy laughs and nervous coughs, and even some tear-filled eyes. And then one student slowly, forcefully, loudly clapped his hands. And pretty soon there was general applause. The humiliated instructor never returned to the podium. Mitch exited in the other direction. And after a while the shell-shocked students just drifted away, leaving the ghosts of the great ancients to continue their dialogue in the silent hall.

Abby was in the class and witnessed those remarkable events, then she called me to describe the scene. She was not all that close to Mitch or me at the time, but she knew of our friendship, and she immediately understood that this would be a defining moment for him. She eagerly shared every detail, and, although I knew Mitch probably better than anyone, I still was amazed. I thought about it for a few moments and then called Mitch's dad up in Orange to tell him the story. Mitch and his father disagreed vehemently about politics. His father was a staunch Democrat who stood squarely in the mainstream African-American political tradition in which the churches played a central role. Mitch was a renegade. But this was a story I thought a father ought to hear. I am glad I let him know, because Reverend Jackson called Mitch that night and told his son how proud he was of him.

"I won't ever agree with those strange ideas of yours," Mitch recalled him saying, "but I am proud of you for standing on your own two feet and saying what you believe."

Even to this day, I really think that call was probably the happiest moment of Mitch's life. It was one of the greatest blessings a father can give—freeing his son to stand on his own feet—and that freedom is what matters most to Mitch.

The controversy continued for several weeks after that, and Mitch's stand on the underlying issue of affirmative action began to pick up a smattering of support. Some African Americans broke ranks and agreed with him, but mostly it was vocal white students who chimed in their agreement, and often in a way that made Mitch uncomfortable. Meanwhile, Mitch's provocative stance drew two distinct sets of detractors on Grounds. There were the thoughtful critics who contended that the persisting effects of past discrimination and the benefits of a diverse learning environment were considerations that outweighed the negatives Mitch had flagged. And there were the fierce guardians of liberal orthodoxy that Mitch had offended. The latter group grew increasingly frustrated at their inability to answer the eloquent black dissenter, and so they responded by lashing out at him even more insultingly and pointlessly.

An interesting sidelight to all this was the "trial" of Mitch, which took place, coincidentally, the day after the episode in Old Cabell. Abby, the ever-vigilant reporter for the *Cavalier Times*, was on the scene there, too, and she supplied the firsthand account.

Mitch had joined the Black Student League immediately upon arriving on Grounds and had relished being a constant source of irritation for the more liberal social activists who generally ran the show. So, when the controversy over affirmative action erupted, a rump group seized the opportunity to force Mitch from the organization. A meeting—which some took to calling a "trial"—was scheduled, and "evidence" was assembled. In a rare display of self-restraint, Mitch chose not to dignify the proceedings with his presence, a decision that undoubtedly relieved his accusers. Of course, they would never admit to the relief; instead, they savaged Mitch for his "cowardice" in not showing up to defend himself.

Most of the serious members of the League, including nearly all of the third- and fourth-year students, had better things to do, and few showed up.

But a good representation of rowdy first-years and some of Mitch's fellow second-years were on hand, seizing the chance to vent their outrage and establish their *bona fides* with the guardians. And so, as a dozen or so members of the group looked on in a small meeting room in Newcomb Hall, several students took turns breathlessly detailing Mitch's offenses. They made it abundantly plain to every clear-thinking person, should one have chanced to drop by, that views of the sort expressed by Mitch Jackson were simply and utterly *forbidden*. Not only did they represent "a turning back of the clock on civil rights," a "reversal of hard-won gains," and so forth. Insidious views like his were by their very nature "hate speech." In arguing that he should be treated like everyone else without regard to his race, Jonathan Mitchell Jackson was, purely and simply, a voracious malignancy eating at the very lifeblood of the University, the Nation, Universal Principles of Justice, and whatever else came to mind.

Dorothy Meade was one of those largely indifferent fourth-years. She had more important work to do, she told Abby, and had planned to skip the inconsequential gathering. But as a founding member of the rejuvenated league and as the newly elected student government president, she decided on the way over to Alderman Library that she had some responsibility in such matters, so she diverted to Newcomb Hall and dropped in to see what was happening. She considered the whole business to be somewhat unseemly—stifling speech, even the disagreeable sort like Mitch's, was not the U.Va. way—but she also knew it was normal, and probably healthy, for younger activists to start out a bit overzealous. Plus, Mitch Jackson and the folks in this particular organization certainly did not have any useful business they could do together from now on, so it was just as well they parted company.

Slipping into the back of the room unnoticed—quite a feat in itself, since her stunning appearance and formidable intellect dominated nearly every room she occupied—Dorothy Meade listened to the rant for five minutes or so until she heard the word "coward." Then she had heard enough.

"Excuse me, Mr. Chairman," she interrupted, pressing forward into the view of all. "But this is one of the silliest things I have ever wasted my precious time sitting through. Lord knows, we all disagree with Mitch Jackson. It doesn't take this meeting to figure that out. His opinions are reactionary—extreme—*crazy!* He thinks the opposite of the way we do on just about everything. But, please God, don't sit here and call this proud brother a coward! He may be an idiot—he *is* an idiot—but from what I see he has more stones than most folk at this University!"

She paused, ever so briefly, to see if anyone was going to dissent, then concluded with a dismissive wave of the hand. "Now get out of here, and go accomplish something useful before Mitch Jackson comes and embarrasses you like he embarrassed that pathetic T.A. yesterday in Old Cabell."

The brief episode received no attention—Abby did not deem it newsworthy, and nothing appeared in the *Cavalier Times*. But Abby shared the episode with Mitch, and down the road it would matter … a lot.

The rest of Mitch's time at U.Va. was generally productive. He remained a pariah to some and an enigma to others on the politically diverse Grounds, but he undoubtedly gained a measure of gravitas from the controversial events. Though he probably needed a boost to his self-esteem less than any other person at the University, he got one nevertheless. And, above all, he was fortified in his sense of moral absolutism.

For Mitch, indecision and ambivalence on important questions were signs of weakness, not intellectual depth. He was never one to say in conversation, "On the one hand, this, and on the other hand, that…." While others deemed keeping an open mind to be a virtue, Mitch regarded it as a mark of immaturity or superficiality—or, worse, a surrender of principle. A serious and well-informed person had clear convictions, Preacher would insist, and was not afraid to declare them whenever and wherever the situation warranted.

Although he had firm and fixed views on a wide range of issues, it was no accident that affirmative action had supplied the spark for a Mitch-inspired brush fire. Ever since junior high, Mitch had talked about going to U.Va. For a kid just up the road in Orange, black or white, it was the ultimate affirmation. And so, for Mitch, that goal had trumped all others. It even had trumped playing college sports, which struck me at the time as a colossal waste of talent. Mitch probably could have gotten a full-ride scholarship to dozens of midsize Division I schools, been a star QB, gotten noticed by the pros, and gone who-knows-where from there. He had the crazy skill combined with smarts, gift of gab, magnetic personality—all the qualities he needed to become a sports star, media personality, or who-knows-what-else.

But that was not what mattered to Mitch.

With the top grades in our graduating class and with board scores even better than mine, he gained a much-prized early admission and made his way, proudly, to Charlottesville. He did not need a leg up because of his race, or because he could play sports, or because of political or alumni connections—Mitch made it entirely on his own academic qualifications. He had pressed me hard to go with him, but I was the one who wanted to go to the smaller liberal-arts school to study history and play ball, not necessarily in that order. In retrospect, there was great irony in that choice given the late-season injury that dramatically changed my situation.

The other thing that drove Mitch to the University was his budding passion for politics. He was not the typical starry-eyed politico, captivated by the glitz and prospect of acclaim. For Mitch, even as a teenager, it was all about ideas—declaring them, fighting for them, carrying them into action. And what better place to engage in the battle of ideas and to prepare himself for a fruitful political future than U.Va.? The great legacy of America's third president, the University had supplied the fertile soil into which profound ideas and aspirations had been planted and from which enormously consequential political careers had flowered. Its distinctive culture stressed *values*, foremost among them personal honor and the unfettered pursuit of truth—the very definition of Mitch's mission. He was eager to add his potent acumen and powerful constitution to that grand tradition.

Mitch had sparred with his father constantly on politics and gained confidence from the verbal fisticuffs. Once, his father had challenged him on his aspiration for a political career. "You have been blessed with remarkable gifts," Reverend Jackson had told his son as he departed for college. "Have you considered what you owe to Christ, and all the good that you can accomplish by using those great gifts as a preacher and pastor rather than a politician?"

"I owe everything to Christ," Mitch had acknowledged, "but, as you always say, the Lord works in mysterious ways. You preached on that just the other day; you said, 'His ways are not our ways.' Well, Dad, your ways are not my ways. Besides, if I'm not meant to concentrate on politics, why have you spent all this time arguing with me about it and toughening up my hide?"

Mitch had smiled with satisfaction as he related to me this personal declaration of independence. But when it came to fire and brimstone, Mitch—*Preacher*—was indeed his father's son. Both were "Old Testament kind of guys," Mitch once remarked. They did not agree on much except that fidelity to the "law" was paramount. For Mitch, this moral rectitude often tended toward intolerance, and though he did not suffer fools gladly, he demonstrated considerably more Christian patience and forbearance toward fools than toward moral relativists.

This attitude destined Mitch for a lifetime of contention and frustration in politics. It may also have destined him to make a difference.

As a political leader, Mitch over time would seem to transcend questions of race, rendering them beside the point in what some would take to calling the "post-racial" era. But I suspect that, even in college, Mitch already was viewing himself, at least subconsciously, as a liberator—a latter-day Joshua who would complete his people's exodus, end their decades of wandering, and lead them across the river into the promised land where they would finally receive the respect due them as full and equal citizens. The exodus had begun with the civil rights movement, and Mitch's hero, Dr. King, had been their Moses. Since then, Mitch believed, a generation had wandered and failed to reach that promised land, and the chief culprit was the liberal coda that pervaded the Democratic Party. It was a kind of false religion that had held people in deadening dependency, perpetuated their economic and political servitude, and undermined their culture and faith. If not the calculated cultivation of dependency, then at least the Democratic liberals were guilty of well-intentioned but wrongheaded policies that had the same effect.

The Democratic liberals had failed to aid the exodus, but what the Republicans and Democratic conservatives had done was far worse. Mitch compared them to the Edomites, Moabites, and all the other hostile 'ites who controlled routes to the promised land—the selfish, haughty tribes who refused passage to Moses and his people. At best they were indifferent to the sojourners' history of oppression, and at worst they were bigots who figured Moses and his people had gotten what they deserved. And so they had stood by as evil men gunned down heroes like Medgar Evers and Jimmie Lee Jackson and Jonathan Daniels, blew up young girls in church, set vicious dogs loose on grandmothers and grandchildren, met demands for the ballot with sly evasions and fire hoses, and paused from the gracious intercourse that typified polite 'ite society to take their turns as jurors and set lynchers and fire-bombers free.

If the liberals had been pathetic, the so-called conservatives more often than not had been evil—at least that was Mitch's take on the generations that had preceded ours. Of course, he would never have conceded the "conservative" label to those racists and their apologists. Mitch saw conservatism's core as the defense of liberty, and liberty—*individual* freedom—exalted character over classification and personal merit over group-based stereotypes. Mitch knew plenty of principled young conservatives who saw the world in that colorblind way, and they attracted him. But he also perceived much of the GOP as unwelcoming, or at best indifferent, to people like him. For too many Republicans and no small number of Democrats, race remained a tool, a tactic, and a constant temptation. Mitch found plenty of offenders in both parties who were willing to play the race card when it served their purposes, and he was sure they all had to be overcome before any truly "post-racial" political order could be achieved.

The first step, though, seemed abundantly clear to Mitch. He and his people had to break free of their current political chains to achieve the true independence that God and Country had promised them. Mitch saw things that way during his time in Charlottesville, especially after the dust-up on affirmative action. Only later did he come to believe that his people's long journey to freedom—surviving and overcoming through Providence and perseverance—had equipped them uniquely to lead people of all races back to the true faith and set them free.

In the meantime, he set aside whatever remaining reservations he had about controversial associations and questionable motives, and became a Republican. It was, he often would say later to curious questioners, "the true party of liberation, from Lincoln to Reagan, even if it sometimes lost its way."

I suppose most people would find Mitch's story to be either inspiring or infuriating, depending on their political persuasion. But at the time I found his deepening political obsession mainly to be inconvenient. I could think of a lot of great ways to spend my time—girls, parties, golf, cards, ball, hunting, fishing, reading history, girls—and politics was nowhere on the list. It is ironic, therefore, that I was the one who made the crucial introduction that landed Mitch in the heart of Neversworld and, ultimately, on that stage at the 1982 Virginia GOP convention. It happened during our sophomore year, when Mitch was on campus for our big Greek Week bash. Bart Bell was there, too, and I connected them. The discussion almost immediately turned to politics, which was inevitable, and Bart was thrilled to learn that Mitch held strongly conservative views and even was considering joining the U.Va. College Republicans. Bart offered to introduce him to the GOP activists in Charlottesville and others around the state, and Mitch's political pursuits took off from there.

How and why the Nevers for Senate high command made the decision a year or so later to entrust the principal nominating speech to Mitch, I still do not know for sure. Given the delegates' reaction to the speech and Nevers' improbable success that day, it looked like a brilliant stroke. But the choice apparently had more to do with necessity than genius. Nevers was a dark-horse candidate; most of the GOP's statewide luminaries were supporting one of his first-tier opponents, and there was no way to match that star power. So, as Bart explained it, Nevers and his team decided instead to go for a forward-looking contrast. With Mitch, they certainly got that contrast ... and a lot more. Given the way Bart's trickery helped Nevers win on the fifth ballot, I doubt that the speech really affected the outcome of the convention. But, for my friend Preacher, it had a catalytic effect that would change his life and, over time, transform politics in Virginia and perhaps beyond.

It is a story that could only happen in America.

Mitch's great-grandfather had been a slave. His grandfather did not know how to read or write. Yet that same grandfather had sat with his son, Mitch's father, every day, listening to him report on what he had learned in school that day and making sure he completed every bit of his homework. Mitch's father had gone to college, an all-black one because it was his only legal option, and then had become a pastor and a political leader in his community, working for the Democrats because they were the one political party that had cared enough to champion civil rights for his generation. Now, it was Mitch's turn. Like his forebears, he would break sharply with the past and claim new ground in pursuit of the promised land of freedom.

Always the contrarian, Mitch was fond of quoting a memorable Martin Luther King Jr. sermon about the power of what Dr. King called "transformed nonconformity." By that, he meant the courage to go against the tide of popularity, to defy the standards by which the world judges, and to stand firmly for a righteous cause or moral principle. Dr. King used the example of the faithful heroes from the Book of Daniel—Shadrach, Meshach, and Abednego—who refused to compromise their religious principles and bow down to an idolatrous image even though their defiance meant a likely death sentence from the king. Bowing would have been the convenient thing to do, the practical thing, so easy to rationalize in the name of getting along and moving ahead. And, yet, they refused to go along with the crowd and instead took their stand.

From that story, that sermon, and other counsel like it, Mitch had gained the inspiration to strike out on his own way, contrary though it was to the path of his forebears. Yet, for all the differences, there were greater similarities. Mitch shared the faith of his fathers and their irrepressible confidence that better days were ahead. And he believed deeply that he was part of a plan.

THE PULL OF POLITICS

While I was at the convention because of Mitch, Chad, and Abby, they were there because they had been inspired. The major inspiration had come not from Ned Nevers, the object of their current labors, but from Ronald Reagan. Though the 40th president was then the oldest man ever to seek the office, his 1980 campaign had a powerful effect on many younger voters, and my three friends were among them. Once they were engaged, Bart had made sure they did not get away.

Most young people today are like I was at that age—turned off by politics. But for the others what seems to make the difference are the players on the stage. I have noticed over time that whenever a young person gets captivated by politics, it is usually because an inspirational leader has cut through the din with a hopeful message and a summons to take part in a larger cause. He can be one of the oldest, like Reagan, or one of the youngest, like JFK. He can be on the Right, like Goldwater, or on the Left, like McGovern. He can be the champion of a great moral cause, like Martin Luther King Jr., or of a powerful idea, like Milton Friedman. For a lot of folks in my parents' generation it was FDR, and, before that, it was his older Republican cousin, Teddy. There have been many—some national and famous; others local and obscure. But the point is, you generally need a human catalyst to get a young person charged up about the political business.

There is an exception that proves this rule, however, and Bart Bell was a living example of it. Sometimes politics itself is enough to get people into politics. When that happens, it is not an inspirational leader or the pull of an idea, a calling to lead or desire to serve, that supplies the main impetus for involvement. Instead, the catalyst is the political process itself or some attribute of it. It may be the glitter and excitement, the thrill of competition, the gratification derived from winning affection and adulation, or the rush from acquiring and wielding power over others. Most likely, it is all four of those in some mix.

None is inherently corrupt. But when they are the principal motivations, whether crassly displayed or concealed beneath a thin veneer of public-spiritedness, you likely are headed for trouble.

That is where Bart was headed, but hardly anyone could have spotted it at the time. A product of the cosmopolitan suburban powerhouse that was (and still is) Fairfax County, Bart was smart and outgoing, creative and energetic, good-looking and positive-sounding. His Hampden-Sydney classmates elected him student body president, which said something. In his case, it was not so much anything that he planned or promised, or that he was particularly popular on campus. It was that he wanted the title more than anyone else wanted it, and he worked harder to get it. That "work" included submarining a couple of rivals with ugly rumors and buying off a couple more, but those things happened in the shoals while Bart accentuated the positive on the surface. He was so obviously destined for a consequential political career beyond Hampden-Sydney and Southside Virginia that it somehow would have seemed short-sighted to deny him the on-campus stepping stone. He was a talented guy who was going places, or so it seemed to most people. Even I tried to indulge that hopeful notion back in those days, but there was always unease. Like a horse spooked by an approaching storm, I just had a bad feeling about Bart down deep inside.

My three friends had no such hesitancy—at least, not at first. Prodded in different ways, each had become attuned to political events by the time Reagan ran for president in the fall of our sophomore year. They got involved in that exciting, transformative campaign and celebrated the Gipper's landslide victory that fall. In the process, they saw Bart in action and were mightily impressed. The tireless senior already was well-connected in statewide Republican circles and appeared to be master of everything. In addition to his on-campus leadership roles in student government and his fraternity, Bart was deputy campaign manager for the "Re-Elect Congressman Nevers" campaign, state chair of the College Republicans, and president of the "Young Virginians for Reagan" organization. The latter two posts took him to college campuses around Virginia where he exhorted students to help with registration drives and phone banks, organized rallies and "lit drops," rubbed elbows with prominent politicians, and got to know virtually all of the talented young GOP politicos in the state.

Bart's role as "deputy manager" of the Nevers reelection campaign in 1980 was mostly symbolic since the Congressman ended up with no serious

Democratic opponent that year. But after winning a third term representing the sprawling Southside congressional district, which ranged from the James River south to the Carolina line and from the southwestern outskirts of Richmond to the foothills of the Blue Ridge, Nevers had decided to go after a seat in the United States Senate two years hence. Bart concluded a deal by which he would work part-time on Nevers' political team throughout his senior year in college. Then he would join the team's skeletal campaign staff on a full-time basis in summer 1981—more than a year before the Senate election—and take on a key organizational role in what promised to be a hard-fought struggle to gain the party's nomination at the state convention the following summer.

How Bart came to be such an intimate and ally of the acclaimed Edward Kenneth Nevers at so young an age is still not altogether clear to me. A politico even before he came to Hampden-Sydney, Bart met Congressman Nevers at a candidates' forum on campus soon after his arrival. To hear them both tell it, the encounter was the political equivalent of love at first sight. Nevers was always in search of new talent, and he was immediately struck by the unusual intensity, maturity, and sophistication of the eager freshman. Bart got his first up-close exposure to a prominent elected official and was thrilled that the high-profile politician paid attention to him. Bart quickly became the ubiquitous super-volunteer in the Nevers organization, always around and willing to take on any task. Back home in the summers, he even ventured across the Potomac to volunteer as a gopher in the congressional office. It took little time for his responsibilities and standing in the Nevers councils to become more substantial. There were older and wiser operatives and advisors, to be sure. But by the time Bart left college and officially joined the adult political world, no one seemed to enjoy the Congressman's personal confidence as much as he.

While the Reagan campaign set the hook, it was Bart who pulled Mitch, Chad, and Abby into the boat and set them on the political course that was to dominate their lives for decades. It was not by happenstance. At Nevers' direction, Bart had surveyed the landscape with the aim of recruiting the best young political talent in Virginia.

"Find strong, healthy, good-looking kids who are smart and well-read," Bart recalled the Congressman commanding. "Make sure they are eager and alert, have common sense as well as book sense, plus the wit and poise to come across well at the headquarters and out on the campaign trail."

Bart knew the type because he exemplified it—and because he understood the Congressman's designs. Already a master-politician, Nevers understood that politics is a team sport and a young person's game. He not only wanted the agile minds, boundless energy, and naïve enthusiasm of the best youngsters for his own campaign—he wanted to deprive potential rivals of those assets. Plus, Nevers was a relatively young politician himself and was looking ahead. By co-opting the best and brightest wherever possible, Nevers was reducing the likelihood that they would develop ambitions of their own that later might collide with his.

Bart's search led him to many who were ready to help, and he enlisted them as regional organizers, local and campus volunteers, and in other roles. But despite the wide net he cast, Bart found none so impressive as my three friends and their special combination of brains, looks, dedication, and esprit de corps. He knew that style and substance were equally important to Nevers, and the trio scored high in both categories. In addition, each brought individual attributes that would become valuable to the Nevers-Bell cause over time. Chad was enterprising, innovative, and an aficionado of the free market—an economic orientation that fit well with the moderate Nevers, who often seemed uncomfortable with GOP social policy but was an exuberant advocate of the free enterprise system. Abby knew media relations and communications and brought intangible but obvious value to the team as an organizer and problem-solver. Mitch was vocal and somewhat unpredictable, with a self-righteous streak that did not sit particularly well with Nevers or Bell. But other Republican campaigns could only dream of having a cool and compelling African-American lieutenant to help them broaden the base and reach across party lines for support, so Mitch was a prize.

Bart recruited the three in 1981 by offering them summer internships in what he described as the Nevers for U.S. Senate campaign headquarters in downtown Richmond. In truth, there was no formal campaign and no real headquarters in place yet, just a musty room with a few phones and some well-worn desks and file cabinets that had been loaned by one of the Congressman's businessman friends. With the spring 1982 nominating contest eight months away and the general election more than a year ahead, a full-fledged campaign operation was still a few months off. But Nevers' political action committee would pay each of the interns a modest stipend, cover room and board in a run-down row house on Church Hill, and reimburse them for gas. The cool part was that they would be on the inside at the start of the Senate campaign and would be playing in the political big leagues with Congressman Nevers and his faithful sidekick Bart Bell. That was an alluring prospect, and it is easy to understand why Mitch and Chad jumped at the chance. Abby came along, too, though her decision to join them puzzled me.

With my friends on board, Nevers and Bart had their hotshot trio. But what they really wanted was a quartet—meaning, they also wanted me. Apparently our encounter the day of my folks' funeral had made an impression on the Congressman. If nothing else, his embarrassment upon later learning that he had expressed profound sympathy over the plight of my nonexistent little sister caused him to remember the *faux pas* and thus my name. But I suspect it caused more than that because no politician likes to be the object of sport, and I was the teenage smart-aleck who, though disconsolate on the day of his parents' burial, had the wit and temerity to make fun of Nevers when he misspoke. If pressed, I could cite any number of other personal attributes that would more than adequately explain why I was his quarry: acute intelligence, noble pedigree, suave demeanor, irresistible charm, perfect physique, and stylish deportment, just to name a few. But, kidding aside, I have pondered the question many times in the years that have passed, and I have always come back to the same conclusion: Nevers' interest in me at that early stage had mainly to do with the conquest. For a brief moment on the floor of the gymnasium at Orange County High, I insolently had exerted dominion over the august Edward K. Nevers, and from that moment I suppose I was destined to become his captive.

In any event, I spent little time wondering about Nevers' and Bart's motives in those days. I readily accepted the summer internship in Richmond because, despite my general aversion to Nevers and his kind of pursuits, I had failed to identify any summer job other than my usual opportunities in Orange, and I could not imagine going back to the house there without my parents. There was a practical consideration, too, in that I needed to make progress over the summer on my independent-study thesis on James Madison, and in Richmond I could do my research at the State Library. But the real reason was that my three friends were now my substitute family, and I wanted to hang with them for the summer even if it meant working for a bogus character like Nevers.

RAPID RISE

Of all the things I eventually would learn from and through Ned Nevers, by far the most important would be this: *People, some of them, really can change.* But that lesson lay well down the road. At the time, I regarded the man as a typical politician—mildly interesting, vaguely annoying, and generally uninspiring.

Nevers was a baby-boomer who hailed from the Valley of Virginia, from a small city named Staunton (pronounced "Stanton") situated at the junction of state Routes 250 and 11 (and now I-64 and I-81). The burg had been significant not only for what passed through it—the Warriors' Path of the Iroquois, Valley Turnpike, and the Central Virginia Railroad, among others—but for its early devotion to humanitarian causes, including institutions (progressive in their day) to care for the mentally ill and to educate young women and the disabled. Those facilities, along with several large hotels and many handsome homes, much of it in the Greek revival style, gave the city a certain gravitas in the 19th and early 20th centuries that had been somewhat diminished by the time Ned Nevers came along. The discredited eugenics movement, in particular, had taken its toll on the local reputation, with forced sterilizations occurring at the state-run Western State Hospital for several dark decades. Notwithstanding this blot, Staunton remained a charming Old South community that boasted, among other assets, a particular aptitude for preparing schoolteachers (at Mary Baldwin College), a country and gospel music group destined for the hall of fame (The Statler Brothers), and, above all, a famous political son (Woodrow Wilson, the eighth Virginia-born president of the United States).

Nevers did not share the Calvinist predilections of the 28th president or his rigid racial views, but he did have one thing in common with Wilson: They both left Staunton destined to make their political marks elsewhere. Wilson launched his White House pursuit from the New Jersey governorship, having come to that post via the presidency of Princeton. Nevers, who one day would seem like a decent bet to become the *ninth* Virginia-born president, returned from exemplary service as an Army captain in the Vietnam War, settled back down with the stunning Hollins girl he had wed soon after finishing VMI, and made his new life in her hometown of Blackstone, a community of several thousand good folks in rural Nottoway County about an hour southwest of Richmond. There, he accepted an agreeable position in one of the local banks—the one whose president, not coincidentally, was the father of the young Mrs. Nevers—and began eyeing the landscape for political opportunities.

Nevers had moved away, but his Staunton roots remained an important factor in his political outlook. At the time of his birth—roughly nine months after his father returned from helping to dispatch Hitler in Europe—Virginia, like the rest of the South, was a solidly Democratic state. In the wake of the Civil War and Reconstruction, "Republican" had been a dirty word for generations of Virginians, and it remained so well into the 20th century. Unlike today's Democrats, however, the ruling party in Virginia then was solidly conservative, and its adherents took their cue (and the name of their organization) from the state's political titan, U.S. Senator Harry Flood Byrd. There were pockets of Republican sentiment, especially in the highland counties where Civil War sympathies had run to the Union side generations earlier, and there were a few urban areas where Democrats with more liberal tendencies had some success. But during the days of Ned Nevers' youth, "Byrd Democrats" still won all the statewide contests and most of the local ones. In fact, the only serious political competition in most of the Commonwealth was in the Democratic Party's primary contests, which were tantamount to election.

Situated between the Byrd bastion of Winchester in the northern Shenandoah Valley and the more mountainous, more moderate, and occasionally more Republican areas to the south and west, Staunton during those days found itself both literally and figuratively in the middle. So did young Ned Nevers, whose father was a Byrd loyalist and whose mother, a contrarian by nature, made a point of casting protest votes for Republicans with increasing frequency and openness during his adolescence. By the mid-1960s, as Nevers moved through high school and on to the Virginia Military Institute down the Valley a ways in Lexington, a new generation of moderate-conservative young political leaders was emerging on the scene. They were the Republican "mountain and valley boys"—young lawyers, doctors, businessmen, and other achievers who recoiled at both the closed, conservative system of the Byrd Democrats in Virginia and the yawning liberalism of the national Democratic Party. Nevers found their middle course appealing, and in the years while he was away at war he took to identifying himself as a Republican whenever the conversation turned to politics.

By the time Nevers returned to Virginia in 1971, a political transformation was well underway in the Commonwealth. Economic expansion and diversification, election law reforms, civil rights legislation, shifting political alliances, rapid suburban growth, party leadership takeovers, and polarizing policy debates (especially on the war, law-and-order, school integration, and economic issues) all had culminated in a budding partisan realignment in the state. The tumultuous times after his return would see conservative Virginia Democrats exit the left-trending party of their fathers in droves and make common cause with moderate and conservative Republicans. It soon would produce an unprecedented and unexpected decade-long string of GOP victories in statewide, congressional, and legislative contests in the 1970s.

That Republican-dominated decade and the stunning developments that would produce it lay just over the horizon as Ned and Sally Nevers settled down for their new life together in Blackstone in 1971. It was a life to be dominated by a dizzying rise to power, improbable setbacks, striking accomplishments, and unspeakable tragedy—but for a time it looked like a political career that would fail to launch. Nevers was barely on the ground in Blackstone before he was contemplating potential pathways into politics. But he quickly realized that he was an avowed Republican in the one region of the state—rural Southside Virginia—that remained singularly wedded to the political, social, and fiscal conservatism and ancestral partisanship of the Byrd Democrats. There were very few Republicans in the town, at least few who would admit to it, and there seemed a real danger that even his father-in-law's vaunted place in local society might prove inadequate to save the young Nevers couple from being ostracized socially for their political heresies.

The situation looked daunting, but opportunity soon knocked, and when it did Nevers exhibited the distinctive mix of brass, brains, and innate political skill that would catapult him into the top rank of state and national politicians with remarkable speed. Upon the sudden death of the Byrd loyalist who was the area's octogenarian state senator in the autumn of 1972, young Captain Nevers—for that is how he now styled himself for political purposes—climbed into his car and drove to Richmond for an unscheduled meeting with Bob Billingsley, the Republican Party's energetic state chairman. There, he volunteered to be the party's first-ever candidate for the State Senate from the Southside senatorial district, and he brashly promised he would win. His campaign in the hurried special election would be well-funded—half by his wealthy father-in-law and half by the well-heeled captains of industry in Richmond (assuming the party chairman embraced his plan and helped deliver the latter). Nevers would campaign across the district day and night, at every stop recalling his military service and decrying the unpatriotic defeatism of the Democratic Party and its standard bearer, George McGovern. Never mind that most elected Virginia Democrats already had repudiated the presidential candidacy of the archliberal South Dakota senator. Never mind, also, that "McGovernism" had nothing to do with any matter before the State Senate in Richmond. The voters of Southside Virginia were more patriotic than partisan, said Nevers. They had no use for that Communist-coddling McGovern regardless of his party label, and they would not say "no" to a decorated Vietnam veteran who had fought for his country when others had taken flight.

With that single-minded, single-message campaign, Nevers pledged to deliver the Southside breakthrough in state legislative elections that the GOP state chairman and other Republican leaders so coveted. Within 48 hours, thanks partly to Billingsley but mostly to the well-heeled and fiercely loyal VMI alumni base in Richmond and Southside, Nevers had gained the funding pledges and vote commitments needed to capture the party's nomination without opposition. Eight weeks later, in the mid-December special election, he won the Senate seat by a margin of 17 votes out of more than 8,000 votes cast. A couple of weeks after that he prevailed in the recount, when his winning margin swelled to 36 votes, a comparative landslide. On January 10, the first day of the 1973 General Assembly session and a month shy of his 27th birthday—Captain Nevers was sworn in as "Senator Nevers," the first Republican state senator from his neck of the woods since Reconstruction.

This most improbable of political feats gained Nevers instant notoriety in Richmond, but he was barely in the state legislature long enough to learn the names of his colleagues, let alone get to know the other influential players who make things happen in the State Capitol. Instead of seeking reelection to a full term in the Virginia Senate in 1975, he declared for the Republican nomination in the Fifth Congressional District, won the party's nod again without opposition, and wrestled his way to a narrow victory in the 1976 general election. He arrived in Washington in January 1977 at age 30 and never looked back—except, of course, to campaign, which he did indefatigably.

Just five years after that arrival on the Capitol Hill scene, Nevers was ready to run for the United States Senate. Flush with a decade of successes in state elections and Reagan's huge 1980 presidential landslide, Republicans suddenly regarded their 1982 U.S. Senate nomination as an extremely valuable prize.

No less than five credible candidates were jockeying for position and preparing to formally declare their candidacies as soon as the November 1981 gubernatorial election had passed. Besides the boyish Nevers, the Senate contenders included one of his older colleagues from the Virginia congressional delegation, the popular Republican Party chairman who had underwritten Nevers' maiden political bid, the sitting Lieutenant Governor, and a two-decade veteran of the Virginia House of Delegates. The five hailed from varied parts of the far-flung state: Nevers from Staunton by way of Blackstone, and the others from Virginia Beach, Richmond, Bristol, and McLean, respectively. Each approached the contest with a respectable bloc of committed support, a mix of assets and liabilities, and a genuine shot at the nomination. All were much senior to Nevers and seemed far better positioned to win. My three friends and I got to know a whole lot about each of them because one of our main tasks for Bart Bell that summer was genteelly termed "opposition research."

When we returned to school in the fall for our junior year, my priorities diverged from those of Mitch, Chad, and Abby. I threw myself into my studies, with history and literature as my passions and admission to law school as my objective—though I allotted ample time to recreation and saw a marked improvement in my golf game. Although I did not advertise it, I also was developing a significant spiritual dimension during this time. There was no sudden conversion, just a growing sense—no doubt influenced by Dr. S. D.'s engaging counsel—that the distant and dour God of my youth had been replaced by a caring and approachable Friend. Meanwhile, my earthly friends burrowed deeper and deeper into the Nevers campaign, a development I watched with a mix of amusement and annoyance. Their political preoccupation and resulting unavailability for activities more agreeable to me continued to be a source of inconvenience. But I have to admit that even I got a little caught up in the excitement as the increasingly spirited Senate contest unfolded.

From late November until the party mass meetings and caucuses started in April, the five candidates went on the road for joint appearances in every part of the state. Almost every night they were attending some Republican county or city committee meeting or some other local forum. The arcane GOP nominating process allowed up to five people to be elected as delegates for every one delegate vote at the state convention, so personal appeals to grassroots party activists and sympathizers were crucial. The contest hinged on whom you could motivate to show up, first for the local mass meetings in the spring that would elect the convention delegates, and then for the June convention in Richmond that would choose the nominee.

All five candidates seemed to acquit themselves adequately in these joint appearances, but it was the affable young Ned Nevers who invariably stole the show. At least, that is how my friends saw it, as did other less-biased observers. I had the same reaction on the handful of occasions when the candidates were appearing down our way and I went along to hear them.

For one thing, Nevers was relaxed and folksy, and he understood the value of two tactics that do not come naturally to most politicians—self-effacing humor and brevity. Nevers had several different versions of his shtick, but he would usually start his remarks at the joint appearances by telling a story about his father, a decorated World War II fighter pilot. He knew that an admiring son's mention of his dad would appeal to these family-oriented Republican crowds, plus the reference to his father's military achievements inevitably would call to mind his own service. He invoked the family's church-going habits, too, for good measure.

"I learned something from my dad, who flew fighter planes over Europe and had two of them shot out from under him," Nevers would say.

> Dad never missed an opportunity after church on Sundays to compliment our pastor on the brevity of his sermons. He figured that a few extra minutes handing out some positive reinforcement would pay dividends the next Sunday and on down the road. So after church he would pull Reverend Hartsock over and introduce him to the first visitor he could find, and he would say, "Here is our wonderful pastor, Reverend Hartsock, and as you heard today, he always delivers a thought-provoking sermon and never misses a good stopping point. It's a real talent, you know. Sort of like landing an airplane. Don't circle the airport again and again, wastin' time and fuel. Just bring 'er right in and set 'er right down. That makes everyone happy and brings 'em back ready for the next mission—isn't that right, Reverend?" And, you know, I never heard Reverend Hartsock say anything other than "You got that exactly right, Major Nevers."

The crowd would chuckle and nod their heads appreciatively. The younger Nevers would pause and give them plenty of time to finish their chuckling and nodding so that everyone noticed he had scored with the story. Then he would clear his throat, look off in the distance thoughtfully, and say something like,

> You know, I think of that story right often during all these joint appearances. Folks listen to us most every night circling the airport in one town or another. It's sort of like the politicians I hear up on the floor of Congress—everything's been said but not everybody's said it, so they talk on and on. It's no wonder people tune politicians out. I once met a woman in a grocery store who wouldn't give me the time of day. So I asked her why so few people paid attention to politics; was it due to *ignorance* or *apathy?* She said, "I don't know, and I don't care."

The joke was a bit shopworn but would always bring another good laugh.

"Well, you're here because you do know and you do care," Nevers would continue.

> You and I are on a mission, and I'm not going to waste our fuel here this evening by circling the tower. I'm going to say right up front that these gentlemen are all fine folks, and every one of them would make a fine United States Senator. I admire 'em all—they're almost like father figures to me. They've each been at this political business for a long time, and God bless 'em for it. But there is only one of us who has never lost an election—only one who's won tough races when he was supposed to lose 'em. And there's only one of us you can count on to go out and hustle and win the U.S. Senate for the Virginia Republican Party this fall!
>
> If you give me the honor of being your nominee, I will bring this beautiful, shining jet fighter of a party home as a winner. But before I bring 'er in and set 'er down, I will put the Democrats through a dogfight they'll never forget. I

will take the fight to 'em on high taxes and waste in government, on preservin' our free enterprise system against bungling bureaucrats and big-spending politicians, on stayin' strong and alert so our kids can live in peace and freedom instead of under the jackboot of Communism. These are life and death issues, and it's not just Republicans who see them like we do—it's right-thinking independents and sober Democrats, too. Down my way in Southside there aren't many folks who call themselves Republicans, but they keep sending me to Congress anyway because they are freedom-loving Americans.

And, you know what—when we all meet up on Sundays outside church like my Dad and Reverend Hartsock and all the other good folks, it isn't Republicans huddling over here and Democrats over there and Independents someplace else. We're all standing there together as *Americans*. And together we thank the Good Lord for our many blessings—for the sermon that was short but made us think, for the Sunday dinner we'll enjoy in peace and freedom, and for the fact that we live in the greatest state in the greatest nation that the world has ever known....

At this apparent ending, with Nevers' voice cresting as he paid homage to "the greatest state in the greatest nation," the crowd invariably would break into warmly appreciative applause. Nevers would bask in the reaction while appearing to want to tamp it down, and then when they quieted he would wind it up with something like this:

I should stop right there, after that very generous response, but my Mom taught me something just like my Daddy did— she taught me to say, "Thank you." Thank you to all of you for being here with us this evening. Thank you for coming to the mass meeting in a few weeks and the convention in June. And thank you for all the hard work that you, the grassroots of our party and the backbone of our Commonwealth, do to make us successful at election time. Without you and all you do, we up here would just be flying paper airplanes...

The crowd would be clapping and smiling as he sat down, and the whole thing would have taken only six or seven minutes. Usually a joint question-and-answer session would follow the five candidate speeches. Nevers always kept his answers short and superficial, interjecting anecdotes and adages and personal touches whenever appropriate. He was a smart man—smart enough to know he was there to ingratiate, not educate.

The exception was when one of his opponents took a swipe at him on some issue. Whenever that happened, Nevers would feign a measure of disappointment and say something about preferring to save the dogfight for the Democrats, then he would meet the opponent's point clearly and forcefully, sometimes brutally. He would conclude by firing a serious shot of his own, almost always in a way that made his rival regret having started the fracas. The audience came away with the sense that this Nevers guy really knew his stuff and it was a good thing he was so doggone nice and conserving his fire for the Democrats because otherwise he probably would dismantle these other candidates nightly with ease. It did not take long before the other four candidates came to a similar conclusion and stopped lobbing volleys in his direction. Instead, they trained their sights on each other, which tended to make them look like petty bickerers while Nevers, wise beyond his years and seemingly statesmanlike, stayed above the fray.

During these engagements, my three friends should have been thrilled by Nevers' success, but I noticed that they frequently came away a bit frustrated. The Congressman indeed had done his homework—or, rather, my three friends had done his homework—but only a small fraction of the extensive material they developed on the other four candidates' past statements, voting records, and other vulnerabilities ever got used in these appearances. It was even less apparent that the policy briefs Chad and I prepared on various issues had any practical value. Over time, we all would learn that it takes a huge amount of work to be ready for those few, brief moments when what a candidate is able to say on the spot matters. We also would learn that a lot of what matters in a campaign happens beneath the surface.

The beneath-the-surface activity was well known to Bart Bell. The subterranean setting, in fact, was where he did his best work, if you want to call it that. At each event, he was evidently ebullient—dapper and smiling, encouraging supporters, confidently predicting success, and striking a statesmanlike pose akin to his boss's, albeit in miniature. But behind this earnest and positive exterior was a natural manipulator who reveled in intrigue. He spun reporters, always off the record, with the latest gossip on the Nevers rivals. If there was insufficient dirt for real, he would simply make up something insidious, injecting it into the campaign's undercurrent like a mosquito injects malaria into the bloodstream. At times, he behaved less like a mosquito and more like a tick, burrowing in deeply and remaining there as long as necessary to cause serious trouble. His sordid methods became fully apparent to us only over time, but we got our first glimpse of them at the Republican convention that June.

TRICK AND TRIUMPH

The convention session was a marathon that began in the morning and lasted into the early evening. But on Friday night before the Saturday voting, many of the delegates and alternates crowded into sweaty hospitality suites at the aging Hotel John Marshall and other nearby venues where lips were lubricated and arms twisted. They then dispersed to their own hotels throughout the capital city and surrounding suburbs for the evening. My friends had various campaign duties, and Chad was responsible for coordinating the quiet dissemination of Nevers campaign flyers under all those hotel doors during the wee hours of Saturday morning. The flyer, no doubt designed by Bart, was a positive-sounding missive in the form of a newsletter. Delegates awakened to read confident-sounding predictions of an improbable Nevers victory and a personal appeal from the Congressman for Republican unity during the nominating convention and in the days after the historically competitive contest was decided. "Congressman Nevers Predicts November Victory if Virginia GOP Honors Ronald Reagan's 11th Commandment ('Thou shalt not speak ill of another Republican')," blared the newsletter's headline.

Uniting the party and winning in November likewise were the themes when Nevers gave his pre-balloting speech to the delegates on Saturday morning. Each of the five candidates was allotted a few minutes to greet the delegates and make a personal pitch before the formal nominations and accompanying floor demonstrations commenced. As usual, Nevers managed to use the time better than his rivals. Some of the lines were familiar: "… these gentlemen are all fine folks, and every one of them would make a fine United States Senator…. I admire them all." And: "…there is only one of us who has never lost an election—only one of who's won tough races when he was supposed to lose them...." But there was also this:

> If you nominate me today, I promise to deliver a strong, positive message that will bring this Republican Party together for a great victory this fall—the moderates and the conservatives, the grassroots and the business leaders, the good folks from the suburbs and the mountain-and-valley boys, the lifelong Republicans and the Byrd Democrats whose party has abandoned them, the people who believe in freedom from Communism abroad and freedom from government meddling in the economy here at home, the folks who believe in the right to life and the right to work and the right to bear arms, the folks who understand that families are the foundation of our good society and that faith and freedom are the fountainhead of every good nation. United we stand, divided we fall! *My name is Nevers and I am never, ever negative.* Join me and we will wage a positive campaign that will bring together Republicans and right-thinking Independents and Democrats for a great victory this November!

After a hard-fought contest over many months, Nevers' appeal for unity resonated particularly well with the delegates. It perfectly fit the sunny, approachable persona that the Congressman had assiduously cultivated during his rapid political rise. Indeed, it was the message and persona that Bart Bell had counseled continually in every setting and situation that my friends and I had observed since becoming involved in the Nevers campaign. Nevers would be the consensus "good guy"—if not the delegates' first choice, then an agreeable alternative once their preferred candidate faltered. For that reason, Bart's clandestine maneuver at the beginning of the fourth ballot struck me as especially underhanded.

The first two ballots had gone predictably. Delegate Dan Dahlgren of McLean, a 20-year-plus legislative veteran and chairman of the powerful House Appropriations Committee, found that his legislative preeminence translated into campaign cash but little grassroots support. So he had bowed out graciously after landing in last place on the first ballot. Dahlgren's exit had been followed after the second ballot by the withdrawal of Bob Billingsley, the Richmond banker and conservative state GOP chairman who enjoyed the gratitude of the party rank-and-file for his selfless service in the trenches but who just did not strike many of the delegates as "electable" in the fall.

The successive departures of Dahlgren and Billingsley had left three candidates in the race as the third ballot began: Congressman Clarence "Bud" Gordon, a former Byrd Democrat from Virginia Beach who had converted to the GOP just three years earlier; Lieutenant Governor Bill Smyth, a lifelong Republican who had grown up just north of the Tennessee line in Washington County; and Nevers. Congressman Gordon, the solidly conservative favorite of the party establishment and expected frontrunner, had led on the first two ballots. In second place, several hundred votes behind, had been Lieutenant Governor Smyth. Smyth's conservative views generally aligned with Gordon's, and the Lieutenant Governor also had the benefit of strong regional backing from the mountain-and-valley moderates in his native Southwest. Nevers, the outlier and long-shot, had turned more than a few heads by finishing in third place, ahead of Dahlgren and Billingsley, on the first ballot. Plus, he had picked up more of the withdrawn Dahlgren's delegates than expected on the second ballot. But he was still a ways back, and, as delegates had returned to their seats for the third round of balloting, most in the hall thought the stage was set for a showdown between the two conservative frontrunners.

When the convention secretary announced the third-ballot results, a murmur of surprise had rippled through the stuffy, packed hall before the partisan chants resumed. Gordon's lead had increased as supporters of the exiting Billingsley went disproportionately into his camp, a development that recharged the frontrunner's momentum and made a Gordon victory seem even more inevitable. The surprise, however, had been Nevers. Having captured many more of the party chief's delegates than Smyth, he now had moved into second place by a handful of votes.

Each political convention is a living organism, guided by facts and reason to a point, but always a volatile mix of adrenalin and emotion, and often given to fits of passion born of the basest human traits. About this Bart seemed to have uncanny insights, and he had this particular situation figured just right. Gordon was leading but remained about a hundred votes shy of the majority needed for nomination. Smyth's supporters were fiercely loyal and were standing firm, but the chemistry of the pulsing arena was now against him. The Lieutenant Governor had suffered a big psychological setback by slipping, ever so slightly, into third place on the third ballot. The moment was right for Nevers to make a move.

As Bart explained later, he had not been sure exactly when or how it would happen, but he always had known it would come down to Gordon, Smyth, and Nevers in some order. And since Gordon and Smyth were generally regarded as the rock-ribbed conservatives in the field, something had to happen to shake things up or one of them eventually would fall heir to the other's support and clinch the nomination. Nevers, the relentlessly positive pol, had positioned himself well, impressing many with his winsome ways and offending no one. But his message seemed a bit vapid to the more ideological partisans who tended to dominate such GOP proceedings. Nevers needed a game-changer to win, and, as the delegates returned to their seats for the fourth round of balloting, Bart was ready.

Chad had been coordinating floor communications and literature distribution for the Nevers campaign, and so he noticed it right away. A bevy of young volunteers who had been assigned to the Nevers count room downstairs and who, until now, had been anonymously working the telephones and calculators in the bowels of the Coliseum, suddenly had fanned out on the convention floor, running from delegation to delegation dropping off those stacks of neon orange flyers that Bart's messenger had told me to give them. The other campaigns had long since depleted their stores of literature, and so, Chad thought, had the Nevers campaign. With nothing much new out on the floor to read for hours, the delegates all seemed to be eagerly grabbing and examining the bright-colored flyers. Chad hustled over to pick up one, and he was confused by what he read—but only for a moment.

The missive appeared to be the handiwork of the front-running Gordon campaign. Congressman Gordon's name was nowhere to be found on it, but what did appear prominently at the top and bottom was Gordon's unmistakable silhouette along with a phrase he had used repeatedly during the springtime joint appearances: "Control of the U.S. Senate is at stake in this election; we are in a life and death struggle for the future of our country; and it is our solemn duty to win this decisive battle here in Virginia." From the look and content, most delegates inferred—*erroneously*—that Bud Gordon's campaign produced the document.

While Gordon's name was absent from the flyer, the name that did appear, and very prominently so, was Lieutenant Governor Bill Smyth's. It appeared before a colon, and after the colon were six or seven bullet points—short statements, devoid of any citations, charging Smyth with a variety of misdeeds, from legislative conflicts of interest and enriching himself personally in public life, to voting for large tax and fee increases on four occasions, to voting against pro-life legislation and supporting onerous firearm restrictions, among other heresies. It was later apparent that all of the allegations either were gross distortions or completely false, but the facts were not the point. The point was that Bud Gordon's campaign had directly and viciously attacked Bill Smyth, or so it seemed to nearly everyone in the hall. It seemed that way to all except the Gordon high command, which would never have done something so stupid, and to the master of this misdirection, our dashing and dastardly colleague, Bart.

Bart had intended to make the Smyth partisans angry at Gordon and Gordon's supposedly negative tactics, setting the stage for a resentment-fueled shift to Nevers. But even Bart could not have imagined what happened next. Enraged upon seeing the flyer, the red-faced Lieutenant Governor Smyth strode over to the Virginia Beach delegation looking for Congressman Gordon. He found him on an elevated perch in the back left corner of the convention floor, and so the angry exchange that ensued was visible to thousands of delegates. A hush came over the crowd; the fourth round of balloting in delegations seemed to suspend as people looked up to see what was the matter; and there in the corner was Lieutenant Governor Smyth, neon flyer in hand, cranium aglow in the lights, gesticulating wildly as a head-shaking Congressman Gordon tried to turn away. Even without the sound, it took little imagination for anyone in the hall to figure that harsh words had passed between the two heretofore collegial conservative leaders of the Virginia Republican Party.

The balloting resumed, and by the time the fourth tally was complete, it was apparent that the Smyth candidacy was doomed. His delegate total did not slip a lot, but he was already suffering from his third-place showing on the preceding ballot, and the negative momentum created by even the modest slippage on the fourth was too great to reverse. Most important, the movement by Smyth delegates, though only about a hundred of them, was almost entirely into the Nevers column. Unthinkable just hours before, the pattern was now set. The fury in the Smyth camp toward Gordon, already palpable, intensified as the Lieutenant Governor's supporters realized his cause was lost. Many cast around on the floor for previously discarded Nevers signs and took to the aisles, joining the Nevers partisans in a loud "Ned Nevers Now!" chant that quickly overwhelmed the "Gor-don Go!" chorus by the frontrunner's supporters. Ready for this moment, the Nevers high command had every volunteer they could muster, including yours truly, swarm the hall passing out bright red and white "Nevers NOW!" lapel stickers that were identical in all but one respect to the "Nevers Next!" versions the upstart's supporters had been donning all day.

It was an amazing, exhilarating phenomenon to experience. The fifth round of voting saw Nevers, the young star and ever-smiling apostle of party unity, surge past the powerful Gordon to victory. Even some of Gordon's grudging converts on preceding ballots, irked by his apparently negative antics, now joined the Nevers bandwagon—*and why not?* After all, Nevers was the one candidate who had been unwaveringly positive throughout the contest.

Bart's "false flag" flyer might have caused a scandal if anyone had discerned his trickery soon enough and had appreciated how effective the ploy had been in manipulating the emotional course of the convention. But such details tend to get lost in the political shuffle and in the inevitable ambiguity of big and complicated events. The vigorous denials from the Gordon camp were predictable, and they fell on predictably deaf ears, especially since the winner of the contest was the refreshing Congressman Nevers who had wisely stayed out of the Smyth-Gordon contretemps. A rehash of the convention sparring seemed impertinent now that all eyes were on Nevers and his general election match-up with the Democratic nominee, former state Attorney General Miles Murphy. But Bart learned an important lesson from the episode—the unwholesome lesson that scurrilous stunts can be wildly successful—and his course was probably set from there. Chad repeatedly asked him about the flyer, and the self-satisfied Bart, grinning from ear to ear, never admitted anything. "Those cocky Gordon people were just too clever by half, and they blew it. Let it be a lesson to you," he smirked.

In the fall, things went decidedly Nevers' way. He and his team conducted a safe, methodical campaign, and they could play it that way mainly because they had the good fortune to draw the right Democratic opponent. It turned out that Murphy had some serious baggage, including questionable contributions from companies with interests in the Attorney General's office during his tenure, and that was the kind of thing Bart was not going to overlook.

Murphy also had too many connections to left-of-center Democrats for the taste of Virginia's moderate-conservative swing voters. Nevers' victory margin was not huge—the winner's advantage rarely is wide in the hyper-competitive two-party system that has existed in Virginia since the early 1970s. But the Republican nominee managed to roll up nearly 53 percent of the vote, and that made it a solid win.

A HEALTHIER DIET

Shortly after the election, Senator-elect Nevers and Bart met with Chad, Abby, and Mitch, and offered them all junior jobs in his Senate office. He even offered to hold the positions open from January until early May, when all three would graduate from college. They had performed commendably on virtually every assignment they received during the campaign, Nevers observed; Bart's advice that they could be entrusted with responsibility beyond their years had been proven correct. Needless to say, my flattered friends jumped at the chance for employment on Capitol Hill straight out of college, even in minor roles. I am sure they would have accepted anyway, but the fact that the positions were offered to them personally by Virginia's new United States senator surely made the elixir more potent.

The young Senator-elect asked me to join them, too, and he dispatched Bart to reel me in—but I declined. Even the excitement of Nevers' upset victory did not leave me much impressed with the business of politics. I could tolerate it in small doses, but a steady diet of the stuff did not appeal to me at all. The opportunity for a government job admittedly was attractive given my strained financial situation, but I was pretty sure that if I yielded to that temptation now I would never make it to law school and to the career as a criminal prosecutor that I then saw as my calling.

Bart, however, would not give up. The Senator-elect had told him to make it happen, and at this stage in his Nevers relationship Bart fretted that any notable failure to deliver might mortally wound his standing. He came back again and again during the spring of my senior year until this exchange finally ended it.

"You cannot say 'no' to a United States senator, Danny," Bart insisted. "You just can't—especially this one. He's the king of the state now, and mark my words, one day he's gonna be running the country. You just don't say 'no' to the man on the throne."

"I thought we got rid of kings here about two centuries ago, Bart. I know I read that somewhere. There was a tea party, and some dudes nearly froze one winter, then the French fleet hung out in the Bay while the Beatles played 'The World Turned Upside Down,' and then—"

"You're really hilarious, Danny. Look, this is *important*. You've got a U.S. senator who thinks you're a wizard. He calls you his 'Madison,' for Pete's sake—says you write better stuff than anyone else around. And, for whatever reason, he likes the way you operate. He expects you to come and do this, and saying 'no' is not an option."

"It's an option for me. This is still a free country—remember?"

"Yeah, well, freedom ain't all it's cracked up to be when you have a United States senator who's on your case. I mean, think about it. Didn't you just ask me a few weeks ago if I thought Nevers would write a recommendation for you to U.Va. for law school?"

"Yes," I said warily. He now had my attention.

"Well, you can kiss that goodbye. I don't think he's going to be real eager to help you out when he offers you a dream job in D.C. and you tell him to shove it. C'mon, Danny, just take the job and work with us on the Hill. You can go to law school in the evenings at Georgetown—"

"That isn't going to happen," I cut him off. "I'm going to U.Va., and the truth is, I really don't need a letter from the great Edward K. Nevers to get me in. I just thought it would be the icing on the cake. But forget it…."

"Look, Danny, you're not thinking straight here. There are a lot of levers of power a senator can pull. You don't need to make an enemy out of Virginia's new political star. It's just not smart."

"Who said anything about making an *enemy* of him, Bart? Geez! Does the guy think he owns people? I guess you're just fine with being his boy."

"Damn straight I'm fine with it, and you should be fine with it, too."

"Look, Bart, I know you want to deliver me to Nevers, and for some reason it's a big deal to him. But it is not going to happen. I don't want a steady diet of politics; it's not the way I plan to live my life. So let's find a smart way to deal with this."

"Well, if you have a way out, I'm all ears," Bart allowed.

After a few moments, I gave him a plan.

"How about you go to the Congressman—er, the Senator—sit him down on that throne of his, and tell him that we talked about it and that I am very flattered by the offer. Tell him that we discussed the best way I can help the team, and we both realized I'm the only one in his kiddie corps who has both the desire and creds to go on to law school. Tell him that I'm open to the possibility of signing onto his team after that if he still wants me, and then I'll have a law degree and maybe I can help in ways others cannot. Yeah, that's it—tell him I'll be more valuable to you all as a lawyer. Tell him all that, and I'll go along with it, and I'll do my best to keep an open mind about the future. And if there are things I can do to help out you guys in the meantime, I will. Honestly, politics isn't for me—plus, between you, Mitch, Abby, and Chad and the rest of Nevers' staff, I can't see what I could possibly add. But present it to him that way—convince him that my detour is in his own best interest—and let's see if it gets us past this."

Bart pondered momentarily before acceding. "Well, my oddball friend, I wish you weren't so stubborn, but under the circumstances what you've laid out makes some sense. You say you don't like politics, but there must have been a schemer in that woodpile somewhere."

I could see his mind continuing to calculate as he refined the way he would present this plan to his king. "Yep, it just might work," he said after the pause.

"Okay, it's your plan now, so go sell it. And if you are half as good as you think you are, you'll be able to get me that recommendation letter, too."

A copy of the flattering recommendation letter showed up several weeks later. It did not matter because I already had gotten a call from the director of admissions at U.Va. Law telling me I was in, but it was like a certificate of good standing. Along the bottom, Nevers had scratched a personal note that made it obvious how Bart had presented the deal.

"Get good grades in Charlottesville, visit us when you can, and finish on time so you can get up here and help us out," he wrote.

A BAD DREAM

It was a beastly hot Sunday in mid-May—Mother's Day—when I paraded out from under the broad canopy of white oaks and ascended the platform in front of stately Venable Hall to claim my hard-earned diploma. In the shadow of that landmark where aspiring young ministers once had been schooled and where I myself had outgrown grief, I felt the deep satisfaction of one who had persevered and prevailed. But as I strode across the platform, my eyes were drawn outward, into the audience where all the proud parents gazed up lovingly at their sons. In that unguarded moment I unconsciously scanned for my own mom and dad before my mind snapped me cruelly back to reality. Shuddering, I turned to meet the smiling, sympathetic visage of President Small, who held my diploma in one hand as he stretched out his other to clasp mine.

The moment was an apt metaphor for the past three years. Elsewhere, I might have been an orphan lost in the crowd, but this caring community had folded me in its arms and kept me straight. It had taught and tested me, yes— but it also had consoled, cheered, counseled, and encouraged. Both Danny the Idiot and Danny the Image were now long gone, and in their place stood a competent, confident graduate, stretched and shaped by a rigorous liberal arts education and by a dreadful dose of life's hard medicine, ready to find his way in the world and do his part. Much more than an education, I had gained an extended new family after my natural one was lost, and I would forever cherish my home on the hill that is Hampden-Sydney.

The problem with that kind of affection, though, is that it hurts an awful lot when you have to say goodbye. The best remedy is to get on with the next thing, and for me that was law school. With my friends moving to D.C., I did what before had seemed unimaginable and returned to Orange for the summer, staying with an older couple from our church and saving some money by working at the plant my father used to own. My thoughts, though, were fixed on the next adventure. In mid-August, I filled up my aging Chevy with all my essentials and anxious energy and made my way down the road a few miles to the entirely new world that awaited in Charlottesville.

It proved to be a challenging experience, but sticking to my guns and going to law school rather than Capitol Hill was definitely the right call. I found the three years there to be more stimulating than anything I had done before. The people were varied and fascinating; the courses were hard but interesting; the professors, with rare exceptions, were classy, clever, and committed. Contrary to what I heard about other law schools from friends and older classmates, the culture was collegial rather than cutthroat, and the students and professors were upbeat, not dour. I discovered that the law is not a set of rules, as I had assumed, but an intricate body of collective wisdom as rich as the history in which it developed. I discovered, too, that the main fruit of law school labors is not a storehouse of legal propositions to be retrieved at will but a linear manner of reasoning that substitutes analytical rigor for loopy, ponderous meandering. At the end of the three years, I could say, like the popular TV commercial of that time, "Thanks, I needed that." It helped me organize my mind in ways I would use for the rest of my life.

The beginning, however, was a *bear*. As a first-semester law student, you really do not know how you are doing in any class until you finish the final exams and get your grades. Its political equivalent is the winner-take-all primary or caucus—there is just one shot, and everything turns on it. If there was a monitoring device that could measure critical levels of stress, students approaching the end of the first semester in law school would be constantly setting off the alarm. Of course, being well qualified, nearly everyone does just fine. And, after that, law school gets much easier—downright fun, in fact—because the uncertainty goes away and you are left with the work and the play, both of which are really great in Charlottesville.

While my time at U.Va.'s celebrated law school produced a cache of happy memories and enduring friendships, I still look back on late 1983, the final weeks of my first semester there, as among my toughest times mentally. Like other trials I would experience, the only way to get through it was to keep your head down, focus, and *do the work*. There was no substitute for that, no easy way around it. "You just have to put one foot in front of the other and head up the hill," my Dad would have said. And even if you had faith to lean on (something I was still working on at the time), there was the stern counsel attributed to my alma mater's namesake, Algernon Sydney: "God helps those who help themselves." Sydney, of course, was a much better philosopher than theologian, but in my father's absence his kick in the rear end was useful.

So I willed myself to work and tried hard not to waste time and energy worrying.

It was in that pressure-packed timeframe that the gathering storm in the office of fledgling Senator Edward K. Nevers unleashed its fury, and I was called in as an emergency responder.

I had not seen much of my friends during that autumn—they were busy with their demanding new jobs on Capitol Hill, and I was fully consumed with law school. But whenever I did see or talk to them it was apparent that all was not well in Neversworld. Moving to the Senate from the House had been a bigger change than anyone, including the young senator, had imagined. In the House by age 30, he had been something of a curiosity—but for his military bearing, he might have been mistaken for a page—and no one had expected much from him there. He had attended diligently to the needs of his Southside constituents and had spent every opportunity back in the district seeing and being seen. The toughest issue he had to confront was whether to vote with his GOP colleagues for free trade legislation or to look out for the ailing textile industry in his district. Nevers had not hesitated on that one; he embraced protectionism. A fellow congressman had urged him to take a principled stand in support of free trade, reminding him of the Irish statesman Edmund Burke's counsel that a representative owes his constituents a vote based on conscience. Nevers replied that in his district there probably were a few people who cared about Burke, but there were a lot more who had lost their jobs or feared they soon would, so he figured he would let their conscience be his guide.

In the Senate, however, anonymity and parochialism were not so easily sustained, especially for a 37-year-old phenom who had confounded the pundits, bested a talented field, and arrived at the northern end of the Capitol exuding a confidence easily taken for cockiness. Now he was in the limelight, and what he said and how he voted mattered to a lot more people.

The first few months had gone well enough, but by the summer and early fall the cracks in the Nevers operation had begun to show. Instead of hiring experienced staffers steeped in the often byzantine ways of the Senate, he had manned his office mainly with young folks from his House staff and senatorial campaign. Politics indeed is a young person's game, and Nevers appreciated the near-boundless supply of zeal and energy that youth brings to the political project. But experience counts when it comes to governing, and, by Labor Day, Virginia's new senator and his team seemed "junior" in more ways than just longevity. First, they screwed up on the major transportation package, failing, despite the Senate's GOP majority, to secure funding for the Northern Virginia transit and highway improvements that had been among Nevers' prominent promises during the campaign. Then in quick succession came a series of more serious missteps.

The Senator first sided with Democrats and GOP moderates on a budget-balancing plan that included a mix of new tax levies and budget cuts. His expression of support appeared to contradict the strong anti-tax pronouncements he had made during the recent campaign, and he was roundly denounced by Republican partisans back home. Wilting under the fire, the startled Senator soon changed his position and sided with Senate conservatives to defeat cloture and kill the measure. He made a similar about-face on a bill to deny funding to states that did not require parental consent for teenage abortions. After voting for the measure in committee, he bowed to arguments about its constitutional infirmity—plus pressure from vocal female constituents—and voted against it on the floor. Even on national defense, where Nevers seemed to know his mind, there was equivocation. He first announced that he would vote with the President on a sale of new military technology to moderate Arab states and then reversed himself under heavy pressure from the pro-Israel lobby. These and a number of lesser stumbles had quickly taken their toll on Nevers' public standing, and his reputation on Capitol Hill took an even greater hit.

In the House, Nevers had been able to bob and weave on tough issues largely without scrutiny, but now the press was all over him. Even the conservative-leaning editorial pages among the state's major newspapers—pages that had strongly endorsed him just a year earlier—joined a chorus now chiding him for indecision, flip-flops, and broken promises. A couple of unflattering notions about the state's young new senator began to take hold. One was that he was in over his head—that his rise had been too meteoric for his or the state's good. The other was that the man simply did not seem to know what he stood for.

Nevers had not previously experienced the withering gale of a media storm or even the occasional cloudbursts that weather more practiced politicians. During his first and only statewide campaign he had glided along with relative ease while his opponent, plagued by a series of damaging revelations, had taken most of the incoming fire. Then had come a wave of fawning, even gushing, post-election stories—Nevers the political prodigy, Nevers the rising star, Nevers the master politician—that would have been enough to turn even the grayest head. He was, as one magazine cover story declared, the "Golden Boy of Virginia Politics." Accustomed to such praise, and no doubt believing he deserved it, Nevers did not respond at all well to the sudden avalanche of criticism that came his way less than a year into his term. Encountering his first real adversity in public life, Nevers was certain that someone else, primarily his staff, was to blame. He grew increasingly irritable, had trouble sleeping, and lashed out unpredictably at his aides on matters large and small. The missteps kept coming, and by the time Abby called me, the situation had become critical.

"I know you are still in the middle of exams, and I hate to call you," Abby said when she finally reached out to me. "Mitch and Chad both said not to bother you. There's nothing you can do at this point anyway. But we're all at our wit's end."

Barely half a year into what had seemed like the dream job for three wide-eyed politicos fresh out of college, my friends suddenly were living a nightmare. Nevers reportedly had been threatening to fire just about everyone, saying they all had let him down. Abby described a terror-filled office in which events had taken a particularly bizarre turn in recent weeks, including several episodes where Nevers—evidently strung out due to lack of sleep—had raged at staffers, including Mitch and Chad, in a manner that struck all of them as irrational.

"The Senator says we need a plan, an agenda. He says we've had all these mistakes and misfires because no one working for him is capable of preparing a plan," explained Abby. "He says no one here understands his positions so we keep giving him wrong advice. I bet we have put together probably three dozen memos on various issues, Danny, and each one has carefully outlined what is coming down the pike and where he should be on those issues. But each time he balls it up and then starts ranting that it's not a plan, that we don't understand what a political plan or a legislative agenda is, that we would not know a strategic plan if it knocked us in the head, that we just don't get it. And on and on. It is *awful*."

Abby sounded like she was holding back tears, so I started to say something. But before I could comment she continued.

"So here we were yesterday; we were all still scratching our heads about the last outburst when Bart came in and said, 'Okay, folks, I'm afraid this is it. The Senator is at the end of his rope. He really believes you people have no idea what he wants—that you don't know or care what he stands for and what he came to the Senate to accomplish. He says you're just here collecting a paycheck and taking advantage of him. I know that sounds harsh, but please don't blame me—I'm just the messenger, and a reluctant one at that. Anyhow, earlier today the Senator fired Chief of Staff Douglas and appointed me as his successor. And I am very sorry that one of my first duties is to let you know that he would like your resignations as well. You have two weeks' notice, and the Senator will write an appropriately positive letter of recommendation for each of you. He feels he needs to make a change to make room for people who share his values and vision. He wants a fresh start as we enter the new year.'"

"You mean he is firing you and Mitch and Chad?" I asked Abby incredulously.

"Yes—us and even the more senior people on the legislative and communications staff," she responded. "Some Christmas present, huh? I think he's canning the political guys on retainer to the PAC, too. He has been riding them just like he's been riding us—no one can seem to please him. It's like the Great Purge, Danny. He's gone off the deep-end."

It was obvious that tears now were flowing at the other end of the line.

"I don't know why I am here, Danny. I did not want this. It seemed fun at first, but now ... now it's just terrible."

"I am very sorry, Abby—I don't know what else to say. I'm just shocked that things have deteriorated so fast. But, listen, hang in there, and tell Mitch and Chad I said not to do anything rash. I don't know what can be done about this, but I have an exam until noon tomorrow, and I will head up there as soon as it's over."

"Are you sure? You really shouldn't do that," Abby said softly.

"I will be there by three tomorrow—let's the four of us plan to meet at that American Café place around that time. Now you take care, okay?"

"Okay" was her barely audible response, but at least it sounded like she had stopped crying.

COMPASSION AS A CAUSE

I have never felt sorry for Abby—not even once—and that is mainly because she adamantly, absolutely refuses to feel sorry for herself. But, at the time, I thought she probably had made a mistake by letting Mitch and Chad, and in-directly Bart Bell and Ned Nevers, pull her into politics.

Abby is now, and seemingly always has been, all about compassion. And since compassion has to find expression, Abby is all about doing good deeds for people. She is into serving her fellow man, especially if that fellow man happens to be a downtrodden woman or a suffering child. But when I first met her, she defined herself mostly by what she was *not*.

She was *not* religious, and she was *not* political.

Her parents did that to her.

The rest of us—Chad, Mitch, and I—came from normal, boring families. Chad's folks were an accountant and a stay-at-home mom; Mitch's dad was a pastor, and his mother took care of preschoolers at their church; my dad owned a small shelving manufacturing operation, and my mother taught elementary school kids. Compared to Abby's parents, their lives were as interesting as watching paint dry.

Abby's folks—although it seems far too quaint to call them "folks" —were radicals before it was cool in the Sixties and acid-dropping hippies before most Americans had ever heard the terms. Her father, a decidedly unobservant Jewish kid from Yonkers, was literally a bomb-throwing anarchist, having rejected the socialism of his own father (a Columbia sociology professor) as tiresomely conventional and embarrassingly submissive. Her mother was a native of Suffolk in southeastern Virginia and, as Abby later discovered from a cousin, a descendant of the Algonquian Indian tribe known as the "Nansemonds." Orphaned as a toddler, her mother had been sent to New Jersey to live with her aunt and her aunt's fourth husband. There, the "uncle" frequently abused the displaced Virginian, and so the desperate young woman who would give birth to Abby fled the hell-hole of a home at age 13 to live on the streets with an older cousin.

When Abby's father and mother were both 17, they encountered each other one weekend at a commune in upstate New York, and it was love at first sight. Or, more aptly, it was sex at first sight, love in anything other than the animalistic sense assuredly having had neither time nor reason to blossom. Her mother became pregnant, and her father predictably disappeared. To Abby's great good fortune, a young Jesuit from Fordham had involved himself with the commune, endeavoring to redeem several lost souls who were his former students. Father Francis took Abby's mother under his wing, asking only that she agree to carry the baby to term and then put the child up for adoption.

Shortly after the child was born, the anarchist returned for some odd reason, and a violent argument ensued. The good Father Francis was pistol-whipped and left unconscious, and Abby's flaky mother fled with her unhinged boyfriend. The priest eventually recovered from his wounds enough to gain discharge from the hospital and inquire of social service workers regarding the whereabouts of the child. He did not know the location of the mother's family, but he did have two crucial bits of information: the last name of the anarchist and the fact that his father taught at Columbia. So, when he learned that the child had not been placed with a family, Father Francis tracked down Professor Weinberg at Columbia and apprised him of his granddaughter's sad fate.

To Father Francis' surprise and great relief, Professor Weinberg immediately hastened to the scene and took responsibility for the child. The little girl bore her mother's last name (Wingo) and had been christened "Abigail Naomi" by Father Francis. Professor Weinberg eventually adopted little

Abigail but did not change her legal name, presumably deeming it best not to saddle the innocent with the surname of her fugitive father. A divorcee and single parent, Nathan Weinberg proceeded to smother Abby with all the loving attention that he had denied her wayward father when he was a boy. Having been given a second chance at parenting, he had resolved to make the most of it.

And so Abby Wingo had a Jesuit priest and a Jewish professor to thank for saving her from a horrific fate that otherwise would have included abortion, abandonment, or infancy on the run with two lunatic parents. The latter would have been an abbreviated fate, because when the hapless pair finally turned up, they were arrested for conspiracy to commit bank robbery. Their plot was foiled because they both had passed out, stoned, while staking out the bank early on the morning of the planned heist. The cops who knocked on their car windows observed the handguns, sacks, and "give us all your money" signs in the backseat and astutely concluded something was amiss. It was not a proud moment for the would-be Bonnie and Clyde, nor was it the blaze of glory that the anarchist probably figured would mark his exit from the field of action. But it did take the two pathetic creatures safely off the streets, and so Abby did not have to waste time wondering about their fate.

I learned all this back during college while hanging out in Mitch's apartment one night with Abby and her roommates. Having only met her briefly before, I did the Virginia thing, which is to ask about her family, where she grew up, and who "all her people" were. I was not perceptive enough to take the hint when Abby replied, "I could not begin to tell you." So I pressed, and at length she relented and told us the whole story.

"Okay, you asked for it," she said with a smile, then took a deep breath and started in.

Forty minutes later, she had recounted all of the facts I have described here plus a lot of other details, all of which she had reconstructed over time from conversations with her father—her adoptive father, Professor Weinberg—and from the only other "parent" she acknowledged, Father Francis, with whom she now regularly corresponded.

When she finally finished telling us who "all her people" were—supplying my first great lesson about never asking a question unless you already know the answer—we were all sitting there with our eyes wide and mouths agape, completely sobered and utterly amazed by the gut-wrenching tale. What amazed me was how Abby had related this incredibly difficult family history without the slightest trace of self-pity or resentment.

If she had wanted to descend into an attitude of victimhood and grievance, Abby certainly had more than enough reason. It was not just her bizarre childhood experiences; it was the ghastly legacy of historic wrongs to which she was heir.

As a young girl, Abby had been shielded by Professor Weinberg from the horrors of the Holocaust for as long as possible. But she would never forget the day her fifth grade teacher told her class about Anne Frank, a young girl very near her own age, and shared brief passages from her diary. Abby had been severely traumatized by the sudden revelation, and from that day forward her utter despair over the depravity of man and his potential for wanton brutality was like an open psychic sore that stubbornly refused to heal.

A wound of a different sort came when Abby was a teenager and Professor Weinberg allowed her to visit her cousins in Virginia for the first time. It was then she learned of her native American heritage, news that surely would have been a source of pride and joy had it not been accompanied by a dark truth: the story of the discrimination endured by Virginia Indians at the hands of the state's Bureau of Vital Statistics for more than three decades following the agency's creation in the early 20th century. Those Virginians whose ancestors were native to the soil before the arrival of English settlers or African slaves in the 17th century found that, beginning in 1924, Virginia's laws rendered their race officially nonexistent. Every person thenceforth had to be classified as white or "colored"—there was no designation for Virginia Indians. Rather than bend to this mandate and disavow their ancestry, many Indian families refused submission to the insidious regime and removed their children from the public schools. Some were sent to school outside the state while many went untaught. Even the consignment of African-American children to separate and unequal schools did not exact such a high price as this injustice.

Now, several generations and a tragic journey later, Abby had come back to Virginia, the land of her maternal forebears. But she had come with little sense of her heritage because whatever of her identity official state policy had not robbed, her troubled childhood had stolen.

That childhood also had left her without any religious roots or conviction. Her father had taught her compassion, but he could not teach her about faith because he did not have any—at least, none he would acknowledge. And even if he had thought it wise as a practical matter to add some religious dimension to her upbringing, he would not have known where to start. What exactly do you do in New York City with a little girl who is half Jewish, baptized Catholic, and raised by an agnostic? The answer, of course, is you do something to give the kid a sense of belonging and hope. But Professor Weinberg, full of love but a prisoner to remorse, simply could not connect the dots.

Abby recalled once returning home after a day at school at which the students, most of whom were children of immigrants, were asked to describe their family roots. The others had all sorts of things to say, but Abby had been stumped, and that night she had asked her father plaintively, "What am I, Daddy?" She had watched his eyes moisten, and now she could hear his answer like it was yesterday: "You are a beautiful rosebud that is going to blossom and brighten up the world," he said, giving her a big hug.

And so that had become her mission in the world—the mission of a rosebud—and it had nothing at all to do with religion.

Or politics....

After his son's lurch toward extremism, Professor Weinberg had faulted himself for not better controlling the political influences to which the boy had been exposed. With Abby, then, he apparently had gone in the diametrically opposite direction, screening out political influences of all kinds and sparing no opportunity to denigrate political passions and even the very idea of civic involvement.

So Abby, a beautiful, brilliant, and sensitive young woman, had arrived at the University of Virginia without a heritage she could trace, without a religious faith she could embrace, and without a political creed she could espouse. More than merely lacking those things, she seemed to *eschew* them. She would brighten the world with her radiant smile, glowing heart, and good works. As a student of journalism and psychology, she would examine people and events, find the good in them, and share those stories with others. And she would keep politics, religion, and all other such debilitating distractions from getting in her way.

That plan worked right up until the time Abby started to hang out with Mitch, Chad, and me. With my two friends and eventually Bart all tugging at her, I suppose it was inevitable she would succumb. What no one could have envisioned then, especially on that day when she called me in despair after getting the axe from Nevers, was how incredibly adept she would turn out to be at all aspects of the political game. She would become a peerless political dynamo—a "natural," as everyone would say. Yet through it all she steadfastly would continue to reject all ideology, whether of the Right or the Left, casting herself oxymoronically as the zealous moderate. For Abby, it would remain all about compassion, and if she made any concession to politics, it was simply to accept it as another venue, perhaps even an ideal venue, where one could find people to help.

Looking back, it is evident how Abby would complete the political picture for me. Chad would share his libertarian ideas, and Mitch would model moral conviction. But Abby would add the essential complement—*compassion*. Even before faith finally broke through the packed topsoil of her life and blossomed, she was already expressing it through her love and care for others.

GOLDEN BOY TOPPLED

After Abby's distress call, there was, of course, no way to concentrate on the next day's Crim Law exam. My thoughts were on my friends and how this fickle, ferocious thing called politics was again screwing up the lives of people I cared about. I kept going over the conversation in my mind, and at one point I tried to reach Mitch or Chad without success. *There has to be more to the story than this*, I thought. *It doesn't make sense.* Things obviously had not gone well for Nevers in recent months, but it was the first year of a six-year term, and no sane person would get completely rattled like this over some criticism in the media.

After a sleepless night and a predictably deplorable exam-taking experience, I headed for D.C. When I reached my friends I am sure I looked rough, but they looked terrible. All three seemed dumbstruck by the sudden turn of events. We talked about the situation for a couple of hours, and Mitch and Chad supplied additional anecdotes and details. They defended not only their own actions but the quality of the work product turned in by their superiors on the legislative and policy staff. Abby likewise made a compelling case for the press secretary and her efforts to ameliorate the negative media coverage. At the end of the conversation I had the same basic information Abby had provided the night before. And it still did not compute.

So I went over to Nevers' office in the Russell Building and asked to see Bart. I was not ready for his sprightly demeanor.

"Don't tell me—you flunked out of law school and you're here looking for a job," he said jauntily as he extended his hand. "You picked the right time to show up here; we happen to have a few openings!"

"I heard, and that's why I'm here," I said glumly. "But I don't think it is a laughing matter, not when my friends are involved."

"Oh, no, it's not a laughing matter at all," Bart said, suddenly sounding earnest. He was a couple of seconds and sentences tardy in his realization that a sorrowful visage was the right mask for this encounter. "Unfortunately, the three of them are just collateral damage. Not that it's any consolation."

"What is really going on, Bart? This makes no sense to me."

The new chief of staff to Senator Ned Nevers ushered me into his surprisingly cramped little office, asked his assistant to excuse herself, and closed the door.

"Look, I am not going to sit here and tell you I'm sorry to be the beneficiary of Derek Douglas' misfortune," Bart started in. "He is a pencil pusher who was an awful choice for chief of staff. He ran this place pathetically; it has been a disorganized mess; and I would be thrilled to see him go even if I were not his replacement. But the fact is, I *am* his replacement, and I intend to get this place working properly—"

"Yes, but what about—" I tried to interrupt.

"Now the rest of this—the Senator's fits and frustration and rants about no one having a plan and no one knowing what he stands for and his firing everyone in sight—that is *all him*. It really is, and I don't understand it myself. I mean, I've been working for the guy for a couple of years now. You know I was his body man during the campaign, and I've been around him more than anyone, with the possible exception of his wife. But I just don't know what's going on inside that head of his. For the last month, he's been having bad dreams and sleepless nights, and he really is completely off his game. Frankly, it's a little bit scary."

"Scary? Somehow I don't think of you as being scared, Bart," I said reflexively. But then I realized he was being candid. Bart's chief asset was his proximity to power, and here he was admitting that he was not as close to the boss as everyone had assumed. It was an admission he would not have contrived.

"Did he tell you what was keeping him awake? Did he tell you about his nightmares?" I asked.

"No. I don't know if he doesn't remember them, or he doesn't want to say, or what. But he just keeps complaining that no one around him understands him, no one appreciates what he's going through, no one shares his vision, blah, blah, blah. It's almost like he wants someone to read his mind and tell him what to think and do. There's no earthly way anyone can do that for him, and I tried to tell him that yesterday morning—in a more tactful way, of course—but he just about bit my head off. I was probably this close to getting canned myself," Bart said, illustrating with his fingers. "I guess we just have to wait and hope he gets over it."

"Well, waiting and hoping might be a fine approach if he had not already given pink slips to half of the staff, including Mitch, Chad, and Abby," I said. "Seems to me something more decisive is needed."

"Well, if you have a bright idea, let me hear it," he replied.

"I don't know how bright it is. In fact, I can think of a hundred other ways I would rather spend my Christmas break. But I do have an idea," I started reluctantly. "Why don't I offer to take the lead in putting together a strategic plan for him over the next few weeks that will include all the pieces—policy analysis and recommended positions, legislative strategy, communications plan—all the things that need to be included in there? You can help guide me on it, and I will tap into the other expertise around here. I mean, only a few months ago he thought I was some wizard he desperately had to have on his team, right? Maybe I can persuade him to let me give it a shot."

"I don't know, Danny," Bart replied, turning the idea over in his mind. "It's likely to strike him as a rather odd suggestion. He thinks you're plenty smart, and for some reason he seems to trust you. But his first reaction will probably be that you're not qualified to do this—that you haven't set foot on the Hill, and that you'll end up giving him some long, scholarly policy paper or legal brief rather than a practical political document he can actually use."

"Well, if that's his reaction, I'll just remind him that all the wise men you've hired on the Hill haven't given him what he wants, so what's the downside to reaching outside the Beltway for some common sense and fresh thinking? Seems like he might buy that," I answered.

"He might. But even if he does, I'm still not seeing how it leads to any change in his behavior. I mean, the staff has put together a truckload of good paper for him already, and he just rejects it out of hand. What do you know about legislative and political strategy that the rest of us don't?"

"Absolutely nothing," I readily conceded. "But what else do you have in mind?"

Bart did not bother to answer me. He headed into the Senator's inner sanctum, as I sat, still confounded. *There has to be more to this story*, I thought. *What is really going on with Nevers?*

My meeting with the Senator did not supply the answer.

Within a few minutes, Bart opened the door and waved me in. I entered Senator Nevers' dingy office and was struck immediately by the sight—not by how unimpressive was the office but by how diminished appeared its occupant. I had seen a lot of wrung-out frat brothers the morning after rowdy parties, and none of them had eyes as red and sunken or faces as pale and palsied as the man lost in the high-back swivel chair behind the desk. It was hard to believe this was the same supremely confident super-pol who had so dominated the Virginia political landscape a year earlier.

He stood but did not reach to shake my hand, and the barest of pleasantries were exchanged before the Senator came brusquely to the point. "Bart says you're willing and able to put together a legislative strategy and political plan for this office over the Christmas holiday—one that accurately reflects my thinking. I have to tell you I have my doubts. I don't need some law review article or some treatise on policy. I need a practical document from someone who has supported and listened to me, believes in me, knows what I stand for. I need a playbook that can prevent all these last-minute, improvisational, ad hoc judgment calls and rookie errors. I need something that will help me get the media back on my side and make us look like we're actually ready for prime time here."

"Yes, sir, and that is what I plan to prepare for you," I responded, sounding as confident and commanding as I could manage.

"Well, may I ask, my dear Daniel, *why* you want to do it? What's in it for you?"

"Sir?" The question surprised me.

"I mean, if it's a job you want, I suspect we can still fit you in."

"No, sir, I am still committed to law school—assuming I survive this semester," I answered.

"Well, it's been a few years since I was in college, but I don't ever recall thinking it would be just great to do some extra work over the Christmas break. Are you just a glutton for punishment, or do you have some ulterior motive?"

"I don't have an ulterior motive, and I am not asking for anything." I replied. "Well, I'm not asking for anything except one thing, which is crucial to make this work: I need access to your legislative and communications staff for the next four weeks. I know you're dissatisfied with their performance and are letting them go, and I'm obviously in no position to second-guess your judgment on that. But right now they're all you have, and if I am going to pull this plan together, I need access to what's in their files and in their heads."

I went on in for the hard ask: "Is there any way you can suspend your firings long enough to give me a crack at this?"

An obvious trace of irritation immediately punctuated Nevers' pained face. "I suppose," he said slowly, "that I can *delay* the dismissals. But if you're here doing the bidding of your college classmates and the other under-performers on this staff, let me assure you that my decision is final. I want a new team and a fresh start. I want people who are loyal and believe in what I believe in. I could probably sleep at night for a change if I just knew that someone with some brains had my back."

I resisted the temptation to ask him what it was that he believed in. "Exactly, sir, I understand that," I said.

"Bart, I gather this is your recommendation and you are prepared to work with Daniel on this project?" Nevers asked.

"Yes, sir, whatever he needs."

"What he needs, Bart, is someone with a practical perspective to work closely with him and make sure he doesn't kill a lot of trees for nothing."

"Yes, sir, I'll work with him," Bart responded. "Danny is very smart and very perceptive, Senator, and we could benefit from a fresh, outside-the-Beltway perspective...."

"That's a good point, Bart," Nevers interrupted. "An outside-the-Beltway perspective could do us some good. It's not like the wise heads here on Capitol Hill have done us any good this year...."

"No, sir, it's not like they have done us any good at all," Bart parroted back in his trademark sycophant manner.

"Thirty days, Daniel—I will look for your draft plan in 30 days, if not sooner," Nevers said, rising and supplying our exit cue. "Thank you for your willingness to assist us."

I concluded things with Bart and then huddled with my friends in the cafeteria down in the basement of the Dirksen Senate Office Building. I was exhausted—it now had been two days without rest on top of the usual exam-related sleep deprivation—and I still had to drive back to Charlottesville to study for two more exams. So I gave them my quick take on things and headed out.

"Look, guys," I said as I was leaving, "You need to know that Bart doesn't think this plan has a prayer of a chance, and he has the best read on Nevers of anyone. We've just bought a little time. So don't get your hopes up—okay?"

"Now that's a coincidence," interjected Mitch.

"What's a coincidence?" Chad asked.

"Danny just said we don't have a 'prayer of a chance,'" Mitch answered. "I haven't heard that expression in years, but I was talking to my dad this afternoon and his parting comment was, 'Remember, son, when you don't think you have a prayer of a chance, a prayer's the only chance you got.'"

"Well, it looks like you will have an opportunity to test the good Reverend's theory," I said to the trio as I headed toward the door of the Dirksen Building and out into the cold.

Moments later I was sitting in the annoying traffic that snarls Capitol Hill late in the day, thinking how glad I was not to work up there, dreading the studying that awaited me in Charlottesville, and wondering what in the world I had gotten myself into.

As it turned out, I survived the exams. In fact, I more than survived them. I did well in all except Crim Law, and I escaped with a B-minus there rather than something more embarrassing. I left for Orange to spend a few days over Christmas with Mitch and his family, then I went down to Suffolk to hunt ducks with Chad and his dad on the Nansemond River. But mostly I was up in Alexandria, working out of Abby's apartment on what my friends took to calling the "Grand Plan."

Mitch, Chad, and Abby worked hard on the document—it actually became a thick notebook—and so did the rest of the Senator's endangered staff. Every potential issue of significance likely to arise in the coming congressional session was researched, analyzed, succinctly summarized, and neatly tabbed. Recommended positions and corresponding talking points were supplied for each topic, as was a plan for media outreach. Polling data revealed the disposition of voters and helped frame the optimal message on each point. I had no practical experience with any of it, but I did have common sense and a logical mind, and to me the materials seemed comprehensive and correct.

The hardest part was the overview memorandum, the primary strategic document. It was supposed to spell out the key themes and specific policy initiatives the Senator would emphasize in the coming months, how he would roll them out, and what each would yield from both a policy and political standpoint. This was the document that I felt obligated to write personally, having promised to lend my "fresh perspective." But I had the devil of a time writing it. By New Year's weekend, I had completed (with lots of input) a 20-page strategic memorandum that was, by all accounts, solid. That was the opinion of Bart, the Senator's legislative counsel, his press secretary, his other legislative, communications, and policy staffers, and my three friends. I, too, thought it was a quality product, if a little bit lacking in imagination. We certainly had invested a lot of time in it. Few people on the Hill, Bart observed, could possibly have gone to such lengths to anticipate, analyze, strategize, and articulate a considered course of action for the coming session.

Yet, something was missing, and it gnawed at me. I experienced a string of uncharacteristically restless nights of my own as my January 9 session with Senator Nevers approached. But, on the evening before that meeting, I slept … and I dreamed.

The custodian typically did not enable me to remember my dreams, and back then the dreams I did remember were usually very enjoyable ones, almost adventures. When I was not studying, I was accustomed to sleeping soundly— and happily. But on the eve of my meeting with Nevers I dreamed about the Senator. And it was not a happy dream.

It began positively enough. Nevers was standing in the bright sunshine along a creek, fly rod in one hand and stringer of bluegill, brook trout, smallmouth bass, and red eyes in the other. The sun radiated off his auburn hair, producing a golden glow about his head, and it illuminated the water behind him so that the whole scene appeared iridescent. Beaming boyishly from ear to ear, Nevers obviously was proud to display his fishing prowess. He was even prouder to be—and now I recalled where I had seen this same image—the political phenom featured on the cover of *Virginia Weekly*, the state's most prestigious and widely read journal of politics, society, the arts, and whatever's in style. He was, as the headline declared, the "Golden Boy of Virginia Politics"—the good-looking, well-spoken man of the rapid ascent, a late thirtysomething powerhouse with a boundless future … king of the hill. The cover story lavished praise on him as the biggest, brightest new thing on Virginia's storied political scene.

That was the scene on the magazine cover and in my dream. But, then, in my dream the unexpected happened.

Someone threw a big object toward the triumphant Nevers, apparently assuming he would catch it. It looked like a rock or box or ball—or maybe it was a Budweiser tossed to him by his fishing buddy. But, whatever it was, it was big enough to change this picture permanently. He was not looking for it, so it startled him, and when he instinctively reached to catch it, he slipped on the slick clay bank, his feet went out in front of him, and he landed back in the creek with a huge, inglorious splash.

In an instant, he was no longer the proud power and unconquerable hero of the photo—he was an object of derision. The people had been divided, fighting among themselves, but now they were all united in laughter, which rose into a loud guffaw, some people roaring and others "hissing and fissing like snakes" in the manner of the "I Love to Laugh" scene in *Mary Poppins*. Everyone, and now it was a throng, was pointing at Nevers and laughing loudly, hysterically—huge, convulsive belly laughs punctuated by insulting jeers. It went on and on as Nevers stood chest-deep in the creek, hair matted to his face, thoroughly humiliated. One after another, the fish slipped from his stringer and swam free.

Nevers could not even climb out of the water, so slippery was the clay alongside the river. But eventually he yielded to the current, which took him downstream a ways to an area where the bank and everything else suddenly was solid rock, the laughter was out of earshot, and Someone extended a hand to help him out of the water and onto his feet.

The dream awakened me abruptly, and it sent my mind reeling.

As I lay there pondering the strange images that had marched through my head, it occurred to me that Nevers' rise in politics had never been about any idea, issue, cause, or calling. It had all been about his personality and style and ambition. The "Golden Boy" moniker and image said it all. Nevers had achieved remarkable political success, but he had not been building something of value to others; he had only been making a monument to himself. And it only takes an instant to pull a monument down.

Grateful for the insight, I lay awake pondering its import and wondering what I should do about it.

By the time morning finally arrived, I had crafted a plan. I called the Senator's press secretary and asked her to see if she could find a copy of the "Golden Boy" magazine cover. I expected her to have to work at unearthing it, but to my surprise she had it handy. It was lying there atop a number of prized articles, cover pages, and photos featuring Nevers that recently had been framed and were slated to fill a large collage on the reception area wall in the cramped Senate office.

I sprinted over to the Hill and darted in to pick up my copy. While there I noticed on the closed-circuit TV that the Senate chaplain was offering a prayer to open the day's session. *An interesting tradition*, I thought to myself irreverently. *Not sure how you square that with separation of church and state, but if anyone needs divine intervention it's probably that bunch.*

At 2:00 P.M., I arrived back at the Senate office for my scheduled presentation. Bart had planned to go in with me, but I asked him to let me do it alone. He balked at this request at first, but when I pointed out that he might want to keep his distance until we knew Nevers' reaction, he saw where his self-interest lay and readily endorsed my plan to fly solo.

I took a deep breath, pled silently for calmness and courage, and entered the Senator's office. With me, cradled in my arms, was the several-inches-thick white notebook that had housed the output from our holiday labors. I proceeded to the sofa and laid the notebook on the coffee table as Nevers emerged from behind his desk to greet me and position himself next to me, ready to sit and inspect my work. He did not look markedly better, and the intervening holiday did not seem to have altered his mood. But at least this time he engaged in a little disarming small talk.

"You know," I began after the pleasantries, "I'm just a kid from a small town who doesn't know *boo* about politics—"

"Oh, geez, don't give me that," Nevers interrupted, managing a forced sort of smile. "You're way too young to be using that 'I'm just a country lawyer' shtick—you gotta at least get your law degree and license before you can engage in that kind of folksy misdirection. By the way, I assume you finished the semester; how'd you do? Are you at the top of your class again, like you were in high school and college?"

"Actually, your soon-to-be-former-employee, Mitch Jackson, was at the top of our class in high school," I replied reflexively. "I was #2. But I think I did pretty well this semester, all things considered."

"Did you ever finish that big paper on Madison you were working on all last year?" he asked, changing the subject and ignoring the Mitch reference. I was surprised and impressed that he remembered my Madison project.

"Finished it and got an A," I responded. "But my undergrad professors have been pushing me to keep working on it and get it published."

"You should do that, Daniel. I mean, the only other things you have going on right now are first-year law school and helping a frustrated United States senator come up with a political agenda and strategic plan. I don't see why you can't squeeze in a book on Madison in your spare time."

"Right," I replied, managing a wry smile of my own.

"Now, Senator, about that strategic plan. You probably don't remember this—I *hope* you don't—but when we first met in Orange a few years back it was right after my parents had died, and I was a bit of a smart-aleck when you expressed sympathy for the little sister of mine who didn't actually exist. I have to warn you that if you thought I was a smart-aleck then, well, just wait until I show you—"

"I remember the scene well," Nevers interrupted, a pained smile creeping across his drawn face. "I was mortified later when Bart mentioned my mistake but amused by how you handled the awkward moment. I said to myself, 'That kid has moxie.'"

"Uh, huh," I grunted.

"Yes, that made an impression. So, now," he said, reaching for the notebook on the table in front of us, "show me what you have done with all your smarts and moxie to help straighten things out for us here in the land of the lost."

Before I could say anything, he had flipped open the notebook, and there on the first page was the *Virginia Weekly* cover featuring his beaming visage and branding him the "Golden Boy of Virginia Politics." It stopped him in his tracks.

"Why is this here?" he asked, stricken.

I took a deep breath. "Actually, it is there because I dreamed about it last night," I answered directly.

"You what?"

"Dreamed about it, you know, while I was sleeping, last night—only I'm afraid the dream didn't stop with the scene in the photo. I dreamed that you fell into the water and were embarrassed—*terribly* embarrassed."

"You dreamed that," he repeated, with a stunned look as if someone had just invaded his own private thoughts. After a pause he silently motioned for me to continue.

"And the dream got me thinking about all the work we had done fleshing out your policy agenda and the key issues that are coming up this year and your political strategy. We put together really great stuff, and it filled a whole notebook this thick. But, Senator, it was full of what *we* think. It wasn't what *you* think. And so I took all of that information out of here. These pages are all blank."

Nevers inspected the notebook, thumbing through nearly a ream of completely blank pages, as if to make sure they really were all devoid of content.

It was at this point, as I had envisioned it, that the Senator would realize the disrespectful stunt and explode. I had rehearsed how, having grabbed his attention, I would quickly deliver my message before I was thrown out of his office. But as I looked at him now, there was not the slightest trace of anger on his face. There was surprise, even shock—but no anger. So I proceeded at an even pace and immediately found myself wandering off script, involuntarily invoking Madison.

"You asked about my research on Madison. Madison was the least self-absorbed of the founders. Others preened for history, but not Madison, even though he out-lived them all. In fact, he at first had no political ambitions; he wrote dismissively of politics to his friend and college classmate. But he eventually got into politics and government because he believed deeply in certain ideas, in certain freedoms, especially the freedom of conscience. He became fascinated with the process of self-governance and immersed himself in the history and theory of it. Once engaged, he put his whole self into the cause of framing a successful republic. He was just a sickly and shy little man, but he was in it for the ideas and the impact."

I paused, partly for effect and partly to gauge his reaction. "Now, Senator," I continued, "of course, everyone cannot be a Madison. But everyone can be in it for the right reasons—everyone can be in it to accomplish something. I wasn't very religious before my folks died, but since then I have spent a lot of time thinking about it, and I really have come to believe that each of us has been put here to make some contribution. Each of us has been given talents for a purpose...."

Nevers was listening now, still stunned, but seemingly taking in my words. So I continued along the general outline I had arranged in my mind.

"I happened to see the opening session of the Senate this morning, and I heard the current Senate Chaplain quote one of his predecessors. He said, 'We all have to stand for something or we will fall for anything.' And that is certainly true of politics. You have to believe in and stand for something, because if the only thing you care about is getting elected and holding office and being famous or whatever, then what is there to make you draw the line between right and wrong? There is no limit to how far you'll go in the name of self-advancement. You'll fall for anything, stoop to anything, say or do anything, because it is all about you and it is all about winning."

Nevers' visage had not changed. But his sagging frame had stiffened, and I could tell I was having some impact. Just where it was heading remained a mystery.

"When I dreamed last night about you standing there in one instant as the darling of the political chattering class and in the next instant falling and becoming the butt of their jokes and laughter, it occurred to me that this is the end that often awaits the powerful. Politicians come and go; they're up and then they're down. Throughout history great powers and kingdoms have risen and fallen. They seem all-powerful in their time; they are the political 'golden boys' of their day; but they are not all-powerful. Patrick Henry at St. John's Church said there is a just God who presides over the destiny of nations, and, if that is true, then it means he presides over the affairs of individual men and women, too, including politicians. He's the presiding officer who isn't term-limited, and his is the only republic that will last. I fundamentally believe that our ability to have a positive impact during our time on the planet begins with acknowledging that we are not supreme and that it is *not all about us*."

Now was clearly the time to tie the message back to the crisis at hand. Plus, I was eager to end this awkward lecturing of a man nearly twice my age.

"Look, most of what I know is what I have read, but to me a statesman is a politician who has a core philosophy and set of beliefs rooted in a sense of obligation. And I don't think there are any shortcuts or substitutes. A senator can change his staff a hundred times and assemble all the smart young politicos and whiz kids that Washington's excitement can lure to town. But at the end of the day no one can write the script for him if he does not have his own core convictions."

"These are the pages, Senator," I said, pointing again to the notebook and resolutely delivering the planned punchline. *"You're the reason they're blank."*

There was an oppressive silence that made seven seconds seem like a week. By any objective standard, I had been presumptuous, even offensive, toward this powerful man who was my senior in age and position. I was ready for an outburst even if—or *because*—I had gotten my point across.

Instead, after the silence, the Senator did something I could never have imagined. He sighed, as if surrendering at last, and smiled.

"I truly have been haunted by this image," Nevers said, flipping back to the magazine cover, "ever since Mrs. Burden showed me how she had framed it to go on our office wall. I have been tormented by it in nightmares and daydreams, and it has driven me almost crazy. But until this conversation I had no clue why it bothered me so much. I see it now. *I see it all.* And, to be honest, I feel like a weight has been lifted from my shoulders."

I exhaled in relief at the reaction. But what followed brought new distress.

"You are truly brilliant, Daniel—*brilliant!* And unbelievably brave, too. I cannot imagine another soul who could come in here and say what you've just said to me. And I think you're right, too—I really do. You obviously have a firm conviction, a center that is strong and true, and that's why I need you at my side more than ever. I need you to help me cultivate that healthy spirit … that good side. Together, we can come up with that core philosophy you're talking about. Think about all the really good things we can accomplish for Virginia and for this country."

I could see where he was headed, and I immediately knew he was grasping the wrong lifeline.

"Whoa there, Senator," I rushed to put on the brakes, "it's not about me any more than it is about you. That is what I meant when I said there are no shortcuts or substitutes. You cannot pull yourself off the pedestal and stick someone else up there instead. It's not about finding someone who has big brains and God on his speed-dial list. You can't grab someone else's principles off the shelf like a can of beans. Misappropriating conviction is worse than having no conviction at all!"

This I had blurted out impulsively—and tactlessly. Now I worried that I might have undone whatever good had been done by the preceding exchange. I paused and searched for the right words as Nevers eyed me with a puzzled, even hurt, expression.

"Senator, I'm sorry. I'm no expert on this—you know that. To tell you the truth, I'm figuring things out as I work through this, just like you are. I guess what I'm trying to say is that I don't have some magic way to make your nightmares leave or make your service in the Senate meaningful. I don't think you will have peace until God gives it to you, and I don't think he will give it to you until you surrender yourself to a higher cause and calling. But the good news is that something inside you is telling you to care and to try. My Mom always used to say, 'God doesn't start a project with us unless he plans to finish it.'"

As I heard myself offer this counsel, it occurred to me that I was speaking from the heart, expressing thoughts and ideas I had never even focused on before—things that were jelling for me even as I was giving voice to them. I suspect they were the product of ideas expressed by my parents, by Dr. S. D., by my three friends, and by many others. No doubt they were informed, too, by lessons from history and literature and maybe even a sermon or two. It was as if the insights had been sifted, refined, and packaged in useful words by a consciousness beyond my own. As I counseled Nevers with wisdom beyond my years and ideas beyond my own convictions, I was undergoing my own process of self-discovery. The remarkable thing is that my "self" had so little to do with it.

That, as best I can recall, is what transpired that day in the office of Senator Nevers. And, at least for a time, it appeared to make a difference.

In the wake of the episode I still declined to join the Senator's staff, but it was apparent I had become a trusted advisor, and the phone calls and summons to the Hill for consultations became commonplace. When asked how I thought he should handle the staff situation, I held my tongue regarding Bart's role as chief—a decision I now greatly regret—but I urged emphatically that Mitch, Chad, and Abby be given new responsibility commensurate with their unusual abilities and dedication. This advice Nevers took to heart, giving all three significant promotions to posts in the Senate office that others had vacated.

Politics, though, is Newtonian: for every action, there is an equal and opposite reaction. So it did not take long before Bart grew apprehensive about the trio's increased clout with the Senator. The new chief of staff's shortsighted solution, which Nevers and my three friends readily embraced, was essentially to outsource them. The Senator corralled some donors as investors, signed on a couple of veterans as mentors, and helped my three compatriots set up a brand new political consulting firm—"JBW Advisors"—with Nevers' political action committee as their primary client. It was the best thing that could have happened to them.

The order of initials in the new business's name was determined randomly, but their respective contributions to the enterprise were anything but happenstance. Each member of the team added something of value. Chad realized his ambition to become a pollster, testing the viability of ideas and messages in the political marketplace. It took him a while to get the methodology down, but he had a mentor who was a wizard, and over time he would become a political encyclopedia without peer, able to recite the voting histories of every

Virginia locality and call to mind (or find in his files) the most minute details about voting behavior across the Commonwealth. Abby, magnetic and outgoing, took the lead on communications and media relations. She not only knew the craft; with her nose for news and knack for befriending, she soon developed personal relationships and a deep reservoir of goodwill with reporters and pundits all over the state. Mitch focused on policy development, applying his formidable intellect to the task of ferreting out what really worked. He also took his insights into the field, recruiting candidates, teaching them and their aides what to say and how to say it, and helping to turn practical ideas (rooted always in his strong philosophical precepts) into political platforms.

While the talented trio that comprised JBW Advisors would influence the course of Virginia politics mostly from behind the scenes, their labors were not entirely shielded from view. Their impact—not just their work for Senator Nevers but their success in helping to elect other Republican candidates—was highlighted later in another *Virginia Weekly* feature article, this one entitled "The Golden Boy's Brassy Trio." At one point in the laudatory piece, my friends were described as a "uniquely talented trio on a crusade for good government, spreading the conservative gospel with the flourish of Cicero and the urgency of Revere." The metaphor was amusing, exposing the reporter's pretension, and I considered penning him a note suggesting that Patrick Henry and Jack Jouett would have been more apt analogues for his Virginia readers. But he would not have understood the reference so there was no point. Meanwhile, the article was duly framed and adorned the lobby of JBW Advisors' much-trafficked office on Union Street in Alexandria, attesting to my pals' remarkably early career success.

Somehow the four of us had survived the converging traumas of first-year law school and a bizarre meltdown on Capitol Hill. It was as if we had been skiing along the edge of a cliff, sustained by the friction that nature's force supplies, the balance the brain mysteriously confers, and the intrepid spirit that propels oblivious young people forward despite the dangers. The political enticements and diversions easily could have pulled me away from law school, and things like my below-the-curve performance in Crim Law might have dissuaded me from my chosen course. But I stuck with it and went on to land a judicial clerkship with a well-respected federal judge based in Alexandria. That experience, along with my Capitol Hill connections, set the stage for a prized appointment the next year as the most junior assistant in the U.S. Attorney's office there in Alexandria, putting me where I long had hoped to be.

Nevers soon settled in, the nightmares stayed away, and he started to get some traction on his committees. While fundraising events and other political appearances were a constant, a senator's six-year term affords the luxury of concentrating on the actual legislative work, and that is what Nevers seemed determined to do. But the palace is never really beyond politics. And if you indulge the dangerous illusion that governing allows you to be a statesman without also being a politician, you can be sure events will snap you back, often brutally, to the reality of how democracy really works.

Chapter Three

Furnace

Ned Nevers had a lot of ground to make up after his inauspicious start in the Senate, and he worked hard at it. Bolstering his public support was important, but Nevers mainly wanted to restore his standing in the eyes of his Senate colleagues. It was not an easy task—first impressions are hard to shake—and events across the nation did not make it any easier. It was a time of continual conflict and, apparent only in hindsight, vital growth.

Political credibility, like personal character, is forged in the crucible of conflict. The furnace melts the cutaneous facade, starves ambivalence of its ponderous oxygen, and refines to its essence what it does not destroy. When you face that crucible—especially when it pits principle against expedience, or, worse, principle against principle—it is good to have a little help from your friends.

I was not there when my three friends faced their moment of truth. But by then they had each other. The intervening events drew them tightly together, readying them for the crucial test.

Brother against Brother

The first time I can recall Chad and Mitch arguing about the Confederate flag was during our Memorial Day weekend getaway in 1986, a little past the midpoint of Nevers' Senate term. In what by now had become an annual tradition, we and a few other friends had rented a place near the beach in Corolla, on

105

northeastern North Carolina's Outer Banks, for some much-needed R&R. It ordinarily was a laid-back, fun time, but the peace of this particular weekend had been interrupted, at least temporarily, by my feuding friends. The cause of their quarrel was a sudden flaring of racial tensions across the country.

It began earlier that spring with sporadic, unexplained fires at African-American churches in various Southern states, including one located in rural southeastern Virginia. These oddly similar but far-flung events drew the concerted attention of state and local authorities, and they aroused concern in the Justice Department's Civil Rights Division and the FBI in Washington. But the church burnings did not become a page-one national story until the lives of a young pastor in Biloxi, Mississippi, Rev. James Clemens, his wife Rachel, and their eight-month-old little girl Leah were brutally extinguished in one of the conflagrations. The ghastly crime and heartbreaking loss produced a wave of revulsion and grief that swept the nation, and events cascaded quickly out of control from there.

Faith leaders convened a series of large, peaceful rallies in multiple cities, North and South, where the message centered on racial understanding, reconciliation, and healing. The rallies were soon followed by marches, organized as peaceful protests, that acquired an increasingly angry air as time went on. It was not long before extremists hurling racial epithets and other incendiary items, literal and figurative, moved in aggressively to exploit the opening. Before summer gave way to fall, the suffocating heat would combine with raw racial wounds and festering economic grievances, organized provocation and random mayhem, to produce riotous conditions and devastating looting in numerous cities, including the nation's capital.

This destructive wave was still building as we gathered for our Memorial Day retreat—ironically, a holiday first conceived as a day for decorating the graves of Civil War dead. Two weeks earlier, the perpetrator of the Clemens murders had been cornered in his home by police and, after wrapping himself defiantly in the Confederate flag, had blown out his brains. Strangely, given the deeply embedded social, economic, and cultural maladies that the spring and summer events brought to the fore, it was the erstwhile emblem of Southern rebellion that quickly became the all-consuming object of political energy. Several senators already were calling for legislation tying federal funding for various state and local programs to the removal of "symbols of hate"—including, by name, the Confederate battle flag—from public property in those jurisdictions.

106

"For the life of me," Abby complained as we took refuge on the beach to escape our contentious companions, "I cannot understand how two people who are so close can be so far apart on something so basic."

The "something so basic" that drove Mitch and Chad apart, of course, was history—not their personal history, though that had contributed to the gulf, but the collective history to which each was heir because of his race and place. It would have been nice if that history had flowed down like a peaceful river whose obliging streams made everyone glad on their way to the sea. But that history also came down from the hills at times like a mudslide. It overwhelmed all logic and deposited in a confused heap the legacy of man's feats and foibles, history's ennobling lessons and its almost unbearable burdens.

The burdens, at their root, came down to *separation*. It is all there in Genesis, whether read literally or figuratively: man separated from God in Eden; man separated from men at Babel. The resulting repair mission was clearly marked and, lest anyone miss it, was expressed most directly in the two "greatest commandments"—to love God with all your heart, soul, and mind, and to love your neighbor as yourself.

The explicit legacy of Babel was one of separation by language. But mankind also had been separated by race and gender, cultural and religious traditions, continents and climes, nationalities and ideologies, and myriad attributes and sympathies, some physical and some emotional, some inherited and some acquired. The command to love your neighbor as yourself was a command to overcome these and all other separating conditions so as to embrace a common humanity. But, because of the other, transcendent separation—the separation of man from God—"neighbors" had less often been the objects of love than of hate, and man's history had less often been about freedom and justice than about oppression and exploitation. Only through a faith-borne grace that remedied the first separation would there be any real hope of repairing the second.

So it was with America's original sin of slavery. So it was with Jim Crow and, later, Massive Resistance. So it has been with all the other struggles for freedom and justice that have marked our nation's journey. And so it is in our contentious republic today and in every place in the strife-ridden world. The burdens all derive from the separation.

Mitch and Chad were joined together by a solid bond of friendship—a relationship, I happily reflected, that had resulted from their initial introduction and interaction through me. By this time, they shared not only mutually rein-forcing relationships with Abby, me, and numerous others, but core values, political principles, and policy goals. While very distinct personalities, they possessed a common perspective and mission. Yet, despite all that united them, these friends persisted in a disagreement that earlier had separated countryman from countryman, brother from brother. The long-past war was a tumor still resident in Southern bosoms, and even when it was not malignant with parti-sanship of one sort of the other, its pathos lingered stubbornly, a vague source of discomfort born of guilt, grievance, and the image of 600,000 corpses—Americans slain by Americans—sacrificed to a convoluted cause.

There were some aspects of the matter on which Mitch and Chad could readily agree—among them, that Confederate symbols had been grievously misappropriated during the 20th century. Mitch personally knew many guardians of Southern heritage and tradition like our friend Chad. None of them, he conceded, seemed like bigots. From Chad's viewpoint, no one had done more to sully the reputation of his Confederate forebears than the red-necks and racists who affixed the Stars and Bars to their clothing, pickup trucks, and other ostentatious items, turning a noble emblem into an instru-ment of intimidation, resentment, and hatred.

My friends agreed, too, with my historical assertion that preservation of a single American republic in the 19th century had been indispensable to Amer-ica's victory over the succession of totalitarian despots in the century that fol-lowed. "We would be two countries, North and South, but we all would be speaking German or Russian," I had quipped, easing the tension briefly during one of their exchanges.

The pair likewise acknowledged the truth of Lincoln's observation that the "monstrous injustice of slavery ... deprive[d] our republican example of its just influence in the world" and made us appear as "hypocrites." Thus, only with its abolition—and the long-sought gains of the civil rights movement—was America finally able to promote democratic development credibly around the world.

Once they moved beyond those fairly modest points of concurrence, how-ever, Mitch and Chad both dug in their heels.

Lee was a gentleman and statesman, the embodiment of fidelity to duty, a military genius, and personal hero to Chad. To Mitch, he was a slaveholding traitor to the country whose uniform he had worn.

Lincoln, for Mitch, was the Great Emancipator—an inspiring leader whose personal growth in wartime paralleled the vital change in Northern war aims from preserving the Union to freeing the slaves. Frederick Douglass had been the *voice* of conscience; Lincoln had been its *hands* and *feet*; and Mitch revered both. Chad, by contrast, thought the 16th president's reputation had more to do with his death as a martyr than his performance, which had been marked mainly by excess and ineptitude. First through the reckless political demagoguery that propelled him to the White House and impelled Southern secession, then through his tyrannical conduct of a war that his mismanagement prolonged, Lincoln had fostered an unnecessary conflict and made the carnage far worse than it should have been—or so Chad saw it.

From Mitch's perspective, Southern apologists contrived all sorts of gallant-sounding explanations for the rebellion but denied the one true and overriding cause, which was the perpetuation of chattel slavery and the racism that undergirded it. To Chad, that simplistic view ignored the sincerity of the Southern fight for self-determination and stout defense of home and hearth. Virginians had no desire for separation, Chad would point out; they initially voted against secession. But when a choice was forced upon them by Lincoln's resort to arms, they viewed the war as a continuation of the struggle for independence carried on some eight decades earlier. "That may have been the perspective of *white* Virginians," Mitch would answer. "My people were in bondage and just wanted the most basic human right—their freedom."

Both of my friends were highly educated students of the war and of the complex set of events leading to it.

Mitch liked to quote the pertinent passages from the secession resolutions, which made abundantly clear that the threat of federal action against slavery was the central cause of the conflict. He could recite from memory Lincoln's second inaugural address, which he regarded as the most important speech in American history. Taken together, the secession resolutions that laid bare the South's motive for rending the Union and the searing benediction offered by Lincoln at his second oath-taking said pretty much all one needed to know about the American Civil War.

For his part, Chad deemed it vital to show that neither Lincoln nor the North were paragons of racial virtue. He likewise would mount a vigorous defense of Southern motives, including the venerated General Lee's. Chad liked to point out that the General's ancestor, Richard Henry Lee—the one who made the motion for independence in the Continental Congress in 1776—had urged the Virginia legislature to abolish the slave trade nearly two decades before independence at a time when New England merchants and towns were still enriching themselves through the transit in human cargo. He had proposed placing so high a duty on slave importation that it would "put an end to that iniquitous and disgraceful traffic within the colony of Virginia." Not to be outdone by Mitch's resort to historical texts, Chad quoted at length from the elder Lee's appeal:

> [W]e encourage those poor, ignorant [African] people, to wage eternal war against each other; not nation against nation, but father against son, children against parents, and brothers against brothers, whereby parental, filial, and fraternal duty is terribly violated; that by war, stealth, or surprise, we *Christians* may be furnished with our *fellow-creatures*, who are no longer to be considered as created in the image of God as well as ourselves, and equally entitled to liberty and freedom by the great law of nature, but they are to be deprived, for ever deprived, of all the comforts of life, and to be made the most wretched of the human kind.... Let us, who profess [Christianity], practise its precepts....

Both Chad and Mitch bolstered their respective cases with colorful stories.

Chad went out of his way to invoke religion in any argument with Mitch, engaging Preacher on his home turf. Chad's favorite story, powerful though perhaps apocryphal, hearkened back to St. Paul's Church in Richmond and a scene there shortly after the war ended. A lone black visitor was said to have surprised the white congregation by standing and moving toward the Communion table. Others remained in their seats and watched with dismay, but Robert E. Lee rose and advanced to the chancel area to join the black man in receiving the elements. The rest of the congregation soon followed the gentle General's lead.

Another evocative account routinely cited by Chad featured the VMI professor, Thomas J. Jackson, before he was "Stonewall," circumventing state law by teaching slaves during Sunday afternoon religious exercises. Like an earlier Presbyterian apostle, Samuel Davies, Jackson regarded the act as his Christian duty because the slaves were God's children.

The ways of Lee and Jackson, Chad would assert based on these and other examples, were not the ways of hatred and bigotry.

For his part, Mitch was a storehouse of anecdotes that personalized Lincoln and showcased his folksy wisdom, especially when it came to casting the country's slavery conundrum in plain moral terms. What is the essence of Christianity if not the Golden Rule, he would ask. And what does the Golden Rule say of slavery? "As I would not be a slave, so I would not be a master," Lincoln famously answered.

Approving enslavement of one's brothers, Mitch said simply, could never be the Christian way.

For Mitch and Chad alike, the problem at bottom was one of empathy.

Chad could not understand why Mitch, who had declared his independence from African-American political orthodoxy in many other respects and whose every success had flowed from relentless personal effort, nevertheless persisted in an attitude of grievance on, of all things, a centuries-old wrong that no one alive today had committed. Had not Mitch railed against the ideology of victimization that held people back, including many black Americans? Yet, he refused to concede that slavery was the result of complex conditions, beginning with the enslavement of Africans by Africans, and exploited in America by Northern and Southern interests alike. Why could Mitch not acknowledge all that was admirable about Southern culture and values? When it came to the Civil War and slavery, Mitch had a chip on his shoulder. *Why couldn't he just get over it?*

Mitch could not understand why a smart guy like Chad, someone who preached empirical objectivity and reliance on reason, was unwilling to acknowledge the plain truth that his forebears had been bigots or, at the very least, docile beneficiaries and willing perpetuators of oppression. Chad was all about advancing personal liberty, or so he said, yet he refused to see or concede the evil affront to liberty that was in his own pedigree. And, being so blinded, he likewise denied the pervasive, persisting effects of that grievous offense on the contemporary condition of many black Americans. From his comfortable *white* perspective, Chad saw slavery as distant and irrelevant. Somehow the fact that the underlying racism had survived emancipation and gone on to manifest in Jim Crow, Massive Resistance, and countless other forms of state-imposed discrimination—offenses neither distant in time nor irrelevant to the present situation—*had slipped past the good ol' boy.*

111

Neither of my friends was able to understand the other's perspective. And failing to understand, it was impossible to take the next, vital step, which was to "bear one another's burdens." Instead, they just went right on talking past each other—something Americans had been doing for a century and a half. Of course, as they talked past each other, they talked past everyone else, too, converting a potentially useful topic into a colossal irritant or, at best, a big bore.

It might have been different if either of my friends had been able to see the other's hero—Lincoln or Lee—as a good man. Neither leader had been perfect; indeed, neither had placed himself consistently on the right side of history or morality. Yet, despite the enormity of their flaws and failings, both had been giants in the context of their times, the embodiment of values and ideas that made them useful exemplars for the American people. Ironically, Americans much closer in time to the horrors and passions of the war had viewed them so, and had celebrated them both. Patriotic icons from Teddy Roosevelt to Dwight Eisenhower had placed Lincoln and Lee, with Washington, among the greatest Americans ever. But here we were, well over a century later, with my two friends so facile and firm in their hindsight verdicts that the passage of time and lengthening shadow of history actually had compounded, not eased, the burdens. Neither seemed to understand that forgiveness is an act that liberates the forgiver, and so, unwittingly, each had tightened his own chains.

Nahum, the Jewish prophet, foresaw "charging cavalry, flashing swords and glittering spears! Many casualties, piles of dead, bodies without number, people stumbling over the corpses," a vision of ancient Nineveh's fate that could as easily have been an account of battlefield horrors in our own Civil War. The problem—unforgiving separation tending toward violent imposition—is a timeless one, and so is the question Nahum asked: *"Where now is the lion's den?"* In what parts of our own lives are we so weighted down by our earthly conceits—our self-certain convictions, preferences, grievances, and resentments—that we ignore the admonition to let go of those burdens and leave judgments to the only one who truly is faultless, the suffering Servant who reconciles us with God and who alone can reconcile us with one another? Even when we are right—*especially* when we are right—the thing that is most important is also the most difficult: giving partisan passions a rest, listening to one another, and letting God's redeeming grace enter in, healing the separation.

All this I can see pretty clearly now, but at the time I was not able to offer my quarrelling companions much useful counsel. I must have been looking for answers subconsciously, though, because something helpful soon found its way to the surface.

A few weeks after the Memorial Day trip, Abby invited Chad, Mitch, and me over to her apartment just off Duke Street for a dinner that she probably envisioned as a peacemaking affair. If that was her aim, the gathering fell short of its goal because Mitch and Chad continued to go at it. But I thought I detected a somewhat improved tone in their back-and-forth, and I was encouraged to hear them agree on one hot topic: While they had very different desires on the fate of the Confederate flag, both thought passing federal legislation to ban it was a very bad idea. Departing shortly after dinner due to an early work obligation the next day, I left the pair engaged in another animated discussion.

"I hate to bug out and leave you with those characters," I said to Abby as she saw me to the door. "I hope you can get rid of them before sun-up."

"Oh, they'll be fine," she said. Then she lifted a small bag from a side table and extracted a hardcover book. "Here, this is for you; I saw it at my corner bookstore this past weekend and thought of you. It's a collection of the letters exchanged between Thomas Jefferson and John Adams after they both were out of politics and managed to reconcile. You don't already have it, do you?" she asked.

"No, I don't. But I certainly know about their correspondence, and I would love to read the actual letters," I replied.

"Well, sometime when you aren't rushing out I'll tell you a really amazing story about what got Jefferson and Adams started writing these letters. I learned about it in one of my Psych classes back at U.Va., if you can believe that."

"I will believe anything you tell me," I replied with a smile before thanking her for the gift and dinner and making my way out the door. I had barely reached the sidewalk before I was thumbing through the volume, and an hour later I was still perusing it as I lay down for bed. One letter in particular caught my eye: Jefferson's pointed missive to Adams about Calvin and the afterlife. For Calvin, Jefferson had general disdain, but for the afterlife he had hope. "May we meet there again, in Congress, with our ancient Colleagues, and receive with them the seal of approbation, 'Well done, good and faithful servants,'" Jefferson had written to his aging friend and former rival.

I slipped into sleep, and the dream-borne image that next appeared was of a similar rendezvous. But the saints this time were sitting around a campfire, and there were three of them. For a while I could see them only at a distance, as if spying from the dark woods nearby. I could not make out what they were saying, but it had the familiar sound of friendly banter. Nor could I see their faces, though for some reason I knew who they were. Earthly contention had set Lincoln, Douglass, and Lee apart as champions of their respective causes—Union, Freedom, and Home. But now they were together, enjoying a permanent peace, their presence attesting that each had won the divine approbation Jefferson coveted … their easy conversation confirming that their earthly separation had been overcome for good.

In my dream, I moved to get a better look and snapped a twig. My surveillance revealed, the trio happily welcomed me into their conversation, albeit as a mute auditor. It was immediately apparent that the heavenly threesome had not abandoned the earthly principles and perspectives that had separated them, but they now saw them in the light of a greater truth and purpose. As the Catechism had forecast, they could "see the checkered web of providence spread out at its full length, and that there was a necessity for all the trials and troubles they met with in time."

The next morning I recalled the nightly encounter and its powerful message of reconciliation, and was eager to share it with Mitch and Chad. But by the time I connected up with them after work the custodian had erased the actual dialogue from my memory. What I did recall was the trio's camaraderie and the dream's benediction, the counsel of faithful surrender from Lincoln's second inaugural address: "As was said three thousand years ago, so still it must be said, the judgments of the Lord are true and righteous altogether."

Mitch and Chad never again argued about the Civil War in my presence after I conveyed the essence of that dream. Perhaps, once it occurred to them that grace had reconciled even the protagonists in that great contest, they decided it was time to extend a little grace to each other. Whatever the reason, the two of them finally started hearing each other that summer. Their dialogue was not heavenly, but it was respectful and candid, and it worked a softening of attitudes. They found they could disagree, often vehemently, without doubting the other's sincerity or questioning his motives. In the process, they discovered they had a relationship of mutual trust that was strong enough to bridge the foul history that had separated them. During a time of renewed national strife over race, Abby and I watched our friends clash and then come together, emerging from the crucible far closer than they ever had been before.

RETHINKING INDIVIDUALISM

Mitch and Chad gained some extraordinarily valuable perspective during that long, hot summer, but they were not alone. I learned some important lessons of my own.

If you had asked when I was in college, I would have said that the American story is mainly about individual freedom and opportunity. But after observing events far and near in the summer of 1986, I had come to believe that the American story is mainly about relationships and reconciliation. Conflict is inevitable, even essential, in a republic of ideas. But where the underlying relationship is valued—where cherished bonds of respect and affection unite people, whether personal friends or fellow countrymen—beneficial boundaries are imposed on the conflict. There are things you will not say and do to win an argument if you care about preserving the underlying relationship. The longer view and larger purpose compel decorum and restraint—and, when we go too far, apology and forgiveness. Uncivil discourse like ours today, and even a civil war like theirs back then, become possible only when people separate themselves into warring camps and let their passions overwhelm this filial principle.

Of course, the American story is about both freedom and friendships—about both individuals and communities—which, it turns out, are mutually dependent. Individuals define and refine themselves through their relationships with other people. Freedom is personal, but its exercise depends on social and political order, which is communal. Belief is individual and occurs in the mind, but practice is communitarian and occurs in relation to others. Faith is a matter of conscience touched by grace, but it expresses itself in love and service to other human beings.

Surmounting the separating causes and conditions, then, is a primary pursuit of free people.

For Americans, the greatest source of separation during the republic's first century was not race, religion, ideology, or party—the familiar contemporary causes of contention. Rather, it was *regional* identity and interest. North and South were trapped in a dysfunctional marriage, and it was the worst kind of dysfunction because both parties were sure they were absolutely, morally right. The realization that my own family embodied resolution of this particular source of separation was a personal epiphany that came as I watched events unfold during that contentious summer midway through Nevers' first Senate term.

At some point during the running historical rehash by Chad and Mitch it occurred to me that the Civil War had received scant attention in the McGuire household during my youth. Despite the official family fascination with history, the domestic squabble of the mid-19th century somehow had not been our thing. It was as if history had proceeded straight from Jamestown, the Revolution, and the "Golden Age" of founding-era statecraft to the 20th century and its serial triumphs over totalitarianism, bypassing the whole disagreeable chapter that was the Late Unpleasantness.

The reason for the omission came to me as soon as I perceived the omission itself. I was the progeny of a mixed marriage, a child of North and South. Among other legacies, that circumstance had made a consistent partisan position—the kind that Chad and Mitch each found so facile—anything but easy. More than a century had passed, but regional perspectives and prejudices endured. Rather than engage an awkward topic, even embrace it for a teachable moment, my parents generally had avoided the subject in the customary manner of their generation: *If you can't say something nice, don't say anything at all.*

That is not to say my dual citizenship had not been celebrated. I learned from the earliest age that my hometown was not just Orange, Virginia, the place of my youth and maternal forebears. It was also Bristol, Rhode Island, the home of my father and his kin. Familial affection, fond memories, and, ultimately, profound ideas would forever link me to both places. I am a son of Virginia through and through, but I claim a Rhode Island heritage, too, and that makes me the literal embodiment of South and North. Even if I wanted to keep fighting the Civil War, I could not—a house divided against itself really cannot stand. But the same is true with or without the separation-surmounting genealogy: *We are all Americans.*

Something positive happens when you decide to dwell on this notion of a shared American identity and narrative. Instead of obsessing on the separation, differences, and grievances, you start to discover the connections and good things you have in common.

My discovery of the intertwined histories of Virginia and Rhode Island is a case in point.

In their early days, the proud, staid "Old Dominion" colossus and the raucous, impudent "Little Rhodie" seemed to have had less in common, perhaps, than any two states. At the nation's founding, Virginia claimed westward to the Mississippi, northward to the Great Lakes, and beyond. Rhode Island was about 1,200 square miles—so small that it would take two of them just to fill up the crater left by the ancient asteroid that created Virginia's Chesapeake Bay. Yet, sometimes acting in concert and at other times contrarily, the two states have played vital roles together in the American story.

In matters of religion, the pair pioneered, transcending mere tolerance to enshrine full freedom of conscience in law. Ironically, the foremost founders of both colonies traced their roots to the same Anglican parish and community (St. Sepulchre's in the City of London). It is not known whether John Smith and the much junior Roger Williams actually shared the same pew, heard the same sermon, or drank from the same Eucharistic cup. If so, those were among the very few things they had in common. Smith, an adventurer, struck out in search of fame and fortune; Williams, a clergyman, sought freedom and truth. But their divergent purposes and paths nevertheless brought both men to the New World, to places where their often controversial labors set in motion events that would loosen and eventually jettison the bonds of religious and political attachment that marked their common points of departure.

Smith came in 1607, made his crucial early mark on the Virginia colony, and left. His consequential edict—"he that will not work shall not eat"—had biblical origins even though little else about his methods conjured up notions of Christian charity. It was some 17 decades later before his successors—foremost among them, Mason, Madison, and Jefferson—wove religious liberty into the state's legal fabric through the Virginia Declaration of Rights and Virginia Statute for Religious Freedom. Williams arrived in the New World almost a quarter century after Smith, but that was soon enough to make him the earliest prominent exponent of religious liberty in America. A separatist who not only renounced attachment to the Church of England but urged strict division of matters civil and ecclesiastical in the colonies, the irascible Williams almost immediately collided with authorities in Boston and Salem as well as nearby Plymouth. He was banished from the Massachusetts Bay colony as winter descended in late 1635, and rather than return to England he found refuge, with the aid of the native Narragansetts and Wampanoags, at the headwaters of the Narragansett Bay. There, in a settlement he dubbed "Providence," Williams set about fortifying his community of faith against external corruptions by fashioning a "wall of separation between the garden of the church and wilderness of the world." More than a century and a half later, President Jefferson would invoke a like image in asserting that a "wall of separation between

Church and State" had been erected by the religion clauses of the First Amendment, whose enactment Representative Madison had accomplished during the first Congress under the new Constitution.

No two people had more to do with the revolutionary American idea of religious liberty than Virginia's Madison and Rhode Island's Williams. I was proud to have a connection to both, and over time I would become fully invested in the idea to which the consequential lives of both men attested: that religion and politics must be at once legally separate and practically interdependent, because politics is about achieving liberty, and liberty is about making choices, and choices are about exercising conscience informed by faith and reason.

The cause of independence also brought Virginia and Rhode Island together. The support of the largest and richest colony was indispensable for independence, so when the time came to command the army, make the motion, and write the declaration, Virginians were tapped for the major tasks. Between the brash Bostonians and the Old Dominion heavyweights, it was easy to overlook the contributions of the Rhode Islanders. Yet, by the time Richard Henry Lee offered his motion for separation from Great Britain in the Continental Congress on June 7, 1776, Rhode Island already had been independent from the Mother Country for a month, the first colony to have so declared. And long before there was Lee's Jackson, Grant's Sherman, or Ike's Patton, there was Washington's Greene. History has largely overlooked the revolutionary commander-in-chief's heavy reliance on General Nathaniel Greene, the plucky, self-taught Rhode Islander to whom Washington repeatedly turned during the arduous, six-year struggle for independence. When asked at one point which of his generals should succeed the commander if he died in battle, Washington unreservedly identified Greene. Indeed, Washington had Greene largely to thank for the failure of Cornwallis's Southern campaign in 1780-1781, a fact the Virginian no doubt pondered as his army joined Rochambeau's French troops—recently arrived from Newport, R.I.—on their historic march to Yorktown and the decisive triumph over Cornwallis that effectively ended the war. A different Rhode Islander, Gilbert Stuart, rendered the timeless image of President Washington that peers back at us from our dollar bills, but Greene likely would have placed the most prominent stamp on Washington's presidential legacy had untimely death not prevented his taking a top role in the Virginian's landmark first administration.

The two states' common cause on independence did not augur collaboration between them on the Constitution, however—at least not intentionally so. But "Rogue Island," as its critics were fond of calling it, nevertheless did its part to aid Madison's enterprise by rendering the Articles of Confederation dysfunctional. It seems odd now, given the little's state big appetite for taxation, but under the Articles it blocked one proposed levy after another, creating a funding crisis for the national government and providing a strong catalyst for constitutional reform in Philadelphia.

Not all the shared history of the places my parents called "home" was cause for pride and celebration, however. Largely unspoken during my youthful forays north to visit my father's family in Bristol, but an unmistakable part of that port community's past, was its role as a key locus for the importation of African slaves. By the middle of the 18th century, Bristol and Newport (just to the south on Aquidneck Island) had surpassed Boston to become the primary slave markets in America. Bristol's merchants, like the region's mercantile interests generally, reaped enormous riches from their sordid traffic in human cargo, a practice that forever linked New England, and especially Rhode Island, to the scourge for which Virginia and the South are routinely derided. I ferreted out these facts on my own, a curious college student unaided by the later-developed Internet, and with these sad discoveries both a measure of my idealism and much of my native Southern guilt vanished, replaced by an overarching sense of sadness.

As a young man fascinated by history, I had uncovered these and other ties that bound my paternal and maternal homelands. But their larger significance, as threads interwoven in a richly diverse American fabric, did not dawn on me until that contentious summer, as my friends gave voice to the regional and racial divisions that nearly had torn our country asunder more than a century earlier. By then, though, my mind was ranging back to an even earlier point in time, before my apprehension of the varied partisan divisions—North and South, Green and Orange, Catholic and Protestant, Republican and Democrat—to which my Daniel and McGuire lineage made me heir. It ranged back to a childhood when I was happily ignorant of all such divisions, whether cavorting carelessly with my friends in sun-drenched Piedmont pastures or biking with my cousins along the narrow streets of Bristol and the breezy shores of Mount Hope Bay.

The youthful memories are vivid still, no doubt refreshed by years of nostalgic reverie. During our family's northern pilgrimages, my cousins and I would bike to the town center from our grandparents' modest home on Sidney Street across from the imposing Blithewold estate. There on the Commons between streets unimaginatively named "Church" and "State" we would play ball with the local kids, make fun of (and, later, flirt with) the neighborhood girls, talk big, and act silly. Because of the tightness and traffic, we were instructed not to ride along the most interesting parts of Thames Street, the hectic, historic thoroughfare that every July 4th famously plays host to America's oldest patriotic parade. Marking the parade route in the street's center were three solid stripes (red, white, and blue) in lieu of the usual orange pair— an attractive nuisance that, together with the illicit character of the activity, made riding our cycles there unusually inviting. We became serial transgressors, and on the few occasions when we were ratted out by a vigilant relative or nosy neighbor, we justified the breach with the claim that we had transited the forbidden zone only briefly to gain access to the nearby waterfront. That somehow seemed eminently reasonable, since Bristol Harbor was the greatest place of all—boats of every type coming and going, hoisting and lowering sails or revving motors you could hear for miles; unassuming fishermen with godlike knowledge of the secrets of the deep; screeching gulls, splashing waves, cool breezes, and long, hazy views; thousands of rocks and shells to throw and plenty of random mischief to commit. There was everything a boy needed to kindle his curiosity and engage his senses, to lose track of time and get into trouble. It was all a grand experience—and that was even before I grew up and also reveled in the remarkable beauty of the place.

Of course, my childhood exploits around Bristol Harbor and Colt State Park, Little Compton and Briggs Beach, and other memorable Rhode Island venues stand out in my memory because they were departures from the norm— special summertime adventures that I looked forward to like Christmas. When they were over, soon to be followed by summer's end and the dreaded return of school, I slipped into a depressed funk of sorts. That reaction seems quite unreasonable now as I reflect on my daily childhood existence in Orange and how wonderful it was. We were not wealthy but comfortable; circumstances were not idyllic but enriching; life was not easy but full of love; and, looking back, there was abundant joy. One of the ironic facets of home is that it is so familiar it loses its appeal. So natural is our tendency, especially as children, to wish life away so we can get on to something extraordinary and different that we often fail to appreciate what we have, or had, until it is only a memory.

Orange County is relatively small now, but initially (in 1734) it encompassed virtually all of western Virginia, which at the time included the lands of present-day West Virginia, Kentucky, Ohio, Indiana, Illinois, and parts of Michigan and Wisconsin. Though my mother's family traced its roots back many generations there, by the time I came along our family's part of it was quite small—a little over an acre and a half right on the southeastern edge of the Town of Orange, the county seat. That was close enough to civilization for me to have a lot of friends to play with and a fairly large zone in which to operate with a measure of independence. Of course, that zone began small and grew as I did, and somewhere along the way I began to take real interest in the history of the place … in my home county's unique role in the founding of the nation. Those paternal walks around Montpelier, the Madison home place, awakened something that still motivates me. Often during our New England sojourns I would brag that my county was home to two presidents (Taylor as well as Madison). In turn, I had to fend off disparaging comments from Granddaddy McGuire, who was quite insistent (and erroneously so) that the place had been named for the same William of Orange whose forces prevailed at the Boyne and pacified Ireland for the English in the late 17th century, victories marked there provocatively each year by parading Protestant "Orangemen." That particular William—the same one who, with Mary, ascended to the British throne in the felicitous settlement that was the Glorious Revolution—was different from the later William IV of Orange, a relatively obscure English prince by marriage, for whom our county actually was named. He was nobody to brag about, but at least I could attest—thanks to my mother's solid research—that our county's namesake did not have the blood of Granddaddy's forebears on his hands.

You cannot dwell on such childhood memories for very long before the childhood lessons also start to appear, and with them come more of the connections.

Apparently, I was something of a big-mouth during our early trips north to visit my funny-sounding grandparents, uncles, aunts, cousins, and other kinfolk in Rhode Island. At least, so I was often told, and my own recollection is not to the contrary. Once, at a very young age, I playfully branded my Northern relatives "damn Yankees." Having heard the phrase uttered back in Orange, I figured it was good for some mischief on our vacation. Excoriation for this "cussing" was expected, and my parents promptly obliged. But my grandparents' reaction was a surprise and stuck with me. "Up here," explained Granddaddy McGuire. "Yankees are old-money Brahmins—Protestants from Boston and the like. *No one here* uses the term 'Yankee' when talking about an Irish Catholic family like ours."

Realizing from my blank expression that I needed some additional context, Granny added, *"They look down on people like us, dear."*

Thus was I first introduced, in the most casual yet unsettling way, to the idea of bigotry. And though it had surrounded me each and every day back home in Orange, somehow the racial stereotypes, prejudices, and separation there had seemed logical, inevitable ... natural. It had always been that way. Here, however, was something different and disturbing, and not least because it applied to me. *Why would anyone look down on my father's family?* My offense was immediate and palpable.

It is striking how suddenly the scales fall from your eyes once you are on the *receiving* end and get even an inkling of what it is like to be unjustly judged.

Memories of that important early lesson came flooding back as I watched the nation erupt in racial discord in 1986. But soon an even more powerful Rhode Island memory, a truly cringe-worthy recollection, came to mind and resonated with the first.

Several houses down the street in Bristol from my grandparents lived a family with a mentally impaired son, probably in his early teens or maybe even younger. I had overheard my grandparents reassure Mom and Dad that the boy was "just a little slow" and posed no danger to me or to my other young cousins. One day, following a severe thunderstorm that washed considerable dirt and debris down the street and into my grandparents' driveway, I answered a knock at the door. I was startled to look up and see the "slow" boy, who then asked, as if somehow I was authorized to answer, whether we needed him to clean the driveway. Turning anxiously from the doorway, I took only a few steps before yelling to my father in the next room, "Daddy, it's that dumb kid from down the street, and he wants to clean Granddaddy's driveway!" My father entered the room immediately and spied the open door and outside it, running away, the kid from down the street. Telling me to wait, he hurried along to retrieve the boy; I saw from the window that tears were streaming down the kid's face as they returned. Dad put him to work on the driveway chore and then gave him a couple of other quick tasks before paying him, no doubt lavishly, for the service. What my grim-faced father—the man

I worshipped and wanted more than anything to please—said to me next I will never forget: "Son, if I had to choose right at this moment who was the better son—who would make a father more proud, that boy or you—I would choose *him*." It cut me to the core, and it cuts me still. Never, ever, to my knowledge, have I said a word to another soul as unkind as what I callously yelled that day in my grandparents' doorway. In that one moment in Bristol, a moment I would desperately like to have back and do over, I learned a permanent lesson about respecting *everyone*.

The custodian pushed that painful memory forward during that summer in 1986, as I watched Chad and Mitch wrestle with some of the most divisive issues of our time. I saw the connection immediately. If we could simply respect one another, accepting that each of us is on a journey charted by a good but inscrutable Providence, then we would be slower to judge, more reluctant to assert moral superiority, and less inclined to claim Manichean certitude in our disagreements. Even our most intense debates, as valuable as they are inevitable in a system premised on competition and choice, could be aired without tearing at the tapestry of our friendships or straining the solidarity of our republic.

This, of course, is a pretty picture of republican harmony, often at odds with the harsh reality on the ground. The truth is that self-governance in a fallen world requires not only basic decency, mutual respect, and forbearance, but also a backstop in the form of shared principles that are embodied in the rule of law. And there will be times in a dynamic self-governing nation when even those principles, or at least our applications of them, collide. It was along such a fundamental divide that North and South clashed—a ghastly affair for sure, but undeniably a fruitful one, for it was in the crucible of that conflict that our national character was forged and our founding ideal of equality before the law was affirmed. Yet, while some great principles were vindicated through that conflict, others were sullied—effects that linger today, often subtly.

Those truths were on display in 1986 for those who cared to look. But, like most Americans, the Ned Nevers of that day did not have much of an eye for subtlety.

The Power of Home

There never was a chance that the United States Congress would ban the Confederate flag, though such an action would have pleased a significant share of the electorate.

To restrict the flag's use by private citizens would have violated the First Amendment in the most flagrant fashion. To restrict its display on the public property of the states and their political subdivisions, by invoking the Spending Power or some other ostensible constitutional authority, would have done unprecedented violence to the core concept of dual sovereignty, sapping whatever vitality remained in the beleaguered Tenth Amendment (reserving powers to the states and their citizens). Even if it were lawful legislation, nothing productive, redemptive, or cathartic could possibly come from forcing such a rule on the few remaining states that had not set aside the emblem on their own. And the collateral damage to the salutary doctrine of federalism would have been enormous.

For years, Nevers had decried "the constant federal overreach that encroaches on the constitutional powers of states and localities and the people they represent"—a standard complaint lodged by conservative politicians, especially in the South. Now the Senate was preparing to vote on an unprecedented and assertion of federal power in an effort to rid society of a singularly divisive emblem, the Confederate battle flag. It would be impossible to square a vote for the legislation with Nevers' longstanding rhetoric, and the fallout from such an about-face would make the Senator's earlier flip-flops pale in significance.

None of that mattered, or mattered enough, to Ned Nevers.

Even our concerted attempt at an intervention fell on deaf ears. I pressed the constitutional objections with all the historical and legal authority I could muster, and Mitch and I together gave passionate voice to the federalism objections. Abby stressed the redemptive value of voluntary solutions crafted at the state and community levels. Chad cited the adverse polling data and urged the Senator to respect the will of his constituents. Even Bart, who usually found ways to undermine us, joined our chorus urging opposition to the flag bill, though his reason was not the greatest. A yea vote on this one, Bart declared, would send as few as eight and as many as two dozen major donors packing, probably for good.

Mitch and I virtually pleaded with Nevers to stand against the tide and challenge his Senate colleagues not to "waste this crisis" on eradicating an emblem. The Confederate flag was not killing people; white nationalists and other racists were. Congress and the Justice Department instead should be channeling the outrage over the Clemens murders into an all-out federal law enforcement push designed to infiltrate and eradicate domestic terrorism, with far-right hate groups as the primary focus. This was not a time for symbolism, we argued; it was a time for decisive action to counter a violent element growing in our midst.

Nevers, however, would not budge.

"It is time," he declared on the Senate floor, "to make a strong and unequivocal statement in favor of racial healing in this country. Even my native Virginia, the former Capital of the Confederacy, has seen fit to consign the Confederate battle flag to proper historical venues. It is time for our sister states and other public bodies to do the same, and, in so doing, to affirm that we will give racial hatred no quarter and racial imagery no sanction in this country."

The sentiment was noble, and the stand, courageous. At that still-early stage in his maturation as a political leader, it made Nevers feel good to do the "right thing" even when it hurt politically (as this stance surely did with the small yet vocal cadre of pro-flag partisans in his Republican base). But despite all his gifts—his smarts and political savvy, his ability to ingratiate and power to persuade, his winsome ways and newfound earnestness—the Senator seemed unable or unwilling to grasp the palpable damage his shortsighted stance would do to the Constitution if enacted.

"Great cases like hard cases make bad law," observed Justice Oliver Wendell Holmes, Jr. "For great cases are called great not by reason of their real importance ... but because of some accident of immediate overwhelming interest which appeals to the feelings and distorts the judgment."

This in a nutshell was the problem with Nevers' position, and all of us who worked for or with him could see it. In the service of the most laudable of ideals, one that "appeal[ed] to the feelings and distort[ed] the judgment," Nevers had trampled all over a basic principle, a core constitutional feature designed to empower citizens and guard their liberty.

I tried to get this point across to the Senator by sharing a family story, and Mitch weighed in by recounting a compelling college lecture. Neither had any effect—at least, neither had any effect on him that we could see at the time.

125

The family story was brought to my attention that summer by my Uncle Seamus in Bristol. It seems that among my McGuire forebears were two brothers who arrived in this country from County Fermanagh and soon thereafter joined the famed Irish Brigade—more specifically, the "Fighting 69th," as General Lee dubbed the Union regiment after watching it repel his Confederate force, likewise comprised of Irish soldiers, at the battle of Malvern Hill. The brothers McGuire eluded death at Malvern Hill and again at Antietam, but only one of them escaped the unimaginable carnage on the sunken road in front of Marye's Heights in Fredericksburg, and that one survived Chancellorsville only to fall finally at Gettysburg. The interesting thing is that both brothers, like many of the Emerald Isle countrymen they fought with and against at Malvern Hill and Fredericksburg, had come to the United States to gain military experience that would equip them to fight for Ireland's independence. Their loyalty to North or South, as the case may be, was steadfast but acquired. What brought them all the way across the ocean to fight was their *home* and a passion to see it free.

It is virtually impossible for Americans in our day, viewing, if at all, through a lens darkened by time and the smoke of contentious causes, to fully appreciate how many on our Civil War battlefields were fighting for the same thing. Today we see the monstrous injustice of slavery and rightly recoil at any stance that would not move heaven and earth to crush it. But, as Lincoln reminded victor and vanquished alike in his Second Inaugural Address, both North and South had profited from slavery, puzzled over it, and allowed the evil institution to persist for generations. For many of my maternal ancestors, the ones on the Confederate side, the fight had less to do with slavery—three-fourths of the Southern white population owned no slaves—than about the defense of *home* and the freedom to live as they chose.

There is little room for this truth in the American historical imagination today, so heavily and completely does the great moral wrong associated with the Southern cause weigh on our modern minds. And well it should, for in this time of rampant moral relativism it is good that at least we can be certain about the evil character of white supremacy and other forms of racism. Yet, as Mitch and I argued in vain to Senator Nevers, sometimes a very good idea can be sullied by association with a very bad one ... and vice versa.

The idea of *home*—not just as a place, but as a powerfully motivating cause, practice, and principle bound up with notions of personal freedom—was the subject of a memorable lecture delivered at the University of Virginia while Mitch was a fourth-year student. The speaker, a best-selling author named Nehemiah Adams, spoke at the Law School, and Mitch ventured over to North Grounds to hear him. Like his ancestor, Charles Francis Adams Jr., who had fought against Robert E. Lee on the battlefield but delivered a laudatory address on the centennial of the General's birth, Dr. Nehemiah Adams was a descendant of the second and sixth presidents and an expert on 19th-century American history. The telling title of his talk was "States' Rights: What if the States Really Had Been Right?"

Mitch was deeply impressed by what he heard that evening—so much so that he obtained a recording of the lecture for me—and my reaction was much the same. We found reason to refer to the powerful presentation on a number of occasions thereafter, but none was nearly as important as in 1986, when Mitch played it for Senator Nevers.

Dr. Adams began his presentation, very oddly it then seemed, by talking about his biblical namesake—"Governor Nehemiah," as he described him—who was among the Jewish exiles still in Babylonia around 450 B.C. Over time, Nehemiah had attained high rank as senior aide to King Artaxerxes, the Persian ruler then in power, and in an act of beneficence the King gave Nehemiah time off as well as the passports, men, equipment, and protection necessary to return to Jerusalem, the home of his forebears, and accomplish the long-delayed reconstruction of the ransacked city's walls. Almost a century had passed since the Jewish exiles were first allowed to return to Jerusalem, yet they had not prospered there mainly because they had failed to erect the appropriate defenses and thus were under constant pressure from various over-bearing rivals in the area. In the Old Testament book aptly named "Nehemiah" there is a lengthy account of how this long-neglected public works project finally was carried out successfully. As Dr. Adams read a series of passages from that biblical account, his point became obvious: "[Jedaiah] made repairs opposite his house.... [Shallum] repaired the next section with the help of his daughters.... [Pedaiah] and the temple servants living on the hill of Ophel made repairs.... [Azariah] made repairs beside his house.... [T]he priests made repairs, each in front of his own house.... Next to them, Meshullam made repairs opposite his living quarters...." And so on. The people, Adams pointed out, were not especially interested in the project when it was for the city as a whole, but when given responsibility for the part of the wall near their homes, they got the work done. Indeed, they got it done even in the face of vicious harassment and marauding saboteurs. "Do not be afraid of them," Nehemiah exhorted his people. "Remember the Lord, who is great and awesome, and fight for your families, your sons and your daughters, your wives and your homes."

Having used the account to illustrate the timeless universality of his no-place-like-home proposition, Dr. Adams then reviewed, succinctly but intelligibly, the history of early America, focusing on the sentiment in the individual colonies and the way the colonists identified with their respective communities as extensions of home and hearth. Especially important in the emergence of America's democratic traditions, he noted, were the town meetings of New England. They were chiefly an outgrowth of religious forms—namely, the participatory modes of ecclesiastical government employed by the Calvinists—and their impact quickly and powerfully extended into the civil sphere throughout the region. The town meetings of New England, like the representative assemblies in the Virginia colony dating back to 1619 and other early forms of colonial self-rule, had imbued the colonists with a sense of responsibility for their own fate and the wellbeing of their families and communities. It had schooled them in the art of government by consent, and for them the "consent" was proximate, palpable, and often quite vocal.

So it was that this homebound perspective—identification with the local community or, in its broadest form, the individual colony—dominated at the time of the Revolution, constantly impeding the effort to fund and equip the Continental Army and, after independence, frustrating the exercise of energetic government on matters that plainly required regional or national action. As explained by Dr. Adams, it was the need for such action, together with the unfolding spectacle of state legislatures trampling on essential liberties, that prompted James Madison and his contemporaries to contrive for a new national charter. To accomplish this, the chief claim that Madison had to overcome was that greater central power would pose an even more ominous threat to the people's liberties. Madison's answer in *The Federalist* turned the prevalent thinking about the virtues of small republics on its head. Liberty would be safe in a large republic, he contended, because of the multiplicity of interests, or factions, that would contend with and thereby constrain each other. When combined with governmental architecture that arrayed interests (both the transitory and institutional ones) against one another, power would be checked, and a dynamic and felicitous balance favoring freedom would be maintained.

"Ironically, in a system of checks and balances that has become a model for much of the world," said Dr. Adams,

> the one "check and balance" that has been most egregiously eroded in modern America—the power of the states to check what we now call "federal" power—is the one the framers viewed as the most impenetrable and least vulnerable. All of their experience said so. The people, after all, saw themselves chiefly as citizens of their respective states. The states were the primary form of government and would remain so under the new Constitution. Indeed, unlike the other checks and balances that the framers *manufactured* when they conceived the new plan of government, state power was not a created device; it was an established fact. And even with the notion of "dual sovereignty"—a seemingly ingenious finesse that would come back to bite everyone eight decades later— all understood that state governments would have plenary powers and that the national government power would be limited in scope. They even added a constitutional amendment, the Tenth, to reiterate the point: *The powers not delegated to the United States by the Constitution, nor prohibited by it to the States, are reserved to the States respectively, or to the people.* All agreed the national government would be the junior partner....

In the most eye-opening part of the lecture, the noted historian then went on to describe the shifting regional and partisan perspectives on state powers—or, "States' Rights," as it has come to be known—during the period between ratification of the Constitution and the Civil War. As Americans entered that period, secession was a time-honored tradition. The Puritans had left England to create their city on a hill; Roger Williams had left the Puritans; and Anne Hutchinson had left Williams. Of course, the American colonies had seceded from Great Britain. In reaction to Adams and the Federalists, Jefferson's Kentucky Resolution of 1798 asserted the states' right to negate unconstitutional federal government actions, and Madison's Virginia Resolution of the same year called on states to arouse the citizenry by laying bare such constitutional encroachments. Once the Jeffersonians gained power at the turn of the century, the New Englanders, who were unhappy about the expansion of presidential authority evident in the Louisiana Purchase, claimed similar powers for the states. Regional hostility to Jefferson's embargo, Madison's trade policies, and the War of 1812 was so intense that the New England states sent representatives to a convention in Hartford to consider secession. The convening states instead opted to assert their power to reject federal legislation, ironically invoking a rationale akin to that set out in Jefferson's 1798 resolution. Southerners were back at it again during the Jacksonian era, with South Carolina's John C. Calhoun championing the states' sovereign right to nullify disagreeable federal actions—in this case, the protective tariff. Calhoun's secessionist talk was rebuffed by the elderly Madison in a final plea for preservation of the Union.

For years, as the "Slave Power" dominated Congress, anti-slavery forces in the North contended their states could ignore federal laws that protected the Peculiar Institution. When, in the infamous *Dred Scott* decision, the U.S. Supreme Court in 1857 rejected federal legislative restraints on the territorial expansion of slavery, upsetting decades of delicate compromises, Radicals in Northern states began invoking the Kentucky and Virginia Resolutions, claiming the right to overturn the *pro-slavery* actions of the Buchanan administration and federal judiciary. The 1858 Republican convention in Maine passed a resolution declaring the states "independent sovereignties," and the party convention in Ohio similarly asserted the state's rights a year later. In Wisconsin, the state supreme court declared the federal Fugitive Slave Act unconstitutional, and when the U.S. Supreme Court overturned that ruling the Wisconsin legislature invoked the Kentucky Resolution in reaffirming its sovereign authority. Even on the eve of the Civil War, authorities in New York City, New Jersey, Oregon, and California were threatening secession on similar grounds.

"The point of all this," said Dr. Adams after the recitation,

> is that claims of states' rights, claims to state sovereignty, claims even to the right of secession, were not the exclusive province of the South and the defenders of slavery in the run-up to the Civil War. They were often invoked by Northern states and the foes of slavery as well, depending on who was in charge of the federal government at the time.

So my question for you is this: *What would we think of States' Rights today if the positions in the Civil War had been reversed?* What if, instead of Lincoln, another pro-slavery Southerner had won the White House in the 1860 election? What if the "Slave Power" had remained dominant in Congress? What if the Northern states, the opponents of slavery, had been the ones who felt compelled to leave the Union and had been forcibly compelled to stay? Indeed, what if, for the past century, the federal government's position had been to support Jim Crow, segregation, and racial discrimination, and it instead had been the states, or some noble cadre of them, that had vigorously and even violently disagreed, demanding an end to discrimination and seeking to vindicate the principle of equality under the law? *In short, when it comes to States' Rights, what if the states really had been right on the issue that mattered most?*

Adams elaborated on the historical plausibility of his alternative-universe scenario, but his point was not to prove its plausibility. Rather, he challenged his students to accept his hypothetical as credible and then reason from there. "If the dissenting states rather than the federal government had been on the right side of history and morality on the issue of equality under the law, would we today have a more robust system of federalism—more in keeping with the framers' design and the original constitutional bargain, more respectful of the democratic choices made in the states, more friendly to local decision-making, with government closer to the people and, as a result, a healthier, more engaged democracy?"

His thesis was that the principle of "federalism" had been sullied by association with discredited ideas and losing causes, but the principle remained sound. *Reverse the association,* he said, *and Americans today readily would affirm the principle.*

He now had everyone's attention, and he proceeded to make the case for "federalism" using, not the discredited states-rights lingo of the Southern segregationists, but the words of various esteemed authorities across the centuries. First he invoked the leading lights of the Founding Era and their vigorous contention over these issues, not only in forging the Constitution but especially in the debates over its ratification. Federalists and antifederalists, northerners and southerners, all had attested to the imperative of preserving state and local autonomy over the vast majority of issues within government's purview, he noted. So, too, had they agreed on the need to check and balance power. Their views and forecasts had diverged only over how well the new Constitution would succeed in accomplishing those goals.

"Of all the checks on democracy, federalism has been the most efficacious and the most congenial…," wrote Lord Acton, the great English expositor of liberty. "The federal system limits and restrains the sovereign power by dividing it, and by assigning to Government only certain defined rights. It is the only method of curbing not only the majority but the power of the whole people…."

It was not federalism's value in restraining power, but its practical utility in cultivating the salubrious habits of participatory democracy, that caused Alexis de Tocqueville, that keen French observer of the early American republic, to applaud government close to the people:

> [I]t is at the local level that the strength of a free people lies. Local institutions are to liberty what elementary schools are to knowledge; they bring it within the reach of the people, allow them to savor its peaceful use, and accustom them to rely on it. Without local institutions, a nation may give itself a free government, but it will not have a free spirit….
>
> * * *
>
> [In some nations where authority is centralized] inhabitants think of themselves in a sense as colonists, indifferent to the fate of the place they live in. The greatest changes occur in their country without their cooperation. They are not even aware of precisely what has taken place…. More than that, they are unconcerned with the fortunes of their village, the safety of their streets, the fate of their church and its vestry. They think that such things have nothing to do with them, that they belong to a powerful stranger called "the government." They enjoy these goods as tenants, without a sense of ownership, and never give a thought to how they might be improved. They are so divorced from their own interests that even when their own security and that of their

children is finally compromised, they do not seek to avert the danger themselves but cross their arms and wait for the nation as a whole to come to their aid....

When a nation has reached this point, it must either change its laws and mores or perish, for the well of public virtue has run dry; in such a place one no longer finds citizens but only subjects.

Dr. Adams also highlighted the role of the states and their constituent communities as the locus of innovation, experimentation, and reform, along with the corollary proposition that too much legislating at the national level tended to put the country in a policy straight-jacket, a one-size-fits-all approach to governing imposed by the sheer breadth of the mandate. A variety of respected voices across the political spectrum had expressed this view down through the decades, Dr. Adams noted. But the idea of the states as *laboratories of democracy* was most often attributed to a leading progressive thinker of the early 20th century, Supreme Court Justice Louis Brandeis, who wrote, "It is one of the happy incidents of the federal system that a single courageous state may, if its citizens choose, serve as a laboratory; and try novel social and economic experiments without risk to the rest of the country."

Dr. Adams next reached to the opposite pole philosophically, quoting Chad's icon, F. A. Hayek. "There need be little difficulty in planning the economic life of a family, comparatively little in a small community. But, as the scale increases, the amount of agreement on the order of ends decreases and the necessity to rely on force and compulsion grows," Hayek wrote in *The Road to Serfdom*. "Nowhere has democracy ever worked well without a great measure of local self-government, providing a school of political training for the people at large as much as for their future leaders," he concluded.

It is only where responsibility can be learned and practiced in affairs with which most people are familiar, where it is the awareness of one's neighbor rather than some theoretical knowledge of the needs of other people which guides action, that the ordinary man can take a real part in public affairs because they concern the world he knows. Where the scope of the political measures becomes so large that the necessary knowledge is almost exclusively possessed by the bureaucracy, the creative impulses of the private person must flag.

In a concluding flourish, Adams declared a pox on the contemporary houses of both Republicans and Democrats. Candidates for federal office from both parties, he charged, had postured and pandered for votes by promising far-reaching and intrusive federal legislation once each gained power. In doing so, they not only had undermined the constitutional checks and balances on which freedom at length depended; they also had eroded the people's very capacity for constructive self-governance. In Washington, D.C.'s dysfunction, in both its partisan polarization and bureaucratic excess, he charged, lay the bitter fruits of divesting local communities, public and private, of the capability and responsibility to work out their differences and chart their own courses.

Mitch's views had been shaped in important and lasting ways by the words of Dr. Nehemiah Adams that evening, and he hoped Senator Nevers would be similarly affected. After playing the recording, which held Nevers' attention throughout, Mitch drove toward the goal line.

Federalism matters—that is, deference to state and local decision-making matters—Mitch argued, not because state and local communities are any more likely to reach the right decisions, but because they are venues where ordinary people own the choices. In seeking to reenergize American democracy, no one is going to be motivated much by abstract talk of "checks and balances" or "laboratories of democracy." But what might get them revved up is the idea of lodging power close to the people based on the practical principle of *home*. Like those lackadaisical denizens of Jerusalem whom Nehemiah finally succeeded in galvanizing, people will rise up, link arms, and put their shoulders to the wheel for the things that matter to them, their families, and their neighbors in their daily lives. They will work in concert with others where loyalties exist and relationships of trust can be forged. The strength of America, Mitch insisted, recalling Tocqueville, is found in families and neighborhoods, in communities where people engage each other and work through differences to get things done, and in a wide range of enterprising direct interactions and relationships that meet individual and societal needs. With the technological revolution making the global increasingly seem local, new avenues for direct personal engagement are being opened every day, Mitch noted, and the principle remains the same: When people are empowered to act in their spheres, on their own interests, and are largely responsible for the outcomes, they strive and achieve. And because they are, on the whole, generous people—at least when an overbearing government is not sapping their means and spirit of generosity—they make common cause with their neighbors and do great good for those around them.

When even this line of argument, powerfully conveyed by Mitch, failed to alter the Senator's stoic visage, I turned, in a final appeal, to Madison. He was the practical founding father, I reminded Nevers, who was able to see a problem from all sides and seek *balance*. He had witnessed state legislatures trampling on minority rights and impeding national action, and he sought to remedy those two ills through the deployment of national (what we call "federal") power—enumerated, limited, checked, and balanced federal power. Not very long thereafter, he had observed excesses committed by the national government and had sought to array a reinvigorated state power in opposition. But such arrangements, too, were prone to excess, and he would close his public life with a plea for unity under the Constitution and preservation of the Union.

Today, with the question of union long settled, I was certain the visionary architect of limited government, balance, and compromise would be deeply alarmed by the perversion of his constitutional design, especially the explosion of invasive rules and restrictions imposed by largely unaccountable federal bureaucrats. The reinvigoration of state and local decision-making—the return of authority to a level within the practical reach of ordinary people, to a place where ties still bind and where the trust necessary for social cohesion and concerted action is achievable—would have been Madison's pressing purpose in the late 20th century. And so, I argued, it should be Nevers' purpose as well. But the Senator would never have any credibility again on that issue if he were to abandon the principle on the high-profile flag vote.

"If we want choices returned to us in Blackstone and Staunton, in our states, regions, and communities," I told the Senator, "then we have to resist the temptation to pick up a federal hammer every time we spot a nail. If we believe positive change depends on active citizenship and a renewed spirit of public and private service, then we have to leave room for people to choose … and even at times to choose poorly."

All of this we passionately conveyed to Ned Nevers, imploring him to refrain from supporting unprincipled feel-good legislation on the Confederate flag. But, in the end, the Senator simply did not appreciate the principle at stake well enough to weigh it against the opportunity of the moment. And the opportunity of the moment exerted a powerful pull on his good intentions.

"Federalism is an abstraction," Nevers replied, "and right now it's a distraction. The whole country, indeed the *whole world*, is looking for a statement about racial healing."

"But what does it profit a man," blurted Mitch reflexively, "if he gains the whole world but loses his soul?"

I looked at my friend in surprise. Nevers just looked at him in bewilderment.

FROM BAD TO WORSE

While much of America was coping with the summertime outbreak of racial unrest and we in Neversworld were trying to dissuade our windmill-tilting principal from facile symbolism on the Confederate flag, Bart was cultivating a new set of friends. In the top staff role for Nevers just a few years, he already was growing restless. In becoming chief of staff, he had gained the prized status that had been his first and strongest desire. But from his vantage point as king of that particular hill, Bart immediately observed that the landscape in Washington was dotted with much larger rises. There were bastions of elevated wealth and citadels of power far greater than that which surrounded a lowly freshman senator, and Bart looked enviously on both.

Of course, Bart endeavored to conceal his self-serving motivations. He constantly was exhorting the staff to be, as he was, "1000-percent committed to helping Senator Nevers be the most influential and effective senatorial workhorse Virginia has ever had." But colleagues and bystanders inevitably pick up on things, so the concealment was not as complete as Bart imagined.

The first thing to arouse my friends' suspicions were the trips.

Bart relished hanging out with K Street up-and-comers, political insiders, and the hardest charging Hill staffers at work or at play. Lunches, dinners, parties, pub crawls, workouts and runs, squash matches, poker games, evening sails on the Potomac, Bullets and Caps games—these and more were standard D.C. fare, marks of the political man in full enjoying life while working the system. Most of that stuff was not my three friends' cup of tea, so they had little ability to relate to Bart's world. But they knew he was a grasping politico with a knack for ingratiating himself, so they were not surprised to see him cozying up to well-heeled lobbyists and hustling to keep up with his racier, cooler peers on the Hill.

What set off warning bells, however, were Bart's trips to increasingly lavish venues and high-dollar events. Bart was proud of his finer tastes, and his prosperous family indulged itself routinely, so some of this activity seemed explicable on benign (i.e., parentally funded) terms. But, by the summer of 1986, it had become apparent to my friends that Bart was enjoying life beyond his means, or beyond what *should* have been his means. Though just 27 years old and aide to a relatively obscure first-term senator, Bart affected a much more seasoned and connected persona. The shtick obviously worked with some of the right people because, even before Congress recessed for the 4th of July, Bart had spent weekends in Palm Beach, Louisville (for the Derby), and Sea Island, and those were just the ones known to my friends. During the recess, he was off to Martha's Vineyard.

Second only to these travels as causes of angst were the increasingly strange grants of senatorial access.

Nevers, of course, wanted to get to know as many influential business and community leaders as possible, and as one of 100 senators rather than one of 435 House members he now had enhanced opportunities. The development of such relationships, especially those calculated to produce political support and donations, was part of the constant campaigning that is a contemporary senator's lot. Plus, in Washington, clout to a large extent is a product of whom you know and can get to do your bidding. So it was expected that Bart would produce a steady stream of prominent visitors for Nevers to schmooze, and this was a duty the Chief of Staff performed enthusiastically.

Just a few years into that role, however, Bart's choices were beginning to raise eyebrows in the Senate office and across the river at JBW Advisors. The majority of meetings were with people you would expect: captains of industry, heads of business and professional associations, veteran lobbyists, and, from back home, party potentates, state and local officials, college presidents, and local business leaders. But scattered in among them were more than a smattering of questionable characters. At first, it seemed like Bart might just be showing off for his fast-lane friends, securing pointless but harmless audiences with the Senator for some "out there" personalities with little to gain from the access. But, by the summer of 1986, there had been at least three instances, and probably more, where Bart arranged meetings for people with dubious *bona fides* and an obvious desire to do business with, or derive some other benefit from, the federal government.

The case of Arch Ayers, the fast-talking young CEO of a new tech firm in suburban Maryland called "Ardabrent" was typical. Ardabrent's proprietary software could "save the Defense Department hundreds of millions," Ayers glibly informed the Senator in his office. All he needed was a favorable introduction and helpful nudge to the major defense contractors, which so far had shown little interest in his company's products. Nevers ignored the request and wished Ayers well, but soon Bart was harvesting campaign support and some recreational benefits, too. "I've lined up another bundler for the reelect," he bragged to Abby. "An entrepreneur named Ayers—crazy-smart IT guy—probably the next thirtysomething billionaire. I've been courting him for months. Even had to go on his boat for a couple of days, which was torture...."

There was nothing demonstrably wrong with such interactions—businesses with federal interests routinely made political donations—but what worried my friends was what Bart could be doing beneath the surface. In the best of circumstances, the combination of travel and entertainment, political action committee donations, and requests for official or semi-official favors represented a potentially toxic mix. The confluence was made infinitely more worrisome by my friends' growing skepticism about the central actor. By now, they had seen more than enough to justify a generalized distrust of Bart: the manipulative stunt at the 1982 convention; the Senate office intrigue and high-handed dealings with subordinates; the dissembling on matters large and small. With Bart, you never really knew what he was up to, but his ethical rudder apparently was out of order so anything was possible.

What most alarmed my friends was when Bart started mucking around in the Senator's legislative business. That same summer produced an especially troubling episode of that kind. Returning to the steamy capital from an abbreviated August recess, members of the Senate Finance Committee began marking up a tax break bill that was supposed to help jump-start growth and boost the sagging national economy. Bart had shown little interest in the legislation before the recess, but he returned from his August sojourn loaded for bear. He excitedly exhorted key staff members and the Senator himself to reverse field and support a controversial tax break in committee.

Alerted by concerned staffers, Chad and Mitch started to nose around. They had rarely seen Bart so passionate about a legislative matter—the urgent, almost desperate, tone of his advocacy suggested he had something personal at stake—and they inferred he was doing the bidding of one or more of his high-flying friends. The duo resolved to share their concerns with the Senator directly, but the sponsor of the particular tax measure withdrew it before the committee mark-up session, so the crisis passed. Learning of the episode afterwards from Mitch and Chad, Abby decided to do what she always did when there was a problem: she went to fix it, which meant she went to Bart.

Was Bart keeping good track of trip costs and gifts for reporting purposes, Abby asked. If he needed some help with the accounting, she would be glad to work with the staff.

"Not a problem at all," was Bart's nonchalant brush-off.

There sure are a lot of new people trying to get the ear of the boss these days, Abby ventured a few days later, making another pass. Could it be that some of Bart's newer "friends" were using him to get to the Senator?

"Not a chance," replied Bart. "I'm no babe in the woods; you don't have to worry about me."

Frustrated, Abby next abandoned the finesse. "Bart, a logical person would look at what just happened here on the tax bill and ask, 'What kind of game is that guy running?' No interest in the subject before recess, and then after recess the boss has to come down your way or it's the end of the world. Talk to me—is there a problem? Do we have something to worry about?"

The answer was hardly reassuring.

"Yes, if I were you, I'd worry about sticking my nose where it doesn't belong. Now, *butt out*. You do your job, and I'll do mine."

TAKING A STAND

In retrospect, the serial conflicts and difficulties of Ned Nevers' first term appear as prelude and preparation for the real test: a near-disastrous situation that developed in the fall of 1988, during Nevers' first campaign for reelection to the Senate.

A lot of water had washed over the dam since the Senator's easy election six years earlier: the shaky start and high-profile misfires soon after moving to the Senate side of the Capitol; Nevers' controversial stance on the Confederate flag midway through the term; Bart's enigmatic behavior and the increasing skepticism it engendered; and numerous lesser controversies that seemed major in the moment. Though my success rate as an advisor was decidedly mixed, I had been in the loop on most of those big matters. But in the fall of 1988, I was immersed in a major white-collar fraud prosecution in Richmond and thus far away physically and mentally from the Neversworld drama. My role in the fraud case was a supporting one, but it was a two-week trial, and the preparation and event were all-consuming.

I heard about the nearly cataclysmic occurrence only after the fact. Most of the details I gathered through Abby, who provided a characteristically thorough journalistic narrative. Some missing pieces I pried out of Bart, who had his own jaded take on things. I also quizzed Mitch and Chad, who supplied eyewitness accounts like dazed survivors who had just been snatched miraculously from the path of an oncoming train.

It began, apparently, when Bart Bell decided that Ned Nevers' reelection campaign might be in trouble.

Of course, Nevers was never really in trouble. His lead in the polls over Second District Congressman Horatio Hobart, a Norfolk optometrist and three-term incumbent, never fell below seven points even during the heat of the fall contest. But the Democrats nationally were waging a spirited campaign to recapture the White House, and it looked like they might have the upper hand. Driven at last to pragmatism after an eight-year exile, they had picked two moderates, a Border South governor and Midwestern senator, for their national ticket. Adding to the GOP worries, commentators were talking about the American electorate's "two-term fatigue" and the early signs of an economic downturn. Bart perceived trouble at the top of the ticket, and he knew that voters can quickly turn surly toward incumbents, even relatively popular incumbents, when the economy heads south and they feel it in their wallets and pocketbooks.

By Labor Day, the professional pundits and wise heads in the national media had pretty much gone chasing like a pack after the notion that something dramatic was about to occur nationally—that a strong Democratic tide, a veritable tsunami, was heading in and would crash onto the political beaches on election day and change the face of the nation. When they get to talking that way, and especially when they have some economic data and poll numbers that lend credence to their thesis, you had better watch out. Most of them lean toward the Democratic side of things anyway, but what they really want more than a particular partisan outcome is a big story. And when they get that talk going—when you start to hear that "wave" word and "sea-change" metaphor— you had better watch out because their punditry has a way of becoming self-fulfilling prophesy.

Bart Bell knew this, and so the more he listened, the more nervous he became. And the more nervous he became, the more worked-up Senator Nevers got from listening to him.

Chad's polls had consistently shown a solid Nevers lead, and that was some reassurance. But Hobart had come up some and cut into that lead after the Democratic national convention, and in head-to-head match-ups Nevers still was south of the all-important 50-percent support level. The Senator had not raised anyone's ire much—with the notable exception of some unreconstructed Confederate partisans—but he remained vexingly ill-defined in the minds of many Virginians. A sizeable percentage told pollsters they had no opinion of Nevers, causing his "hard reelect" number—the share of voters who said they would vote for the incumbent regardless of his opponent—to remain stubbornly under 35 percent. These were not numbers calculated to put minds at ease in the front-runner's camp, so the Senator and Bart, and even the trio of young campaign hotshots who were my friends, were all like cats on a hot tin roof.

It was in that fretful environment that a very bad idea took hold in the mind of Bart Bell.

Bad ideas tend to take hold when you want to stay in power, or at the right hand of power, more than anything else in the world—and I mean, literally, more than anything else. Bart, though not even 30 years old yet, literally shuddered at the prospect that he might be forced from his prized rung on the political ladder.

He had heard rumors about Hobart's extra-marital adventures several years earlier, and had made a mental note of the tantalizing tidbits. At the time, the Norfolk Democrat had seemed unlikely to merit Bart's attention, but in politics one never knows who or what might end up crossing your path. Always attuned to "character" questions, Bart by now had been on Capitol Hill six years, long enough for the sifting and kneading of political dirt to have become his consuming passion. And the best dirt was sexual. Where there was sex of anything but the most mundane marital variety, there was the opportunity for scandal. Where there was the opportunity for scandal, there was the possibility of leverage. And where there was the possibility of leverage, Bart Bell wanted to understand it, control it, and use it—or at least threaten to use it.

The cliché is that "knowledge is power," and there is usually more than a little truth in clichés.

Horatio Hobart's early campaign ad, the obligatory "bio" spot, showed the smiling candidate laughing and playing with his three children in ostensibly candid clips. There was the happy and shapely brunette, age 15, dressed in jeans and a suitably conservative top, the sandy-haired 12-year-old boy flinging a red frisbee with evident skill, and the 8-year-old small fry jumping to catch the disc so he could toss it to his dad, who received it with a joy-filled expression and almost blinding dental gleam. They were the portrait of the winsome, well-adjusted family. Their wholesome images passed across the screen crisply and quickly before the scene changed to more weighty matters of state, leaving scarcely enough time for even the most discerning of viewers to notice that something was missing.

The something was *Mrs.* Hobart.

Bart knew that Mrs. Hobart was absent because she had, less than a year earlier, filed papers putting in motion the process of becoming the *former* Mrs. Hobart. And he was sure there was a story there. The question was … what story?

Bart was still working on that one when he decided to go to the Senator and tell him it was time to start playing hardball if he wanted to hold onto his seat. Bart knew just the right buttons to push. He knew how to sell the Senator on something—how to help him rationalize giving the instruction that Bart desperately wanted him to give.

"I told the Senator that Hobart's a complete and utter fraud," Bart told me later. "And I stand by that—he's a liar and a cheat. You know that as well as I do."

"I do?"

"Yes, if you are paying attention at all, you do. He pretends to be this paragon of familial virtue, and it's all a hoax. And if he lies about that, he lies about other things. I told the Senator that if half of the rumors about Hobart turned out to be true, he would be a colossal embarrassment to the state. I said we couldn't just sit idly by in a bad election climate and let the fraudulent son-of-a-bitch waltz in and grab *our* Senate seat. It would be bad for Virginia. That's what I told the Senator—*we can't let him do that to Virginia.*"

"And…?" I nudged.

"And … he told me to go get it done. He said if there is shady conduct or bad behavior by Hobart that is going to come out, it would be better for the people of Virginia if it came out before the election, so they can make an informed choice."

"He said that?"

"Yes, he said it," Bart replied. "Or, maybe I said it and he agreed with it, and that means he said it. But it doesn't matter who said it because of the other thing he said, which was that I should go get it done. And I don't apologize for that...."

Bart did not apologize, not then, not ever—not even after it was apparent how badly he had screwed up. In fact, as long as I knew him, Bart never apologized for anything. If you apologize, you are admitting you did something wrong. And before you can admit you did something wrong, you have to understand the thing you did was wrong, and why. And to understand that, you have to believe there really is something that deserves to be called "right" and something that deserves to be called "wrong." And Bart did not have such a belief—or, if he had it, he had fully suppressed it because it was an obstacle to getting done the things he needed to do.

Bart might have apologized sometime if he thought it would help him manipulate a situation to his advantage, but he always seemed to find other ways to maneuver without ever having to fake contrition. And that was just as well, because Bart could fake a lot of things, but humility was not one of them, and contrition requires humility.

Anyway, Bart had wrangled the "get it done" instruction from the Senator, and with that instruction had come the unspoken corollary: "... and don't tell me how you do it." The Senator did not just want plausible deniability; he wanted actual deniability. He somehow had convinced himself that the more vague the mandate to his chief of staff, the more innocent the act. But that self-delusion, as the Senator would learn later, was the worst possible thing you could do with an amoral lieutenant like Bart Bell, because Bart Bell then did in your name whatever he thought would be most effective, and your name was sullied by proxy without your ever even knowing it.

The bottom line, though, was that it was the Senator's responsibility. He had given the instruction, and the instruction was to undermine his opponent's political standing by sullying his character. Of course, he did not view it that way. Maybe he was genuinely offended by Hobart's superseding hypocrisy, which he had witnessed frequently in meetings of the Virginia congressional delegation and in other encounters. Maybe he believed the rumors that Hobart was a fake, a fraud, a philanderer, and even a predator. Maybe he actually bought Bart's line—"This is Virginia, by God, and Virginians deserve better than to have the reprehensible Mr. Hobart representing them in the United States Senate." Maybe he truly believed it was his duty to expose the callow fellow before the people made a big mistake.

But I do not really believe it was any of those things. The thing happened because Ned Nevers, like Bart Bell, was afraid he was going to lose the election.

So, Bart had gotten the order, and had gone hunting. He had unearthed a lurid array of rumors but had found the corroboration elusive. Then one day he arrived early at the campaign office to find a brown envelope that had been shoved under the door overnight—or so he claimed. In it was a private investigator's report recounting the details of Horatio Hobart's extended liaison with a young male member of his congressional staff—one "Hap Lapkin." Bart had studied the report, which was full of credibility-enhancing specifics (times, dates, places) and had done what he regarded as the requisite due diligence. That consisted solely of checking House of Representatives employment records and confirming that a young man named Harrison Lapkin had indeed been on Hobart's congressional payroll for three years.

Convinced that he had the smoking gun, but knowing that the manner of its disclosure would be all-important in nailing the intended target, Bart apparently had contemplated the matter for several days. Then he called in his crack team of political operatives—Chad, Mitch, and Abby—and took all three into his confidence. He did so reluctantly, because broadening the circle of knowledge obviously was dangerous. But he made the calculated judgment that the one he wanted to do the deed would consult with the other two anyway, and so he might as well persuade them as a group.

Persuasion, however, was not his purported purpose as the group convened. Bart took his seat in the large chair at the end of the conference room table, the one used by Nevers when he attended political meetings at the headquarters. After describing the anonymous and unsolicited transfer of the data into his possession and his own "research" substantiating the report's central fact, Bart directed Mitch to deliver the report into the hands of one of Mitch's trusted confidants at the Fredericksburg-based Christian Conservative Association (CCA). Bart figured those folks not only would be grievously offended by the conduct in question but could be counted on to protect the source to their dying breath. In that manner, the damning documents would find their way into the public domain from a third party without any traceable connection to the Nevers campaign.

Bart delivered the instruction unexcitedly, intending to convey the impression that the proposed course of action was self-evidently the correct one. He wanted to make it clear that the matter was being put to the group for execution, not for deliberation and debate in their usual manner. Of course, there was nothing "usual" about this situation or the directive, and so a spirited discussion ensued.

"Give us a break!" exclaimed Abby. "This man has three children who apparently love him very much, and you want us—or Mitch, at least—to tell them and the whole world that their father is some kind of lech?"

"I want you—or Mitch, rather—to help tell the people of Virginia the truth," Bart replied evenly.

"You really expect us to believe that story about the brown paper envelope being slipped under the campaign office door in the dead of night?" asked Mitch. "C'mon, Bart, do you think we are idiots?"

"I told you how I received it," Bart answered firmly.

"What do you know about the reliability of the investigator?" asked Chad.

"It is a firm down in Norfolk. It's in the phone book—"

"Oh, well, that settles it," Chad replied sarcastically.

"Look, Chad, I would love to tell you that I have checked them out with the Norfolk PD, the FBI, the CIA, the Secret Service, and the Better Business Bureau, but I thought it best not to go advertising that this material was in our possession. And I am afraid I don't have a lot of personal experience investigating the credentials of private investigators," Bart replied.

This was perhaps Bart's most truthful statement, though over time he would become quite experienced in such matters.

"What if it's not true?" Abby pressed.

"It is *obviously* true—look how well documented it is…," he said, shoving the material in her direction. "But it will be the CCA that takes the heat, not us, if it is turns out to be inaccurate in some minor respects. The main thing is, it gets out the truth about Horatio and his seedy behavior. If it's not accurate in that central allegation, then someone has gone to a great deal of trouble to perpetrate a hoax…."

"Yes, and that someone would not be you, would it, Bart?" Mitch asked insolently, blurting out the suspicion that was foremost in the minds of all three. "All I see in this report, just thumbing through it, is a lot of rumor and innuendo."

"That's downright offensive, Mitch," responded Bart. "I give you my word that I have not concocted any of this."

"Did you hire the investigator?" Chad asked bluntly.

Bart had maintained an understated, business-like demeanor, but now he sensed the time was right to lay down the law.

"Look, dammit, I did not come here to debate this or be interrogated by you all," he said forcefully, pressing forward in the big chair. "We have the goods on this phony, and here you are, grilling me like I am somehow the suspect. I told you what I want you to do, and I expect you to do it. This campaign is not a democracy. You are employees of this operation, and the Senator and I have been damn good to you. We've made you what you are, and we have entrusted you with major responsibility for the success of this campaign. This election is on the line—it isn't fun and games anymore. *There is a real possibility we can lose!* And we have just been handed credible information that shows our opponent is unfit for the United States Senate. So we have our job and we have our duty, and we are going to get it out there, and get it out there fast. And unless one of you bright guys has a better idea, having Mitch get it to his buddies at the CCA is the best way to do it."

"Why all the intrigue—why not just slip it to a reporter off-the-record?" asked Chad.

"He doesn't want to do that because he knows the source will become an issue," answered Abby. "Even if the person we give it to protects his source, other reporters will immediately ask us directly about whether it came from us. Bart is worried that if we can't convincingly deny we're behind the distribution of this sleaze the story will turn and focus as much on our 'dirty tricks' as on Hobart's alleged exploits."

"Bingo, Ms. Wingo—that's exactly why we need to do it my way," Bart resumed. "Mitch will get the info about Hobart and his Capitol Hill cruising to the CCA guys, and they will be appropriately outraged by it and will get it to the press. And then our hands will be clean, and we will all be proud of what we did, because we will have gotten the truth out to the people of Virginia and kept a fraud and quite possibly a predator from becoming the next junior senator from Virginia."

"And I will tell you one more thing," added Bart, his face now red and his indignation palpable. "This is not a close call in terms of legitimacy. Maybe it's not legitimate to get into a guy's personal life, and maybe it doesn't make it legitimate even when you add in the fact that the guy is pathetically exploiting his cute kids on TV and making them unwitting accomplices to his lies. But you cannot tell me it's not a legitimate campaign issue that a member of Congress is sexually involved with someone half his age *on his congressional payroll*. That, by definition, is sexual harassment, and if you or I or Ned Nevers did it, we'd be sued or prosecuted. Why should Hobart get a pass?"

"If that's so, then why isn't the right thing to turn the information over to the FBI, or at least the Ethics Committee—the people who are there to investigate this kind of thing?" Abby asked.

"Because that will take forever, and it will be too late," responded Bart. "Look, the guy needs to be exposed *before* the election. What he's been doing is offensive as hell—and the people of Virginia deserve better."

"Oh," said Mitch, "now I get it. This is all about the people of Virginia. For a minute I thought it was about doing whatever it takes to save Ned Nevers' hindparts...."

"And what if it is about that?" shot back Bart. "What the hell are you doing here if you are not here to do whatever it takes to save Ned Nevers' hindparts? This is about *loyalty!* When you signed onto this team, you accepted the fact that Ned Nevers is up there on that pedestal, and you promised to serve him, didn't you? And you have done right well as a result, haven't you? And what I am telling you now is that the Senator expects you to salute smartly and carry out his orders."

"*His* orders, Bart, or yours?" countered Mitch. "Did Senator Nevers give these orders?"

"In so many words," Bart answered lamely, immediately realizing he had allowed the conversation to range in the wrong direction.

"We don't want it in 'so many words,'" interjected Chad.

"We want to hear it from him," added Abby quickly. "We *need* to hear it from him."

The contentious meeting ended shortly thereafter, and Bart next did the only thing that he could do under the circumstances. He briefed the Senator on the unsolicited receipt of the investigator's dossier and the much-coveted proof it supplied.

I can see that scene in my mind's eye.

Bart would have reported solemnly that the dossier verified Congressman Hobart's long-rumored infidelity, but more than that, it disclosed some personal practices that were not only, ahem, "untraditional," but also probably "illegal." Bart would not have elaborated, but he would not have needed to, because his arching eyebrow, cocked head, and leering smile would have conveyed that the goods he had on Hobart were really damaging and probably very kinky stuff indeed. Then, to close the deal with the Senator, as he had unsuccessfully tried to do with my three friends, he would have stressed that the most serious aspect was Hobart's flagrant abuse of his office in his sordid bid to gratify his appetite. Bart would have given the Senator every reason to conclude that the most high-minded option, the most noble course, *the best thing for Virginia*, was to run the play Bart was proposing.

The virtue of his position thus established, Bart would have donned a long face and reported with grievous disappointment on the embarrassing weakness displayed by the Senator's favored trio of campaign operatives—Chad Braxton, Mitch Jackson, and Abby Wingo. Having defied Bart's directive on the Senator's behalf, the three, regrettably, now needed to hear from the Senator himself. They needed his firm and unequivocal command if they were to carry out the plan that Bart had developed for effectively disseminating the Hobart information through an independent third party. It was a shame, Bart would have said, that their lack of commitment to the Senator's reelection and lack of gratitude made such a meeting necessary—the Senator deserved better than to be dragged, personally, into this unhappy business. But, alas, it was a necessity....

Nevers would have become highly irked, if not really angry, by this point. Bart's manipulations would have produced their intended effect: The Senator would have been persuaded about the depravity of his opponent, the ironclad quality of Bart's proof, and the imperative—*for the good of Virginia*—that the information be disclosed in some appropriately indirect manner. He also would have become quite miffed if not indignant that the young people he had elevated and entrusted with his campaign could be so irresolute when the Senator's very political survival was on the line.

The scene I envisioned was generally true, as it turned out, but there was more. Senator Nevers did believe Bart had the goods on Hobart, and he believed that Bart had come up with a characteristically clever and competent plan to get that information out on the street. He believed it was his solemn duty to make the people aware of this unfortunate news so that a sleazy character like Horatio Hobart did not become their next senator. And he was irate

148

at my reticent friends. But the Senator also had another notion: He presumed that Bart was lying to him protectively about how he had received the dossier on Hobart. Indeed, he took private comfort in assuming that Bart, who was very good at what he did, had lined up a reliable investigator who had unearthed this damning truth....

They gathered in the campaign office in Crystal City the next day. The mere fact that the Senator would not have the conversation in his official Senate office spoke volumes to the trio of consultants, who arrived expecting the worst. In that, they were not disappointed.

"Bart tells me you are reluctant to proceed with the plan for the disclosure of the information about Congressman Hobart's flagrant abuse of his office," Senator Nevers began, standing with his hands on the back of his outsized chair and peering out the window laterally at the behemoth that was the U.S. Capitol, which rose like a statue above the other alabaster buildings across the Potomac.

My three friends were seated at the table, and he turned his gaze from the citadel of power to face them with a fiery ferocity they had not seen before.

"I want you to know that I expect you to do it. I *demand* that you do it! It is not an illegal or improper request, and unless a request is illegal or improper, you are bound to do it. Your unwavering loyalty to me—let me repeat: Your *unwavering loyalty* to me—*requires* that you do it." His teeth were clenched, jaw set, and voice rising. "If you cannot adhere to that simple standard, then I don't want you working for me. Do you hear me? And if you don't work for me, I fully intend to see that you don't work for anyone else in this business. *Do each of you understand me?*"

He paused and then added in a softer voice with a slight hint of conciliation, "If you have a problem with this, I want to hear it now, so we can put it behind us."

By prior agreement, Mitch delivered the response for the three. The acid must have been palpable in his throat, and his knees probably felt as if they would buckle—anyone else's undoubtedly would have. But Mitch's did not. By everyone's account, his voice was firm and sure.

"Senator, we admire and respect you, and we are thankful for the opportunity you have given us. But this is not something we need to talk further about. We understand what you are ordering us to do, and we cannot do it. We have thought about it, debated it among ourselves, prayed about it—we've hardly slept at all these last two days. If you feel the need to punish us, drive us out of your campaign, drive us out of politics, or drive us clear into the ground, so be it. The Good Lord will watch out for us, whatever may come. But, regardless of what the future holds for us, we need to say this to you: What you and Bart want us to do is *wrong*. And as much as we respect you and feel a sense of duty to you, there is a higher duty we owe, and *we will not betray it*."

If the three harbored any illusion that Mitch's courageous soliloquy would weaken Nevers' resolve, soften his heart, or tame his fury, their hope was quickly dashed. The Senator immediately went into a blue rage, and ordered them to leave the office immediately and not come back. Punctuating their hurried exodus, he shouted, "Just try to get a job in Virginia, you bums. Just try! I gave you everything—I trusted you with my political future—and this is how you repay me?!"

They did not hear the rest of the rant because the shaken trio was hastily exiting the building. But I learned from Bart that, after they left, the seething Senator issued three emphatic orders.

First, he directed his chief of staff to get a new plan to him within 24 hours for the dissemination of what the Senator sterilely termed the "Hobart data."

Second, he told Bart to have recommendations about a replacement campaign team on his desk by the same deadline.

And, third, he told Bart to "see to it that those kids are politically *out of action*. Put out the word that they are untouchable, and anyone who helps them will have to answer to me."

Bart was enthusiastic about the first directive and resigned to the necessity of the second, but he found himself in the improbable position of counseling against the third. Having labored mightily to jack up the Senator for this confrontation and having achieved more degrees of heat than he ever intended or imagined, Bart sought to cool the raging inferno and talk sense to his irate boss.

"Hadn't we better soft-pedal the punitive aspect until after the election? We don't need news stories about a campaign in disarray, plus you never know what those guys will say to the media if they feel desperate. We have bigger fish to fry. Let me talk to them and develop some benign party line about their 'reassignment' that gets us all past this and…."

"Forget it!" Nevers cut him off. "They are untouchable—*untouchable!*— and I want everyone in the business to know it. This is no time to go soft, Bart.

When people think you're so weak that your underlings can pick and choose which instructions they will obey, no one will fear you and no one will obey you. There will be no end to the chaos."

"Normally I would agree with you—"

Bart tried to argue the case further, but there was no point. The Senator's mind was set, and he ended the exchange with a raise of the hand and a scowl that his chief of staff recognized. It was the look of the stout old woman who stands in front of the school bus and commands approaching vehicles to stop on pain of death so that the little ones can cross the street. Nevers wanted the little ones to cross the street, all right. He wanted them off the bus and out of school, out of his sight, and out of his life. He was genuinely outraged that the young people he had recruited and cultivated and placed ahead of more experienced and battle-tested operativess were now being disloyal to him. It was an affront to his senatorial dignity, an intolerable display of ingratitude, a rank betrayal....

Leaving the headquarters building for their separate cars, my three friends, who were now unemployed ex-campaign somebodies with a scarlet letter on their foreheads, resolved to meet up across the river at their favorite Union Street watering hole. Unknown by the other two, but included in her private narrative for me, was a detour by the distraught Abby into the synagogue on Seminary Road just up the road from her Alexandria apartment. She told me she was not sure what had moved her to go there—she had driven by it and thought about stopping for over a year—but in the aftermath of the disastrous encounter on the Hill she had the impulse to stop in and acted on it. Even without knowing how that brief diversion would later transform her life, it was apparent that this sorry series of events was going to have some salutary byproducts.

In fact, events took a positive turn almost immediately.

The three rendezvoused in Old Town, and they barely had time to order their drinks before Joe Baraldi, another young campaign staffer, entered the popular haunt.

"Okay, how bad a dive did our poll numbers take?" he asked.

"Why do you say that?" replied Chad.

"Well," Joe said, "because you three are here drinking at 4:30 in the afternoon and looking like somebody just ran over your pet dog, plus I just came from the campaign office and Bart Bell was sitting there in the Senator's chair looking like he had seen a ghost."

Apparently that is exactly what Bart had seen, or something resembling it.

Shortly after my three friends unceremoniously exited the premises and the Senator issued his heated instructions and departed, Bart dropped into the big swivel chair behind the Senator's little-used campaign office desk. Thumbing distractedly through the small stack of campaign mail marked "Personal" there, his eyes fell upon a plain business envelope with a Virginia Beach postmark and no return address. It was addressed by hand to the "Mr. Nevers for Senator Office."

Exercising his prerogative as chief of staff, which entitled him to invade every conceivable aspect of the Senator's public and private space, Bart tore open the curious package and started reading. As he did so, I can well imagine his body stiffening like a cadaver as the blood drained from his face and his jaw dropped somewhere around his ankles.

The handwritten letter read:

> *Dear Mr. Nevers,*
>
> *I cannot tell you my name, but my sister works for a PI here in Hampton Roads. I voted for you last time, but I am not promising to do it again because a lot of folks are out of work down here and something needs to be done. But that really doesn't matter because what is wrong is wrong.*
>
> *My sister told me something I think you need to know. Her boss does some pretty low-rent PI work around here. She has only been working for him for about six months, but she has picked up on some things. She keeps her ear to the ground, if you know what I mean. Anyhow one of his buddies is a big wheel in politics down here. I don't know his name but a few weeks ago she overheard her PI boss talking to that guy about making up a phony PI report that accuses Congressman Hobart of being some kind of sex maniac or something. The guy said he wanted my sister's boss to make it real convincing with a lot of details in it, and he was going to give him some things to go in there that would help make it sound true, but it was all supposed to be just made up. And he said they were going to get this phony report to your campaign people and see if they could trick you all into using it to slime Hobart. He said with all the rumors out there about Hobart, they had to do something*

because people were starting to believe them, so the best thing to do was make it look like you all were making up the stuff and spreading it around. It seems like a sorry plan to me but I don't know how politics works.

What made me mad is that when all this hits the fan, my sister's boss is supposed to say that it was someone in your group who gave him all the nasty information and asked him to write the report. He is going to lie about that and I guess they are going to pay him some good money to do it. He is supposed to say he never saw the guy before or since and doesn't know who he was, but it was someone who said he was working for your campaign who gave him all the dirt he put into his report on Hobart.

That's the deal. My sister doesn't know I am sending you this. She wasn't planning to do anything because she is scared, plus she says if you fall for a cheap trick like that you will get what you deserve. I am not sure what I think about that but I have seen a lot of bad things happen to good people and I just think a person should know if somebody is out to get you. I would want somebody to tell me if my shoe was on that foot.

Politics sure is a rotten business. Well, that is it and I am sorry I have to keep my name secret but I think I have to do that for my sister. If this gets to you please do something about jobs down here because people are hurting and no one seems to care. The politicians and all the other big people just seem to be in it for themselves. God Bless You.

The letter was signed, simply, *"An honest person."*

It took, I would guess, just a few brief moments for Bart Bell to realize that his pathetic little political life and all his selfish plans had just flashed before his eyes. The adrenalin must have been pumping the way it does after your attention slips and you barely dodge a massive car accident.

Bart quickly gathered himself and raced across the river, over the trestles, under the mall, and back into the Senate garage, arriving shortly after the returning senator. He went directly into the imperial solon's office, where he found the Senator still fuming from the heated exchange not 40 minutes earlier. He set the note before him.

"What is this?" the Senator asked as he began reading. He sat silently and read half of it before exclaiming, "Oh, my God—you mean you really did get this PI report anonymously? Are you kidding me, Bart? You trusted a note slipped under your door?"

"Oh, that's rich!" Bart blurted. "So you assumed I was behind this report all along, and you were fine with that?"

"Well, I sure thought you had more sense than to believe something that is shoved under the door in the dark of night. Good heavens, Bart, what were you thinking?"

"Well, I bet it's still true, or something close to it—maybe something worse!" Bart replied lamely. "Look at the lengths they went to try to trap us and divert attention from whatever Hobart has really been doing. It must be some really bad stuff...."

"'*May* be, *must* be, *woulda, coulda, shoulda!*'" exclaimed the Senator. "You don't *know* there is anything at all there, Bart, except a guy with a loose zipper, apparently, and a lot of rumors. Your paranoid mind and carelessness could have cost us this election. Do you know how devastating it would have been if that bogus report came to light and was traced back to us—and it surely would have been traced back to us. They had prepared a road map to make sure it was traced back to us! My goodness, those guys are clever...."

"Devious is more like it," Bart replied.

"Yes, very devious, and they almost had us," the Senator said, still shaking his head in surprise. "Now, let's unwind this fast. Get those three kids back over here right away. I need to apologize to them and try to get them back on board. And put this note somewhere safe. We may need it as evidence in the future, but don't speak of it to anyone."

"Yes, sir," Bart said, turning to leave.

As he started out, he heard the Senator say to himself, "Thank God for those three kids. I should have listened to them. They just took one heck of a brave stand. *What was I thinking?*"

Bart paused when he heard these words, and turned back to the Senator. He said to Nevers the same outlandish thing he impressed upon me in recounting the remarkable series of events later.

"That's why I recruited them for you, Senator. Strong and courageous, good character, sound judgment. I saw it firsthand when we were in college, and I wanted them on your team for times just like this," Bart said, shamelessly.

"Sure, Bart—right. Absolutely. You have been on top of this at every turn. Thank you so very much," Nevers replied, or something to that effect. The sarcasm seemed obvious to me from the recounting, but, amazingly, Bart seemed to have taken it as affirmation. In fact, hearing him later cite this episode as proof that he enjoyed the Senator's complete confidence gave me my first faint inkling that Bart actually had a screw loose up there somewhere.

When he reached me that evening, however, Bart was still frantic. His purpose was to gain my help in persuading my three friends to remain on the Nevers team despite the day's acrimonious exchanges. As part of the narrative, he breached the Senator's directive and told me in confidence about the anonymous note—I suppose it was his way of casting himself and the Senator as victims rather than culprits in the intrigue. It was the first I had heard of the day's chaotic events, and even without hearing the other side from my friends, I flatly refused to get involved.

"You and the Senator made your bed on this one," I said, lacking a more creative analogy. "Now you can lie in it."

Speaking of my friends, they had arrived at the Senate office a short time after Bell tracked down their whereabouts. The slightly inebriated ex-nobodies were treated to a most deferential and conciliatory conversation with their suddenly less-than-imperious master, who made a point of asking Bart to leave the room before he began speaking with them.

The Senator complimented their courage in sticking by their guns and in trusting their inner moral compass, regardless of the dire consequences. He complimented Mitch on his faith, and he apologized for trivializing it. He said he was wrong to demand they do something contrary to their consciences, and even worse to threaten them. He said something about needing more rest and also needing to have them around more to help him stay focused on doing the right things. He asked for their continued work on his campaign. In fact, he said he was now persuaded beyond any doubt that they were the strongest, smartest, most principled, most creative, and absolutely the best team anyone in his business had the good fortune to assemble, and so he wanted them to assume an even larger role in his operation after the election was over. Most important, he said this: "You know, guys, I don't think of myself as an especially religious man—at least, I don't like to talk about it. I go to church and so forth, but I have never seen much evidence that God gets involved in our political business down here. At times like this, though, I can almost believe in miracles."

There was something miraculous here, all right. But it was not the letter that saved Nevers and Bart from themselves. The truly miraculous thing was the clarity, integrity, and courage—the *faith*—of my three friends.

Mitch, Abby, and Chad were faced with a situation, like so many in politics, that offered a near-endless supply of opportunities for rationalization. If the various justifications advanced by Bart and the importuning by Nevers were not enough, then there was the plain matter of my friends' self-interest. One can summon all manner of "higher purposes" to be served by protecting his own interests, especially when the interest at stake is survival, real or supposed. Indeed, surviving for the purpose of future good works is a seemingly noble end that can justify even the most insidious means.

My friends made a contrary choice. I attribute it to their growing faithfulness and a commitment to principle stronger than reason alone can produce. Their mutual trust and collaboration also mattered, for my friends were then at different points in their journey, yet their stand together gave them strength. It is not easy to hew to your convictions and trust that God has a good purpose when you do not understand the plan and when every earthly thing you have counted on seems to be in jeopardy. It is not easy to take responsibility for making the moral judgment rather than indulging the easy view that the decision is someone else's to make, above your pay grade. My friends' deliverance came in the form of an anonymous note, an intervention of unknown origin, but they made their stand without any promise or expectation of that intervention. They emerged from this fiery furnace with their standing with Senator Nevers enhanced and their career opportunities improved, but they had no reason to anticipate those outcomes. Nor could they, at that nadir in Nevers' office, have imagined how this experience would bolster their confidence, kindle their faith, and fortify them for the even more tumultuous times to come.

In Abby's case, the traumatic experience not only affirmed her inner moral sense but more or less ended her long-running argument with religion. The young rabbi she met that day at the synagogue would, in time, become the center of her world. And seemingly from that first encounter and the simple prayer he offered for her protection, she would exhibit newfound respect for the ancient faith of her forebears. Her compassion would flow not only from a good heart but a regenerate spirit.

It is hard to say what impact the episode had on the principals in the Nevers-Bell political operation. For Bart, it should have been the alarm that awakened him to a second chance, perhaps the last chance to avert his descent. But he seemed to sleepwalk right on through it.

For Senator Nevers, I am inclined to invoke Churchill. The event was not the end, and it was not even the beginning of the end. But maybe it was the end of the beginning. Sometimes you have to see the worst of worlds, even the worst of yourself, before you can choose to change.

For me, the episode was instructive despite my absence. It was about decency, but more than decency—about integrity, but more than that, too. Though it was a trial I did not experience personally, it did as much to prepare me for what was to come as anything in my own past or future. I saw the power of faith in action—the young and vulnerable confronting the powerful, clad only in the armor of truth.

Like every crucible, this furnace had refined: exposing character weaknesses in some, fortifying strengths in others, and creating new bonds of trust. Most significant for my friends and me, it had moved our notion of principles and standards from the comfortable confines of abstraction to the ferocious arena of choice and consequence. That was the way of the world and perhaps its purpose, too. It certainly was the way of the political world, which would keep trying to exert its dominion over us. Like every wide-eyed young person whose illusions are shattered in the awkward, awful theater of good amid evil and evil amid good, we were growing in understanding even as we were struggling to find our way.

CHAPTER FOUR

AWAKENING

I began work as counsel to Senator Edward K. Nevers on the first day of June in 1993.

Somehow, despite my determined resistance, Politics finally took me captive and pressed me into service. How it happened is not easy to reconstruct. One is not transported from a contented domain to a contentious one—from Jerusalem to Babylon—without the forceful interplay of a lot of complicated factors. I certainly did not wake up one day after some dream-borne revelation and say, "Wow, I think politics is the right thing for me after all. Why don't I just ring up Ned Nevers and see if he still has that job for me on Capitol Hill?

I was a free man—a fact I had pointedly impressed on Bart a decade earlier—or so I continued to believe. But there are points in your life when things converge consequentially, and many of them are outside of your control. Take the aging flag I am peering at now, across my office, in the glass case on the wall. It is from the 17th hole at the Sandy River Links. The club pro there wrote the words "HOLE IN ONE" in all caps and added the date of the event, both of which are faded now. It is a trivial thing, I know—but not a random thing. It is there on my wall because this trivial thing brings a smile to my face every time I lay eyes on it. It reminds me of a sublime moment of convergence.

It all started with my birth, of course—though events obviously were in the saddle long before that. Then I went up for a pass one night and came down without a football future. Next, I went to college with a bunch of kids who had spent their summers hanging out at country clubs with nice golf courses. My best friends got caught up in politics so I needed something to do. My parents were killed so I was not heading to Orange on any of my weekends. A wealthy foreigner years earlier had decided to build a links-style golf course a few miles outside of Farmville, and it was now in operation. Business was slow so they gave H-SC men a cut rate to get people on the course.

On this particular Saturday the sun was shining when I woke up. Two golf-crazed fraternity brothers were less hungover than usual and decided to join me in heading out early. The breeze was sporadic, light, and from the southwest. The greens were wet and receptive from the previous day's rain. I had excellent hand-eye coordination, but my self-control was still a work in progress, as evidenced by the destruction of my five-iron following an errant shot the previous week. Having not yet replaced that go-to club, I had no choice but to use a seven-wood off the tee. I had great confidence in my seven-wood in the fairway but less so on the tee, so I pretended I was in the fairway. I was in a good frame of mind because I had sunk a 25-foot putt on the 16th green. I was focused because I was one hole up with two to go. I was relaxed because we had only bet one beer. The heavy hacker on the adjacent 14th tee duck-hooked his drive and loudly heaved a familiar epithet as I was lining up for my shot, rather than three seconds later when it would have been during my backswing. My backswing was full that day because I was focused on it, thanks to the way one of my buddies was trash-talking the other about how short his was. My hips slid out a tad ahead and I came across the face of the ball, sending it high and fading right. I had underestimated the wind so the fade was helpful. The ball landed six inches short of the green, on the fringe, and took an unusual 45-degree bounce to the right, probably due to the depression around the sprinkler head. The superintendent had placed the hole that morning in what would become my ball's path—not 15 feet north or seven inches west. And the ball's third bounce took it directly into the bottom of the cup rather than an inch to the left where it would have rattled off the flagpole.

I could go on with a dozen or a hundred more factors that converged in my grand golf feat. The tort professors teach their students to call the most immediate agents the "proximate causes" and to pay less heed to the longer list of actual but remote contributing causes. It is a good thing they make that distinction, even if it is an amorphous one, because if you take the chain of causation to its logical "*but for* this or that" extreme, you end up with a limitless list of things. But here is the point. Whenever I look up and see that 17th hole flag on my wall, a smile forms reflexively on my face, and it reminds me of the life lesson it holds. In that moment Shakespeare is apt to come mind because Shakespeare has a line for everything. He was impoverished by his lack of exposure to golf in general and to the sublime character of a hole-in-one in particular, but he nevertheless mused thoughtfully about converging causes and employed a series of serviceable analogies of his own. "[M]any things ... may work contrariously," the Archbishop of Canterbury observed in *Henry V*, "as many arrows, loosed several ways, fly to one mark; as many several ways meet in one town; as many fresh streams run in one salt sea; as many lines close in the dial's centre. So may a thousand actions, once afoot, end in one purpose, and be all well borne without defeat." Which is how my memorable day on the links ended, thanks to all the converging factors: *without defeat.*

Down the road, years removed from that celebrated hole-in-one, my wife Martha and I would join faithful friends in pondering the intricate tapestry woven from life's converging threads. Our small group of confiding believers would wrestle with the mind-numbing, age-old question about the interplay of God's sovereignty and man's will, of divine providence and human freedom, in the weaving of all things corporeal. We would resolve little, but in resolving little we would affirm much. For at the end of the day, we would all agree on one thing that even the "lucky" Irish half of me finally had to concede: The tapestry is a magnificent *creation*, a monumental mystery that randomness— *luck*—can never convincingly explain.

So I do not take much credit for things anymore—though the framed golf flag still brings a smile. And one of the things for which I take virtually no credit is the decision to plunge into politics. It took a convergence of causes that I could never have conceived and am still struggling to understand.

THE CASE THAT KINDLED

Since one has to start somewhere, it seems appropriate to trace the proximate causes of my decision to work for Ned Nevers to an election—specifically, the presidential election of 1988. It produced a change within the White House and, about eight months later, a change in the Office of the United States Attorney for the Eastern District of Virginia. My boss and mentor was out, and another lawyer with closer political ties to the new chief magistrate and his team was in—a move that, owing to my naivete, struck me as most unjust. Partly out of misplaced loyalty and partly in response to his flattery, I decided to follow the suddenly ex-U.S. Attorney to his former haunt, a top-tier law firm in D.C.

As a junior litigation associate at a premier Washington firm, I was paid what then seemed like a king's ransom and labored in a way resembling medieval torture. As it turned out, I had little substantive contact with the aggrieved mentor I had followed into private practice—a fact that revealed my hasty misjudgment in departing the U.S. Attorney's Office. But things worked out well nevertheless. I largely was spared the usual mundane litigation apprenticeship—Bates-stamping, reviewing, and redacting documents, distilling dry details from voluminous deposition transcripts, researching arcane legal issues, and drafting motions—for two related reasons. One was that I had some actual, albeit modest, courtroom experience. The other was that, alone among the associates, I volunteered when the call went out for help on an unusual case.

Some months before my arrival, the firm had agreed to the *pro bono* representation of a young woman named Susanna Samuels who had been denied admission to a tax-exempt Christian college because of her Jewish faith. My fellow associates all wanted to stay away from such an uncompensated engagement, lest it reduce their effective billing rates and diminish prospects for partnership. But I was naïve about those matters, too, and was intrigued by the issue presented in the case. My examination of Madison during undergraduate studies had flagged the general topic of church-state relations as worthy of deeper investigation should the opportunity sometime present itself, and my Con Law (constitutional law, that is) fascination at U.Va. had provided a further catalyst. Then, too, one can hardly breathe the Charlottesville air without acquiring a reverence for all things Jeffersonian, and nothing is more Jeffersonian than the Sage's quarrel with religion. So, when I heard the hunt was on for a junior associate to help with pre-trial discovery and legal research, I immediately volunteered.

I worked on the case for the better part of a year, and in the end we gained justice for Ms. Samuels, whom the college chose to admit rather than jeopardize its prized tax exemption. The justness of the outcome in a broader personal, practical, and legal sense was ambiguous, but no jurisprudential ground was gained or lost because a settlement rather than a decision ended the litigation. Most important for me, I became altogether enthralled with the strange bedfellows that are the religion clauses of the First Amendment.

It may seem odd to jump from a hole-in-one near Farmville, to document reviews in D.C., to Jefferson and the provenance of the First Amendment. But I said this chapter was about strange convergences, so here is some of what I learned on the latter subject thanks to Suzanna's case and why it mattered.

It was Mark Twain's pal, Charles Dudley Warner, a lawyer and novelist of some renown, who coined the familiar "Politics makes strange bedfellows" phrase. Warner's forebears were Puritans, perhaps rendering his authority on such temporal matters suspect. But the accuracy of his aphorism is nowhere better demonstrated than in the relationship between Thomas Jefferson and the evangelical Christians who backed his efforts to end state sponsorship of religion. Their progeny, the "establishment" and "free exercise" clauses of the First Amendment, likewise coexist and collaborate in the most awkward way.

Historians have made a cottage industry out of assessing, or trying to assess, Jefferson's religious views or lack thereof. Indeed, those views were the subject of intense controversy in his own time. In the pivotal 1800 presidential campaign, he routinely was attacked as an infidel and even an atheist. To his friend Benjamin Rush, he wrote during that autumn:

> [The clergy] believe that any portion of power confided to me, will be exerted in opposition to their schemes. And they believe rightly; for I have sworn upon the altar of god, eternal hostility against every form of tyranny over the mind of man. But this is all they have to fear from me: and enough, too, in their opinion....

Jefferson's apprehension of the historic ills wrought by power-hungry men in religion's name was acute. He abhorred in equal measure religious and political absolutism, since both were means of controlling others by imposition rather than enlightened application of reason. For ceremonies marking the 50th anniversary of Independence Day, he wrote what would prove to be his last letter and reflected on the significance of the fledgling American republic:

> May it be to the world, what I believe it will be, (to some parts sooner, to others later, but finally to all,) the signal of

arousing men to burst the chains under which monkish ignorance and superstition had persuaded them to bind themselves, and to assume the blessings and security of
self-government.... All eyes are opened, or opening, to the
rights of man. The general spread of the light of science has
already laid open to every view the palpable truth, that the
mass of mankind has not been born with saddles on their
backs, nor a favored few booted and spurred, ready to ride
them legitimately, by the grace of God.

Earlier he had reached from Paris with this counsel for his nephew, Peter
Carr:

Fix reason firmly in her seat, and call to her tribunal every
fact, every opinion. Question with boldness even the existence of a god; because, if there be one, he must more approve of the homage of reason, than that of blindfolded
fear.... Do not be frightened from this inquiry by any fear of
its consequences. If it ends in a belief that there is no god,
you will find incitements to virtue in the comfort and pleas-
antness you feel in its exercise, and the love of others which
it will procure you. If you find reason to believe there is a
god, a consciousness that you are acting under his eye, and
that he approves you, will be a vast additional incitement; if
that there be a future state, the hope of a happy existence in
that increases the appetite to deserve it; if that Jesus was also
a god, you will be comforted by a belief of his aid and love.
In fine, I repeat that you must lay aside all prejudice on both
sides, and neither believe nor reject anything, because any
other persons, or description of persons, have rejected or believed it. Your own reason is the only oracle given you by
heaven, and you are answerable not for the rightness but uprightness of the decision.

Jefferson eschewed Calvinism and was "of a sect by myself, as far as I
know," he wrote to Philadelphia clergyman Ezra Stiles Ely in 1819. Yet, it was

Calvinists, Baptists, and other Christian dissenters—the era's most ardent religionists—with whom Jefferson made common cause on behalf of religious liberty. They provided the political impetus for his Virginia Statute for Religious Freedom and celebrated its passage. They importuned his friend Madison to carry forward an amendment to the new Constitution embodying a guarantee of religious liberty. Even Jefferson's famous "saddle[d] ... booted and spurred" line apparently was borrowed from a Puritan soldier martyred just before England's Glorious Revolution. And it was in correspondence with the Baptists in Danbury, Connecticut—a letter he closed by reciprocating his correspondents' prayer—that Jefferson employed the metaphor destined to be used, and misused, in 20th century Supreme Court jurisprudence: "a wall of separation between Church and State."

The "strange bedfellows" created by the struggle for religious liberty each found its cause encapsulated in a portion of the First Amendment to the United States Constitution, which prohibits both the establishment of religion and abridgement of its free exercise. That these words can bed down next to each other and, despite frequent disturbances to their rest and intercourse, remain intact if not always in harmony is perhaps the most profound discovery from the American experiment. It bears on that experiment's enduring if unexpected lesson that religious faith tends to thrive as religious coercion subsides. It also affirms the necessity of preserving the two principles in healthy tension going forward. For if the protection accorded either is eroded—a risk mainly for the free-exercise promise due to the strongly secularizing tendency in today's society—then state-fostered pressures favoring or disadvantaging religious belief and practice likely will follow.

Jefferson lived long enough to see that both faith and reason could, indeed *would*, prosper in an atmosphere of religious freedom. How he received that news is a matter of debate. He at first seemed surprised that, with reason "fix[ed] ... firmly in her seat" under the new Constitution, and with his Jeffersonian Republican party fixed firmly in the seat of national affairs, a wave of religious revival nevertheless swept the new nation in what became known as the Second Great Awakening. Yet, he did not seem to deem the development so disagreeable as he approached his own rendezvous with the worms and evidently something beyond the worms. In the previously mentioned late-in-life correspondence with John Adams, he mused about being "lookers-on, from the clouds above" as succeeding generations labored at the business of democracy. "May we meet there again, in Congress, with our ancient colleagues and receive with them the seal of approbation, 'Well done, good and faithful servants.'" The Apostle of Reason had taken to quoting Jesus, whose doctrines but not divinity he had embraced, perhaps less eager to occupy a "sect by [him]self" as the prospect of the end or eternity approached.

The discovery of this fascinating history, together with the contentious real-world applications it occasioned, was more than enough to kindle a new passion for me. The law firm job left me precious little free time, and I spent much of it with Mitch, Chad, and Abby, variously Irish bar-hopping around D.C. and Northern Virginia, playing touch football on the Mall, catching an occasional Orioles, Skins, or Bullets game, meandering through some Smithsonian history museums, and occasionally succumbing to Abby's entreaties for more refined entertainment at the Kennedy Center or the Folger. But I found myself increasingly using my spare moments to dig further into the history and jurisprudence of the Constitution's religion clauses. The D.C. gig was just a quick way-station on my life's journey, but the law firm job and *Samuels* case conspired to make me wonder, if only briefly, whether I should consider a career as a First Amendment scholar, practitioner, or both.

That seed began to germinate in the late spring or early summer of 1990 when a favorite law professor, recently ensconced as dean, called to ask whether I would be interested in coming down to Charlottesville one evening a week to teach an upper-level seminar on the religion clauses of the First Amendment. Dean Harwood had followed the *Samuels* case, and he thought a practitioner's perspective might be interesting for third-year students. I dutifully consulted my law firm masters, and, after issuing the obligatory warning about further detriment to my effective rate and prospects for advancement, they gave their assent. So, quite suddenly in the fall of 1990, I became "Mr. McGuire," at age 28 an adjunct member of the U.Va. Law School faculty.

Leading the seminar was challenging and enjoyable. The brilliant students pushed me intellectually, and I somehow managed to stay awake after the adrenalin gave out on my way northward along dark, hilly Route 29 each week after class. But it was definitely a luxury that my demanding day-job did not afford. So, despite positive evaluations from students and a tempting offer from the Dean, I decided not to reenlist for similar duty during the spring semester.

I would teach again sometime—of that I was certain—but at a point when my legal career was on a surer footing.

Then, in late January, another unexpected event intervened, the kind whose life-changing implications are immediately apparent despite the development's seemingly random character. Kerry Dorgan, my revered Con Law professor and a robust fixture on the law school faculty for three decades, was stricken in his sleep and died of coronary complications a few days later. He was barely in the ground—indeed, it was at his wake—when Dean Harwood pulled me aside and asked whether there was any way I could pick up part of his course load. One thing led to another, and in a matter of weeks I was back in Charlottesville, now a former practitioner and full-time professor, completing Mr. Dorgan's courses on constitutional law and civil procedure and filling his faculty slot on an ongoing basis.

It is all a blur now, and although it happened too fast for much deliberation, I was very much aware at the time that it made little sense as a career move. This was a time when other top performers in my law school class were well established at their large firms, looking forward to admission to partnership within a few years. Others were moving into lucrative in-house positions with their key corporate clients or were engaged in laudable pursuits with their chosen nonprofits. If they were teaching—and several were—they had arrived at that lofty perch impeccably credentialed through prestigious Supreme Court and lower-court clerkships. Compared to them, I resembled an itinerant working stiff. Though something of a curiosity to colleagues and students alike, I really enjoyed the work and, by all the accounts, became good at it.

A CHANCE ENCOUNTER

When I was not teaching or counseling students, I generally drifted away from the modern-looking North Grounds setting where the Law School was located to the genteel environs of the Lawn and its spirit-renewing connection with things ancient and fundamental. Going to those graceful grounds that spread out before Jefferson's Pantheon-inspired rotunda was less often a conscious choice than a general impulse. But, whatever the forces that took me there, the effect was vital. I worked out many issues while jogging over those well-worn bricks and strolling in reflective solitude in the cool shade.

Most important, it is where I met the girl of my dreams. She just fell at my feet—*literally*.

I was minding my own business, snoozing on a bench near Pavilion IX, when she rounded the corner and the heel of her tennis shoe touched the puddle near me. Her legs and torso went airborne and her flailing arms grabbed my shoulder in an unsuccessful attempt to cushion her fall. It jarred me from my unplanned nap, and in the momentary disorientation my initial reaction was irritation. But then the full dimensions of the situation dawned on me. The sprawling victim was a good-looking female … who had slipped and fallen next to me…. The cause of her calamity was my bottle of water, the contents of which had trickled onto the ground when my hand relaxed … which occurred because I had dozed off while cooling down after my jog … which happened because I had been up all night grading exams … which was a consequence of my dubious decision to go out to Breckenridge skiing with Chad, Abby, and several other Neversworld apparatchiks over the holidays rather than stay back in Charlottesville working.

It was one of those perfectly explicable chains of events—the proximate causes were easy to trace if one cared about such things—and it was *all my fault*.

While the situation seemed awful at first, it quickly proved positive … and in a life-changing way.

I helped Martha up, showered her with the most profusely pathetic apologies, and helped her to the clinic where, to my enormous relief, she was diagnosed with only a deep thigh bruise. Somewhere along that way I made a diagnosis of my own: *She was the most beautiful person I had ever met.*

As first dates go, it left quite a bit to be desired. But then everything has to start somewhere. In our case, what started was a romance that is still budding. The 25-year-old schoolteacher I married the following autumn was thrilled about life, alert to its fragility, grateful for its blessings, outraged by its injustices, and determined to right the world one child at a time. She was also the most poised and positive, smart and sensible person I ever had encountered. She remains all that to this day, but she also is my passionate partner, constant confidant, and best friend. I thought I had broken her hip the first day we met, and that was an awful feeling. I resolved never to break her heart.

We were married on a bright, warm September afternoon in 1992. Our wedding day was as perfect as one can be without having your parents there to enjoy it with you. Astride always-busy McCormick Road, a hundred yards and change from the Rotunda, the Gothic Revival chapel managed to seem unself-consciously modest despite its glaring contrast with the adjacent Academical Village's classicism. Its interior lighting and acoustics were poor; its austere wooden benches, uncomfortable. Yet, probably no place within hundreds of miles had hosted more nuptial ceremonies. Generations of brides had stridden down the center aisle of University Chapel to greet their grooms and enter matrimonial bliss in a Cavalier tradition that traced to the late 1800s.

As I entered the front of the church, heart pounding and mind racing as I imagined the logistical failures that could mar the carefully staged pro-duction, I was struck by the simple, radiant beauty of the place. Soft rays of light filtered through the stained glass and mingled with the floral pastels, creating a perfect visual accompaniment for Mozart's resonant strains. Its calming effect was palpable. So, too, were the smiling faces and irreverent murmurs of my college and law school buddies. By the time Martha entered, my composure was returning and the sight of her completed the recovery. She always made things easy and fun, and 20 years and three kids later, that is still the way she works.

We danced that afternoon to Louis Armstrong's "A Kiss to Build a Dream On," and it indeed seemed like we were living a dream. It still does.

There was but one discordant note that day. Absent from the many friends who assembled in the chapel and then gathered for merriment at the Boer's Head Inn on that warm September afternoon was one First Lieutenant J. Mitchell Jackson, U.S. Army Reserves. While we all were enjoying the com-forts of home and the grand occasion's camaraderie, he was in decidedly dif-ferent circumstances.

Mitch never directly explained it to me, but I have always assumed that the controversy that enveloped him in Charlottesville—and his political self-discovery there—had a lot to do with his joining the Reserves in the first place. Duty and tradition (his father and grandfather had served) also had much to do with it, no doubt. So did the inspirational example of the Tuskegee airmen; one of them was from Orange, and Mitch's father had told him the story at an early age. But joining ROTC also was a way Mitch could flip the bird at the pointy-headed liberal activists who had become the bane of his existence. When he heard that some of them were agitating for banishment of ROTC from Grounds, I think it probably registered with Mitch that if the libs were so passionately against it, he should be emphatically for it. And once he decided he was for something, it was just like Mitch to figure he ought to go and do it himself rather than just talk about it.

Whatever the combination of causes, Mitch enthusiastically joined Army ROTC in his second year in Charlottesville. He was commissioned a Second Lieutenant in the U.S. Army Reserves after taking his degree, and maintained his active reserve status while working for Senator Nevers and then as a young principal in JBW Advisors. Within weeks after the Iraqi dictator invaded his country's oil-rich neighbor in the summer of 1990, the President vowed the aggression would be repulsed and the dictator removed. Mitch's unit was activated, and after six months of training and some stateside duty, Lt. Jackson and his men shipped out for Kuwait in February 1992, bound for Iraq and what would prove to be an eight-month deployment.

Those days were before the advent of ubiquitous cell phones and other forms of personal communication from the war zone, and so all we ever heard from Preacher came through the mail—or, more typically, via a phone call from his dad, with whom he corresponded religiously. Mitch presumably played down the dangers for his father's benefit, but the daily news reports about the war left little doubt about Mitch's circumstances, and his letters gave worrisome clues of horrific firefights, frightful near-misses, and the agonizing loss of comrades in arms.

My good friend was at *war*—a condition in which Americans, with few exceptions, had not found themselves for decades. Only yesterday, it seemed, Mitch and I had been running back and forth on football fields, acting like we were doing something important, masters of the only world we knew. Now the world was the master; Mitch was halfway around it fighting for his country; and I was at home, unable to do much other than worry.

Mitch was due home for good in October—his return was a little over a month away when Martha and I tied the knot—but a heavy mixture of unease and guilt hung over me during that time, feelings that were heightened by the wedding celebration. *I was in Charlottesville dodging rose petals while Mitch was in Iraq dodging bullets and grenades.* Maybe that was a bit of an overstatement— I sure hoped it was an overstatement—but the danger and hardship inherent in his situation were palpable, and the contrast between his selfless service and my self-enjoyment could hardly have been starker. Despite the excitement of the engagement and the joy of starting a new life with Martha, I was gripped by anxiety not only about Mitch's wellbeing, but by my nagging sense that I owed my country something more. Increasingly prominent in the mix, too, was my growing disdain for the academy, whose leftward lurch was evident in the anti-war hysteria that had begun to issue from campuses across the country, including my own.

By the fall of 1992, Americans had become deeply divided over the war. Shortly after the invasion, the President vowed not only to liberate Kuwait but to capture and punish the brutal Iraqi tyrant who had waged chemical warfare on ethnic minorities in his own country and destabilized the entire vital region through his aggressive pursuit of weapons of mass destruction. It was a decision on which the course of history pivoted. To do less than rid the region of this detestable dictator, the President declared, would only delay the inevitable and set the stage for a future war. So he directed his commanders to take Baghdad and see to the securing of the entire country by American and allied forces. This was accomplished with amazing swiftness in 1991, owing both to American technological superiority and the courageous soldiers who made up "the most effective fighting force the world has ever known," as Senator Nevers liked to say. But a year later the occupation plainly was not going as well. Late in the spring of 1992, the President ordered the deployment of 25,000 additional U.S. troops to counter the insurgents' increasingly violent and effective tactics.

As another presidential election approached, skepticism about the war effort mounted in the media and within the ever-ready corps of pundits and "experts." The decision to go to Baghdad and replace the government there, rather than merely to expel the Iraqi invaders from Kuwait, was re-litigated with growing vehemence. An increasing number of congressional Democrats, including some who just 20 months earlier had voted to send American soldiers into harm's way, now were claiming to have been misled and were faulting the administration's war aims and prosecution of the conflict. Senator Nevers, an increasingly influential member of the Senate Armed Services Committee, stoutly supported the President's policies, as did most others in Virginia's bipartisan congressional delegation. But as the war dragged on and deployments lengthened, military families began to second-guess the strategy, and popular support began to flag even in defense-focused, military-friendly Virginia.

The pitched national debate over the war provided a loud and disagreeable backdrop during those first months of our marriage. This was a time when Martha and I each had to give a little to establish our new mode of life together.

We did that well. But outside the newly established and harmoniously adaptive McGuire household there seemed to be little middle ground anywhere—not in Iraq where Mitch was fighting a shadowy but lethal enemy; not in America where a bitter presidential campaign was raging; and not at the University of Virginia where I tried but failed to keep my mind on teaching.

OBNOXIOUS LIBERALS

I had been immersed in academia for only a few months when I began to question whether it was the right place for me. It was not that I found my colleagues on North Grounds to be politically objectionable. In fact, I did not find them to be particularly political at all. Strong views would find their way into publications and sometimes even into classrooms, of course, and the preponderance of opinion undoubtedly was a tad left of center. But robust exchanges were valued most, and the U.Va. Law faculty nurtured a self-image and reputation for being among the most tolerant and balanced, politically and jurisprudentially, of all the leading national law schools.

That was all well and good, and in normal times the relatively cloistered and refined law school setting might have shielded me from the more objectionable political aspects of life on a typical American college campus. But the early 1990s were not normal times. The country was consumed with an increasingly controversial war, and so the general run of faculty, the dutiful academics devoted to teaching, scholarship, and research, receded into the background while the intellectual chauvinists with the loudest voices and most provocative messages seized the spotlight. Largely insulated from the ardors of daily striving and real-world experience that afflict the unwashed masses, these over-bearing professorial pontificators expressed their facile radicalism with the greatest certitude, exuding contempt for those with contrary views. Perhaps it was unrealistic to expect the more mainstream voices in the faculty and administration to rise in resistance to the one-sided vitriol. But for an intellectual elite that fancied itself heir to the "liberal" tradition of truth-seeking inquiry, the suffocating imposition of a narrow and often extreme set of ideas—with the bully known as Political Correctness standing menacingly by to fend off dissent—struck me as stunningly hypocritical.

Of course, the leftward lean of the academy is hardly a new development, nor is it confined to matters of war and peace. Contemporary liberalism or

172

progressivism, at least as I have come to understand it, is a hodge-podge of political positions routinely associated with the American Left but with a dogma of material equality at its core. Few now dare call it "socialism," the word having become an epithet after a century in which the real-world refutations of its utopian premise stacked up disagreeably like so many corpses in concentration camps and gulags. But the essential redistributionist idea is alive and well and stubbornly holds sway in academia and other effete circles as a matter of intellectual fashion.

I was and remain puzzled by this phenomenon, but it was no mystery to my friend, Chad. His oracle, F. A. Hayek, had written a prominent article on the subject, and during my professorial days Chad would call me every so often and read another quote from it. Apparently his aim was to save me from a life of desuetude and disfiguration as an academic—an ironic mission since it was Chad who later would embrace higher education as his principal project. At the time, I reminded Chad that Hayek himself was an academic, as, of course, were the other Austrian school economists whom my friend revered and regularly invoked. But I nevertheless got his message.

Hayek and Chad were concerned with economics, of course. But the thing you notice if you study history is that countries with economic freedom tend also to be the places where democracy and civil rights flourish. Likewise, economic and political imposition tend to go hand in hand. The odd thing is the denial or indifference that always greets this empirically unassailable proposition in left-wing intellectual circles. Dictators and despots always come for the intellectuals first, but somehow the specter of potential new Hitlers and Stalins on the world scene never seems quite real enough for the elites on the Left until it is way too late. In fact, the whole train of human history right up into the modern period is a long succession of tyrannical exploiters and oppressors, yet the prospect of such despotism always seems to arouse the intellectuals less than the actions of their own freely elected government.

Liberty—the ordered kind that yields justice and fulfillment—is the great pursuit of mankind. But somehow the thing just keeps sailing right over the intellectuals' heads.

So it was during the Gulf War.

A patently malevolent dictator with achievable ambitions for regional hegemony in a strategically vital part of the world had committed brutal aggression against a defenseless neighbor and had savagely denied his own people the most basic civil liberties. All that was undisputed. So the response of the angry, arrogant Left was to decry the warmongering by—you guessed it—the *American* military and administration. Some universities even bowed to the radical nonsense by closing ROTC programs and barring military recruiting on campus. Thankfully, mine was not among them.

Many people, of course, had honest objections to the President's war strategy and even to the war itself. Open debate on the wisdom of war is not only inevitable but healthy in a peace-loving republic, and I had no patience for those who tried to stifle thoughtful dissent by invoking a mindless patriotism. "'My country, right or wrong' is a thing no patriot would ever think of saying...," observed the witty Brit G. K. Chesterton. "It is like saying, 'My mother, drunk or sober.'"

Appreciating the inevitability, indeed the desirability, of contrariness when it comes to war-making, I had paid little attention to the strident antiwar sloganeering before those sharply polarized times in 1992. But now I not only began to notice; I deeply resented the increasingly hysterical criticism of the war effort emanating from the nation's campuses. It occurred to me that I had witnessed this spectacle before, notably during the defense build-up by President Reagan back when I was in college. Then, it had not been only the strident left-wingers on campuses but supposedly respectable voices in Congress and the media who had bitterly denounced Reagan's peace-through-strength strategy, branding him a "dangerous dunce," "a militaristic madman bent on global nuclear annihilation," "a war criminal without parallel in modern history," and so on. Of course, the policies of that much-maligned dunce, madman, and war criminal were now broadly credited with producing victory in the Cold War and liberating hundreds of millions of human beings, so the anti-Reagan vituperations of that time were conveniently forgotten.

But now the nuts were back, and this time it was personal.

This time, my close friend happened to be one of those in the field, risking his life for the freedom and stability these bozos blithely took for granted. Mitch had left everything to do his duty in the hot sands of the Persian Gulf region while in comfort back home his sacrifice was not only trivialized—it actually was *denigrated*—by beneficiaries of his service. No longer was such liberal lunacy merely irksome to me. It was downright *offensive*.

My instinct was to get as far away from it as I could. But one day I got closer to it than I planned.

I was traversing the Lawn in my usual manner, accompanied only by my thoughts in that peaceful little world we inhabited together, when I was jarred by a bullhorn that boomed with a voice I recognized but for a moment could not place. I maneuvered through a passageway and beyond the brick walkway to spy a small antiwar rally underway on the nearby steps of the Rotunda. There, holding forth in high dudgeon was Jeremy Cox, a fellow Con Law professor, visiting from Berkeley, and one of the more aggressive liberal provocateurs on the law school faculty. He was gesticulating wildly and intoning harshly about the "illegality" of the Gulf War. The small but rowdy crowd was loving it, and the more they cheered and fed his ego, the more extreme Jeremy's ravings became. It was time, he exclaimed at one crescendo, "to stop America's rape of this innocent nation for its oil and bring our storm-troopers home—*now!*"

Most war critics, I had noticed, were careful to show respect for the troops even as they trashed the war and the ruling war-makers in the most virulent terms. But Jeremy observed no such niceties. He was a true believer, and from his particular ivory tower the servile instruments of death and destruction in Iraq were war criminals, pure and simple.

"These young men and women don't have to be there. No one drafted them. No one forced them. No one tied them up and bound them and took them to foreign soil! *You're* not there. *I'm* not there. But *they* are there because they *choose* to be there!" he screamed. "They are willing killers in an illegal war waged by America's fascist president. They are the eager pawns of his right-wing government. They are the blissful instruments of the military-industrial complex's merchants of death who rain down their blood money on campaigns like so much napalm in the jungle!"

Napalm? Jungle? Jeremy no doubt wanted to be viewed as a deeply intellectual and principled radical, yet here was a glimpse of his transcendent superficiality. He must have sensed that the napalm/jungle reference threatened to expose just how little there was to him other than a highly romanticized infatuation with the Sixties, so he quickly updated his imagery.

"They are gun-toting, missile-firing, sand-blasting rats of the desert—bloodthirsty war criminals just as much as any stupid, knuckle-dragging, right-wing warmonger of a politician in Washington. I know it's not *fashionable*—he sneered as he dragged the word out mockingly—to criticize the troops, but they are the ones who are doing the fascists' bidding, and people are *dying* because of it!"

175

Then Jeremy uttered the lines that sent me from a state of seething contempt into crazed action. "The next time you have some spare time," he actually told this young crowd, "why don't you head over to a bus station or a train station or an airport, and find some of these young soldiers who are returning from the war zone, and tell them how much you appreciate their service. And then, when they meekly thank you with that fake humility of theirs, you just scream in their faces, 'I'm lying! I don't really appreciate your service! In fact, I despise you, and I despise all you've done and all you stand for. You're a disgrace to this country and to humanity itself!'"

In the brief tussle that ensued I was blocked before reaching Jeremy. What I would have done had I reached him is unclear, for I had not formed a rational thought; I had just lunged. I might have punched him. I surely would have yanked him away from the microphone and showered him with some unflattering epithets. There is even a slim possibility I would have gathered myself sufficiently to demand equal time at the microphone, as silly and futile as that would have been. But it does not matter what I would have done because my sudden approach was spotted by one of the vigilant bearded radicals in my path—clearly *not* a college student—who knocked me aside and then elbowed and kicked me a couple of times before a campus cop who was eyeing the scene nearby grabbed me by the collar and shoved me on my way.

The rally was so unexceptional that no reporter had bothered to cover it, and the abortive scuffle went unreported. Jeremy, unwisely, complained to the law school dean about my attempt to "stifle the exercise of his First Amendment rights," whereupon our astonished superior put both of us on probation—me for a lunge that could be construed as an attempted assault, and Jeremy for "remarks tending to bring discredit upon the Law School and/or University."

The episode was completely out of character for me: *"Hey, I don't like what you're saying so I think I'll just beat the *$#/^! out of you."* I had jumped to forcibly silence the disagreeable, an offense I routinely decried when the perpetrators were illiberal campus liberals whose tender faculties required protection against unfriendly opinion. But such was the ugly tenor of those tumultuous times that even my impulsive actions hardly seemed out of place. The stateside situation was bad and would get worse, but what happened in America is not nearly as noteworthy, at least for purposes of my story here, as what happened next to Mitch in Iraq. A week before his scheduled departure from the war zone Mitch's right leg was shattered by an IED. The doctors' only option was to remove the leg to save his life. And so what was left of my suddenly broken friend returned home to a hero's welcome.

I do not know what awful visions Mitch saw during the difficult days that followed. He would not talk about anything much. But in my recurring nightmare, he would shout, "Dreamer, go long!" and I would dutifully oblige, sprinting away. Looking over my shoulder, I would see the high-arching pigskin spiraling toward me with the usual pinpoint accuracy. But just before the ball sailed into my outstretched arms, I would catch a tele-scopic glimpse of Mitch's face, his larger-than-life smile turning to horror as his entire back leg exploded to bits beneath him. I would scream "Noooooo!"—utterly helpless—as the ball tumbled pointlessly to the ground beside me. And there on the sidelines, with a smoldering RPG cra-dled in his arms, ready to slither anonymously into the chaotic crowd, was a smugly smiling Jeremy Cox.

DIRTY LITTLE SECRET

If Mitch's fate and the fall's jagged emotions had not been not enough to awaken my dormant political passions and shake me from my self-absorbed course, another set of converging events likely would have sufficed. The im-probable agent of those developments was a ten-year-old boy named Lorenzo Washington.

Now, Lorenzo's story ends well—at least, it has gone well so far. But Lorenzo is one of the fortunate ones; he beat the odds. Most kids like Lorenzo do not get that chance.

My introduction to Lorenzo's situation came in the early summer of 1991. Classes had ended, and I had closeted myself at my apartment working on a law review article about recent court decisions applying the religion clauses. I heard a gentle tapping, which I first thought was coming from the adjacent unit. But it persisted, sporadically and faintly, until it finally occurred to me that someone was knocking at my own door downstairs. I descended quickly and opened it to find a young woman, unremarkably clad but wearing desper-ation on her face. She looked the right age but I guessed correctly that she was not a student—at least, not at the University.

"Are you Daniel McGuire?" she asked.

"Yes, I'm Danny," I conceded quizzically. "What can I do for you?"

"My name is Bonita Washington. I used to live in Orange. You might re-member my older sister Sandra. She was in your class in middle and high school—or part of high school, I guess, until she quit because of the baby."

I did remember, vaguely. "Oh, sure, I remember Sandra. Why don't you come in and have a seat," I said, pulling back into the foyer and gesturing to the spartanly appointed space that was my dining room. "Can I get you a Coke or something?"

"No, thank you. The doctor at the clinic said I should stop drinking so much soda. Hasn't your doctor given you a talking-to about that?"

"Yes, I guess, but I just ignore him. How about some water?"

"I'm really just fine," she said as she settled into a seat across the table. She was beginning her story before reaching the chair.

"I know it's strange to have someone like me just show up at your door, but I hope maybe you can help my son. His name is Lorenzo, and he is a very good boy."

The smile that lit her face momentarily erased the telltale lines of pain and sadness.

"He's ten years old—well, almost ten. He just finished the third grade. But, Mr. Daniel, he still cannot read hardly a lick. I have been to the school so many times they won't see me anymore, and every time they just say he doesn't work hard enough and doesn't want to learn. As far as I can tell, they're just saying he's stupid and they can't do anything for him. It is frustrating—my Lord in heaven, it is frustrating! I mean, they have just given up on him, and they don't want to hear anything more about it."

"I'm surprised by that. I thought Charlottesville had pretty decent schools, at least for a city school system," I replied, immediately realizing how cavalier that must have sounded.

"Oh, he isn't in any school up here," the young mother said. "I mean down in Richmond."

"You mean you came all the way up from Richmond to see me! What in the world for?" I blurted.

"Yes, I saved up my money and came on the bus, and then I walked the rest of the way. I did it just to see you, Mr. Daniel McGuire. Now don't you feel like a special somebody?" Her smile returned, this time accompanied by a mischievous twinkle of the eye.

"I mainly feel confused, to be honest. Why me? I mean, what do you think I can do for you and—what's his name—Lorenzo?"

"Yes, Lorenzo—you got it. Lorenzo Washington. He doesn't have a middle name because I don't have one so he doesn't need one, either." The smile flashed again, but then she quickly turned to business. "My coming here is not as strange as it might seem. My sister Sandra still lives up in Orange. She heard from some of her folk that Mitch Jackson has a big job up in D.C., so she said maybe Mitch could help me figure out something to do for Lorenzo. So I called his daddy the preacher—he is *such* a good man, that Preacher Jackson— but he said Mitch was off fighting the war…. So then Sandra told me about you and Mitch being good friends and playing ball back in the day when she was in school. So I called back Mitch's daddy and asked, 'Do you know a man named Daniel McGuire who went to school with your son, and do you think he would help Lorenzo?' And he said he sure did know Danny McGuire—he told me you were a fine young man. He even offered to call you for me. But I said, 'No, thank you, sir. I'm gonna take it from here.'"

"The rest," she concluded triumphantly, "I got from calling 411 and then putting my foot in the path."

I was dumbstruck. "Geez, I wished you had just called," I mumbled. "I mean, I'm sorry you had to go to all that trouble to come here."

"Oh, that's all right. A mama trying to do what's right by her little boy doesn't think of it as *trouble*, Mr. Daniel. She just does what she has to do…."

With that, she had me.

"Besides, if I had just called on the phone I bet you would have said, 'Now there is one crazy sister,' and you would not have given me the time-a-day."

"I suppose that's right," I muttered lamely, my mind searching for what to say or do next. Then I excused myself and did what I have done so many times since then … whenever I have a practical problem that stops me in my tracks. I called Martha.

The events that flowed from this improbable encounter would give me a sudden introduction to a devastating reality—the failure of education and denial of opportunity to hundreds of thousands of young people in inner cities across America—and to the dirty secret of why this outrage stubbornly persists.

I had been vaguely aware of the problem prior to delving deeply into Lorenzo's plight, but like most comfortable Americans I had turned a deaf ear to it. It was just another of those sad but inevitable facts of life, sort of like famine in a far-off land, even though this particular impoverished land lay just down the street. And, while I am embarrassed to admit it, I guess I just unquestioningly had assumed that "those kids" were not capable of more.

But over time I learned the truth.

There is more to it, I discovered, than just the vices of monopoly and bureaucracy—though those are plainly ingredients in the failure. The main cause is crassly political. Many urban public education systems in America today have become, to a large extent, public employment programs and spoils systems that are integral to the political apparatus that dominates the city government. Supported by education unionists and other political beneficiaries within and beyond the city's borders, this machine zealously opposes all threats to the educational hegemony on which its strength depends.

And the chief threat is the dangerous idea that inner-city young people can learn as well as anyone else if they are just afforded quality instruction.

Of course, for many of these young people, quality instruction is available only *outside* the defeatist, problem-plagued political behemoth that is the city school system. But if that secret were to get out—as it surely would if educational success stories outside the school system were allowed to blossom and spread—then the whole self-perpetuating political structure would come crashing down. Once people figured out that their tax dollars might actually be invested in schools that taught rather than churned ... once people of goodwill realized that these kids actually could learn and prosper ... once parents and their kids found that the cycle of hopelessness actually could be broken ... well, then, *anything* could happen. One thing that surely would happen is the power of the political machine would be broken. So, on the altar of comfort for some and power for a privileged few, a generation and more had been sacrificed. The greatest number had been consigned to a hopeless and bitter struggle, and, for many, there was the hell of gangs and guns and drugs and prison and death.

Of course, even the most self-interested among us would never admit to others, let alone to ourselves, that we have struck such a Faustian bargain. So an ideology of self-justification emerged to cover up this dirty little secret, and even a lot of well-meaning people unwittingly embraced the ideology. It held that tax dollars must go only to the public school system, no matter how futile or wasteful the expenditure, lest those with impure motives be allowed to succeed: the racists, the religionists, the bad people from that other party, those hostile to the very idea of public education. Even the most modest expenditures outside the monopoly threatened to send the system careening down a slippery slope into the arms of these malefactors. There was simply no end to the villainy that would be unleashed if education dollars went someplace other than the demonstrably failed urban public school system.

Kids might learn and have a future of hope, but, hey, at what cost?

I had none of this perspective when Bonita Washington knocked on my door that warm summer day. I was a product of the Orange County public school system. My mother had devoted her life to teaching in those same public schools. And Martha had committed herself to that calling in Albemarle. I certainly was not part of the political crowd that routinely bashes public education and champions "choice" without ever having set foot in a public school. To the contrary, I was a proud product of and advocate for public education, and remain so today. But at the time the question of what to do when public schools persistently fail had not arisen in my personal experience.

As a student of history, I believed deeply in the idea of universal education and understood its indispensable connection to the success of American republicanism. Whether one approached it from the secular perspective of a Jefferson, the evangelical fervor of a Davies, or the merger of both strands like a Madison, all could agree—all *did* agree—that freedom and opportunity depended on education.

With my introduction to Lorenzo, however, I was transported from the pleasant valley of my own privileged experience and the mountaintop idealism of the founders to the hostile real-world terrain inhabited by a poor city kid in late 20th-century America. And it got me thinking....

Fortunately, Martha had a suggestion, and ultimately a solution, for Lorenzo.

Though employed in comparatively affluent Albemarle, Martha several years earlier had encouraged the missions committee at her church to launch a volunteer mentoring and tutoring program for kids struggling in both the county and city schools. The emphasis was on underprivileged kids in Charlottesville. Other city and county churches soon joined the effort, and the program now was plainly having an impact, especially for elementary school kids who had fallen behind in reading. In the course of this project, Martha had connected with others involved in similar nonprofit programs in Richmond and around the state, and had plugged into their informal network. I did not know much about any of this at the time, but at least I had the presence of mind to call for help as Bonita described Lorenzo's disheartening situation. Martha pretty much took over from there.

She and I drove Bonita back to Richmond that evening and picked up Lorenzo from her friend on Church Hill—the part of town, ironically, where Patrick Henry proclaimed the choice as "liberty or death." Lorenzo was a cute, eager little kid whose broad grin gave no hint of the bleak future that awaited him on his present trajectory. From there the four of us went down the hill to Shockoe Bottom for pizza. We were joined by Mike Balenger, the youth minister at Faith Covenant Presbyterian Church, and the director of the church's small day school, Chandra Jones. Over dinner the pair explained how their church had launched the school a few years earlier for the express purpose of helping young inner-city kids who were falling behind in reading and other key subjects. Once caught up after two to four years, they transitioned the kids back into the public schools. What happened at that point was, they acknowledged, a matter of great concern, and something they hoped to help address more over time. But at least a kid who had learned to read and write well had a fighting chance to succeed.

"We want you in our school, Lorenzo, if you are willing to work hard," Rev. Balenger said, talking to the youngster as if he were an adult.

"My mama says I'm smart and I just need some help—isn't that right, Mama?" Lorenzo responded brightly.

"That's right, baby," Bonita replied.

Chandra, whose compassionate gaze could easily have been mistaken for his mother's, immediately reached to hug the boy. "Well, we're going to give you that help, young Mr. Lorenzo. That's exactly what we're gonna do with you."

My own education process commenced that day, and I was truly shocked at what I came to understand about public education in impoverished settings. Literally thousands of kids received social promotions, failed to master even the most basic subjects, and dropped out as soon as they were old enough. There were notable exceptions, of course—some wonderfully inspiring stories of overcoming written by teachers who refused to give in or allow their students to give up. But there were many more victims of "the system," and they included not only the neglected students but a lot of very capable young teachers who began with a real sense of purpose but soon were overwhelmed by the entrenched nonperformers in neighboring classrooms who lowered expectations, the suffocating bureaucracy that treated any suggestion for improvement as an affront, and the inevitable unruliness and disrespect that characterize settings where failure and futility are foreordained.

My distress was compounded by the proximity of a completely different education reality. Thousands of kids were doing just fine in the suburban public schools just a few miles away. How could good and decent people blithely accept such a palpably unfair state of things? For that matter, how had *I* accepted it for so long?

What really outraged me, though, was a subsequent conversation with Mike Balenger in which he related the hostility that he and his fellow pastors at other churches—with both black and white congregations—had encountered from the school system's managers. After several years, the collaborating churches' success in providing remedial instruction and preparing kids to reenter the city schools as high performers was undeniable. The initiative also had brought substantial charitable resources to bear on the city's difficult educational mission, supplementing public funding. The churches felt they could expand their impact through a closer partnership with the city schools through which kids with remedial needs could be identified early and encouraged to enroll in their programs.

"We were not seeking any financial support from the school system," Mike explained with an incredulous tone. "We just asked for their active cooperation and partnership with us in identifying which kids most needed our help and then making their parents aware of the option. But they gave us a stiff arm, big-time! Treated us with contempt ... actually told parents not to listen to us. They know the good we do, but it doesn't matter because, to them, we're just a threat: if we succeed, it shows *they* could and should have succeeded."

I just shook my head. I could not for the life of me figure why concern for those kids did not trump every other stupid, selfish impulse.

"You know the story of the Good Samaritan?" Mike continued. "It's like the folks in the education establishment are not just passing on the other side of the road, ignoring the suffering traveler. They're actually in the bushes throwing rocks so the Samaritan won't stop and help, either."

"It just isn't right," I kept muttering to Mike. I could not think of anything else to say.

It did not take long before I perceived a connection ... and a conflict. One set of events in my life had inspired a mostly theoretical fascination with the problem of church and state. The challenge there, it seemed to me, was keeping and protecting each entity in its own sphere—the public and the private, the secular and the religious, each kept at a safe and respectful distance from the other. But now, with my sudden introduction to Lorenzo's plight, I saw the practical side, and almost immediately the situation looked very different. The practicalities—the interests of the Lorenzos across Virginia and America—appeared to cry out for collaboration, not separation.

The result was something of an internal wrestling match. And it was not long before the tussle found its way into my law school classroom. I was already attempting some new teaching methods when it occurred to me that this was the sort of struggle that would have fascinated, and probably divided, Jefferson the theorist and Madison the practitioner if they could have foreseen the future. So I decided to present the varying perspectives to my students and tease out the issues in a creative way.

It was a decision with unexpected repercussions.

The thought process behind my pedagogical innovations was straightforward enough. As a law student I had done well, but I had never been particularly thrilled with the standard method of legal instruction, which involved examining court decisions. Now I was the teacher and had the opportunity to try something different. Mimicking the methods of my accomplished academic colleagues was calculated only to highlight my comparative shortcomings, so I decided instead to play to my strengths and innovate. What I knew well was history, especially constitutional history, plus I had a few eventful years of real-world experience in criminal then civil practice. So, for my Con Law course, I decided to abandon the traditional approaches—lectures and "Socratic" explications of case law—in favor of a series of provocative guest presentations. The "guests" appeared only vicariously, however; I played the roles and presented the perspectives, staying in character for all or most of the class sessions. Sometimes two or more "guests" would appear in a single class, offering contradictory views. At other times only one would attend, and the students would be the ones to probe, debate, and rebut. Some of the visitors' views were welcomed by the students; others met with fierce resistance. But it was entertaining, in part because it provided a departure from the usual drill. I was rewarded with levels of student enthusiasm, engagement, and participation that were envied by a number of my colleagues.

Most of the battles joined by my "guests" were predictable for anyone familiar with the fault lines in constitutional jurisprudence: The "living Constitution" enthusiast dueled with the originalist; the champion of executive power clashed with the defender of congressional prerogative; the advocate for an expansive federal role sparred with the proponent of reinvigorated federalism; the vigilant protector of public safety and national security battled the stalwart defender of civil liberties; and so forth. Various notables stopped by to explain or defend themselves, as circumstances warranted. Marshall held forth on judicial review; Madison reconciled his call in Philadelphia for a federal veto over state legislation with his later support for state-inspired resistance to the Alien and Sedition Acts; Taney sought vainly to explain why the territorial expansion of slavery deserved constitutional protection; Lincoln had a go at justifying suspension of the writ of habeas corpus and arrest of pro-Confederate members of the Maryland legislature; FDR rationalized his attempt to pack the Court; Warren, Blackmun, and Powell defended their *Miranda*, *Roe*, and *Bakke* handiwork, respectively, against dissenters decrying robed policymaking; and there were numerous others.

Three of the class sessions were devoted to the religion clauses of the First Amendment, and the first two of those went great. All hell broke loose after the third.

I opened the first class with a "debate" between Jefferson and Lincoln over the propriety of proclamations declaring national days of prayer and thanksgiving, a point on which they diverged decisively. Viewers of *post mortem* events from "on high"—a notion to which both men seemed to subscribe—the two guests offered sometimes conflicting, sometimes coinciding views on a range of later controversies, from the propriety of school prayers and congressional chaplains to the national motto ("In God We Trust") and nativity scenes on public property. At one point during the discussion, Jefferson chided Lincoln for the hyper-religious character of his Second Inaugural Address, calling it the "most thoroughly theological discourse ever delivered by a Chief Magistrate in this country." In reply, Honest Abe jocularly rescinded his famous "all honor to Jefferson" declaration and recalled the Sage of Monticello's checkered wartime governorship. "In my experience, ravages of war and apprehensions of mortality tend to focus the mind," said Lincoln. "As I recall, you quite readily declared a day of thanksgiving and prayer as the Virginia magistrate. An entreaty for the Almighty's aid no doubt seemed quite sensible when the Redcoats were marauding through your countryside looking for a rebel governor to hang." Irked by the reference to a sore subject but characteristically gracious, the Virginian rejoined, "Mr. President, I concede it is exceedingly rare, but I must say in this instance your historical reference is flawed. The depredations of Colonel Tarleton, to which you implicitly refer, were inflicted on our country a considerable time *after* my thanksgiving proclamation. Perhaps you have not seen my letter to the good Reverend Miller in 1808 explaining why, as president rather than governor, I considered myself enjoined by the First Amendment from issuing such a proclamation...."

The second session zeroed in further on the Establishment Clause, and its centerpiece was a four-way conversation between the two hugely influential Scots, David Hume and Adam Smith, and their junior Virginia contemporaries, Patrick Henry and James Madison. After introductory comments by Madison highlighting the influence of the "Scottish Enlightenment" and Presbyterians' covenant theology on the American Revolution and later constitutional design, the four offered divergent perspectives on the efficacy of collaboration versus separation in regard to church and state. Hume, the irreligious one in the quartet, made the most expansive argument for state sponsorship of religion. His rationale was utilitarian: established religion tended to dull the passions of practitioners and thus curb zealotry and excess. Smith, a more traditional ethicist and apparent believer, confessed to some ambivalence but came down on the side of a generally free religious marketplace. Both agreed on the underlying economic proposition: religious observance would be more robust if pastors had to attract worshippers to the pews with motivational messages rather than relying on the force of law to pack the house no matter how lame the preaching.

Henry, who early on had made his name in Virginia by opposing the compensation claims of Anglican clergy in the Parson's Cause, now argued that the people should be taxed for the general support of religion. This "bill establishing a provision for teachers of the Christian religion," or "general assessment," as it was known, would promote religious education and practice. This, he argued, was essential for social harmony and the cultivation of republican virtue, and it would not favor any particular denomination or sect (that is, any particular *Christian* denomination or sect). Even this went too far, said Madison, echoing the persuasive *Memorial and Remonstrance* through which he (writing anonymously) had turned the tide against Henry's proposal and set the stage for passage of Jefferson's Statute for Religious Freedom.

The perspectives offered by this foursome, I noted in a concluding summary of recent Supreme Court jurisprudence, had echoed on down through the present. Missing in the four-way exposition, I acknowledged, was an advocate for keeping church and state strictly separate as a means of diminishing the former and aggrandizing the latter, though that motive was routinely ascribed to contemporary First Amendment enforcers by frustrated religionists.

That concluding observation provided a segue into the third class, which is where I took on the vexing matter of motive—religious affinity or hostility—in constitutional analysis.

The final class session opened with Jefferson and Madison enjoying a glass of Madeira on the second floor of Pavilion VII (now the Colonnade Club) before joining students in the library downstairs for a "guest" lecture. Their cordial exchange touched generally on contending approaches to constitutional interpretation, with Jefferson offering what we might today call a "strict constructionist" view and Madison arguing for a more nuanced approach (though he was quick to distinguish his method from "the Hamiltonian heresy that anything the Congress or President does is 'necessary and proper'"). Discussing the religion clauses, Jefferson unsheathed the "wall of separation" metaphor from his letter to the Danbury Baptists and argued for a rigid demarcation between the religious and civil spheres. Ever deferential to his more senior friend, Madison endorsed the Sage's theory but averred that myriad circumstances could arise in which some form of collaboration between religious and governmental institutions might be deemed felicitous by the people. In such circumstances, Madison ventured with a grin, the *dead hand of the past* ought not to thwart the popular will by assigning the constitutional provisions in question a more sweeping effect than their authors envisioned.

The pair soon realized the time and ambled downstairs. There, they and a dozen or so students welcomed a visitor from the future, an irascible professor of constitutional law named "Calvin Pope." Professor Pope began his lecture, shockingly, with a recitation of the Apostles Creed and a forthright declaration that his purpose was to proselytize. It was an affront that might well have sent the University's first rector toward the exit had Madison not leaned in to whisper, "It's a test, my friend—one of those errors we must tolerate so long as reason is free to combat them." It was well that Jefferson stayed, because Professor Pope soon confided that his preceding declaration was bogus and that he actually was a firmly convicted atheist. The about-face left everyone in a state of confusion regarding the Professor's motives—which, of course, was his purpose—and from there he commenced nearly an hour-long explication of his interpretation of the religion clauses.

In his provocative conclusion, Professor Pope argued that the Establishment Clause was violated by state constitutional provisions that prohibited aid to religiously affiliated schools (what those familiar with the bans' origins call the "little Blaine amendments"). He went farther still, indicting the secularist orthodoxy in law and policy that had made many public school environments "hostile to religion." He contended that when a state or local government undertakes to provide public schooling it has a constitutional obligation to provide "a fair and neutral forum therein for the advancement of religious and irreligious beliefs." In the absence of such a forum, the federal constitutional violation could be cured only by providing students with *non-discriminatory access to educational alternatives, public or private, where their rights could be vindicated.* He added, for good measure, that the educational guarantees in many state constitutions created similar entitlements under state law. His bottom line was as clear as it was controversial: If students were not afforded a truly level playing field on matters of religion in the public schools, they had a right to redirect their share of tax dollars to a private school of at least comparable quality where a balanced forum was provided.

With the "guest" lecturer's presentation complete, I asked my students first to explore whether the lecture was itself a constitutional violation. Was Professor Pope guilty of abusing our state-funded educational forum to advance pro-religious views? What were his true motives, and did they matter in the constitutional analysis? Was there legal merit in his presentation, and did the presence or absence of objective merit matter if his motives were impermissible? What was the correct constitutional boundary; was actual coercion of religious belief necessary to establish a violation, or was the taxpayer-paid professor's endorsement of religion enough to cross the line? A vigorous discussion ensued, and to the extent I could discern a consensus, the students' view was that Pope's motives were irrelevant, unknowable, or both, that his presentation was legally plausible but generally unsupported by precedent, and that, whatever effect the lecture might have had on other audiences in other settings, there was no actual coercion here because U.Va. Law students are an unusually canny lot and thus impervious to undue influence by their professors, especially silly, imaginary ones.

I deferred discussion of Professor Pope's overall conclusion—the one calling for remedial access to publicly funded private school options—because I reserved that topic for one of two essays on the course's final exam. There were audible groans as some of the students apparently contemplated how much work it would take to prepare such an essay, but I thought I also detected some excitement about the project. In any event, the big news was that the exam would be of the "take-home" variety, and that announcement was a certain crowd-pleaser and pressure-reliever.

Leaving the law school that afternoon, my reaction to the three sessions on the religion clauses was almost triumphant. I had used my unconventional method of instruction to especially good effect, it appeared. The sessions had required an enormous amount of preparation and rehearsal on my part, but I had pulled off each of the "guest" presentations convincingly enough, and the students plainly had been energized and intrigued. The classroom discourse had been unusually animated even in comparison to others during this same course, and I indulged the hopeful notion that the experience might inspire one or more of these super-bright young people to delve deeply into the fascinating and important topic of church-state relations.

So satisfied, I was particularly unprepared for what I read roughly 40 hours later on the editorial page of the *Charlottesville Dispatch*. There, under the trite heading, "When the Far Right Goes Far Wrong," was a ferocious denunciation of "Professor Pope a/k/a Monsignor McGuire" for "brazenly promoting his personal religious views" in a lecture that "obviously was better suited for a church sanctuary than a university classroom." I had, the editorialist bemoaned, "opened the class by exhorting students to recite the Apostles Creed and closed it by conferring on every American a constitutional right to a proselytizing parochial school education at taxpayer expense." Apparently mistaking me for a Catholic (the only non-offensive error in a piece riddled with them), the author allowed colorfully that "at least I was pimping for the Pope rather that purveying the Elmer Gantry-like prattle of the fundamentalist

Christian Right." But, it added quickly, the effect was the same: "The Far Right's campaign to tear down Mr. Jefferson's wall of separation between church and state and, in the process, to tear down the system of public education he helped to inspire, continues unabated. That's old news. What's new is that the University of Virginia School of Law now apparently has joined the fight—on the *wrong* side."

That was only the first of several editorials and letters on the subject in the local papers. Most repeated the mischaracterizations and piled on with even more indignant indictments, while a few writers defended me for the wrong reasons. Worried about the bad light in which my alma mater and employer was being cast, I wanted to respond. But it was not readily apparent how I could answer the criticism in the media given the complexity of the topic, and the Dean counseled emphatically against the attempt. Instead, after a couple of days he issued a statement, accompanied by the full text of my presentations on the religion clauses, that read simply: "Professor McGuire's presentations on the Constitution's religion clauses were grounded in a rich appreciation of the history and context of the provisions and were well within the bounds of appropriate academic discourse on their meaning. Over three days of lectures, Professor McGuire presented a range of views on the complex subject of church-state relations, and, contrary to published reports, he engaged in no inappropriate importuning of students regarding religious matters."

I was pleased to be so defended but mortified that a defense was necessary. To my mild surprise, my colleagues on the law school faculty were uniformly supportive and encouraged me variously to "ignore the papers," "hang in there," and "stay true to myself." Beneath the surface, though, I was sure I could detect some snickers, and perhaps deservedly so. After all, I was the upstart who had arrived after modest public and private practice and who, with less than a year's experience in the classroom, had concluded that I knew more about how to teach the law than all the experienced professionals and renowned scholars who comprised the faculty of this leading national law school. The hubris in my behavior was undeniable, though I had just tried to use my limited gifts in creative ways.

Ironically, the thing I took from these unexpected trials in Charlottesville was an added measure of confidence. Becoming an object of public criticism was a new experience for me, and it forced me to confront the dichotomy between what the crowd thought and what I knew was right. I decided, as one faculty colleague urged, to stay true to myself and disregard the crowd. That timely counsel was, I realized, an echo of the University's founder: "In fine, I repeat that you must lay aside all prejudice on both sides, and neither believe nor reject anything, because any other persons, or description of persons, have rejected or believed it. Your own reason is the only oracle given you by heaven, and you are answerable not for the rightness but uprightness of the decision."

The insight struck me as supremely important … until an even more important one impressed itself on my conscience.

"That is true as far as it goes," I heard my "guest" Lincoln replying, it being his lot to finish things Jefferson had started. "But in addition to reason there is this inexplicable thing our embattled countrymen call 'grace.' From time to time, you will have to yield to the possibility that a greater purpose is at work beyond your faculties of reason."

A TIMELY CALL

Such a purpose indeed may have been at work in these converging events. The passions triggered during these years in Charlottesville were not political—at least, they had little to do with politics as a *process*. They had everything to do with issues—with public *policy*. Whether it was sparring at the law school over the proper reading and application of the Constitution's religious freedom promises, or confronting the absurdity of the peace-at-any-price mantra of the radical Left, or arriving at the distressing realization that whole generations of inner-city school children were being sacrificed because of an often incompetent, self-serving political machine, I had come face to face with problems and policies that all had one thing in common: *They deeply offended my sense of Justice.*

They had something else in common, too. The solutions all seemed to be *political.*

This is where Martha—one of the least political people I knew—really had the pivotal impact on me. It is hard to step back, take stock, and make a big decision well. You reflect on what your information and experience tell you about it. You consult your trusted friends. If you're believing, you pray about it. And, if God has blessed you with a soul-mate, you let her look inside you and say honestly what she sees.

I had been pretty thick about it, but Martha finally helped me see that I had been looking for the right thing in all the wrong places. Someone would promote Justice by prosecuting criminals, and someone would promote Justice by practicing law, and someone would promote Justice by teaching law students. But maybe, just maybe, I was meant to promote Justice by getting involved in politics and government.

As I surveyed the range of influences on me—the historical lessons, the parental examples, the entreaties of friends, even the self-serving importuning by the Senator and Bart—it finally dawned on me that my primary response to all these influences had been *resistance*. And why was that? For a long time I thought I was resisting threats. But now I began to wonder whether I really had been resisting opportunities.

It was during this fertile time of reassessment that I received a pivotal call from Chad and Abby. They called to relay word of the impending departure of Senator Nevers' chief counsel and to urge me to seek the job. Unaware of the converging factors that already were stoking my political interest seriously for the first time, they made the case for my return to Washington largely based on two things: Bart and Mitch.

Bart, they reported, was a source of mounting worry. Always tending toward the covert in his dealings, the Chief of Staff was now spending even more of his time in high-flying circles, attending extravagant parties, hanging out with wealthy donors, luxuriating in ever more lavish venues, and, in general, engaging in a lot of "stuff" other than Senate business. Since my friends always had regarded Bart's hands-on engagement in Senate business as a mixed blessing, these diversions might have been a welcome development. But, as Chad described the situation, it became clear that Bart was not weighing in any less; he was just weighing in more selectively and surreptitiously. The instances were infrequent, but whenever Bart wanted to influence Nevers on some key vote, constituent request, or political item, he would swoop in unpredictably, bypass the key staffers as well as Chad, Abby, and the political team, and importune the Senator directly just before the needed action. The approach precluded any practical opportunity for others on the staff to discern who the real beneficiaries were and to assess whether the action would put the Senator at risk.

Chad stressed to me that he was not alleging outright misconduct by Bart; he had no sound basis for such an assertion. To the contrary, Chad always had assumed that Bart knew the applicable laws and ethics rules and was careful not to run afoul of them. But the Chief of Staff's high-handed approach and secretive manner long had caused unease among senior staffers, who occasionally had ventured over to Alexandria to quietly share their concerns with Chad or

Abby. The guy who should have been on top of things was Charlie House, the longtime Hill staffer who had been the Senator's legal counsel for a decade. But Charlie had seemed most intent on reaching retirement without controversy, a goal he now had achieved, and his laid-back, hear-no-evil/see-no-evil attitude had done nothing to reassure the rest of the team.

"We need to protect the Senator," Chad said. "He is now in a position of real influence on the Hill on key issues, from fiscal policy to defense, and we are doing a lot of good work on things that really matter for Virginia and for the country. I don't say that Bart is doing anything wrong, but you can never tell where he's coming from or what kind of game he's running. And one of these days he's going to get the Senator in trouble."

I listened attentively, waiting for the inevitable, which came quickly.

"The bottom line is this, Danny. We desperately need a sharp legal counsel on staff, and you are the one person the Senator respects and Bart can't ignore. There's an opening, and it's too good an opportunity to miss."

Abby agreed with Chad, and said so. But after he made his case she turned the discussion to a more personal consideration.

"Danny, the other thing you have to consider is Mitch—he *cannot* stay in Orange. He will waste away there, and one day he will just give up. He belongs back in D.C., on the Hill—at *work*."

It was not the first time since Mitch's return from Iraq that the three of us had shared concerns about his recovery. We understood why he had to go back to Orange. With the death of Mitch's mother shortly before his deployment, his father had been at home alone. Reverend Jackson was sustained by an attentive congregation that cared for him like family, but he was home alone nevertheless. Mitch's tour in Iraq and severe injuries had made the elderly pastor sick with worry, and various maladies had set in. Mitch's presence in Orange comforted his father while, in nearby Charlottesville, he had access to the top-flight prosthetic therapists and orthopedic specialists at the U.Va. Medical Center. In addition—and here I knew Abby was right—the presence of Martha and me in Charlottesville, eager and available to help as needed, provided further impetus for Mitch to settle in back at Orange.

Abby was also right about his future. Mitch had things to accomplish, and he would not accomplish them in Orange. If he did not get back in the saddle quickly—if he became sedentary and content at home—there was a chance he would never get on the horse again.

"If you and Martha come up here, he will come, too. I *know* he will," Abby said earnestly. When he gets to the point that he's up to it, he will want to be where the three of us are—*back in the game.*"

I could probably add a few other factors to this litany of converging causes. No single one was determinative, but collectively they were compelling.

I had rejected politics with both head and heart, through the exercise of informed judgment as much as emotional impulse, in reason as well as resentment. And yet, as I serially pursued what I conceived to be higher callings, I always seemed to be circling the political abyss. I whirled past law school to a prosecutor's office, and from there to a law firm, and from a law firm back to law school. At each venue something unwanted or at least unexpected propelled me onward until, in the spring of 1993, I reached the place where the course of my life converged with the path taken by my historical icons, familial forebears, martyred parents, and starry-eyed friends.

The great Athenian statesman, Pericles, is supposed to have said, "Just because you do not take an interest in politics doesn't mean politics won't take an interest in you." Whatever the statement's provenance, the proposition was nowhere more dramatically demonstrated than in the life of the father of American politics—Madison. "I do not meddle with Politicks," the youthful James Madison had written to his fellow Princeton alum, William Bradford, as the two friends exchanged ideas about their prospective vocations. Yet, "Politicks" had captured Madison, making him not only one of his country's most consequential founders but the epitome of the *partisan statesman*—master of doctrine and tactic, ideals and realism, action and equipoise.

Now that same "Politicks" had captured me. Madison's contributions were monumental; mine would be modest. But they belonged to the same tradition, born of the same ethic. From Athens to America, liberty's dependence on self-government had pressed ordinary citizens into service through political action. Not politics for its own sake—as an instrument of selfish ambition or adulation—but politics for a greater good. And not for the good of the government, but for the good of free people.

The Athenians, Pericles actually did declare in his famous funeral oration, "regard those who take no part in civic duties not as unambitious but as useless." Whatever might later be said of my life and labors, I resolved that the word "useless" would have no place in the narrative.

UNHEEDED WARNING

Several months later, with my transition from law professor to Capitol Hill functionary complete, my new duties took me to the western Virginia hills. There, on the front porch of The Homestead, I found Senator Edward K. Nevers in fine form, puffing on a pungent Cuban, rocking effortlessly, and regaling a mostly random mix of fawning friends, including several notable Virginia captains of industry.

The Homestead was a place of special significance. Nestled in the Allegheny Mountains near Virginia's western border, the stately red-brick hotel with its massive, twelve-story clock tower dominated the hilly, tree-bathed landscape of the little town of Hot Springs from nearly every vantage point. The bucolic village's name signaled its distinctive geological feature, though it was Warm Springs some five miles north on Route 220 that afforded the more temperate and hospitable baths for those seeking relief from rheumatism and other ailments. Among the distinguished guests since Jefferson "took the waters" in 1818 were 20 or so of his presidential successors. The surrounding county was known as "Bath," for the English resort city with the same moniker, and traced its American lineage to John Lewis, a larger-than-life Ulster Scot who settled in the area in 1732. Western Virginians would recall the Lewises—John and his son Andrew, an acclaimed Revolutionary War general—with reverence not unlike that accorded John Smith and the Jamestown settlers by the easterners.

The sprawling hotel and surrounding resort claimed provenance nearly as old as the first non-native visits to the springs, a fact that only the most oblivious could escape given the presence of the signature digits—"1766"—on everything from the hotel telephones, stationery, and matchbooks to its acclaimed restaurant and even the immaculately trimmed topiary out front. Older than the Republic, the resort was founded—partly by another son of John Lewis—during that brief but crucial interlude between two wars when Virginians began to see themselves as Americans. The frontier crossroads had been close to the action in the first conflict, the global one during which the Redcoats and Colonials collaborated to secure English America's western border. Known parochially as the French and Indian War, that conflict had paved the way for the more familiar ensuing one by supplying two of the Revolution's most vital agents: George Washington and the British government's resolve to make the colonies help pay its war debt. More than two centuries of American history later, after myriad expansions, sales, facelifts, and reorganizations, the proud hotel gleamed as the radiant fall colors came alive and what passed for the Virginia glitterati came "to see and be seen," as the saying goes, in the fall of 1993.

This was the place each autumn where Senator Nevers and his top aides—a clique that now included me—feted major donors during what was billed as a "weekend retreat for insiders." There was no price of admission per se, but all in attendance understood their prized invitation to the vaunted assemblage and its cozy access had been procured by someone's substantial beneficence—either their own, their company's, or the other poor suckers' on whom they had put the squeeze. It was a place where the unseemly imperative of American-style political fundraising made uneasy peace with the genteel Virginia way of doing things.

The great advantage of this approach was that it was the kind of political event that everyone—from the donors and activists to the officeholders and apparatchiks—genuinely seemed to enjoy. Here in full flower in a single venue were Virginia's distinctive natural beauty and cultural elegance, her perpetual politicking and relentless social climbing, her grand ambitions and rugged realities, and her enduring ethic of intensity at work and play.

It was, of course, the latter pursuit—*play*—that received the greatest attention, and of the varied pastimes golf was by far the most prominent. The resort's courses entreated and then humbled all types of players, from professionals to presidents. The first tee on the aptly named Old Course was reputedly the most venerable in America, the first to play host to a president (McKinley) who hit the links while in office. Down the road a few miles was the Cascades Course, and the resort's favorite son, Sam Snead—the winner of more professional victories than any other golfer in history—once said that if you can play Cascades you can play anywhere. Decades later, Slammin' Sammy's presence remained palpable, but I preferred to conjure up the comical image of President William Howard Taft—massively out of place on the links but never one to let governing get in the way of his golfing.

I had only been on the job a few months when the Senator, reversing Bart's contrary instruction, informed me that my presence was desired at this year's mountain soiree. Before the war, Mitch had been the golfing partner of choice for the CEOs with low handicaps, and in his absence no other Neversworld representative was able to fill the bill. The Senator seemed glad to again have a worthy lieutenant he could deploy to bolster—and monitor—the most athletically competitive of his wealthy supporters. He apparently had an added reason to want me along for the weekend, although so far he had given no such indication.

On my solo drive to the resort the scenery had been preoccupying. I opted for the back way from Staunton through Buffalo Gap to Millboro Springs via Route 42 and across Warm Springs Mountain on Route 39, retracing the turnpike that earlier generations, bent on progress, had financed with tolls and bonds. The primary alternative routes—up breathtaking Goshen Pass from Lexington or past Falling Springs Waterfall en route from Covington—arguably were even more impressive. But Nevers was a Staunton boy, and he seemed to take the matter of the route quite seriously, so I had come the way he recommended.

To the extent the scenery permitted reverie en route, my thoughts had run to the *contrasts*—namely, how well Senator Nevers was doing compared to the rough patches I had witnessed at earlier points in his Senate tenure, and how much my own frame of reference and interests had changed over that time.

Virginia's Ned Nevers was not a household name by any means—not yet anyway. But the two-term senator was clearly at ease with himself and gliding along comfortably, confidently, occasionally now even a bit haughtily. A consummate politician, he was increasingly so regarded by a widening circle. He had mastered a range of important policy topics, and what he said and did on those issues now mattered. His advice was sought frequently by colleagues. Even the President coveted his help on key legislation. His endorsement and the services of his captive political consulting team were much in demand. And, his pronouncements garnered serious attention on news broadcasts and talk shows. Completely gone, I reflected, was any lingering trace of the strung-out first-termer who had been so utterly rudderless at the start and so paranoid about potential defeat. If anything, I thought, he seemed a bit nonchalant about the next reelection campaign, which was now barely a year off. But no credible Democratic opponent had appeared on the horizon, and everyone—including Chad and Abby—said Nevers was a shoo-in for a third term.

Virginia's senior senator was in a groove, and I was in it with him.

I had allowed myself some uncharacteristic self-congratulation as I sped along the route to the weekend gathering. It was a great time to join his team

... a brilliant career move. I was a little thankful but even more self-impressed. Big things lay ahead, and I would be there to play an important role and perhaps make some lasting imprint. My parents would have been proud of me. My close friends would be alongside me. I would be marching in the path trod over two centuries by the heroes who had inspired me....

I was a convert to politics, and there's nothing like the zeal of a convert. *It doesn't get any better than this*, I thought.

That was my mindset as I pulled in front of the grand hotel, climbed out to stretch, and received what I now recognize as the inevitable greeting.

"Welcome, sir. It's a beautiful day at The Homestead. Will you be checking in?"

I had barely nodded in reply when I heard a familiar voice boom at me from his rocking chair on the porch. "'Bout time you got here, Danny-boy. What took you so long? You didn't let them talk you into comin' by Covington, did ya?"

"No, sir," I yelled enthusiastically. "Staunton, Buffalo Gap, Augusta Springs, Craigsville, Goshen, Millboro Springs, Warms Springs Mountain. And I got gas before I left Staunton, just like you told me!"

Ugh. I had only been at this gathering of heavyweights about 30 seconds and already I was coming across like some pathetic little suck-up. I made a mental note not to fall into that trap again during this high-brow weekend.

I went over to greet the Senator and the guests he had clustered around him. Some were rocking, some were standing, and the others were perched awkwardly on the porch railing. Nevers was holding court, clearly reveling in the affections of his admiring subjects and enjoying the presence of an attentive audience.

My mother would have said he was "full of himself."

As I approached, one of the guests—obviously a bank executive—was telling the Senator how much the banking community appreciated his recent handiwork on the big financial services bill. "I don't know how we can ever thank you enough," the dapper man said to him earnestly.

"Well, we just did the right thing on that bill, but I'm glad you like the way it turned out," Nevers responded. "You know, I always love it when someone says, 'I can't thank you enough.' Reminds me of the old judge down in Southside who sentenced a young man to two 35-year terms, running consecutively. The boy cried, 'But, Judge, I won't live that long!' And the judge said, 'That's all right, son. You just do the best you can.'"

At that, Nevers heaved a hearty laugh and the rest of us chortled with him. The point—the Senator *always* had a point—would sink in with each of these folks, some sooner and some later.

Though I had no standard by which to judge, the weekend seemed to go quite well. Certainly it appeared to be "Mission Accomplished" based on the positive reaction of the attendees. My own experience was made immeasurably better by Bart's last-minute withdrawal due to a chest cold—or so he had claimed. The only downer was our foursome's second-place finish in the golf tourney on Saturday, a result I attributed to creative scorekeeping on the part of the notoriously shark-like Congressman Johnny Bondurant and the obvious ringers he had assembled. But my ego's surface scratch from the golf results did not diminish my enthusiasm for the festivities, and I was looking forward to playing a real round on the Cascades course before returning to D.C. on Sunday afternoon.

That plan changed early Sunday morning when I received an unexpected call from Senator Nevers' young personal assistant, Raj Hummar.

"The Senator has decided to have breakfast delivered to his room instead of going down to the main dining room, and he is hoping you will join him," Raj said in his standard monotone manner. "Give me your order, and I will call it in with his."

I showered quickly and headed to the president's suite in the tower. As I entered, Raj exited with a nod to the adjacent room where our breakfast plates had just been set out on the coffee table and the Senator was seated in a plush chair, reading the newspapers and sipping coffee. He seemed far less regal and "full of himself" than during our Friday afternoon encounter, but he was still plainly in command.

"Morning!" I said jauntily. "Just you and me? Where's Mrs. N.?"

"On the tennis court by now, I suspect. You know Sally—can't slow *her* down," he said, sipping from the massive mug emblazoned with the ubiquitous quartet of digits and a sketch of the tower we now occupied. "Glad you could join me. Trust you've had a good weekend. Heard lots of compliments on your presentation yesterday morning. Facing all those super-bright law students over the last couple of years must have made you pretty good on your feet," he said.

"Glad to hear it was well received. You can't make a review of Supreme Court decisions but so interesting," I responded. "As for the weekend, it's been fantastic ... although—"

"—although you're ticked off that y'all came in second in the golf thing yesterday," Nevers said with a broad smile. He already had heard of my competitive failure and had no difficulty completing the sentence for me. "Don't let it worry you. Simpson and Ramos had a great time playing from where your drives ended up—that's what matters. Besides, Danny, you do know that Johnny Bondurant cheats, don't you? He's incorrigible—has to win, period. The guy isn't gonna walk off the green with four people missing a makeable putt—he'll just take as many tries as he needs. Y'all never had a chance."

The Senator laughed and added, "Don't ever let yourself get caught in a card game with the guy. I hear he wins at cards *without* cheating."

"Really? He strikes me as a loser who probably can't do much of anything without cheating," I said, laying bare both my hyper-competitive side and my disdain for the arrogant son of privilege who was the youngest member of the Virginia congressional delegation.

"Well, consider yourself warned on the cards," Nevers concluded, before ruminating further on the golf. "I thought you guys might go low enough yesterday to surprise Johnny, but I see he took ample precautions. He didn't get this far by half-measures," the Senator joked.

A notably more serious expression then crept onto his face as he turned and stirred his coffee ponderously.

"Listen, I trust you completely, plus now you're my lawyer. I want to let you in on a little matter. Not a big item at all … no big deal, really. I have debated even bringing it up at all, especially since things could hardly be going better. But since you're on the team now, and … well … in light of some of our history—"

I thought he was about to confide some legal fix he was in, probably along the lines Chad had been fearing. But I soon realized, to my great surprise, that he was alluding to a subject that had not been broached by either of us, even elliptically, for the decade that had passed since the event.

"—you know, I mean the nightmares I was having way back when I first came to the Senate. Well, it actually was one big nightmare that kept recurring, as you probably remember. And they're back, sort of, I mean, at least one of them is back … well, not one of them but one *like* them … or one like *it*, because there really was only one like that …."

He was babbling and stopped abruptly. I was starting to shift in my seat, and my expression must have betrayed me.

"Oh, for goodness' sake, Daniel, it's not like that! It's one bad dream, right? I mean, I have lots of dreams—some good, some bad—just like everybody else. It's just that this particular one, well, it was especially vivid, and, you know, it reminded me of that nightmare way back then...."

I did not know what to say. Fortunately, the Senator kept talking.

"Let me explain. It's a little embarrassing but more silly than anything. Anyway, I know I can count on your discretion based on ... well, I know I can count on you, so here goes. It's Saturday night about a month or so ago, and Sally and I are keeping the grandkids and we decide to watch this new cartoon movie they've been wanting to see. It was about this king or emperor who lords it over everybody and behaves like a jerk, then falls under a spell and turns into a llama, loses his kingdom, is put out to pasture—a really cute, funny little movie. It had a happy ending. The llama turned back into the king ... the king was now humble, appreciated those who helped him, learned his lesson ... you know, good moral to the story and very funny ... Robbie and Kristin loved it. So that was no big deal—just a movie...."

"Uh-huh," I murmured, waiting for the punchline.

"But that night I went to sleep and dreamed that I was standing under a big oak tree—you know, a huge stately old one full of foliage with lots of colorful birds in its branches and animals resting in its shade—when *lightning struck*! The tree crashed over my head. Birds and animals scattered. And when I climbed out from under the branches and debris, I looked around, and you know what I was, Daniel? I was a *horse*! I mean, I was a freakin' talking horse ... you know, like Mr. Ed. You know, 'Helllooo, Wilbuuurrr....'"

At this, I gasped involuntarily and emitted a guffaw like a mini-burst. I had not been at all ready for him to go imitating Mr. Ed talking to *Wilbuuurrrrr*....

"Sorry," I recovered, "I know it's not a laughing matter...."

"Well, of course, it's a laughing matter! I would laugh at it myself—the absurdity of it! Me, the senior senator from Virginia: 'A horse is a horse, of course, of course....'"

He actually was singing the TV show ditty. "That's not fair—now you're *trying* to make me laugh," I complained, seizing the opportunity to exhale and grin broadly while it was diplomatically acceptable.

"Yes, well, now listen to the rest of it. This horse—which is me; I am *still* the doggone horse! He climbs out of the wreckage of this old tree that has been destroyed, and looks around. And the whole scene—all the branches and debris and the horse—are all in … *the grand lobby of the Jefferson Hotel*.…"

I bit my lip and squeezed the arm of the chair hard enough to turn both it and my knuckles white.

" … So I got up—I mean, the horse got up—and sort of shook off the leaves and everything, you know, like a wet dog shakes off water. And then this guy—Willllbuuurrrr, I suppose—leads me by the bridle over to this podium where I am supposed to speak. And, so I step up to the microphone, and say, 'I'm sooorrrry, Willllburr, and I'm sorry to all the rest of you.…'"

I was biting my lip extremely hard at this point.

"Then some smart aleck in the audience yells out, 'Why the long face?'"

Blood was now beginning to flow from the hole in my lip.

"People were laughing at that wisecrack and obviously they were all laughing at me, but Wilbur patted me on the neck and said, 'That's okay, Mr. Ned, just ignore them—everybody's gotta be a comedian these days. You just go on about your business.' So I went ahead and made the announcement, you know, that all the votes had now been counted and *we had lost the election*. It was a concession speech, Daniel! I have never given a blasted concession speech in my life, as you know. But here I was, a horse speaking into a microphone, saying, 'It was a real horse race, but I'm afraid we came up a few lengths short.…'"

I had to say something quickly or I was going to laugh in his face again.

"You didn't really… I mean, the horse didn't really … say that part about it being a real horse race, did he? C'mon, boss."

"You think I'm making this up, Daniel? I'm not making any of it up—*not a bit*. And it would all be very funny if it were not such a vivid dream that reminded me of that nightmarish scene back in 1989 where I slipped and fell in the river and everyone was laughing at me."

"Well, I can see how it would be upsetting," I said, trying to heed his serious turn. "Have you kept dreaming about it, like you did with that earlier dream? Or did you dream it just that once?"

"Just that one time," he responded, "though I keep thinking about it."

"Hmmm," I exhaled, buying time.

"Oh, and I forgot to mention the man on the balcony in the Jefferson," Nevers added.

"The man on the balcony?"

"Yes, on the balcony. I don't think he actually was supposed to be a man. I think he was like the supervisor, you know, the one observing and presiding over this whole scene in the lobby from up in the balcony. He had sort of a glow around him...."

"Okay, let me see if I've got this now," I said. "You watch a cartoon movie with your grandkids and then have a dream in which there is this huge oak tree, full of branches and birds, and lighting strikes it, and it crashes down, and when the dust settles you are a horse who climbs out of the rubble and gives a concession speech in the lobby of the Jefferson Hotel under the attentive supervision of some mysterious angelic figure. Is that the deal basically?"

"Yes, I guess that about sums it up."

"Well, it's really quite simple," I said, avoiding a grin. "It's an archetypal dream that is very common—you know, like the one where all your teeth fall out, or the one where it's final exam day and you never opened the book all semester, or the one where you can fly. Everyone dreams of being a talking horse making a concession speech at some point. It almost always happens when you mix pizza and Scotch...."

I was chortling now, proud of my cleverness, but I noticed that the Senator seemed mildly amused at best. "Yes, well, I'm glad I can supply some entertainment for you. I thought maybe you would tell me there's some profound message for me in this dream. You know, like maybe the big guy upstairs thinks I'm a horse's ass...."

Surprised again, I emitted another mini-burst.

"That's a pretty creative interpretation," I said, regrouping, "but it's not exactly what I was thinking. For one thing, the dream seemed to be focused on the other end of the horse."

"Ah—good point. Then, tell me, my ever-so-wise advisor, what if anything does it mean?"

"I don't have a clue," I responded. "But I'm thinking that, if I were you, I would watch that cartoon movie again and see what it was in there that set me off. From what you've said, it seems like the obvious message is that a little humility once in a while is a good thing."

"No doubt about that," he said, shrugging agreeably. Then, after neither of us said anything more for a few awkward seconds, the Senator signaled that this odd little consultation session was nearing its end. "I guess that's it," he said. The discussion meandered through a few inconsequential subjects before

I was dismissed and the Senator headed toward the tennis courts to applaud his bride's performance.

It was a sign of Senator Nevers' cresting self-confidence during this timeframe that the dream gave him only a little pause. For my part, I obviously found the whole thing quite amusing at first. But when I got back to D.C., I rented the movie. And, as I reflected on it, a more serious supposition set in.

The movie was about pride and the comeuppance that awaits the haughty. That much I already knew from the Senator's brief description. But as I watched the cute flick, I began to ponder its application to the Ned Nevers whose Senate staff I had just joined. The Senator *was* proud—quite "full of himself." He did take his success for granted. He did view his accomplishments as his own doing. And he did seem to think he was politically untouchable.

And then it hit me: Maybe a still, small voice inside of him was trying to warn him, trying to deliver a message before it was too late. Maybe I had done him a huge disservice by making light of his dream. Maybe I had missed an opportunity to drive a key point home. I was here to counsel and help him— *maybe I had blown it.*

So the next time I had a brief moment alone with the Senator back in D.C. I tried to do my duty, albeit belatedly and hurriedly. "I rented that movie about the llama. Maybe I should not have made light of your dream," I said. "Maybe there's a message in both the movie and the dream—you know, the proud king getting kicked off the throne. Maybe it's not a coincidence you dreamed it. Maybe the 'big guy upstairs' wants to get your attention."

Nevers had obviously decided the dream was pointless, and he now seemed put off by my comments. "What are you saying? You think my noggin's gotten too big and I'm headed for defeat next year? Listen, Danny, you're a great guy with a great head on your shoulders, but you don't know squat about politics, and you're flat wrong on both counts: My head *ain't* too big, and I *ain't* gonna be put out to pasture anytime soon!"

With that, he was up out of the big chair and off to his next appointment, slapping his next back, touching his next donor, earnestly greeting his next constituent, adoringly stroking his next baby's head, giving his next stock speech, shaking his next hundred hands. It was a race, always a race, and he didn't have time—didn't *make* time—to put it all in perspective. He just naturally assumed he would be out in front of the field for as long as he wanted.

How the Mighty Fall

It took about ten months before things really came apart.

It was then that the chief counsel to the President of the United States finally resigned, admitting that she had advised the Under Secretary of Defense to mislead a congressional committee about the re-direction of funds to the unpopular war effort. Already suffering from the second-term syndrome—buyer's remorse, over-exposure, depletion of ideas, third- or fourth-tier talent, and general malaise—that routinely retards worn-out administrations and sends presidential approval ratings plummeting by the midterms, the embattled President now saw the bottom fall out politically. A few of his fellow partisans—the ones who had taken nothing for granted and labored for months like their seats depended on it—survived the strong, scandal-fueled downdraft.

Senator Nevers was not one of them.

In retrospect, the signs had all been there—and I do not mean the dream. The unexpected Democratic sweep a year earlier in the contests for governor, lieutenant governor, and attorney general was one leading indicator. The President's seriously sagging poll numbers were another. Then, in May, just weeks before the filing deadline, the sacrificial lamb that had been unopposed for the Democratic nod for Nevers' seat suddenly withdrew. In his place, enticed by the significant shift in the polls, stepped a popular former governor who months earlier had rejected his party's entreaties to take on the seemingly invincible incumbent. The economic numbers got worse all spring and headed south big-time in June and July. Then the war-funding scandal hit, and what had been a swelling tide became a surging wave.

Chad and Abby had become alarmed by early spring and had pleaded with the Senator and Bart to devote more schedule time and resources to the campaign and seek more help from the GOP's national senatorial campaign committee. I had chimed in as best I could, though neither Nevers nor Bell saw campaign tactics as my area of expertise. Mitch even came up from Orange several times to weigh in, but it had little effect. I am not sure any of it would have mattered anyway, but by the time the Senator and his distracted chief of staff finally woke up to the reality of the political tsunami that was approaching, it was way too late.

With six years between elections and with most senatorial business beyond the ken of the average voter, the typical incumbent U.S. senator really has to work at keeping his name ID up, his base of support motivated, and his political stock high. Even the most talented politician is challenged by this electoral fact of life. Nevers, one of the most talented politicians around, never seemed to grasp that voters could not be counted on automatically to swarm to the polls and send their impressive senatorial veteran back to Washington. It did not matter what polling data Chad presented or what ad scripts and press announcements Abby prepared. The august Edward K. Nevers kept giving speeches about how *he* had gained enormous seniority and clout inside the Beltway, how *he* had looked out for our military bases and brought home the bacon to Virginia, how *he* had built this new bridge or that new post office, how *he* knew all the issues backwards and forwards, how *he* was the high-profile leader with the great future that Virginians were really lucky to have in Washington. He was a truly majestic Senator, and if you did not already understand that, he was quite ready to educate you.

That shtick might—*might*—have worked in a different political environment, but in 1994 it was fatal. The last thing voters were in the mood to do that year was reward another proud politician.

The upset defeat caught the Senator completely by surprise. "I never thought," he said dejectedly, "that this could happen to *me*." He just knew he would win despite all the rapidly accumulating evidence to the contrary. He always had won in the past, and he would win now. When finally confronted with the one factoid he could not dismiss—an election tally that showed he got fewer votes than the other guy—the Senator became distraught to the point of illness. He left Washington for his farm in Nottoway and was rarely heard from during the waning weeks of his term. He did graciously thank his team, and he made a few calls to put in good words for his soon-to-be-jobless staffers with other members of Congress and some business allies. But mentally he had checked out even before he finally retreated to Nottoway for good in January. He wanted no visitors for a long time, and for the most part he had none. I was the most persistent in trying to see him, but Sally finally advised that he was under a doctor's care and a visit was impossible.

"Daniel," she confided, "I trust you will keep this in strictest confidence, but it appears that Ned has had some sort of emotional breakdown. He seems relatively happy here on the farm even though he doesn't know a thing about farming. But he goes out and spends time with the animals. He feels so rejected, you know. He keeps saying, 'Well, at least the animals still like me.'

And I kid him and say, 'How can you be so sure about that, Ned?' And we have a good laugh about it. But he's just not himself."

The vision that mischievously popped into my head was Mr. Ned chatting up a bunch of fellow horses, but I immediately reproached myself.

"I am sure he will get better," the dutiful love of Ned Nevers' life opined reassuringly, "and I will let you know as soon as he does. For now, please just keep him in your prayers."

"I certainly will do that. But please call on me if there is any way at all I can help. I am not a fair-weather friend—I want you both to know that," I responded.

"I know, dear," she said.

I felt terrible for the Senator. *Whatever his faults*, I thought, *he didn't deserve this*. It inevitably reminded me of my Granddaddy Daniel's sudden defeat back when I was a little kid. And that brought painfully back to mind my own considerable losses as a young man.

My first major trauma was the injury that took football away from me. I thought that was as awful as things could get until I lost my parents and learned what real loss is like. Self-pity had come knocking on both of those occasions, and I had let him in. He even had been my closest companion for a while. But I finally had figured out—in the first instance, with the help of my parents, and in the second, with the aid of Dr. S. D. and my three pals—that self-pity was no friend at all. In fact, he was the enemy ... the most insidious enemy ... and I was determined not to let him use this sudden setback to gain a new foothold in my life.

My Nevers-linked reversal of fortune was sudden and severe, all right. But, in truth, things were much better for my friends and me than we might have expected under the circumstances. Chad and Abby by now had a very solid reputation in the political consulting world and enough business in the pipeline to make it through the next election cycle even without their sidelined mentor's help. Among the Nevers Senate staffers, I was one of the fortunate ones. There were not many Hill jobs available on the GOP side after the party's historic shellacking in November, but my law degree and Nevers' timely phone call were enough to land me one of them. I went to work as legislative counsel for Bill Wiegand, a first-term Wyoming senator who had the good fortune not to be up for reelection during the 1994 debacle. Yet, even with that comparatively soft landing, I marveled in my distress at how wrong I had gotten it. After years of resistance, I finally had climbed into the cockpit of Ned Nevers' shiny jet fighter—just in time to experience the crash.

THE WINDOW OPENS

For striking convergences with stunning consequences, history has few to surpass Virginia's "Red Letter Year." Generations of school children in the Old Dominion dutifully have learned to apply this label to the momentous year 1619, the Jamestown colony's 12th, because in that single portentous span representative government got its rudimentary start in British North America, the first Africans were brought forcibly to these shores, the Virginia Company in London recruited female settlers to populate the colony, and the first official Thanksgiving observance in America was held along the James. Each development represented a crucial beginning in its own right as well as a milestone in the continuing journey toward fulfillment of the American ideals of democracy, opportunity, and inclusion.

I cannot help but think of that historical convergence when I look back now on the events of Memorial Day weekend in 1995. I would come to regard it as my own "red letter" weekend because it was then that many lines closed in my dial's center, and I first experienced the freedom that comes from submission. It was an *awakening*—no less dramatic a term will do—and it marked a new beginning for my journey. Not even my hole-in-one was more improbable, or more sublime.

The scene was Wintergreen, a ski and golf resort nestled in the Blue Ridge Mountains southwest of Charlottesville, and the occasion was another springtime getaway with my friends. Almost seven months had passed since the election, and all of us were still a bit dazed and dull, so no one had taken the initiative to organize the annual outing. Into the breach stepped Martha, who decided, despite our affinity for Corolla and Sandbridge, that a change of scenery might do everyone some good. A couple that included Martha's former roommate at the University of Richmond owned a nice vacation home overlooking the Wintergreen resort from its highest peak, known as Devils Knob. During our several ski-season visits they had encouraged us to use the place for a weekend getaway sometime. A quick call from Martha revealed its availability over Memorial Day, so on relatively short notice my three friends joined Martha and me there for some mountaintop relaxation and reflection.

Having struggled for half a year to come to grips with the train wreck I had just witnessed, I came to this tranquil weekend with some new insights as well as questions. Events had deposited me in the political world just in time for me to see firsthand how hard the mighty fall, and I wanted to understand what it all meant. My thoughts had returned repeatedly to the movie, the dream, the Senator, the defeat, the breakdown, and—most important—the peculiar problem of pride in politics.

You can call it "pride" or any of its other familiar names. The phenomenon certainly is not unique to politics, yet in that realm it seems especially pervasive ... and seductive. Even the most grounded political leader or public official is going to be tempted and tested by it, because all the ingredients are there. You were chosen by the people as their leader, a sign of superior standing. Your title conveys gravitas. Staff members wait on you deferentially. Constituents stand in line or hover nearby just to speak with you and shake your hand. Most around you utter flatteries. Reporters covet your comments. Interested parties solicit your favors. Colleagues seek your counsel. Few are willing to tell you when you are wrong. You wield power daily and consequentially. And, the more comfortable you get in that role—indeed, the more you gain the self-confidence that is a prerequisite for success in the political world—then the more likely you are to indulge the dangerous illusion of self-sufficiency.

That illusion, I had come to realize, is the essence of pride. Pride is not haughtiness, arrogance, self-importance, or thinking yourself better than others. Those are all just symptoms. The essence of pride is the illusion of self-sufficiency.

My reflections on the peculiar problem of pride in politics led me to a corollary proposition that is especially controversial in today's secular society: the importance of faith in politics. The only real answer to pride, I had become convinced, is a sincere humility. I am referring here not to the skin-deep, false humility that is a familiar artifice of politicians, but to a genuine humility, the kind that is unavoidable once one comes to an honest conviction about the power and love of God, shipwrecked man's dependence on divine rescue, and the imperative of responding to this lifesaving provision with gratitude and loving service to others.

All of the major religions teach humility, and it is the central tenet of my own faith. Micah, the Old Testament prophet and statesman, put it simply: "[W]hat does the Lord require of you? To act justly and to love mercy and to walk humbly with your God." Jesus drove the point home for his disciples: "Truly, I tell you, unless you change and become like little children, you will never enter the kingdom of heaven. Therefore, whoever takes the lowly position of this child is the greatest in the kingdom of heaven." Cultivating that child-like dependence on God has always been the chief concern of the Christian faith. And a child-like dependence on God is the antithesis of a god-like reliance on yourself.

This message poses an especially formidable challenge to Americans, like me, who are steeped in a tradition of rugged individualism. But, in truth, it is a hard message for any political leader or activist to hear, and even harder for one to heed. Nothing about it comes naturally. If humbling oneself like a child is contrary to human nature—and certainly it is—then the idea of humility seems hopelessly out of place in politics, where human nature comes to the contest on steroids. Even for those who have the right aspiration, the follow-through inevitably falls short. That is why Madison, having breathed in deeply what biblical and secular authorities teach about the nature of man and what man's experience teaches about the nature of self-government, sought to fashion a political system that took both virtue and vice productively into account. If the pursuit of self-interest was an inevitability, indeed a necessity, so, too, was the possibility of sacrifice in service to higher ideals. Indeed, republicanism succeeds when a preponderance of people come to identify their own interests with those higher ideals. This identification comes only through humility. And humility—real, genuine, honest-to-God humility—comes only through faith.

There has been, of course, no act of humility in American history more complete or consequential than George Washington's resignation as commander in chief after leading Americans to independence. Such a supreme act of self-denial, George III predicted, would make him "the greatest man in the world." In Washington's June 1783 final communication to the states as commander in chief, a pronouncement he then believed would be among his last testaments in public life, he wrote of the connection between humility, faith, and the future of his nation:

> The great object for which I had the honor to hold an appointment in the Service of my Country, being accomplished, I am now preparing to resign it into the hands of Congress.... But before I carry this resolution into effect, I think it a duty

incumbent on me, to make this my last official communication, to congratulate you on the glorious events which Heaven has been pleased to produce in our favor.... I now make it my earnest prayer that God would have you, and the State over which you preside, in his holy protection, that he would incline the hearts of the Citizens to cultivate a spirit of subordination and obedience to Government, to entertain a brotherly affection and love for one another, for their fellow Citizens of the United States at large, and particularly for their brethren who have served in the Field, and finally, that he would most graciously be pleased to dispose us all, to do Justice, to love mercy, and to demean ourselves with that Charity, humility and pacific temper of mind, which were the Characteristics of the Divine Author of our blessed Religion, and without an humble imitation of whose example in these things, we can never hope to be a happy Nation.

Tocqueville captured the essence of Washington's message succinctly. "Liberty," he wrote, "cannot be established without morality, nor morality without faith."

While church and state are kept separate for good reason in this country, faith and politics are inseparable in a healthy democratic society precisely because the former supplies the humility on which the latter absolutely depends. The Athenians, who first gave birth to a system of liberty, understood that freedom's great enemy is hubris—the belief on the part of a person that he has the wisdom, the strength, and the right to rule over others. The Athenians also believed that the crucial choice between humility and hubris was a matter of personal decision rooted in morality—a capacity for virtuous self-restraint that our Creator gave us when he set our minds free.

The same understanding lies at the heart of our conception of liberty in America. Even Jefferson's landmark charter of religious liberty, the Virginia Statute for Religious Freedom, ascribes our freedom to divine consent, invoking "the plan of the Holy author of our religion, who being Lord both of body and mind, yet chose not to propagate it by coercions on either, as was in his Almighty power to do...." There is a dual humility in those words that is vital to appreciate, if easy to overlook. First, there is the humility of a people who acknowledge the sovereignty of God even as they declare regulation of religious belief and observance to be beyond the proper reach of civil authority. But there is also the humility exemplified by God himself, who has the sovereign power to command our thoughts and actions yet instead gives us freedom.

Though we welcome that freedom, it can and often does produce startling and disagreeable developments. Having seen its dubious exercise by the sovereign people of Virginia in the last election, for example, I was not all that happy that God had delegated his franchise. But my reflections on this notion produced an epiphany of sorts. It occurred to me that this idea of divine humility, or divine forbearance, truly is central to the capacity of free people to live in harmony and constructive community. For if God, who is sovereign and really does have all the answers, nevertheless leaves it to men and women to make choices and even to err, how can we—fallible beings who are not sovereign and do not have all the answers—not accord our fellow citizens the same respect?

From there, it had been a short journey for me to several crucial conclusions that I would try out on my friends this weekend: First, that humility born of our trust in God is what gives us the grace to respect the ideas of others even while vigorously advancing our own. Second, that humility born of gratitude for God's beneficence is what drives us to jealously guard our freedom and the fruits of our labors and then freely sacrifice them to be a help to others. And, third, that humility is the antidote for pride in religion itself, since it is our awe at God's unlimited power that gives us the boldness to proclaim the faith we fervently believe while at the same time accepting that a sovereign God is great enough to work through the varied faiths of others in ways we do not understand.

So, whether we are talking about our politics or our religion, the state or the church, the wonder is that a God who could command our thoughts nevertheless created our minds free. In so doing, he displayed the very humility he desires from each of us. It is a humility that varied faiths derive from belief in a higher power—one that, for me as a Christian, was perfectly and permanently displayed at a place called Calvary.

This is highly personal stuff, and heavy, too. Plenty of people are made uncomfortable by it, so they say it has no place in politics. But you really cannot understand the American story without this perspective. And my own story, especially the hard decisions I would make down the road, will not make much sense without understanding these beliefs and how I came to them. I came to them during an altogether unexpected and unwelcome low point in my life. I came to them through disappointment and doubt, conversations with devastated friends and colleagues, and the rich store of balance and perspective—*wisdom*—that often goes untapped until hard knocks come along and make us pay heed. Most important, I came to them because seeds of faith planted long before this now had found fertile soil in which to grow.

Ned Nevers' unexpected ouster by the Virginia electorate had supplied the stimulus for these reflections on politics and pride, faith and humility. But there was more. His defeat also had brought front-and-center the idea that God is at work in the affairs of men, that he is not a passive observer of history but an active participant. His hand can be seen not only in those "glorious events which Heaven has been pleased to produce in our favor," as Washington put it, but also in the inglorious experiences that challenge, humble, correct, and refine us. I will forego a foray into the vexatious thicket that surrounds the question of how divine providence and free will intertwine, but during this searching time I had come across an observation by John Calvin that struck me as applicable, perhaps, to the sad-seeming case of Edward K. Nevers. "When God ... wishes to lead us to repentance," wrote Calvin, "he is compelled to repeat his blows continually, either because we are not moved when he chastises us with his hand, or we seem roused for the time, and then we return again to our former torpor. He is therefore compelled to redouble his blows."

Perhaps God had reached the end of his rope in the long-running case of *Nevers v. Pride.* Unable to get through to the proud Senator through sound counsel, night terrors, interventions like the faithful stand taken during an earlier campaign by Mitch, Abby, and Chad, and who-knows-what-else, perhaps God now had delivered the only blow that Ned Nevers, the master politician, would heed: sudden, ignominious *defeat.*

That seemed like a harshly judgmental assessment on my part—and presumptuous, too, for none of us can know the mind of God. Plus, bad things happen due to people's choices, and it seems like a dodge to lay them all at God's doorstep. But then the positive flip-side also had dawned on me. The Senator did believe there was a "big guy upstairs," as he put it. And if the big guy actually was disciplining and correcting him through this God-awful political debacle, then maybe he still had some things he wanted to accomplish through this broken man who had been a political master.

That last encouraging note, along with the other insights, were on my mind, and I was looking forward to kicking them around with my friends and Martha on the mountaintop.

On the way out of the driveway en route to Wintergreen, Martha stopped so I could grab the day's mail. Thumbing through the inch-thick stack, I was delighted to spot a plain business envelope with a familiar Hampden-Sydney return address. I eagerly opened and read the missive, which Dr. S. D. had punched onto two crammed pages using his trademark Royal typewriter:

> *Dear Daniel:*
>
> *Considering it as ever my duty to enhance your understanding of the true genius and grace that gave rise to our republic, and which must attend its survival if that be the Almighty's purpose, I wanted to relay to you a recent product of my research that has excited me and provided no small amount of inspiration for further inquiry.*
>
> *You are, of course, fully informed concerning the profound impact that the Reverend Samuel Davies had on that pivotal patriot, Patrick Henry. My latest discovery relates to his evident influence on the even more consequential General Washington.*
>
> *Your reading on Davies probably has disclosed, and perhaps we also discussed, Davies' role as a military recruiter during the French and Indian War. He was praised by Governor Dinwiddie as the most effective recruiter in the colony. He exhorted young Virginians to join the fight against the French interlopers in the Ohio Valley and their Indian allies, yet he cast the frontier conflict as part of a much larger, global contest. The French were not simply rivals for strategically important territory; they were committed ideological foes. Their dedication to papal and monarchical absolutism was considered as antithetical to Anglo-American values of political liberty in their day as was Soviet Communism in ours. Speaking at a time no farther removed from England's Glorious Revolution than World War II is from our own day, Davies understood the far-reaching stakes of the titanic struggle during which he lived.*
>
> *It is my thesis that Davies' worldview, especially his belief in political liberty's dependence upon moral purpose and divine favor,*

had a profound impact on Washington. First, we can safely assume that Davies' martial exhortations fell impressively upon the appreciative ears of young Colonel Washington, whose budding military career and ambition for glory depended upon a supply of militia recruits. After Washington miraculously survived the bloody encounter along the Monongahela that took the life of General Braddock, Davies sensed—two decades before the revolutionary struggle—that destiny held the young Virginian in its grasp. To a company of new Hanover County volunteers on August 17, 1755, Davies observed, "As a remarkable example…, I may point out to the public, that heroic youth, Col. Washington, whom I cannot but hope Providence has hitherto preserved in so signal a manner, for some important service to his country."

Washington knew Davies' eldest son, Colonel William Davies, and relied on him in several major roles during the Revolution. After the long struggle was won, the General spent much of his post-war life exhorting for political unity and invoking the active aid of an engaged Providence in a manner reminiscent of Reverend Davies. And, as you well know, President Washington concluded his service with an appeal for Americans to eschew political divisions for the sake of the larger national purpose. "Let me now … warn you in the most solemn manner against the baneful effects of the spirit of party," he declared famously in his farewell address.

So here is my discovery, and I am embarrassed to have missed it earlier. Washington's farewell appeal for avoidance of excessive partisanship in the political realm contains echoes—with so stark a similarity as to exclude the possibility of mere coincidence—of an earlier entreaty by Davies that Christian believers transcend their denominational differences. "My brethren, I now warn you against this wretched mischievous spirit of party," Davies had implored during a memorable sermon. "A Christian! A Christian! Let that be your highest distinction!"

Davies had been summoning believers back to the true faith and warning them not to fall victim to religious partisanship. Washington was summoning patriots back to the Spirit of '76 and

warning them not to let political partisanship become their preoc-
cupying aim. The two men and their messages were inextricably
bound, just as they are today and ever shall be, because political and
religious liberty are mutually dependent.

I am committed to further research into the influence of the
remarkable Reverend upon the indispensable General. But, lest you
think my purpose in writing today is purely historical, let me point
to an aspect of some relevance to your present situation. Washington
survived defeat, learned from it, and went on to great accomplish-
ment. Likewise must you learn and proceed. Do not give up on your
Senator Nevers, for I "cannot but hope Providence has hitherto
preserved him for some important service to his country." Nor can
you overlook the powerful positive influence that Washington's at-
tending agents, among them the good Davies, so evidently exerted
on our nation's greatest leader and thus on our national affairs. In
either role, leader or attendant, lies a noble pursuit if pursued with
noble purpose.

Devotedly,
Dr. S. D.

I read the letter to myself, then read it to Martha. And, hours later, after
I had finished building the fire and mixing drinks, I settled in and read it to
my friends. It lifted our spirits there on the mountaintop and was the stimulus
for an unusual series of conversations.

I am struck, in retrospect, by how the wide-ranging discussion that
evening kept finding its way back to religion. This was quite a new experience for us. Faith is a private thing—at least, that is the way most of us had
been raised—and politics and government are domains our culture fences
off as strictly secular. So, like most folks of our age and occupation, my
friends and I generally avoided religious topics, especially matters of personal
belief. Mitch, of course, was an obvious exception; he could be counted on
to leaven any conversation with apt quotations from the Bible, Dr. King, or
his pastor-father. But even Preacher's predictable interjections became a kind
of background noise, like a cardinal's repetitive chirping, that we largely
would tune out.

This evening, however, was different.

The conversations triggered by my reading of Dr. S. D.'s letter went in a variety of directions. Martha, Mitch, and Chad were off to the side chatting about something—a recollection of Dr. S. D. at Hampden-Sydney, I think—when Abby sat down beside me in front of the fire, tapped on my knee with resolve, and said, "Look here now, I want to ask you something."

"Have at it," I said, intrigued by her uncharacteristic seriousness.

"Dr. S. D., and, for that matter, Davies and Washington and a lot of other religious people—they're all very smart people, or they were. Well educated—wise to the world. Not simple minds, that's for sure. Yet, somehow they manage to see the 'hand of Providence' in every event. I mean, nothing is ever just a coincidence; nothing is just an accident. Even terrible things—no matter how bad it gets—God is behind it all. At least, that is the way they see it. I just find that fascinating. It seems like it could make you really mad at God, on the one hand, you know, when things end up being unfair. But, on the other hand, it also could be kind of comforting if you could convince yourself to really believe it. But it all seems so, well ... *convenient*."

"Wow. Okay. I hear what you're saying," I replied. "I guess I would answer by turning it around on you. Have you ever seen an event or series of events that was just too amazing, too much of a coincidence, for you to believe it was just happenstance?"

"Oh, sure, I guess. Hmmm ... yeah. Lots of times, probably." Then she remembered something specific and her visage brightened. "Did I ever tell you that story about Benjamin Rush, the Father of American Psychiatry, and his dream?"

I knew the name well—a Pennsylvanian named Benjamin Rush was a member of the Continental Congress, signer of the Declaration of Independence, and friend and ally of Jefferson and Madison. I assumed that was a different person but mentioned him anyway.

"That's the one," she said. "He was a major player in the Revolution and in government all during that time, but he was also a medical doctor, and late in his life he became interested in mental illness. Today he is regarded as the 'Father of American Psychiatry.'"

The comment catapulted me back to our college days, when I had enjoyed making sport of Abby's major in Psychology, deriding all the mind-reading and

Freudian dream-decoding as hocus pocus. Now she seemed poised to resume that shaky terrain, and I lapsed good-naturedly into my former role as sarcastic skeptic.

"Are you sure about that, Abby? I have read a lot about that period, and Rush's name comes up pretty often. If he was a nationally acclaimed shrink, it seems like someone would have mentioned it."

"Well, maybe you need to diversify your source material," she rejoined with a smirk. "I assume you know that the second and third presidents, Adams and Jefferson, both died on the Fourth of July...."

"Of course. That was widely viewed at the time as a miraculous event," I took over knowledgeably, as if reclaiming my personal domain from an interloper. "Here were the two titans of independence passing away, many hundred miles apart, on the same day. And it was not just any day—it was the Fourth of July. And it was not just any Fourth of July—it was 50 years to the day after the Declaration of Independence, on which they had collaborated. Their deaths that day not only marked the end of an era in the minds of Americans; most seem to have interpreted the stunning coincidence as a divinely ordained event—an affirmation by God of his providential hand in the rise of the American republic. I can point you to a good book on Jefferson if you want to read about it...."

"Actually," Abby interrupted, "I *have* read about it, and apparently I know something about it that you don't know."

"I'm sure there are many things I don't know. But, fortunately, you are here to enlighten me."

"Yes, I will be happy to. You see, Dr. Benjamin Rush was a contemporary and friend of both Jefferson and Adams. And, of course, the two of them—Jefferson and Adams—had a falling out."

"You *think?*" I intruded again with reflexive sarcasm. "They had a little difference of opinion over which of them should be President in 1796 and again in 1800, not to mention whether to go to war against England or France, whether criticizing the government should be considered treason, what the role of the federal government should be, and a number of other modest topics...."

"Yes, well, if you can stop showing off and just let me tell you my story, it might actually be interesting to you." The reprimand got the attention of the others, who now were listening as Abby drew in a breath impatiently and continued. "Now, Dr. Rush thought it was a tragedy that these two great patriots who had been such good friends and worked together on such a great cause were alienated from each other because of all the vicious politics that went on back then. And he took it upon himself to get them speaking to—well, corresponding with—each other again late in life."

I knew Jefferson and Adams had been reconciled and had a very rich correspondence in the years before they died. In fact, thanks to an earlier gift from none other than Abby, I had read most of their letters. Still, a dismissive wisecrack seemed more suitable than an admission.

"I suppose your point here is that the world is a much better place because of shrinks...."

"No—I mean, certainly—but that's not the point," Abby continued. "Rush had sided with the Jefferson partisans against Adams, but Rush and Adams got back together and started corresponding about...well, just guess what they started corresponding about!"

I had no clue, so I just waited.

"Their *dreams*. Rush had become fascinated with how the mind works, and he was a century ahead of Freud in analyzing dreams. He and Adams started writing to each other about their dreams. Adams had all these stormy emotions and insecurities that came billowing out in embarrassing ways; he was consumed with worry that history would not give him his due. But he and Rush started describing their dreams to each other, and the letters got pretty crazy, and it really helped Adams loosen up. He even started to poke fun at himself."

"Now there's an interesting take on history: 'How the shrink helped the statesman get his groove back.' I think your Psych prof should have stuck to that psychoanalysis mumbo-jumbo, Abby, and left the history to the experts."

She ignored me and pressed on. "Rush wanted his old friends Adams and Jefferson to be reconciled—he thought it was terrible that they were embittered old adversaries. So he started writing to them both and maneuvered them into a correspondence with each other, and his little plan worked. But get *this*: What prompted Rush to do this in the first place was a dream—a dream he described at length in a letter to Adams long before those events."

She seemed confident she knew what she was talking about, but it sounded like an old wives' tale to me.

"The dream happened at a time when Adams and Jefferson were still completely estranged, but in Rush's dream, he saw a passage from a history book that described the Adams-Jefferson reconciliation. It not only reported that they were reconciled; it said they had years of active correspondence of which the world later took great note. And then it said they 'sunk into the grave nearly at the same time.' That's the future history that Rush, in his letter to Adams, said he had foreseen in his dream. He was writing at a time when Jefferson and Adams had not been communicating for a decade and were still regarded as bitter enemies, yet he described their reconciliation and their years of important correspondence, and he even described their tandem deaths—all based on a dream that he dreamed *17 years before* those events."

"Now," she exhaled triumphantly, "is that something or what?"

"It's something all right," I allowed, not even attempting to hide my skepticism. "I'm not sure you have the history right, but it seems like you've answered your own question. If some coincidences are just too coincidental to be accidental, then at least some of the time something else must be going on...."

As an aside, by the way, Abby had the history right after all. I researched it the next week and found, to my amazement, that her story was characteristically correct in every relevant detail. The "dream correspondence" of Adams and Rush did exist, and there in 1809 was a letter describing the night vision in which Rush foresaw the later rapprochement between Adams and Jefferson and their departure "into the grave nearly at the same time."

It struck me then as a most curious matter, another layer of coincidence piled inexplicably on the happenstance that both men—the "North and South Poles of the American Revolution," as Rush called them—departed this earthly tent on the 50th anniversary of their most important handiwork. Later, as I continued to read and discover, I would add several layers of personal connection to this pile of coincidences. For example, I learned that Benjamin Rush was greatly influenced during his own college years by Princeton's president, Samuel Davies—the same Samuel Davies whose descendant and namesake, Dr. S. D., had provided life-changing counsel to me at Hampden-Sydney and in the years since. It was Rush who some years later wrote and journeyed to Scotland to persuade Reverend John Witherspoon to accept the Princeton presidency—a crucial event, since Dr. Witherspoon became not only a signer of the Declaration of Independence but one of the most powerful voices of the Revolution. Rush's recruitment of the pivotal parson was an important factor contributing to American independence, but it held special significance for me once I learned that Witherspoon probably had given Hampden-Sydney

College its name as well as its first president (in the person of his son-in-law). He also had exerted an outsized influence at Princeton on one of his Virginia students, James Madison—the same Madison whose name I bore, whose birthday I shared, and who became the object of my lifelong interest and study.

Coincidences of this sort may be regarded as truly remarkable or remarkably trivial, but the discussion that evening was neither. It evolved into a frank exploration by five sincere friends and confidants of the possibility that there existed a presence and purpose other than, *greater* than, that which any of us could comprehend in nature, and what its character might be.

Many people I know, including a lot I count as good friends, worship avidly at the altar of Coincidence. For a time I myself was among those faithful. But, as I shared with Chad, Mitch, and Abby on that mountaintop evening, I had come to regard the central tenets of that faith—randomness, luck, accident, and the like—as just too far-fetched and fantastical for my logical mind. Causes kept converging consequentially; effects kept culminating in crucial events; and chance just struck me as a very implausible explanation for it all. I discovered that, as the saying goes, I did not have enough faith to be an atheist.

The real clincher for me had been provided some months earlier by Martha. "I can believe that many things in this world are products of some massive atomic accident," she had told me one evening, "*but not love*. You cannot explain love—a bond so strong and so deep, so powerful and yet so subtle, so real and yet so mysterious that it can produce sacrifices even to the point of giving up one's own life—in any sensible way except as a divine creation."

Yes, something had *created* this love. And before the something could create it, it had to understand it. And to understand it, it had to have experienced it. And to experience love is to share it, because that is what love is—the giving and the receiving. And if only a loving creator was capable of creating this earthly love, then these other strange concepts I had been taught over the years also began to make more sense. The notion of eternal life, for example … because what would a loving father do but gather his children back to himself? And the idea of an attentive and engaged Providence … because what would a loving mother do when her children were away? Would she send them on their journey and then turn her face away in indifference? No, she would want to watch over them—*she would want to be with them*. A parent's love would have it no other way. And that, of course, is exactly what my faith teaches that the living God has done: through the inscrutable intricacy of his all-encompassing Providence; by the presence of his Spirit; through the mystery of prayer; in the person of his Son: *Emmanuel, God with us.*

Thus had I *reasoned* my way finally to faith, as I confessed awkwardly to my friends that pivotal evening. But not really, because this odd thing, *love*—this missing link that Martha had provided—was the key to my whole chain of logic, and you cannot reason your way to love; you have to experience it. That had been my great blessing, learning about love by being the object of it … from Martha, my parents, my friends, my mentor Dr. S. D., and so many others. I was one of the "lucky" ones who had been surrounded by it.

The Greco-Roman democrats and republicans whom our founders so admired had figured out a lot of it. They understood that freedom and justice are dependent on a shared moral sense of necessarily divine origin. But, as St. Augustine illuminated in *The City of God*, even the wisest of them, even Plato and his adherents, had missed the crucial link that is love. Their deity was not a transcendent yet approachable Father who longed to be in active fellowship with his children; theirs instead was dutiful, defined, and detached. Their moral sense, their *virtue*, was grounded in the elusive hope of validation by generations hence rather than in the awful immediacy, unblemished integrity, and unrelenting love of an ever-present Parent.

Abby listened intently as I laid out this case. Then she returned, in all her innocent, piercing candor, to the question she had wanted to ask in the first place.

"If all that is true, if God is all about love, then why does he allow his world to be a place of such terrible suffering? Why do such awful things happen to so many good people? Like Senator Nevers losing the election? But worse than that—like Mitch losing his leg in Iraq? And … well … like you, Danny, losing your parents so young? If God is like a loving parent, how in the world could he take your own parents away from you when you needed them most?"

The room fell silent, seemingly in shock, and I rose and headed to our bedroom. I suppose the others thought the question had hit too close to home, but I did not leave to conceal my emotions. I went to retrieve the book my parents had given me as a young boy, the one I almost never had opened until after they died. Tucked in that Bible, which now went wherever I did, was a slip of paper Dr. S. D. had given me back in college when I had posed a similar question.

I returned and read it: "The decisive act of creation was the creation of our freedom. Without freedom, there is no choosing. Without choosing, there is no error. Without error, there is no evil. Without evil, there is no suffering. Without suffering, there is no fear. Without fear, there is no trust. Without trust, there is no hope. Without hope, there is no work. Without work, there is no purpose."

Then I remembered what Dr. S. D. had said when he handed me that paper: "This is *part* of the answer to your question, Daniel. Call it the logical part. But none of it, none of our suffering, makes any sense without love. The entire identity and object of our faith is redemptive love, sacrificial love—*suffering love*. And, of course, suffering love is a phenomenon that cannot occur unless both suffering and love exist in the world. It is what our Savior did for us; it is what we are called to do for others."

So that was how we dealt on that mountaintop with the most fundamental questions about fate and faith. And, as I look back, it is apparent that this was a crucial passage on my journey. Though little mindful of the change, I had progressed from a superficial regard for my maternal Presbyterian heritage to an actual belief in its tenets, whereupon my rejection of concepts like coincidence, accident, and luck was complete. I still happily claim the "luck of the Irish" whenever it suits, and I still cannot help wishing people "Good luck!" whenever it fits. But I do not really believe in the idea of luck anymore. And the time I fully realized it and shared my belief was that night at Wintergreen.

Of course, the rejection of luck is, and was for me, only a beginning. The questions get harder from there, not easier. As Abby suggested, it is a facile source of comfort to see in every agreeable event the helping hand of some generous Providence. And if there is a superintending power that deserves credit for the good things, who gets the blame for the bad ones? If freedom—that is, the gift of free will—is the culprit because it opens the door to wrong choices and hence to evil, then why does Providence retract our freedom by intervening to protect us from some earthly evils and not from others—from the consequences of some of our wrong choices and not others? Why are some right choices rewarded in this life and others only in the next? Why must some people cry out in agony, "My God, why has Thou forsaken me?" while others enjoy prosperity as the fruit of earthly obedience—or, even more confounding, in spite of their earthy *dis*obedience? Why do good things happen to bad people, and why do bad things happen to good people, and, by the way, why does anything happen at all? Or is it just a dream? These are not all the right questions—some may not even be good questions—but they are part of the mystery that began to occupy and even inspire me once I moved beyond the truly absurd notion that everything here is a product of randomly colliding particles of matter.

No one over the years had been more cocksure or dogmatic on these very issues than Mitch, but during the course of the evening on Devils Knob he evinced a degree of deference that surprised me. The extended recovery from his battlefield injury had given Mitch lots of time to reflect. And, though he never voiced it, I have to believe he wrestled mightily with the apparent contradiction between the divine favor he long had trusted and the shattered leg he recently had forfeited. His comments throughout the evening gave some hints of the continuing struggle within, but what impressed me more was the gentleness and grace he exuded as he conceded the inexplicability and encouraged the rest of us to "trust in God's plan." Here was a person whose faith had been tested far more severely than mine, more severely than just about anyone I knew, and who now gave voice to his convictions in a compelling yet amazingly humble way. I knew my friend well, but this was something new and powerful.

Chad had been uncharacteristically quiet as we kicked around these very personal ideas by the fire. So after a while, when no one else had pressed him, I decided to give him a shove. "Okay, Chad, what's with this Silent Cal routine? Don't you have a dog in this fight between the hand of God and the fickled finger of fate? Or maybe you've got a third possibility—you know, like the Invisible Hand of the free market."

This, it turned out, was like poking a bear. Or maybe the better analogy is to breaching a dam. Chad could wax on knowledgeably about most any topic, and would do so often to a tiresome degree, but matters of faith seemingly were not in his repertoire—until now.

For the next 30 minutes, maybe longer, Chad held forth without significant interruption, and in summary here is what he had to say. Yes, he supposed he believed in God, if that is what I was asking, though he could never recall uttering those words before. He recalled the liturgical numbness and religious indifference of his youth and said he definitely had reasoned his way from there to a general conviction that a higher power indeed was at work in the affairs of men. This higher power certainly was not to be confused with the Invisible Hand of the free marketplace, however. Whoever and whatever God was, he presumably had more permanent matters with which to concern himself than the production and consumption of widgets and the determination of equilibrium price. Yet, there was a connection, since economics is the science of human behavior, and the laws of economics are rooted in the laws of human nature, and human nature, being both original and immutable, must be of intentional design.

That, however, was about as far as one needed to go in worrying with religion, Chad averred. At least, that is what he had thought for a while. The divine origin of human nature was a proposition at once logically self-evident and scientifically unprovable, and therefore it should not long detain a serious man from more useful—*i.e.*, empirical—pursuits. Besides, from Chad's perspective, Christianity had declared itself content with a mere confession of belief. As he understood it, one needed only to embrace the unobjectionable if bizarre notion that Jesus of Nazareth actually was the Son of God and Savior of the World, and the religious piece could be safely salted away. Like other contentious matters that preoccupied the world's varied religions, the divinity of the carpenter's son was another of those notions not susceptible to empirical proof or rebuttal and thus unworthy of undue time and attention.

Chad's attitude reminded me of Ben Franklin's stance on the subject. Asked in his later years what he thought about Christ's claim to divinity, Franklin candidly confessed to some lingering doubt on the matter but said it was "a question I do not dogmatize upon, having never studied it, and I think it needless to busy myself with it now, when I expect soon an opportunity of knowing the truth with less trouble...."

If Chad's religious faith was largely perfunctory, his belief in the goodness, and therefore godliness, of the free market was passionate. It was, he emphatically reminded us, the most efficient way to achieve "the greatest happiness for the greatest number," borrowing Francis Hutcheson's famous formulation. And to what higher purpose could God or man aspire than that?

Enterprise and exchange rendered things of value to people. Value derived from meeting human needs and supplying human wants in ever more creative, efficient, and desirable ways. The free market existed to facilitate exchange, and exchange occurred only when both parties perceived a benefit from the transaction. The principle of comparative advantage ensured the optimal exchange by the optimal parties. The happy products of the process invariably were individual happiness and societal progress.

There was no such thing as selfishness, Chad insisted. Or, to state it better, there was nothing at all wrong with a person invariably and relentlessly pursuing his or her self-interest. Quite to the contrary, people pursuing their interests is what made the whole system work. Establish a system, Chad argued, where there exists economic liberty, where rules (laws) assure fair exchange and protection of property rights, and where people hew to a shared set of basic ethical precepts, and the pursuit of self-interest within such a system inevitably will produce the greatest possible individual and societal happiness and progress.

One needed only to consider the history of free countries—that is, free economies—to see the proof of this proposition, Chad contended. To charges of capitalist exploitation and overreach, he responded with an admission rather than denial, acknowledging that every human activity is a reflection of human nature and thus susceptible to the full range of machinations, from good to evil. With great force, he argued that the good had far outweighed the evil— that the creativity and productivity of free people engaged in commerce had brought the world out of darkness, and that every modern aspiration, from justice and democracy to freedom from disease and want, depended upon fidelity to sound market principles in the future.

"If ideals such as freedom, justice, democracy, relief from poverty and disease, and so forth, are what you think 'all God's children' should have," Chad declared, "then you have to agree it's the free market that does the Lord's work. Economic opportunity and prosperity create the conditions in which all those other good things can happen. Without free markets, people would be engaged in a constant struggle for subsistence and survival, leaving no time or means for the higher purposes to which man aspires."

That was Chad's central argument, well grounded in a substantial body of knowledge and opinion, and it had undeniable force. But, even now, I do not think Chad has quite finished working out his own peculiar brand of economic religion. His belief in the efficacy of the free market was then and is now unshakeable, regarded as immutable truth. But over time Chad would come to perceive a practical dilemma posed by poverty's persistence amid prosperity in democratic societies. He would ponder whether liberty—ordered liberty, with its vital protection of property rights and free commerce—could long survive alongside poverty in a country where the majority rules. Might it actually be in liberty's long-term interest to place some of the fruits of its material prosperity at the disposal of the community, through taxation or philanthropy or both, in order to "promote the general welfare," as the Constitution put it, and buy political peace? It was, he thought at first, a matter of principle, demanding a "yes" or "no" answer, and the answer was "no." But over time he would begin to wonder whether it was more a matter of practicality, requiring the striking of some felicitous balance.

What I noticed that evening (and have observed many times since) was that, even with his cavalier attitude toward religious doctrine and practice, Chad was not beyond the influence of an inspired conscience. Unlike some of his libertarian soulmates who took every Ayn Rand utterance as gospel, Chad flatly rejected the Randian agnosticism that compelled dogmatic disregard of the basic distinction between statist "looters" who confiscate others' wealth in the name of altruism and generous souls who give freely and voluntarily from their own abundance. He was and would remain closer to Adam Smith, whose *The Theory of Moral Sentiments* argued that "to restrain our selfish, and to indulge our benevolent affections ... can alone produce among mankind that harmony of sentiments and passions in which consists their whole grace and propriety."

From his impressive Wintergreen soliloquy, I got the sense that Chad was, like so many of his role models, coming to faith almost in spite of himself ... or at least in spite of his creed. But that was only the beginning of the complication. Confronted by two fundamental truths—the efficient market's reliance on self-interest and the transcendent selflessness of the Nazarene—Chad would stubbornly refuse to shrug off the seeming contradiction. He would always seem to be searching for that reconciliation as he traveled along on his journey. And he would not be alone.

The evening had many other highs along with a few lows. Its usefulness began to decline as the night wore on and the casual pace of alcohol consumption quickened (by everyone except Martha, who, I noticed, had foregone her usual few glasses of wine). We all were worn out, and the discussion ended around midnight, close on the heels of Mitch's apt but unfortunate comment about these being "times that try men's souls." The invocation of Thomas Paine, even the familiar line from *The Crisis*, was enough to send me off on a mini-rampage that chased everyone away for the evening.

Paine was an ass, I declared, and not just because of his scurrilous attacks on Washington and other excesses. He had famously gushed that "[w]e have it in our power to begin the world over again," supplying one of the Republic's truly foolish lines. There is, I exclaimed, only one power in heaven and on earth that can "begin the world over again"—the rest of us, alas, are constrained by the laws of nature and lessons of history. That is why Madison spent months at Montpelier before the seminal 1787 convention immersing himself in the collected wisdom about politics and governance from classical times to his own day, readying himself for an indispensable role in the conclave that would set America's course. It is why General Washington had Addison's *Cato* performed for his troops as they camped during the long winter at Valley Forge. And it is why even Jefferson, reflecting on the content of his revolutionary Declaration, cited the influence of "Aristotle, Cicero, Locke, Sidney, etc." These republican builders were not tearing the world down to begin it over again; they were unearthing bedrock principles on which a solid new foundation could be set.

This was a very important, even profound, point—the central distinction between the American Revolution and its calamitous counterparts in France, Russia, and elsewhere. But you would not have known it from the indifference my friends displayed as they meandered about, rounding up car keys, wallets, glasses, etc., gesturing goodnight, and making the way groggily to their various bedrooms. I did not mind—it was not the first time I had made this point, and it certainly would not be the last. But as I spread the coals to kill the fire, the import of the evening began to sink in.

We cannot despair over our setbacks, for nothing happens truly by accident. Suffering and disappointments humble us; obstacles are there to be overcome; things are meant to change. We are here to live and learn. Errors and evils will come, a fact of life I would have to embrace in the even tougher times ahead. We cannot, despite Paine's flourish, "begin the world over again." But through grace we can *begin our lives over again*, and that is the true freedom.

First Thanksgiving

I awakened early the next morning, before the sunrise, to take advantage of the magnificent vista and greet the new day at its start. To the east at first was but a yellowish glow on the horizon. Below it I could see the dark profile of the mountains while, above, wispy white clouds that I could almost touch partially obscured the flickering stars, which seemed bigger and brighter here than anywhere else I could recall. Settling into a rocking chair on the porch,

I found myself giving silent thanks for the glory of the dawn, the beauty of the place, and the peace of the moment.

The sun, like a master painter, still unseen, then began to reveal its original work of the day before my eyes. White clouds soon were discernible below in the spaces between the mountain ridges, a morning fog helping to extend the sleep of those nestled beneath its blanket. The dull glow of the horizon turned to a series of blue, pink, magenta, purple, and lavender pastel lines and layers created by the cirrus and cumulus clouds stacked up for miles to the east. Soon the addition of morning light changed the dark space occupied by the mountains into a rich green landscape in which the irregular pattern of treetops and some rock cliffs were visible in the foreground, with the hazy blue outlines of other ridges beyond. I noticed that the fog was not stationary, as it had first appeared, but now seemed to march with great purpose up each cut between the mountain ridges, only to disappear suddenly at the same level on each hill. I strayed momentarily from my wide-eyed witness of the unfolding vista to muse that perhaps the fog's purposeful march but inevitable end was a commentary on life. If so, I thought, life is a march that takes place surrounded by beauty that is too seldom noticed.

The pace of the painting now began to hasten as the sun, still behind the scenes, began to work its magic on the clouds overhead. The cotton balls which had appeared white against the evening sky now began to appear dark blue and gray against the crystal blue morning dome, and on the lower side of each the sun painted a variety of colors—pastel shades of purple and pink at first, and then increasingly brilliant splashes of golden yellow and orange.

There was enough light now to track the movement of the clouds at different levels, and, combined with the changing colors, it added to the drama of the impending appearance of the sun itself. When that finally occurred—when the top edge of the reddish-orange ball suddenly peaked through on the multi-layered horizon—the clouds floating in the foreground and those suspended above all greeted the Source of Light by putting on rims of bright golden lace, as if returning a bright smile or a sharp salute. The scene in all its uniqueness and brilliance seemed to last only a few moments before the sun was up fully and gleaming brightly, transforming the tranquil scene into another busy day.

By that point I was no longer viewing the painter's work in progress. Now I was deep in prayer, giving thanks to the Author of this masterpiece, confessing that nothing in my life made me worthy of such blessings, and placing myself as fully and completely as I knew how in the hands of the God who had put me here and surrounded me with such indescribable beauty and grace. Humbled and seeking, I asked for forgiveness, for help and guidance, for calmness and courage and purpose and patience in the days ahead, so that I would be a faithful trustee of the gifts God had given me and accomplish whatever purposes he had for my life. I prayed for the grace to trust God's will, whatever it was, and for his will to be done.

I prayed for others, first and foremost for Martha, without whom I could not imagine living. I prayed for my friends, for the ailing Senator, and for others I cared about. I prayed for people who were sick and grieving and in distress and for those who sought to help and heal them. I prayed for our church and community, our state, and our country, seeking God's forgiveness for our collective and individual failures, asking his blessing on our collective and individual pursuits. I prayed with all the sincerity I could muster for my antagonists—Bart's was the face that came into view—and for the people who made me crazy on a daily basis. I hoped these prayers were genuine, but doubted.

And then I turned to thanksgiving. Reflecting on my many blessings, I gave thanks for the unwavering love and redeeming grace of Jesus Christ and for the increasingly evident manifestations of his Spirit in my life. I gave thanks for Martha's unconditional love, for my mother and father and their ever-present example of love and faithfulness, for my close friends, and for all the other saints and angels that God had sent to light my path. These thoughts were the most humbling. I gave thanks for America and for Virginia, for freedom and justice, and for the struggle and sacrifice of all those who made freedom and justice possible. I prayed for the preservation of peace where it existed in the world with freedom and justice and for reform and deliverance where it did not. I prayed that good people would not to be overcome by evil, but that the evil would be overcome by the good. I gave thanks that God was watching over it all, and I asked for help trusting in his providence. I prayed about other people and other things in the stillness of the morning. And, then, my soul refreshed, I left the porch and mountaintop vista to engage the day.

This, I now recognize, was my own first thanksgiving. The new conversation God began with me that day would continue, and it would be a conversation grounded in gratitude.

Like the Red Letter Year of 1619, there were three other things about this time that would remain worthy of recollection.

First, it was the day Mitch surprised us with the fantastic news that he was running for Congress. We were all geared up to pound on him some more about joining us in D.C., but before we could even start in on him good, he stopped us cold: "Y'all think you are so smart. How exactly am I supposed to run for Congress in the Seventh District if I am living in Northern Virginia?"

The second thing was Ned Nevers. Later that same afternoon, he tracked me down. It was the first call I had received from the Senator himself rather than Sally in the seven months since the election. He sounded upbeat, even excited, and invited Martha and me to swing by the farm on Monday. He had made a "profession," he said, and wanted to share it with us.

Ned Nevers never liked to write anything down, but he had written out a statement of faith that he shared with the trustees of New Hope Methodist Church upon his rejoining the church as an active member. In it, he testified unabashedly to what he had come to believe about the sovereignty of God and the sinfulness of man, about forgiveness in Christ and the power of the Holy Spirit, about the impact of pride in his life and the hope he now had. "God," he declared, invoking the Book of Daniel, "was able to put down those who walk in pride, no matter how powerful." He described his privileged but troubled journey unselfconsciously, in deeply personal terms like one who no longer felt constrained to preen for an audience. God obviously had been at work through his political humiliation and emotional turmoil, through his embrace by the New Hope pastor and congregation, through Sally—heck, for all I knew, even the animals had played a part, lending a sympathetic ear as he talked things through. But whatever the combination of causes, the Ned Nevers I encountered plainly was a new man, and to both Martha's and my eyes and ears the newness unquestionably appeared genuine.

Sitting on the front porch sipping Sally's iced tea—prepared to traditional Southern specifications and thus far too sweet for my taste—the Senator and I chatted refreshingly about a wide array of topics, with his religious awakening prominent among them and politics seemingly the only taboo topic. I certainly was not going to bring up that sore subject. But shortly before we departed, Nevers sprang from his chair and went indoors, then emerged moments later with a well-worn copy of the political classic *All the King's Men*.

"Have you read this?" he asked rather excitedly.

I examined the spine, thought for a minute, and answered. "In college—I think I had to read it in my American Lit class. I can't say I really recall much about it, though. Why?"

"Well, you need to read it again," he said. "Here, take my copy, and don't mind my hen-scratching and dog-earing. Read it and then bring it back to me when you come for your next visit, and we'll talk about it."

"It's about politics," I muttered, mostly to myself.

"Indeed it is," Nevers answered. Then the smiling former senator said something that made sense only later, after I had reread the great novel. It echoed something the Boss had said in that story: *"You know, Daniel, when this conscience business starts, ain't no telling where it'll stop...."*

I was still pondering that one on the drive home when Martha broke the silence and delivered the red letter weekend's biggest news—the kind that makes every other thing in your life suddenly seem trivial. A gift from God was on the way—a brilliant new thread for his tapestry—and, amazingly, he was entrusting her to us.

PART TWO

FAITH

1997 - 2005

CHAPTER FIVE

RENEWAL

You have some choices when you find yourself exiled, politically or otherwise. You can disengage, ascend to the self-certain mountaintop, and look down on everyone. You can disengage and descend into the solitary muck of resentment and self-pity. Or, you can suck it up, engage where events have placed you, and work to make life better for your family, your friends, and your community. My newly kindled faith counseled the latter course:

> This is what the Lord Almighty, the God of Israel, says to all those I carried into exile from Jerusalem to Babylon: Build houses and settle down; plant gardens and eat what they produce. Marry and have sons and daughters.... [S]eek the peace and prosperity of the city to which I have carried you into exile. Pray to the Lord for it, because if it prospers, you too will prosper.

The flourishing of the city—*Shalom*, as the Hebrews called it—can be pursued in many ways, varying according to our circumstances and calling. For better or worse, my place now was in *politics*. So, if I intended it for the better—if I meant to contribute to the "peace and prosperity of the city" and the renewal of all things—then I needed to get onboard and get going.

Which is what I did during the 1997 Nevers for Governor campaign.

The thing I discovered during that campaign is that politics actually can be a lot of fun. Traveling across the Commonwealth aboard what we privately took to calling the "Neversaydiemobile"—a large rolling campaign headquarters known to ordinary folks as an "RV"—I experienced the rich variety of Virginia's remarkable people, culture, and communities.

I found myself irresistibly ranking the events and venues. My food favorite was the Oyster Festival in Urbanna, where I ate heartily and watched our candidate shuck oysters with townspeople like he had grown up on the river rather than in the hills. A close second in the food rankings went to the Pork Festival in Emporia; there I indulged myself from booth to booth, neglecting my campaign duties and returning several times for more stew and spareribs despite the oppressive mid-summer heat. The entertainment, predictably, was tops at the Fiddlers' Convention (officially, the "Old Fiddlers' Convention"). People came from far and wide each year to hear the mountain music played to raucous perfection, and the politicians, of course, followed the people. The prize for the most spectacular vista went to the Meadows of Dan atop the Blue Ridge plateau; we pulled over several times to take in the breathtaking scenery en route to Galax to hear the fiddlers. Surveying the handiwork of local artisans and shopping was a big part of these events, but that generally held little appeal for me except when it came to the amazing waterfowl carvings on display at the Easter Decoy Festival at Chincoteague. The award for the most interesting mix of people went to the "United We Stand" rally, our late campaign "coalitions" event at Sully Plantation in diverse Fairfax County. The most inspiring and memorable occasions—I rated them a tie in generating goose bumps— were the christening of the USS *Harry S. Truman*, the latest Nimitz-class aircraft carrier constructed at Newport News, and the Independence Day celebration and naturalization ceremony at Monticello.

The campaign was a jigsaw puzzle of such festivals and functions interspersed among speeches to groups and gatherings of all kinds, fundraising breakfasts, lunches, receptions, and dinners, walking/talking/listening tours of towns, stores, schools, shopping centers, manufacturing plants, and farming operations, "meet and greets" in settings of all kinds, media interviews and editorial board visits, huddles with key business and community leaders, civic and social group gatherings, prayer breakfasts, Wednesday night church suppers, Sunday morning church services, and, in the final fall phase, debates, news conferences, and rallies.

I have described the RV as a campaign headquarters, and it did serve as a rolling command post, receiving and executing directives from the real HQ in Richmond. But it was also a place of fun, camaraderie, and easy banter, a setting where the walls normally erected around a candidate—or which the candidate erects around himself—come down and you enjoy each other's company. You enjoy it, that is, if the candidate and his people actually like and trust and are comfortable with each other, which was the case with us. We were happily barnstorming the state together and were good at what we were doing.

At least, we were all pretty good at it, with the notable exception of our helmsman Dawson, a well-meaning but hopelessly under-qualified middle-aged volunteer who did not seem to fit in anywhere else. Apparently the task of wheeling a ten-ton mass of metal, fiberglass, vinyl, and chrome around the state's byzantine road network with the campaign's most precious cargo on-board was something anyone could do, and so that anyone was Dawson. He became a continual source of amusement, annoyance, and actual fright as we routinely got lost, knocked into gates and walls and an occasional storefront, banged into and bounced over curbs at corners, rolled back over the fenders of several lesser vehicles, and even gouged our grand tour-mobile on a jagged rock as we took a hairpin mountain turn too closely.

This rolling "hey y'all" with Virginia's fine folks in all their warmth and variety, traversing a Commonwealth that keeps surprising you with its beauty and history, surviving a harrowing experience or two, enjoying the company of the guy who will be governor but right now is not—that is the stuff you remember and reminisce on for years. You wash out of your recollection all the anxious moments and discordant notes, though there are plenty of those, and it all becomes just a grand memory.

Of course, it is not just a frolic—it is an education and an inspiration, too. You meet remarkable people whose stories of struggle tug at your heart and whose perseverance humbles you, bringing home how easy you have had it. Many people like that stand out from the 1997 campaign, and some of them changed the way I view the world. When all the fuss and fanfare subsided, those people and their stories were the reason you hauled yourself out of bed after a few hours of fitful sleep and raced into action for another 18-hour campaign day.

One of those people, Mrs. Nellie Moulton, was fanning herself on the sagging front porch of her tiny, ramshackle home late on an unseasonably hot

April afternoon as our RV rattled past, taking a back-roads shortcut through pines and peanut fields from Zuni to Smithfield in southeastern Virginia. I spotted her there and pointed her out to Nevers, who surprised us by directing Dawson to stop and turn around. The order was executed with difficulty, and our oversized RV soon pulled into what passed for a driveway next to the small house, creating a most incongruous scene if anyone had chanced along to see it.

Nevers disembarked first, but instead of bounding out in his usual energetic way, he moved deliberately so as not to unsettle the elderly lady. Following closely behind, I noticed that another white-haired woman was emerging from the front door as the smiling ex-Senator gently removed his baseball cap in a show of respect and greeted the lady we would soon know as "Miz Nellie." The frail but dignified woman remained seated, rocking at the same slow, purposeful pace without any discernible change of expression, and responded to Nevers' greeting with a simple but perky, "How do you do?" Then she arched her head upward, in the direction of the apron-clad presence exiting the front door, and said, "My goodness, Sallie. You had best find every cup you can. From the size of this man's motor bus, there must be an army in there, and every one of them is bound to be thirsty in this heat!"

Our army consisted of only four, but we each accepted a cup of lukewarm water with gratitude. The unplanned stop, which I assumed would be a momentary greeting, ended up being a half-hour-long visit—and, even at that, we seemed to be rushing off. Mrs. Nellie Moulton, we discovered in those 30 minutes, had spent a century and two years on the planet, had outlived her husband, both children, and her one grandchild (an especially sad tale that brought a tear to Nevers' eye). She was living in this, her home of many decades, through the aid of her longtime companion, Mrs. Sallie Burrows, and the attention of nearby neighbors and some churchgoing friends.

The companion, "Miz Sallie," at age 85 a comparative spring chicken, was herself a widow without surviving family. When she went to pour the water for us, I offered to help and followed her inside. She moved at a glacial pace, with evident difficulty. Watching her quivering hand empty one of the plastic gallon jugs and reach for another, it dawned on me that the house had no running water.

Solomon Moulton, Miz Nellie's husband, had lived only until the Depression, when a logging accident had extinguished his hopeful young life just three

238

years into their marriage. He had grown up not far from this very place, she explained, and his father had been born a slave on the nearby Hardaway farm. "Solomon's father and his family stayed to work the land after gaining their freedom," Miz Nellie said softly, still every bit the exile despite her hundred-plus years. "Here is where the Good Lord saw fit to plant us, so here is where we made our stand. I'm sitting now, and sit right here I will until he calls me home."

"Amen to that!" exclaimed Miz Sallie, before mischievously adding a moment later, "It is taking him a right good while, though. You don't reckon he's forgotten about us, do you, Nellie?"

With that, the two old ladies enjoyed a good laugh, and we said our good-byes.

Only a year later would I learn that Nevers had tracked down Miz Nellie's pastor shortly after our visit and had sent a sizeable personal donation with the request that it be used for her care. He had asked that the gift's source remain anonymous but that he be kept informed as to her and Mrs. Burrows' wellbeing.

"Miz Nellie," the Governor of Virginia would say at her graveside service two years later, "was of this good place ... of this good land. Virginia was not always true to her, but she was always true to Virginia. And we will be her faithful heirs as stewards of this blessed place—*so help us God.*"

A Revamped Team

Before meeting Miz Nellie on that memorable afternoon, we had done our duty at the granddaddy of all the festivals, the legendary "Shadplanking." The springtime ritual was so steeped in political lore and lubrication that generations somehow kept coming despite the bony fish. The nearby town of Wakefield, like most of the other burgs along Route 460 and the Norfolk Southern line east of Petersburg, had been given its name more than a century earlier by the railroad builder, William (Billy) Mahone, whose wife found inspiration for the town names in Sir Walter Scott's novels. Mahone's remarkable body of work later included service as a general in the Confederate Army, heroism at the Battle of the Crater, artful coalition-building that brought Republicans briefly to power in recently reconstructed Virginia, and a short stint as a United States senator before his machinations caught up with him. It was a colorful bit of history unknown to most of the latter-day politicos who ventured into the pines to consume beer, bourbon, and political gossip on that unusually hot April day, but it reminded me of life's familiar patterns and the inescapable connection between history and politics. Outside the RV, shaking hands and jawing amiably with a seemingly endless string of well-wishers, was yet another son of Virginia who was heir to her considerable benefits and burdens—another, like Mahone and countless others, who rose from the ashes of defeat to satisfy an insistent destiny.

That destiny was determined to make Ned Nevers the 68th governor of Virginia.

Once committed to the idea of a return to politics, it did not take Nevers long to get his political groove back. Politicking is like riding a bicycle: once you have mastered the basic art, the ability to balance all the competing forces comes right back as soon as you climb on again and start pedaling. So once the decision was made, Nevers hit the campaign trail at a torrid pace and never looked back. In some ways it was like nothing had happened. But, of course, a lot had happened, and it was a different man—a *better* man—who was running for governor under the familiar "Virginia is for Nevers" brand.

The campaign traced its beginning to the immediate aftermath of the 1995 state legislative elections, when a delegation of party leaders and senior GOP politicians ventured to Nottoway to solicit the Senator's political return. By then the inevitability of the phoenix's rise already had become apparent to most of us. Ned Nevers' personal renewal and recovery—it was more of an epiphany—preceded the return of the political bug. But the two were unavoidably linked. The Senator had too much political talent to waste, and now that he saw politics as an avenue for accomplishment more than self-aggrandizement, he desperately wanted a second chance. A Robert Penn Warren devotee from reading *All the King's Men* during his Nottoway hiatus, Nevers had dwelled at length on the dying lament that Warren's tragic "Boss" had conveyed to his young understudy: "*It might have been all different, Jack. You got to believe that.*" Nevers saw himself in that picture, and he did not want his own life's political labors to end in such a puddle of regret.

Politically, the circumstances were just right for a Nevers comeback. With the Democrats' 1993 sweep of the three statewide elective offices, there was no logical GOP standard bearer for governor—no sitting Republican lieutenant governor or attorney general waiting in the wings for the gubernatorial contest four years hence. Nevers' political stock with Virginia voters remained high, as opinion surveys regularly attested, and he looked like the Republican with the best chance to win. While some partisans faulted him for not doing more to preserve the party's grip on its prized U.S. Senate seat, most accepted the conventional wisdom that the GOP collapse in 1994 owed to factors beyond Nevers' control—most notably, the precipitous decline in the incumbent president's standing among a majority of Americans and Virginians. By 1997, that impediment for Republicans was gone, and Democrats controlled the White House, Congress, and dozens of statehouses, including Virginia's. Under these adverse circumstances, even Virginia GOP activists who pined for a more ideologically pure conservative at the reins were willing to get on board the Nevers bandwagon.

If Nevers had needed a draft, the arrival of a diverse delegation of respected partisans at his farm in late 1995 amply would have sufficed. That such a delegation could be assembled was surprising, given the factional fault lines that routinely beset the Virginia GOP. But there was more than positive feeling about Nevers behind the visit. Rumors then abounded that the ambitious Seventh District congressman, young Johnny Bondurant, was poised to jump into the governor's race, thereby avoiding a tough re-nomination battle against a war hero and conservative favorite (Mitch Jackson) who was rumored to have eyes on his seat. As it turned out, even the cocky Bondurant understood the obstacle posed by the influential party leaders' determined resistance to his potential candidacy. More persuasive still was his recognition that surrendering his congressional seat without a fight would look craven. So Bondurant took on Mitch's challenge while still hoping to preserve the option of a gubernatorial bid the following year. He went on to lose the June 1996 congressional primary so decisively and ungraciously—his attacks on Mitch had an unmistakable racial tinge—that he posed no real political threat at all to Nevers by the time the gubernatorial campaign was to begin in earnest.

It was a remarkable reversal of fortune. Broken, humiliated, and out to pasture just a couple of years earlier, the irrepressible Ned Nevers now was the consensus nominee of his party for Virginia's highest office.

The experienced candidate assembled a strong team that was spearheaded by Chad as campaign manager and Abby as communications director. The two possessed invaluable practical experience and made an especially formidable duo, with Chad serving as the chief strategist and painstaking planner while Abby handled the media and turned up everywhere as the ubiquitous fixer.

What made Chad so unique as the senior partner in this managerial arrangement was his uncanny insight into the crucial bloc of ballot-casters known as "swing voters"—those ordinary citizens, numerous in the Virginia suburbs, who will vote for candidates of different parties from election to election and even in the same election cycle. Chad had mastered both the mechanics of identifying these voters and the art of motivating them. The former, accomplished through meticulous polling and examination of prior election returns, had become more difficult in the increasingly polarized environment as the number of self-described "independents" grew but the number of true swing voters declined. Once identified, the challenge was to motivate these people to come out and vote for your candidate by conveying the right mix of themes, values, ideas, images, and character traits. In a hyper-competitive state like Virginia, the ability to get these up-for-grabs voters onto your side and into the voting booth was the campaign gold standard.

Had the ball bounced differently for Chad, he could as easily have been a standout success in business, applying his economic ideas and behavioral insights to commercial transactions. Instead, he had focused on the *political* marketplace, where he found that he not only could advance his economic principles and ideas but could do so by deploying the data-driven analytical tools and marketing techniques that so fascinated him. It was, as he often would say through the years, "the perfect fit for me ... so long as I can find good candidates who believe in freedom and reason."

While Chad the empiricist approached campaign tasks like a mad scientist mining the data for the gems locked within, Abby supplied an indispensable complement in the form of empathy and intuition. She could relate to many of those all-important swing voters because she was one of them: a professional woman moderate in her politics and eager to see good things done for folks.

In campaigns past, Mitch had supplied a key ingredient that now appeared to be missing in this brew. He spoke for the Republican base, especially the culturally conservative part of it, the activists who found their political passion not in the sterile, materialistic domain of the free market or the muddled moderation of the perpetually conflicted, but in the stark, clear confines of the morally virtuous. A spirited and uncompromising approach to an actually quite varied set of "social issues" typified this faction, or coalition of factions, within the Republican Party. Prominent among these issues, and second only to the abortion issue for most, was education—the setting where values either would be taught and perpetuated or neglected and undermined. Mitch more or less belonged to this wing of the party, and he had his finger on its pulse. Although he now was back in Washington, learning the ropes in Congress and discovering that the job looks a lot different—and *harder*—when you are the guy out front, he nevertheless made time for regular strategy calls with Chad and Abby and weighed in energetically with Nevers whenever the situation warranted.

Completely absent from the 1997 Nevers gubernatorial team was the powerful figure who had hung menacingly over Nevers' Senate tenure like a billowing nimbus cloud, our old recruiter and erstwhile "friend" Bart. Even before the Senator's unceremonious ouster became an electoral fact, his chief of staff had scurried away like the proverbial rat leaving the sinking ship. Bart had new friends now—rich, influential, and fun-loving friends—and he probably figured that his association with a politician on the verge of being cashiered by the voters looked uncool to this crowd. More to the point, Bart had been plotting the launch of his own political career forever, and now he had both well-heeled friends ready to stroke checks and an open state Senate seat in western Fairfax squarely in his sights. So, a week before voters dealt Nevers their brutal blow, Bart abruptly left the doomed senator's staff to accept a lucrative position in a real estate development firm owned by one of his high-flying buddies.

Always possessing a knack for timing, Bart did himself and the rest of us a favor by exiting when he did. Two months earlier, my friends and I had resolved to make a frontal assault on him with Nevers as soon as the election was over. The final straw had been a confidential call from one of my law school classmates, an altogether credible Wall Street lawyer, who had succumbed to a client's entreaties and tagged along on a weekend jaunt to Bimini. There, he had chanced to encounter Bart Bell—an obviously inebriated and out-of-control Bart Bell—bragging to a bunch of party-goers that he had "a U.S. senator in my pocket" whom he could "deliver whenever and on whatever I choose." There was no mystery about whom Bell claimed to control, but the name of the putative marionette was not mentioned in my law classmate's hearing. Though resting on hearsay and inference, the case against Bart was compelling. Whether he was guilty of criminal conduct or ethics violations, we could only guess, having no hard evidence that rose to that level. But Bart plainly was engaged in a reckless pattern of conduct that could be tolerated no longer, and we were determined to make Nevers see that.

Bart saved us that trouble by bailing on Nevers, and he never looked back. He never contacted Sally while the Senator was ailing … never ventured down to Nottoway for a visit after Nevers recovered. In fact, as the Senator remembered it, he and Bart spoke only once between Election Day 1994 and the gubernatorial campaign nearly three years later. That one occasion came after Chad turned down Bart's request for access to the updated donor file from Nevers' Senate race. With Bart's own campaign for the Virginia Senate at full throttle just months after Nevers' loss, he called down to Nottoway frantically asking the Senator to overrule Chad and give him access to the valuable fundraising list. Still disconsolate from his own defeat, Nevers indifferently granted the request. He probably regretted that decision almost as soon as he made it, but I confess that the relationship between Bart and the Senator always puzzled me. One thing I did detect was a palpable discomfort on Nevers' part during the campaign for governor whenever he shared the stage with Bart at political rallies in Northern Virginia. He seemed to stiffen every time he obligatorily acknowledged "my longtime colleague, State Senator Bell."

Nevers was a classy guy who tried to take the long view, and so he dutifully concealed whatever his true feelings were about Bart. I had no such high-minded inclination. What I saw, quite clearly now, was a narcissistic ingrate who had wrung all the personal benefit he could from his connection to the Senator and who then had abandoned his mentor and patron without the slightest hesitation or remorse. It was a betrayal, pure and simple, and I resolved never to give the self-centered jerk the benefit of the doubt again. He was a soulless political animal, and I wanted nothing whatsoever to do with him. My judgment was a harsh one—the beginning of a pattern when it came to Bart—but whether it was too harsh, I cannot say. It is something, I suppose, I will forever be debating with myself.

My own role in the Nevers for Governor operation was an unusual hybrid: part-time policy director and full-time traveling confidant. Given the way his last campaign had turned out, it would have been understandable if the Senator had harbored some doubts about putting the Chad-Abby duo at the helm again. But Nevers never voiced any such qualms, as far as I knew, nor should he, since the pair plainly was not the cause of the 1994 debacle. Nevers did want some changes, however, and one of them was for me to be a full- rather than part-time participant in the campaign and by his side out on the stump.

I was flattered by this invitation but reluctant to impose the resulting hardship on my family. Our spirited little Meg was displaying "terrible two" attributes well before her second birthday, and Martha already was struggling to juggle her teaching and parenting duties while I maintained a typically demanding Capitol Hill work schedule. She would be a veritable single parent for seven-plus months if I did what Nevers asked. Characteristically unselfish, Martha did not hesitate a moment when I shared news of Nevers' offer—she insisted that I accept the job. So I parted ways gratefully with Senator Weigand and his weird western issues and returned excitedly to the more familiar terrain of the Old Dominion. I assumed the chief policy position on the campaign and set about recruiting an unusually talented staff of whiz kids to do the serious research and policy work back at headquarters while I was out on the road.

It was there at Nevers' side that I gained my first real introduction to retail politics, and I found it fascinating.

CAMPAIGN CONVERSION

On the campaign trail, skill and energy count for a lot, and so do planning and organization. But, in the end, the candidate is there in the arena, standing relatively naked before the media and masses, and *context is everything*. I got my best lesson on this subject—and my first up-close glimpse of Ned Nevers' true political genius—during a bizarre and little-noticed episode that spring.

Unopposed for his party's nomination for governor, Nevers had a luxury seldom afforded to statewide candidates in a competitive state like Virginia. Having waged and won a closely contested campaign for the GOP nomination in his maiden statewide bid in 1982, the experienced politician knew the value of the gift he had been given this time. He also understood the price Democrats would pay for failing to put their affairs similarly in order. The incumbent, Governor Jasen Williams, was the last chief executive to be barred from seeking reelection by Virginia's unique one-term rule—a constraint that Virginia voters had finally cast off via a constitutional amendment earlier in the decade. Without an incumbent or other consensus nominee, Democrats were treated to a costly primary campaign battle between their two strong gubernatorial contenders, the sitting lieutenant governor and sitting attorney general. While the contentious Democratic pair spent their substantial resources trashing each other over the airwaves and rending their party with acrimony and intrigue, we on the Nevers campaign seized the chance to get a head-start on the general-election effort.

In addition to fundraising, we decided to use the spring for a two-pronged approach: solidifying the party's base in rural areas and reaching out to traditionally Democratic audiences in urban areas. Both tended to get short shrift in the fall when the hunt was on for the crucial suburban swing votes that decide Virginia elections, so we used our "spring break" to give them some quality attention.

The rural part of our program took us one day to Augusta County, the sprawling Republican bastion in the Valley of Virginia roughly midway between Roanoke and Winchester—Nevers' stomping grounds before he went off to war. Our schedule called for us to be up before daybreak and on our way to one of the county's largest dairy farms, where the candidate would tour the operation, have his photo taken while engaged in some "hands-on" business with the cows, and then meet with a contingent of local farmers over breakfast. After that, we would be off to a nearby carpet fiber manufacturing plant before heading into the town of Waynesboro for a fundraising luncheon and then a sit-down with the local news media. The dairy farm was an appropriate venue from which to pay homage to agriculture, the backbone of the state's economy since Jamestown, and the fibers plant provided an opportunity to celebrate the expanding opportunities created by the rapidly diversifying rural economy.

Nevers handled both events very well, although it was apparent to me that he did not relish the time spent underneath the Stokes family's prized Holstein. I had been around my grandfather's dairy farm enough to know that milking cows is another of those things that is like riding a bicycle—once you know how, it is easy. The corollary principle, though, is that if you do not know how, you cannot fake it, and you are apt to look pretty silly. That is just how Ned Nevers looked, and he knew it.

The contorted expression on his face beside the lower reaches of the cow is the image that comes to mind as I think of all that day's comic, manic, and ultimately inspired moments. It was one of those days when events careen and converge with such speed and irony that all you can do later is shake your head and smile—or, as was appropriate that day, laugh out loud.

It began innocuously enough. Ned Nevers was hamming it up with the farm family over "the best scrambled eggs that ever crossed [his] lips" and making sport of his manifest lack of cow-milking prowess to good, self-effacing

246

effect while, unbeknownst to him, the political establishment was having a cow back in Richmond. The subject was the latest development in the strange controversy engendered by Governor Williams' proposal to amend a breast-feeding bill. By the time Nevers had finished touring the manufacturing plant down the road in Lyndhurst, about 90 minutes later, a cub reporter from the Waynesboro paper was waiting for him, armed with a question he did not expect.

Context, as I said before, is everything. As Nevers hurried to the car that would take him, a little behind schedule, to his fundraising luncheon, the context was benign enough. The plant tour had been like 20 others he had done, or maybe it was 200. At least it had supplied something of a return to normalcy following the early morning encounter with the uncooperative cow, which was still fresh in his mind. That experience had pushed even the nimble Nevers outside his comfort zone and had stoked his general annoyance over the varied indignities to which candidates for office routinely are subjected as their staffs come up with ever-stranger ways to secure "man of the people" photos.

The young newsman who intercepted Nevers as he approached his car was operating from a decidedly different context. Dispatched by his editor to inquire about the issue that had just flared in Richmond, the lad's mission was to reach Nevers and get a comment—the content of the remark mattered not at all—and then report back promptly. That success would ensure the big-time politician's comments were on the wire well before his scheduled meeting with the local media—a daily, two weeklies, and some radio stations—after lunch. It assuredly would starch up the cub's standing with his overbearing new boss.

In Richmond, the context was complicated. Weeks earlier, the General Assembly had passed and sent to the Governor a rather innocuous little bill that obligated local governments to take special steps to publicize any ordinance they enacted requiring breast-feeding mothers to cover themselves during the feeding process. New mothers certainly should not be caught unawares, the argument went, and so the bill had passed without notable opposition and little or no media interest.

Virginia's Constitution empowers the chief executive not only to sign or veto legislation passed in the General Assembly's regular January-March conclave, but also to recommend amendments for consideration at a brief follow-up legislative session held every April. Governor Williams—apparently influenced by the thoroughly liberated First Lady Anna Benet-Williams, who was something of a zealot on the subject—had plucked the innocuous breast-feeding bill from obscurity and proposed a far-reaching amendment. The Governor's proposal would make it *illegal* for local governments to impose any restrictions whatsoever on the prerogatives and public activities of breast-feeding moms. The right to breast-feed babies in public was, according to the statement crafted for the Governor by one of his exuberant staffers, a matter of fundamental privacy rooted in the luminescent penumbras of the sacred state and federal charters as well as the time-honored rights of parents to control the upbringing of their children, or some such grandiose notions.

Nevers had been asked about this tempest in a teapot when the Governor's amendment first surfaced. He had deflected the issue with relative ease, declaring that while he was second to none in his admiration for mothers and babies, he saw no pressing need or public clamor for Governor Williams' proposal. The legislature ought to study it for a year, he suggested.

The theretofore dormant issue of female modesty had been broached, however. And on this cool spring morning, while Nevers had been talking up cows and carpets in Augusta, a bizarre new twist in this controversy had been unfolding back in the "holy city," as Virginians from the state's more remote reaches derisively dub the capital. The Reverend Joe-Bob Throckmorton Jr., second-generation pastor of a large fundamentalist congregation in central Virginia and one of the Christian Right's more unpredictable televangelist icons, had been holding forth in the State Capitol on, of all things, the timely subject of bare breasts. Standing in the stately Rotunda as Houdon's heroic Washington cast his marble gaze ahead with a trace of disbelief, Pastor Throckmorton had trained his own stern sights on a most egregious example of exhibitionism, one committed daily in every community in the state, one that threatened the moral fiber of every Virginia school child, one, in fact, that was sanctioned by none other than the Commonwealth of Virginia itself! The purveyor of this pornography, he exclaimed—as if he alone had been treated to the sudden and shocking revelation—was nothing other than the Commonwealth's own official seal, the sacred emblem on the state's venerated flag.

The lady appearing thereupon was, alas, a tramp.

Apparently everyone had been so preoccupied with the foot of the noble lady, which rested impressively on the throat of a vanquished tyrant, that they had overlooked her uncovered breast. A dot and half-circle marked the spot, and indeed he was right about what it depicted. Pastor Throckmorton had no doubt but that it was the work of a latter-day voyeur, or at least some kind of imp, who had luridly or mischievously altered the state emblem at some point without official sanction. All that was needed now was for the Governor and General Assembly to make things right by erasing the offending image, or perhaps by shifting the robe of the esteemed Roman goddess due east by a degree or two. That would protect the virtue of Virginia's youth, the apple of the Commonwealth's eye, from this naked assault on its moral wellbeing.

These strange events were completely unknown to Ned Nevers and me when the young reporter breathlessly approached us at the car and mumbled the query prescribed by his editor: *"What's your position on the breast on the seal?"*

This question, which surely would have seemed strange in the best of circumstances, landed awkwardly and imprecisely on the candidate's unready ears. It sounded to him, he later told me, like the kid had asked, "What's the position of the breast on a seal?" Nevers' first thought was that this must be a high school student working on a term paper or something: "You have no idea the crazy things people say or ask me about...," he insisted defensively. In the haste of the moment, having recently dealt with the rather inconvenient positioning of the milk-bearing gland on mammals of the bovine variety, the question somehow seemed no less bizarre to Nevers than anything else he had been dealing with that morning. Of course, the jump from cow to sea lion was so plainly a *non sequitur* that Nevers would have been alerted that something was amiss had the situation afforded even an instant to reflect. Normally, in fact, he would have stopped briefly for the typical campaign-style handshake, introduction, and exchange of superficial pleasantries, and that would have been enough of a pause to align the reporter's context with his own. But Nevers was hustling, already late and anxious not to keep the well-heeled worthies in Waynesboro waiting. He assumed that if the boy was a real reporter he would corner him after lunch at the press availability anyway—plus the kid did not seem serious. So Nevers deflected the curious young man's apparent attempt at humor with an equally lame attempt of his own just before bounding into the car.

"A seal, huh?" he responded, clapping his palms together flatly to show he had the right critter in mind—a gesture the kid no doubt missed. "Well, I'm certainly no expert on the subject, but it has been my general observation that Mother Nature usually puts the equipment where it needs to be. I can tell you from recent experience that anything's better than having a cow over it!"

The ex-Senator chuckled with satisfaction at his ability to come up with a clever play on words, then added, almost to himself, "But on a seal? Who cares about that? The cute little things are just fun to look at."

The puzzled young reporter, I noticed, did not smile.

It took about 15 seconds to realize we had a problem. That's how long it took our driver, a friendly young kid named "Ray," to utter the words, "Senator, Ms. Wingo just called while you were in the plant, and she wanted me to let you know right away that...."

Before Ray had finished his succinct report on Rev. Throckmorton's news conference, I was replaying the reporter's question and our candidate's reply in my mind. The young reporter, I now understood, had been asking about the puritanical televangelist's indictment of the bare-breasted female image on the state seal, and Ned Nevers had responded irreverently with words that now flashed like a distress signal across my mind: "Mother Nature puts the equipment where it needs to be ... anything's better than having a cow over it ... the cute little things are just fun to look at...."

"*Oh—my—God*," I blurted, followed involuntarily by a nervous giggle.

"Turn the car around," Nevers abruptly instructed, casting a ticked-off glance in my direction. He, too, had quickly replayed the question and response in his mind. "We obviously can't let that answer stand."

It only took a couple of minutes to go back, but Nevers obviously used the time to focus. When we pulled back up alongside the kid, the seemingly unflustered pol hopped out and extended his hand. "Hey, son—excuse me, what did you say your name was?"

"Billy Thrasher, Senator, with the *Waynesboro Gazette*," he responded. I was encouraged that, at least from my vantage point, the kid seemed flattered to be the object of additional attention.

"Billy, okay, Billy—call me Ned; that 'Senator' stuff was a lifetime ago. Look, Billy, I turned around and came back even though we are late for another event in town because I realized that I had completely missed the point of your question. You popped me right before I got in the car, and I hadn't heard about the events this morning at the State Capitol and this whole issue of the state seal, and so I had no clue what you were asking. I gave you a flippant comment that probably made no sense to you, and you deserve a serious answer to your question. So now that I have the context, let me strike my wise-crack and give you a real response. In fact, I'll tell you what, Billy—if you work with me on this, we will give you something that will light up the wire as soon as you put it out. It will make you a hero with your editor...."

"Yes, sir," he said eagerly.

"Here's my comment, Billy. Take it down word for word: 'I have enormous respect for my good friend, Pastor Throckmorton, for his many, many good works and his sincerely held convictions. But on this issue he could not be more off-base. The Virginia seal is a classical image that has inspired generation after generation as our Commonwealth has helped bring the nation and indeed the whole world out of the darkness of tyranny into the bright light of liberty. Young men and women, citizen soldiers and other selfless souls, have served under that banner, fought under that banner, *died* under that banner. It is not a symbol of declining moral standards; it is a symbol of eternal principles of liberty and justice. It stands for the rejection of tyranny, and tyranny is what we must always oppose, whether it is tyranny over the body imposed by an overbearing king or tyranny over the mind imposed by a well-meaning pastor. If I am governor, we won't censor our seal, and we won't change our flag— not one bit, not for anyone, not now, not *ever!*'"

The message was delivered with a firmness and passion, an arching of the brow and gritting of teeth, that were rare for this man. It was the kind of intensity you cannot fake. But I also immediately understood what the Senator was doing, and it was *brilliant*. He was seizing the moment to separate himself from the holier-than-thou Pastor Throckmorton, delivering a deserved reproof that the younger, more libertarian audience in the suburbs would fervently applaud. At the same time, his display of patriotic passion and resolve would go over just fine with the conservative base in rural areas and elsewhere.

It was one of those moments you cannot script, one of those fleeting opportunities, shrouded in danger, that a less experienced and more tentative candidate probably would have missed. Heck, I had missed it, and even at that stage I thought I was pretty sharp.

Nevers was a new man, for sure, but the change in his motivations did not mean his basic methods had been altered. He was still a master of the political art, still amazingly quick on his feet, still quite willing to throw a sharp elbow when the situation warranted. He was also, I noted, still given to shop-worn rhetoric, lame attempts at humor, and the occasional good-ol'-boy relapse. As he climbed back in the car, he let fly a couple of characteristically bad puns that made me wince. "Danny, my boy, in the immortal words of Bob Hope, 'Thanks for the mammaries.' Next time, we have to do a much better job of staying *abreast* of the developments in Richmond"—he paused as I groaned on cue—"but I do think we can turn this particular near-miss into an opportunity."

Ray probably was too young to understand the Bob Hope reference, but the kid giggled about the business all the way to town anyway. Meanwhile, Nevers was quickly back to work, diagramming the rest of the play for me. I correctly guessed the first instruction.

"I assume you want me to get your 'good friend' Pastor Joe-Bob, on the phone for you," I ventured.

"Yes, but I want to wait until we get to town so I can use a regular phone. This bag phone keeps going in and out on me. Call ahead and get me a private place where I can call from as soon as we get there—*before* we go into the luncheon. And while I'm dealing with the good Pastor, you call our friend, Congressman Jackson, and tell him that I want to move forward on that school choice plan of his. You guys need to finish polishing it up for release in a week or so, two at most," he instructed.

I had anticipated his other moves but this detour surprised me. "I thought you wanted to have the brain trust do some more thinking about the school choice thing and maybe test it further when we go back into the field for the next survey," I said.

"Things just changed a bit," he responded. "Plus, I already had pretty much decided to do something on it—it's the right policy. It's the *politics* I've worried about. You guys just need to help me package it right when we roll it out. Tell Mitch I'm trusting y'all's judgment on both the policy and the politics, so you'd better not let me down."

"Got it. And do you want me to ask Mitch for help with Pastor Joe-Bob and his friends on the state seal matter? I don't think he has any particular re-lationship with Throckmorton, but he's obviously close to a lot of the Pastor's conservative allies."

"No, I don't think so," Nevers replied, shaking his head. "Let's let nature take its course when the press calls the good Congressman for a reaction on the great state seal debate. I'm pretty sure I know how he'll react. Remember, Mitch took that flag with him to the Gulf. He will say whatever he feels, and it will be from the heart. What I want him focused on is our school choice plan. He will be getting lots of calls on it from his allies before the day is out."

Our calls took place in parallel, as diagrammed.

Mitch was delighted to hear of the Senator's decision on school choice. "It will define his governorship," he triumphantly predicted. I responded that we had to win the election first, and then Mitch could explain to me how we would get it through the Democrat-controlled legislature. But I shared his enthusiasm for the initiative, and congratulated him on laying the groundwork with the candidate, not only in recent months, but over a number of years.

Nevers seemed satisfied after his conversation with Throckmorton. He did not recount it to me word for word, but he gave me a pretty clear picture.

"I told him that I had two things to go over with him—one that he would like a lot and another that he wouldn't like nearly as much," Nevers recapitulated. "I went with the thing he would like first. I told him that, after many weeks and months of work, Congressman Jackson and I would soon be unveiling an education choice plan that he—Pastor Joe-Bob, that is—and many of our allies in the conservative movement would like a lot. I thanked him for his input and encouragement on it, and he said that it was his privilege to assist and that he was sure there would be a great outpouring of support for it, and for my candidacy, among evangelicals and the pro-family crowd. That part went great."

"And then?" I asked.

"Then I told him that I had had to disagree with him pretty firmly in the press on the issue du jour, the state seal. I told him I wished he had called ahead to let me know he was coming out with that statement—that I was blindsided by it and maybe I could have been a little more gentle in replying to the media if I had been given a heads-up and some time to frame a more diplomatic response. But there was no harm done, I said. We just had to agree to disagree on that one and work together on things we agreed on, like school choice. And he said, 'Fine, thanks for the call,' and hung up."

"You feel okay about that?" I asked.

"I feel just great about it. When the press tells him what I said on the seal, he will be furious—no question about that. But I have him boxed in. He knows he doesn't want to get into a spat with me right now, in the middle of a campaign for governor, and when everyone else in the conservative movement soon will be focused on our bold education initiative and not his silly hissy-fit over the seal. Now, what was Mitch's reaction to moving forward on school choice?"

"Ecstatic, I would say. He said it would define your governorship."

"You can take that a couple of ways," Nevers said, alluding to the political risk.

"Yes, I know. But whatever else comes of all this, at least the doorknobs now are safe," I said impertinently.

"The doorknobs?" asked Nevers.

"Yeah, the doorknobs at the State Capitol. My mom used to take kids there on field trips, and, of course, I went, too, when I was in the fourth grade. The thing that amazed and always stuck with me was that somebody went to the trouble to imprint the state seal on all the brass doorknobs in the State Capitol," I said.

"You know, I have been there a hundred times and I never noticed that," Nevers said.

"That's okay," I answered, "I have looked at the state seal a hundred times and never noticed there was an exposed nipple."

"You serious?" he asked.

"You mean, you had noticed it?" I responded, incredulously.

"How could anyone miss it, Daniel?" he said with a mock leer as we turned into the restaurant, and the applause began.

When the day started, it had seemed sure to be a quiet news day and a routine one out on the stump. But, by lunchtime—we were *very* late for the luncheon—it had become one of the decisive moments in the campaign. Even in the middle of that hectic day it was apparent how the various disparate contexts had merged in the nick of time: Nevers on the dairy farm; the cub reporter on his first assignment; Pastor Throckmorton on his soapbox; Mitch Jackson on his mission to save kids from failed schools. They had come together—an unexpected twist that some might attribute to dumb luck and others to a divine sense of humor. It all had clicked because, at bottom, Ned Nevers was a really gifted politician.

Until that bizarre spring day, the campaign had delayed making a decision on whether to roll out any kind of school choice plan. It presented a tactical conundrum, and we were all over the map on it. Mitch was certainly in favor of trumpeting the issue aggressively in the campaign; he had been a passionate supporter for some time and was already out front on it publicly. I had become really fired up on the issue, too, mainly as a result of the mentoring that Martha and I had done in the Charlottesville and Alexandria schools and the incredible progress we had watched Lorenzo make over the years. (He was in high school now, near the top of his class, and thriving.) Abby, in contrast, was at best ambivalent. She took seriously the argument that letting tax dollars flow to private schools would divert scarce resources and "skim off the cream," as the critics said, leaving the public schools as the hopelessly underfunded preserve of the poorest students and weakest teachers. She also worried about the problematic interplay of church and state in such a sensitive domain as education.

Chad was the most important. No typical campaign manager, he was both a pollster and policy wonk with a hand in every aspect of our campaign platform. I was the one with the "policy director" title, but it mainly was Chad, for example, who crafted Nevers' signature plan for "Economic Freedom, Opportunity, and Recovery"—a comprehensive set of proposals that included individual and business tax cuts, regulatory and tort reform, creation of "enterprise zones," and a host of other measures designed to restore Virginia's temporarily sagging status as a job-creating leader among the states. When it came to education, however, the wizard in charge of Nevers' campaign was less knowledgeable about the facts and less sure of the politics.

Instinctively supportive of consumer choice, Chad understood the inherent tendency toward lethargy, inefficiency, and corruption in monopoly settings. He also saw how teacher unions—and even, as in Virginia, associations without collective-bargaining rights—often acted as defenders of mediocrity rather than catalysts for excellence. Most of all, he recognized the enormous obstacles to innovation posed by unwieldy and large unaccountable government bureaucracies. Intellectually, Chad had absolutely no doubt that the way to improve education was to empower parents and students as consumers. They would demand quality, and the marketplace would meet those demands, as it always does in a free society. In such a competitive environment, the religious affiliation and motivation of some of the private schools would pose no serious concern, since parents would be free to choose schools just as they were free to choose churches. Indeed, the religious aspect was a strong argument *favoring* school choice, as Chad saw it, since school establishment and church establishment were first cousins in their stultifying effects, and the freedom to choose a school would liberate students, parents, and everyone else in the enterprise from adherence to any orthodoxy, secular or sectarian.

Understanding all this did not decide the question for Chad, however. His immediate job was to manage a winning campaign, and he was concerned about the political blowback.

The conservative party base would love it if Nevers were to make school choice a key plank in his platform—that much was plain. But the GOP nomination already was sewn up, and Chad knew that in the fall general election the issue would be at best a two-edged sword. Not only would such a proposal arouse the public education establishment, including a legion of local teachers, in fervent opposition to Nevers' candidacy. There was also the problem of the all-important suburban swing voters. They were generally happy with their public schools and were especially susceptible to the diversion-of-resources, cream-skimming argument. Plus, to be crass about it, the problem with the inner-city schools was not the suburbanites' problem, and to be even crasser about it, a lot of them were not at all eager to see those African-American inner-city kids venturing out to private schools in their neck of the woods anyway. This latter point struck me as highly offensive and probably true only of a small cohort of diehard racists. But when I challenged Chad on it, he showed me the poll numbers that backed up his disturbing claim.

Of course, the candidate is the one who gets to decide these things, and Ned Nevers by this time had come to believe that drastic action was needed on education. He was not keen on spending tax dollars on private organizations of any kind, but the public schools in many urban centers across America were hopelessly dysfunctional. Even in more prosperous areas their outcomes were decidedly mixed. He felt for the young people who would have no chance to succeed, and he fretted over the threat to the social fabric of the country. What worried him most was the threat to the nation's economic strength and competitiveness globally. Once the land of opportunity envied and mimicked worldwide, the United States now was being outperformed educationally by dozens of other countries, and it would not be long before educational mediocrity produced entrepreneurial lethargy—before failing schools resulted in a floundering economy from which the country might never recover. For Nevers, all the familiar plaints about diversion and skimming and slippery slopes and the rest were just so many excuses and distractions. The ship was sinking, and someone had to take charge and plug the leak. Nevers was determined to do so even though the public schools in his state were comparatively strong, and he was convinced that being governor would afford him that opportunity.

But with his political advisors not yet of one mind on the wisdom of predicating a gubernatorial bid on the issue or even making it a prominent campaign plank, he had been holding back.

The reality, of course, is that governors have limited time and political capital to invest in producing change of any kind, and they invariably choose to spend that time and capital on the things they promise during the campaign. So it mattered a great deal whether Ned Nevers made education choice a significant plank in his campaign platform. We will never know what would have happened if not for the strange series of events that spring day in Augusta County, which forced his hand. But Ned Nevers made his decision then and there to champion a school choice initiative, and, as Mitch astutely predicted, it would define his governorship.

Really good policy sometimes gets made that way, and I suppose really bad policy does, too. The speechwriter writes a speech; the candidate answers a question at a press conference; an interest group survey is filled out; a donor is mollified; a voter's letter gets answered—it happens a thousand times in every campaign. Positions get staked out in one situation or another, for one purpose or another, and then that drives what happens in office. Casual observers of politics, especially those who disdain the whole business, routinely criticize this phenomenon. Some believe it is all a charade and that campaign promises not only can, but should, be disregarded once in office. "We elect people to be statesmen, not politicians," goes the familiar refrain.

But campaign commitments—even the improvised ones—are an integral part of the American political system and, really, of any truly representative process. They are endemic to democracy itself, because it is during campaigns that a bargain is struck between the people and their chosen representatives. The commitments made at election time are the politician's side of the bargain, or at least a big part of it. Edmund Burke, the great Irish statesman, famously said that a representative owes you his "enlightened conscience." He was certainly correct, and so a politician with a good conscience will make only the promises he intends to keep and will do his level best to keep the promises he makes.

Critics of contemporary politics and politicians perceive in this a worrisome new malady, as if promising and pandering constitute the current generation's distinctive character flaw. By contrast, our forebears from golden ages past are credited as selfless statesmen who would never stoop to such tactics.

But such notions are downright silly and display not only naiveté about representative democracy but ignorance of American history.

Take, for example, the Bill of Rights in general and the First Amendment in particular. There is no more cherished aspect of our constitutional system than the litany of fundamental civil liberties known as the Bill of Rights. For those Americans who are turned off by politicians' plays for electoral support, the most consoling component of our constitutional arrangement is this set of provisions that spell out freedoms that are placed beyond the reach of political majorities. Yet, without politics—and, specifically, without a timely, campaign-inspired conversion and commitment—we likely would never have had our beloved Bill of Rights as part of the Constitution.

Historians generally agree there was no one in that First Congress besides Representative James Madison of Virginia who could have forced the issue onto the crowded legislative agenda and maneuvered the proposed constitutional amendments through to passage in 1789. It was a painstaking piece of legislative craftsmanship, carried out during the hectic first year under the new governmental arrangement, and it was an assignment that Madison had never sought. The reason he nevertheless took on the task and accomplished the feat was largely political.

Madison believed that inclusion of an enumeration of individual rights in the new Constitution would be at best superfluous and possibly dangerous. In a federal government of limited rather than plenary powers like he and his colleagues had fashioned in Philadelphia, all rights were reserved to the states or to the people except those that were specifically forfeited through an explicit grant of federal power. Thus, a listing of liberties would inevitably be incomplete, and the presence of some rights on the list might wrongly imply the intended negation of others. When a fellow member of the Virginia delegation—the well-respected George Mason, author of Virginia's Declaration of Rights—complained near the end of the deliberations in Philadelphia about the absence of a declaration of rights in the new charter, neither Madison nor other prominent delegates were willing to lend their support or prolong the proceedings. Mason went on to vote against the Constitution there, and he joined Governor Patrick Henry and other "anti-federalists" in opposing its ratification, with the lack of a bill of rights among their chief criticisms.

There is no persuasive indication in the historical record that Madison ever really changed his view of this question on the merits. But politics soon trumped the merits.

Virginia's support for the new Constitution was crucial to the new plan of government's success—so crucial, in fact, that Washington himself pressed Madison to stand for election to the ratifying convention so he could supply responses to the issues raised by opponents. "[E]xplanations will be wanting— none can give them with more precision and accuracy than yourself," the General wrote. His secretary, Tobias Lear, conveyed Washington's sense of Madison's importance, calling him "the only man in this State who can effectually combat the influence of Mason and Henry." But as Madison lingered in New York writing his *Federalist* essays, the opponents of ratification made surprising headway even in his home area, and Madison realized, almost too late, that his election as a delegate to the ratifying convention was in doubt.

Objections to the new Constitution emanated from varied quarters, but among the most significant were the Baptists, a significant voting bloc in Orange County and its surrounding precincts. Like the Presbyterians, another major group dissenting from established Anglicanism in Virginia, the Baptists regarded an express guarantee of religious liberty as utterly essential. They appreciated Madison's crucial role in passage of the landmark Virginia statute on that subject—legislation that elaborated on the principles enunciated earlier, with Madison's help, in Mason's Declaration of Rights. But the exclusion of a like guarantee from the new federal charter caused them grievous concern, and Madison apparently had endorsed that omission. Madison arrived back in Orange on the eve of the voting and found his father and friends in agreement that his election to the convention was in serious jeopardy.

The reclusive candidate responded by doing something he had never done in any prior contest: He went to Orange Courthouse and delivered a campaign speech. "I was therefore obliged at the election which succeeded the day of my arrival to mount for the first time in my life, the rostrum before a large body of the people, and to launch into a harangue of some length in the open air...," Madison wrote to a friend. He won, and the politicking was just beginning. In the ratifying convention, his meticulous scholarly and practical presentations at length overcame the fiery denunciations of Henry. But having bested the age's preeminent elocutionist, Madison next experienced in full measure the political ingenuity and vindictive designs of the state's popular chief executive. Intent on blocking Madison from the new Congress, Governor Henry had the congressional districts gerrymandered before the "gerrymander" moniker was even coined, and he recruited a war hero, the tall and handsome Colonel James Monroe, to oppose the diminutive Madison in the first congressional contest under the new plan of government.

Even with ratification secured and the congressional contest looming, Madison remained at best lukewarm about adding a list of liberties to the Constitution by amendment. He saw some tactical advantage in supporting amendments in the first Congress if that would undercut the anti-federalists' continuing demand for a second constitutional convention. He also knew the views of his friend Jefferson, who had written to him from Paris that "a bill of rights is what the people are entitled to against every government on earth, general or particular, and what no just government should refuse, or rest on inferences." While denying any hostility to the idea of such a bill, Madison responded to Jefferson that he had "never thought the omission a material defect, nor been anxious to supply it by *subsequent* amendment, for any reason other than it is anxiously desired by others." Soon, however, the anxiousness in Virginia's new Fifth Congressional District, particularly among those same Baptists, supplied ample impetus for an unequivocal pledge of support.

After denying his detractors' persistent charges that he opposed all constitutional amendments, Madison eventually put his campaign promise into writing. If elected, he would work in the first Congress so "that the clearest, and strongest provision [will] be made, for all those essential rights, which have been thought to be in danger, such as the rights of conscience, the freedom of the press, trials by jury, exemption from general warrants, etc." Moved chiefly by political exigencies, he had promised to make the project of adding a bill of rights to the Constitution his own. And though he might easily have made a token effort and then yielded to the strong resistance in a First Congress dominated by Federalists who shared his belief in the inefficacy of such "parchment barriers," Madison pursued the project with tenacity until he gained a hard-won legislative victory for his earnest constituents.

However unenthusiastically, Madison had made a pledge, and once it was made he moved heaven and earth to keep it.

Such stories may seem a digression, but the parallel is an important one. Nevers was no Madison, and his school choice initiative paled in importance alongside a bill of rights. But the matter was one of personal integrity, and in that there was no daylight between the first Virginia congressman and the 68th Virginia governor. The politics of the moment had a hand in making the promise, but principle commanded keeping it.

There was an important lesson in this for me. The significance of the moment in which we find ourselves acting on the political stage—or on *life's* stage, for that matter—is not something we can control or foresee. We may be tempted to cast an envying eye back on those who were part of the gifted generation that accomplished our nation's founding, or on the heroic generation that turned back the tide of 20th-century despotism, and to wish we had been born to such opportunities for achievement and veneration. Yet, humility counsels against such envy—first, because great hardship attended those great opportunities, and we cannot know whether we would have been equal to the moment; and, second, because for all we know our moment may matter even more. We cannot see into the future to know the significance of our time and deeds. In the great chain of causation grand consequences can flow from seemingly benign or mundane events. What we can control is our response to the circumstances in which we find ourselves.

Our moment, *this* moment, presents an opportunity to act based on integrity, to keep our commitments, to embody the Golden Rule and live out our principles, to advance the cause of liberty. It is our chance to love and serve others as we would want to be loved and served. The truth is, there is no better moment in which to live than the moment in which we have the gift of life. So we need to make the most of it.

Ned Nevers had come to understand this, and now he helped teach it to me. It was a good thing to learn, but also a dangerous thing, because principled decisions and promise-keeping integrity mark the surest road to happiness but not necessarily the shortest.

PERSEVERANCE

The Nevers campaign ended with an election-eve fly-around and series of airport rallies in all the major media markets in the state. Nevers by now was comfortably ahead and the outcome was not seriously in doubt, though we were all bundles of nervous energy, excitement, and worry anyway.

We had run a great campaign, muscling through despite our opponent's relentless harping on the mortal threat that our school choice plan—a plan to make sure every child got a good education—supposedly posed to the very survival of public education. In running the standard anti-choice play used by the education establishment elsewhere, the other side had failed to come to grips with a distinctive aspect of our proposal: the fact that we had coupled our school choice proposals with measures that would *increase* investment in the public schools. To insulate us against the expected charge that our choice plan would siphon resources away from the public schools, but also because we deemed it good policy, the Nevers education platform called for new investments to reduce class sizes in the early grades so that young students received more individual attention, to expand pre-kindergarten programs targeted at at-risk kids, and to develop regional alternative schools for chronically disruptive students so that teachers could more easily maintain orderly classrooms and troubled youths could receive specialized services. Each of these sound proposals, along with our support for increased pay for public schoolteachers based on performance, was popular in its own right. As a practical political matter, the presence of these planks in our platform made it impossible for the other side to argue convincingly that Nevers had some secret agenda to drain resources from public education.

We had handled the thorny education issue well, but that was only a modest factor in the campaign. The other side had been disabled throughout by infighting and leaks that reflected the still-festering wounds from their bitter primary struggle in the spring. Even without those self-inflicted gashes, our opponents would have found themselves in a nearly impossible situation given the steering currents that favored the Republican side. Democrats had swept to power in Washington a year earlier, plus they now controlled all three statewide offices and the legislature in Virginia—a degree of one-party domination that goes against the grain in the evenly divided Commonwealth. Virginians, especially the suburban swing-voters, are an independent-thinking lot who, consciously or subconsciously, like the checks and balances associated with divided government. They are Madisonians without knowing it. So the Virginia gubernatorial elections that follow a year after presidential races tend to behave like early midterm contests, which means the president's party has an uphill climb.

By the eve of this particular race for governor, these and other dynamics had collaborated to aid the Republican nominee, and the entire state political establishment knew that Nevers was going to win. A master politician with a new lease on life, he had done everything right in his campaign and also had won the favor of the fickle political gods who control the gales.

The well-attended and carefully choreographed final-day events went off without a hitch until mid-afternoon, when the stop at the Newport News airport was disrupted by a loud, fist-shaking protester whose yells at first interrupted and then eventually drowned out the candidate. Things were briefly chaotic until the miscreant was whisked away by a couple of over-exuberant local gendarmes. It was hard for many of us in the audience to tell what the fellow had been shouting, but the man behind the podium was able to look him in the eye and hear him very clearly. The heckler appeared to be a homeless person, and Nevers immediately recognized him as another strung-out veteran of the Iraq war.

The bitter feelings produced by the war were still raw, and this kind of disruption was hardly unfamiliar to anyone who had been around political events over the past several years. I had seen politicians, including Nevers, deal adroitly with antiwar protests and other such outbursts time after time. A candidate who is hounded by protesters too often and effectively will have difficulty delivering his message, but most skillful politicians know how to use occasional hecklers and hostile questioners as foils. I expected the same from Nevers here.

The crowd was chanting "Go! Go! Go!"—not at Nevers, as in "Go on to victory!" but at the offending protester, as in "Go away!" or "Go to hell!" As they are trained to do, the campaign's young operatives and volunteers (college students and teenagers known as "CRs" and "TARs") had swarmed to the location of the disruption to screen off the media and incite a chanted "Nevers Now!" rejoinder from the crowd. It was the classic response—except that Nevers now departed dramatically from the standard script. With the disruptive veteran now out of sight, Nevers raised his hands and with a familiar tamping-down motion asked for the crowd to quiet. The noise gradually subsided and then disappeared completely. You now could hear a pin drop, but the Governor-in-waiting just stood there, looking down, then to the side thoughtfully, then down again. The silence lasted only a few moments, but it seemed like an eternity. It was odd and very awkward.

When Nevers did speak, it was as if he was talking to himself and perhaps a trusted confidant or two—certainly not to a political crowd.

"I, uh, well ... I think ...." He cleared his throat, and looked down and then up again. "I think it's important that we not judge that fellow...."

There was an audible murmur of dissent in the still-agitated crowd, which he stilled with a gently dismissive wave of the hand.

"No, no, folks ... we shouldn't judge him ... we shouldn't. That fellow served his country, and he feels his country has let him down—and it probably *has* let him down." Nevers paused. "You can't look at somebody like that and dismiss him as filthy and homeless, a junkie, crazy, out of control, or whatever. You have to look at him and see a *soldier* who has borne the nation's burdens."

There was a return of the awkward silence until Nevers resumed, and when he finally did so, it was not in the mode of a speechmaking politician. Instead he spoke in the slow, ponderous manner of a guy who is sorting things out for himself, indifferent to whom is listening.

"You know, when I came back from Vietnam, I put on a brave face, but inside I was angry—I mean, *bitterly* angry. I was angry to have fought in a war that nobody back home seemed to support. I was angry that we went, and I was angry that once we went, our leaders did not do what it took to win. I saw my friends, scared young boys who overnight became brave warriors, maimed, mauled, blown to bits—and for what? When I saw video of those helicopters pulling people off the embassy roof in Saigon, I was angry and embarrassed for my country. I hated the antiwar crowd in Congress that had cut off the funds and left our allies without a lifeline. But I also hated Nixon.... I mean, I *really* hated Nixon, because he had blown it completely with Watergate. That scandal really was the reason the war in Vietnam ended the way it did, not with the Communists being contained but with the bad guys winning a huge Cold War victory and humiliating us. If Nixon had just been honest rather than covering up the boneheaded stuff his political hacks did, he would not have been run out of office; there would not have been a total collapse on the Republican side; and the surrender crowd in Congress would not have had their way. Nixon took himself out, but he took a lot of other good people out with him, including a lot of good people in South Vietnam who were massacred as soon as we pulled out. But no one ever said anything about those people. And no one ever said so much as 'thank you' or 'to hell with you' to those of us who had been over there trying to help them. It was like everyone just wanted to pretend the whole thing never happened...."

He was meandering, and the folks in the crowd were starting to murmur and look around anxiously at each other. I had the frightening sensation that we were witnessing a slow-motion meltdown.

"Anyway," Nevers said, as if returning to present realities, "we shouldn't judge people without knowing their story."

He paused, gazed out across the crowd as if to confirm they were still there, and then went back inside himself.

"You know, I don't hate Nixon anymore. I'm not a fan, but Nixon was just like the rest of us—he had his angels and his demons and was just trying to find his way. I remember what he said to the White House staff the day he left the presidency in disgrace. He had been reading about Teddy Roosevelt, and he recalled how devastated Roosevelt had been when his beautiful young wife died. He thought the light had gone out of his life forever. But Nixon said that was not true—that life's setbacks are only a beginning, always. Because only if you have been in the deepest valley can you know how magnificent it is to be on the highest mountain. And I think there's some real truth in that. Sally and I heard the same message this morning as we were driving and listening to that countdown of the top songs of the seventies. I guess that dates us a bit, doesn't it, Sally?"

The comment afforded a slight break in the tension, and the nervous crowd seized the excuse to chuckle more heartily than Nevers' remark warranted.

"Anyhow, like a lot of folks, I had my easy times with 'my back turned toward the sun,' but 'when the cold wind blows it will turn your head around.' It happened for me in the 1994 election; the voters turned me around with a cold wind. In fact, it was more like a gale."

Some more anxious chuckles emanated from the sympathetic audience.

"Talk about things 'in pieces on the ground'—I was about as broken up as a person can be. But if you remember the song, you also remember the next verse where he asks Jesus for help because he 'won't make it any other way.'"

"Well, that's my story, too."

"Now, I am not running to be your priest or pastor; I am running to be your governor—and a governor for people of all faiths and no faith at all. But you can't tell who someone is and where they are going if you do not know where they came from and what they stand for. And the truth is, I would not be here tonight if I hadn't had some help, you know, from a power greater than myself, pulling me back from the edge of a very high and dangerous cliff. Believe it or disbelieve it—like it or hate it—that's what I believe and that's who I am. At least, that's who *I've become.*"

I don't think the Senator intended that as an applause line. He was still talking more to himself than anyone else. But the crowd sensed an opening and clapped approvingly.

Like many effective communicators, Nevers normally acknowledged and encouraged his audience's concurrence with a perceptible up-and-down motion—an agreeable nod—of his head as he spoke. But I noticed that now he was shaking his head right and left, negatively. It was not exactly the way you normally want your candidate to connect with his people.

"Well, thank you all very much, but I don't deserve your applause," Nevers said to the restless crowd. "What I want to say to you is that all of us are trying to find our way; we are all struggling just like that sad young man they just escorted out of here. And we are going to find that veteran when this rally is over, and thank him and listen to him and learn his story and find a way to help him. And I would just ask all of you to lend a helping hand to people like him whenever you have a chance. We need to help all kinds of folks who face hardship, not just our veterans. But our veterans especially deserve our thanks and our help, and there are too many of them who are falling through the cracks. They deserve better."

He turned his shoulders and for a moment I thought he was going to leave the podium without saying anything more. It seemed he had forgotten the purpose of the event as well as his manners. But then he turned back to re-engage. *That's a relief,* I thought. *Now presumably he will end with an appropriately motivational closing and thank-you, and we can get out of here unscathed.*

I was wrong, at least partly, because he had more to say. And what he now said, while uncalculated and unlike any of the day's scripted lines, was probably his most powerful message of the campaign.

"In closing, I guess I would like to leave this one further thought with you," Nevers resumed. "Tomorrow is one moment among many in the grand tradition of free people choosing their own way. That's our great blessing as Americans and a blessing that is the birthright of all people everywhere. But when the campaigning is over and the people have chosen, then the hard work of freedom really gets underway. Politicking is a sprint; governing is a marathon. It requires patience and determination and goodwill. It requires us to rise above our differences and, at times, to rise above our own interests. I am not running for governor just to hold an office or have a title. I tried it that way before—"

Oh, no, don't go there, I cringed. *Even if it's true, this is no time or place to say it....*

"This time, it is going to be about what I can *give*, not what I can take."

Another long pause and deep breath ensued at the podium. It was the last of many in this odd, soul-bearing speech. When he emerged, it was Ned Nevers again—the renewed and inspired Ned Nevers—exhorting the faithful as their leader. And, though he could not have planned this unusual moment, he clearly had been thinking about the wrap-up message he now delivered:

> Earlier in this campaign, you may recall there was a little dust-up about the state seal. Well, that episode prompted me to take a fresh look at the seal, and I discovered something. The familiar image of the seal is on the obverse side, but there is an image on the reverse side, too. It is an image of three figures standing, talking, and—I like to think—planning how they are going to work together to get things done. The Latin word on the reverse seal is *Perseverando*, which means, "by persevering."
>
> That's the secret of Virginia and America, isn't it, my friends?
>
> It is not just overcoming what we do not like—the *Sic Semper Tyrannis* of the front of the seal. It's also the *Perseverando*—the perseverance in getting things done on the back of the seal.
>
> It's the perseverance in integrity when tempted to cut corners, and the perseverance in principle when tempted to take shortcuts.
>
> It's the perseverance in freedom even though free people don't always act as we like, and it's the perseverance in faith even though the truth doesn't always overcome our doubts.
>
> It's the perseverance in our relationships even when getting along is hard, and the perseverance in serving others even when it requires sacrifice.
>
> It's the perseverance in strength so we do not fall victim to evil from without, and the perseverance in humility so we do not fall victim to evil from within.
>
> Above all, it's the perseverance in love even when people sometimes can be so doggone hard to love.
>
> Tomorrow the voters choose … and if they choose us, then we will begin … and once we begin, we will persevere until we succeed.

We will persevere and succeed for the hard-working, tax-paying entrepreneurs and innovators and their families and their employees, for the investors and risk takers, the job creators and job performers, for those who have work and those who seek it. Because none of our other hopes and dreams will come to pass unless we fulfill our Commonwealth's promise as a leader in creating opportunity for all.

We will persevere and succeed for the young people of Virginia, the school children of our Commonwealth who are our common blessing and our common hope. No matter their race or place, no matter their advantages or disadvantages, from the inner cities to the most rural reaches of our state, every one is precious—and we will keep our promise to each of them.

And, finally, we will persevere and succeed as free and generous people of unparalleled compassion—a commonwealth of character in which we care not only when it's easy but when it's hard ... not only for the up-and-coming but also for the down-and-out. Because deep in our hearts, indeed the depths of our souls, we know the truth that our loud and angry brother has reminded us again here this afternoon: *In the city of God we are all his children, and we must cast none of our brothers and sisters aside.*

Thank you for being here, and thank you for your help. May God richly bless every one of you and this wonderful Commonwealth.

He turned away. Then, no doubt feeling a bit foolish, he stretched his neck back toward the microphone and indecorously bellowed, "And don't forget to vote!"

"Every Child Counts"

For republican enthusiasts the inaugural ritual is without peer. Marking the peaceful and orderly (to a point) transfer of power according to the people's will, the rite affirms for attentive citizens their status as masters rather than servants of their government. In the latter decades of the 20th century, representative democracy was in such sudden ascendancy around the globe that few folks paused to consider how truly extraordinary was this sort of ritual in mankind's long history of imposition and oppression. For the Virginians present on January 17, 1998, this was less of a problem. Surrounded by marble and bronze likenesses of George Washington and the nation's other freedom-fighters and founders, huddling around a temple to democracy that Thomas Jefferson designed, and carrying on a tradition dating to the liberated Commonwealth's first governor, Patrick Henry, those on hand to see Edward Kerr Nevers sworn in as the state's 68th chief executive knew they were part of something profound and unique.

Barring the unexpected, Nevers would be the last to serve as Virginia's governor during the 20th century. He also planned to be one of its most productive. The century had witnessed momentous challenges and major reform movements, awful injustices and uplifting innovations. During its dynamic decades the Commonwealth had been transformed from the domain of a privileged and monochromatic few to one of America's most democratic and diverse societies ... from a staid, one-party preserve to a competitive political hotbed ... from an economic laggard to a national pacesetter. Even these inaugural festivities— the grand ceremony on the steps of the South Portico of the Capitol, the 19-gun salute, the parade down Grace Street and through historic Capitol Square, and all the rest—were largely a 20th-century innovation. And when this latest quadrennial display of pageantry was done, Governor Nevers would rest his head on the pillow in the history-laden Executive Mansion across the Square and ponder how he would make productive use of his precious time and keep his commitments to the people who owned his new home.

The words that echoed down the hill and around Capitol Square were all exceptionally well chosen, with Nevers' new favorite—*perseverance*—prominent among them. But the lofty sentiments and elegant phrases of the inaugural address would be invoked less often in the coming months than the simple words the Governor chose the following day, as he sat unceremoniously on a chancel step in the front of the sanctuary of nearby Monument Avenue Methodist Church surrounded by the youthful congregation's preschoolers and kindergarteners. Having welcomed the new first family into membership a few weeks earlier, the Pastor invited the Governor to take to the pulpit at the first Sunday morning worship service following his inauguration. Not wanting to disrupt or draw attention to himself, Nevers declined the invitation. But, after some brief reflection, he made a counter-proposal to the earnest minister. At his previous church home in Nottoway, Nevers had enjoyed delivering the children's sermon whenever the need for a volunteer arose. The gentle grandfather had been such a hit with the little ones who gathered at his knee that he had become a regular in the role, at least until the campaign finally took him away seven days a week. If a similar need existed at Monument Avenue Methodist, the Governor told his new pastor, he would be happy to pitch in from time to time.

About 20 boys and girls sat or kneeled around the coatless giant on this particular Sunday, and they all leaned forward eagerly as he pulled a handful of coins from the pocket of his trousers. "Which one of these is the most different?" Nevers asked them.

A few answered, "The big one!" referring to the Kennedy half-dollar. But most exclaimed, "The brown one!" or "The penny!"

"Yes, the penny. It's a different color from all the rest, isn't it?"

Several who had guessed correctly shook their heads up and down emphatically, in triumph.

"Whose picture is here on the face of this penny?" the Governor asked.

"It's *God!*" one of the eager little boys shouted, showing off. The congregation laughed heartily, and Nevers waited for the commotion to subside.

"That's a good guess, since we are here in God's house, but actually it's Abraham Lincoln, our country's 16th president. He freed the slaves, and that's something you will learn about one day. Now, look closer here—do you see some words written there?"

They squeezed in even tighter, and the Governor took his time, letting each draw close for a look.

"God actually is on the penny—right here in these words across the top. They say, 'In God We Trust.' It's our country's motto, and it means you can depend on God, just like you depend on the parents or grandparents or others who brought you here this morning. He takes care of each of us, so we don't have to be afraid."

As he was saying this, the Governor reached into his other pocket and pulled out a plastic sandwich bag that contained several dozen loose pennies and a partly filled 50-cent penny roll. He poured the contents out on the floor and picked up the roll.

"Now, everybody pick up some of these pennies. Let's make sure everyone has at least one penny…. Okay, now, everybody got some?" They were all nodding.

"Now if you have a penny or two, that's a good thing. You can do something with it by yourself. But if you share your pennies with me, and I put them in this roll…." He stretched out his hand as they all contributed, fully loaded the roll, and then folded it closed and showed them the result. "If we choose to put our pennies together, we can make this with them, and do you know what this is worth? It's worth this"—he held up the big, shiny half-dollar—"the biggest and best coin of the whole bunch!"

There were "oohs" and "aahs" as the young ones smiled and nodded agreeably, comprehending none of the math but something of the concept.

"Now that we have put our pennies together, and we have this valuable penny roll, what do you think we should do with it?" Nevers asked excitedly.

"Roll it!" yelled a couple of kids. "Throw it!" shouted another. "Spend it!" hollered others in unison.

"Noooo," said the Governor playfully. "I have another idea. I think we should put it away and *hide* it." He took the roll and reached to set it out of sight behind the cloth skirt that was draped around the slightly raised chancel area.

"No, that's silly!" exclaimed one little girl, removing the thumb from her mouth for the first time to register the forceful protest.

The Governor smiled broadly. "It *is* silly, isn't it?" he said, retrieving the penny roll. "God didn't give us the pennies to put them where they would do no good, did he? That would be like having a shiny new red fire engine and not taking it to the fire, or like having a bright light and putting it under a bucket where no one can see it. Jesus said, 'Let your light shine so that men and women will see your good works and give thanks to the Father.' We need to do something *useful* with these pennies, don't we?"

"Yeah!" shouted the chorus of excited kids.

"Okay, well then, we are going to do something good with the pennies this morning. We are going to put on a little show for your parents and all the other nice grown-ups here." The Governor turned choreographer and proceeded to arrange the kids in clusters of three or four each, speaking as he set the stage and distributing handfuls of pennies to someone in each group. "Now each little group of you will have your own hometown name, and when I tell you your name, I want you to repeat it back to me so I'm sure you know it—okay? … You guys here are 'Hanover,'" he said, speaking to the first group. "Now, *who* are you?"

"Hanover!" they roared back.

He went through the same exercise until each of the groups was tagged with a name that, not coincidentally, matched one of the local government jurisdictions in the Richmond metropolitan area.

"Okay, now let's start the show. Ready, parents?"

The congregation responded with child-like enthusiasm.

"Ready, kids?"

The children made a point of outdoing the adults in volume.

"Here's the deal. How many of you like to read books and maybe have a bedtime story read to you before you go to sleep at night?" They all shouted and raised their hands.

The Governor then reached into a bag and pulled out a sizable stack of small children's books of various shapes and colors. "Well, here's what we are going to do. Your group can turn in your pennies and trade them for some bedtime story books that you can take home with you from church today. They're yours to keep, for real!"

The children gasped then murmured with delight, smiles abounding. "Now, everybody has some pennies, right?"

They nodded affirmatively, many raising their penny-filled fists to prove it.

"Okay, one group at a time, as I call you. Hanover …."

One by one, the groups came forward, exchanging their pennies for handfuls of books, until only the City of Richmond group was left. As the final group approached, Nevers hung his head. "Uh, I am so sorry, but we're out of books. That's too bad—tough luck, really. Maybe I could give you this church bulletin for your pennies instead…." They were shaking their pouting, downcast faces. "Well, look," he said, "it's not all that bad. If you don't have a bedtime story book, maybe you can, you know, just sing a song to yourself at bedtime … or count sheep … or cry yourself to sleep. I don't know—you'll think of something. All the books are gone. It's not my fault. I'm sorry."

"But we have pennies!" shouted one distraught little girl in the Richmond group.

"I know you have pennies," said the Governor, "but that doesn't mean I have books."

There was a painful silence. Then, slowly, hesitantly, first one, and then another, and then a third, fourth, and fifth child from the other clusters came toward the Richmond group, books in their tiny outstretched hands, offering up their own prized new possessions to right the wrong.

"Thank you for doing that," the smiling grandfather said to the children after a few moments passed in the hushed hall. "There were enough pennies for everyone to have several, and there are enough books, too, if we share. It doesn't matter what our hometown happens to be, does it? *Everyone* should have a book and a chance to hear a good story."

The Governor motioned the young people toward him. "Come here and kneel with me, and let's have a little prayer before we go back to our families...."

"God, thank you for giving us the pennies. Thank you for showing us that our pennies are more valuable when we choose to join them together. Thank you for teaching us not to hide our pennies, but to use them for something good. Thank you for bedtime stories, and for the books that have the stories in them, and for the pennies that buy the books, and for the young people who have so much love in their hearts they're willing to share their books with those who don't have any...."

I thought I detected a catch in the Governor's voice, but after a moment he continued. "Lord, on this new morning so full of promise, thank you for showing us that it doesn't matter what your hometown is or what part of town you're from—*everyone* needs a book and a bedtime story, a chance to listen and a chance to learn. And, even though all of us aren't grown up enough yet to understand it, help us to realize that we *all* need to see ourselves there on the face of that penny—trusting in God and working to free the slaves. Because none of us is truly free while our neighbor is not. In Christ's name, amen."

When the Governor emerged from the church, only one reporter was so lacking in decorum as to intrude upon the tranquil scene. It was Jerry Snelling of the Associated Press. "Governor Nevers, it sounded like there was a message in that children's sermon for the members of the General Assembly who aren't supporting your school choice plan."

Both Snelling and the Governor knew that a substantial number of lawmakers, most likely a majority, were in that category. The more adamant among them already were expressing their opposition in strident, almost apocalyptic terms. Senator Howard Morris, the Democratic leader in the upper chamber, had declared the legislation dead even before it was introduced. "We will ring that chicken's neck as soon as it gets here," he had said with characteristic disdain.

Nevers' response to Snelling, which went out on the AP wire along with a detailed account of his parable, would be invoked frequently during the vigorous political debate of the next several years. "The thing is so obvious even the little children understand it. They understand that *every child matters*," the Governor told the reporter. "Some of the supposed adults around here haven't achieved that same level of understanding yet, but we're going to help them out. We're going to fill their minds with child-like wonder at the possibility of doing the right thing for a change—as in, making sure *every child* gets a good education."

That evening, after all of the other close friends and political allies departed the governor's mansion, I had a few moments alone with the exuberant but exhausted new chief executive before calling it a day myself. I couldn't resist asking the question.

"Those kids stepping forward to share their storybooks this morning ... that really was an amazing moment—it made for an incredibly powerful message. I couldn't help noticing that your granddaughter was one of the first to share. Did you, uh—?"

"Did I what—have a little insurance policy?" the smiling Governor interrupted. "My goodness, Daniel, what do you think I am—some sort of manipulator? Don't be such a cynic. Next you'll be suggesting that I invited Jerry Snelling to church today."

I smiled back and left it there. "Well, you zinged the legislators pretty good in that interview after church," I said. "It'll irritate some of them big-time, but I expect you'll say worse things to them before this particular battle is over."

"You mean, I'll have to bash 'em like the Boss?" Nevers asked as he strode over to the shelves where his favorite books, including *All the Kings Men*, now resided. He flipped past several dog-eared pages in that volume before lighting on the one he had in mind. He affected a Southern drawl and was pretty convincing: "Folks, there's going to be a leetle mite of trouble back in town. Between me and the Legislature-ful of hyena-headed, feist-faced, belly-dragging sons of slack-gutted she-wolves. If you know what I mean...."

We both laughed—it was clear he was itching for the fight. "Yeah, just like that," I said. "... only the more genteel Virginia version."

The next evening the Governor went to the chamber of the House of Delegates, an august body that traces its roots to Jamestown in 1619, making it the oldest continuous representative assembly anywhere. There he delivered the traditional gubernatorial address to a joint session of the Virginia General Assembly and to those relatively few Virginians in TV land who were not pre-occupied with the standard game-show, cable-news, and Hollywood-gossip fare at seven o'clock. He covered his whole gubernatorial agenda in detail with little flowery rhetoric, and he lavished far more time on his economic growth plan than on his education initiatives. But when he came to the subject of education in general and school choice in particular, his entire physical bearing seemed to change. His body stiffened, his jaw set, and his eyes glared with steely intensity, signaling that every ounce of his fiber would be committed to this fight.

He began with a long litany of his key proposals:

Tax credits for families of students attending private and parochial schools and for businesses and individuals donating to scholarship-granting charitable organizations...

A state constitutional amendment allowing issuance of elementary and secondary school vouchers modeled on the successful tuition assistance grant (TAG) program for students attending Virginia's private nonprofit colleges...

New financial incentives for charter schools and a streamlined, state-level process for their approval...

A new statewide school district to offer virtual (online) course and diploma options...

Grants for a significantly expanded cohort of children defined as "at-risk" to access early reading and childhood development programs by public and private providers...

Statewide and regional public-private partnerships through which businesses and schools would collaborate on internships, job "pipeline" programs, and career and technical education opportunities, especially in the so-called "STEM" fields (science, technology, engineering, and math)...

Capital and operating fund investments to expand the availability of Governor's schools, STEM academies, and regional alternative schools for students with chronic disciplinary issues...

Funding for creation of optional new structured-study academies with longer school days, a highly disciplined environment, emphasis on character development, and special financial incentives to attract teachers and principals well-suited to such programming...

Funding for student transportation and cross-subsidies to dramatically expand transfer options, within and across school district lines, to Governor's schools, STEM academies, regional alternative schools, new structured-study academies, local magnet schools, and other specialized programs...

A public-private partnership and tax credits to finance the renovation of older school facilities, acquisition of new equipment, and internet access...

Updated academic content standards and a new testing regimen to identify shortcomings in student performance where intensified remedial attention was needed...

Funding to lower pupil-teacher ratios in public elementary schools, especially those with higher percentages of "at-risk" students, and for increased "wrap-around" and tutoring services for the most disadvantaged children...

Access to more public school system resources and programs for home-schooled students...

A "star teacher" program for accomplished instructors who were willing to trade tenure for significantly higher pay opportunities...

A peer and student review plan and performance pay for teachers, coupled with state-funded teacher pay raises...

Forgivable college loans and other incentives to attract new teachers to jobs in distressed urban and rural school systems, and measures to reduce teacher turnover there, including training and mentoring programs to prepare teachers for the distinctive challenges of those classroom environments so they stay and succeed once there...

A mechanism for the state education board to assume control of chronically failing local schools and even whole school systems, and a "Marshall Plan" to turn around their performance, including teacher support, mentoring, lesson plan assistance, retention incentives, rigorous evidence-based assessment of student and teacher performance, and provision of "turnaround" expertise in the principal's offices...

And, perhaps most creative, a combination of revenue-raising strategies to fund the ambitious program, including monetization of various state assets, privatization and taxation of liquor sales, legalization and taxation of gaming enterprises, large tax deductions for businesses and individuals contributing to the program, and two new taxes that, because they were revenue-neutral overall, generally avoided tax-hike objections: a corporate income tax surcharge, the proceeds of which would cover all of the business tax deductions under the plan; and a statewide sales tax increase sufficient to offset the aggregate "cost" of the personal income tax credits and vouchers under the plan.

Together, these and other quality-enhancing provisions would comprise the most comprehensive education reform and choice program anywhere in the country, a full mobilization of all available public and private resources—the public school establishment, the business community, faith-based organizations, nonprofit charities, and for-profit educational providers—to lift schools out of mediocrity, to create equal opportunity and more diverse school environments, and, above all, to dramatically improve results for students.

Anticipating the charge of radical experimentation, the Governor repeatedly stressed his plan's reliance on policies and practices that already were producing tangible gains in student performance elsewhere. The program, whose initial development Mitch and I had spearheaded during the transition, would import the best practices from around the country, including but not limited to those that Nevers had touted during the campaign.

"If we really care about our young people and have faith in their potential," the new leader of the oldest state passionately intoned in passages echoing Jefferson and the Virginia Constitution, then we will seize upon the success of states and localities that have had the boldness to serve as laboratories in this vital realm of education. On other issues, at other times in our history, Virginia has been the leader and the innovator. But, sadly, not so in the realm of school choice. We have invested in more of the same, and we have more of the same to show for it: static, mediocre results and, in too many places, a culture of failure that dooms kids to falling behind, giving up, and dropping out—to getting caught up in gangs, tripping out on drugs, and ending up in prisons if not morgues. Surely we are not so callous as to turn a blind eye to these tragic stories playing out daily in neighborhoods not so far from our own. And even if some consciences are immune to the injustice, none of us can deny this hard truth: *Too many of our young people are emerging from our high schools unprepared for the rigors of college or the world of work.* Unless we act, these young people will be unable to access the well-paying jobs of the new economy, and the American Dream will be beyond their reach.

Taking head-on the familiar charge that support for private educational options was an invitation to re-segregation based on race or ethnicity, the Governor surprised his audience with the provocative words of an outspoken ally. "To those who say that providing young people of all races with access to successful schools will somehow turn back the clock on civil rights, I offer this answer from Congressman Mitch Jackson, a true hero and role model for all our young people:

> If you don't have a solution, then you're part of the problem.
>
> If you're all about equal opportunity but all you can offer is an equal opportunity to fail, then you aren't for equality—you're just for failure.
>
> If you say you're for education but you keeping putting politics first, then you're not helping the kids—you're just helping yourself.
>
> Access to a good education is the great civil rights cause of our time. Either we will set our "eyes on the prize" for a

new generation of young people, or we will consign a new generation to slavery. And this time the overseer's lash will be in *our* hands.

The Governor let Mitch's harsh words hang as an audible murmur rolled around the House floor. He then went on to extend an olive branch, announcing that he would appoint a bipartisan commission to flesh out the details and forge consensus prior to the plan's introduction a year later, in the 1999 legislative session. In this, Nevers was making virtue of necessity, positioning the delay and resulting dialogue as a magnanimous gesture even though insiders knew it was a time-buying bow to political realities. The first legislative session of the Nevers administration would be occupied fully with the Governor's far-reaching economic proposals, the key elements of which, especially the business and individual tax cuts, faced substantial political hurdles of their own. The votes to pass the promised education plan were nowhere near in place, nor were the revenues to pay for it, and it would take a concerted, months-long campaign of public pressure and private jawboning to produce anything approaching a reasonable prospect of passage. Lest anyone on Nevers' right flank take to questioning his resolve in the meantime, however, the indubitably conservative Congressman Jackson and I, newly ensconced as the Governor's chief of staff, were placed ostentatiously at the helm of the new "Every-Child-Counts Education Reform Commission."

What we could not have imagined then was that three legislative sessions and a hard-fought General Assembly election would have to pass before our sweeping education reform plan would finally make its way into law. Its key elements would survive substantially intact, a result owing chiefly to Governor Nevers' stubborn refusal to make concessions to gain a political "win" if it meant sacrificing elements that he deemed vital for the program's practical success. The long-running battle would take a severe toll on lesser policy initiatives, on our relationships with legislators, and on the physical and emotional wellbeing of the Governor's top team members and their families. Few people who have not experienced the ardors of this kind of change-oriented public service appreciate its intensity or cost. By the time the fight was over, we well understood the meaning of "perseverance" and knew why Ned Nevers had invoked the term so often. But if the effort was exhausting, the victory was even more exhilarating. I hearkened back to that first day in Charlottesville when Bonita Washington showed up at my door, desperately seeking help for her son anywhere she could find it. Now maybe the salvation of young people like Lorenzo could be the norm, not the exception.

While introduction to Lorenzo's plight first had pricked my conscience, my inspiration during our long legislative struggle for education reform came mainly from Martha. Less than a year into the Nevers governorship, our second child, a strapping baby boy we named "Martin Lafayette McGuire," arrived on the scene. We could not afford to forfeit Martha's income, so my amazing wife's complicated life now consisted of a full teaching load plus caring for our newborn Marty, our three-year-old Meg, and the most dependent one of all, her frequently embattled, inevitably exhausted, and generally absent husband. I shared in the household duties when I could but constantly failed to hold up my end of the deal. Martha not only refused to complain; somehow she also found time to have an impact politically. Believing deeply in our cause, she organized fellow teachers into a vocal grassroots advocacy group that she cleverly named "School Teachers Rallying for Excellence in Teaching, Choice, and Hope for Kids," or "STRETCH for Kids." And stretch she did, traveling around the state to meet with teacher and parent groups, speaking at rallies, and providing compelling committee testimony in support of our proposals. Only a true believer could have done all that, and seeing the tireless, positive way she went about it motivated me. Both of us were convinced that the public schools and the private ones, the teachers and especially the students, all would benefit if somehow we managed to succeed.

Learning the Ropes

To say we learned a lot of lessons during the Nevers administration would be the most colossal kind of understatement. The fact is, despite all our concerted efforts to convey competence to the world watching from outside the Governor's domain on the third floor of the Capitol, we were truly an amateurish, unprepared lot when we reported for duty that January. Each of us was a politico with some limited governmental experience, and we had made the most of the frenzied transition period. But state government is a creature unto itself, and we were not the least wise to its ways. Thrown immediately into the deep end, as each new gubernatorial team is, we found ourselves obliged to do the butterfly and backstroke when we were barely equipped to dog-paddle.

Eventually, of course, the remarkable economic, educational, and other policy successes of the productive Nevers years would speak for themselves, vindicating our endeavors fully. But it easily could have gone the other way.

As I reflect on it now, I think the secret to our success was our ignorance of the alternative. We were in it to win, and at times we skated close to the edge, placing the Governor's political standing needlessly, even recklessly, at risk. We were a very young team by any standard, and this circumstance made mistakes common ... and occasionally comical.

One of the funnier episodes, at least in retrospect (at the time, I was not much amused), came right after our busy first legislative session. It involved one of the young-gun policy staffers whom I personally had recruited: a super-smart, super-confident kid named Billy Fessler. Billy had graduated from William and Mary in the spring, worked for the campaign as a policy researcher and writer in the summer and fall, and then joined the Governor's policy shop in a junior capacity when the new team was put in place in January. There he was assigned to cover legislative and policy issues for several of the cabinet secretariats, including the one the Governor had tapped Chad to head: Commerce and Trade. Because of that assignment, Billy happened to tag along with Chad and several other state officials in early March as they toured the power company's impressive pump-storage facility in Bath County.

The delegation listened intently as the facility manager explained how the state-of-the art generating plant worked. During hours of peak or high demand for power, the water ran through the hydroelectric generator, producing electricity. The water was captured in a reservoir below, pumped back up to the upper reservoir during times of slack demand, and then allowed to run through again during hours when demand was high. The arrangement provided a clean, low-cost way to generate power.

Spotting an opportunity to be funny—always a dangerous notion—Billy raised his hand right after the technical explanation, and deadpanned, "I think we understand all that. *But how many times can you run the water through there before you get all the electricity out of it?*"

The kid undoubtedly was proud of himself. Chad—*Secretary Braxton*—thought it was very funny. By all accounts, the power company officials on-site laughed heartily. But the press corps back in Richmond chose instead to treat the question as serious, and seriously *stupid*. The Democrats around Capitol Square had been pushing the narrative that the Governor's team was full of inept young novices and numbskull political hacks, and their message was beginning to gain some traction thanks to a few high-profile miscues during our maiden legislative session. This apparent gaffe provided ample fodder for derision in line with the opposition's theme.

"We don't want to pile on," said the state Democratic Party's sharp-witted spokeswoman mischievously. "We're actually glad they're getting some on-the-job training on how the scientific world works—it's something they don't hear about in that right-wing ivory tower of theirs. Maybe it will turn out to be a teachable moment and someone also will clue them in that the earth's not flat."

The ridicule bothered the rest of us, but the Governor shrugged it off. "Much ado about nothing—the kid was obviously kidding," he said, being charitable.

Though the episode was a silly one, the impact was not entirely benign. Voters seldom tune in to what people in government are doing, and when they tuned in for this one the impression created was not positive. This, after all, was an official visit by a delegation of senior state officials who had traveled there at taxpayer expense, presumably for some worthwhile purpose. It was not exactly a good answer to say that among those representing the Nevers Administration on the mission was a twentysomething *wunderkind* who thought he was a comedian. The minor flap blew over quickly, of course, but not before impressing indelibly on our minds the wisdom of refraining from trying to be funny when you are on duty, especially when your duty is to run the executive branch of a government that employs 100,000 people and spends $20 billion annually, much of it extracted from hard-working taxpayers.

Another of the valuable lessons we learned was about civility and the value of building personal relationships across party lines.

For a team whose lead players had come of age politically on the sharply discordant shores of the Potomac, the more genteel and collegial environs we encountered along the James took some getting used to. It was not that the players were smarter, better informed, more passionate about policy, or more fervent in their partisanship in one capital than in the other. Nor were people in one venue any more determined to get their way. The Washington players, of course, were in the political big leagues, performing before an attentive national and even international audience. But in Richmond, as in other state capitals, the fans were closer to the field—that is, the politicians were closer to the people—and many of the state-level decisions had more apparent and immediate impact on the daily lives of citizens than those in remote D.C.

Whatever the combination of reasons, the Virginia Capitol largely had been spared the near-perpetual partisan polarization and political bile-spewing that had become commonplace in Washington's corridors of power. Things were just calmer here—more friendly, more deferential, more imbued with a spirit of cooperation and compromise, more mindful of tradition, especially the ethic of disinterested public service, and, yes, more *productive*—than in the more consequential capital two hours to the north.

As chief of staff, I found myself continually immersed in diplomatic efforts to advance the Governor's ambitious legislative agenda, and more often than not my responsibilities involved reaching across the aisle. One of the interesting discoveries I quickly made was that while legislators of the governor's party tend to have very high (indeed, virtually insatiable) expectations concerning the favors that should come their way from a friendly administration, the members of the opposing party seem flattered and appreciative just to receive some respectful attention from the "Third Floor" (the colloquial term long affixed to the Office of the Governor based on its physical location). Once alert to this phenomenon, I used it to advantage. While others on our staff attended assiduously, if often futilely, to the desires and demands of our Republican legislative allies, I concentrated on the Democrats who owned the majority.

My primary collaborator proved to be none other than the powerful Speaker of the House of Delegates, Josiah Percival II. A moderate, pro-business Democrat from the "inner suburbs" of Northern Virginia, the erect, erudite, and (in private) earthy Si Percival had been at the legislative business a long time and mainly wanted to get things done. He correctly surmised that Governor Nevers was similarly minded, and he also took note of the new chief executive's lopsided win at the polls. A lawyer by profession (and, by all accounts, an extremely effective one in his day), Percival had no great interest in ideology. He did have to tend to his political knitting, though, and that meant maintaining an often tenuous alliance among the African-American members of his caucus from Hampton Roads and central Virginia, the female progressives from Northern Virginia, and the centrist rural "yellow dog Democrats" from the Southside and Southwest. To a large extent, Speaker Percival was a vestige of Virginia's past, the beneficiary of historic political alignments that were eroding decisively as the century raced to a close. In time, a more familiar liberal-conservative divide would take hold and overwhelm even his durable power base. But, for now, all the wise hands and smart-money donors were still firmly attached to the Speaker and, through their largesse, to his political action committee. The self-evident reality was that no productive business would be concluded during the Nevers administration on any subject—not the Governor's economic growth agenda, not his education choice proposals, *nothing*—without the powerful Speaker's assent.

Speaker Percival and I spent many hours bonding over drinks—his typically an 18-year-old Glenmorangie on the rocks, and mine a more pedestrian (and light-as-possible) Makers Mark and ginger ale—in his mezzanine-level hideaway in the Capitol, his spacious sixth-floor office in the nearby General Assembly Building, and occasionally at the nearby Commonwealth Club. He presumably was a master at reading his adversaries, so I took as a given that he would garner far more than he gave up in the course of these well-oiled encounters. He treated me like a wayward son—*"How in thunder's name did you end up as a Republican anyway?"*—and relished schooling me on the ins and outs of the Capitol scene. I gleaned a number of useful tidbits from this engagement, including the strong impression that Si Percival was sure he would make a far better governor than anyone else in the Commonwealth and was still fairly confident it would happen. *If so*, I thought, *it had better be pretty darn soon.* At age 62, Percival was at the peak of his legislative power but getting up there in years for a statewide electorate that seemed to fancy youthful energy in its executives.

When it came to his attitude on our legislative agenda, Percival was not especially hard to read. I inferred—correctly, as it turned out—that he would readily support most of the Governor's fiscal and economic initiatives. Those proposals allowed him to strike a bipartisan, statesmanlike pose while not unduly arousing the more liberal players in his caucus. The opposite was true of our education plans. Although he liked a good deal of what he saw there, I reasoned that he would need a major concession from us before showing any flexibility publicly, given the sizeable bloc of Democrats who were die-hard foes of anything that smacked of school choice. But Percival always wanted a deal, or so everyone said, and he wanted to be the one to craft it. Here there could be substantial credit to claim, both within his party (for forcing us to make concessions) and with the general electorate (for reaching across party lines to achieve progress). He might resolve to block us instead—that was always a possibility—but I concluded he was savvy enough, powerful enough, and, above all, proud enough to play the architect rather than the obstructionist.

The Speaker had a reputation as a master vote-counter—in fact, he was seen inside Capitol Square as the best vote-getter, vote-counter, and vote-keeper in modern memory. Given the longevity of many of the senior lawmakers, that was saying a lot. Prodded by the Governor to probe for the secrets of his success, I took on the daunting task of trying to figure out what made him tick.

"Mr. Speaker, I am new to this game and you're universally regarded as the best there's ever been," I said obsequiously soon after taking on my legislative liaison role. "What's your secret—you know, how do you consistently get your way on legislation? Is it just the power of your office?"

"Oh, hell no, Daniel," he replied. "No one gets anything done by 'just the power of their office.' It comes down to *persuasion*. And persuasion is all about understanding what is going on in the mind of the person you want to persuade. Human nature being what it is, everybody has something they *really* want. It's something they want to have, or something they want to avoid, or something they want someone else to have or avoid...."

A lecture ensued, just as I had hoped.

"Didn't they teach you anything at that fancy D.C. law firm? You were a litigator, right?"

"Yes, for a while—a very junior one."

"Well, what did they tell you about winning over a jury? Surely they taught you that you gotta do more than show the jury *how* to get to the result you want. You gotta make them *want* to get to that result. And the 'want' and the 'how' often are two different things."

Percival paused, apparently reminiscing, as a smile crept onto his face. "I had a young lawyer once, a smart, idealistic kid, who thought he was going to get his client off by having the jury disregard a key piece of evidence because it was obtained through trickery—basically, the police had lied to him. Because of the inevitable discovery rule, the court would not exclude the evidence, but this kid wasn't going to let that stop him. He was hell-bent on convincing the jury to acquit his client because of that police misconduct. He showed me his draft opening statement, and it went on at great length about how justice in this country requires that juries deny convictions in such cases so that police won't cut corners and trample on personal liberties and all that bunch of malarkey."

Percival obviously liked story-telling and enjoyed having a new audience for this tale, even if I was an audience of one.

"So I told the kid, 'Look, son, you can be a liberal crusader on your own time, but your poor schmuck of a client can't afford for you to be an idiot on his. I mean, which of those jurors do you reckon got out of bed this morning thinking that their highest calling is protecting losers like your client from the police? Was it the hairdresser? Maybe the hog farmer? How about the pharmacist ... or the hardware store owner? Hell, son, they're all counting on the police to protect them from thugs like your client. And if that takes cutting a corner or two, how much do you think they really mind it?'"

The Speaker took another purposeful swig of Scotch, at least the third since our conversation began, and carried on.

"I told him, 'Bad behavior by the police might—I stress, *might*—be the way that jury can justify handing down a not-guilty verdict if it is looking for an excuse to let your client off. It may be the *how*, but it sure as hell ain't the *why*—it ain't gonna be the reason they *want* to vote for acquittal. The want has to come from something else, and that is what you gotta figure out, first and foremost, and then build your argument around that. Make 'em like your client or feel sorry for him, or make 'em like or feel sorry for you, or make 'em hate the prosecutor, or hate the victim, or hate the whole blasted process. Whatever it is, whatever it takes, get them on your side—make 'em *want* what you want. Then, once you've done that, yes, you can give them a legal roadmap to your destination. But before you do that you gotta give 'em a reason to want to get in that car and drive!'"

"So I guess the same is true of getting someone to vote the right way on a piece of legislation," I prodded gently, trying to nudge us back to the topic at hand.

"Absolutely! But you would be surprised how many people around here don't understand that. Some of them have been around here a decade or more and still don't understand it. They keep trying to *educate* folks. Well, education is nice, and it's necessary, too. But have you ever tried to educate a kid who doesn't want to be in the classroom? You just beat your head against the wall."

"So the key is to motivate them—I see that," I said. "But isn't the motivation going to be the thing itself—you know, the merits of the bill?"

"Well, it might be," said the Speaker. "In fact, it's that way most of the time, but those are the *easy* votes to get. The member sees the merit, or can be shown the merit, and there is no countervailing rationale or pressure, so they vote with you. Those are easy votes to get, though you gotta be careful because they also tend to be soft votes—you know, hard to hold onto when the cruel winds blow. But you didn't ask me how I get easy bills passed or killed. Anybody can do that."

"So, for the hard votes, I guess that comes down to the power. You're able to pressure them because you're the speaker," I interjected. "That's what makes them want to vote with you: you make them an offer they can't refuse."

"No, sir—that's not the way it works," he replied firmly. "If I were to go throwing my weight around as speaker, telling everyone to vote with me or else, I wouldn't be speaker very long. It doesn't work that way here. Maybe a few times each session I can make that kind of appeal to the caucus or to individual members, but those are special cases."

"So, then, what makes people want to vote with you?"

"Any of a thousand things—ten thousand!" he answered. "Everyone and every situation is different. There are personal reasons, political reasons, philosophical reasons, selfish and expedient reasons … great reasons, ornery reasons, flat-out inexcusable reasons. There are noble motives, vindictive motives, ludicrous and laughable motives. Before you can figure out how to make somebody *want* to be with you on a bill, you gotta understand who and what they're thinking about when they're in the shower in the morning—who and what are on their mind when they aren't managing where their mind is going. You say you want to know my *secret*? Here's the secret: What's important to them probably has nothing to do with that bill, and there's a fair chance it has nothing to do with you, either. So what you do is you look and you think, and then you listen and you think, and then when you're finished doing that you look and listen and think some more, until you figure out what it is that they want and that you have … or, more likely, what it is that you can either go get for them or go keep them from getting. And you offer that up if they will help you on that little bill."

Percival, I eventually learned, had been a page in the U.S. Senate in the early fifties, and after college his first job had been back on the Hill as a junior Senate staffer. That was when Lyndon Johnson ruled the roost as majority leader and had his way with everyone and everything that came through that body. Only several years later, when Johnson's excellent biographer laid bare the story, did it occur to me how much of Percival's means and methods resembled the legendary LBJ's. But Percival was a stickler for propriety, and that was obvious from his concluding admonition.

"Now, that thing you offer up, it has to be *legal*, son—never, ever, *ever* be a party to someone trying to leverage you or this process or their office for personal gain. And don't look the other way if they try to, either. No one around here tries that with me because they know if I ever hear anything like that I'll personally get their ass kicked out of here in the next election, if not before. But within the bounds of proper horse-trading, that's what you do. And the key to it is what?"

The master was now quizzing his student to make sure I actually was learning.

"Well, I guess—"

"*Information*," he said, quickly answering his own question. "The key to it is information. If you're gonna be good at this, you gotta invest the time, and you gotta have other people who work for you investing the time, to figure out what makes these guys and gals tick."

The conversation ranged over a few other topics, and then I departed to make my report to Governor Nevers. He knew Speaker Percival more by reputation than experience, and he would be investing plenty of his own time to build a relationship and figure out what made the legislative kingpin tick.

"Nothing new or revolutionary there," the Governor said in response to my report. "It just confirms what we already knew: We're up against a master. We aren't going over or around him, so we have to find a way to go *with* him."

THE GREAT DEBATE

At the opposite pole from my cozy, private collaboration with the Speaker was Mitch's running public debate with the woman who quickly emerged as leader of the forces opposing the Nevers education agenda, State Senator Dorothy Meade. She was the very same "Dorothy Meade" who had led the Black Student League at the University of Virginia and had been student government president there during the Mitch-inspired dust-up over affirmative action. Now, as then, African-American ancestry and a U.Va. education seemed like the only things in the whole wide world that Congressman Jackson and Senator Meade had in common.

Meade was serving her second term in the Virginia Senate, having won her first bid for public office easily in a majority-black district centered in Norfolk. Even before she threw her hat in the political ring, however, she was well known in Democratic Party circles beyond Hampton Roads and even beyond Virginia. A hard-charging civil rights lawyer who reveled in battling the patriarchal white power structure, Meade had been prominent in numerous high-profile controversies involving racial and/or gender discrimination alleged against major corporations. She fought for her causes with an intellectual force and ferocity that few could match. An unapologetic progressive, she bristled continually at the clubby ways of the Virginia Senate and especially abhorred the routine collaboration between the chamber's white Democratic moderates and its substantial GOP minority. But if there was one thing she found even more displeasing than a white Virginia Democrat who consorted with the Republican enemy, it was a black conservative like Mitch Jackson.

Given Mitch's rather demanding day-job in Washington, most regarded his designation as co-chair of the Governor's education commission as a largely symbolic gesture. But immediately after Nevers concluded his opening address to the joint assembly, Meade rushed to button-hole every reporter she could find and deliver the same pointed message: She was challenging Mitch Jackson to a series of debates throughout Virginia on the school choice issue.

"If Congressman Jackson has so little to keep him busy in Washington," she taunted, "then let him come out into the community with me and defend the Governor's radical plan to starve the public schools of Virginia and hand their money over to a bunch of lily-white academies. I want to hear him defend the indefensible, and the people in the community deserve to hear it, too."

Mitch would have had little choice but to take up the cudgels even if he had not welcomed the assignment. In fact, it excited him like nothing had in years, and he eagerly accepted.

"I welcome the opportunity to discuss these issues in the light of day with State Senator Meade," read Mitch's public statement the next morning. "She is an exceptionally talented communicator, and she needs to be. As an architect of today's educational failure factories and an apologist for the defeatist status quo, she has a lot of explaining to do."

What ensued over the next eight months was a dramatic series of encounters that some folks soon took to comparing, rather too grandly, with the Lincoln-Douglas debates. In actuality, of course, Lincoln and Douglas never debated in the contemporary sense; they each speechified at great length in the other's presence. But the more things changed the more they seemed to remain the same. Slavery had supplied the primary subtext for the duo's famous 1858 encounters, and the tragic truth was that much of the same imagery and even a variant of the same issues were still relevant in these exchanges 14 decades later. The fact that both of the contemporary debaters were African-American elected leaders did much to highlight the intervening progress and remove race as a sword or shield in the discourse. But the persisting consequences of the nation's original sin were never far from the surface as the Jackson-Meade show played to standing-room only crowds in varied settings across the Commonwealth and even garnered cable-news coverage beyond the state's borders.

To their considerable credit, Mitch and Dorothy kept their debate on a relatively high policy plane. Both could turn a phrase like a stiletto, and both were passionate champions of their respective—and utterly irreconcilable—positions. Still, they came grudgingly to respect each other's intellect and motivation. Their appearances became a fruitful forum for the airing of just about every conceivable argument for and against the proposition that the Jeffersonian ideal of universal education, which all embraced, could best be achieved by having public and non-public providers share, and compete for, the resources supplied by taxpayers.

In one typical exchange, Meade hammered home the two-fold proposition that educating kids is a core function of government and that "the people" would lose control if someone other than government were allowed to run schools:

> Congressman Jackson is always talking about the brilliant "private sector," as if all the really smart, motivated folk are on that side of the fence and all the other poor, dull, dim-witted folk work for the government. Tell that to the police officers and the firemen! Tell that to the engineers who design the roads and bridges! Tell it to the researchers at our public universities! Heck, tell it to Mitch Jackson! Last time I checked, poor old dim-witted Uncle Sam was signing his paycheck.
>
> This notion that education has to be sold on the private market like some widget or wiener is a truly foolish notion.

If that's true, why not outsource the entire government to Exxon or GE or Oscar-Meyer? We don't do that because certain things like a good education are not niceties you get if the mood strikes you or if some extra change is burning a hole in your pocket. *They are rights we possess as citizens.* And who do you want protecting your rights—someone who is elected or appointed to serve the people so that everyone gets a fair shake, or someone who is in it to make a profit for themselves and their cronies, so they give you as little as they can get by with?

I am not willing to surrender the future of our kids to Mitch Jackson and the greedy profiteers who bankroll him, and you shouldn't surrender to them, either!

Mitch was more than capable of parrying Meade's thrusts with a philosophical discourse, but he generally resisted that temptation and instead grounded his case in practicality:

Senator Meade says you should worry about someone taking away your rights, and she has a point. You want to know how our rights are taken from us in America today? They go out the door with that teenage kid who never learned to write a simple, coherent sentence or add two numbers bigger than five. No one with a sane mind will ever give him an honest job, so he goes out on the street and commits petty crimes, runs drugs, joins a gang. Then one thing leads to another, and pretty soon it's a drive-by shooting or an armed robbery or a fight that ends up in guns blazing. And if he is lucky enough to stay alive, he ends up in an orange suit sitting in a six-by-eight cell experiencing one of those fine government institutions that Senator Meade is so pleased about.

No, folks, losing your rights isn't when someone from the private sector does something for you that actually might work for a change. Losing your rights is when your whole life becomes a hopeless hell because everyone who is supposed to give you a hand up lets you down—when your teachers just assume you can't learn so they don't really try; and even if they want to try, they can't get the classroom under control long enough to get anything done.

Losing your rights is not only when the teachers give up on you; it's when somebody already gave up on the teachers. Because, hey, why bother to make sure the teachers can teach if you've already decided the students can't learn?

But here's the thing: As much as you'd like this to be somebody else's problem, it's not—it's your problem. The rights that are disappearing in America today are your rights. When most of us were in school, this country was a world leader in education; we were the place of ideas and inventions. Now we are around 17th in science and 28th in math. You want to talk about rights disappearing in this country? They disappear every day we fail to pass on the American Dream to a new generation. They disappear when failing schools lead to failing communities, when a failing workforce leads to a failing economy, when being 17th or 28th is accepted as our fate, and so we become a failing country!

Getting a crowd wound up was something that Mitch did well, and he also knew how to get Dorothy Meade going. Whenever he invoked the "American Dream," and he did so often, it sent her into orbit. I did not agree with hardly anything Meade said—it all smacked of pointless class warfare to me—but her spirited rebuttals were invariably entertaining, and they won over many an audience:

Inside the beltway, which is where Mr. Jackson spends his time these days, they throw around this term "American Dream" like it's candy. You heard him just now. They have this vision of the fine life—you know, in the 'burbs, with two-point-four children and a dog that doesn't shed, a Volvo wagon or two out front, a Weber grill out back by the pool, and four or five bedrooms in between, not because anyone is sleeping in them but just so the help has something to keep 'em busy. For these high-living folk a tough day is a "bad hair day," and a hard decision is figuring out whether to serve goat cheese or brie on the veranda.

I mean, sure, it's great to stand up here and say everyone ought to have a shot at the good life, at the American Dream. Goat cheese doesn't float my boat, but, whatever your thing is, you ought to have it—right? Well, see, here's the problem with that. The "dream" right now is only working for the rich people in America. Report after report shows that the rich are getting richer; they're zooming right along while the rest of us—the middle class—are stuck in the parking lot with a flat tire. We can't get moving at all, and so the wealth gap in this country keeps getting wider and wider.

Congressman Jackson talked about international rankings and how America has slipped in math and science compared to other countries. Well, here's somewhere else we've slipped: it's called "economic mobility." It's the chance that someone in poverty or even the middle class has to climb up out of the basement and enjoy some of the good life upstairs. And you know where the U.S. ranks on economic mobility today? Behind Canada, behind the UK, behind much of supposedly stagnant Europe.

So, Congressman Jackson, don't tell these fine folks that the way to correct the huge and growing income inequality in America is to take those same corporate profiteers who are already living large on the backs of ordinary, hard-working folk, and give them control of our schools on top of everything else they own! How does letting them make even more money make one single school better? No, sir—Jesus chased the money changers out of the churches, and it will be a cold day in you-know-where before we let them set up shop in our schools!

Meade's adept theatrics might have chastened a less talented and confident foe, but Mitch kept provoking her so he could punch back.

"Wow! She's great, isn't she?" he would say to the audience with a broad smile as he rose swiftly to respond.

If you want to start a revolution, Senator Meade's the one to call. If you want to get people mad at "the man" for holding them down, she's got the speech already written. But if you actually want to make something better, like actually improving a school, she's got nothing for you.

Let me say it again: she's got *nothing*.

She can tear down the house with the best of them, but give her a hammer and a nail and tell her to go build something, and she is totally useless.

She stands right there, knowing a lot of these schools are failing, knowing these kids are going to suffer because of it, knowing—in her heart, in her head, *knowing*—that the world is going to miss out on the light that should have shined brightly from each of these young stars because her failure factories and the streets are going to snuff that light right out of them. And all she can do is stand there and stoke the anger and reap the political benefit from everyone's frustration and mistrust.

Fix it!? Fix it!? Don't ask Senator Meade to fix it! That's not her department. "Fix it" is over on aisle 27. Senator Meade runs the "Excuse it" department over on aisle one ... unless she's filling in over in "Blame it" or "Resent it."

Look, I could spend the next 30 minutes talking about the American free enterprise system, how it has met human needs and produced opportunity and innovation without parallel in human history. I could show her class-baiting rhetoric for the snake oil that it is. Maybe we'll do that later. But you don't have time now for an ideological argument, and neither do the school kids of America.

You want to know why economic mobility has declined in this nation? It's our failing school systems. Before you can move up, you have to learn how to do something useful— you have to learn how to add value. You have to *learn*, period. And unless we stop allowing politicians like Senator Meade to divert us from the real issue—the deeply uneven quality of our education system—then we are never going to get serious about giving our young people the hammer and nails they need to build something useful, something valuable, and lift themselves up....

The sparring pair proved themselves to be remarkably talented, and the two relative unknowns reaped enhanced statewide name recognition and political standing from their engagement. Most commentary lavished praise on both, finding it impossible to declare either the winner. But it would become apparent to most Capitol Square denizens—some sooner and some later—that the encounters had lopsidedly benefitted the Nevers cause on school choice. The debate coverage focused more attention on the issue than had occurred even during the gubernatorial campaign, and it gave the subject heightened importance and immediacy in the public mind. Inertia, not organized opposition, is the main enemy of most legislative initiative, and the impetus supplied by the Meade-Jackson show became a vital agent in overcoming that inertia. From the time of the debates forward, there was a sense that the issue had to be addressed and decided by the General Assembly. This meant that it could not be bottled up in committee and quietly buried there by the Democratic majority.

Another effect, also beneficial to our side, was that the exchanges largely removed the bugaboo of race from the discussion, which was no small feat given Virginia's sordid history of racially segregated schools. Mitch's conservative ideas might not command general support in African-American political circles, or even in the community at large, but his racial motives could not be credibly impugned. He was a bona fide war hero and a living, breathing example of what it takes to overcome extreme adversity. No one would dare lob his way any of the epithets ("Uncle Tom," etc.) that often were flung intimidatingly at other black conservatives. By now, of course, it was apparent that such tactics were not going to deter Mitch anyway, but that was not the point. Having Congressman Jackson out front on the issue enabled other dissenters to speak their minds without fear of denigration or reprisal. Parents from around Virginia and from other states, many of them African Americans, came forward to tell stories—like Lorenzo's—about how access to educational alternatives had thrown lifelines to their children.

The debates also had an impact in the politically important suburbs. Given the generally high satisfaction level with the public schools there, it had been frustratingly difficult to generate any sort of intensity on school choice in suburban households, no matter which line of argument was advanced. Suburban conservatives were told reform was needed because throwing more tax dollars at failing schools would only worsen the waste while changing little—a charge there was evidence to support. Per-pupil spending already was higher in places like Richmond than in surrounding jurisdictions, thanks to a statutory formula that channeled state taxpayer funds disproportionately to economically impaired areas. For more socially minded suburbanites, there was the Nevers-Jackson appeal for equity and opportunity for kids in distressed urban and rural settings. And for suburban voters of all political stripes, there was the Governor's urgent call for educational excellence as the key to Virginia's prosperity and America's global competitiveness in the 21st century. But none of those lines of argument had produced any real grassroots passion that could translate into serious constituent pressure on suburban lawmakers.

To our rescue in suburban precincts, however, came Dorothy Meade. Aggressively progressive and fiercely partisan, she became the embodiment of the case against the Nevers education initiative, and that did not help the antis' cause in the suburbs. Nor was her class-warfare rhetoric appreciated by that crowd. The smarter pitch would have been one coming from the suburban perspective itself—from a Republican or at least an independent or Democratic moderate who highlighted the strengths of the local schools that suburban families knew firsthand and regarded highly. Defending those public schools against a money and brain drain well might have garnered suburban sympathy. Instead, the Meade-Jackson debates raised the decibel level and positioned the contest largely along the familiar liberal-versus-conservative divide, bringing us growing suburban backing as the eventful first year of the Nevers administration drew to a close.

Finally, there was the youthful appeal of the fresh faces that squared off in the Mitch and Dorothy show. One of the fastest growing demographic groups in Virginia during this time consisted of younger, well-educated business and professional types who tended to be more multi-racial in hue and habits, more apt to reside in urban settings, less captive to the desegregation-era stereotypes and syndromes of their elders, and less interested in that generation's polarized politics. Chad's polls showed that these younger voters were among the most entertained by the exchanges between Mitch and Dorothy, and they remained engaged on the issue thereafter, bringing a potent new political dynamic to an otherwise tired old fight.

EARLY SUCCESS

The school choice "debates" stoked interest, and our "Every-Child-Counts" commission laid essential groundwork with stakeholders, but the first year of Ned Nevers' governorship was mainly about economics, not education. The self-declared "Job One" for the new administration was job creation. Leading the charge, second only to the Governor himself, was his true-believing, tax-cutting, free-market guru, Secretary of Commerce and Trade Braxton. As the primary architect of the Governor's plan, it was logical that Chad would pilot the legislative effort. This arrangement worked well enough during the regular session, which convened right before the inauguration and ended just eight weeks later, in mid-March. That frenetic, two-month span, however, afforded barely enough time for the frazzled freshmen who comprised the new chief executive's team to introduce ourselves around, learn the basic procedures, and discover what lay behind all those heavy wooden doors with the seal-stamped knobs. Recognizing these realities before his senior staff did, the Governor prudently rejected Chad's more aggressive game plan and advanced only the least controversial components of the economic package in the January-March regular legislative session. The items requiring the heavy lifting, most notably the tax cuts and tort reform proposals, were reserved for a special session to convene in late spring.

A compromise set of business and individual tax cuts, more modest than we preferred, finally passed both houses and were signed by the Governor in late October 1998. Included in the package were our regulatory reform initiatives, a significantly expanded enterprise-zone program, a swap that replaced growth-inhibiting local business taxes with a local levy on retail sales, and several tax- and grant-funded inducements for job creation in targeted industry sectors. Tort reform, however, lay prostrate on the legislative battlefield, routed by a bipartisan coalition of trial-lawyer lawmakers who claimed, not without some justification, that Virginia's legal landscape already disfavored civil claimants. Despite the sound and fury that attended the tort-reform tussle and the wholesale defeat that ended it, the special session was widely viewed as a major success for the new administration. Most of our package had passed, including meaningful tax cuts, enabling the Governor to claim credibly that he had delivered on one of his two major campaign promises.

While passage of our economic plan yielded political dividends and boosted Virginia's economy (or, so the later fiscal evidence would suggest), the effects of the extended first-year legislative engagement inside Capitol Square were more mixed. Chad was especially unhappy, having dissented from the late concessions that secured the package's passage. He was even more upset that the Governor inserted me in his place as the lead negotiator opposite the Speaker. The longstanding bond that Chad and I shared would survive this rough patch, but what should have been a time of close collaboration on a major project followed by celebration over its success instead was a period of personal pain for the two of us. Nor would the relationship with my college roommate and longtime friend be the only personal tie of mine to be strained.

I came into the Governor's Office rather grandly imagining that my role would be roughly akin to a prime minister's, but sometime during that first year it dawned on me that the main job of the chief of staff is to deliver bad news to friends and allies and to massage the easily wounded egos of cabinet members, legislators, favor-seeking donors, office-seeking supporters, and sundry other actual and would-be public servants. These tasks required patience, calmness, and fortitude, attributes that I usually managed to display despite the chaos without and tempest within. But there were times when the pressure got the best of me and I flamed out brilliantly. The most notable of those came during the pivotal phase of the economic negotiations when our hapless first education secretary—a former federal functionary whose superficiality already had been diagnosed by everyone in Capitol Square—insisted on interrupting a crucial negotiation session with Speaker Percival so he could tell me, for probably the 15th time, how aggrieved he was over all the press attention that Mitch Jackson was getting on the school choice issue. My brusque retort so offended him that he refused to speak to me for weeks, a condition I gladly would have allowed to persist if the Governor himself had not shamed me by convening a make-up session.

It was a rocky first year in other respects, too, and by far the biggest vicissitude was the run-on special session on taxes. Our team had hoped to finish that business by Mother's Day, or by Memorial Day at the latest, whereupon we would salt away the economic accomplishment, the Governor would take a statewide victory lap via RV in the summer, and, propelled by the legislative momentum and forthcoming commission report, we would roll into the major encounter over education that all expected in the 1999 legislative session. Instead, we were lucky to complete the tax thing by Yorktown Day (mid-October), and in the meantime we had to endure hearing after hearing and recess after recess. Ironically, Speaker Percival had wanted a speedy resolution, too. He and his high command sensibly preferred to engage us on the Democrat-friendly turf of education policy rather than on the GOP's favored economic ground, and the Speaker was personally eager to avoid being branded an obstructionist, especially on tax cuts that his business friends generally applauded. But bicameralism thwarts many a well-laid plot between executive and legislative branch collaborators, and when it came to wanting a swift end to the special-session business, there was a crucial odd man out.

That man, unfortunately, happened to run the Virginia Senate, and he was someone to whom Ned Nevers had taken an immediate and visceral disliking.

Derided as "His Haughtiness" behind his back even by fellow Democrats, Senator Howard Morris was renowned for the defect that my boss could least brook—superciliousness. His majority in the 40-member upper chamber was tenuous, resting on a bare two-seat partisan advantage, and his grip on the Democratic caucus was even shakier. But what the mercurial Norfolk mortician lacked in ability and actual clout, he more than compensated for in petulance and chutzpah.

Nevers knew the type well. And, having received due comeuppance from the voters for his own arrogance several years earlier, he now had zero patience for the character flaw in others. Indeed, Nevers had come to relish opportunities to deflate the egos of those around him. He usually managed to accomplish that work in a good-natured way, but he was serious about it. During the transition, he summed up his criteria for appointments in an earthy nine-word directive to Abby and me: "Find me very smart people who are not assholes." Personnel was Abby's bailiwick as secretary of the Commonwealth, and she made the colorful command her secret motto, confounding Capitol Square monitors with a curious new vanity plate—"VSPWANA"—on the aging Accord coupe she parked near the Capitol's west entrance. Nevers also made humility a litmus test for inclusion in his cabinet. In considering candidates for those key posts, he insisted on personally taking the finalists to dinner, ostensibly for one last interview but actually so he could observe firsthand how they treated the wait-staff. Tellingly, the only cabinet member to evade this lens, owing to his ever-so-busy schedule in D.C., was our soon-to-be-ex-education secretary.

Given the chasm that existed between their political views, party loyalties, and especially their ways of treating people, it was just a matter of time before Nevers and Morris collided. In fact, it took no time at all. The day after Nevers first addressed the General Assembly in joint session, Morris got carried away at one of his shrill news conferences and issued the extraordinary public demand that the Governor and his team come to the Senate leader's office in the General Assembly Building and explain their "outrageous" school choice proposals. We all assumed that Nevers would simply ignore the impolitic demand. Instead, he surprised us by directing his scheduler to arrange the meeting, and at 9:10 the next morning, a contingent that included the Governor of Virginia, three cabinet secretaries, the chief of staff, the budget director, several budget analysts and policy aides, two Executive Protective Unit (EPU) state troopers, a stenographer, and a student intern marched from the Capitol's third floor over to the "GAB" in a line resembling a mother duck and her sizeable brood heading for a nearby pond.

Once inside the made-over corporate headquarters that now contained the solons' offices, our group crowded into an elevator, spilled over into a second, and made our way to the sixth floor, where a leadership suite housed the office of the Senate majority leader and other top lawmakers. But instead of heading west off the elevator toward the glass doors that marked off the leadership's domain, the Governor directed the entourage eastward toward the snack bar. Several of us sought to correct the apparent wrong turn, only to have the Governor bark, "You all come over here and get some of this ice cream. Daniel and I were up here making courtesy calls last week, and I had the best chocolate cone that's ever crossed my lips." Already 15 minutes late for the scheduled 9 A.M. session but no doubt moving at exactly the pace the Governor intended, we followed his instruction and placed our orders. Even the pudgy intern, who at first demurred on account of his diet, left with cone in hand. The EPU troopers alone were allowed to abstain.

As constituents, lobbyists, and sundry other befuddled bystanders cleared a path, the duck-like procession next proceeded down the corridor, past the elevators, through the glass doors, 15 paces west, then 28 paces south to the Senate leader's corner office. We were almost a half-hour late, and each participant—from the Governor down to the pudgy intern—was licking feverishly on an ice cream cone in a futile bid to avoid dripping on the carpet. The Governor entered first, of course, and greeted Senator Morris like a long-lost friend. As the stunned Senator reached for a handkerchief, presumably to remove the sticky residue left by the hearty gubernatorial handshake, Nevers turned back toward the door and waited for his entire entourage to squeeze into the office. Then, he pivoted back to face Senator Morris and uttered words that would have made me spit ice cream onto the floor if it had not already been flowing there from the remnants of my rapidly melting cone.

"Well, Senator, we're all here, just as you demanded. And it's like the fellow said when he came home drunk late at night and passed out on the front stoop. He woke up the next morning, and his wife was scowling down at him, demanding to know what he had to say for himself. 'Ma'am,' he said, 'I don't have a prepared statement, but I will be happy to take your questions from the floor.'"

We all laughed at the boss's joke, but the jocularity was momentary. An icy glare from Senator Morris froze away our smiles like warts. A brief conversation between the Governor and Senator ensued—I cannot recall anything consequential being said—and then our group departed in the same manner as our arrival. I was glad not to be the one bringing up the rear, especially when the door slammed inches from the intern's backside.

Despite his opening disclaimer, Nevers, of course, had made a quite a statement with this spectacle, and it was definitely of the prepared variety. We would pay a steep price for the classic smack-down in our future dealings with the Senate leader, and the prolonged special session on our economic program would be just one of the costs. In the episode's aftermath, I would have to play the good cop and spend excruciating hours with the insufferable egotist, distancing myself from my "crazy" boss in an effort to build some semblance of a working relationship with the influential lawmaker. But the truth is, the Governor that morning took the first really significant step toward passage of his school choice bill. Behind Morris' back, from that day forward, friend and foe alike would be laughing at his expense. Not only had the boss carved his initials onto another tree in the forest that would become the legend of Governor Ned Nevers. He had neutered one of his main detractors.

Senator Morris dearly would have loved to kill our economic plan, especially the tax cuts, but he never came close to having the votes for that, and by October he also had run out of excuses—and Democratic support—for his stratagem of delay. The first year of the Nevers administration ended soon thereafter with nearly all commentators declaring the wily chief executive a legislating mastermind.

With all the accolades, it looked for a time like we might follow the impressive tax cut victory with a quick breakthrough on school choice. The positive editorial reviews of year-one combined with favorable poll numbers to give the impression that Nevers had a strong political and legislative head of steam going into the 1999 legislative session. The impromptu Jackson-Meade debates had turned a spotlight on the school choice issue, generating increased support in our suburban base. Our education commission had completed its work, delivering a well-crafted, nominally bipartisan report that added policy details, compelling statistics, and evocative anecdotes. Several middle-of-the-road Democratic senators, looking ahead to midterm elections in swing districts that Ned Nevers had carried handily a little over a year earlier, were signaling their receptiveness to key elements of the plan. Our grassroots allies were mobilizing constituents to turn up the heat on wavering GOP moderates. Some in the politically influential teachers association, a key Democratic interest group, reportedly were open to compromise if it would get a substantial teacher pay raise enacted. Two legislative sessions (one of them a marathon) had schooled and toughened our policy and legislative teams, readying them for the really challenging work ahead. By year's end, we even had an impressive new secretary of education on board, one who did her homework and became a major contributor in the lobbying process.

Perhaps most important, we had a good fix on what Speaker Percival most "needed" or "wanted" at the moment: *taxpayers' money*. The just-passed tax cut legislation had reduced the state's projected revenues. The two-year appropriations act adopted the previous winter would have to be trimmed. And the Speaker and his top lieutenants had pet projects and spending items they had promised, promoted, passed in the 1998 regular session, and now meant to preserve. Percival had tried to make a deal on the budget during the special session, but he had forfeited most of his leverage by publicly endorsing the tax cuts, and the Governor thereafter had flatly refused to open the Pandora's Box of budget deliberations. We had the votes to pass the tax cuts in the special session and defer the budget issues until the General Assembly returned for its next regular session in mid-January, so that is what we did.

Nevers opened that 1999 session with a celebratory but resolute "State of the Commonwealth" address that lauded the Democratic majority for its cooperation on the economic package. Until its more controversial education passages, in fact, the speech actually generated more bipartisan applause than had greeted the Governor's speech from the same rostrum a year earlier. Within another week, we had completed the arduous process of finalizing our package of education bills and getting them all introduced, most with a bipartisan list of patrons. We knew we had a big uphill climb. Passing a school-choice package in a Democrat-controlled legislature during a midterm election year certainly was not for the faint of heart. But things seemed to be coming our way.

For the briefest of moments, success actually seemed within our grasp. But it was only a mirage—fortunately.

I received the scintillating call from Speaker Percival late one afternoon in early February.

The House Appropriations Committee, like its Senate counterpart, was just starting the weighty work of framing out a slightly scaled-down version of the state budget. The Governor had submitted his proposed reductions a month earlier, as required by law, and legislative budget-writers were now beginning to parse them to see what they could accept and what they would reject or revise. Though not currently a member of the influential House money committee, Speaker Percival was something infinitely better: the committee's former chairman and the man who every two years appointed its chair and members. So he called the shots.

The Speaker summoned me to his office for a drink. His usual way, even when he had something major on his mind, was to affect an easy, matter-of-fact manner. But this time was different. He was delivering a blockbuster of a message and wanted me to appreciate how big—and fleeting—was the opportunity.

"The stars may have just aligned for a deal on both education and the budget," he said, "if you guys are smart enough and nimble enough to jump on it."

As it turned out, we were probably less "nimble" that evening than at any time, day or night, during Nevers' entire governorship. But that was beside the point.

The Speaker was all business and very convincing. He could put the deal together in the House of Delegates, he said. That chamber, with its 12-seat Democratic advantage, presented the heaviest lift for us, so this was stunning news. And, with a little outreach by Governor Nevers in the Senate, Percival declared, a thin bipartisan majority could be assembled in that body as well. But time was of the essence.

"We have to strike tomorrow and lock down the key votes before the other side gets wind of it and goes ballistic. Everyone assumes these things—both education and the budget—will drag on for weeks, so they are not ready. No one really has their ducks in a row yet. Believe me, the only way this deal ever gets done is like greased lightning! I need the Governor's commitment tonight; I need him to call three or four swing senators first thing tomorrow; and I will do the rest."

This was the coolest, headiest thing you can possibly imagine. Here I was, a novice but quick study, making law at the very epicenter of political power in Virginia, plotting a grand bargain with the legendary deal-maker, the pre-eminent power-broker of a state that gave birth to power-brokers, deal-makers, states, and everything else that has to do with democracy.

All this, and the Speaker was asking so little of us ...

Except that I did not know what he was asking of us. Nor, for that matter, did I know what he was proposing to give us in return. I was struggling just to contain my excitement. And if I had succeeded in that struggle, perhaps it would have occurred to me that something was amiss when the Speaker pulled out a six-page, typed term sheet that contained five pages about specific budget provisions and just a single sheet devoted to our education plan. The most sweeping set of education reform and funding proposals ever submitted by a Virginia governor, the subject of two dozen newly introduced bills and 18 separate budget amendments, had been reduced to about a dozen bullet points on a single typed page.

"We cannot do the constitutional amendment on vouchers," he said as he rushed through the punch list on the final page. "Can't get the votes, period. But all the other big things the Governor has proposed are on here. Need details on some. Some will have to wait a while for serious funding, but you knew that when you decided to push a tax cut. I can tell you this, Daniel. You all will never get another deal anywhere near this good...."

I thanked him, promised a speedy reply, and hastily departed. My mind was spinning. Back on the Third Floor, I asked the EPU trooper on duty to connect me with the Governor. I emailed Abby and asked her to assemble the legislative team as soon as possible. Next I planned to call Mitch. But first I had to read through Percival's paper ... and think.

My solitary deliberation was interrupted almost immediately. "I spoke with First Sergeant Macauley," the young trooper said as he entered my office from the adjacent conference room. "He is with the Governor. He said to ask you whether you are calling about a life and death matter, because, if not, the Governor is *unreachable*."

"Huh? He's what?" I blurted. "I've only been at this job for a year, but I am pretty sure the words 'governor' and 'unreachable' don't get to show up in the same sentence. Get Scotty Macauley on the line for me right away, please."

The nonplussed trooper turned to make a second call to the leader of his detail, a Nevers favorite. Then I remembered Nevers' supposed whereabouts.

"The Governor is at his farm in Nottoway. How can he be *unreachable* in Nottoway?" I shouted into the adjoining room.

"No, there was a schedule change three hours ago," the agent replied. "The Governor is in Suffolk … at the hospital."

Moments later, Macauley was on the line.

"Scotty, where are you, and what's going on?"

"Louise Obici in Suffolk," he muttered over the crackling line.

"Who is Louise Obici?" I asked.

"She's not a who—she's a what. We are at Louise Obici Memorial Hospital in Suffolk."

"Okay … whatever. Put the Governor on the line, please."

"Is it a life-or-death matter?"

"Don't ask me questions, *dammit*—just put him on the line!" I snapped.

It was the first—and last—time I ever lost my cool with a member of the Governor's protection detail, and I immediately regretted it.

"Strike that—I'm sorry," I said, exhaling deeply. "Look, Scotty, we have an urgent matter here. Not to be melodramatic, but it happens to be the main thing Ned Nevers wants to accomplish as governor. So if he is unreachable, I need to know why that is and when I can to talk to him."

"Danny, I don't have a clear fix on when that will be. The Governor got a phone call, and said, 'Let's go to Suffolk,' and we came over here right away. He's been in there with this elderly patient ever since. A pastor's been in and out, and there's another older woman in there who I guess is a visitor, though she seems pretty out of it herself. Last time I looked, the Governor was holding the patient's hand. She appears unconscious, but I don't know. Abby had me interrupt the Governor about an hour ago. He gave me that look—you know the one—and said, 'Unless someone has a life and death matter, I don't want to be interrupted again.'"

"Wow. It must be a relative. I didn't think Nevers had any living relatives who are elderly…," I pondered aloud.

"It's unlikely that she's a relative," Macauley replied.

"And you say that because...?"

"Because she is African American, and the Governor does not appear to be...."

"Ahhh." I was just beginning to connect the dots when the veteran trooper added a couple of key clues, solving the puzzle.

"I heard the Governor call the one lady 'Miz Sallie,' but the name on the plate here outside the door is 'Moulton,'" he said. "'Nellie Moulton'."

SAVED FROM DISASTER

I will never be quite sure what it was about Miz Nellie that so moved Ned Nevers. "Salt of the earth," is all he said the one time I probed. But he was by her side at the end—which took a very long time—and I have no doubt he is with her now.

She may well be the unsung hero of the Nevers administration. We will never know, but it is quite possible that the ten-plus hours it took for her to pass on to her Great Reward were ten-plus hours that saved us, and a lot of Virginia schoolchildren, from a truly disastrous deal.

Nevers did grant me an audience during that night's vigil—a short phone call after he had reviewed the faxed copy of Percival's terms. In the meantime, I had a chance to calm down, clear my head, talk to Mitch, Chad, and Abby, and reflect. So I was not surprised by his eventual response.

"If it is such a good deal tonight, it will be a good deal tomorrow," he said. "My priority is here, and I'm not going to be railroaded. Besides, you cannot tell from this paper what Percival is actually agreeing to on the education stuff."

Had we reached the Speaker earlier in the evening, full of excitement and eager for a deal, intense overnight negotiations undoubtedly would have ensued. We would have required a lot more specifics on our "education stuff," and Percival might well have come our way with a palatable package, or so it might have seemed. It sure would have been tempting to strike a bargain. In just my brief time with the Speaker that evening, I had experienced the incredible rush that comes when you mix adrenalin, power, and whatever you call those deal-chasing hormones. Yet, even the best deal Percival could have delivered at that time would have been a disappointing compromise, preempting and preventing the real "win" that loomed ahead if only we—there it was again—*persevered*.

Percival had declared, erroneously, that we would never get a deal any-where near as good as his. When Dorothy Meade got wind of it the next day, she was sure she had never heard of a deal anywhere near as bad. The Speaker had been wrong about several aspects of this particular play—foremost among them, underestimating Senator Meade—but events quickly proved him right about one thing. Time indeed had been of the essence, and all hell did indeed break loose when the deal went public before the votes were locked down. Meade did not have the whole scoop, but a leak from Percival's inner circle had alerted a friend of a friend that a budget-and-education trade was in the works, and that word was sufficient to send Meade to the microphones with a full-throated attack. Within hours, a veritable *Who's Who* of the Left, representatives of every Democrat-aligned interest group imaginable, were parading before the salivating Capitol press corps to denounce the rumored sellout and to im-plore lawmakers to "Save Our Schools." Dozens of Democratic legislators from the House and Senate quickly joined in what became a political stampede.

By day's end, any potential for a bargain had evaporated, and Percival, nat-urally, had evaded responsibility.

"I believe in bipartisan cooperation when it is good for our schools, and I am the first to fight when it is not," Percival declared emphatically to the re-porters who hastily assembled outside his Capitol office. "My job here is to try to fashion agreements for the people where that is possible and wise. But if the Governor and his ideological young lieutenants believe for a moment that their radical education program is acceptable to the party of Jefferson, the party of universal education and equal opportunity for all, then they have a lot to learn. Personally, I'd like to see those lads start talking less and listening more."

Of course, I had been listening—to Percival—and it almost had taken us off the rails. He knew it as well as I did, but that had not kept him from taking a public potshot at us.

"You must come by for a drink," the Speaker intoned soothingly on my voicemail that same evening. "I always enjoy your company, and we cannot take this public business personally."

I took a pass and did not return the call.

The remainder of the 1999 session became a polarized spectacle as both sides shifted from legislating to honing arguments for the fall showdown at the polls. The budget got done with difficulty, but that was about the only thing. Except for a few technical bills, all of our proposals on education were killed or withdrawn, as were our education-related budget amendments. The rest, including the teacher pay raise, were partisan pokes that the Governor item-vetoed with relish. Angry words and partisan diatribes filled Capitol Square.

The brutal shredding of the Nevers legislative agenda produced an avalanche of public and private criticism, much of it directed at our young staff. Geniuses as freshmen, we now were derided as sophomore flops. I took the criticism personally, and one evening in early spring I dutifully proffered my resignation to the Governor.

"Quit if you want," Nevers replied, taking the tender at face value and misreading my motives. "But if you go, go away completely and don't come back. My team is for the stouthearted, persevering types. I won't have you hanging around, demoralizing these other young people. *They* are soldiers."

PULLING ALL OF THE LEVERS

Everything seemed new when the General Assembly returned for the 2000 legislative session. The millennium had arrived two weeks earlier without the much-feared "Y2K" blackout, and GOP reinforcements recently had arrived courtesy of Virginia's evenly divided electorate. The Senate's narrow partisan division remained unchanged, but when the Governor rose to deliver his third address to a joint legislative session, five more Republican delegates gazed up and cheered lustily. It was a fully deserved response because the Democratic advantage in the House of Delegates had been trimmed to only a pair of seats—an outcome that far exceeded GOP expectations—and the chief causes were the heaps of campaign cash from the Nevers political action committee and the canny operation overseen by the Governor's political MVP. All of us had pitched in, and no one had invested more hours than the barnstorming Nevers. But Chad Braxton had been the genius behind the gains, and everyone knew it. In the few places where it had made sense to make the contest a referendum on Nevers, Chad's missives (mailed, emailed, and phoned) had done the trick. But most of the pick-ups had come from recruiting the right candidates and exploiting local issues, a strategy that required mastery of nuance about scores of candidates, communities, and controversies. With the Democrats in charge of one branch and a Republican at the helm of the other, both sides had been well funded. The difference had been the campaign wizardry, which meant it had been Chad. The feat was all the more impressive because the political mastermind was also the commerce secretary, and either job alone was sufficient to occupy someone more than full-time.

We followed the campaign success with what surely would be regarded—if people were able to track such things—as one of the best legislative operations that Virginia's centuries-old assembly ever had witnessed. By now, we had made most of the mistakes needed to complete our education, and we knew what we were doing in every respect: the grassroots operation; the media plays; the partisan and cross-party appeals; the lobbying and hearings; the horse-trading on bills, budget items, and whatever else we could bestow; how to use the Governor's prestige and persuasion for maximum effect inside Capitol Square and out on the hustings; how to massage the Speaker into a friendly position; how to isolate Senate Morris and inoculate against Senator Meade; whom to cajole, whom to threaten, and whom to ignore; what voice had the ear of which legislator; which members you could buy and which would stay bought (figuratively speaking, of course); and all of the other tools and tricks of the lawmaking trade.

Like the proverbial sausage-making, it was not a pretty sight. But it worked.

Everyone had learned along the way, but probably no one had learned more than I. And the main thing I had learned was how to rise above my naive idealism, kind heart, and genial nature to fight like hell using every legal lever within my reach. Instead of worrying about the collateral damage, I focused entirely on what it would take to win. I drew the line where the Governor and the Speaker both had drawn it—I never engaged in, encouraged, or, for that matter, encountered a corrupt bargain—but that left a very broad field in which to operate. If there was a member who feared or could be made to fear something remotely plausible from our administration, I used the threat to full advantage. If there was someone who needed help with something, I made sure we delivered it. No matter was too trite or insignificant—not a pothole, not a photo or proclamation, not even a personally inscribed copy of Sally Nevers' recipe book—while, at the other extreme, even the tallest orders brought serious attempts at accommodation. There are improved bridges and interchanges and new school wings and upgraded municipal sewage systems and renovated labs and all manner of other useful things scattered around the Commonwealth today as a result of budget-related deals that helped get our education plan passed.

As the Governor's primary messenger, I expressed our position in urgent, adamant, even apocalyptic terms, demanding loyalty from everyone whom Nevers and his extended regime had ever helped on anything. "There is," I said repeatedly, "no tomorrow on this issue. We win or lose on education in this session. And Governor Nevers is counting on you to help him win."

A case in point was my dealing with the Republican legislators, several of whom had a well-established pattern of asking us for help whenever it suited and then slinking away on the tough votes. Once I was confident the Governor would back me up, I went to the Senate and House Republican caucuses and declared that, since Ned Nevers had staked his governorship on the passage of his education package, there would be no free passes this time—no tolerance or forgiveness for those who strayed from the partisan fold.

"This time it is like voting to override a veto. Breaking ranks on this one is the unpardonable sin," I declared at a joint meeting of the Republican members who comprised each chamber's partisan minority. "We have not come this far to fall short now. You guys would not have your new committee seats or your increased numbers and leverage without Ned Nevers' help, and now he needs your support. I am not threatening anything—each of you will make your own decision. I am just giving fair notice, and this comes from the Governor himself, that those who do not stand with us on this package, and I mean the entire package, will be *dead to us* politically and every other way we can think of."

"Who turned you into such a hard-assed SOB?" asked crotchety old Delegate Abe Harrell of Buchanan, one of the more unpredictable and unreliable of the bunch.

"*You did*, Delegate," I replied reflexively, before adding, to an avalanche of guffaws, "and since you did such a good job, I figure I ought to make the most of it."

The school choice controversy reached a fever pitch that session, and, since we held nothing back, the cost in personal as well as political terms was enormous. Virginia's Capitol had witnessed a lot of fights, but few of those could have been more acrimonious or suspenseful. The outcome on several of the key bills was in doubt right until the end, but we prevailed by a vote here and two votes there, somehow squeezing out wins on all the major points. There were compromises, of course ... a *lot* of them. But none represented a substantive surrender on an issue we thought mattered. We even mustered the votes to send the constitutional amendment on vouchers to the voters—a proposal they went on to approve by a lopsided margin in the referendum a year and a half later.

The final act in the drama came just before the key action in the Senate. We knew we were within a handful of votes at that point, and we thought we had them—but there were no guarantees. Into that eleventh hour of opportunity stepped, to our great surprise, our most formidable foe.

"Look, maybe you'll get the votes to pass this thing; maybe you won't. But even if you get the votes, you don't want it to be a lily-white bill," Senator Dorothy Meade said during a huddle she initiated in the Governor's corner office. "You need it to pass with some African-American votes, and that means you need to do business with me."

She paused, letting the stunning news register that she was here to negotiate—or something like that.

"I am not going to beat around the bush," she said. "Here's my price: I want double the amount of new money for smaller class size in the at-risk schools. I want $350 million in bond money for school rehab in distressed jurisdictions. I want a sum-sufficient appropriation for bus transportation for kids exercising inter-district transfer options—no limits; the state pays whatever it takes based on the number of students opting in. And I want a bipartisan oversight commission in which teachers designated by the state education association have at least one third of the membership. I can't deliver more than my vote and maybe a couple of others, but that will make all the difference in how this bitter pill goes down with the broader community. So you give me what I need, and I will vote for your precious package."

Nevers leaned backed, suppressed a smile, and began to hem and haw about several of the particulars, as if to negotiate. Meade cut him off immediately.

"You must have misunderstood me, Governor. I'm not here to negotiate. You can ask your chief of staff about that—negotiating is not my thing. I'm sure you know that I get zero out of this. Politically, the best thing for me to do is holler and kick up a fuss, call you everything but a gentleman, and if I lose, I'll have gone down fighting. That is what my base wants me to do, and they will love me for doing it. So if you want to bounce me out of here without a deal, I will land right in that briar patch and say, 'Thank you for doing me a fine favor.' No, I'm not here to bargain. I am here trying to make some good out of this sorry situation. I have something you need, and I figure you are smart enough to realize you need it. And you have something I could use to make things just a little better for folks who don't have much. So you decide—take whatever time you need. But from what I understand, these outbreaks of statesmanship are like 24-hour viruses; they run their course and then you come to your senses...."

"I'd say you have full command of your senses," Nevers cut in. "And I don't need 24 hours to think about it. You've got a deal."

Moments later, with the matter settled and Meade gone, the Governor and I sat back to take in the surprising twist.

"I would have bet the farm," I said as soon as the door closed, "that Dorothy Meade would play to her base to the very end. She's absolutely the last person I expected to cut a deal."

"I can't say I saw it coming, either," conceded the happy dealmaker-in-chief. "But I always knew she had an independent streak and wondered when it would make an appearance. She waited until the last minute and then used her leverage for maximum effect. It was a strong play."

"I guess so. I just assumed she'd go down with guns blazing as a matter of principle."

"I bet the principle thing actually cut the opposite way for her," ventured Nevers. "She had a chance to make the package better, and she took it. These hardliners in both parties who go down with guns blazing always talk a good game about principles—as in, 'I'm doing the stalwart, stand-up thing by holding the line, and you're a weak-kneed low-life who is violating your principles by caving.' But the reality is just the opposite. That uncompromising guy puts himself on the sidelines during the negotiations, passing up the chance to make the bill better from the standpoint of his principles. I'm sure sometimes there's a high-minded purpose, but for a lot of these yahoos the only higher purpose is to keep the base happy and make sure they don't get challenged in the primary. Where I come from, that's not called 'standing tall'—it's called 'selling out.'"

"Well, obviously I agree with you," I sighed. "I spend three quarters of my time trying to reason with members who are great at fighting but clueless when it comes to governing. But before you nominate Senator Meade for sainthood, let's keep in mind that she and her theatrics have generated mountains of misinformation and prejudice on this choice issue for the last three years."

"No question about that," the Governor replied. "But it is also true that she could not have come in here tonight and cut a deal if she had not spent years kicking our butts from one end of this Capitol to the other. No one in her base can ever question *her* commitment to their cause."

"You're right about that," I conceded reluctantly. "She's Nixon going to China."

"No, no, wrong analogy—wrong president!" Nevers corrected. "This is like Reagan at the Brandenburg Gate: 'Senator Meade, tear down this wall!' She folded like Gorbachev, and we just liberated a lot of young people."

When the victory came shortly thereafter, Nevers appeared every bit the conquering hero. But despite the success and all the accolades, he steadfastly refused to gloat—with one private exception. When the bipartisan delegation of legislative leaders came to the Governor's office at the end of the 2000 session to deliver the ceremonial message that the General Assembly had concluded its business and was prepared to adjourn *sine die*, the satisfied Governor greeted the solons warmly and thanked them for finally approving his school choice initiative. Then, unable to restrain his inner Churchill, he leaned in close to the hyper-partisan Howard Morris, the kingpin who had promised to wring our school choice plan's neck upon arrival. "*Some* chicken...," he whispered into the bemused Senator's ear, "*some* neck."

Once the blood cooled following this fight of fights, it was possible to appreciate more fully the value of the process itself, including the conflict. The multi-year legislative push had provided an object lesson on the crucial and often complex ways that politics and governance, ambition and service, intertwine. For the first time I had experienced how it all works on the inside—the intriguing interplay of personalities and policy, politicians and lawmakers, lobbyists and legislators. I had listened to Speaker's Percival's maxims then seen them in practice: politicians trading votes and bartering support based on their wants and needs and the give-and-take of the political process. It is popular these days to decry such influences, as if the ideal were some pristine process in which philosopher-kings endowed with super-human judgment work their will with absolute detachment and beneficence. But nothing could be farther from reality, especially in a part-time "citizen legislature," and the Madison in me found this quite refreshing. "Ambition must be made to counteract ambition...," Madison observed in *The Federalist No. 51*. "This policy of supplying by opposite and rival interests, the defect of better motives, might be traced through the whole system of human affairs, private as well as public."

The beneficial collision of interests occurs in legislative corridors just as it does in markets, in courtrooms, in political "debates" like Mitch's and Dorothy's, and in myriad other consequential settings. The proverbial truth is that, "as iron sharpens iron, so does one person sharpen another." Thus, by design or default, we employ adversarial arrangements in a wide range of human interactions, from the negotiation of deals and adjudication of disputes to the two-party political system that has grown organically in our country and the dynamic factions and situational alignments that spring up in the legislative process. We employ these devices in large measure because the deciders—judges, jurors, legislators, voters, or whoever—possess neither the relevant knowledge nor the time and means to obtain it on their own, and so they depend on others to supply the information and make the case. We regulate the engagement through rules, restrictions, and disclosure obligations so that it is fundamentally fair to the participants and to those they represent or assist.

Understanding this context is a prerequisite for legislative success. I only casually observed in Washington, but came to fully appreciate in Richmond, how thoroughly lawmakers depend upon interested advocates. If you ask them, nearly all will readily acknowledge that fact, and they likely will add that the best lobbyists, whether dispatched by the executive branch or by some other interested party, are those who not only make the case knowledgeably for their own side but also air the countervailing considerations. It is in this practice of full disclosure alongside vigorous advocacy that trust is built. So that is what we tried to do in the Nevers administration, and we got better at it as we went along.

To say that this complicated and contentious arrangement is generally beneficial is not to say that it is efficient, pleasant, satisfying to behold, or rewarding to experience. Jefferson designed the Capitol to classical specifications, but it was Madison who appreciated the architecture of human nature. He knew that the ordinary course of human events would inevitably give rise to faction, and he sought to align various institutional powers with the contending interests so as to check the excessive accumulation of power and its tendency toward overreach. This arrangement set up an inherently inefficient and untidy process—the price paid for restraint. Madison understood it could result in productive governance only if the participants shared an overarching vision rooted in a commitment to honest public service and republican principles. "If there be not [virtue]," he declared at the Virginia ratifying convention, "[n]o theoretical checks—no form of government can render us secure."

In Virginia, this shared sense of honorable obligation is strong, and breaches of decorum and ethical standards are relatively rare. It is possible to get good and important things done. Yet, legislative machinations here are no less tortured, cutthroat, petty, or painful. Once re-situated on an executive perch, even an experienced legislative hand like Governor Nevers found the process of dealing with a 140-person General Assembly mind-blowingly frustrating. On one occasion I was complaining about the slow pace of progress on our bills, and I worried aloud that we were going to suffer "death by a thousand pricks."

"One-forty," Nevers deadpanned. "The maximum number is 140."

I laughed and then added that he should know, having been one himself for most of his political career.

The frustrations we experienced during Nevers' first term had been acute, at one point even prompting me to offer my resignation. But despite our stunning failure in the 1999 session and the necessity of an intervening election before we finally succeeded on our signature initiative, most of the adversity never seemed to register with the Virginia electorate or observers beyond the Commonwealth's borders. To the outside world, Governor Ned Nevers always appeared clearly in charge and rather effortlessly successful. Virginians have a habit of liking their governors—a residue, probably, of the one-term limit that endured for more than a century and ensured that each executive left office before wearing out his welcome. Opinion surveys routinely showed that Virginians liked Governor Nevers even more than most of his popular predecessors.

One reason for Nevers' success was his almost innate understanding of "political capital" as an executive resource. Governors fail by trying to do too much or too little, by asserting themselves too early or too late, by being too heavy handed or too light. Some are so self-certain as to be tone-deaf, oddly oblivious to the sucking sound that signals the siphoning of executive clout through precipitous or excessive pursuits. At the other extreme, some want so desperately to be loved that caution overwhelms initiative, and their capital is wasted in the manner of the biblical talents—by being buried rather than advantageously invested—and ultimately is forfeited. Some simply fail to grasp the truth that success breeds success and defeat breeds defeat, so the choice of which battles to fight is pivotal. Some governors, of course, are victims or beneficiaries of circumstance, but most make the beds they lie in, and there is no way, really, to teach how to make this particular kind of bed. It is a knack you get by observing intently, reading newspapers and history books, sometimes by trying and erring, and, most of all, by keeping your pride and passion in check so that your basic decency and good common sense have room to operate. It is not all experience, either. There are some gifted young gubernatorial prodigies, and there are some ineffectual dons who have been at it a long time. But, generally, as in Governor Nevers' case, executive success comes when you have a capacity—native to a degree, but honed over time—for reading other people, when life's journey has taught you a bit of humility, and when you are certain enough about what you want to accomplish that you can focus all your faculties and powers on producing those results.

Nevers' big advantage was that his ego was in check, thanks mainly to the voters who showed him the exit in 1994. Absent some hard knocks, it takes an unusually perceptive and circumspect personality in the governor's chair not to fall victim to the position's propensity to aggrandize. It does not help that governors have all the trappings of executive power—a mansion, a limo, body-guards, audiences that automatically rise whenever they begin and conclude their remarks, and so on. Staff members, especially the younger ones who always find their way into significant posts, breathe the rarified air, too, with two principal effects. One is they tend to give the governor such deference that they may shrink from pushing back adequately when he is off-base. The other is they tend to assume that, as His Excellency's designated emissaries, they are endowed with special gravitas and their requests to legislators, staffers, agency heads, etc., are imbued with irresistible force. This typically is foolishness because governors and their apparatchiks come and go but the power structure in the legislature and executive branch agencies is in place for the long haul. Once you realize this—and Nevers and I heard it loud and clear from various predecessors whom we consulted during the transition—then you start looking for the real levers of gubernatorial influence and how to operate them. They inhere in the "bully pulpit," as TR called it, in the full panoply of constitutional and statutory prerogatives, and also—perhaps mainly—in the soft exercise of one-on-one persuasion aided by the perks and accoutrements, the trappings of power, friendships, and favors. Finally, there is, at least in Virginia, the mantle of history. Unless the governor dissipates the resource by haughtiness and overreach at one extreme, or by timidity and fecklessness at the other, it is not easy to say "no" to the successor of Henry and Jefferson.

Principled Politics?

Another major asset that Ned Nevers possessed by the time he became governor was a certain balance in perspective. At earlier points in his career, I had seen him fall on his sword over some perceived matter of principle while, at other times, he had indifferently cast principle aside for expedience. Recollections of failings in both categories came immediately to mind when Nevers asked me, shortly after the education reform victory, to write a speech for him to deliver at a leadership conference at his alma mater, the Virginia Military Institute. The assigned topic was "Principled Public Service." The exercise would illumine for me the insight and judgment that Ned Nevers had gained over the course of an up-and-down career in public service, and it would go a long way in honing my own view of the way the political world should work.

My draft of the speech began, as any Virginian's on the subject rightly would, by invoking Mason's Declaration of Rights for the proposition that "no free government, nor the blessings of liberty, can be preserved to any people, but by … frequent recurrence to fundamental principles…." The Framers left this reminder, my draft asserted, because they understood that neutral principles, if revered by the people sufficiently to withstand transitory temptations, could help provide a durable bulwark against governmental overreach. They understood that the greatest threat to ordered liberty would always be well-intended passion—people so eager to accomplish some indubitable good that they would knock down all the obstacles, including those erected to guard liberty. If the Framers' era had featured alternating current, they might have analogized the role of principles to that of a circuit-breaker, interrupting, or at least impeding, the flow of power for laudable ends through destructive and self-defeating (i.e., *unprincipled*) means. The draft went on to explain that there are moral principles rooted in something beyond this life, and there are practical propositions that have been elevated to the level of principle because of what living has taught us over time. Both types of principles play the same role that a healthy discipline plays in a virtuous life—the role of restraint in service to a larger purpose.

Next, my draft made the unremarkable observation that, since people are not born with political principles and do not come by them naturally, education and practice are essential. Indeed, this form of "virtue," as the Framers understood it, arises only when people are taught the essential ideas, habitually identify their own interests with them, and perceive a personal stake in preserving the republic for their own good and that of their neighbors. The ideas and habits to be cultivated, of course, are the ways of sensible citizenship—civic values, including political participation, community engagement, mutual respect and civility, and honest public service—as well as the core tenets of our national creed: freedom of conscience, speech, expression, and the entire constellation of civil liberties; equal justice under law and equal opportunity; property rights and free enterprise; limited government accountable to the people through representative processes and institutions; the rule of law; judicial independence and integrity in interpreting the law; the checks and balances supplied by federalism, separation of powers, and other salutary doctrines; service to the nation, peace through strength, collective defense with powers that share our values; and so on.

Especially given the centrifugal force applied today by mass democracy, advanced technology, and contemporary culture, a concerted effort was needed, my draft argued, to cultivate awareness and adherence to these foundational principles of American freedom among young people. Indeed, the digital age poses a particular danger since its depersonalizing tendency creates a thirst for meaningful relationships that, if not satisfied through the constructive community of free people, may seek relief instead from belonging's false prophets—utopian socialists, bigoted nativists, beguiling autocrats, and other sirens who supply connectedness by demonizing those outside the group as "the other." Regrettably, this pressing need to renew our American community around shared republican principles had not generated much educational ardor among those who benefit most from the liberal democratic order, I noted. To the contrary, much of the learned elite in the academy and media seemed to regard such topics as old-fashioned if not downright chauvinistic. Instruction on civics, history, and social studies thus had gone out of fashion, and it had become increasingly hard to find young people who really understood much about the American system of government. It had become rarer still to find young Americans who saw themselves in the larger narrative of our national striving for "a more perfect union."

These points, though a bit provocative, were definitely the right place to start a speech on principled public service, and Nevers made few changes when he looked at my first draft. But, as he and I worked on that speech together, a more nuanced perspective emerged. It centered on the notion that, despite their obvious merit, principles are volatile, perilous products.

Dr. Nehemiah Adams' memorable lecture back during my college years had alerted me to one of the greatest sources of that peril: the danger of misappropriation. In showing that the idea of "states' rights" could as easily have wound up on the right side of history and morality—that it could as easily have been aligned with, rather than against, the higher principle of equal justice under law—Dr. Adams had demonstrated how a salutary tenet can be pressed into service for wholesome or unwholesome ends. It can be so pressed by people with the best of intentions or the worst of intentions. Even when the right outcome at length obtains, the result of the misappropriation can be to sully, weaken, erode, or even eviscerate the principle through a negative association in the public mind. This was, for me, a very sobering thought, because if it could happen with something as intrinsic to the Framers' design as federalism, then it could happen with anything. So we made that point in the speech.

Next Nevers suggested that we address another danger that principles pose—the peril of absolutism. I was well attuned to this point thanks to my longtime fascination with Madison. Compromise is an essential element of the American constitutional scheme. In contrast to the parliamentary approach and to other systems that periodically permit even greater concentrations of power in a single individual, party, or faction, Madison's scheme of diffused and checked power almost always propelled the national government toward a brokered result. And while there is obvious danger in the surrender of principle to expedience, there is at least equal danger in the elevation of mere prejudice or preference to the status of principle. Once gaining that exalted status, ordinary matters of policy and opinion—"disputable matters," as the apostle Paul described them in his missive to the faithful in Rome—would become impervious to compromise. By elevating matters of taste to tenet, whether selfishly or just shortsightedly, politicians would make productive self-governance elusive and, in the process, cheapen the very idea of principled behavior. So we made that point in the speech, too.

The final point came entirely from the Governor, and I now regard it as one of the most important lessons he ever taught me. Even the most salutary moral or practical principle—patriotism and maternal love were the evocative examples C. S. Lewis used—can become an idol, a consuming ultimate objective that supersedes and obscures our higher calling. Indeed, the temptation is greatest because the values in question are so inherently good. "The false religion of lust," Lewis noted by way of illustration in *The Great Divorce*, "is baser than the false religion of mother-love or patriotism ... but lust is less likely to be made into a religion." During Nevers' desperate, searching, and ultimately redemptive time back in Nottoway after his Senate defeat, he had dwelled at length on what was truly important in his life. The answer that came was faith in God, and close behind that were his love for his wife and family, his personal integrity, and the imperative of practicing the Golden Rule in his dealings with others. Individual matters of state or church, politics, policy, or even religion, as important as they were—as fertile a ground for principles and as central a position as they occupied—were still only means to an end. And no person, purpose, or even principle could be allowed to assume God-like importance without devastating consequence.

That was the way Ned Nevers concluded the speech at VMI, and it was the way he tried to govern. He kept his eye on the ball, made sure his ego stayed in check, found practical ways to advance his principles, and treated the job like a sacred trust granted to him by the people. Nevers had come a long and winding way, but now he knew himself, had a clear mission, and was able to draw the line.

Though he was a wily veteran and had become an insightful, earnest man, there was great irony in Ned Nevers' governing success in Richmond. He had set his sights early on the nation's capital and had been generally successful there for most of the 18 years. He seemed to be at the pinnacle of his power during the 17th, yet the disastrous 18th had forced the most fundamental kind of reappraisal, redirected his efforts, and propelled him into a new and unfamiliar arena. It was here, at the *state* level, that Nevers finally had discovered his purpose and found his voice. During most of his time in Washington, the back-to-back Republican administrations had been working to devolve power to the states, seeking to reinvigorate the founders' vision of federalism and giving state and local governments broad new latitude to diagnose problems and craft solutions at a level closer to the people. Senator Nevers had generally supported those efforts but was hardly a true-believer; indeed, he was a moderate who often had bristled at the controversies that the persistent conservative reformers had generated. Yet, now he was the beneficiary of those principled labors. That salutary trend had converged with the development of ambitious state-level policy goals, a cooperative political environment, and, perhaps most important, the refinement of his own character. A man and a moment met, and great good seemed to result.

Governor Nevers' accomplished administration was the product of these converging forces, and time would tell the value of his reforms for the Commonwealth's citizens. But it was already apparent that his tenure would be the catalyst for a new type of activism in state capitals. As Nevers' reform-oriented administration increasingly earned national accolades, the previous managerial model—go-along-to-get-along governorships typical of times when all the serious business was done in Washington—fell into disfavor. Nevers also put his own distinctive mark on the state capital iteration of the Reagan "revolution." While other Republicans talked of markets and capitalism as if they were ends in themselves, Nevers talked about them as indispensable means to the larger and nobler end of a free, just, and productive society. While other figures waxed abstractly about individualism and liberty, Virginia's governor talked about what free people could accomplish by working together in their neighborhoods and communities. The Virginia that Nevers envisioned was the local version of Reagan's "shining city on a hill," a true *commonwealth* in which the creative and compassionate capacities of free people were unfettered, a wholesome society where opportunity and service went hand in hand.

To make sure everyone got the message, Nevers was constantly stepping outside his official role to set a positive example of hands-on community engagement. He practiced what he preached. One day he was stacking cans at the food bank; on another he was painting the home of an elderly shut-in; on yet another he was showing some middle school boys from the city how to cast and catch a fish. The press came sometimes, especially early in Nevers' term, but none were mere photo-ops. Whatever he did, and it was hundreds of things, the Governor gave the person and project his complete attention and put himself into the task fully. Whenever possible, Nevers' scheduler made sure the activities included a meal, not because the Governor had a big appetite (though he did), but because Nevers wanted to relate to people where they were, and he knew the best way to connect and show respect was to pull up a chair and commune over food.

"You don't make people feel accepted and valued by flying in with a hammer or a check like, 'Here I come to save the day!' You do it by sitting down, asking how you can help, listening, and letting them know you are honored to eat with them," he said more than once to skeptical staffers.

Of course, not every setting or situation was conducive to such an encounter. Nevers' preference for partaking created some unpredictable scenes that unnerved the staff, and these situations seemed to amuse the Governor no end. The occasional anxious moments were a small price for us to pay because we were among the biggest beneficiaries of his example. He never had to tell his staff to follow suit; it happened naturally. And so we became tutors and mentors, legal-aid lawyers and business advisors, handymen and handywomen, camp counselors, hospital candy-stripers, and much more. We developed a heart for service and made permanent friends. A lot of folks benefited from our good efforts, but no one gained more than we did ourselves.

ILL WIND

As the 2001 elections approached, I viewed our remarkable first-term successes with something approaching euphoria. For most of my life, I had doubted that anything positive really could come from the cynical game-playing that seemed to dominate contemporary politics. But now, having given three, going on four, of the most intense years of my life to the pursuit, I had become a confident believer in the possibility of politically impelled progress. The pendulum for me had swung widely—as widely as one can imagine— and it left me with a skewed perspective. Of course, that was not apparent at the time. Kipling said the mark of a man was the ability to "meet triumph and disaster, and treat those two imposters just the same." I had absolutely no idea what he meant.

There was, however, a flashing warning sign during this time, if we could have slowed down long enough to notice it. It came to the Governor's office one day in March 2000—right on the heels of our big legislative victory on the school choice package—in the person of State Senator Bell. Bart no doubt regarded himself as one of the Governor's valued allies; at least, that is how he desperately wanted to be perceived as our success became more and more evident. In truth, however, he had been virtually irrelevant. Preacher once asked Chad, Abby, and me if we could think of a single thing Bart had done that had made a difference in passing any of our major legislation, and we literally could not think of one. Bart asked for things a lot, but it was all get and no give.

When the Governor and I sat down with Bart on that blustery March day, neither Nevers nor I had any idea what was on his mind. We assumed he wanted some additional favor. As he spoke, I must have looked totally stunned, because that is how the Governor looked despite having spent a whole career honing the ability to conceal his reactions.

"I am going to run for lieutenant governor next year, and I would like your support," Bart said to the Governor forthrightly. "I have it on good authority that Lieutenant Governor Townsend will not be seeking reelection—or, if she is so unwise as to run, she will lose. I am getting in early and staking a claim to the nomination."

Ann Townsend was no political powerhouse, by any means. She had gained the nomination for the second spot on the 1997 Nevers ticket with barely a third of the primary vote, the beneficiary of an unusually crowded and remarkably unimpressive GOP field. She then had squeaked by in the general election by a few thousand votes, upsetting her far more accomplished Democratic opponent almost entirely because of Nevers' lopsided win and lengthy coattails. But if she was not a compelling political figure, she at least had carried out her meager duties—limited largely to presiding over the Senate—with competence and dignity. As Nevers' nominal number-two, she continued to benefit from the Governor's popularity. No one, until this unexpected conversation with Bart Bell, had talked seriously of replacing her on the Republican ticket when the three statewide offices came open again in 2001.

"This comes as a surprise, Bart," Nevers said evenly after a moment's reflection. "I don't question your political savvy, but what exactly leads you to believe that Ann won't be running?"

"Let's just say that she was not well vetted by her previous opponents. No one, it seems, took the prospect of her election seriously. But, as you know, I have some skill at that sort of inquiry, and my friends and I have gained access to some very disturbing personal information...."

Not knowing what Bart was up to, I was not about to let this unguided missile of a conversation go any further in the Governor's presence. "Okay, that's enough," I interjected immediately. "I'm sure whatever 'information' you have is very interesting, Bart, but I don't think we need to delve into it here."

"Cool your jets, Danny," Bart rejoined derisively. "I know what's appropriate and what's not. I used to have your job, remember? Let's just say that the federal government tends to frown on it when people have income they don't report. And the working stiffs who actually pay their taxes don't like that sort of thing, either."

I rose out of my seat. "Bart, I *said*...."

"Thank you, Bart," the Governor interrupted, averting the impending faceoff between his present and former chiefs. "I will take your request under advisement, but at this point, I think it is very unlikely that I will be coming out against Ann anytime soon—even for a friend as old and trusted as you are. That's not the way I do things."

I escorted Bart out of the Governor's office the back way, through my office. Once in my quarters, I closed the door. "Bart, if you ever pull a stunt like that again, I swear I'll make sure you never set foot in that office," I said, managing to control my anger with effort.

"Steady there, choirboy," Bart answered smugly. "I merely wanted to give you and His Excellency the courtesy of hearing about it from me first. You wouldn't have been happy if you had read about my candidacy in the papers, now would you? That's not 'the way I do things'—especially with 'friends as old and trusted' as you and the Governor."

With that, he left, and I sat down. The notion of Bart Bell being a heartbeat away from the governorship registered with me for the first time, and it was immediately disconcerting.

Apparently it registered with the Governor, too. He had to leave immediately for another appointment, but I caught up with him over in the mansion that evening. He greeted me in the library, book in hand. Of course, it was another apt passage from *All the King's Men*, this one about Tiny Duffy, the Boss's lieutenant governor.

"The beauty about Tiny," read Nevers, quoting Governor Willie Stark, "is that nobody can trust him and you know it. You get somebody somebody can trust maybe, and you got to sit up nights worrying whether you are the somebody. You get Tiny, and you can get a night's sleep."

We laughed heartily at the coincidence—life imitating art—and then put the matter aside. We were too busy with the people's business to waste energy on Bart and his schemes.

CHAPTER SIX

GRACE

On September 11, 2001, just two months before Governor Nevers' re-election, war came to America's shores. For a time it submerged lesser differences and focused attention anew on the recurring threat posed by evil ideologies that seek to impose their will by lethal means.

In the 20th century a parade of bloodthirsty despots had marched across the global landscape, massacring multitudes, consigning hundreds of millions to lives of servile terror, and wreaking havoc on liberties, economies, and psyches in the rest of the world. Without a united America, forged in the crucible of its own civil struggle during the preceding century, the whole of humanity might well have succumbed to Nazi or Soviet oppression.

Barely a year into another century, a different radical ideology, this one masquerading in religious garb, had emerged to hoist the ugly standard. In a shockingly short span on a brilliantly sunny day it had brought more darkness and death to American soil than all the others despots combined. Not since the bloody battle of Antietam, fought by Americans against Americans on the 75th anniversary of their Constitution, had so many perished here on a single violent day.

The stunning events of that September brought the political season in Virginia to a screeching halt. Continuity of leadership suddenly became the priority, and this reinforced the Virginia electorate's already evident intention to return to office both the gubernatorial incumbent and sitting attorney general. Nevers became the first Virginia governor since the advent of popular election in 1851 to win two consecutive terms, and he did so with an electoral margin of nearly 18 percentage points—a modern high. His Republican running mate, Attorney General Harry "Bud" Cheasley, likewise won soundly.

The newcomer in the mix, the one with the lean and hungry look, was the state senator from western Fairfax. His seemingly long-shot bid for the GOP nomination for lieutenant governor had been rewarded by the incumbent's unexpected and still-unexplained retirement announcement, which occurred barely three months before the Republican state convention in Norfolk. By then, it was too late for anyone to mount an effective challenge to Bart, who already had a political operation in place and was assumed by many to have the backing (never voiced) of his erstwhile patron, Governor Nevers. Once on the Nevers ticket, he coasted to a comfortable win with his running mates in November.

The Governor was keeping his old job, but he was suddenly occupied with a whole new set of issues. As a former U.S. senator, acknowledged expert on foreign affairs and defense, and governor of a state that was hit by the terrorists, Nevers was a logical person for the national media to seek out for comment in the aftermath of 9/11. With his landslide reelection two months later, speculation about a possible presidential bid in 2004 naturally ensued. Its ferocity surprised all of us and, to be honest, turned our heads a bit. From then on, the Senator-turned-Governor was constantly in demand, appearing frequently on the national television talk shows and receiving a veritable blizzard of speaking invitations from political, business, and foreign affairs organizations around the country.

It would have been tempting for Nevers to grab the national political baton and run with it. But the Virginia economy had been hammered by the extended closure of the Dulles and Reagan airports, sudden deployments from Hampton Roads, and other 9/11 after-shocks. These factors combined with an already weakening national economy to produce a significant budget shortfall in the Commonwealth. New and pressing homeland security issues also shot to the top of the agenda for state chief executives, and this was especially true for the executive whose state bordered the national capital and was home to the Pentagon and other key federal installations. So the work was heavy in Richmond, and gubernatorial forays out of state had to be few and far between—at least for now.

One exception was the Governor's address to the World Security Congress in Chicago shortly after his second inauguration in January 2002. The reelection campaign and work on the state's next biennial budget had proceeded in earnest and in parallel from Labor Day to Election Day, making for an exhausting autumn. Then, as soon as we put the finishing touches on our budget proposals, which the Governor unveiled in mid-December, we turned to the preparation of three major speeches: the "WSC" address on the war, the inaugural address, and the annual "State of the Commonwealth" message to the joint session of the General Assembly. All three high-profile speeches were to be delivered within a week of each other, requiring simultaneous drafting and adding an extra layer of intense activity to the holiday-ruining workload that always precedes the legislature's mid-January return to Richmond. After receiving the Governor's broad direction, I took the laboring oar in preparing the first drafts of the inaugural and legislative speeches. Nevers personally drafted his major speech on the war, relying mainly on input from Mitch and a few trusted former colleagues in Washington.

In domestic matters, Nevers had long struck a judicious, center-right pose: invariably pro-business; vocal in support of free markets; socially conservative but in an understated, non-threatening way; and, especially during his time as governor, a practical problem-solver with a knack for tackling complicated issues like education reform and forging common ground among disparate interests. But when it came to national defense and foreign policy, issues on which Nevers long had been passionate, he had no interest whatsoever in cultivating such a "moderate" image. The World War II and Cold War defense build-ups had turned Virginia into one of America's foremost military bastions, with more federal defense spending in the Old Dominion than any state other than California. Upon his arrival in the Senate, Nevers had gained a prized appointment to the Armed Services Committee and had begun earning a creditable reputation as a defense hawk and foreign affairs expert. His intervening tenure as a governor had diverted his focus but not diminished those credentials, so the notables who gathered for the World Security Congress in Chicago, plus the attentive political establishment in Washington, greeted his presentation in the windy city as a significant policy pronouncement.

As Nevers framed it, America's new war was but the latest manifestation of a classic struggle between the forces of freedom and tyranny, light and darkness, good and evil. The aftermath of 9/11 was thus a decisive time of choosing. Either America and its democratic allies would engage the forces of violent Islamic radicalism systematically around the globe, offering an unambiguous articulation of American ideals and stamping out the violent movement with overwhelming military and intellectual force, or our nation's leaders would huff and puff, maneuver and temporize, back and fill with diplomatic delays and empty threats, conveying weakness and irresolution and ultimately encouraging more attacks. The jihadists, Nevers declared flatly, wanted nothing less than the overthrow of Western institutions and values by violence and intimidation, and they would not stop until they had successfully detonated a nuclear weapon on American soil. That day, he warned apocalyptically, will be the "new 9/11—the day that will truly live in infamy and plunge the world into a darkness it has never known."

While stoutly supporting the President's campaign to root out Al Qaeda in Afghanistan, Nevers fretted that the Democratic chief executive was underestimating the magnitude of the global threat and missing an opportunity to rally the American people for the broader battle that loomed. This was no "war on terror," Nevers insisted. The foe was radical Islam, the violent perversion of a great and noble faith tradition. "Let us define the enemy not by the tactic of terror but by the twisted ideas and evil people who constitute it," he declared.

> Despite their covert and cowardly ways, they are not an anonymous foe. They are real people, committed to a real ideology, with real resources, real weapons, and real state sponsors, and with a mission for which they are quite ready, even eager, to become martyrs. Let us call them who and what they are, and let us meet them head-on with the full might of the American nation and the righteous resolve of the American people. Let us require that every nation choose whether to stand with us or with our enemy, and let us then attach clear and dire consequences to that choice. Let us make the world safe for peace-loving people everywhere by denying the bloodthirsty radicals safe haven anywhere.

The powerful speech generated news coverage across the country and seemed to signal the first crack in post-9/11 solidarity on war aims. The hawkish

Virginian, commentators suggested, was urging a significant widening of the conflict. He was also, according to the chattering class, positioning for a presidential run.

While Nevers was calling for a global campaign against violent Islamic radicalism and the rest of us were focused parochially on the new legislative session, Bart Bell was without any major obligations. As lieutenant governor, his chief duty was to serve as the State Senate's presiding officer, a role for which Bart required little schooling since he had served in the chamber and knew its rules. Though the position straddled the executive and legislative branches and gave statehouse denizens cause to refer to him rather grandly as "Mr. President" (as in, President of the Senate) and as "Governor" (the "Lieutenant" qualifier was dropped in salutations), the job carried little real power. His duties were almost entirely ceremonial, and, except for casting an occasional tie-breaking vote, his biggest decisions involved choosing among speech invitations, social functions, and meeting requests. No longer an actual "member" of the Senate, he was relieved of the duty to patron legislation and attend lengthy committee sessions. Rather than offer legislative recommendations of his own, Bart happily deferred to the popular Nevers administration on the substance.

This did not mean, however, that Bart lacked activity or focus. One subject alone dominated his thoughts and occupied his efforts: the General Assembly's unfinished work on congressional redistricting.

Required to redraw both the state's legislative and congressional district lines decennially based on new federal census data, state legislators naturally concentrated their energies first on their own districts. The line-drawing for the state legislature took on special urgency because of the Commonwealth's odd-year election cycle. From the time the census data was released in early spring, the Virginia General Assembly had only about six months in 2001 to design and enact new districts and secure the requisite Voting Rights Act "preclearance" by the U.S. Department of Justice before House of Delegates elections would be held in November. The two legislative houses crafted predictably self-serving configurations for their districts that mainly protected incumbents of both parties. After some executive-legislative contretemps, the new maps were approved in both legislative chambers, signed into law, and approved by the Justice Department. A truncated state election process followed. This all was accomplished with enormous effort and many political bruises, and in its aftermath a collective exhaustion and preoccupation with the autumn election season set in. As a result, agreement on a new plan to reapportion the state's 11 congressional districts in time for the 2002 federal elections was punted to the next General Assembly, which would convene early in the new year.

The redistricting task was the province of the "Privileges and Elections" committees of the two legislative houses, and Bart had no official role in that process as lieutenant governor. Indeed, he had not even been a member of "P&E" while serving as senator and had no expertise of value. His sudden interest in the subject of congressional redistricting thus generated immediate— and altogether justified—suspicion. Bart denied any personal interest, and indeed he had no desire to fashion a congressional seat for himself. But he was not without a plan and motive wholly rooted in personal ambition. His purpose, it later became apparent, was to craft a southeastern Virginia district that would attract the interest of Attorney General Bud Cheasley, an intensely popular figure in his native Chesapeake and a formidable political force throughout the populous Hampton Roads region.

As the two junior statewide elected officials who had emerged from the 2001 balloting, Bud and Bart immediately had been cast as rivals for the 2005 GOP gubernatorial nomination. Should such a contest occur, Cheasley would bring to it considerable assets, including a superior equitable claim by virtue of his two-term service as attorney general, a strong downstate political base, a sizeable stable of enthusiastic donors, and the ardent backing of a grassroots coalition that included a rather unusual mix of evangelicals, conservative GOP partisans, and business leaders. Absent some malign discovery like that which apparently had submarined Ann Townsend—a most improbable prospect given Cheasley's sterling reputation—Bart understood that he would need to co-opt and divert Bud rather than take him on frontally. An intermediary thus approached Cheasley at Bart's behest over the Christmas holiday with this query: If a suitable district were fashioned, would the Attorney General consider running for Congress?

A congressional seat now versus a shot at the governorship three years hence was a choice calculated to confound a thoughtful man like Bud Cheasley. The governorship was unquestionably the state's top political prize, but a seat in the United States Senate was not far behind it, and one well-worn path to the Senate was through the House of Representatives. Some politicians seem more attuned to state issues while others tend to have a national (i.e., federal) focus, and Cheasley was in the latter category. He had been an activist attorney general during his first term and relished wading into frays over contentious national issues, especially anything involving God, guns, abortion, property rights, or other items high on the social conservative wish list. He appeared to be in a reasonably strong position for the 2005 gubernatorial nomination, but three-plus years was an eternity in politics, and Bell was not without some substantial resources of his own. One of them—more apparent than real—was Bart's relationship with Governor Nevers. Bud assumed, incorrectly, that the relationship was still a relatively close one, and so the impact of a possible Nevers endorsement on the Republican nomination process had to be taken into account. Then, too, there was the chance—a bit far-fetched, to be sure, but increasingly a subject of national speculation—that Nevers might set his sights on the Presidency and, if successful, make Bell governor through succession. More than either of these, though, was the intimidating reality that must have preyed on Cheasley's mind: Bart Bell had a reputation as an anything-goes political slasher, and he would spare no effort or tactic to achieve his goal once he fixed on it. Cheasley would not run from a fight, but he did not need to go looking for one, either. So he decided to go to Washington instead.

After the two men sealed their deal, Bud Cheasley came over to share his plans and ask for my help in securing an agreeable district. I thought it odd that he asked to see me rather than the Governor, but I chalked that up to his being a class act and not wanting to put Nevers in an awkward spot if, for whatever reason, the Governor did not want to help. Bud said nothing of Bart's role in his thought process, but it was not difficult to discern the maneuvering that had occurred behind the scenes. Within weeks, Bart's otherwise inexplicable interest in the congressional line-drawing came to light and confirmed my suspicions.

"Wow, that's a surprise," I recall saying to Bud when he first laid out his congressional scenario for me. "I always figured you were a lock to be the next governor of Virginia. You would make an excellent one, too. I know the boss feels the same way."

"Thank you, Danny," Bud replied. "It's an honor to serve with you guys, and you know my enormous affection for the Governor. But I've always had an interest in federal issues and a bit of the congressional bug. If the district they create is solidly Republican, like I think it will be, the time is right for me to head north. Plus—"

Here he seemed to hesitate.

"—you've got a strong ally and good potential candidate for governor now in Bart. We didn't have that when Ann was LG, bless her heart. I think with Bart in line here, the place for me is D.C."

I was tempted to offer a vigorous rebuttal, telling him how much he was assuming in error, but I managed to bite my tongue.

In June, the Justice Department gave its approval to the new congressional district lines, and Bud Cheasley surprised no one with his formal announcement. Earlier, when legislative agreement had been reached on the new districting configuration—including an open seat in southeastern Virginia that Nevers had carried by 15 points the previous year and in which Republicans now sported a ten-point generic ballot advantage—the Attorney General had privately signaled his interest and cleared the field. As expected, he was nominated without opposition in August and elected easily in November. Mitch welcomed the arrival of reinforcements in Washington, but my reaction—and, I suspect, the Governor's—was pretty much the opposite. Bud's exit made Bart the clear heir-apparent to Nevers.

To his credit, I suppose, Governor Nevers never told me what he thought of Bart Bell at this point in their careers. My contempt for Bart had become impossible to conceal, and at the time I assumed the Governor just wanted to preserve peace among his various lieutenants and keep us all focused on the tasks at hand. Knowing what I know today, I wish Nevers had confided in me because I might have taken some action—though I am not sure what—to avert the approaching disaster. But, the truth is, I had little time to devote to the seemingly remote question of who would be the *next* governor because, as chief of staff, attending to the business of the *current* governor was all I could handle.

Then came an otherwise normal summer day, shortly after Bud Cheasley publicly confirmed his plan to redirect to Washington, when my life changed forever.

"Danny," said the Governor, "it now appears that I will have the opportunity to appoint an attorney general to complete Bud's term. Bud wants me to appoint his chief deputy, and I understand why he wants that. But the constitutional responsibility is mine, and I am going to appoint you."

It was not an offer or an invitation to discuss. It was an announcement, even a command. My normal reticence instantly kicked in, and my immediate instinct was to push back. But I was so utterly surprised by his words that for several moments I literally had nothing to say. Then, almost like an out-of-body experience, I watched myself reply, "Governor, I am honored by your confidence. I will be happy to serve the people of Virginia and you in that role. It's not something I sought or even had imagined, quite frankly. But I am ready, willing, and able to take it on."

Bart's self-serving machinations had set the events in motion, but I do not know what his real reaction was when he got the word after the November election that I would be the new AG. We clearly were not allies or pals; we struggled even to remain civil at times. On the other hand, what Bart most wanted was a caretaker attorney general who would not be a rival for the gubernatorial nomination in 2005, and I certainly fit that bill. Whatever his true feelings about the appointment, he made a game effort to take credit for the whole turn of events. He acknowledged his role in Cheasley's departure and implied that he had my "elevation" in mind all along.

"I always figured the Governor would turn to you once Cheasley was out of the picture," he said to me during an aside at a mansion reception. "You're a lawyer's lawyer, Danny, and the best around. You'll make a better AG than Cheasley ever did. After that, who knows? The Virginia Supreme Court? The Fourth Circuit? Maybe even higher! You have a great future, Danny, and we'll make a great team. Who would have imagined it way back when! Two Hampden-Sydney boys—'Governor Bell' and 'Justice McGuire.' That has a certain ring to it, don't you think?"

"It has the ring of unbridled ambition," I replied brusquely. Then I reflexively added, "But I appreciate any help you've provided."

Those latter words had barely left my lips before I regretted them. It reminded me of my parting comments—a similar expression of gratitude—the day Bart first introduced me to Ned Nevers in the Orange County High gym a lifetime earlier. Then, I had meant what I said, at least a little. Today, I did not mean any of it, and I felt cheesy for saying it.

Before the General Assembly came back to town in January 2003, I had removed my meager belongings from the third floor of the Capitol and resituated myself in the newer part of the Pocahontas Building, a nondescript, white, shoe box-shaped structure at the foot of Capitol Square. A former bank building, the complex recently had been remodeled to serve as the new quarters of the Office of the Attorney General and the Virginia Lottery, a pairing that struck me as wonderfully ironic. There was irony aplenty, too, in the vista that I enjoyed from my comparatively cavernous sixth-floor office. The Capitol supplied a daily reminder that I remained in Governor Nevers' direct line of sight and supervision from his perch atop the hill.

Other changes occurred as the state's second-term chief executive completed a top-level reorganization. It had begun months earlier when the Governor shifted Chad to the Finance secretariat from Commerce and Trade. Nevers' most trusted advisor on matters of fiscal and economic policy, Chad had learned a lot and was the one the Governor wanted in charge of the budget as the state's long-running boom began to bust and revenue shortfalls mounted. Anticipating my departure, Nevers had designated Abby as my deputy in the summer and then elevated her to chief of staff when I left. I knew those two positions—chief of staff and secretary of finance—were the two most powerful in the executive branch aside from the governor himself. I thus left the administration with confidence that Ned Nevers was in excellent hands.

The temporarily downtrodden Democrats, meanwhile, were doing a bit of repositioning of their own. Speaker Percival's cresting interest in the governorship was well known, but the Virginia political establishment was stunned in early 2003 when State Senator Dorothy Meade announced she was forming a political action committee to aid the party's legislative candidates during the autumn campaigns and—she made no secret of this—to lay the groundwork for her own run for governor two years hence. Democratic and Republican pols greeted Meade's de facto declaration with derision. The stated reason for the negative forecast was her unabashed liberalism; the unspoken reason was her race. Among those disparaging her chances in public was Speaker Percival. "I like a powdery snowball's prospects in the southern Sahara right much better," he ventured injudiciously.

So it was that the key players, by early 2003, were all pretty much in place for the stunning events that would make the Commonwealth of Virginia the focal point of national and even international notice over the next half-dozen years. During that time, the Old Dominion's creative governance and competitive politics would engender continuing interest and admiration from beyond her borders. Accolades and top rankings for being a well-managed, business-friendly state would cascade in. The 400th anniversary of the first permanent English settlement in the New World at Jamestown—"America's 400th Birthday"—would be observed with pomp, pageantry, and poignant remembrance in 2007. Various natural disasters—a drought that dried up the river in my native Orange and parched the Piedmont, a hurricane that drew a direct bead on Hampton Roads, wildfires, tornadoes, tremors, and sundry lesser travails—would strike the state, layering a set of meteorological anxieties on top of the terrorism worries. But all of those happenings would pale in importance alongside the unspeakably tragic events that were soon to flow from the confluence of God's inscrutable providence and Bart Bell's apparent malevolence.

IF NOTHING ELSE

I quickly discovered that being attorney general of Virginia is very different from being chief of staff to the governor. While both are incredibly demanding jobs and involve you in just about every facet of state government—an attribute of the attorney general's office seldom appreciated by people who have not served there—the AG has the added burden of being a constitutional officer of the Commonwealth and prominent public figure. As chief of staff, I had been like a doctor on call 24/7, and the constant state of being ready for anything had been more exhausting mentally than I had realized. When I became attorney general, my existence became somewhat more predictable, and that was a great improvement. But the new job also took me out on the road daily addressing various groups, and the travels and frequent dinner functions meant that I typically was getting home after the kids had gone to bed. This aspect was most disagreeable to Martha and Meg, now a first-grader, and they made little effort to conceal their disappointment over my serial evening absences. The boys—Marty, age 4, and his brand-new little brother, Jonathan Maples McGuire—were less judgmental, but their obliviousness about what they (meaning, we) were missing provided little consolation.

While the changes in Richmond in recent months has been substantial—Chad, Abby, and I were all adjusting to demanding new regimens—nothing compared with the stress of post-9/11 Washington, D.C., and the transformative events Mitch had been experiencing. A policy expert, canny communicator, wounded warrior, and member of the House Armed Services Committee, four-term Congressman J. Mitchell Jackson was now an influential and increasingly visible figure in the capital of a nation at war. His expertise on military matters surpassed most of his colleagues, and he became a trusted workhorse on those issues, but what concerned Mitch most was the toll the new pressures took on the solidarity of the American body politic. Religious radicalism and the distrust it engendered were the latest threats to national cohesiveness, but they threatened a wider metastasis. Once unleashed, racial and ethnic passions tended to range broadly in search of new objects of fear and loathing. The first impulse of an afraid and angry America would be to turn away from the world; Mitch worried that the second impulse would be to turn on each other. I knew his mind on these matters, or thought I did, so I really should not have been all that surprised when Mitch shared some unexpected news with me over Memorial Day weekend in 2003.

"Danny, I have decided it is time for me to give a speech on race," he declared.

Mitch had been invited to speak at a late-June gathering of religious scholars and commentators at Montpelier, Madison's handsome mansion back home in Orange. The organizers had suggested that Mitch address "Religious Liberty and Diversity in 21st Century America," but Mitch—*Preacher*—had decided to add his own twist. "My remarks," he informed his surprised but gratified hosts, "will be entitled 'Race, Religion, and America's Mission.'"

As odd as it might seem now, Mitch to that point had never given a serious speech on the sensitive subject of race in America. Elected to Congress from a majority-white congressional district in Virginia's Piedmont region—a feat that made him only the second black Republican elected to Congress from the South since Reconstruction—Mitch always had viewed himself as the representative of constituents of all races, faiths, and creeds. He never missed an opportunity to stress that "my ideas work for everyone." He paid homage to civil rights leaders, particularly Dr. King, whenever the opportunity presented itself, and he was a frequent visitor at predominantly African-American churches and community gatherings, but he eschewed emphasis on issues that would pigeon-hole him as an "African-American congressman." He was "part of a new generation of post-racial politicians," opined one prominent national commentator who chronicled the success of black candidates, both Republicans and Democrats, in majority-white districts in the South and across the country. Mitch was proud of his heritage and cognizant of its burdens, but his public persona was not defined principally, or even significantly, by his race.

Many times since his controversial encounters in college, and even *after* his arrival on Capitol Hill, Mitch had been goaded with insults suggesting that he was a "traitor to his race" because of his conservative views, and he always had managed to ignore the jabs. Dorothy Meade had tried to play the card in the early days of their school choice debates, but she had abandoned it after observing Mitch's disciplined refusal to take the bait and the apparent negative reaction to the tactic by audiences, black and white. Standing above the racial chasm—and at times, I felt, *avoiding* it—was both a principled stance and a politically beneficial one for my friend. It was so much a part of who he was and how he went about the business of politics that I was truly flabbergasted when he told me of his speech plans.

"Some things have clarified for me," Mitch explained. "For a long time, I did not want to speak of the 'black experience' because of the double standard. I mean, you know what I'm saying. If a white person today talked about how proud he was of his white heritage, the intelligentsia would come down on him like a ton of bricks, branding him a racist, a white supremacist. There isn't a 'White History Month.' There isn't a national uproar when some innocent white kid is shot by somebody who happens to be black. White people are tired of being called racist, and they are tired of watching people play the race card—*I get that*. The double standard is real, and it is wrong. But here's the thing: Racism in America is real, too; it is still a major fact of life. And history is real. Many people have had to overcome things, but only one race of people in modern times had to overcome the indignity of being treated as property, as sub-human...."

As I watched Preacher talk, I could see the pain on his face, and I could hear a bit of the conflict within.

"I can see both sides of it," he continued. "I just have never viewed it as my mission to talk about it. I have viewed it as my mission to *rise above it*. Plus, you know me; I want to make it on my own. I don't want or need anyone's sympathy, help, or approval."

This last point, I knew, was at the heart of it.

"But now I realize there are some things white people in this country can't say to people who look like me. I mean, when they say it, it comes across like an old sea captain who crashes the ship on the rocks and then stands there berating the crew for not passing the buckets fast enough. Folks don't want to be lectured by someone they blame for their problems. Plus, white people can't really relate to the black experience—or, at least, no one is gonna believe they can—because they haven't been there."

I listened intently to my friend, and what I heard made perfect sense. But it still saddened me because I was one of those white people who inevitably could not relate, and that meant there was a gulf between us that all the years and friendship, all the trials and mutual support, all the trust and confidence, still could not bridge. There was a separation that persisted despite everything. But Mitch understood this, too—and in ways I did not. That is why he decided to speak not only about race, but also about faith. It is the only way the separation can be fully cured.

Sometime during the run-up to the conclave at Montpelier it fortuitously occurred to Mitch that this was not a talk only, or even primarily, for a high-brow group of scholars assembled on an erstwhile plantation. So on a sunny Sunday a few days before he was to speak at Montpelier, Mitch drove down to Gloucester County in southeastern Virginia and shared his remarks with a group of aspiring young African-American political activists who were attending a weekend conference there.

For much of the 20th century, Holly Knoll, the stately Georgian-style manor house on the York River, had played host to African-American leaders who gathered to exchange ideas and lay plans for social change. It was a fitting role for the historic site, which derived its name—Capahosic—from the native peoples whose paramount chief, known to history as Powhatan, made his capital just upriver at Werowocomoco. Before releasing the captured Captain John Smith in 1607, the Chief even had suggested that Smith and his English interlopers settle at Capahosic, the better, presumably, to keep an eye on them. Smith had spurned the offer, but three centuries later Dr. Robert Russa Moton took up residence on the site and made it a place of consequence. After concluding his two-decade tenure as principal at Tuskegee Institute, the Virginia-born educator and author retired to Capahosic and began welcoming leading African-American thinkers and doers, a practice that continued long after his death. It was there that Moton's successors conceived the United Negro College Fund and later planned the desegregation of lunch counters. On a bench under the magnificent, 400-year-old live oak in front of the manor house, Dr. King was said to have drafted portions of what later became his "I have a dream" speech. Rescued from dilapidation early in the 21st century, the historic setting was again the locus of transformational discussions, and Mitch had attended several previous gatherings at the restored conference center. Unlike on those occasions, however, this time he had something important to say.

The "something important" that Mitch imparted, first at Capahosic and then at Montpelier, began as it would end—in an uncharacteristically personal and revealing way:

There comes a time to talk candidly about the pain in our lives, the suffering that we experience and that we see others experiencing. Because most of what divides us today in America, and in the world, has its roots in somebody's suffering, past or present. We have seen how painful legacies can become powerful weapons in the hands of those bent on evil. But we know that suffering can be a source of good as well. Indeed, the apostle Paul went so far as to tell the Christians in Rome that they should "rejoice" in their sufferings, because suffering produces endurance, and endurance produces character, and character produces hope.

Taking Paul's advice to heart, I have come to perceive my own legacy as a source of advantage. Not as the world sees advantage, for the world sees advantage in material wealth or political power. But true advantage lies in the character, and so the spirit and soul, of a person. And if character is refined in a crucible of suffering and trial, then the African-American experience in this country since that first arrival in 1619 here in Virginia—an experience marred by slavery and systemic discrimination—must have supplied an advantage in terms of the refinement of character.

You see this phenomenon in the spirituality that pervades the African-American community today. It is a common characteristic across a range of political viewpoints. Our people were oppressed and reviled, maintained in ignorance as a means of subjugation, exploited, and, to rationalize this treatment, dehumanized—regarded as less than a person, like a dog. But they were not dogs; they were people—*God's children*. So they turned to God for strength in their great and continual distress, in the utter hopelessness of their condition. And, having so turned and sustained themselves from generation to generation through faith in a God who would deliver them, if not in this life then the next, they are not liable to turn away so easily. Not so easily as other people whose worldview has been forged in strength more than weakness ... in comfort more than hardship.

All across America today there is an effort by the secularists to wipe from the face of our society every vestige of religious imagery and religious belief. Indeed, we are told again and again that religious contention is the primary cause of world conflict, and that if we will but rise above our ignorant reliance on divine deliverance and instead embrace faith in human reason and potential, then all our peaceful dreams will be fulfilled. But this falsehood is not a dominant ground of belief in my community. We still celebrate our spirituality and our faith, not in man, but in a God who has ordained freedom, justice, and love. We have seen his deliverance, leading us out of the depths of oppression by his mighty hand. And it may be the calling of our community to lead America back to faith, back to the righteousness that has exalted this nation.

Consider the power of this story: A young man is sold into slavery by his own people and transported to a foreign land. The enslavers intend it for evil, but God can outflank evil and make something good. Over time the slaves' numbers grow even as their condition worsens. And then God sends deliverance; he performs mighty miracles, and the people are freed. But their freedom does not lead them directly to the promised land. Instead, they undergo decades of additional hardship, reviled by their neighbors, without the benefits enjoyed by other peoples, wandering somewhere between the condition of slavery they left behind and the full enjoyment of their birthright—the promise of freedom. At times they are so frustrated and disappointed at what seems like a cruel hoax that they are tempted to turn back and give up, or lash out in anger. But they are reminded by their leader that God has shown his mighty power by delivering them from bondage, and that if they will but trust him, deliverance will come to them at last.

This is the story of Joseph, sold into slavery in Egypt, and of Moses, whom God chose to lead his people out of bondage and to the edge of the promised land. But it is also the story of the *White Lion* that first brought Africans to the Virginia colony for sale, and of a modern Moses—Dr. Martin Luther King Jr.—who echoed Moses in words delivered the night before his death: "I've looked over. And I've seen the promised land. I may not get there with you. But I want you to know tonight that we, as a people, will get to the promised land."

Now, if you read the Old Testament—and we don't read it enough—you see a subtext to this story. Again and again, God tells his people to recall the miracles by which, through his mighty hand, God led his chosen people out of bondage, to a land flowing with milk and honey. He wants them to reflect on that crucible of experience—how he delivered them from the depths of oppression and hardship; how he refined them and molded their character; how he forged their faith. He wants them to recall their own exodus from slavery so they themselves do not become enslavers, but instead become contributors to his divine project of liberation.

Above all, he wants them—and us—to ponder the purpose: *For what have we been set free?*

You see, the people of the exodus were God's chosen people. But they were not the chosen because they were superior. They were the chosen because they had experienced God in a way others had not. They had been driven by their suffering to trust God to the very depths of their souls. And having trusted him they experienced his miraculous deeds. And having experienced his miraculous deeds, their faith was fortified, and they gave testimony to it, and they became a force for the spreading of that faith throughout the world and across the ages.

So God used slavery—he used hardship and suffering and oppression and dehumanization; he used the very depravity of mankind—to lead men and women back to him.

What, then, shall we say of our story and our time?

Having been led out of servitude into the promised land of freedom and opportunity by the mighty hand of a loving

God and by God's human instruments, including the struggle and sacrifice of those who came before us, will we bear witness to it? Will we lead America back to faith? Will we put that faith to work healing our homes and neighborhoods and communities? Will we put that faith to work restoring a sense of possibility and moral purpose among our young people? Will we put that faith to work rekindling not only a spirit of individual opportunity but also of personal responsibility and community obligation?

Because only if the answer to these questions is "Yes!" will we reclaim the American Dream and make it real for those who have been left out, for a generation that not only is not yet living that Dream, but is in danger of losing even the ability to understand it....

Now, I realize some of you may be uncomfortable with this emphasis on religion. And if that is the case, then I encourage you to treat what I've just said as a historical analogy and reflect on the same concept as it relates to the principles for which our nation stands—the principles of freedom and justice.

We know that despite this nation's founding promises of liberty and justice for all—despite the Jeffersonian declaration of equality and unalienable rights—a race of people were denied those blessings. America did not honor its promise to our forebears. And so our people have been overcoming for centuries. Yet, we do not see ourselves as victims; we see ourselves as victors. For in overcoming this adversity, in persevering on our own pilgrimage to the promised land, we have helped refine our nation's faith and affirmed the power of its founding ideals.

And so, whether we take from our history the mission to spread our faith in divine freedom and love or the mission to spread the American gospel of political freedom and universal rights, we are drawing from the same experience—the same story of believing, struggling, persevering, overcoming.

Indeed, in our experience these moral missions merge, and the distinction between the secular and the sectarian appears artificial and meaningless. "We will win our freedom," Dr. King wrote from the Birmingham jail, "because the sacred heritage of our nation and the eternal will of God are embodied in our echoing demands."

So I would argue that we have a special trust and a sacred mission. We have been given special influence on the culture and politics of the nation. And so we must take our character refined in adversity and the deep spirituality of our people, and lead America back to faith. Faith in God. Faith in ourselves. Faith in the possibility of men and women of goodwill, from varied backgrounds and creeds, working together. Faith in the great ideals this country so boldly and radically proclaimed and promised at its founding. Ideals that we have affirmed in the centuries since, with God's help, by overcoming all who would deny that promise and make America, and each of its children, less than God intended us to be.

So that is the mission, but hear me on this: It is not merely an African-American mission; it is the mission of *all* Americans.

Just as Moses told his people, "Love those who are foreigners, for you yourself were foreigners in Egypt," so is America a nation of immigrants, a country of hope-filled wanderers from many lands and legacies searching for a better life for ourselves and our families. Adversity and hardship have been our constant companions, faith and perseverance our only hope, whether we arrived on the Godspeed or the White Lion, at Plymouth Rock or Ellis Island, whether we toiled on a steaming, hot plantation in eastern Virginia or in the harsh and unforgiving hollers of Appalachia, whether ours were "pilgrim feet whose stern, impassioned stress a thoroughfare for freedom beat across the wilderness" or the shoeless, bleeding feet of native mothers carrying their starving children on the Trail of Tears.

You see, our expedition is unique, but our destination is universal. And we shall overcome … all of us … so long as we recognize that these varied journeys of hardship and pain did not deliver us here to stand apart, dwelling on our diversity as grounds for grievance. They delivered us here to stand together, reflecting on our shared ideals and common hopes … not tearing each other down, but lifting each other up.

Our national motto was never "out of many, many." Our struggles have brought us together to be together. *E Pluribus Unum*—out of many, *one*.

Have you ever asked yourself why Dr. King, who felt so profoundly the injustice of America, nevertheless believed so deeply in the promise of America? It was because he saw America's purpose—the advancement of freedom—bound up in God's plan of liberation.

In that speech the night before his death, Dr. King imagined how he would have responded if God had given him a choice to live in any era of human history. Canvassing the greatest times of ferment and achievement, he nevertheless settled upon the present:

> I would turn to the Almighty and say, "If you allow me to live just a few years in the second half of the 20th century, I will be happy." Now that's a strange statement to make because the world is all messed up. The nation is sick. Trouble is in the land. Confusion all around…. But I know, somehow, that only when it is dark enough can you see the stars. And I see God working in this period…. The masses of people are rising up. And wherever they are assembled … the cry is always the same—"We want to be free."

Dr. King lived in his moment, as we must live in ours, but his truth was eternal. The cry is always the same: *"We want to be free."*

It is a universal desire, hard-wired into our hearts by the God who created us in his own image of perfect freedom.

It is the birthright of every person. But it is something else, too: *Freedom is the community's ultimate affirmation of individual dignity and worth.*

This communal statement may sound humanist to some ears, but history teaches the opposite. Humanism gave us power, not freedom, as the unifying principle, and even today it routinely seeks to impose its will by claiming a greater, better wisdom.

The truth—inconvenient for some—is that the political history of the world pivoted on a religious event. For the Christian faithful, the Cross brings saving grace. But all the world changed when Jesus of Nazareth died willingly, not for his family or his tribe, not for the powerful or a favored few, but for all mankind—to set each child of God free.

This was the revolutionary idea that triggered a movement and transformed a world: the idea that every individual human being counts, that all are equal in God's eyes, and that humanity's transcendent purpose is not power, but freedom and—through it—love.

So thorough has been this transformation that, today, no religious or political belief system can claim a monopoly on this idea. And no human institution, even the church to which I belong, can claim exemption from the errors to which all flesh is heir. Indeed, we deny the very universality of this freedom when we give quarter to religious pride or prejudice.

My friends, in these unsettled times it is right and good that we Americans close ranks. But sometimes we take a good thing too far and close some other things, too. We close minds, and we close doors.

We make this American fortress our idol and hide behind its walls.

But is this what Scripture teaches us? No, it says to "[l]ove those who are foreigners, for you yourself were foreigners...."

Is it what American history teaches? No, "my country, 'tis of thee, sweet land of liberty" is not just the "land where my fathers died"; it is also "land of the pilgrims' pride." And as pilgrims ourselves we are called to let freedom ring "from *every* mountain side."

Now, this is a great and powerful calling, one that demands that we open our hearts. But it does not demand that we stop using our brains.

Dr. King compared freedom to a promissory note, but he made clear it was not a blank check.

We were made free in the image of God, and his image of freedom includes justice. And so there are standards that come with the status. And there are obligations that come with the rights. And there are duties that come with the privileges.

We want America to be that shining city on a hill, that beacon of hope for mankind. And, for that to work, not only must we be welcoming, but those who journey to join us must be accepting.

It is their duty to abide by our laws, to embrace our community's essential ideals, and to exhibit the same tolerance and respect for individuals of other faiths and creeds, cultures and communities, that we exhibit in welcoming them and theirs.

Ours is a covenant community. Our Declaration of Independence declares it. Jefferson, of all people, wrote that God ordained it. And it is our duty to preserve the moral capital of our community, without which freedom itself cannot long survive.

You see, my friends, diversity, like suffering, can be deployed for good or for ill. Diversity's virtue lies in the understanding it cultivates, the character it elevates, the unity it necessitates.

But we are not called to celebrate every difference, to promote diversity for diversity's sake, or to treat every varied value as morally equal to every other. We are called to be discerning and embrace those from distant lands and varied faiths and many creeds who share our core values and who, with us, are committed to holding universal human rights inviolate.

Even the most gracious host understands you don't let just anyone into your home.

Even Christ, who dined with tax collectors, cast money changers out of the temple.

A country can be welcoming—"give us your tired, your poor, your huddled masses yearning to breathe free"—without being complicit in its own destruction.

So there will be some who refuse our extended hand and others from whom prudence demands we withhold it. For the rest, from across this land and beyond, let us embrace the richness of our many stories and struggles, places and faiths. Let us display the same generous, grateful spirit and acceptance that we seek from those who journey to join us, and let us treat them as we would hope to be treated if the roles were reversed … for this is not only the Golden Rule but the historical truth.

I, for one, am full of hope for my country. I believe there is a great awakening coming in our land, an awakening of the human spirit through a new birth of freedom and faith. It is a song of reconciliation that will erase old divisions and alliances, and transform not only how we govern and renew our city but how we govern and renew ourselves. A song of victory, not victimhood. A song of generosity and hospitality, not selfishness and shunning. A song of love and faith in a God who meets each of us where we are, whatever our race or place, and rescues us from the slavery, wreckage, and ruin of our natural lives.

On this deeply personal of topics, a topic that I have never addressed before, I want to conclude with an expression of thanks. And for a proper expression of that gratitude, I close with these words from the testimony of a personal hero of mine. They are from the *Narrative of My Life* by Frederick Douglass:

I look upon my departure from Colonel Lloyd's plantation as one of the most interesting events of my life. It is possible, and even quite probable, that but for the mere circumstance of being removed from that plantation to Baltimore, I should have today, instead of being here seated by my own table, in the enjoyment of freedom and the happiness of home, writing this Narrative, been confined in the galling chains of slavery. Going to live at Baltimore laid the foundation, and opened the gateway, to all my subsequent prosperity. I have ever regarded it as the first plain manifestation of that kind providence which has ever since attended me, and marked my life with so many favors. I regarded the selection of myself as being somewhat remarkable. There were a number of slave children that might have been sent from the plantation to Baltimore. There were those younger, those older, and those of the same age. I was chosen from among them all, and was the first, last, and only choice.

I may be deemed superstitious, and even egotistical, in regarding this event as a special interposition of divine Providence in my favor. But I should be false to the earliest sentiments of my soul, if I suppressed the opinion. I prefer to be true to myself, even at the hazard of incurring the ridicule of others, rather than to be false, and incur my own abhorrence. From my earliest recollection, I date the entertainment of a deep conviction that slavery would not always be able to hold me within its foul embrace; and in the darkest hours of my career in slavery, this living word of faith and spirit of hope departed not from me, but remained like ministering angels to cheer me through the gloom. This good spirit was from God, and to him I offer thanksgiving and praise.

A few days later, I was relaxing with the Governor in his third-floor office. Most of our work was done, and we were catching up on the news before he headed over to the mansion and I left for home.

"I got a chance to read Mitch's speech today," he said.

"What'd you think of it?" I asked.

"Oh, an inspiring speech … a powerful, powerful message. He has a remarkable gift," the Governor responded. Then, after several moments' pause, he added, "Really surprised me, though."

"I know. For all these years he has avoided giving a speech on race," I agreed.

"No, I don't mean that," said Nevers. "He had that speech inside him and it just had to come out. It was only a matter of time."

"Yes, I can see that," I replied. "I guess the big surprise was that he asked Chad to help him on the speech."

"No, I really was not surprised at all to hear that."

"Okay, I give up—*what*?"

"It was just that Mitch has always been about Old Testament justice. Yet, that was as good a New Testament sermon as I've ever heard."

I pondered the comment in silence for a few moments. The speech had dwelled at length on an Old Testament analogy. What was the Governor talking about?

"I gather from your silence you disagree," he said finally.

"I wouldn't say I disagree. I'm just reflecting on what you mean."

"Well, it won't surprise you that the same point is made here in *All the King's Men*," he said, reaching for the heavily dog-earned volume on the credenza.

"I should have assumed so," I said. "But what possible connection can there be between that book and Mitch's speech?"

"It's what Jack said toward the end—righhhhht here," he said, flipping successfully to the passage he had in mind.

"I am a student of history," Nevers quoted the narrator, Jack Burden, as saying, "And what we students of history always learn is that the human being is a very complicated contraption and that they are not good or bad but are good and bad and the good comes out of bad and the bad out of good, and the devil take the hindmost."

I looked at him with what must have been the blankest of expressions.

"It was Mitch's main point, Danny—the one hovering above the whole speech—the message that things aren't black or white ... good or bad. They are black *and* white ... good *and* bad. It took Mitch a while to see it, but not nearly as long as it took me. It isn't relativism, where good and bad are indistinguishable. It is *redemption*—the notion that even out of the worst possible situation, from the depths of human misery and depravity, great good can come. Our purpose doesn't lie in the suffering inflicted and its legacy of guilt or grievance. Our purpose comes from the deliverance received and its legacy of obligation—the obligation to show our gratitude, forgiveness, and love by helping others. That is what bridges the divide. It's what turns these awful burdens into blessings. But Mitch is right—it requires a journey of *faith*."

This was a wholesome and hope-filled proposition—the essence of who and what Ned Nevers had become—and the Governor's enthusiasm was evident. So, too, had been Mitch's. But at the time I had only a superficial sense of what they meant. Despite some painful losses, my life really had not forced me to come to grips with many harsh realities, and things seemed to be going along just great at the time.

I might have been less nonchalant about the evening's conversation if I had focused on the import of Nevers' parting comment.

"Well, if I accomplish nothing else in my life, I will have done something good by giving Mitch his start in politics," the Governor said, mostly to himself. "He has the potential to change this country."

A Good Walk

On a Sunday earlier that spring, I had arrived home after attending church with Martha and the kids, looking forward to a rare, family-focused Sunday afternoon. For that reason, I had been less than thrilled by the voice message that awaited me.

"Danny, it's me. If you're around this afternoon, give me a call. I have a good walk in mind, and I need your services as guide. My schedule has been cleared all afternoon for bill review, and I'm thinking of heading out at three or so for Hollywood Cemetery. *Dying* to have you along—otherwise I'll be bored *stiff*. Ha-ha. Call me when you get this and let me know if you can join me. I'm flexible on the time."

The Governor's idea of a "good walk" was one in which either of two things would happen, and frequently both: I would provide some historical color as we traversed the noteworthy terrain, and he would talk through some issues that were weighing on his mind.

The origins of the practice probably traced to 1997 when we were on the campaign trail together. Now and again we would come to a town or just a place along the road where some event of historical note had happened. This was Virginia, of course, so it happened a lot. My recollection might be triggered by a historical marker we sailed past, or the name of a town or street, or some other sight. But whenever something came to mind I would tell the story. The candidate and the rest of the traveling party relished making fun of me as an encyclopedic repository of utterly useless Virginia trivia. The more they razzed me, the more I got into it. I would even do a little quick research about some of our impending venues as time permitted so that I would be well armed with anecdotes.

This penchant for history-telling no doubt came from my mother. She did it for a living and did it so well that she was the most popular teacher in the school. Her passion was such that she could teach all day and still have enthusiasm and energy enough to tell me a good story or two at night. When I was little, she and my father would take me on an occasional Saturday or Sunday afternoon excursion to a president's home or a battlefield or some other famous locale, and there I would learn about the events that shaped Virginia and so America.

When Nevers became governor the schedule was a killer, especially at first, so "good walks" were rare. But when he did have a chance to get out, he almost always wanted to go to a historical site, and so it was inevitable that I came along. We walked over to the John Marshall House and White House of the Confederacy, both just a few blocks away from the Executive Mansion. We meandered astride the canals that were part of Washington's grand plan for inland commerce and crossed the river to traverse the Richmond Slave Trail beginning at the Manchester Docks. We walked around the Tredegar Iron Works, the major Union Army objective during the Civil War, and Belle Isle where Union soldiers suffered and died as prisoners of war. We went up to Church Hill and St. John's, an Episcopal church where re-enactors still send chills up the spine with the immortal words of Patrick Henry. We took a boat ride downriver to Henricus, site of the early English settlement where

Pocahontas was baptized and married John Rolfe, and where the 1622 uprising led by her uncle, Opechancanough, killed hundreds. We went out to Hanover County to see the Polegreen Church site where Samuel Davies inspired Patrick Henry's oratory and to Hanover Courthouse where Henry first gained renown in the Parson's Cause. There were many more excursions than these, including others out into the surrounding countryside, once Governor Nevers became comfortable with his duties and the pace became more manageable. He would often say the outings were therapeutic, and I had no doubt that was true for both of us.

Against that backdrop, the invitation to join the Governor for a stroll through Hollywood Cemetery had not seemed as strange as it otherwise might have. The landmark's significance as the resting place of a venerated Virginia elite was undeniable. Beneath its statuesque oaks, granite monuments, and well-trimmed turf lay three "presidents" (James Monroe, John Tyler, and Jefferson Davis), Governor William "Extra Billy" Smith and five one-term Virginia governors, J.E.B. Stuart, George Pickett, and 21 other Confederate generals, and sundry others of fame and consequence, including Matthew Fontaine Maury, Dr. Hunter Holmes McGuire (no relation, as far as I knew), Major Lewis Ginter, Bishop Francis Whittle, Ellen Glasgow, Virginius Dabney, Jim Wheat Jr., and Douglas Southall Freeman, just to scratch the surface. Even more numerous were the comparatively uncelebrated whose lives, loves, and labors were remembered by God and a few fast-fading mortals at most. Among the humble rest were the 18,000 Confederate war dead to whom the cemetery's signature stone pyramid was dedicated, a woeful number whose cold gray sacrifice history had forever united with the blue-clad fallen in a timeless testimony to man's capacity for nobility, fidelity, vanity, and cruelty.

The cemetery was a statuary garden with narrow driveways that traversed formidable hills and modest stream beds in indiscernible patterns, occasionally supplying breath-taking vistas of the James River below and invariably confounding casual visitors. Our visit had come during the time of year when the dead habituated in their naps despite the enlivening signs of spring, especially those welcome harbingers of perennial rebirth, the dogwoods. That had made it nearly an ideal place to rest and to contemplate. Unfortunately, it had not been sitting and reflecting, but walking and talking, that the Governor had in mind—and I had known from experience that the setting was not particularly conducive to either. It was not for that reason alone, but also because of the vast amount of weekend catch-up work awaiting me on the sixth floor of the Pocahontas Building, that I had groaned as I listened to the Governor's message. Then I had called the mansion to say I would be there by three.

As we walked along that afternoon, I occasionally pointed out a notable grave and offered a brief vignette, playing what I thought to be my primary role in the proceedings. But it soon became apparent that this was no typical "good walk." On the ordinary sojourns, the Governor was attentive, inquisitive, and animated on the historical subjects, and if he wanted to consult or command or just vent on a more timely topic, it did not take long for him to get to the point. But, on this day, he said little. We strolled mainly in silence, and a bit awkwardly so, until the Governor broke the quiet.

"Daniel, I struggle with the purpose of all this. Why are we here? We work so hard to pass this bill or that one, to recruit this or that business, to change this or that way of doing things. But it's a drop in the bucket, really—*less* than a drop in the bucket. It's a footprint in the sands of time, and sandy footprints all wash away. I know what we're doing here *is* important. It's important to try to make things better for folks, to keep our commitments and succeed for them if we possibly can. It's a great gift, a great blessing, to be in a position to do that. But this all will pass, all of it—the good and the bad. Governors come and go. Attorneys general come and go. Elections come and go. Even legislators come and go, thank goodness...."

We chuckled together, recalling the battles.

"There is really only one permanent thing," he continued. "It's the place these folks have gone—this rest they've won, or that's been thrust upon them. I believe what we do here matters because I believe God put us here to matter. But in the end, we all end up like this. And somewhere above there is a God who decides if we will have a place of rest with Him. Sometimes I wake up at night in a cold sweat, quivering in fear at that thought, because I know I have failed to do so many things I could've done with all that's been given to me. And I have done some things that were not right. If I could just do it over, I could do so much better...."

The Governor had opened a window into his soul. After that spring day, I spent many minutes thinking about what I *should* have said at that moment, when I had the chance. I should have cut in and said, "Boss, I agree with everything you said right up to the point about worrying about the past and wishing you could do things differently."

I should have said what I truly believe on that subject, even though it is easier to preach than to practice. I should have said, "There's no use worrying or wishing, because we *can't* do things over. We have done what we have done, whether we are proud of it or ashamed of it."

I should have said, "The next time you wake up quivering, you need to stop right there and thank God for his forgiveness, for the redemption that we have through the Son who died for us, *because that's all any of us has*. We have all fallen short, everyone since the beginning of time. It's what we do with that fact once we realize it—*if* we realize it—that matters. It's a sign of our faith that we don't waste time wishing we could do things over or worrying about the past. We acknowledge our shortcomings and failures; we accept God's grace; and move on. We resolve to do the best we can. We draw on all we have learned. And we trust in him to help and guide us."

I should have said, "I know you know all that, Boss. I know it's there in your head. But the peace you seek only comes when you believe it in your heart and trust it in your soul."

I should have offered that candid ministry to my friend, to the man who was sometimes my mentor and at other times my charge. I should have sensed that his spirit was troubled and that this was a moment that mattered. I should have been ready—prepared to speak the truth "in season and out of season," as Paul counseled his understudy, Timothy. I should have seized the chance while Ned Nevers was here in the flesh, still searching, still needing, still within reach of my aid. I should have been bold, amazingly bold, as I had been with him on some notable occasions before.

But God gives us the words when we need them. And, looking back now, I do not think the Governor needed to hear anything more from me. I think I was there to hear from him.

SUBTRACTION

It was about four months later—during a brief Fourth of July getaway with my family—when I emerged from a frolic in the surf with the kids, caked with salt, sand, and bits of shell, to unexpectedly encounter the expressionless visage of a young Virginia Beach sheriff's deputy at the water's edge.

"General McGuire?" he asked to confirm.

"Yes?"

"Sir, I need you to come with me to the patrol car, please. There's an urgent call for you from the Governor's Office."

I cast a puzzled glance toward Martha, who had baby Jon in her arms and already was summoning Meg and Marty from the water's edge, then hustled over to retrieve my cell phone from her beach bag. The dead battery explained the deputy's presence.

Once at his car beyond the dunes, the deputy patched through Abby, whose crackling, cryptic message was audible enough. I raced into the cottage and flipped on the TV to see the soul-shattering bulletin: "Virginia Governor Presumed Dead in Boat Explosion." A lesser headline added: "Officials Not Ruling Out Terrorism—Security Tightened for Other Presidential Prospects."

With aerial footage of a debris-strewn area of the Chesapeake Bay and bobbing boats in the background, the newsman summarized the information then available:

> Here's what we know at this point: The Virginia State Police have now confirmed that the Governor of the Commonwealth of Virginia and former United States Senator, Edward K. Nevers, perished with all four others onboard a recreational fishing boat in a fire and explosion about an hour and 20 minutes ago. A State Police vessel nearby saw the smoke and had just begun to race to the scene when the huge explosion occurred, destroying the Governor's vessel. The damage from the explosion and fire was so total, according to officials, that it was immediately apparent there were no survivors. Officials currently are on the scene preparing for what they describe as a "recovery operation."
>
> The Virginia First Lady, Mrs. Sarah Nevers, was not aboard the boat and has been notified of her husband's death.
>
> Reportedly accompanying the Governor and also presumed dead were a Virginia Beach business executive and personal friend of the Governor, the businessman's teenage son, a personal aide to the Governor, and a member of the state of Virginia's executive protection unit. Names are being withheld pending notification of family members.

Meanwhile, with the terrorist threat level still at Orange, officials in Washington are reacting to the breaking news with caution. While they will not rule out terrorism in the blast, a senior official at the new Department of Homeland Security, speaking on condition of anonymity, tells us the Department was not aware of any known threats to Governor Nevers' safety or any indication of increased terrorist threats against people or sites in Virginia. The official noted that fires, explosions, and other accidents on recreational boats are rare but do occur. Still, the official would not rule out enhanced personal security for other potential presidential candidates and senior officials. Nevers, a former two-term U.S. senator and frequent commentator on national affairs, including the war on terrorism, was among a handful of additional Republicans thought to still be considering a bid for his party's presidential nomination next year....

A range of emotions swept over me like so many crashing waves, making it impossible to think and hard even to breathe: shock, disbelief, anger, sadness. An urgent, desperate plea that it might all be a mistake, that the reports somehow were wrong, that the Governor had not been on the boat after all. Then the enormity of the personal tragedy—the shattered families, and the awful wondering about who the other victims were. Which EPU trooper? Which member of the Governor's staff? In my former role as chief of staff, I would have known who was with the Governor at every moment of the day, but not now. They were all like family to me, and it occurred to me that, whoever they were, they probably were there because of me—because I had hired them or assigned them. And then my thoughts ran to Sally—sweet, saintly, long-suffering Sally—having endured so much to reach this happy time, and now the love of her life suddenly taken from her.

My mind was racing, emotions running wild, half-formed thoughts and prayers cascading, all out of control. I knew I had to rein it in.

I tore myself from the TV and glanced outside, looking for Martha and the kids. Instead, there now appeared a swarm of police vehicles with flashing lights and a gathering crowd of curious neighbors.

"Deputy, will you please get Mrs. McGuire and our three children and gear up from the beach," I asked the uniformed man standing in my doorway. "I have to get rinsed off and head out."

"Where to, sir?"

"Richmond … I think," was my tentative response. A quick call to Abby confirmed my assumption that there was nothing to be accomplished at the accident and recovery scene, and that my place was back in the capital city.

As I hung up the phone, a young state trooper entered.

"Trooper Watchford, sir. Colonel Mobley just radioed. We've been directed by Governor Bell to get you back to the Capitol. Just let us know when you are ready and we will roll out."

The incongruous words—*Governor Bell*—sliced like a cold dagger. It was the first time the thought had crossed my mind, and I shuddered.

My shower was the briefest of events, but as I stood beneath the refreshing water in solitude something resembling a sense of calm returned. I had work to do. "Thy will be done," I said finally, uttering the words I had repeated so often by rote and now struggled to accept. I needed focus and I needed help, and getting into an argument with God over why he let this happen was not calculated to produce either.

Within minutes, I was racing along I-64 in a State Police cruiser, one of the few unmarked vehicles in a streaking, squealing swath of grey and blue. I had a legal pad in my lap and, most of the time, a phone to my ear.

My thoughts immediately ran to terrorism. It was the cause that one automatically assigned to otherwise unexplained acts of destruction and violence during those days, and it seemed very plausible given Nevers' outspoken comments on the subject and his widely touted presidential aspirations. I found myself playing the "what if" game, wishing that Nevers had made public what he had already disclosed to his senior staff and key advisors several weeks earlier: that he was *not* running for president. Perhaps that would have made him less of a target. Perhaps it would have saved his life.

I forced myself to focus on the tasks at hand, scratching an outline on my pad. The investigation into the disaster's cause was one such task, but only one. There were security measures to implement … families to console, especially Sally … staff members to reassure … a new and inexperienced chief of staff to assist … a gubernatorial funeral to plan … and—the dagger again—a *transition*.

I was on the phone with Abby discussing the latest information and reviewing my list of action items with her when Bart Bell's cell phone number flashed up.

"Abby, this is Bart calling. I need to take it," I said.

"Yes, call me back as soon as you can," she said.

I was about to switch to the incoming call when I heard her faint voice again, so I put the phone back to my ear. "Danny," I heard her say. "It's not 'Bart' anymore. It's 'the Governor.'"

I pressed the green button without responding, and said, "This is Danny."

"Danny, it's Bart. How are you holding up?" asked the voice at the other end earnestly.

As mentioned previously, the proper way to address a lieutenant governor is to call him "Governor," just as the proper way to address a lieutenant colonel is to call him "Colonel." I had used the formal salutation in addressing Bart before, but always with a smirk. Now the title was no longer honorific, and the circumstances were the most sober imaginable.

"I'm okay … *Governor*. How are you doing?"

"I am very sorry, Danny. I know how close you two were. I know it's like losing a father for you. I'm sorry. It's just awful—so devastating for all of us."

I did not know what to say, but I took the uncharacteristic display of feeling as genuine.

"Yes, it's tragic for everyone," I replied. "Do we have any more information?"

He rehashed the state of play, offering nothing much new of note. Reinforcing my own assumption that terrorism was to blame for the day's tragedy, he emphasized the precautionary steps he had taken regarding increased security, not only for himself and me, but for Speaker Percival, the Supreme Court justices, and several other prominent state officials. Then he turned the discussion to next steps.

"Danny, I need your advice. I think it's important for me to reassure folks, don't you? I think I need to go on television and provide some context and direction. Abby recommended that I call in the press for a briefing, along with her and Colonel Mobley and maybe the head of the FBI field office or some other appropriate federal official. And that might be the way to go if we were responding to a hurricane or something, but I don't think it's the way you respond to the sudden death of a governor. I'm thinking that I should leave the police details to the police, and I should speak to the people live from the Governor's Office, to show that things are under control and that we are not going to miss a beat."

"*Not going to miss a beat,*" I grimaced. *I sure hope he doesn't say that.*

There was something deeply disconcerting about the way Bart made his point, but I had to agree with his conclusion. Virginia had lost its leader, suddenly and violently, perhaps by accident, perhaps as the latest casualty of the war on terror. The extraordinary insecurity that everyone felt as 9/11 unfolded was still palpable. The people needed to be reassured that their lives would go on unmolested, that their sturdy institutions were capable of withstanding this latest shock, that a steady hand was at the helm.

"I agree with you completely," I said. "You're the governor. You need to speak to the people of Virginia as their governor."

"I appreciate your support, Danny," he said at the end. "We will get through this together."

The next call I took was from Miguel Angiolo. The chief deputy attorney general and my principal aide, Miguel was, at 32, something of a phenomenon. A brilliant young lawyer, he had been discovered by Bud Cheasley, who had made him his chief counsel. Upon becoming attorney general, I surprised just about everyone by promoting Miguel to chief deputy rather than installing one of my governor's office protégés in the top spot. I had taken over as the appointed successor to an attorney general who had been elected by the people and who was beloved by his team, and I wanted to send a message of continuity. When passed over by Nevers for the AG spot, Bud's chief deputy had decided to go to Capitol Hill with the new congressman, so Miguel was the next in line. More important, I had interacted with the impressive young man on several matters and regarded him as wise beyond his years.

Had I paused to ponder it, that impression would have been strongly confirmed by Miguel's behavior on this frenzied day, because he responded by coolly and calmly analyzing what needed to be done, then sharing his guidance with me without waiting for my instruction or request. We had been working together only a few months, but his recommendations invariably accorded with my own thinking and even anticipated it. This was already our fourth or fifth conversation, and the crisis was not yet two hours old.

"I have just gotten off the phone with Ms. Wingo and have some additional recommendations for you," he said solidly. "We know you want to see the First Lady as soon as possible, so we recommend you proceed straight to the mansion, and then from there to the emergency operations center in Chesterfield rather than to the Third Floor. I've been coordinating with Gary Williams"—he was referring to the Governor's legal counsel and policy chief, one of my recruits—"as well as Ms. Wingo. As you know, our interagency working group on continuity of leadership has not completed its report, but a number of states have completed theirs, and we have several of those plans in hand and are consulting them. The crisis management team has been alerted as best we can, and we have the State Police out retrieving them, but it will take some time. Unfortunately, Secretary Harris"—Tom Harris was the experienced cabinet secretary responsible for public safety and emergency preparedness—"is in Canada on a fishing trip. The Mounties have now reached him, and he will participate by phone. Colonel Mobley"—I admired the no-nonsense, 30-year veteran who had risen through the ranks to become superintendent of the State Police—"is in touch with the Secretary from the command center, and is coordinating with the key folks in the field...."

Miguel canvassed the others who were being rounded up, with one glaring omission.

"And the Lieutenant Governor?" I asked.

"The ... *Governor* ... has been at the command center almost since the beginning. He was spending the weekend at home in Midlothian, and the EPU troopers were able to reach him quickly and take him there."

"Okay—"

"And, speaking of the EPU guys, I know you will want to reach out as soon as possible. They've been nothing short of heroic, but they have to be devastated. They've lost not only the Governor but a beloved fellow trooper and leader...."

"Scotty Macauley was a prince," I said, gritting my teeth and forcing back another wave of emotion. "I want to call his wife and also call Billy Thrasher's mom and dad before coming to Chesterfield. I really would like to go by the Macauleys' home, but I know—"

"You just don't have time to do it today, General—I'm sorry. If you want to take these down, I have the phone numbers for Mary Beth Macauley locally, and for Mr. and Mrs. Thrasher up in the Valley and Mrs. Sargent down at the Beach. I don't know which of them you will be able to reach, but Colonel Mobley has confirmed for us that all family members have now been notified."

Scotty Macauley had been on the elite State Police protective detail for the past five governors, his easygoing manner and magnetic personality masking the sobriety and severity of his duties. Billy Thrasher, the cub reporter in Waynesboro who never had any idea how thoroughly he could have skewered us back during the campaign, was still in his twenties. He had come east to work in the press office midway through the first term. His fondness for fishing had been his undoing, since that had gotten him the assignment to fill in during a weekend reprieve for the Governor's usual traveling aide, Bobby Pugh. I did not know Ben and Gail Sargent well, but the well-heeled couple had been frequent guests at the mansion and, though almost a decade younger, were cherished friends of the Nevers. Gail now was not only a widow but a mother shorn of her only son—the cruelest possible twist.

"I need you to confirm the Governor has reached them before I call them...."

"I have already confirmed it," Miguel replied efficiently. "He has a checklist that he and Mr. Barnhard"—Hardy Barnhard was Bart's top aide, a thirtysomething sycophant who was now in way over his head—"have put together, and he has been working down through the list methodically. He took a call from the President a short time ago, and has been in touch with both Senators, the Speaker, and a proper list of others. He is very cool-headed and organized. By the way, General, you might need to speak to Ms. Wingo...."

Miguel went on to recount how Abby, while impressively steady and businesslike under pressure, had so far been unwilling to proceed from the Capitol to the emergency operations center.

"I understand where she's coming from. She wants to be with the rest of the staff. Her maternal instincts have taken over and she wants to be there for them. But I agree we need her at the EOC—I'll call her...."

Several conversations with Abby, Miguel, and Colonel Mobley later, our cruiser pulled into Capitol Square, and I immediately noticed that the federal and state flags, flying a few yards apart atop the Capitol, were at half-staff. I later learned that the President had ordered the tribute even before Bart had issued his like order—one of Bart's few oversights that day. The trooper pulled quietly through the gate and around the encircled fountain to deposit me at the foot of the front porch, just feet from the door of the cream-colored Federal-style mansion. I hastened up and in, and was immediately escorted to the second-floor living quarters where Sally was waiting with one of her grandchildren.

We hugged, as her caring words—"Are you alright, dear?"—drowned out my feeble "Sally, I'm so, so sorry."

Always dignified and elegant, she now exhibited a peace and assurance that could only have come from a profound personal faith. This did not surprise me once I considered it, but it was nevertheless striking to observe.

So, too, was her overarching concern for others. Her own family was just beginning to gather, and they would require and receive all her motherly affection and consolation. But her chief concern seemed to be, not her own brood, but the Macauleys and the Thrashers and Gail Sargent. "Their loss is as great as ours," she said quietly, "and yet all the attention will be on Ned. I feel so sad for them. I need to call them right away." No one had yet provided her with the phone numbers, so I pulled the scribbled note bearing the numbers from my pocket and gave it to her.

"Ned died doing what he loved, Daniel. He grew up in the Valley but he loved that Bay more than just about any place in the world. He called it 'the source.' He would say to me, 'Sally, it had to start somewhere. Before there was the United States of America, there was Virginia, and before there was Virginia, there was the Bay....'"

I had never heard him say those words, but as Sally repeated them I understood.

"You know, he called me last night before he went to sleep," she recalled. "He said he was reading because he was too excited to sleep, and I asked him what he was reading, and he said, 'Well, it's the most marvelous thing. The Sargents have a little bookcase here in their guest room, and guess what the first book was that I laid eyes on.' The one that came to mind was *All the King's Men*, because he goes around quoting that ghastly book all the time, as you know. But I was tired and didn't feel like guessing, so I said, 'Ned, just tell me. It's too late for guessing games.' And he said, 'I'll give you a clue, and you'll only need one guess—it's my favorite novel.' And I said, 'Oh, it must be *A Tale of Two Cities*, then.' And he said, 'Bingo! I'm reading it until I fall asleep.' And we said our 'Good-nights' and 'I love yous,' and that was the end of it...."

"Oh, dear," she added with a sigh, "I am going to miss him so."

The next day, with all the crisis management business subsiding, I went to see Sally again. We talked about funeral plans. And although it was only the first of several such discussions, she had already made the most important decision. "Danny, you do what you all have to do—what is right and proper and befitting a governor—here in Richmond. But when you're done with him, I want him back. I'm taking him to Staunton and burying him beside his parents and ancestors, just as he always wanted. And we're going to take a little detour through Nottoway and drive past the farm on the way."

She also had an immediate request, with which I readily complied. She said she did not want to impose, but she really would appreciate it if I would go to Virginia Beach to retrieve the Governor's personal belongings. She did not want to ask one of her children to do it, and she did not feel comfortable asking anyone else.

I headed east directly from the mansion. When I called to tell Martha about my unexpected mission, she thought I needed company and urged me to let her come along. It was a thoughtful suggestion, but I insisted on driving myself and going solo. There were more calls to make, but mainly I wanted some time alone to think.

As I traversed the tree-shrouded interstate between Richmond and Hampton Roads for the third time in three days, I reflected on how suddenly and drastically the world had changed since our merry band of beach-bound McGuires, thrilled to have a little time off together, had ventured down the same highway barely 48 hours earlier. It had been an enormous shock and had all happened so fast. With so many things to attend to and so many people to consult, console, and direct, there had been no time for reflection.

My thoughts ran back to the previous evening's televised address by Bart. By all assessments, including my own, it had been just the right message. I had watched it with Martha, Chad, and Mitch, who had raced down from D.C. to lend support. From my vantage point in the Pocahontas Building, I had been able not only to see the address over the airwaves, but to look out across the night, up the hill, and see the light shining brightly from the third floor window of the Governor's conference room where I knew Bart was executing his solemn task.

The speech was carried live on all the local stations and on the cable news channels nationally. After an exterior shot of the temple-like Capitol that closed in slowly on the illuminated flags flying at half-mast above, the screen faded to an interior view of Houdon's Washington in the Rotunda, and then faded again to a vividly colored version of the Commonwealth's distinctive seal. The seal was on the screen only for a moment—though long enough for the ideas of "freedom" and "perseverance" to impress themselves once more on my mind—before it faded a final time to reveal the Commonwealth's new governor, seated at what appeared to be a desk but was actually a conference table, youthful-looking yet distinguished and confident, every hair in place, jaw resolutely set, cheeks suitably rosy, eyes glimmering, and every sinew and cell, I now realize, marshaled for deception.

Good evening, my fellow Virginians.

I am speaking to you tonight from the governor's office in Mr. Jefferson's Capitol, the place where so many important decisions have been made that have shaped the future and secured the promise of this great Commonwealth. Decisions made by leaders who earned the trust of Virginia's citizens and used the gift of office for great good.

Tonight we mourn the loss of one of those leaders.

For those of us who served close by his side, he was more than that. He was a mentor, a role model, a confidant … a friend.

For the citizens of Virginia, he was the epitome of the selfless public servant. He served us with ferocious bravery in war … with compassionate creativity in peace. Over three decades, he and his devoted wife Sally, our beloved First Lady, sacrificed their ease and comfort to make life better for the rest of us. Their long labors have borne abundant fruit, and will continue to bear fruit in the lives of Virginians for many years to come.

We pray for Sally and for the Governor's children and grandchildren, that they—and all of us—may find strength and solace in this shining example of a life exceedingly well lived.

We remember, too, this evening four other proud sons of Virginia—Ben Sargent and his son Jimmy, First Sergeant James "Scotty" Macauley, and young Billy Thrasher. We mourn with their heartbroken families and friends, for they, like our Governor, have left us too soon.

But there is more than mourning in Virginia this evening. There is resolve, and there is hope.

Our Governor did not devote his life to an office; he devoted it to an idea.

He did not belong to a fleeting moment; he belonged to a great tradition.

He did not seek to be served; he sought to serve others.

Tonight, I pledge to you that this government will honor his memory by following his example.

And I ask each of you to do the same.

It is our incomparable blessing to live in the greatest state in the greatest nation in the world. Our economy is among the Nation's most vibrant, and our government is among the Nation's best managed. Our leaders, in both parties, are honest and committed. Our institutions are tested and sturdy. Our communities are caring. Our people are resilient. Our future is bright.

Together, as the Governor so often counseled us, we will persevere.

We will mourn each of the lost and console one another.

We will remember with grateful hearts the fruitful lives of those who walked among us.

We will pick up the pieces and begin building again.

And, together, we will give America a portrait of uncommon courage and grace under pressure.

After all, that's what we do—*we're Virginians.*

May God bless our Commonwealth and every one of you during these difficult days.

It was a short speech—no more than 500 words from the way they appeared on the two-page text distributed by the press office—exceedingly well-crafted, even elegant, and quintessentially gubernatorial. I marveled at the creation of such a masterwork within hours of the crisis, amid the chaos. Still, it was not perfect, I thought. The question of what had caused the tragedy and what the ongoing threat might be, the object of so much discussion and speculation during the hours since the disaster, went curiously unmentioned.

And then something else dawned on me, something that I confirmed as soon as I was able to pull the car over, retrieve the crumpled text from my coat pocket, and reexamine the text: *Bart had given the entire speech without ever mentioning Ned Nevers by name.*

That name, unsurprisingly, was on every other lip in the Commonwealth for days. The noble captain, congressman, senator, father, grandfather, children's sermonizer, storybook reader, governor, would-have-been-president, and who-knows-what-else was recalled in the most flowery and flattering terms, cast in the most heroic of lights, and lionized beyond all recognition. Old soldiers fade away, as MacArthur famously said, and old politicians vanish from the collective consciousness like ghosts, but a martyred leader has the staying power of a statue.

The dark walnut coffin that bore the fallen leader's earthly remains lay in repose in the Capitol Rotunda as thousands filed past in quiet tribute, some pausing to touch, some bowing their heads in prayer, others whispering or gazing about awkwardly. It was an honor that few had been accorded, beginning with Williamsburg's George Wythe, the renowned lawyer, judge, scholar, teacher of Jefferson, signer of the Declaration of Independence, and, ironically, a murder victim.

Nevers' casket, draped in a blue Virginia flag bearing the state seal, was borne up the steps of the South Portico by an honor guard comprised of Capitol Police, State Police, and National Guard officers in dress uniforms, their polished boots and buckles glimmering brightly in the sunshine. From there, the coffin was deposited on a bier directly in front of the life-size likeness of Washington, the Commonwealth's most prized artistic work and the only statue for which the preeminent Virginian and American ever actually posed. Flanked by white-gloved Capitol Police officers at parade rest, the recumbent Governor lay not only beneath the heroic Washington's gaze, but also in the sight of Madison and the seven other Virginia-born presidents whose marble busts occupied niches in the Rotunda walls. With Washington in the center, only seven of the eight niches presently were needed for presidents. The eighth was occupied by Houdon's bust of the Commonwealth's revered friend and Washington's de facto son, Lafayette. For a while it had seemed that Nevers might be destined to displace the young Frenchman and occupy the final alcove as the nation's ninth Virginia-born chief magistrate, but that was not to be. Instead, he would take his place among the 16 most recent Virginia chief executives whose portraits adorned the balcony overhead, on the third floor, where each had labored long—and, for the most part, remarkably well—as governors of the Commonwealth.

When the time came, Nevers departed Capitol Square for the last time aboard a horse-drawn caisson, his casket now covered by the Stars and Stripes. The procession made for a magnificent scene while posing a security nightmare. The route, largely along Grace Street and then Monument Avenue, was lined by admiring citizens who were assembled 15 to 20 deep in places. Those hoping to attend the funeral service, but not counted among the invited dignitaries and friends, exceeded the available pew space in Monument Avenue Methodist by thousands, causing the adjacent streets and nearby spaces to fill with an odd mixture of citizenry ranging from the fervently grieving to the mildly saddened and merely curious.

Inside, everything was arranged just-so. Defying protocol at Sally's insistence, Martha and I sat with the Nevers family and intimates on one side of the church, while Governor Bell, the Vice President, members of Congress, other governors, and various state and federal dignitaries were appropriately arrayed across the aisle. The funeral was an apt service of worship and remembrance, and I maintained with effort my stoic demeanor throughout—with one exception. I was not then familiar with a hymn entitled "I Cannot Tell," but it apparently had been among Ned Nevers' favorites. Only when the organist began to play did I realize that the melody was the Londonderry Air, more commonly recognized as the tune of "Danny Boy." That was the song my father had sung to me at bedtime and among those I now sang, with due adjustments, to my own little ones every night when I could get home in time. It belonged to me, and I belonged to it—and the reality that many others likewise revered it made it no less my singular possession. Hearing it now, without warning, caused a sensation I cannot describe. Although Bart had said it and others had expressed a similar sentiment, I now realized that the event in which I was participating ... and for which I had so steeled myself ... was the funeral of my second father. The resulting avalanche of emotion was more than any self-erected barrier could contain.

The funeral service was the official function, but Sally and I both felt the staff needed something more. They were the Governor's extended family, and there were several hundred of them. They not only comprised the officer corps of state government; they were the enlisted men and women, too. And they included not only those serving current tours of duty, but those who had been honorably discharged from the administration, those who had been in the Nevers brigade on Capitol Hill in D.C., and those who had never served in government but had manned the campaign ramparts over the years. So, on a Sunday afternoon less than a week after the funeral, Monument Avenue Methodist was full again, this time for a special service of worship and remembrance reserved for the close-knit *political* family of Ned Nevers. The preponderance of the politicos in attendance were those engaged recently in the Nevers endeavors, so they were generally quite young.

I have not labored over the drafting of any inaugural address, State of the Commonwealth message, campaign speech, commission report, op-ed column, legislative bill, law review article, term paper, exam, or even love letter with a greater sense of anxiety, obligation, and inadequacy than seized me in the preparation of my remarks—my *sermon*—for that Sunday. Had Sally not asked me to do it, I likely would have found some excuse, some way to avoid, evade, or demur. But that is not really true, either. There were things that these crestfallen, leaderless friends needed to hear, and I was the only one able to say them. At least, I was the only person I was sure would say them. And so I prepared and delivered these remarks, hoping to turn the overwhelming sadness into a semblance of hope:

> A lot of folks in this room have helped candidates fill out campaign questionnaires, usually from interest groups and sometimes from reporters. If it's from a reporter, it's usually for a bio piece, and so there will be these penetrating questions aimed at exposing who the candidate really is as a person. You know, such clever queries as, "who is your personal hero," and "what's your favorite dessert," and "what novel or play do you like the best," and "what's the last movie you saw," and "what's your most embarrassing moment," and—my all-time favorite—"if you were an animal, what animal would you be?"
>
> On that last one, the Governor once told me he had always wanted to write, "A skunk, and if you're smart you'll run like hell...." But he always thought the better of it. I'm sure it's one of several things he's having fun saying to reporters up in heaven—assuming, of course, that some have made it there.
>
> These last few days have been a bit like writing the mother of all bio pieces. We have all learned some things we

did not know about Ned Nevers. We now have puzzle pieces ranging from favorite novels and hymns to some weightier matters, and I'm going to try to put a few of those pieces together this afternoon.

If you will turn with me to John's gospel, chapter 9—it's at page 1270 in your pew Bibles—you will read about a young man, blind from birth, whom Jesus encountered and healed. He gave him his sight. I will read from several passages in this chapter, beginning with the first three verses:

> As he went along, he saw a man blind from birth. His disciples asked him, "Rabbi, who sinned, this man or his parents, that he was born blind?" "Neither this man nor his parents sinned," said Jesus, "but this happened so that the works of God might be displayed in him."

Now, we are happy—aren't we?—because we know the end of the story: The fellow was miraculously healed. But let's pause to think about what his birth must have been like. Imagine his parents, full of excitement and anticipation— what great joy! Against all the odds, despite the terribly high infant death rate of those days, they had a son, a seemingly healthy little baby boy.

And then imagine how things turned terribly wrong. Imagine how their great joy turned to shock and sorrow when they discovered that their beautiful little baby could not see.

What an awful twist ... a raw deal! Why did it happen to an innocent little baby? Why such a heavy, heartbreaking blow to such an adoring mom and dad?

How could a loving God be so cruel?

A blind kid in ancient Palestine would not have much of a life. Others would cast him aside as worthless. In fact, John tells us exactly what his life became; he became a beggar. He sat in the village square all day and begged. But, today, some two thousand years later, we are still talking about this young man's life; we are still telling his story. Why? Because God's works were "displayed in him" through the miraculous restoration of his sight.

Then there was Fanny Crosby. Her blindness came when a "doctor" of dubious qualifications applied burning hot compresses to her eyes when she just was six weeks old. She had good reason to be bitter, just as we have good reason to ask, "Why do such awful things happen to good people?" But she was not bitter. She saw beauty in her blindness, and she went on to write thousands of beloved hymns, many of which fill that hymnbook in front of you and nourish souls every Sunday.

And there was young Jimmy McCrury. We don't know the cause of his blindness. It was some great tragedy, no doubt. And yet, as the legend goes, Jimmy McCrury, the blind fiddler, went from town to town playing a melody that would become beloved by generations, by millions. When the lyrics were added later, the tune became "Danny Boy."

But we need not journey back two thousand years or stray into the mists of Irish legend for such stories. Just down the street from here stands one of the oldest investment banking firms established in this city. Its investments over the decades have created opportunity for thousands of Virginia families and businesses. Its leader, a great son of Virginia named Jim Wheat Jr., contracted an eye disease and lost his sight at age 24. He faced a fork in the road—he could have given up. But instead Mr. Wheat became more determined and more focused. Without vision as a crutch, every other faculty became sharper, incredibly sharper, especially his memory and his mind. And he achieved great things.

"Sweet are the uses of adversity; which, like the toad, ugly and venomous, wears yet a precious jewel in his head...."

You see, God specializes in giving by taking away. He adds by subtracting. He took away the sight of each of these people in order to give them—and us—something infinitely more valuable.

It is like the tree that draws strength from the drought. When the rain is withdrawn it puts down deeper roots.

Some of you may recall the story of Gideon. He's one of the great heroes of the Bible, but at the time he didn't feel like a hero. In fact, he was a skeptic and sort of a chicken; he wanted out of it altogether. So God bucked him up by giving him a really powerful army—right? Well, no. In fact, Gideon had about 32,000 soldiers at first, but before the battle God whittled that number down to 300. Why? Because the fewer the soldiers, the sweeter would be the victory—and the more apparent God's role in it.

And, then, after leading his people to an historic victory, Gideon followed God's example of adding by subtracting. He refused to be king. Instead of stepping up to take the credit and the power, he stepped aside.

It reminds us of another story, doesn't it? It's the American story. A few blocks from here in St. John's Church, George Washington sat in a pew not unlike these and heard Patrick Henry say something like this:

> They tell us, sir, that we are weak; unable to cope with so formidable an adversary. But when shall we be stronger? … Besides, sir, we shall not fight our battles alone. There is a just God who presides over the destinies of nations; and who will raise up friends to fight our battles for us. The battle, sir, is not to the strong alone; it is to the vigilant, the active, the brave.

Washington went on to lead his ragtag colonials in battle for eight long years against the greatest fighting force in the world. They lost far more engagements than they won, but somehow they managed to hold on. And we have the testimony of the hero himself as to how the weak miraculously overcame the strong: "No People can be bound to acknowledge and adore the invisible hand, which conducts the Affairs of men more than the People of the United States," said

Washington. "Every step, by which they have advanced to the character of an independent nation, seems to have been distinguished by some token of providential agency."

Forced to confront the reality of their weakness, they had found the source of their strength. And, then, like Gideon, the battle won, Washington himself gave by taking away. He was the conqueror and so, inevitably, the king—that's how it had always worked; that's what the people wanted. But Washington knew better. Instead, he stepped aside and allowed a republic to blossom....

Our Governor loved no poet more than Shakespeare, and no play more than *Henry V*, and no passage more than King Henry's speech on the day known as the Feast of St. Crispian. It was the day before the great battle at Agincourt, and Henry's Englishmen were outnumbered five-to-one by the French. Henry's cousin Westmoreland wished aloud that the odds were more even.

"No, my fair cousin," replied Henry. "If we are marked to die, we are enough to do our country loss; and if to live, the fewer men, the greater share of honor. God's will, I pray thee, wish not one man more."

And thus they went, into battle and into history: "We few, we happy few, we band of brothers."

These heroes—Gideon, Washington, King Harry—prevailed against the odds, just as did the blind beggar and blind hymn writer and blind fiddler and blind investment banker. God's story intersected with each of their stories; he added by subtracting; and they became victors. But God does not promise earthly success even when we trust in his math. Sometimes people step out in faith, stand against the odds, and pay the ultimate price. Think of the brave Spartans at Thermopylae, the farmers who fell at Lexington and Concord, the stout patriots at the Alamo, the ordinary citizens who did an extraordinary thing aboard Flight 93.

As these heroes gave their lives, God gave us something of incalculable value: their stories and inspiring examples.

Now, what are we to make of these lessons?

Our Governor has been taken from us—suddenly, tragically, inexplicably. Are we supposed to believe that this awful accident or despicable act was God's will? What good can possibly come of it? Is this another example of God adding by subtracting—giving us something better by taking away someone we loved and served and now miss so much? How are we supposed to make any sense of it?

It's fine to have all these storybook tales of people God lifted up, but we're here and now, in the real world—and instead of lifting us up, hasn't God just let us down?

My answer likely will surprise you, because there's only one honest answer to those questions: *I don't know.*

But "I don't know" is not such a bad answer, really. It's actually a liberating answer, isn't it? Try it. Turn to the person on your right and say, "I don't know." Now turn to the person to the left and do the same. "I don't know." It's a relief, isn't it?

If you turn back to the ninth chapter of John's gospel, at verse 25, you will see something interesting.

The Pharisees, the establishment religious leaders of the day, did not like this idea of a miracle worker in their midst. It was a threat to their authority and control. So they grilled the young man about what happened, and they even went and cross-examined his parents about whether this was really their boy and whether he really had been blind since birth. And then they came back and grilled the young man some more. They wanted him to denounce the mysterious healer as some kind of fraud or charlatan or sinner. At verse 25, he answers them simply: "Whether he is a sinner or not, *I do not know*. One thing I do know. I was blind but now I see!"

What was that again?

"Whether he is a sinner or not, *I do not know*. One thing I do know. I was blind but now I see."

As punishment for his impudence, the young man is driven out of the synagogue. The self-appointed guardians of worldly wisdom can't tolerate his presence and the witness it bears. Even his parents distance themselves from him. But through their self-serving acts of subtraction, God will accomplish an awesome addition. For Jesus hears that the young man has been driven out and abandoned, and so he goes and consoles him; he reveals his true identity to him; and, at verse 38, the young man declares, "Lord, I believe," and is added to the ranks of the faithful.

At the funeral service here a few days ago, we sang one of Governor Nevers' favorite hymns. It was unfamiliar to me until then. But the melody actually is the work of that blind fiddler, and the lyrics echo the words of that blind young beggar. We all sang it together—people of varied faiths and beliefs—because we were here to honor Ned Nevers, and this was *his* testimony, a song he loved because it said what he believed.

I am grateful to Barry O'Grady for sharing it with us this afternoon, and for adding a little something special before the lyrics of the hymn. Barry is a 14-year-old member of the choir here at Monument Avenue Methodist, and the First Lady tells me there was nothing the Governor enjoyed more on Sundays than hearing young Barry sing solos....

I took my seat as the gifted boy stepped forward and sang these words, his angelic voice transporting the assembled to a place beyond time:

Oh, Danny boy, the pipes, the pipes are calling
From glen to glen and down the mountain side
The summer's gone and all the flowers are dying
'Tis you, 'tis you, must go and I must bide.
But come ye back when summer's in the meadow
Or when the valley's hushed and white with snow.
'Tis I'll be there in sunshine or in shadow.
Oh, Danny boy, oh Danny Boy, I love you so!

* * *

I cannot tell why He, the king of Heaven,
Should leave the peace of all eternity,

Why God himself should lay aside His splendor
To leave the Father's side and come to me.
But this I know: our silence filled with singing,
And all our darkness fled from heaven's light
When Christ the Lord, so human yet so holy,
In love was born a child for me that holy night.

I cannot tell why He, the joy of Heaven
Should give himself to suffer for my sin,
Why Holy God should love me in my shamefulness,
Why He should die to draw my soul to Him.
But this I know: that Christ the Lord is risen,
And praise His name, He's risen now in me!
Because He lives, I'll rise to life eternal!
He took my guilty heart and I'm forever free!

I cannot tell when He will rule the nations,
How he will claim His loved ones as his own;
And who can tell the holy jubilation
When all His children gather 'round His throne.
But this I know: all flesh will see His glory,
And skies will burst as all creation sings.
The Son will rise on one eternal morning
When Christ, the Savior of the world, is Lord and King!

After a few moments of silence I took a deep breath and resumed.

"Thank you for blessing us with your gifts, Barry. I know your #1 fan is smiling above. Now, let's all wipe away the tears and see where we are," I said, returning to my notes.

> We see that God has a history of adding by subtracting
> … of giving by taking away.
>
> We trust that he does this for a purpose, and have seen
> him bring great good out of tragedy.
>
> How and why and when and where he does these things,
> *we don't know.*

What good he will bring out of this awful tragedy, *we cannot tell.*

But this we do know: Ned Nevers came to believe deeply in God's presence and purpose in his life—and he wanted us to believe with him.

So what are we to do with that? What, indeed, are you and I to do?

My friends, we have the answer. We've had it since his first inauguration day, if not before. What did the Governor keep telling us to do when he was here with us? What did he discover on the back of the state seal one day and make the theme of his new political life?

That's right: he told us to *persevere.*

In the few minutes remaining this morning, let me point you to three chapters of the Bible that talk about perseverance. It's almost as if, by his constant preaching about perseverance, the Governor was pointing us to these chapters—so let's look where he was leading.

You can remember these three chapters by remembering the Biblical number "12," because it happens that each is the 12th chapter of a different book of the Bible—Romans, Hebrews, and Daniel—and they're easy for this sanctuary full of politicos to remember because they correspond to three ancient political capitals: Rome, Jerusalem, and Babylon.

First, Romans 12:

It's a wonderful passage, full of guidance about how to live and treat others and use our distinctive gifts. It says to "persevere in prayer." It says to become a servant—to make your life a "living sacrifice" to God. And it says this, which I most want you to remember—it says:

> Do not be conformed to this world, but be transformed by the renewing of your minds, so that you may discern what is the will of God—what is good and acceptable and perfect.

It turns out that one thing perseverance means is this: "Don't be conformed to the world. Don't let the world intimidate, distract, or divert you."

We know what that's about, don't we? The world is a know-it-all. The world demands certainty—scientific proof. If it can't be proven by science, it doesn't exist.

The world is wise, and the world is sure its wisdom is coextensive with all there is—even though it happens to be only what we presently know. So this conventional wisdom is irresistible, or it's supposed to be.

Values? Right and wrong? Well, those are subjective terms; you can't prove anything about those. Plus what is right for one person may not be right for another person—it depends on the situation, right? The important thing is to let each person be true to himself or herself, and to show tolerance for everyone's viewpoint.

Mystery and faith? Justice and mercy? Providence and prayer? What superstitious nonsense! How unworthy of the enlightened minds of modern men and women! Surely we have come too far, we've made way too much progress, for mankind to lapse into such anti-intellectual self-delusion and darkness!

The world wants sensible certitude, and when the world does not understand something, it denies its existence.

And when people persist in believing in the something despite the denials, the world derides it, makes sport of it, tries to embarrass and even humiliate it.

And when—despite all the denials and derision, all the sport and humiliation, all the secular wagon-circling and sarcastic mocking—it turns out that not only does belief in the something stubbornly persist among the masses, but it starts to reveal itself powerfully in the lives of ordinary individuals like Ned Nevers, well, the world desperately wants us to focus on something else.

But that is not what Ned Nevers would want. God changed his life, and he would want us to know it. And he would want us to open our hearts and renew our minds so that God can change us, too.

But there's a catch. In order to do that—in order to appreciate how a divine presence transformed Ned Nevers—we have to pull him down from the pedestal and understand that he was, as he once said, "just like all of us, trying to find [his] way."

He was an imperfect soul, as are we all.

His favorite novel was Charles Dickens' *A Tale of Two Cities*. And that seems fitting since those two cities also were two political capitals—London and Paris—and Ned Nevers' life, at least the political part of it, was likewise a tale of two capitals—Washington and Richmond.

In the one, he was powerful but lost. In the other, he surrendered to a power greater than himself and was found.

He lost an office and lost his way. But in the aftermath of that loss, he regained his soul and found his voice.

More addition by subtraction.

Last week, I went to Virginia Beach at Mrs. Nevers' request to retrieve the Governor's personal belongings. She had spoken with him the night before his death, and he could not sleep. He was excited about getting up early and going out on the Bay. And so he was reading *A Tale of Two Cities*, which happened to be in his bedroom there at the Sargents' house. When I went to the room where the Governor had spent the night, the book was still lying on the floor next to the bed, and it was open to this passage. It is the passage where the unlikely hero of the novel, a washed-out lawyer of wasted potential named Sidney Carton, is likewise unable to sleep, so he goes on a walk. Soon he will do a "far, far better thing" than he has ever done before—he will go to the guillotine in another's place—a surprise that still awaits the reader. But here is what Dickens writes of the hours before his character's ultimate act of sacrifice:

> "There is nothing more to do," said [Carton], glancing upward at the moon, "until tomorrow. I can't sleep."

It was not a reckless manner, the manner in which he said these words under the fast-sailing clouds, nor was it more expressive of negligence than defiance. It was the settled manner of a tired man, who had wandered and struggled and got lost, but who at length struck into his road and saw its end.

Long ago, when he had been famous among his earliest competitors as a youth of great promise, he had followed his father to the grave. His mother had died, years before. These solemn words, which had been read at his father's grave, arose in his mind as he went down the dark streets, among the heavy shadows, with the moon and the clouds sailing on high above him, "I am the resurrection and the life, saith the Lord: he that believeth in me, though he were dead, yet shall he live: and whosoever liveth and believeth in me, shall never die."

That's the end of the passage. But I read on, following Sydney Carton on his nighttime stroll as the Governor must have done that evening, and I imagined how our leader must have faded into the fog of Dickens' dreamy words—"The strong tide, so swift, so deep, and certain, was like a congenial friend in the morning stillness...."

Sleep finally must have come. The book must have fallen to the floor. And in the early morning darkness our joyful, child-like Governor must have fumbled for his clothes and raced out, undoubtedly a few minutes late as usual, maybe more than a few minutes, rushing back into the arms of his congenial friend the Bay, back to what he called "the Source."

His journey, like Sidney Carton's, was a journey of faith. He had "wandered and struggled and got lost, but ... at length struck into his road and saw its end."

And in his renewal is hope for the rest of us, because the Good Shepherd does not give up on any of his lost sheep.

That testament to perseverance in faith brings us to the second of the three chapters on perseverance—the one in Hebrews 12.

Of course, before there is Hebrews 12, there is Hebrews 11, and it's like a biblical hall of fame. The entire chapter is an honor roll of those who put their faith into action. "By faith," Noah did this, and Abraham did that, and Isaac did the other thing. "By faith," Joseph did this at the beginning of the 400 years in Egypt and "by faith" Moses did that on the way out. "By faith the people passed through the Red Sea," and "by faith the walls of Jericho fell," and "by faith [various judges and prophets] conquered kingdoms, administered justice, obtained promises, shut the mouths of lions, quenched raging fire, escaped the edge of the sword, won strength out of weakness," and so on.

It is after that long and impressive recitation of faithful feats that the unknown author of the letter to the Hebrews begins the 12th chapter this way: "Therefore, since we are surrounded by such a great cloud of witnesses...."

In other words, since we have the benefit of so many stellar examples of faith in action, not just from the Bible, but from our history and even from our own lives....

"Therefore, since we are surrounded by such a great cloud of witnesses, let us throw off everything that hinders and the sin that so easily entangles. And let us run with perseverance the race marked out for us...."

The message from the life of Ned Nevers is that God will use us for a good purpose if we do our part—if we run with perseverance the race that he has marked out for us. The God who has begun a good work in us will see it through to completion, just as he completed a very good work in Ned Nevers.

"But," you say, "his work was not complete! We were in the midst of doing so much good, and he was our leader, and now all is lost. And how cruel of God to do that to him and to us!"

And that's natural—we're all tempted to feel that way. But we have to understand that God's work in and through Ned Nevers really *was* done—it was complete, according to God's plan. It is only *our* work—yours and mine—that remains.

If the Governor were here, he'd repeat one of his favorite adages: "Don't cry because it's over; smile because it happened."

He'd say, "Take pride in all we've accomplished together. But temper your pride with even greater humility, because none of us has done anything alone. Everything good has depended on help from each other and help from above."

He'd say, "Together we have laid a strong foundation; now you go build on it. It's never too late to make a difference and make your life a testament to faithfulness and service. Look how I turned my life around—turned defeat into victory—turned selfish ambition into productive service. Now you go turn this tragedy into triumph. Use this experience, the mountaintop of excitement we shared and this valley of loss you now feel—use it all for good. Learn from it; let it mold you; and let it inspire you to live out the next great chapter in the story God is writing with your life."

Above all, he would repeat the words of comfort that the author and perfecter of his faith spoke to him on the night before he died, through the pages of his favorite novel: "He that believeth in me, though he were dead, yet shall he live: and whosoever liveth and believeth in me, shall never die."

Governor Nevers would say all those things to us today. But there is one thing he would *not* say: He would not say it is going to be easy, or obvious.

Listen again to the admonition of Hebrews 12: It speaks of setting aside the distractions and diversions. It speaks of avoiding the sin that "so easily entangles." Perseverance, you see, is more than a test of endurance. It's a test of character, too.

There was another book that became a favorite of the Governor's—a book he rediscovered during the "involuntary vacation" between his D.C. and Richmond political jobs. He took to quoting it so often that he about drove the First Lady crazy. But something in that book spoke to him, and I am pretty sure I know what it was.

The book was the great American political novel *All the King's Men*. It was about another governor in another capital at another time, one who found his way late in his career— just in time, as it turns out. Because soon thereafter he was murdered by an aggrieved idealist named Adam Stanton. The story of Governor Willie Stark is seen through the eyes of a trusted aide, just like many of you, and here's how the aide described his boss's journey:

> It is the story of a man who lived in the world and to him the world looked one way for a long time and then it looked another and very different way. The change did not happen all at once. Many things happened, and that man did not know when he had any responsibility for them and when he did not. There was, in fact, a time when he came to believe that nobody had any responsibility for anything and there was no god but the Great Twitch…. But later, much later, he woke up one morning to discover that he did not believe in the Great Twitch any more. He did not believe in it because he had seen too many people live and die…. [He] could see that Adam Stanton, whom he came to call the man of idea, and Willie Stark, whom he came to call the man of fact, were doomed to destroy each other, just as each was doomed to try to use the other and to yearn toward and try to become the other, because each was incomplete….

I think the author, Robert Penn Warren, came as close to the truth about politics here as anyone can hope to come. There is a thing in the world called Idea—you may call it the "political ideal." And there is a thing in the world called Fact, which you may call "political practicality." And they are enemies out to destroy each other. Yet, the great irony, as Warren's character explains, is that they are not only and always at war with each other. To the contrary, each will try to use and even become the other, because each is incomplete without the other.

Let me bring it down a notch with an illustration. You are facing a choice in your political pursuits. You have in mind some worthy goals; you want to get elected in order to accomplish some good things; so let's call you the man of Idea, the candidate of high ideals. And yet you face a dilemma. It seems the best way to achieve your worthy goal is to cut corners, not a lot but a little—maybe shade the truth a bit about your opponent, maybe promise to do this or that thing in office at odds with your convictions because you need that big endorsement or contribution, or maybe it's any of a hundred other things you don't think are just right. So let's call you the man of Fact, the man who understands and bows to those things we will politely call "political realities." But can you be both the man of Idea and the man of Fact? Should you be both? How do you draw the line so that the "political realities" don't overwhelm and destroy your ideals?

It is true, isn't it, that the man of Idea is incomplete without the man of Fact? After all, what good does it do to have great ideas and worthy goals if you never get elected and have a chance to implement them? Or, conversely, where is the satisfaction in getting elected if you have no higher purpose than the pursuit of power itself—if it's all about what you can get rather than what you can give? The fact is, to accomplish anything, the ideal has to be married up with the practical, the theoretical with the real, the intent with the action. We cannot pitch our tent on the glorious mountaintop of lofty ideals and wholesome intentions; we need to be Madisonian about it. We need to come back down to earth, get down into that dusty and harsh arena of contention and competition, and battle for what we believe in, all the while keeping our heads about us and our passions in check. We must work to win yet not get so caught up in the contest that we forget our standards or surrender our values or sacrifice our principles. We must maintain a healthy balance.

And one thing we must know before and above all else: *We must know where the line is that we will not cross.*

The great discovery, the source of redemption, in *All the King's Men* is the realization that the ends don't justify the means, that there is not a Great Twitch presiding over the happenstance of life with moral neutrality and ethical indifference. Rather, there is, as Patrick Henry declared at St. John's Church, a just God in heaven who presides over the destinies of nations ... and of individuals. And he is not only our judge; he is our maker, defender, redeemer, and friend.

Here's how I see it—and please hear me on this: God summons us to reach out in love to serve others—and for some that calling to service is through politics. And those he summons he also equips; he gives us the brains and train-ing and friends and counselors and tools to practice the po-litical art with skill and energy, cleverness and competitiveness. And those he summons and equips, he also challenges. He challenges us by leaving us free and thus sus-ceptible to trials and temptations, and especially to the sub-tle, seductive notion that our own advancement justifies taking a shortcut here and shortcut there. And those he summons, equips, and challenges, he also sustains, helps, and refines. He provides his Word, and he supplies exam-ples and counselors, and he gives us a still, small voice that reminds us there is right and wrong and that helps us dis-cern the difference. He makes us ask and answer the hard questions about who we are, and what we believe, and where we are going to draw the line. And in doing this, he refines our character. He refines our character not only as players in politics but as people in the world.

I wish I could tell you it was easy. I wish I could tell you it was easy for Governor Nevers, and that it will be easy for you. But it is not easy. Being in the arena is not easy. Drawing the line is not easy. But that's what proceeding from freedom to faith to purpose is all about. It's about making choices. It's about placing your life and labors in the hands of a power and purpose greater than yourself. It's about growing in understanding and perspective, stepping out in faith, and doing your best to do the right thing.

Let me close by borrowing from one final Ned Nevers' favorite—one more piece of the puzzle—his favorite musical. Of course, it is *Les Misérables*, a show he saw again and again. More than once I heard him point out how the great chorus changed from the beginning of the show to the end. At first, what you hear the people sing is the stirring song of the idealistic young freedom fighters: *Join in the fight that will give us the right to be free!* But, then the cruel realities of life come crashing down with all their broken dreams and shattered lives and humbled hopes. In the end, the people are still singing, but now they are climbing heavenward, from darkness into light, their swords exchanged for ploughshares, their chains about to be broken.

So there is the perseverance in faith and prayer of Romans 12. And there is the perseverance in struggle—in principled, practical service—of Hebrews 12. But there is something else, too. It is the perseverance in hope of Daniel 12.

You see, no matter how true we are to our calling, no matter how valiant our labors, we have no promise of truth or justice, health or happiness, in this life.

You can do everything right as God helps you see the right. You can work tirelessly to bring about good through what government does and through what you keep government from doing. You can play the game with surpassing skill and unwavering integrity. And still the political system and the people who populate it may let you down.

Remember the cry of the mob: "Give us Barabbas!"

There will be bad people who prosper, and there will be good people who suffer. There will be wonderful people we love and lose: princes like Billy Thrasher and Scotty Macauley and Ben Sargent and Ned Nevers. And if we ask why, only the blind beggar's answer will echo back: *I don't know.*

But this we do know even in our confusion and doubt: In God's time ... for his people ... the tables will turn: What has been subtracted will be added, what has been taken will be given, and there will be infinitely more. Those who lost their sight will see a brilliant new Creation; those who lost their liberty will gain a perfect new Freedom; and those who lost their lives will rise to an eternal life of Love.

It is the promise of Daniel, chapter 12—the promise of a far, far better place. Here's what it says:

> Many of those who sleep in the dust of the earth shall awake, some to everlasting life, and some to shame and everlasting contempt. Those who are wise shall shine like the brightness of the sky, and those who lead many to righteousness, like the stars forever and ever....
>
> Happy are those who persevere....

My dear friends, we have heard the people sing, and now we hear the drums beating for our Governor. They are beating a song of triumph for one who fought the good fight, finished the race, and kept the faith.

But they're beating for us, too, because here we remain—we few, we happy few—still together, still striving, still joined in the fight that will give us the right to be free.

Let us persevere, then, together—in faith, hope, and love. When tomorrow comes, let us rise no longer mourning what we have lost, but living lives worthy of all we have gained. For it has been our great gain to witness God's amazing grace at work in the life of a prodigal politician: a man who once was lost, but now is found ... was blind, but now he sees.

As the piper took the cue and began to heave out the haunting, hopeful strains of the old slave trader's song of redemption, I closed the book and strode down the steps. All the week's awesome energy and emotion were now utterly spent, and there was nothing left for me except to dissolve in Martha's waiting arms.

CHAPTER SEVEN

HANDWRITING

I f only I could have departed with Governor Nevers—not the world, but that precinct of it dominated by politics—I could have left with my sunny disposition and idealism intact.

I had seen what great good a well-motivated person could accomplish when skilled in the art of politics, refined in the crucible of service, and renewed by faith. Now, in that ennobling lesson's wake, I would see the evil side, too. The next season of my education, when selfish ambition owned the throne, came with shocking suddenness. An awful bitterness and brutality attend a bad person's lust for power, and I experienced them firsthand.

Nevers had barely completed his first night's encampment on the quiet hill in Staunton's Thornrose cemetery before Bart was moving remorselessly to take the reins of power fully in hand back in Richmond. The new governor was the first and only to gain the office upon the death of his predecessor since Virginia governors and lieutenant governors were first popularly elected just before the Civil War. Publicly, he continued to pay homage to the fallen leader, basking in the afterglow of Nevers' near-universal popularity and pledging to complete the sainted executive's unfinished work. Privately, Bart ruthlessly began to sweep away each significant remnant of the prior administration, installing his personal allies and purging every unhappy reminder that his office rightfully belonged to another.

It began with Abby, who was offered the directorship of a junior agency and told to exit the Governor's Office by sundown.

Utterly gone, and never more than a chimera, was the "we will get through this together" spirit that Bart had conveyed to me in that conciliatory first call after the tragic news broke. Bart had gained what he had coveted most (or perhaps second-most)—the governorship. As the attorney general, I was at best a problem to be managed and at worst a threat. Bart assumed the worst, so the conflict commenced immediately.

For reasons that now seem obvious, one of Bart's first orders of business was to fill the vacancy that his elevation had created in the office of lieutenant governor. The position once had real clout, but to go back that far you had to reach into the pre-revolutionary era when royal governors resided comfortably in England while their lieutenants wielded authority in the colony. In the modern era, lieutenant governors routinely joked that they had only three functions—presiding over the Senate, breaking occasional tie votes, and checking the governor's pulse. It was the latter aspect, presumably, that made Bart eager to insert his loyal if unimpressive lieutenant, M. Hardesty "Hardy" Barnhard, into the state's second-highest constitutional office.

There was a catch, however: Virginia's law on the subject was anything but clear.

By one statutory interpretation, the post was to remain vacant until the next gubernatorial election, with the Senate's president pro tempore (currently the Norfolk Democrat, Senator Howard Morris) assuming the presiding officer duties, and with the attorney general occupying the next spot in the gubernatorial line of succession. By another interpretation—one resting on the governor's general authority to fill vacancies in executive branch posts unless otherwise specified in law—the appointment was Governor Bell's alone. Indeed, by this reading of the law, the appointment did not even require confirmation or election at the next succeeding session of the General Assembly in the manner of other significant government positions.

Unsurprisingly, the new chief magistrate preferred the latter interpretation, which gave him *carte blanche* to install a deputy of his choosing until a special election could be held. Having looked into the matter and spotted the legal ambiguity, Bart figured the smart strategy—particularly for a popular new leader seen as doing his best in trying times—was to act swiftly and with certitude. He thus signed the Barnhard appointment the day after Nevers' funeral and summoned the Chief Justice to the Governor's Office to administer the oath.

"It is only prudent," the earnest new governor announced to the assembled reporters with the statuesque old jurist and attractive young Barnhards at his side, "that we fill this vital position promptly. Recent events have taught us that fate is full of cruel twists and the world is full of dangerous people. We should not long leave a gap in our line of succession."

The justification was palpably disingenuous, and the dubious legal basis for the action was never mentioned. But what Bart lacked in authority he more than made up for in chutzpah, aided by the element of surprise. So the thing happened quickly, with all the majesty of a trip to the kitchen for a coffee refill, and was done.

For me, what happened next was even more unsettling—and revealing. Within minutes after the Governor announced the Barnhard appointment, Miguel strode into my office with a letter in hand. "You are not going to believe this," he said coolly.

I unfolded the letter, recognizing at once the familiar gold embossed light blue stationery of the governor.

"Dear General McGuire," read the short missive,

> *This is to inform you that, pursuant to Virginia Code section 2.2-510(1), I have issued an order appointing John Manning Jr., Esq., of the Manning, Manning, Terkel & Parson law firm as legal counsel to represent the Commonwealth of Virginia, the Governor of Virginia, the Lieutenant Governor of Virginia, and all other state government entities and officials in connection with any and all matters arising from or related to my action today in filling the vacancy in the Office of Lieutenant Governor. This action is based on my determination that you are unable to serve as counsel with regard to these matters because of a conflict of interest arising from the attorney general's presence in the gubernatorial line of succession.*
>
> *Sincerely,*
> *Bart Bell*
> *Governor*

Miguel waited to comment until I looked up, utterly stunned. "This is quite serious," he said.

"You think?" I rejoined sarcastically.

"As you recall, the question of whether the lieutenant governor vacancy could be filled was one of numerous issues we identified before the funeral, but it was not an immediate concern. I don't think we anticipated that Governor Bell would act so precipitously, and without consultation."

"We did not," I confirmed.

"But it is obviously a very important question—"

"Obviously—"

"—and so I began researching it over the weekend. And my preliminary conclusion, General, is that the Governor lacks the authority to fill the vacancy."

"*Lacks* the authority?" I repeatedly incredulously. "You're telling me that the Chief Justice just swore in a lieutenant governor whose appointment by the Governor is invalid?"

"I am telling you there is a substantial possibility, if not probability, that a court would hold that a vacancy in the office of lieutenant governor is to remain open until the end of the term, with the Senate president pro tem discharging those duties, rather than being filled by the unilateral appointment action of the governor."

"Well, then, we need to get up the hill and spread the word," I said without thinking.

"Before you do anything like that, General, I encourage you to step back and consider what is going on here. This is only the sixth day since Governor Nevers' death—"

Only day-six, I mused. It seemed much, much longer.

"—yet this is a carefully calculated move. Governor Bell is at least two steps ahead of us, maybe more. He obviously recognizes the legal vulnerability of his action, and he has moved—quite decisively and deftly, I'd say—to block you from challenging it and to install a lawyer friendly to his position as the Commonwealth's counsel for the litigation that will follow. Legally, his position that you have a conflict is not frivolous—he may well be right. And, in any event, it will *look* like he is right. His action not only appears logical and reasonable; it has the legal imprimatur of the Chief Justice. If you challenge what he's done, it will seem completely self-serving."

Miguel's political insight was undoubtedly correct, but I fervently hoped a closer look would prove his legal analysis wrong. One thing Virginians surely did not need after the previous week's gut-wrenching tragedy was an unseemly partisan power struggle at the top. The line of succession was the farthest thing from my concern, but partisans on both sides would regard it as important. Of even greater significance, the Senate was almost evenly divided, with the Democrats still possessing only a razor-thin, two-seat advantage over the Republicans. I was reasonably certain that Senator Morris and his Democratic colleagues were not going to let Hardy Barnhard stroll up onto the rostrum as the gavel-wielding, tie-breaking Senate president without a fight.

As we anticipated, spirited litigation ensued over the Governor's questionable appointment. I remained on the sidelines legally, although I did run a good play a few days later, after strategizing with Mitch, Chad, and Abby as well as Miguel. I called in several reporters and suggested that Virginia would be well served if the Republican governor and Democratic legislature could come together in a spirit of bipartisanship and moot the legal controversy by convening in special session to enact a statute establishing that vacancies in the office of lieutenant governor are to be filled by gubernatorial appointment subject to confirmation by the General Assembly, just as vacancies in the attorney general position are filled between legislative sessions. The legal cloud then would be removed; the General Assembly presumably would confirm Mr. Barnhard's appointment; and all would be right with the world. Despite the evident merit in this suggestion, both sides predictably rejected it. The popular new governor had no interest in submitting his mediocre confidant to the scrutiny of a confirmation process, and Democratic partisans wanted to avoid installing Barnhard—or, for that matter, *any* Republican—as the incumbent lieutenant governor heading into the next statewide election just two years away.

The chief consequence of this controversy, at least for me, was to expose my rift with Bart—not entirely, but enough for discerning Capitol insiders to see daylight between us for the first time. Privately furious, the Governor shook off my suggested compromise nonchalantly in public and professed our continued solidarity as keepers of the Nevers flame. Of course, he was the heir to real power, the experienced political professional who was governing confidently and coasting toward a presumed reelection in 2005, while I was merely the caretaker AG, a political amateur and obvious short-timer. At least, that is the way Bart viewed it, and he never missed an opportunity in the ensuing weeks and months to cast me in that light. His devices for putting me in my place ranged from the substantive—excluding me entirely from his policy pronouncements; quietly torpedoing my legislative initiative to combat illegal drugs; second-guessing various actions by my office; calling on me to trim my budget—to petty indignities such as not inviting me to receptions at the Executive Mansion and failing to recognize me at political events. He even took to jocularly calling me "Dan, Dan, the Generalissimo man" when we found ourselves together in public settings, a trivializing reference that I had to receive amiably even as audiences large and small chuckled at my expense.

Far more disheartening and detrimental, however, was Bart's systematic dismissal or demotion of virtually all of the talented political protégés that Governor Nevers and I had recruited for positions of significance in the administration. In addition to Abby's swift ouster as chief of staff, Chad was unceremoniously cashiered as secretary of finance. Given the opportunity to resign ostensibly of his own accord, or so he was told, Chad was soon the object of a concerted rumor campaign suggesting, utterly falsely, that both Governor Nevers and Governor Bell had found his performance to be inadequate. Bart's seedy operatives fingered Chad as the minister largely to blame for the state's errant fiscal forecasts as the economy slowed. He was a useful scapegoat, and it separated the new executive from his predecessor's regime in the one area—the state budget—that might be a potential vulnerability as the 2005 election approached.

It is hard to express how painful it was to watch the successful Nevers administration dismantled brick by brick over a period of months while the usurper on the throne continued to claim the Nevers mantle, to invoke the Governor's legacy whenever it served his purposes, and to exploit the deceased leader's popularity. As I watched the spectacle with many other deeply chagrined veterans of the former administration, I began to hear them say with increasing frequency that I was the true heir to Governor Nevers and had an obligation to pick up the fallen standard and run in 2005. This was not a welcome suggestion; and, insofar as it meant taking on Bart for governor, it was absurd. He was a skilled politician riding high in the polls and, from the vantage point of most Virginians, honoring Nevers' memory and carrying on his work. Challenging him for the GOP gubernatorial nomination would be a fool's errand.

Yet, the suggestion that someone had to stand up to Bart and stand for the principles and ideas that the party had championed under Ned Nevers landed on fertile ground. And once that need became clear, it was evident as a practical political matter that I was the only one in a position to do it. That is not to say that I was altogether reluctant to put myself forward or that my motives were invariably pure. I deeply resented Bart's serial indignities and his arrogant belief that he could run roughshod with impunity over me and all of Governor Nevers' other loyal lieutenants. Principles, policies, loyalty to Governor Nevers, my competitive nature—even pride, if I am honest about it—were all in the mix. And so I edged ever closer to seeking reelection as attorney general. I concluded that doing so was the one available move that could transform me from caretaker into playmaker, from factotum to force-to-be-reckoned-with in the political arena, and thus give me the clout to carry on our important work.

The daily grind under Bart's new regime was nightmarish: friends and colleagues disconsolate over the loss of their leader and now their jobs; an investigation that brought more questions than closure; an overbearing and unpredictable governor wielding power for power's sake; and a demanding day job that was a minefield. But that daily torture was more than matched by the terrors the custodian sent along to visit me during my fitful evenings.

The worst came in September, following another long and frustrating day spent coping with fallout from the latest high-handed maneuver by Bart. After an hour of tossing and turning, I surrendered to the unhappy truth that I was not going to fall asleep and probably would keep Martha from sleeping if I stayed put. So I went downstairs, crashed on the couch, and channel-surfed for something to take my mind off work. Finding a history program (the kind I never got to see while sharing TV privileges with Martha and the kids), I settled back to watch and soon fell asleep. The program was another that relied on the Nazis' own film footage chronicling their detestable day in the sun. This one was a documentary on Hitler's rise to power and the role his vilification of the Jews played in that rise. I was not awake to see more than a few minutes of the program, but I still recall my last waking thought: *It is incredible that this happened barely a generation ago, in a supposedly sophisticated country, in a supposedly enlightened era, in a world supposedly superintended by a loving God….*

What happened next confirmed the truth of John Adams' observation that a dream can be a "mighty Power." Writing to Benjamin Rush in that strange correspondence Abby unearthed, the revolutionary statesman described a mind "not shackled with any rules of Method in Arrangement of Thoughts…. Time, Space and Place are annihilated; and the free independent Soul darts from Suns to Suns, from Planets to Planets … to all the Milky Way, quicker than rays of Light."

My sleeping soul darted that night, but it was not the free independent frolic from sun to sun and planet to planet that Adams had described. It was from one cruel crime against humanity to another, from one maniacal tyrant to another, from one blood-soaked age to another. Hitler and his gas chambers ... Stalin and his gulags ... Pol Pot's killing fields ... Bin Laden's murderous missions ... Antiochus Epiphanes deifying himself and slaughtering Jews ... Nero exculpating himself and slaughtering Christians ... Crusaders gaining indulgences for themselves by slaughtering Muslims ... Islamic radicals slaughtering New Yorkers of every race and faith. Like a slideshow in hyper-speed, the awful images came lightning fast—one marauding animal after another, ravenous beasts drunk with power and the lust for more, full of envy and hate, thirsty for blood. Yet, not all were despicable dictators, so easily and universally deplored. Some even were regarded as local heroes. I saw a bigot in Birmingham turn police dogs on demonstrators ... a judge in Salem hang a woman for witchcraft ... a bureaucrat in Richmond deny education to Indian children because their parents would not renounce their heritage and label them white or black. I saw a soldier massacre civilians in the name of duty and a guard torture prisoners in the name of justice. I saw an Army recruiting center bombed in the name of liberty and an abortion clinic bombed in the name of life. I saw conservatives pledge fidelity to freedom and then blindly sacrifice it for security, and I saw liberals betray liberty by silencing those with contrary views.

Each rapid-fire image—and there must have been hundreds of them—revealed another injustice committed by a person in power, or in pursuit of power. Each person wielded a political club and claimed a higher purpose, whether secular or sectarian. And each, wittingly or unwittingly, seemed to be an instrument of evil.

In my dream, I was watching as if in a theater, and the person on my left—who turned out to be *Bart*—grasped my arm and said, "Watch this!" Then the scene slowed to normal time, and all the images seemed to merge into one. There was a great throne, and before it stood an awful creature, like a mythical beast, boasting contemptuously. His words cut like a knife for all who were attending court, causing them unimaginable emotional and physical agony. He spewed his bile for what seemed like an eternity but was only a season. Then, the person on my right—who turned out to be *Miguel*—grasped my other arm and said, "Watch this!" Suddenly, the court was bathed in light, and when the light subsided there was a radiant prince standing before the throne in the place where the awful creature had been.

Stunned by all this, I awakened. The still-vivid nightmare was confusing; it should have been a source of hope, but my overwhelming reaction was terror. So much horrid oppression, torture, fear, and pain inflicted on the innocent down through the ages, with so much more sure to come. And the dream made it seem like Bart had been on the scene forever....

ROCK BOTTOM

I have found that good days rarely follow sleepless nights, and the next day was certainly not among the rare ones.

I had a 10 A.M. meeting with Governor Bell to update him on several litigation matters and settlement proposals that required his approval. He kept us waiting for 35 minutes, but once underway it was all business—the Governor behind his stately desk, Miguel and me in the two winged-back chairs facing him, and a pair of young lawyers (Bart's chief of staff and counsel) on our flank, awkwardly sharing the small antique bench in front of the window. After our brief task was concluded, Bart asked his aides and Miguel to exit so he and I could speak privately.

"Danny," he started in without beating around the bush, "I know some folks are urging you to run for reelection as AG. And it's certainly okay with me if you want to do that. In fact, I'll make sure we clear the field for you within the party; I'll do that for you if your heart's really in it. Really, I will—*honest*. But I can't believe that's actually something you're up for. I mean, you're a great behind-the-scenes guy, but being the candidate is something else entirely. You've seen the toll it takes on a person, especially on a young family like yours. Plus, you've never had the passion for politics. You haven't had to play the kind of hardball it takes to succeed in this business. And, you know, it's my job now to lead this party, and the AG position is important, and we need a candidate who is totally committed and ready for everything the Dems will throw at us. I mean, you've never liked the political game. I remember we had to drag you kicking and screaming into that first Nevers for Senate campaign way back when. I have this clear memory of you standing there bored and bewildered on the floor of that convention. You were looking around with an expression that said, 'Man, I would rather be just about anywhere other than here....'"

Bart chuckled at the recollection while probing my expressionless visage for clues.

"Anyhow," he continued seriously, "I have to be convinced that you are really up for this challenge in order for me to support you, and, frankly—"

Without any calculation I cut him off.

"Was there ever a time, Bart, when it bothered you even a little that his whole career was premised on a lie?" I asked.

"What are you talking about? Whose career? You mean Nevers? What lie? 'Premised on a lie' how?"

"That flyer, the one at the 1982 convention, the one that got him the nomination, the one that sent him to the Senate—it was a lie."

"How can you say that, Danny? That's ridiculous. Why tarnish his memory that way? You ... we ... none of us knows what happened with that flyer. It was just a dumb piece of paper, and it is ancient history. Nobody cared about that flyer anyway. I had practically forgotten all about it. So has everyone else."

"It was a lie, pure and simple. I know it, and so do you," I persisted.

"I don't know anything of the sort. But so what if it was a lie?" Bart said, changing course aggressively. "You have all your quaint notions of what is fair. You have these lofty, impractical standards. You've been sleep-walking through politics for years now. You obviously were sleeping through Dr. Weston's class when he talked about Machiavelli."

"Oh, I know all about Machiavelli—the good and the bad," I replied. "If anyone was asleep during history class, Bart, it was you. History draws a straight line from your hero Machiavelli to the political Darwinism that says 'might makes right'—from *The Prince* to Robespierre and the Terror, and on to Stalin and Hitler and the death of millions."

Bart had a blank look. He had started the Machiavelli talk—superficially, the way everyone does—so I resolved to finish it.

"Machiavelli was brilliant, but when it served his personal ambitions he wrote that a political leader should subordinate his sense of morality to the ends of the state. Any tactic is okay as long as it serves the purpose of gaining and exercising power. It usually starts with a little lie, a little shortcut, and then it's a bigger lie, a bigger shortcut, and where it goes from there no one can predict. No one, that is, except history. History has it figured out. History says your morally indifferent approach to politics more often than not ends in corruption and tyranny, even horrendous crimes against human life itself."

Bart's puzzled expression now gave way to red-faced disgust.

"Wow, that's a bit melodramatic, don't you think? From one little convention flyer to the death of millions—I had no idea I was capable of such atrocities!" He was up now, exposing the faded seal on the governor's chair, and raging. "I will really have to watch myself! Maybe I should move this flag over in front of the fireplace so I can look at *Sic Semper Tyrannis* every day and remember not to run amok with the people's liberties! I'm sorry that flyer offended you, Danny—I *really* am. I promise nothing like it will ever happen again…. Oh, wait—it actually *will* happen again if I decide it needs to happen … so I am not promising you *shit!* If you're so good and I'm so bad, don't you wonder why I'm running things here in the Capitol and you're down there in the Pocahontas Building playing with paper clips? It's almost like there isn't any justice in the world…."

I ignored Bart's taunting and tried to make some more historical points, but he cut me off.

"You're so erudite, Daniel—so very brilliant! If I could just sit here and be lectured by you all day and soak in even a smidgeon of that brilliance, I could probably amount to something one day. But, unfortunately, *I have a state to run.*"

It was almost comical how this powerful little man could be so juvenile. If he were actually a child—that is, if his actual years matched his stage of moral development—he would have put a finger in each ear and hummed loudly.

"I am not sure why I even brought up the convention flyer," I reflected. "I guess I was looking for some hint of remorse at the injustice you did to Ned Nevers in the process of advancing his career—or, rather, in advancing your own career through his. But it was silly of me to expect that from you after all these years."

"Oh, screw you, Danny McGuire!" Bart erupted. "You stand there like some saint, looking down on me. You've always looked down on me. Well, look who's on top and looking down now! You're in politics just like I am. You're looking out for yourself just like I am. There's no difference between us!"

"Bart," I answered calmly, "we could not be more different. Your basic character makes no distinction between right and wrong. Mine leaves no room for peace between them."

"Well, we will just have to see who wins, won't we?" Bart said, gritting his teeth and motioning toward the door. With that, my colleague since college, the malevolent new governor of Virginia, turned his face to the window and his back to me.

"Thank you, Governor," I said out of respect for the office as I left. There was no reply, only the bitter silence of a seething man who now regarded me as his mortal enemy.

"Well," I said to Miguel as we traversed the balcony of the Rotunda en route to the steps and exit, "that was clarifying."

I had planned no such encounter, had not even imagined it possible. But as my heart pumped and the adrenalin coursed through my weary frame, I suddenly felt strong—and an enormous sense of relief.

In the weeks and months that followed, my friends set to work helping me build the complicated political edifice necessary to win a statewide campaign. Mitch made phone calls to key conservative donors and movers-and-shakers. Chad worked his business community contacts to the same effect, turning down lucrative offers from several financial firms and large companies so he could return to political consulting and manage my campaign. Abby joined the AG's office as director of administration, tending to the integration of my official duties and political activities. Miguel assumed even greater responsibilities for managing the office's legal portfolio and, with the help of our superb team of deputies, took much of the attorney general's daily decision-making load off of me. I hit the hustings practically full-time, speaking at political events, party meetings, and civic gatherings of all stripes, calling and meeting with the captains of industry, potential donors, and party officials—doing all the things I had watched Nevers and other pols do over the years and had been so very glad I did not have to do.

I hoped for the best but had no clue what to expect. So I was stunned by the expressions of support that flooded in once I let it be known that I was running for reelection. Volunteers and donors came out of the woodwork; endorsements and commitments streamed in; and potential rivals laid back. I knew that a lot of fellow partisans—not just Nevers administration alums but many others—were deeply uncomfortable with Bart's methods and the company he kept. But he was the governor, a very popular and powerful governor, and few in the party or the business community could afford to invite his displeasure by siding with me. Fortunately, they did not have to. Bart plainly hated me at that point and would have derailed my candidacy if he safely could have. But to oppose me overtly would have meant exposing a breach within Neversworld, a conflict within the court of the late lamented king. Bart knew that his claim to the throne—i.e., his case for reelection—rested in large measure on being seen as the heroic leader's rightful heir. An open effort to derail my nomination as attorney general would disclose a schism and would inevitably trigger an unseemly and risky debate over which of us truly had possessed Ned Nevers' confidence and enjoyed the affection of his closest allies. The facts were not on Bart's side, so it was in his interest to maintain the facade of solidarity, at least through the election.

Bart was not the only one in a box, however. I was now a candidate for re-election on a ticket that Bart Bell was certain to lead. The irony was inescapable. I was running for statewide office, something I had never aspired or expected to do. I was doing so largely because I regarded Bart as an unworthy pretender who would not—indeed, *could* not—champion the party's principles and carry our creative conservative reforms forward. Yet, I was joined at the hip with Bart politically. With the Democrats ready to seize any opening, my own election very likely depended on Bart's continued popularity and success. There seemed to be something fundamentally dishonest in that equation, and it nagged me constantly as I campaigned around the state, obligatorily touting the "Bell-McGuire team" and professing our commitment to complete Ned Nevers' unfinished work. I never really made peace with the proposition, but I did manage something of an armistice by reminding myself of my own message at Monument Avenue Methodist weeks earlier: The ideal and the practical are at war with each other, but they also need each other, and no one said reconciling them would be easy....

Meanwhile, although it hardly seemed possible, things got noticeably worse in the wake of my heated encounter with Bart. More heads rolled, and these deeper in the ranks of the administration, as Bart and his lieutenants demanded avowals of fealty from even junior appointees and found ways to purge anyone with more than casual ties to Nevers, Mitch, Chad, Abby, or me. The customary business meetings between the Governor, AG, and our top lieutenants ended entirely, and only the most essential matters were the subject of communication, always curt, between our two offices. Bart and I did not share the stage together at official or political functions unless it was altogether unavoidable, and then it was a huge strain. I renewed efforts to secure passage of several key reform measures, only to have the governor's office either hijack my initiatives by including them in Bart's legislative package or dispatch operatives to quietly submarine my proposals in legislative committees. Some of Bart's actions seemed calculated to make himself look good at my expense, and some were driven by his acute paranoia, but most were just petty and vindictive. For Bart, it was all about who was on top; he had the power and wanted to show it. And with the Democrats posing little threat—poll after poll showed Bart cruising to reelection in the fall—he had the luxury of concentrating his destructive energies on me and anyone he thought was aligned with me.

There was more going on with Bart than just his negativism toward me, however. Those who encountered him during this time found him remote and distracted, constantly on edge, fidgety, erratic, often angry. He evinced little enthusiasm at official functions or on the stump, delivering scripted speeches that said all the right things but displayed no passion whatsoever. Around the Capitol word began to circulate that the Governor was constantly out of sorts about something or someone; he would deliver random tongue-lashings even to legislative allies, cabinet secretaries, and members of his inner circle. That circle seemed to draw ever tighter, too, as Bart trusted few and confided in fewer. Meanwhile, the mansion parties—some very raucous affairs, according to the rumors—became more and more frequent. And when his racy friends were not hanging with the Governor in his official residence, they were entertaining him elsewhere, safely beyond the prying eyes of Capitol Square. It was increasingly obvious to insiders that something was badly amiss. Bart was out of control, but not yet so out of control that the public could see it.

It did not help the new governor's state of mind when a bitterly divided Virginia Supreme Court finally ruled that the appointment of Hardy Barnhard as lieutenant governor had been invalid. The decision came in November, and by then it probably was not a huge surprise to anyone except Bart and Hardy. Though most of Virginia's legal and political elite initially assumed the governor's general appointment powers were broad enough to settle the question in Hardy's favor, that thinking had shifted sharply when the Justices issued an interim order blocking the November special election that the general appointment statute would have required. Once it reached the merits, the Court held that the existence of a specific statute addressing vacancies in the office of lieutenant governor—the one providing for the Senate president pro tem to discharge the duties—trumped the more general gubernatorial authority to fill vacancies. "It would strain both language and reason," the Court declared, "to suppose that the General Assembly intended to give itself complete or shared authority in filling vacancies in the attorney general position, the Commonwealth's #3 office, but intended to give the governor a blank check when it comes to filling the #2 office, an office with major legislative responsibilities." Reacting to the Chief Justice's dissenting opinion that assailed their "unprecedented activism," the Court's majority pointedly rejoined, "Our colleague is willing to construe the laws of the Commonwealth as constraining the governor's authority more when he selects the lowliest agency head in the bowels of his own executive branch (which requires confirmation by the General Assembly) than when he selects the officer who will preside over the Senate and who, as we have seen, may be imbued with the vast executive authority of this state in the flash of an eye. We are unwilling to take such a preposterous flight from reason and experience."

Though he was ousted instantly by the judicial decree, I thought Hardy responded to the devastating development reasonably well. He reaffirmed his plans to contend for lieutenant governor in the 2005 election and thanked various people for assisting during his brief tenure. Bart, however, was *ticked*, and he did not make much of an effort to conceal it at his post-ruling news conference. The Supreme Court had "become increasingly political in recent years," he observed derisively, and so their "partisan ruling was not all that surprising." He snarled, "You'd like to think that in perilous times such as these the justices would put partisanship aside and act in the best interest of the Commonwealth, but that obviously did not happen here." Bart was not finished until he had promised retribution. "At least these hacks don't have life tenure like the federal justices, so there will be accountability...."

For me, this whole bizarre period was a colossal cluster of stress, sadness, soul-searching, anger, frustration, and second-guessing. These were truly tormenting times. I had been awakened for the first time to the actuality of an insidious force—a self-absorbed, power-hungry, amoral energy—dominating daily life, including the politics and governance of my state. Worse, there was the distressing sense that this dominance was not short-lived or exceptional, but sustainable and, in the course of human affairs, even inevitable. In moments of exhaustion, when self-pity tried to sneak in once again, I would marvel at how fast things had changed and how comparatively simple it had all been when Ned Nevers was alive. We had been on such a high, doing so much good. Why did it have to end?

Hey, that question was for you, God, in case you couldn't tell: Why did it have to end?

The answer to this question came first through Martha and my friends: they answered it by refusing to waste time on it. Never enamored with political life, at least as she conceived it, Martha nevertheless jumped in with both feet.

Her performances on the stump consistently outshined my own, and her irrepressible spirit energized everyone around her, me foremost among them. Chad and Abby were equally amazing. They had suffered a sudden reversal of fortune far more severe than my own; their status in the eyes of the political world had been dramatically diminished. Yet, they approached the task at hand without a trace of resentment or the least distraction. I was astounded by their grit, and during one of our Saturday afternoon strategy sessions on the side porch of my house, I asked them how they did it.

"What are you talking about?" Chad replied impatiently, obviously irked by the question. "What do you mean, 'How do I stay focused after all that's happened?' I stay focused the same way you do, for the same reason you do: because this is our *work*. Sure, I could be doing something else; all of us could be doing something else. But we're doing this because we believe in something. For me, it's all about *freedom*—you above all people should know that. And freedom isn't predictable; freedom by its very nature is risky. If we expect that right will always win and that all will go swimmingly, then we don't understand the state of the world or the nature of the human condition or the price of freedom. Hayek said—yes, Hayek; that's your cue to roll your eyes, Danny—"

"Okay," I obliged.

"Hayek said, 'Freedom granted only when it is known beforehand that its effects will be beneficial is not freedom.' That's the simple concept that people can't seem to grasp. I'm not one of those guys who goes around railing against the entitlement mentality of the other party and half of society, and then expects—in fact, feels *entitled*—to have everything go my way. I don't expect every good run of success to be followed by another and another, and I certainly don't expect 'the system' to be rigged in my favor. That's what those other guys expect, okay? It's not me. *It's not me.* What Hayek says to me is that the fight for freedom is every bit as unpredictable as freedom itself. Bad things happen. So, yeah, we've taken a body blow—the kind that knocks your breath right out of you. But it didn't kill us, so let's not sit around whining about it. This is a great contest, the fight of all fights, and I'm in it for the long haul. And you'd better be, too, Danny. *You'd better be, too.*"

Chad's passionate response silenced us until I finally broke the tension.

"Okay, you're right—let's get back to work. But if it's all the same to you, Chad, my wide receiver days are over, so I'd like us to concentrate on *delivering* some body blows rather than absorbing more of them."

404

"I'm all for that," he answered emphatically, as we returned to our planning.

I resolved not to let self-pity, or even pity for my friends, cloud my thoughts again.

ONE THING

My problem was that the blows were coming from multiple directions, and the usual source—the Democratic opposition—was the least of my worries. Despite our surface alignment, Bart and his people would be coming at me. But how? And from where?

I answered the phone a few days later, anticipating correctly that the "unidentified caller" was Mitch.

"Dreamer, you know I got your back, but you guys down there gotta do a better job of guarding your flank," he said.

Having my back, I assumed, referred to my support from the party's conservative base. No one was more influential in that faction than Congressman Mitch Jackson, and he had been working tirelessly to line up support for me. But my flank?

"Roger that," I replied. "But I'm gonna need a new vector, Victor. Can you clue me in on what flank I have to worry about?"

"Three guesses, and the third one is a floor of the Capitol," he answered.

"Ahh, well, no shock there—what in particular?"

"My chief of staff got a call from Sam Garnett down in Orange. You may remember him; he owns a hauling business out near Unionville."

"I don't think I know him."

"You've met him; he says it was just once, in passing. But you know the family. He's that kid Lorenzo's uncle. Bonita Washington is his sister-in-law."

He paused, as if waiting for a reaction. I didn't have much of one, so he continued.

"The other day he called my guy here, and he said he wanted me to call him back on a 'secure line.' I figured he'd been watching too many spy movies or something, but I was down in Orange for an event this weekend, so I went by to chat with him in person. I didn't like what he told me."

"I'm listening."

"He said that some folks from Richmond had been up there asking around about you and Bonita and 'your relationship.'"

"Our *what?*"

"Yeah, you heard it right. Somebody is doing some digging. This is like third-hand at best, okay? But Sam said some white dude in a suit with a low-numbered license plate had been up there talking to a bunch of folks and asking questions like, 'How long have Bonita Washington and Danny McGuire known each other?' and 'What's the nature of their relationship?' and 'Have you ever heard anything about Bonita Washington and Danny McGuire being romantically involved, you know, as in having an affair?'"

At this, I laughed out loud. But the seriousness of the matter was quickly apparent.

"Okay, good ... it's a joke and you're on top of it. Glad to hear it," Mitch offered.

"It's a joke, a very *cruel* joke," I replied. "But I wouldn't exactly say I'm on top of it. In fact, this is the first I've heard it."

"Obviously, it's not true...." My friend knew me well but he had succeeded in life by never assuming anything.

"Obviously," I confirmed. "But I can see right away how the rumor might have started. Clearly somebody is tailing me...."

"Whoooa, Danny, I'm not liking the sound of that. Talk to me now—give me the story."

"It's ... uh ... not a problem. I mean, it's not a political problem. I mean, it's easy to answer the affair thing—that didn't happen. But I have promised to honor a confidence...."

"Oh, it's an attorney-client thing?" Mitch asked, sounding relieved.

"Not exactly. Actually, not at all. It's not an attorney-client confidence, but it's a solemn promise I am bound to keep."

"Okay, enough of this, Danny. Enough! Have I ever breached a confidence of yours? *Ever?* Tell me the situation so we can deal with it."

He was right, and I relented. "You have to keep this in strictest confidence, Mitch. I mean it—you have to give me your ironclad word."

"You got it."

"It's a very bad situation," I disgorged. "Bonita is very sick, and Lorenzo doesn't know about it. At least he has no idea what's wrong or how serious it is. He's off at school in LA; he got a full-ride scholarship to study music at

USC a few years back, and he's still out there—a senior now, I think. But it's AIDS, Mitch—Bonita has AIDS. She contracted it several years ago. Her boyfriend was killed, caught in the crossfire at some shooting, and she was deep in depression. She lost her job and she was afraid she wouldn't be able to pay for Lorenzo to go to college. And she made some very bad choices. If she had only asked for help, we would have found a way to take care of it ... but we were not part of her life at that point, and we should have been. We wanted to help—in fact, we had already started raising money for a scholarship for Lorenzo through a local nonprofit—but you can't just parachute in without knowing what is going on in someone's life. And we did not know. It's clear now that Bonita didn't believe there would be enough money for Lorenzo to go to college, and she was determined that he would be able to follow his dream ... so she did what she thought she had to do. The tragic thing is, he got a big scholarship and didn't need any help after all. It's all just terrible. She took a turn for the worse about six months ago, but she wouldn't tell anyone at her church or anyone else—she's desperate to keep her illness secret so it doesn't get back to Lorenzo. She says he means more to her than life itself and that knowing what she did would destroy him. He would blame himself because she did it for him. The one saving grace is that she finally called Martha. And so we got her moved to a new house out our way; one of the churches near us owns it and gave her a break on the rent, and Martha and I are picking up the rest. We were going by there a lot, basically every day, until we were able to arrange for some sitters. We took turns, but it was mostly Martha. I went by after work a fair amount...."

"So that's the deal," Mitch said finally. "Bart's henchmen are following you around, and they follow you to her house, probably more than once, and in their dirty little minds they think they've got the goods on you because you must be having an affair. So they start digging, trying to find out how long you and Bonita have been at it. Geez, what a pathetic bunch of creeps. See what I mean about watching your flank?"

"Well, I certainly see it now. But how are you so sure it's Bart's people?"

"Well, they may be malicious but nobody ever accused them of being particularly smart. The license plate number was 893. My guy here ran it down through a friend at DMV. It belongs to one of Bart's high-flying friends and funders, and the guy's son works in Hardy Barnhard's office."

"Yeah, that's not real bright. If you're gonna roam around spreading BS about the state's chief law enforcement officer, you might not want to do it in your daddy's Bentley and hand out your business card. But knowing who it is doesn't solve my problem. I have to figure some way to squelch this thing without the whole world finding out about Bonita's situation."

"I will handle it," Mitch said definitively.

"Handle it how?" I asked.

"Simple," he replied. "As soon as I get off this call, I am calling Hardy Barnhard."

"And?"

"And he will understand two things before I get off the phone. One is that you and your wife have *both* been visiting Bonita Washington, so there's no dirt to be found there. The other is that I am onto his games and if I ever hear so much as a hint about him trying to screw you over again, I will make sure that the entire base of the Republican Party knows what a sleazeball he is. When I'm through, he won't be able to get elected precinct captain on Assateague Island, let alone lieutenant governor."

"Well, that probably should get the point across. Even a mule can understand a two-by-four to the head. I appreciate it, Preacher."

"No thanks needed. But I mean it, Dreamer: *Watch your flank!* It may have been a ham-handed maneuver by Hardly Barnyard this time, but you can't count on them to make mistakes. These guys play for keeps—Bart, especially."

The silly business would be dealt with fully by Mitch. But I had promised full disclosure to my bride in all things, and had made a similar commitment to my friend and manager when the campaign commenced, so the next day I told both Martha and Chad about the episode. No one else needed to know; my pledge to guard Bonita's secret was paramount. But our antennae were now up, scanning for signs of trouble, and there would soon be plenty of ominous signals to pick up on the darkening Virginia landscape.

As far as I knew, my young lieutenant, Miguel, was unaware of the growing dangers, but with his sensor trained on me he accurately detected a distinct disquiet in my soul. So, on a Friday afternoon in early March, just eight months before the election, he did something unusual. Until now, our relationship had been all business. But on this day he invaded my personal space, inviting Martha and me to join him at the Sunday services of Good Shepherd Church, a youthful, multi-ethnic congregation on Richmond's Church Hill. Miguel was a member, and one of his college friends—now a dynamic young minister in D.C.—would be preaching there on Sunday.

I did not jump at the invitation. Martha and I were comfortable attending our more traditional church in the West End. We enjoyed the weekly fellowship and were reluctant to skip out even for a single Sunday. I had found particular strength and solace there during more than a year of constant strain under the Bell administration, when it seemed the lions were circling continually, poised to devour me at any moment. I looked forward to Sunday school and the worship service as a way to refresh my spirit and rekindle my resolve. Plus, I had bought into the candidate thing only so much—and not to the point of being willing to spend my Sundays campaigning in other folks' churches. I suspected that Miguel had some such political purpose in mind.

But my young counselor was insistent.

"You *have* to hear him," Miguel said emphatically. "I know what he is going to say, and it speaks to your situation. It's almost like he's coming here just for you."

The scene at Good Shepherd that Sunday was unremarkable. It was the message that mattered. After a prayer and reading from the unfamiliar Book of Habakkuk, here is what the gifted young messenger had to say:[1]

> *In the third book of J.R.R. Tolkien's* Lord of the Rings *series,* The Return of the King, *Pippin is a hobbit, and he comes into service of Denethor, who is the Steward of Gondor. Now, if you know anything about hobbits, you know they are agrarian creatures, and they live incredibly tranquil lives without conflict. There is very little war or violence in their society. But Pippin and Frodo and his friends have been thrust into a living nightmare where everything around them, everything that was stable and familiar, has been crumbling away. And so there is this really poignant scene where Denethor is in despair, and he asks Pippin, his little friend the hobbit, to sing to him one of his hobbit songs, to bring him comfort.*
>
> *And Pippin responds: "But we have no songs fit for … evil times, lord."*
>
> *This little creature, who has only ever known good times, does not know now how to navigate such times of evil.*

---

[1] Author's note: This text is borrowed, with only minor adaptation, from an actual sermon delivered by Reverend Corey Widmer at Third Presbyterian Church, Richmond, Virginia, on October 16, 2011. The author acknowledges with gratitude Rev. Widmer's permission to use the sermon in this volume.

This is the kind of situation that the prophet Habakkuk is in. He is in what the Book of Ecclesiastes calls "evil times."

Evil times are not just a month or a couple of years of hardship. Evil times are whole seasons, generations of darkness, where societies move into periods of turmoil and there is little hope of relief. An evil time like that was happening in Habakkuk's country—in Judah. Moral and spiritual deterioration among his own people. Injustice and lawlessness in his own nation. Serious military threats of destruction all around. And there was no hope that any of this was letting up.

And so, the big question of the Book of Habakkuk is this: How do we navigate, how do we face, evil times?

I think as Americans we tend to believe that times just always get better ... and that things will be better for our children than they were for us ... and that home values will always go up ... and that our investments, even with some little dips, will always be on the rise....

Can we just level with each other here? This is not true. The Bible does not promise this. History does not demonstrate this. Even in our time, with all that has been happening, we don't actually know whether things will be better for our children than they were for us.

So the question becomes, what are we going to do about this? How do we navigate evil times? And not just times in society and history, but even times that you might face personally—how do we face them?

Habakkuk gives us a roadmap because he faced such times. It's an amazing contemporary book. So let's look at what we learn from this book about how to navigate evil times: We see that (1) he questions God; (2) he trusts in God; and (3) he rejoices in God....

So the first thing we see Habakkuk doing is questioning God.

He does it a lot: "How long must I cry for help?" "Why do you not save?" "Why do you make me look at injustice?" "Why do you tolerate wrong?" "Why do you tolerate the treacherous?" "Why are you silent while the wicked swallow up those more righteous than themselves?"

We immediately see that Habakkuk, for some reason, feels the freedom to do what we often feel we cannot do in times of trial. He actually feels the freedom to ask God these hard, challenging questions.

I think a lot of us, when we face evil and hardship, feel we have to offer more answers than questions. Especially for Christians, it's almost like we feel we have to explain evil, or we have to make it seem less bad than it is. And so we say things like, "God must have a reason," or "there's a silver lining to every dark cloud," or "everything works for good," or "all our pain is meant to teach us something," or—when someone dies—"God must have needed another angel." But these kinds of comments are laughable, because what these comments do is sentimentalize evil. They make things that are actually bad, and that God thinks are bad, seem like less than they really are.

When we look in the Bible, we don't see all these trite platitudes that try to explain things. What we see in the Bible instead is people who are shaking their fist at God because they see that God's goodness is not meeting the reality of what they see in the world. They recognize that this world is not the way it is supposed to be, and so they ask God questions.

Job asks, "Why does the Almighty not judge? Why must those who know Him look in vain for his justice?"

Jeremiah says, "Why is my pain unending and my wound grievous and incurable?"

In the Psalms, David says, "I cry to you for help. Why, Lord, do you reject me? Why do you hide your face from me?"

Jesus: "My God, my God, why have you forsaken me?"

You see, it's not the Christian response to say, "Oh, well, God must have a plan," with a smile on your face. It is the Christian response to say undeniably, "This is <u>not</u> the way the world was meant to be."

Do you ever wonder why Jesus was always crying all the time, and weeping all the time, and feeling grief all the time? Do you ever wonder about that? I'll tell you why: because he was perfect, and the less self-absorbed a person is, the more in touch he will be with the pain and brokenness of the world.

411

And so that's what this means. Habakkuk and Jesus asked questions boldly. And so can we.

But here's the key—here's what I want you to see about his questioning. It's directed to whom? It's directed to God.

Habakkuk doesn't start blogging about his questions. He doesn't write a cynical editorial for the local newspaper. He doesn't form a little society with his friends called "The Questioning God Society." What he does with his questions is he brings them straight to God in prayer. The whole Book of Habakkuk is one long prayer, actually, between one man and his God. And so, yes, he questions, he shakes his fist at God, he asks about these inexplicable things that he doesn't understand. But he never, ever, ever considers leaving God.

That's because he knows that God is good even when he doesn't understand him.

The questions flow in and out of the relationship. It's sort of like this: You know how you are most prone to say what you really think or feel to the person you are closest to? It's why your spouse or your best friend is tired of your complaining all the time. You're most prone to tell people you're closest to how you really feel.

That's the sense that you get with Habakkuk and Jeremiah and David. It's that they had such a close relationship with their God that they felt free to pour out their questions and protests to him.

Here's the lesson: It's okay to have questions. It's okay to have doubts. It's okay to have concerns about things you don't understand. But here's what I want to say to you: Do not let your questions drive you from God—drive you from church, drive you from obedience, drive you from community. Let your questions drive you to him. Let them enrich your prayer life.

The people that I have known who have the richest prayer life and deepest relationship with God are the people who have suffered. And they have taken their questions in their time of suffering and they have brought them to their God. He can handle them—he really can.

And so that's the first thing we learn about how to navigate times of trial, times of evil: We can question.

Second, we can <u>trust</u> God.

At the beginning of chapter one, verse five, after Habakkuk asks all these questions, God answers them. And here's what He says: "Look at the nations and watch, and be utterly amazed, for I am going to do something in your day that you would not believe even if you were told."

Now, if I was Habakkuk and God had said that, I would be like, "Yes! God is going to answer my prayers! You know, I've been complaining; I've been saying there's all this violence, please do something about this!" And God says, "I am going to do something you won't believe." And Habakkuk is so relieved that God is going to bring resolution.

But I left out the next verse, where God goes on to say, "I will do something you would not believe. I am raising up the Babylonians, those ruthless and impetuous people, who will sweep across the earth to seize dwelling places not their own." And then God goes on to describe how he is going to use this ruthless and terrible nation of Babylon to destroy his people, Judah.

And Habakkuk responds: "Oh God! Are you not from everlasting?"

To paraphrase: "What??? You call that an answer to prayer?! I thought you were in control! I thought you were God! I pray that you bring relief to the violence and the corruption of my society, and you answer by saying you're going to bring <u>more</u> violence and <u>more</u> corruption? And you're going to drag our society and our people into exile? What kind of an answer is that?"

And God responds, in chapter two: "I told you that you wouldn't understand." But then he says, "Though the answer lingers, it will come … wait for it." And he ends with that famous statement in verse four: "The righteous will live by faith."

What is going on here?

God is teaching Habakkuk an important lesson that all of us have to learn at some point. It's a very basic lesson but it's a difficult one. And it's this: God's timing and plan and agenda are often very, very different from our own. And often it appears to be inexplicable to us.

413

Have you ever heard somebody talk about "all the pointless evil in the world"—about how "pointless it all seems"? Have you heard someone say that?

Here's the problem with that statement. Behind it is an assertion, an assumption, that if there was a point to this evil, I would see it. If there were answers to all the suffering in the world, then I would know them. It is expressing such tremendous faith in your own personal omniscience ... in your own cognitive faculty to discern the coherence of the universe.

But why, friends—why? What makes you think that if there were a point you could see it? I mean, you're a human being. And God is God.

And so what God is saying to Habakkuk here is, "Yeah, okay, you're protesting. But I am going to do something here you aren't going to believe. I am going to raise up Babylon, this ruthless and violent nation, to bring more violence, to drag your nation into exile, and this is actually serving my purposes for salvation. And what I want you to do, Habakkuk, is I want you to live by faith. I want you to trust that my purposes are getting worked out even when they seem inexplicable to you. And I want you to trust that more than you trust your own ability to understand."

What's amazing about this, just as an aside, is that we have the luxury of seeing what Habakkuk couldn't see. One commentator I read this weekend said that because God's people were carried into exile, the Jewish people were scattered all over the ancient world. And most of them did not return to Jerusalem—most of them stayed in diaspora. As a result, Jews established synagogues all over the ancient world, and by the time the Roman Empire came around there was a synagogue in most every Roman city. So when we get to the Book of Acts and Paul begins to spread the Gospel and go on these missionary journeys, what does he do? The first thing he does is go the synagogues where the Jews and the God-fearers (the pagans, who had come to trust in Yahweh) were. And so those synagogues all across the ancient world become sending points for this new missionary movement of the Gospel.

So if God had not brought his people into exile ... if he had not allowed the Babylonians to inflict violence on them ... if he had not allowed his people to be dragged all across the face of the earth ... then the Gospel never would have spread.

God was working his purposes out, but how could Habakkuk ever have seen it?

In 1951, the Communists who had come to power in China cracked down hard on the missionaries. And I have a friend who was a missionary in China at the time who got expelled. And he said, "Everybody went crazy. They were, like, 'How could God have done this? How could God have allowed this to happen? A hundred years of missionary work down the drain! God has abandoned China!'"

But what do we know from history? We know that because of this the Chinese took their faith into their own hands, and Christianity became indigenous to China. As a result, over the last 60 years China has become one of the most vital and fastest growing Christian movements in the world. People say that within the next 50 years there could be 300 million Chinese Christians, the largest population of Christians on the face of the earth.

Was it a waste? Of course not. God was using what some people saw as pointless evil to carry out his purposes.

So this is the hard question we all need to ask and answer: Are you willing to obey God and trust him even when you are not given an explanation—even if you are <u>never</u> given an explanation? Are you willing to trust that his purposes are good even when it seems like the great engines of his purposes are being thrown into reverse in your life?

You see, without faith, suffering is destructive. But, with faith, it becomes an opportunity—an opportunity of grace.

So give up your presumed omniscience, please. It is way too burdensome. <u>If you want a God that is big enough to deal with the evil in the world, then you also have to accept a God who is big enough to do things that you don't understand</u>.

So we can trust him—that's the second thing we can do to navigate through evil times. We can question God. We can trust in God even in his inexplicability.

And, then, finally, we can <u>rejoice</u> in God.

Many people have called Habakkuk a miniature Book of Job because some of the themes are so similar. (And if you want to read one or the other, I would recommend Habakkuk because it's only three chapters.)

What happens in the beginning of Job is really interesting. God is having a conversation with Satan, and God is talking to Satan about Job. He says, "Have you considered my servant, Job" and what a great servant of God he is?

And Satan says, "Hah! You think that Job serves you for nothing? Job doesn't love you; he loves your <u>stuff</u>. He serves you for all the riches and the wealth and the family that you've given him. But I tell you, God, you take away his stuff—his family, his riches, his land—and he will be out of here, because Job doesn't serve you because he loves you. He serves you because he loves your stuff."

This is a great test. Satan knows us very well. He knows that almost all of us tend to associate the goodness of God with what we have gotten from God.

Just this week, a friend of mine who has been unemployed for a while came by to tell me he had gotten a job. And the first thing I said, without thinking about it, was, "That's awesome—God is good!" And he is good. But then I began to think, what if he hadn't gotten a job? What if he had stayed unemployed forever? What if things got worse instead of better? Would God still be good? Is it possible to have access to God's goodness even when God does not give us what we want?

The answer is, yes. And Habakkuk was able to discover that. Look at chapter three, one of the most beautiful passages in the Old Testament. He says, "Though the fig tree does not bud—"

Actually, let me translate this into our contemporary jargon instead: "Though I lose my job, and my health fails … though my loved one dies … though the economy is tanking … though the election does not turn out the way I hope … though my friends don't appreciate me … though my children are estranged … though everything appears to be going wrong in my life … still, I will rejoice in the Lord.

Is this possible? How is this possible?

This is a secret that many people in Scripture and in history seemed to have learned, but I don't quite understand. And I pray that I will, and I hope that you will, too.

I think David understood it. In Psalm 27, he said, "Though an army besiege me, my heart will not fear; though war break out against me, even then I will be confident. One thing"—one thing— "I ask from the Lord, this only do I seek: that I may dwell in the house of the Lord all the days of my life, to gaze upon the beauty of the Lord."

Here's what I think the secret is. Please try to listen carefully.

The secret to whether you are able to navigate times that are evil in your life all depends on what your "one thing" is.

What is your one thing? What is the one thing that you cherish and value more than anything else? Because that will determine how well you are able to navigate evil.

If your one thing is your health, you will not be able to navigate cancer or a health crisis.

If your one thing is family, you will not be able to navigate the loss of a child, the loss of a spouse.

If your one thing is economic security, you will not be able to navigate loss of a job or an economic crisis.

If your one thing is beauty, you will not be able to navigate aging, you know, wrinkling.

If your one thing is anything but God, it can be threatened. It can be taken away from you. And if that one thing is taken, then your life can be taken along with it.

But if your one thing is God—if he is the thing you value most; if he is the one you want the most; if he is what you delight in the most—then what is most important to you can never be taken from you. Nothing ... no storm, no disaster, no crisis, no crash, no fallout can take it away.

Then you will be able to say like Habakkuk, "Though there are no grapes on the vine ... though the olive crop fails and the fields produce no food" ... though everything is crumbling around me ... "I will rejoice." Why? Because I still have the one thing. I still have God.

417

Here's the thing. Don't treat God like you would never want to be treated.

You would never want to be in a relationship where you discover that the other person is only in the relationship because of your benefits—because you are rolling with cash, or because you have something they want—and then as soon as you start to lose those things, they're out. You wouldn't want to be treated that way, and God doesn't want to be treated that way, either.

So, every time you are in crisis, every time you are in pain, every time you are in a time of evil, it's an opportunity. God is coming to you, and he is saying, "Are you in this for me, or for you? Will you trust that I am the good thing in your life, and not what I have given you?"

You see, it's not just about getting clarity to our problems, or getting answers to our struggles. It's about our relationship with God himself. As Habakkuk says, it is God that enables us to go up on the heights, to be in the mountains even when we're in the valley.

So how do we face evil times? We question honestly, bringing our pain to God. We trust in God's timing even when it's inexplicable. We rejoice in God's goodness more than what God gives us.

I know this sounds difficult, but let me give you a word of encouragement. We are in a far better position than Habakkuk or David ever was. That's because they had a promise of the messiah, Jesus. We have the knowledge of who he actually is and who he has been for us.

We know he took on our abandonment, our separation from God, so that no matter what, in every situation and scenario in life, we can be absolutely guaranteed of God's love. So that nothing can separate us—neither death nor life nor angels nor demons nor the present nor the future nor any powers nor anything else in all creation can separate us from the love of God in Christ Jesus. So that when all hell breaks loose upon your head, when all is stripped from you, when everything you dreamed about is taken, you still have the one thing you actually need....

I pondered the message for days after that Sunday morning, and my reflections sent me, oddly, to the book that had so intrigued Ned Nevers late in his life. A political novel seemed an unlikely source of insight into life's great mysteries, and within its pages the marginalized character known as the "Scholarly Attorney" seemed the unlikeliest source of all. Yet, I vaguely recalled reading something the man had said, something similar to that Sunday's message, and I went searching for it. There near the end, lying modestly alongside the main story in *All the King's Men*, were these words that the strange father figure had recorded:

> The creation of man whom God in His foreknowledge knew doomed to sin was the awful index of God's omnipotence. For it would have been a thing of trifling and contemptible ease for Perfection to create mere perfection. To do so would, to speak truth, be not creation but extension. Separateness is identity and the only way for God to create, truly create, man was to make him separate from God Himself, and to be separate from God is to be sinful. The creation of evil is therefore the index of God's glory and His power. That had to be so that the creation of good might be the index of man's glory and power. But by God's help. By His Help and in His wisdom.

It was a confusing statement, to be sure, but both that passage and the gifted young pastor's sermon seemed to say what I had been taught years earlier by Dr. S. D.: the price of freedom is error, hence evil, a price that can only be paid redemptively, through suffering love. Viewed through a glass darkly, this notion would remain stubbornly out of focus in this life, but it was clear what to expect in the meantime. Everyone who seeks to live a life of faith "will be persecuted," Paul wrote to young Timothy, "while evildoers and impostors will go from bad to worse, deceiving and being deceived…." His words echoed the terrible truth that horrified Habakkuk: power would belong to "guilty people whose own strength is their god."

So this condition—*my* condition, *our* condition—might be utterly inexplicable but it was thoroughly foreseeable. God had ordained it; the prophets had foretold it; the apostles had forecast it; history and literature

419

had confirmed it. And nearly everyone who endeavored to fight the good fight would experience it.

Perhaps I should have taken some consolation from this, but I did not. The pain to be suffered by so many good people was too terrible. My dreams continued to distress me by night, and Bart and his minions continued to torment me by day. The worries mingled oddly with the daily highs and lows of campaigning. At times, I felt physically ill; depression nearly overwhelmed me; and I was tempted to give up. But I did not give up—or give in. Instead, I kept the problem in my mind, persevered in prayer, and went on with my work.

I had learned a lot during the good times—campaigning and governing with Ned Nevers, mastering the art of the possible, getting things done. But there never was a time of more dramatic personal growth in my life than during this period between Governor Nevers' death in July 2003 and the November 2005 election. And while it is tempting to offer the hackneyed statement that "nothing could have prepared me for what was to happen next," the reality was just the opposite: *Everything* had prepared me for what was to happen next.

9/11 had brought home for us the persistence of evil, but even that attack on American soil seemed distinctively foreign in origin and alien in character. Ordinary people do not do such things, our modern minds want to believe. Yet, evil still stalks like a lion looking for someone to devour; human nature still craves power above all else; and the collaboration of those forces produces a will to *destroy*—to destroy liberty, justice, even life itself. It is when we are most satisfied with our lives and circumstances ... most secure in our ideas and institutions ... most self-impressed with our patriotism and exceptionalism ... most sophisticated and self-sufficient, embarrassed by the very notion of a superintending God whose moral compass orders the Universe ... that we are the most vulnerable to this evil.

So it was in Virginia. And almost no one saw it until the handwriting was on the wall.

Revelations

In early June, I received the Republican nomination for attorney general at the Virginia GOP's state convention in downtown Richmond's aging Coliseum. The program lavished praise on Governor Bell and paid moving tribute to Governor Nevers, whose statewide political career had been launched 23 years earlier in the same hall. It was all very well done, a political show that well served its campaign purpose. And, as Bart's folks fully intended, I was essentially an asterisk at the affair, completing the Bell-Barnhard-McGuire ticket by filling up a space, and little more.

A week later, our opponents were nominated at a similar conclave in Norfolk. Senator Dorothy Meade, having gained the Democratic nomination for governor by default, entered the race a whopping 35 points behind Bart in the latest polls. In the contest for lieutenant governor, the Democrats' strongest political figure, Speaker Percival, was matched against our weakest, Hardy Barnhard, yet Percival still trailed by double digits. My opponent for attorney general was a civic-minded attorney with a nice way about him, a legal practice that would be aided by the visibility, and no serious thought of winning.

There was little doubt about the outcome of the upcoming elections, making the campaign seem almost perfunctory. Then came the news that changed everything.

It was a typically flaccid, oppressive day in late July, the kind that makes the Virginia capital feel quintessentially Southern. I was eating breakfast with Martha when my traveling aide, Raj Hummar, made his way under the dogwoods and approached the side porch door. Having been awarded an extra 15 minutes thanks to a campaign schedule that put me in central Virginia for back-to-back days and saved me the packing time, I was relishing the few added moments with Martha. Spying Raj's arrival, I glanced at my watch and then at my schedule. The ever-punctual "body man" was 30 minutes early.

"Excuse me, folks—good morning, Mrs. McGuire," Raj said. "General, I know I am early, but Chad asked me to bring the new schedule out to you and get you underway as soon as possible."

"What new schedule?" I asked as Raj extended his hand with the one-page document.

Amazingly, the entire day's events had disappeared overnight. In their place was a lone appointment: "Conference (OAG, 8 A.M.): MA, John Smith."

"OAG referred to the Office of the Attorney General. "MA" was Miguel. "John Smith" was a mystery.

"Okay, let's go," I replied, puzzled. Something was up.

"Don't ask me; I'm just the campaign manager," Chad replied irritably when I reached him as we made our way downtown. "It's a heck of a disruption; we've almost finished notifying everyone who was on today's schedule. All Miguel would say was, 'Make it happen ASAP—I'll take responsibility for it. It's official state business.' So we did. Sure hope it's important...."

When we reached the Pocahontas Building, Raj pulled into the ground-floor loading deck from Bank Street in the usual manner. But instead of heading upstairs to my office, I was intercepted there by Miguel, who motioned toward his car, an imported something-or-other sitting ridiculously low to the ground with barely enough room for two. I climbed in awkwardly, still bemused, and we sped off. Our destination, Miguel disclosed, was his girlfriend's apartment on Rowland Street in the Fan, an eclectic neighborhood of college students, yuppies, derelicts, well-to-do and struggling folks that had gained its name many decades earlier from the radii that parted in fan-like fashion as they spread outward from the city's downtown core. As we proceeded along one of those streets, stopping occasionally for traffic lights and dodging indifferent jaywalkers, Miguel briefed me on the "John Smith" who would be joining us for the clandestine session.

The person's name actually was John Smith, as the schedule had stated. He was John Gabriel Smith, a 35-year veteran of the Virginia State Police, recently retired, and someone I knew as "Gabe." Longtime stalwarts of the executive protective unit, Gabe and Scotty Macauley had been best friends since they attended the Academy together. After Scotty and Governor Nevers died, Gabe had exercised his option to retire from state government. Most people thought it was the pain of the double-barreled loss, and indeed that was part of it. But soon there were wholesale changes in the detail, something that had never occurred as previous governors came and went. The makeover went beyond the executive protective unit, too. Even Colonel Mobley, the much-admired State Police veteran who had risen from the rank of trooper to superintendent under Governor Nevers' seven predecessors, was suddenly out. In his place, Bart installed a former sheriff from Hampton Roads, an agreeable ally and putative law enforcement "professional" who had no tie to the State Police agency and its insular culture.

Once at our destination, we exchanged pleasantries economically and grabbed seats in the sparsely appointed den. Miguel set the stage for the conversation.

"Trooper Smith has briefed me on some disturbing information, General. The pieces of this puzzle have come together only gradually over the last 24 months, and I think it's safe to say that some very recent information has greatly increased Trooper Smith's concern—"

He looked to Gabe for acknowledgement and received a nod back.

"—and has left him no choice but to come to us." Miguel took a deep breath and then continued:

Before I ask him to brief you, I would like to characterize this meeting for the record. There actually is no written or electronic record being made of this discussion, but I want to make sure we are all in accord on these legal points.

First, there is no ongoing investigation of these matters by the State Police. As we all know, Virginia law bars the Bureau of Criminal Investigation from investigating any elected official, including the governor, without the prior approval of the governor, attorney general, or a grand jury. No request for investigation has been made, and Trooper Smith—*former* Trooper Smith—has acted and is acting wholly in his personal capacity as a private citizen.

Second, if we conclude that the facts related by Trooper Smith afford a reasonable basis to believe that a crime has been committed, then we must determine what our legal duty is relative to the reporting of that information to law enforcement authorities. It is my position that, in the absence of a pending state investigation, we—that is to say, the Attorney General and I—have no legal duty, at least until such time as we determine there is probable cause to believe a crime has been committed. Upon such a determination, however, a duty may arise, and we then must consider whether an investigation is warranted, and, if so, by whom. In addressing the latter issue, we must determine whether transmission of Trooper Smith's information to certain state authorities here in Virginia will aid the enforcement of the law or hinder that enforcement. We must act in the manner best calculated to accomplish the former.

I make these statements in advance because it is important that we all understand our legal obligations and act accordingly....

I had waited as patiently as possible, but it seemed like Miguel's preface was a recitation of the strikingly obvious, and he was taking forever to get through it. All I knew at this point was that the trooper had some evidence of corruption in state government, apparently involving Bart. The suspense was killing me.

"Good grief, Miguel, let the man speak," I said finally, then turned to the experienced ex-trooper. "I don't know what you've got, Gabe, but I want you to tell me everything you know. You can be absolutely confident that we are going to do the right thing with the information, no matter the consequences. That means, by the way, no matter what the consequences are for *you* as well as no what matter the consequences are for *me* and no matter what the consequences are for *anyone else* implicated by the information or involved in whatever action follows. I know you're a pro, and you understand that. But those are the ground rules. Now, fire away...."

"Trooper Smith," Miguel said, further delaying the information flow and now really irking me, "before you start, you need to know that I have *not* briefed the Attorney General on what you have shared with me. He knows only that it involves some misconduct—*alleged* misconduct—on the part of Governor Bell. This is going to be a shock, so please walk through it from the beginning, step by step, carefully and chronologically."

"Miguel, the man was conducting investigations when you were a gleam in your mother's eye," I said. "He will tell us what he knows the way he wants to tell us. Go ahead, Gabe."

"Actually, General, Mr. Angiolo is correct. This *will* be a shock, and I need to go through it very methodically. He is also right that chronologically is the best way."

"Go ahead, then. But drop the 'General' stuff—we've known each other too long."

"Yes, sir," he said. He then looked down at his typed notes and began an expressionless recitation that would have made Joe Friday proud:

On Monday, March 24, 2003, during the evening hours, I was in the governor's conference room on the third floor of the Capitol when I overheard a conversation between Governor Nevers and Lieutenant Governor Bell. You, of course, had moved down the hill to the Pocahontas Building a couple of months earlier, and Ms. Wingo occupied your office—or, rather, the chief of staff's office—at the time.

The circumstances of my hearing this conversation were as follows. It was towards the end of the bill review period, and the Governor had been going through bill folders in his office, mostly by himself, for several hours. Everyone except Ms. Wingo and the Policy Office staff across the hall had left for the evening, and Ms. Wingo had gone over to the General Assembly Building to meet with Speaker Percival and several other folks regarding some last-minute amendments they wanted on a piece of legislation. In fact, it was a call from Ms. Wingo that prompted me to go toward the Governor's office from the reception area. She called to say they were making progress but it would be a while longer before she returned, and she wanted me to pass that word along to the Governor. I told her that the Lieutenant Governor had gone in to see Governor Nevers a few minutes earlier, and I asked whether she wanted me to interrupt their meeting to give the Governor her message. She told me to give them another five or ten minutes or so, and then if the LG was still in there, to go ahead and interrupt because the Governor would probably welcome the interruption anyway.

I waited about ten minutes and then concluded I should deliver the requested message. As I made my way into and through the conference room on the way to the Governor's corner office, I heard raised voices, so I stopped. I understood there were only two people in the room, and, given who they were, I did not perceive the situation to be one posing any danger to the Governor. My initial thought was that it was the kind of conversation I should *not* interrupt and that I should return to my post in the anteroom. My second thought was that it might be the kind of conversation I *should* interrupt and that I should proceed into the Governor's office. My third and fourth and fifth thoughts were somewhere in-between, and so I waited in the conference room for a few moments, debating what to do. It was during that time that I heard a discussion which, with the benefit of hindsight, appears relevant to the matters that bring me here today. As you well know, General, we in the EPU hear all sorts of private things, and it is part of our code that we do not repeat any of them. I am also very much aware that my actions in lingering in the conference room and listening to the conversation could rightly be criticized. If you do *not* want me to violate the Governors' confidence by discussing their conversation, I will stop here. But it is my sense that you need to hear it.

"I will trust your judgment on that," I replied.

"I want you to understand that, given the circumstances at the time, there was no reason for me to make notes of what I heard in the conversation," Gabe continued. "My recollection of the conversation is quite vivid, but I cannot substantiate it with contemporaneous notes."

"I take it, then, that nothing in the conversation itself gave you reason to believe that there either had been or would be any illegal or inappropriate conduct?" I asked.

"That is correct," he replied. "Nothing specific or actionable, though there was a troubling allusion to past conduct."

Miguel interjected. "The significance of the conversation goes only to the motivation—the *apparent* motive—for subsequent actions. It will become more evident as he completes the presentation."

"Well, let's proceed," I said, with a measure of reluctance. "I don't like listening in on confidential conversations between governors, but I trust your judgment."

"Thank you," Gabe replied. "I will give you the gist of the conversation because it is obviously impossible for me to recite it verbatim. However, there are a few key statements and phrases that I recall specifically … you know, the more graphic ones."

"Okay," I said, with a tone of "get on with it" in my voice. Having resolved to listen in, I now was eager to hear what the fuss was about.

The gist of the conversation was that the Lieutenant Governor wanted to become governor—*expected* to become governor—either when Governor Nevers ran for president in 2004 or after he completed his second term as governor in early 2006. And he wanted Governor Nevers' support and public endorsement. It was pretty clear that the Governor had pushed back on that, or something of the sort, because when I started listening the LG's voice already was raised, and he was doing all the talking. It was sort of a diatribe.

He said things like, "I have been a loyal soldier, and done everything you have asked me to do, and you *owe* me!" And, "You know as well as I do that you wouldn't be here without the things I did for you." And, "I know where all the bodies are buried, and if you think I am going to stand by while you cast me aside, you're crazy!" He said several harsh things like that, and then he said all Governor Nevers had to do was publicly endorse him as his successor and he would be "quiet as a church mouse" during the presidential campaign or whatever Governor Nevers wanted to do next. The Governor wouldn't have any part of that, and the more he resisted, the louder the LG got. At one point—and I remember this vividly—the LG said, "I protected you when you were in the Senate, back when you couldn't figure out your head from your ass. I did a lot of things so you didn't have to dirty your hands—sordid things, unethical things, maybe even some illegal things—and you knew damn well that I was doing what needed to be done!"

It was at that point that Governor Nevers raised his voice sharply—something I had never heard him do—and he told the LG to "*forget it*" … that it "*wasn't going to happen*" … that he would "*never be governor.*" He said it loud and clear. He said, "By God, Bart, if I have anything to do with it, you will never be the governor of this state!" He said the LG's threats

427

only made him absolutely determined to prevent him from moving up. And when the LG said the thing about having done unethical or illegal stuff in the Senate, the Governor said, "I sure hope that's not true, Bart—*for your sake*. My conscience is clear; I never, *ever* asked you to do anything improper—*not once*. But the fact that you can stand here of all places and admit to doing such things—to breaking the law or being willing to break the law—just makes it abundantly clear that you are unfit to ever hold this office!"

As the heated words went back and forth, I eased back toward the reception room door. I figured the Lieutenant Governor would come storming out at some point, and I didn't want to be caught listening. But their voices were so loud they remained audible even when I was diagonally across the conference room, some 20 or so feet away from the entrance to the Governor's small corner office. Moments after I left the conference room, the LG did in fact exit. The heavy wooden door banged loudly as he left, and he went out of there so fast I don't think he even noticed me sitting at my post. I went immediately in to check on the Governor and to deliver Ms. Wingo's message. He was seated at his desk, red-faced but otherwise calm and collected, and he thanked me for the update on Abby. He said he would be ready to go to the mansion for the evening in a few minutes, and would have a box of bill folders that needed to go over with him. And that was the end of it.

My mind now was racing.

Bart had *threatened* the Governor—had tried, essentially, to *blackmail* Nevers into endorsing him for governor. Nevers not only had refused to supply the endorsement; he had sworn to do all he could to thwart Bart's ambitions. That was a total game-changer for Bart....

Bart had spoken of improper, even illegal acts, while in the Senate. I could only imagine what Bart had done and what kind of dossiers he had stashed away as leverage. Governor Nevers would have gone through the same thought process upon hearing Bart's words, and I wondered how clear his conscience really was. He would never have sanctioned illegal actions or violations of the Senate ethics rules—I was confident of that. But there are sins of omission as well as commission, and in the wake of this exchange Governor Nevers must have wondered what Bart actually had done, how far he had gone, and how much responsibility he (Nevers) bore for enabling those misdeeds by making Bart his chief of staff and allowing him so much latitude.

My thoughts also ran back to the Governor's cessation of the presidential campaign discussions that same spring. There had been a lot of talk for a while, some of it serious, and then Nevers had largely clammed up on the subject. The buzz had continued but Nevers himself had seldom engaged on it as the critical months for pursuing such an enterprise had slipped by. Finally, the boss had simply confirmed privately what all of us in his top echelon already had concluded based on the timeline—that he was *not* running. I had assumed Nevers just decided at some point that he was not up for the hassle, but now I wondered what impact this dust-up with Bart might have had. The Governor's conscience may have been clear, but that did not mean the closet was empty— with Bart, you never knew. And if the price of pursuing the Presidency was bending to Bart's pressure and acquiescing in his advancement, then there was only one moral decision that Governor Nevers—the *redeemed* Ned Nevers— was capable of making....

These thoughts swept across the austere landscape of my anguished mind as I sat there, and they would continue to tramp back and forth in the vexing days thereafter. But, at some point, as Gabe's account sank in that morning, it suddenly dawned on me that this was not about Bart and some corrupt little deed he had done while in Washington or even in Richmond. I was not here, as I had previously assumed, because Bart somehow had violated his public trust and was about to face the music. Miguel's earlier reference to motive and the awful implications of the events described by Gabe finally merged, and I was struck dumb with horror at the realization: *This was about the death of Governor Nevers.*

"I, uh, gather there is more…," I said grimly.

"There is," replied Miguel.

"Let's take a short break. Too much coffee this morning," I said, as Miguel pointed me toward the bathroom.

Once behind the closed door I splashed cold water on my face and stood there in front of the mirror for several moments. A cascade of emotions—with anger probably dominant but fear close behind—swept over me. There was also a clear sense that what I learned in the next few minutes would change everything, and that I needed to steel myself for all that would follow. After a quick prayer and a deep breath, I returned to the waiting messenger.

"General, when I decided to retire, I felt burned out and dejected," Gabe said as we resumed, "but I also felt particularly uneasy about Governor Bell. I knew something of the company he keeps and the kind of parties he frequents. All of us in the detail were aware of that to some degree, and I just did not want to be put in that position. I didn't need it at this point in my career...."

This part did not surprise me. I knew that Bart had been running with a wild crowd off and on since his latter days in D.C., and that his activities had triggered alarm on the part of office insiders, including Mitch, Chad, and Abby. Yet, Bart kept his private life very private, and I had no knowledge of anything improper—just vague rumors and innuendo of uncertain substance.

"What exactly troubled you?" I asked.

"The usual things that happen at jet-set parties—heavy-duty booze, drugs, sex, et cetera," he replied.

"Should I ask what the 'et cetera' refers to?"

"Just *more* booze, drugs, and sex," he answered.

"I don't think that Governor Bell's recreational activities are especially relevant here," Miguel asserted, trying to move the narrative along.

"Actually, they are relevant for two reasons, Mr. Angiolo," said Gabe. "One, I want you to understand why I left the EPU. And, two, there are some associations and relationships in that crowd that appear relevant to the events in question. But, if you don't mind, let me proceed in sequence."

"Go ahead," I said, "I'll try not to interrupt you anymore."

Gabe nodded appreciatively and then resumed his stone-faced account:

> During the period from early July, when Governor Bell took office, until approximately Labor Day of that same year—2003—the entire protection detail for the Governor was changed. Most of this occurred after Superintendent Mosley stepped down on August 1st and Superintendent Anderson took over. The transfers were all involuntary, though everyone reassigned from the EPU was given strict orders not to talk about it. Most of their replacements were

relatively young troopers with few connections to any of us who had been in the unit before, or they were entirely new hires from outside the force. But one of the new officers in the unit is someone who, for reasons no one would suspect, I happen to know very well. Needless to say, I'm going to carefully protect his or her identity. But I mention it so you know the information I have concerning the goings-on inside Governor Bell's inner circle is reliable even though I am not in a position to observe it personally.

On or about October 20, 2003, as best I can recall, my EPU source contacted me and asked whether I was familiar with someone named "Gerard Benedict." He described the man as a "businessman from Nevada and New Jersey who has substantial interests in Virginia Beach, among other places." I told him that I did not know the name. He suggested the man's activities might be of some interest to me.

As of that time, I had no reason to suspect any particular misconduct by Governor Bell beyond the recreational activities I mentioned earlier. I had a nagging sense that something was not right in the whole situation, you know, surrounding his rise to the governorship. But I certainly had not formed any conscious sense or suspicion about the circumstances of Governor Nevers' death—

There it was—the first explicit reference confirming the reason for this conversation. Miguel cast a quick glance in my direction. I looked back without expression, intent on evincing no emotion, as Gabe continued.

After some extensive investigation I was able to determine the following about Mr. Benedict:

He and his varied enterprises were very substantial contributors to the Bell for Lieutenant Governor campaign four years ago, and have been far more so in his current campaign. He and they also have funneled large amounts of funding to the Governor's political action committee and to the state Republican Party. The donor information is

431

publicly available, of course, but it took me quite a number of months, given my lack of access to investigative resources, to identify the various entities and associates through which Mr. Benedict operates. Even so, it's likely I have only touched the tip of the iceberg.

By the way, Mr. Benedict's associates also made contributions to then-Senator Nevers' unsuccessful reelection campaign in 1994 and to the "Virginia is for Nevers" campaign committee in the 1997 governor's race. My suspicion is that Mr. Bell secured those contributions, but that is purely speculative.

What is *not* speculative is that Bart Bell, Gerard Benedict, and various other people with ties to Mr. Benedict struck up a fast friendship sometime in the early 1990s. As best I can determine, this began around the time that Mr. Bell, then chief of staff to Senator Nevers, assisted Mr. Benedict with a major business transaction in Virginia Beach. An article in the *Norfolk Times-Post* on July 3, 1992, describes the Virginia Beach City Council's approval of zoning for a new luxury hotel to be owned by one of Mr. Benedict's businesses. Mr. Bell, Mr. Benedict, and several members of the City Council appear in a photograph accompanying the article, and the article quotes Benedict thanking Bell "for coming down from Washington despite the hectic Senate schedule to express support for the project on behalf of Senator Nevers."

Beginning around that time and continuing through the present day, Mr. Bell has been a frequent guest of Mr. Benedict and his associates on recreational trips and at various dinners, parties, functions, and so forth. These include, by the way, one African safari, two sailing trips in the Bahamas, two Super Bowls and one trip each to the Masters and Wimbledon, what appears to have been a raucous dinner involving the vice president of Argentina and a number of prostitutes in Buenos Aires, numerous trips to Vegas, extended stays at other casinos and resorts, and various other pricey and occasionally exotic outings. Because of the varied entities used by Mr. Benedict as well as my current lack of access to pertinent records, it is impossible for me to say whether and how thoroughly the activities of this sort were disclosed by Mr. Bell under applicable federal and state ethics laws, but for obvious reasons that has not been my prime concern. Suffice it to say there is little indication that Mr. Bell was especially diligent in meeting his disclosure obligations before he became governor. Since then, he's stayed closer to home but has still maintained what I will just call "a very active social life" in which the Benedicts have figured prominently.

Mr. Benedict's *legal* business activities are quite diverse. He and his affiliates own top-tier restaurants and hotels up and down the East Coast, with the greatest concentration in Florida and New Jersey, as well as in several western states, including Nevada and California. They also own several large resorts and a wide array of high-end retail establishments and other businesses, including being sole or substantial owner of what is probably the leading manufacturer of yachts and luxury boats in the country—one of Mr. Benedict's particular passions, apparently. There is much more that I could add about his legal activities, but it is not especially pertinent.

Mr. Benedict's *illegal* activities are more noteworthy. According to my sources in the FBI, he has been identified in recent years as a substantial figure in organized crime. In fact, there is reason to believe he is one of the most senior figures in the Kulakovski organization, which is a name I'm sure you recognize.

As I pieced this and other information together over many months, a very disturbing picture emerged. It is now clear to me that Governor Bell has the strong political and financial support of—and a significant personal relationship with—one of the most influential organized crime figures in the country.

I had listened to the narrative with rapt attention, absolutely thunderstruck by what Gabe laid out, waiting for the connection ... and now it came:

On March 18, the day after the Virginia Supreme Court issued its decision holding that Governor Bell's appointment of Hardy Barnhard as lieutenant governor was invalid, I read a news article in which the outside counsel appointed by the Governor to handle that case—John Manning Jr.—criticized the ruling. The article identified Mr. Manning as managing partner of Manning, Manning, Terkel & Parson. That name rang a bell, presumably from something in my research, but for the life of me I could not recall or retrace why I recognized it or where I had seen it. It gnawed at me off and on for days, and then the days turned into weeks, and still nothing. I looked into the firm, of course, and found that it's a mid-size, mostly East Coast law firm with Virginia offices in Arlington, Richmond, and Virginia Beach—about 30 Virginia lawyers in all. Still, it didn't click.

And then one morning about three weeks ago, I woke up with a crucial thought in my head. It was the name "Terkel"—*Harrison Hays Terkel*. That was the name I had seen before. I began retracing my steps until I finally figured out where I had seen it. Before they joined forces with the Manning firm, Harrison Terkel and Benjamin Parson had their own wills and trusts practice in Philly. Terkel was the executor of the estate of one Madeline Cox as well as the trustee of her testamentary trust, her attorney, et cetera. As a result, Terkel's name and his firm's name appeared on various public filings when a privately owned firm called "Sorrenzo Services Ltd.," in which Ms. Cox had been one the primary shareholders, was sold to a publicly traded company in the early 1990s. I had run across the transaction while searching for various businesses with the name "Sorrenzo," which by then was turning up with some frequency in my search for businesses connected to Benedict and/or the Kulakovskis....

"Wait a minute," I interrupted, "I'm afraid you've lost me. So you've got this organized crime guy I've never heard of, Bart's big donor and pal. And you've got this lawyer, Harrison Terkel, who has some connection to the principal stockholder in a company tied to those mobsters. And you've got John Manning, the lawyer Bart put in charge of the Barnhard case, who has since partnered with Terkel. I guess that's something. But I'm not sure you can draw any conclusion from it, except maybe that it's a small world...."

"Smaller than you think, General," said Miguel. "Tell him who Madeline Cox is, Trooper Smith."

Gabe obliged, delivering a roundhouse punch that collided with my gut with more brute force than the hit that changed my life at age 17.

"After some further investigation, I was able to determine that Madeline Cox is—or, rather, she *was*—the second wife of Gerard Benedict's son, Gerard Jr., who goes by the name 'Freddie.' She was a model, apparently a fairly successful model, and she kept her professional name when they were married. They were married only three years and had no children. She was just 32 when she died in 1992. The significant thing is the manner of death."

"Yes?" I said, bracing.

"*A boat explosion, cause unknown....* Happened just offshore, south of Atlantic City."

There was only silence as I exhaled heavily and sat back, struggling to process what I had just heard. After several moments, Miguel spoke.

"General, Trooper Smith can continue if you want, but the rest is detail. It's clear from his subsequent research that there actually are numerous ties between the Manning firm and the Benedicts and Governor Bell. The Terkel role in Mrs. Benedict Jr.'s estate and the Sorrenzo transaction just happened to be the one that tipped Trooper Smith off. So, basically, what we have is this: One, we have a relationship of some considerable depth and duration between Governor Bell and a key organized crime figure, Gerard Benedict Sr. and his son and lawyers. Two, we have a heated argument between Governor Nevers and then-Lieutenant Governor Bell—an argument over Bell's past behavior and political future—only a few months before Governor Nevers' sudden death. And, three, the manner of Governor Nevers' sudden death appears similar to the manner of the divorced former Mrs. Benedict Jr.'s suspicious death about a decade earlier. It's entirely circumstantial, and it certainly doesn't prove anything in and of itself. But it is not logical to believe it is mere coincidence, either. We have to decide what to do about it."

"Gabe, who else knows what you have shared with us here this morning?" I asked.

"I presume you mean who knows about it other than the three of us plus the thug in the governor's mansion and his murderous friends?" Gabe replied, indulging his feelings for the first time this day.

"Yes, that is what I mean. Who knows about what you have uncovered? Have you confided in anyone—your former EPU colleagues, your confidential source, your wife, some other confidant, *anyone*?

"General, unless they've bugged me or hacked into my personal computer—and I've taken precautions there, plus I don't think they have any reason to suspect me—then *no one else knows*."

"Your source in the EPU, the one who gave you the heads-up about Benedict—what do you think he knows?"

"I don't know what he—*or she*—knows. Obviously, the fact that the Benedicts are bad actors is known. But beyond that, I doubt it. I mean, it took me more than a year of digging to figure out what I've laid out for you here. There's no reason to believe anyone else has put it together."

"What about the BCI or FBI?" I asked. "Don't take this the wrong way, but it seems a little odd that you as a retired trooper could put this together but neither the investigative bureau of the State Police nor the feds have done so."

"That's certainly a fair point," Gabe replied. "Believe me, I've been poking around—very gingerly, of course—especially with my contacts in the BCI. But there is no indication anyone is focused on Bell and this O.C. connection."

My expression must have betrayed my skepticism, because Gabe proceeded to share his own ruminations on this obvious question.

"Remember, General, everyone had a single-minded focus on terrorism for months. I get a strong sense from the BCI boys that terrorism was the feds' sole working theory for most of the past year, and it was only after they drilled one dry well after another that they finally, grudgingly, gave up on it. Where they are on the cause of the explosion now, no one is saying. Maybe they're all over it; maybe they're stumped. It's not like Governor Bell's connections with Benedict are a state secret, but, then again, unless they have some indication of prior misconduct or a motive, they probably have no reason at all to focus on Bell. To all the world he is Governor Nevers' longtime lieutenant and bosom buddy—no one heard what I heard coming out of that office. As for the BCI guys, the same is true of them, only they have much more reason not to dig into it. They're legally barred from investigating the sitting governor without express direction from the governor, attorney general, or a grand jury, and I assume you haven't given them any such green light. Plus, with Bell's folks now running that place, nosing around about the sitting governor would be a great way to find yourself out writing speeding tickets in Grundy."

Gabe's speculation on why none of the other dogs were barking struck me as plausible—and quite disturbing. If accurate, it meant the burden was entirely on us.

"Alright, then," I said after a couple of moments, "Let me take five minutes or so to get my mind around this. Then we need to talk through our next steps."

The two heeded the cue and headed toward the hallway. Then something occurred to me.

"Gabe," I said, prompting him to look back, "that was one heck of a piece of police work. You've just complicated our lives enormously, but that was one heck of a piece of police work."

"Thank you, sir," he replied. "I *had* to get to the bottom of it, you know, for Scotty and the Governor. As for complicating your life, don't blame the messenger."

DESPERATE MEASURES

Even with the additional details filled in thereafter by Gabe, the information was so fragmentary that my legal responsibilities were murky and so was the appropriate course of action. I could exercise my statutory authority to launch a formal state investigation, but given Bart's control of the state's law enforcement apparatus, confiding in the State Police was at best a dicey option. I could appoint a special prosecutor to oversee the probe, force recusals by Superintendent Anderson and others with ties to Bart, and set in motion a completely independent investigation. But it was not clear that the information I possessed was sufficient to justify such a step. More important, it would tip off Bart, and it was also likely to leak out, causing a public furor.

The obvious alternative—the best way to assure a rigorous yet quiet investigation—was to go the federal route.

From the periodic updates provided to me by the U.S. Attorney for the Eastern District, I knew that the Justice Department's investigation was ongoing and that, as Gabe suggested, the terrorism theory had dominated their work for months. Beyond that, my experience had been the same as Gabe's: Both the FBI and U.S. Attorney were incredibly tight-lipped about the whole matter. Publicly, all they had been willing to say recently was that the case was still under investigation, the exact cause was still undetermined, and there was no indication of any terrorist involvement. The latter point, acknowledged about nine months into the investigation, had been sufficient to squelch most media interest, since just about everyone assumed the explosion was either the work of terrorists or an accident. Whether the Justice Department had any inkling about the matters unearthed by Gabe was anyone's guess, but they had made no attempt, publicly or privately, to steer interested parties toward the possibility of domestic wrongdoing.

The question was how to get our information into the right federal hands. Having been a junior federal prosecutor myself and dealt with them over the years, I knew that the presidentially appointed United States attorneys (the chief prosecutors for each judicial district) typically were part law enforcement pros and part politicos. The current one for the Eastern District of Virginia seemed to have more of the latter propensity and less of the former, and I was not at all comfortable entrusting her with such a politically explosive matter. Instead, I wanted to take the information to Main Justice, as the Department's primary office in Washington is known. I called my friend and former law school classmate, Rick Angelotti, the Connecticut attorney general, for advice. Though of different parties, we had teamed up on a couple of matters since becoming AGs in our respective states, and I knew he was wired into the Democratic administration in Washington, including DOJ. I did not tell Rick what my issue was—only that I had a politically sensitive matter of the highest order and needed to know who in the Justice Department was a straight arrow I could trust. He identified several options, and among them was the one I hoped to hear.

I could *definitely* trust Attorney General Cyrus, Rick said.

When you are talking about the political crime of the century—a governor killed by his successor's underworld friends, perhaps with the successor's active complicity—it is hard not to be melodramatic. Not since the three big assassinations of the 1960s—two Kennedys and King—had there been a politically motivated murder of this magnitude in the United States. In those instances, the cause of death had been clear even if questions persisted regarding the perpetrators. Here, the information was sketchy, the case for foul play was circumstantial, and the political sensitivity was acute. The victim and his successor were of one political party; the overseers of the federal law enforcement apparatus were of the other. The beneficiary of the crime, the current Governor of Virginia, was a popular figure in the midst of a political campaign, cruising toward reelection. His opponent, Dorothy Meade, had been enthusiastically endorsed by the just-reelected President of the United States. Any federal investigation of Bell, even the slightest insinuation that there were questions about his public conduct, let alone a role in Nevers' death, would produce a huge hue and cry in Virginia and beyond. The motives of the President and his Justice Department would be assailed as crassly political.

For those reasons, I knew that what I had to say to the Attorney General would be extremely unwelcome news—unless, of course, he already knew it. I called him directly and told him over the phone that I had information regarding criminal conduct of the most urgent and sensitive nature, and that the information was known only to me, my deputy, and a retired State Police officer. He proposed that we come to Washington immediately to brief him, and he advised that, unless I objected, he was going to have the FBI director and Assistant AG in charge of the Criminal Division join him for the meeting. The phone conversation was brief and stilted, owing chiefly to the medium of communication. But once he mentioned the heavyweights he was pulling into the meeting, I had a sense the Attorney General knew the reason I was coming.

Even in a time of crisis such as this, I could not help but be impressed by the fifth floor of the Justice Department and all the history I knew had taken place there. At one end of the marble-floored corridor with its high ceilings, vivid murals, and chalk blue walls paralleling Constitution Avenue were the offices of the Solicitor General of the United States, the official who represents the U.S. Government in the Supreme Court. At the other end was the Attorney General's suite of offices. Its most impressive feature, the high-ceilinged, walnut-paneled conference room, was our destination. The formidable room seemed large enough for a half-court basketball game, and it may have been so used during the tenure of Robert Kennedy, when it served as his personal office. The space reminded me of a cross between an old-style judge's chambers and the dining room of a Newport mansion. In any event, we did not have long to assess the setting before the Attorney General entered, issued a solemn greeting, and bid us to rise from the places we had taken around the massive conference table and follow him around the fireplace into his much smaller, adjacent private office. Five somber faces, at least three of which were mounted on exceedingly weary frames, filed in obediently behind him.

One thing was immediately obvious: You would never want to get into a high-stakes poker game with these three particular embodiments of federal power. Polite and professional, their stoic visages betrayed absolutely nothing during the entire time we were there. We described the information that Gabe possessed and how he had come to possess it. FBI Director Johnson asked if we had time for Gabe to provide the information again for a stenographer following the meeting. Attorney General Cyrus thanked us for coming and said he knew this was especially difficult for me because of my close relationship with Governor Nevers. Assistant AG Saunders, the savvy former prosecutor who led the Criminal Division, said not a thing at any point. And then we left. They volunteered nothing about the status of the federal investigation, and we did not inquire. As he escorted me out of the office, the Attorney General said only, "We will be in touch, General. I know you understand the need for *total* confidentiality. Thank you again for coming."

I am not sure what I thought "being in touch" was supposed to mean; I certainly expected something to happen before the election. But it did not. The silence was deafening, and only Gabe seemed unsurprised. "They won't want to touch this thing with a ten-foot pole, especially before the election," he had predicted as we left DOJ that day, and apparently he was right. The official Labor Day kickoff for the campaign's final stretch followed a few days later. More days and then weeks passed, with Gabe and Miguel continuing their super-secret "research" while I campaigned nonstop, dutifully masquerading as a proud member of the Bell ticket, feeling smarmy and waiting for some unspecified but inevitable disaster to befall us.

A key additional fact fell into Miguel's lap at OAG during this time, and it would lead later to important discoveries about the motivation behind Nevers' murder. While waiting for a meeting on another topic to get started, an assistant attorney general—the one responsible for providing legal advice to the state's Department of Conservation and Recreation—happened to mention that she had been in Virginia Beach the previous weekend and had gone down to False Cape State Park for the first time. So named because the shoreline juts out into the ocean just enough to deceive unwary mariners into thinking they are approaching Cape Henry, which actually lies 20 miles to the north, the isolated park was accessible only by foot, bike, boat, or the park's seasonal tram. It remained one of the few truly pristine coastal areas on the eastern seaboard proximate to a population center. When a colleague asked why in the world she had foregone the Beach's many creature comforts to commune with the mosquitoes, the lawyer said she actually had a business reason for wanting to see False Cape firsthand. Several people in her client agency had mentioned persistent rumors that a big resort development company had its eye on the land, she said, a notion which "would have seemed quite far-fetched except for the strange visit we had a few years back by those two silk-stocking lawyers who claimed to be doing general research on how to create a perpetual park. When we got into the discussion, all they really seemed interested in was the origin of False Cape and whether there were any unrecorded covenants or agreements that restricted the state's use of the land."

That comment amid the banter landed hard on the waiting Miguel's ear, but it was the lawyer's next remark that caused his heart to skip a beat.

"Ironically," she said, "they were from the same law firm that Governor Bell designated to represent the Commonwealth in the litigation over the Barnhard appointment."

This additional puzzle piece was hugely tantalizing. Did Bart's mob friends have their eyes on one of Virginia's most isolated but potentially valuable pieces of Atlantic coastal real estate? Could that be the reason they wanted Bart in the governor's mansion? Had Bart made a deal with these devils?

The situation was maddening because there was nothing immediately to be done about it. The apparent federal inaction was persisting, as was the slow drip of factoids that could mean a whole lot or absolutely nothing. It produced a distressing realization for me as the campaign's final weeks neared: *The timing simply did not work.* Bart was headed for a fall—this I firmly believed. But first he would receive the highest honor the people of Virginia were capable of bestowing: election as their governor. That was an awful prospect. This, after all was *Virginia*, with its enviable ethic of honest public service tracing back to Washington and Madison and before. The state had long been among the least corruption-tinged in America. That was now about to change in a mindboggling way, and the people who voted to make Bart Bell governor would forever be scandalized by their misjudgment. I possessed the information that could somehow prevent it.

Ten days before the November 8th election, I was presented with the opportunity to act, and I made the dubious decision to seize it.

Through Gabe and his EPU informant had come incredible stories of increasingly bizarre gubernatorial behavior. In public, Bart managed to deliver his preprogrammed lines at carefully choreographed events without noticeable difficulty. His handlers had him off the public campaign trail by mid-afternoon every day, limiting him to private fundraising receptions and small private dinners thereafter. Having defied precedent, a phalanx of incensed media and civic organizations, and conventional wisdom by steadfastly refusing all invitations to debate his Democratic opponent, Bart and his team had purged the campaign of virtually all unscripted and substantive interaction. Consistently sporting a 20-point lead in opinion polls, they could get away with this protective approach, and they did. But if the public side of things was deftly squared away, the private side was spiraling out of control.

According to Gabe's source, Bart's seedy friends were now almost nightly regulars at the Executive Mansion, and on at least one occasion the small but raucous cast of partiers brazenly included none other than Freddie Benedict, the kingpin's impeccably coiffed, fun-loving son. Haughty, haggard, and apparently high during these rowdy gatherings, Bart was given to making the most outrageous comments imaginable on all manner of sensitive subjects. Nothing was so serious, secret, or sacred as to be beyond the bounds. Not only his Democratic opponent—"that skinny black woman"—came in for frequent bashing, but so did ostensible allies like me. He even spoke contemptuously of Governor Nevers, finally abandoning the farce, if only in private. Like a runaway freight train, Bart was careening toward a huge wreck, and the only question was how many innocent people he would take out on impact. If there was any way to force his hand before the election—even at this late hour—I felt some obligation to try.

The opportunity suddenly presented itself during the weekend before Halloween, when Chad reported to me that the Bell campaign had purchased 30 minutes of election-eve television time on an impressive statewide array of broadcast and cable channels, including multiple outlets in the hyper-expensive D.C. media market. The production and airtime would cost the campaign millions, and it was the height of wasteful self-indulgence. But they had money to burn, and the candidate wanted to see his mug on the big screen, Hollywood-style.

"All indications are it is going to be a very effective piece of propaganda—maybe even enough to help him squeak by on election day," Chad reported sarcastically. "They hired an Academy Award-winning documentary producer based in LA to work with the Riley Group, the local agency that does top-tier national TV ads."

"Have our people had any involvement in it?" I asked.

"Not much. Abby supplied some of our ad footage and some photos for the brief segment regarding the ticket—and I mean *brief*. She's actually been over to the agency and looked at the rough-cut. Our friend Janie Suttle works there now—she's a real talent; got her campaign communications start with us at JBW Advisors way back when. The piece must be largely finished because Janie is in the process of finalizing the list of credits. She invited Abby to come over on the QT and take a look, and Abby was extremely impressed. She said the part about Governor Nevers was short but made her cry. Said the stuff on Bart was almost enough to make her vote for him—if she didn't hate his guts for firing her, that is…."

"It must really be a good piece of propaganda, then," I said indifferently.

Then Chad added the nugget that got the wheels turning in my head.

"Abby says Janie is rushing to finish it up because Bart has invited the producer, a couple of big donors, and some close friends for a private screening at the mansion on Monday. It's Halloween—that seems kinda fitting, don't you think?"

"Hmmm. That's interesting," I said, the wheels beginning to turn. "Will I be here in town that night?"

"If you're thinking about going to the mansion, I wouldn't hold my breath waiting for an invitation," Chad said as he reached for the updated schedule. "Okay, here we go. Yes, you are in Richmond that evening; it says you're at the Jefferson Hotel for the Manufacturers Association reception, and then you have dinner there afterwards with Bob Horrow, Dan Ashford, and several of the other manufacturing CEOs. Why do you ask?"

"Just wondering," I said, already thinking about my next call.

I slipped out into the parking lot, beyond earshot. "Gabe, this is Danny," I said quietly. "See what your source can tell you about the party and movie screening that His Excellency has planned at the mansion for Halloween evening. Also, find out if your guy is going to be on duty at the mansion that evening…."

"Want to tell me why?" he asked.

"Yes, maybe—depending on what you find out. Call me as soon as you can. I'm headed to Pocahontas to see Miguel."

The plot I hatched was elegantly simple … and definitely a long-shot. Hamlet had crafted a similar scheme to "catch the conscience" of the murderous King Claudius. But even with life's tendency to mimic art, the Shakespearian parallel supplied little cause for optimism. Miguel and Gabe were rightly skeptical of my plan, but when I asked if they had a better idea, they demurred. Miguel worried a little that my scheme, if successful in provoking a reaction, might somehow interfere with the federal investigation. But he thought the whole idea was so far-fetched that it posed little real risk, except perhaps bringing the mob down on my head. I actually considered that possibility, as well as the risk that the Justice Department might object. But after so many weeks responding to the most outrageous sort of information with callow inaction, I desperately wanted to do *something*.

Maybe, if Bart was impaired enough after his All Hallows' Eve self-indulgence, he would have a telling reaction. And if he didn't react at all, it might suggest his knowledge and involvement were limited….

I called in Abby a short while later and gave her these instructions: "In this envelope is a short list of names that need to be added to the credits at the end of Bart's election-eve video, but just for the advance screening at the mansion on Monday night. Tell your friend Janie that some of these are folks who will be at the mansion, and that the Governor will want to acknowledge them in this way. Tell her it's a surprise, and ask her to include the names as prominently as possible among the credits—you know, up-front, right after the producer and the other big-shots who will probably be there for the screening. Do it as late as safely possible, so you minimize the risk that she will tell anyone about it in advance of the screening. Do you think she will do it?"

"Yes, probably. Want to tell me what this is about?"

"No."

"Okay."

"Will she do it without telling anyone in advance?"

"Yes, if I ask her to—she trusts me completely. But will she get in trouble over this?"

"No, she won't. Neither of you will get into trouble. But to make sure, tell her that *after* the credits roll—that's very important: *after* they roll—if someone wants to know who the thoughtful person was who supplied those additional acknowledgements, she should speak right up and say it was Attorney General McGuire."

Abby, Mitch, and Chad later would vehemently protest my decision to keep them in the dark about Gabe's revelations and my subsequent actions. But it was not a question of trusting or protecting them; it was a question of propriety. I could not properly share the sensitive investigative information beyond law enforcement channels, and if it were later disclosed that I had done so, not only could I rightly be faulted for a breach of duty, but they and I would be accused of political scheming. Thrust into a confusing frenzy, considering an action with more far-reaching consequence than I could have imagined, I was without my trusted sounding board.

My crazy scheme would not have worked 99 out of 100 times, but this was the one. Had there been more time for deliberation, I probably would have chickened out, concluding that the better part of wisdom was to hunker down, avoid controversy, and wait for the feds to come riding to the rescue. But the opportunity and inspiration had come out of nowhere, at a moment of cresting frustration and near desperation. Abby's friend Janie was in just the right position, as were Gabe's EPU informant, the sleazy friends who fed Bart's ego and habit, and, of course, Bart himself. The justification was self-evident: "A Prince, whose character is thus marked by every act which may define a Tyrant, is unfit to be the ruler of a free people." And so I did it.

After the evocative film faded to black, a hand with quill pen scratched out noisily on parchment the name of the executive producer, director, and several others in quick succession. Everyone was watching because several of the work's creators were among the favored few in attendance. Some were already starting to offer congratulations when the hand successively scratched out the added names:

Manning Manning Terkel & Parson
Gerard Benedict and Madeline Cox
Kulakovski Pyrotechnics, Inc.
False Cape Spa and Resort
Virginia State Police and the Federal Bureau of Investigation
Attorney General Daniel M. McGuire

The events of the next ten hours would become the second-most investigated episode in Virginia's modern history, behind only the events surrounding the death of Edward K. Nevers on July 5, 2003.

As recounted by Gabe's source and later by others in attendance, Bart literally leapt to his feet and screamed when he saw the hand scratch out the shocking indication that the crime had been discovered. His words do not bear repeating here, and it would be hard to do so anyway, since witnesses later offered varied accounts of the exact epithets hurled and the order in which they took flight. The Governor's stupefied guests (with the notable exception, presumably, of slick-topped "Freddie") had no idea what had so aroused and discombobulated the Commonwealth's usually cocksure CEO and sent him stomping through the foyer like a crazed ten-year-old, loudly demanding to know my whereabouts. It so happened that one trooper on duty that night knew that I was at the Jefferson, and so the black vehicles always at the ready between the Executive Mansion and Patrick Henry Building were soon racing westward.

Most folks who enter the lobby of the stately, five-star and five-diamond Jefferson Hotel find the surroundings unusually impressive. If not the imposing statute of the lanky, erudite Virginian whose elegant penmanship made poetry of the nation's first principles or the bronze alligator situated near where live ones once resided in the Palm Court, then it was the adjacent Grand Ballroom that caused the wonder, with its huge faux marble columns and the grand staircase that may or may not have been the inspiration for Rhett Butler's in *Gone With the Wind*. Rescued from decay in the 1980s and enhanced by several ensuing renovations, the century-old hotel had become a premier Richmond landmark and favorite venue for high-brow events of all types. Governors were there very frequently, but it is safe to say none was ever on more of a mission, more oblivious to the opulence and resident crème de la crème, or more driven by abject fear than was Governor Bart Bell on this evening.

Despite his compromised physical and emotional condition, Bart evidently had gathered himself enough on the way over to hatch a semblance of a plan. And so, upon arrival, one of the accompanying troopers quickly approached the efficient man at the registration desk, verified the availability of the Governor's Suite—a courtesy routinely extended to the chief executive unless the elegant space already was occupied by a VIP—and gained possession of the key. The Governor and trooper then headed for the elevators, while the other accompanying EPU trooper (the one who knew Gabe well) strode briskly around the mezzanine-level ballroom balcony to retrieve me from the Flemish Room, where I was still mingling with the manufacturers.

"General McGuire, excuse me, sir. Excuse me, folks," he said, clasping my elbow in an unusual manner and deftly separating me from the two business executives who had been regaling me. "I'm Trooper Willis with the State

Police. Please come with me." He waited a second or two until we were out of earshot, then whispered, "The Governor is upstairs in a suite waiting for you."

"Upstairs *here*?" I asked, puzzled.

"Yes, sir, we need to head there now, but please listen to me very carefully. Your plan worked."

"My plan?"

"Oh, geez, you don't know me. I am Gabe's friend, the one on the inside."

"Ah, so you are," I said, pleased to know the identity of the good rat at last.

"Gabe read me in completely this morning—*everything*. I am still amazed."

"What happened at the mansion? Why's the Governor *here*?"

"Your plan may have worked a little too well. The Governor freaked out and immediately demanded to know where you were, so I told him. I thought he was going to have us retrieve you but instead he had us race over here." The trooper was talking in a hushed, only partly discernible voice as we tried to make our way back around the ballroom's mezzanine toward the elevators. It would have been hard to talk anyway, but we encountered a steady stream of Virginia's upper crust heading in the opposite direction, and each required a smile and greeting. Finally, we ducked into the bathroom and feigned attending to business until the last two occupants exited.

"Has he said anything to inculpate himself?" I desperately wanted to know.

"No, not yet. Of course, his reaction itself speaks volumes."

Disappointed, I heaved a vulgarity as Willis continued.

"Look, he is in a very agitated state, and there's no telling what he has in his system and what he's going to say or do. He calmed down some on the way over here, and he clearly has something up his sleeve—something he wants to say to you. I'm going to do my best to get into the adjacent room so I can listen in. I also sent Gabe a message to get over here. But if you're going in, there's a good chance you'll be on your own."

"Yes, my word against his."

"*Hell*, General McGuire, I wasn't even talking about that. I'm talking about your *safety*."

"I think I can take him if he wants to rumble," I said, managing a nervous smile.

"It isn't funny, sir. If he really was involved in this thing with the boat accident, he's a very desperate man."

"Let's move," I said, "before he changes his mind and scurries back to the mansion."

When we arrived at the suite, two other troopers had joined the first, and all three were standing in the hallway with the suite door closed. So was the Governor's traveling aide and another late arrival, his chief of staff. Bart was in the suite alone.

When I opened the door to enter, it was if a dam burst; everyone in the hallway hastened in behind me. Bart dismissed them all, and told the two staffers to go home—that he was going to visit with me for a few minutes and then turn in for the evening. As the others headed for the doorway, Trooper Willis made a game effort to slide into the adjoining bedroom instead of the hallway.

"Outside!" the Governor boomed at Willis. "I don't know why we have so many damn troopers here anyway. Leonard, you stay and drive me back to the mansion," he said to the hand-picked head of his detail. "The rest of you, head back now."

As soon as the room cleared, Bart sat in an armchair, and I followed suit, occupying the one directly facing him across about an eight-foot-wide sitting area.

"Danny, Danny ... you and I were such good friends, and we've had such pointless problems recently. There's no reason we shouldn't be good friends again. I know my folks haven't always treated you well these past two years, but all that is going to change. What's past is past. What matters is where we go from here."

He paused, apparently trying to clear his head. He did not seem to want a response, and I was determined to stay quiet and let him say as much as possible—including, I hoped, something incriminating.

"I have some good news and a proposition for you. We all know we're headed toward a huge landslide and sweep on Tuesday, including you and Hardy. But I'm not going to sit on that political equity—I'm going to cash it in with a run for the Senate in 2008. Hardy will become governor, and he will have his one year in the sun, but Hardy does what he's told. And you know what I am gonna tell him? I'm gonna tell him that he and I are going to back you for governor in 2009. I want to have that understanding with you—I will write it down and sign it, and so will Hardy. What do you think of that?"

"Is that all you have to say?" I asked.

"That's a pretty attractive offer, I'd say. *What*—is there something else you want? Name it. *What?*"

I stared back at him, waiting, and noticed for the first time that he was a bit palsied. It seemed like more than nerves.

"For God's sake, Danny, we have to work together. I am offering to get out of your way, to get Hardy out of your way, to back you with all the political muscle I have. My friends will be your friends; my resources will be your resources; *my job* will be *your job*. You have all these things you want to accomplish. I am offering to put you in a position to do every single one of them. I am offering to put you in the driver's seat, just like when—"

He stopped mid-sentence.

"'Just like' what, you little bastard?" I said rising from my chair. "Just like when I was chief of staff? Just like when Ned Nevers was governor? *Just like things were before you and your goons blew him to bits on that boat? Just like that? Is that it—just like that?*"

Bart came out of his chair, too, and I was ready for him to lunge at me. I wanted him to scream, *"Yeah, just like that!"* and then do who-knows-what. I didn't care what else he did. I just wanted to provoke a reaction: an admission ... a denial I could poke holes in ... an attempt to justify himself ... *anything*.

Instead, all Bart did was shake even more violently and then yell at the top of his lungs to his protector outside, "Leonard, get in here!" His face was now completely flushed. "You're insane, you know that? *Insane!*" he snarled. "You could have it all…. We *both* could have it all."

"I don't *want* it all," I shrieked. "All I want is justice, and I'm going to have it—your days are numbered!"

He started past me toward the door and then paused, his face close to mine, and pressed words through his tightly clenched teeth: "It's too bad you weren't on that boat with him, you self-righteous son of a bitch."

I turned my lips to his ear and replied, "It's too bad for you I wasn't."

I followed him out of the suite and watched as Leonard—First Sergeant William Leonard Harris of the Virginia State Police—retrieved his charge, and they ambled down the hall together. Trooper Willis followed a few steps behind. Gabe and I just stood there in the hallway, stunned, and watched them go.

Four hours later, at approximately 2:15 A.M., I was in the attorney general's office with Miguel and Gabe struggling to figure out what our next move should be, when I heard several noises and then a bit of a commotion down the hall. At this hour it obviously made no sense for anyone else to be in the office, let alone on the restricted sixth floor. The three of us rose to investigate, and we immediately encountered five state troopers, three in uniform and two following in plain clothes. Gabe instinctively moved forward to engage the first of them. But before anyone said anything, Gabe and I both noticed that one of the plain-clothed officers, the one bringing up the rear, was Trooper Willis. He looked pained.

"General McGuire, we need you to come with us. We need to take you to the Governor's office," the dour, uniformed man in front declared.

"On whose orders, Trooper?" I asked firmly.

"On Colonel Anderson's authority, sir," he said, surprising me. I had expected him to say "the Governor's."

"I am the *Attorney General of Virginia*, Trooper. I don't take orders from Colonel Anderson."

"No, sir, you don't. But I do. The Colonel ordered me to place you under protection."

"That's convenient. Why do I need to be under protection?" I asked defiantly.

"Because, General, there has been an accident ... or ... uh ... an incident ... you know, an event. It's Governor Bell, sir. He's at the hospital. At last report, he was in a coma. It appears to be an overdose of narcotics, sir."

My legs went limp, and I sank into the chair by the door as Trooper Willis pressed forward. "Sergeant Harris is at the hospital, and for now I am in charge of the protective detail," Willis said. "We think the best place for you to be is in the Capitol ... in the Governor's office. Let's get going, sir."

An enormously complex, ambiguous, and tragic situation in the very cradle of American democracy now had become absurdly more complex, ambiguous, and tragic.

CRISIS MANAGEMENT

When the sun finally peeked over the Oliver Hill Building and cast its energizing glow on the Governor's corner office, we were some 30 hours into the day that had begun as Halloween but now was November 1st—exactly a week before voters would go to the polls to elect a governor.

Those voters did not know it, and no one yet could prove it, but their previous governor had been murdered. Their current governor lay near death in the VCU Medical Center a few hundred yards away. And the man who would become their "acting governor"—once Speaker Percival and Senator Morris arrived to execute the necessary documents—sat in that suddenly radiant corner of Jefferson's Capitol absolutely exhausted, his head spinning, beset with alternating feelings of anger and guilt, nearly distraught.

A Supreme Court decision that did not seem all that momentous when handed down just a few months earlier—the one that left the lieutenant governorship vacant—had the effect of making me the very unfortunate person in whom now resided the executive power of a very troubled Commonwealth.

"General, with all respect, I need you to snap out of it."

I looked up.

"What has happened in the last ten hours has happened—there will be a time later to understand it and to assign responsibility for it. We've got some crucial work that needs to be done right now." Seemingly no worse for the wear, Miguel said this in a firm but compassionate way that I appreciated.

He continued, "I have the final draft statement for your review and edit before the Speaker and Senator Morris arrive. We want them to review and approve it, too."

The draft, captioned "Statement of Acting Governor Daniel M. McGuire," read:

> A few moments ago, after consultation with the medical personnel attending Governor Bell and independent medical advisors, Speaker Josiah Percival, Senator Howard Morris, and I executed the necessary legal document certifying that Governor Bell is incapable of carrying out his duties as Governor of Virginia. Due to the pre-existing vacancy in the Office of Lieutenant Governor, this action has the effect of making the Attorney General the Acting Governor.
>
> As my first action, I have called a special session of the General Assembly to convene tomorrow at 10 A.M. At that time, I will address the General Assembly in joint session, and will ask the members of the House of Delegates to elect an acting governor. I take this action with the bipartisan

concurrence of the General Assembly's two most senior leaders, Speaker Percival and Senate President Pro Tem Morris. We three have concluded that this step is prudent and appropriate, so that the position of acting governor will not be under a legal cloud arising from the happenstance that the Attorney General, in certifying Governor Bell's incapacity, may have an actual conflict of interest, and the Speaker, as a candidate for lieutenant governor, may have at least the appearance of a conflict of interest. The Constitution provides for the acting governor to be elected by the members of the House of Delegates if the lieutenant governor, attorney general, and speaker of the House of Delegates are unable to succeed to the office via the statutorily prescribed method of succession. By confirming the action that Speaker Percival, Senator Morris, and I have taken today—by a vote of the House of Delegates and supportive resolution of the Senate—the General Assembly will remove any uncertainty regarding the executive authority of this state.

There are many unresolved questions at this hour. We will work resolutely to bring accurate information forward as soon as possible, and we will continue to act in concert with the bipartisan leadership of the General Assembly.

In the meantime, I encourage you to lend comfort and support to your fellow Virginians. If you are able, I ask that you take a moment today to visit your church, synagogue, mosque, house of worship, or other place of reflection, or to simply repair in quiet humility to a peaceful corner of your home. As we pray fervently for Governor Bell's recovery and return to this office, I ask that you pray also for me as I fulfill the duties incumbent on me as acting governor during these tragic times. And let us all give thanks that we live in a free land where the rule of law is a rock, and where our institutions and ideals are as sturdy and resilient as our people.

I delivered the statement, without revision, to the cameras in the Governor's conference room as Speaker Percival and Senator Morris stood at my side.

My address to the General Assembly the next morning was concise. I echoed the points made in the previous day's statement and announced that I was appointing a bipartisan panel of highly distinguished leaders to preside over a full and unfettered investigation into the circumstances surrounding Bart's collapse. The group's mandate was broad enough to include the circumstances of Governor Nevers' death, too, though I did not mention the latter aspect in my speech. A short while later all 91 delegates who made it to the Capitol in time unanimously elected me acting governor. Beforehand, the Republicans and Democrats caucused separately in their customary manner, and I took the unusual step of attending each caucus meeting—joining the ruling Democrats as well as my fellow Republicans—to pledge cooperation and ask for support during the uncertain days ahead.

There was harmony, but it was skin-deep.

Beneath the thin veneer of public spiritedness in a time of travail there were some inescapable political realities at work and some intractable partisan forces at play. A statewide election and contests for all 100 delegate seats were less than a week away, and both sides had a lot riding on the outcome. Republicans were counting on extending their dominance of the executive branch and wanted the wave to sweep in enough GOP delegates to change control of the House. Democrats were concentrating on defending their legislative bastion, but they also entertained some faint hope of thwarting the statewide Republican sweep and delivering the lieutenant governorship to their revered House speaker. No one thought Dorothy Jean Meade—liberal, black, and way back in the polls—had a chance of winning, but her candidacy was a source of pride for African Americans, and their strong turnout could produce some unexpected wins for Democrats in other close contests.

That had been the story just 24 hours earlier, before the world changed. Now, the leading candidate for governor, the incumbent and prohibitive favorite, lay senseless in a hospitable bed, dying. It was way too late to name a new candidate or change the ballots and voting machines. If a majority of votes went to Bell and he died or remained incapacitated thereafter, then either Hardy Barnhard or Si Percival—whoever won the race for lieutenant governor—would succeed to the governorship. No one in the political world had a clue how the voters would react to these still-unfolding developments, and by the time you took a poll it would be too late to really impact anything anyway.

When a leader dies or some other tragedy strikes, all of the politicians immediately assume a solemn, statesmanlike pose, as if personal interest and partisan advantage were absolutely the farthest thing from their minds. Meanwhile, behind closed doors and over the telephone, they immediately start huddling and angling for personal interest and partisan advantage. Even if genuine sorrow could quell such maneuvering—and it never does—the circumstances here would have supplied precious little of that balm. No one in the political establishment in Richmond really liked Bart—*no one*. And the fact that he appeared to be the victim of his own deeply flawed judgment and personal demons left even less room for sympathy. I was only mildly surprised, therefore, when a delegation of senior Republican lawmakers in both houses asked for a private meeting with me shortly after the vote confirming my status as acting governor. They had politics on their minds.

As I waited for them to arrive, I peered out across the south portico at the sea of large, media logo-bearing trucks with huge white satellite dishes that lined the circular drive in front of the Capitol and even filled up Bank Street down at the foot of the hill. They were in every conceivable space on the other three sides of the building, too, beaming Virginia's "breaking news" to a riveted national and international audience. It is not often that major political figures die in office, and the sudden violence and specter of terrorism surrounding Nevers' death earlier had triggered worldwide coverage. Now, less than two years later, another Virginia governor had fallen, and the circumstances—a drug overdose—were even more juicy. In this curious little corner of America, governors seemed to be dropping like flies—"rather like Catholic popes and Soviet dictators back during the Reagan era," one British wag observed—and so there was round-the-clock coverage.

I pondered the scene from the conference room window and stayed in that room so I could greet the solons with a handshake as they filed in and took their positions around the antique mahogany conference table. The standard protocol was for the governor to wait in his office next door until all the visitors were in their places and then make a properly gubernatorial entrance. In addition to avoiding that ritual, I chose to sit at the foot of the table, near the door, rather than at its head.

"Gentlemen, ladies, please sit down and tell me what's on your minds," I said.

Delegate Jack Jepson, the House minority leader, obviously had been designated as the spokesman for the dozen or so GOP heavies, and he spoke first.

"Governor ...," he began purposely, pausing on that word for effect, "thank you for seeing us. We know you are dealing with a thousand things. You gave an excellent speech, by the way. I think it's remarkable how you have handled things so smoothly, especially with the Speaker and Howard Morris. They can be a handful."

"Thank you, Jack. It helped enormously that those two and I got to know each other fairly well during the Nevers administration. There is a level of trust there, and I believe they both want to do the right thing. It's just an extremely awkward and difficult situation, particularly with the election at hand and the Speaker and me on opposing tickets. You could not have dreamed up a situation like this," I said.

"Well, as you might have guessed, the election is what's on our mind. Of course, our primary concern is Governor Bell's recovery...."

"Of course."

"But we don't have the luxury of postponing discussion of the election. Decisions have to be made, and made quickly. And we have a suggestion for you to consider."

"A suggestion? On what?" I asked.

"We would like to hold a press conference—in fact, we plan to do it this afternoon if you give us the word—urging you to stand for election as governor on Tuesday as a write-in candidate." I was already pushing back from the table in disbelief when he added, "Now, before you react, just hear us out."

The highly regarded delegate from Rocky Mount was a savvy legislative veteran. Unlike some hayseed members with few political smarts and a purely parochial perspective, Jepson was a seasoned operative with a good strategic head on his shoulders and, he thought, an excellent chance of capturing the seats needed to make him the new speaker of the House. On the verge of that success, the political gods had just thrown him a high hard one, a real stinker, and he was determined to find a way to salvage the at-bat.

"If you allow yourself to be put forward as a write-in candidate, it will be the closest thing to an incumbent we can field for governor in these circumstances. We think there might actually be a strong sympathy vote. Plus, there is a great reservoir of goodwill from the Nevers days, and you are as closely associated with that good feeling as anyone. The alternative, if I may speak candidly, is *untenable*. The people of Virginia simply are not ready to make

Hardy Barnhard the chief executive of this state. We were joking this morning—it's a bit of gallows humor, I know, and entirely inappropriate. But Senator Swoap here said, 'I don't know what will be less appealing to the voters on Tuesday—casting a ballot for a candidate who is actually brain-dead or one who just acts like it.'"

Grimacing, I instinctively played the governor's role—as the adult in the room. "That's funny in a *sick* sort of way," I scowled. "You let that kind of tasteless wisecrack get into the papers and you won't have to worry about winning the election at all."

"You're right, I should not have said that," Jepson hastily backtracked. "But the point is, we have to give the people something positive to focus on and rally around. This thing with Governor Bell not only *is* terrible; it *looks* terrible—you know, the overdose and all. And our Republican voters are going to be very confused and conflicted; meanwhile, the Democrats are going to turn out in big numbers. It's not just the governorship I am worried about; my job is to look out for the House. If we go into this election without a message, without a plan, and without a candidate at the top of the ticket, we will be courting disaster. *You are the one who can do it.* After the last 24 hours, you already look like a governor. People will respond to your steady hand at the helm. They will trust you to carry on the work of Governor Nevers and get things done."

I waited to make sure he was through.

"That's it," he said. "That's the case. We all agree on this course of action, and we are prepared to go out and announce it, right folks?"

They all conveyed strong assent.

"Look, I regard you all as great friends and allies, and I appreciate your sentiments," I replied, sitting erect. "I guess, after the last two days, nothing should surprise me, but you have surely done it here. This is the most unexpected and, frankly, bizarre idea I can imagine. Bart Bell is still alive; he's the governor—and our nominee for governor. I cannot possibly allow myself to be put forward as a rival candidate. It smacks of the most naked kind of ambition. I can't possibly do it. I *won't* do it."

"Danny, your buddy Bart is across the street dying. That's a fact, boy—a fact, plain and simple. You need to man-up and look at the big picture here… ." This time it was my putative friend, the rotund and plain-spoken gentleman from Grundy. "I say this with all due respect, of course."

"Of course, Senator. You always do."

"Look, Governor," Jepson said, quickly retaking the floor. "This is not your idea; it *can't* be your idea. But you think about it. In fact, I suggest you connect with your good friend, Congressman Jackson, and see what he thinks—"

Mitch was heading to Richmond as soon as they finished voting on the supplemental defense authorization bill that afternoon. These guys appeared to have a read on his opinion even before I did.

"—and, in the meantime, we will just go about our business, and we will get together again sometime later. Thank you for your time."

With that, they departed, and I turned to other pressing matters in the still-unfolding crisis. I should have foreseen the chaos that almost immediately would ensue.

First, Jepson and his crew promptly held their news conference announcing the names of nearly three dozen senators and delegates who were supporting their draft-Danny McGuire movement.

A short time later, State Senator Johnny Bondurant and a much smaller cadre of Barnhard enthusiasts rushed before the cameras to denounce my "naked power grab."

"Not only is Governor Bell still the nominee of this party," Bondurant indignantly declared, "but Hardy Barnhard is his rightful successor in the event that, God forbid, our Governor does not recover. Every loyal Republican should be disgusted by Mr. McGuire's power grab. He will be the party's ruin—just do the math. If Barnhard and McGuire—I mean, Governor Bell and McGuire—split the Republican vote on Tuesday, the result is going to be the election of the most liberal candidate ever to hold public office in Virginia, the *kind of person* we don't want as our governor."

Bondurant, the blustering bigot, was back at his old games—and delighted to be relevant once again. But while he was a scurrilous person, he had a political point of considerable merit. No thanks to me, a McGuire-versus-Barnhard battle had suddenly erupted. And unless I acted quickly to quash it, Republicans might well divide their votes for governor on election day....

Speaker Percival arrived for a previously scheduled meeting just after the dueling news conferences concluded. The Capitol was suddenly ablaze with political gossip, rumors, and excitement.

"The lunatics are running the asylum, Danny. You'd better take cover or they're gonna run over *you*," he said knowingly.

CHAPTER EIGHT

CHOICE

Bart Bell was buried in a municipal cemetery near Centreville on a bleak and disheartening November morning. At the request of the three surviving family members—his infirm mother and two older sisters—the graveside service was private. By then, more than a week had passed since his death, long enough for every inch of his body to be painstakingly scrutinized by the state's chief medical examiner and an independent forensic expert, and long enough, too, for Virginia's roiled electorate to go to the polls and choose another chief executive.

I received word of Bart's death from Abby at 4:30 A.M. on Thursday, November 3—five days before the election. By the time the expected news finally came, I was no longer numb to the ongoing crisis. I had spent much of the night awake, lying in bed perusing mental images of those early, generally happy times when Bart and my three young friends had been swept up together in the exhilarating current and chaos of politics, tugging me along with them. I reflected on how oddly intertwined our life's journey had been since then and wondered how things could have gone so terribly wrong with Bart. Even before our values so evidently diverged, there had always been a gulf between the two of us, something inexpressible that gave me pause and seemed to unsettle him, too. I pondered briefly how I might have done things differently—how some better choice on my part might have helped redeem his life—but no answers came. A better person might have dwelled on that subject, but I had neither the inclination nor the time.

Bart had been the master of his fate. My job was to clean up the mess he left.

The immediate effects of Bart's death ranged from minor to monumental. In the former category was my change in title. According to the Virginia Constitution, I was now "governor" rather than "acting governor," and I would be in that role until the end of Bart's term—*Ned Nevers'* term—on January 14, 2006. That development meant that other, more consequential adjustments had to be made. Among them were wholesale personnel changes in the governor's office, including my swift reinstallation of Abby as chief of staff. Since I vacated the office of attorney general upon becoming governor, a successor was needed, and I appointed Miguel. As soon as Bart's things were appropriately packed and removed by the frazzled staff, Martha and I took up residence in the Executive Mansion. I was reluctant to move in at all but was persuaded of the value of projecting as much "normalcy" as possible.

The circumstances of Bart's demise were the subject of both state and federal investigations, which proceeded apace in more or less coordinated fashion. Despite the press of other duties, I spent a substantial amount of time with a cadre of investigators—two from the FBI and two from the Virginia State Police's Bureau of Criminal Investigation—describing the pertinent events in minute detail. Ignoring the advice I would have given anyone else in a similar situation, I participated in these interviews without counsel present. In some of the sessions I was questioned alone while in others, including discussion of Nevers' death and our response to it, Gabe, Miguel, and I were interviewed jointly. One disturbing development of unknown significance was the news that Trooper Jamie Willis had been placed on administrative leave pending completion of the investigation. It could have been just a routine move—he was the last to see Bart alive, as it turned out—but the investigators' questions hinted at some ongoing issue over how and why Governor Bell had ingested the substance that eventually killed him. The general assumption was that Bart either had committed suicide or accidentally overdosed, but that supposition was being critically examined. Meanwhile, I directed Colonel Anderson to reconstitute as nearly as possible the EPU detail that had served during Governor Nevers' tenure, with Gabe Smith in the lead.

Of course, the most momentous developments arising from Bart's death were the political ones. The proximity to the election created an extraordinary, even bizarre, situation. Bart's passing on Thursday, November 3, just a few days before the election on Tuesday, November 8, meant that a dead man's name would be on the ballot as the Republican nominee for governor. Since the events of Halloween evening, there never had been more than a theoretical possibility that the GOP nominee might make a miraculous recovery and resume his rightful place as governor—and, if voters so chose, as governor-elect. Virginians traditionally have not bestowed their highest elective honor on drug abusers, at least insofar as anyone knows, and so even a medical miracle presumably would not have been enough to reelect Bart. But now, the main reason I had given earlier for refusing to seek the office as a write-in candidate—respect for the still-animate governor and nominee—was gone, and the pressure on me to take the plunge suddenly became intense.

I sat down with Chad, Abby, and Mitch to discuss the matter on Thursday morning, just a few hours after getting word of Bart's death, and heard what can only be described as a compelling case. All three agreed, for somewhat differing reasons, that I should declare my candidacy, and do so *immediately*.

Abby's case was rooted in compassion and idealism.

"There's so much you can accomplish, Danny—all the things we started under Governor Nevers," she said. "You know how proud he would be to have you as his successor, seeing those initiatives through, really institutionalizing them for years to come, and *building* on them, taking them the next step. All of his dreams—*our* dreams—for making Virginia the national model for education, for helping people lift themselves up and find good jobs and opportunity, and all the rest. You could do so much to help people, especially at-risk kids and young people who desperately need it. Plus, there's your unfinished agenda as AG. You can move forward with the anti-drug initiative that Bart blocked. Just think about how the people will respond to that issue after what has happened."

Abby was excited and animated in a way that I had not witnessed since before the Nevers funeral. Even with the recovered effervescence, her tone took on almost a pleading character.

"It's the opportunity of a lifetime, Danny. You didn't seek it; it came and found you. But you cannot run from it or shirk it. There's too much good you can do," she said firmly.

Chad's case was rooted in liberty and competition.

"Abby's right—this situation is not of your making, but it's up to you now to make the most of it. It's a gut check for you, buddy." Rather characteristically, Chad was framing the issue as a personal and philosophical moment of truth—a crucial choice at the crossroads of a great ideological struggle.

"There really are just two parties, like Jefferson said: the party that trusts people and the party that doesn't—the party of freedom and opportunity and the party of regulation and entitlement. And I'm not talking about Republicans versus Democrats: *Hardly Barnyard* doesn't have a clue about what's really at stake any more than Dorothy Meade does. She would aggressively trample on liberty based on some misguided pursuit of 'social justice'; Hardy would stumble all over it through indifference and ineptitude. Either would be a disaster and would undermine all we've been working for these past two decades. This is a fight that matters—a battle over big ideas. And you've gotta have faith in the system and compete aggressively within the rules. The rules allow you to run as a write-in candidate, and, with the right message, they'll allow you to *win* as a write-in candidate. It's not your fault that two governors died, but it's your duty to take advantage of the circumstances to advance the things we've been working for."

The stakes extended beyond Virginia, he added for good measure. "If you pull this off, it will mean four years of creative conservative leadership in Virginia when the country desperately needs that kind of energetic, positive example."

Mitch's case was rooted in morality and justice.

"I would only add one thing to what's been said," he said slowly, for emphasis. "Dr. King often said 'even though the arc of the moral universe is long, it bends toward justice.' What he meant is that God has a plan—a plan that is just and that is in harmony with the moral universe he created. And when the time comes to fulfill your destiny as part of that plan, justice *demands* that you do what God put you here to do."

This was the core of Mitch's personal faith and philosophy.

"It's not like someone is saying to you, 'Hey, dude, here's a cool idea; why don't you run if you feel like it?' It's a duty that arises from your situation. Remember Esther, the beautiful Jewish girl who became queen in Persia just as an evil functionary was plotting to exterminate the Jews. Remember what her uncle, Mordecai, said to her? 'Who knows whether you have come to your royal position for such a time as this.' Well, here we are in a time of great crisis. God has put you in a position to redeem Virginia's moral leadership, remove the stain of corruption, and restore the Commonwealth's good name. You're in this spot for a reason, and it's no accident. *Nothing* happens by accident."

The three continued for some time in their distinctive but mutually reinforcing veins of encouragement and insistence. I listened intently throughout.

When they seemed spent, I responded with a string of practical questions that had been troubling me as I pondered the possibilities.

"Wouldn't I just split the Republican vote and elect Meade, as the Bondurant and Barnhard people have been saying?" I asked.

"Not with the right message and appeal for support," replied Chad authoritatively. "You're already the governor. People see you as guiding the ship through the storm, and you're the logical choice going forward. It's logical also because of your close ties to Governor Nevers. It's just an educated guess—we don't have any survey data to back it up—but my gut says the voters are already feeling acute embarrassment over the Bell episode and would love to go back to the good old stable times under Governor Nevers. You can make that subtle appeal."

"That's my sense, too," said Abby. "Hardy is closely linked to the Bell regime, but you are mainly associated with the Nevers administration. Our ads in the AG race have emphasized that connection well. Plus, I just don't see Hardy getting a lot of votes. Remember that he's not on the ballot—not for governor anyway. For him to become governor, he has to win the LG race *and* people have to pull the lever for a gubernatorial candidate who is dead because of a drug overdose. I just don't see many Republicans, let alone independent voters, doing that second thing. It may sound crass, but it's the reality."

"In a three-way race, Meade will get the base Democratic vote—33, at most 36, percent—and that's it," said Chad. "The irony is she probably could have positioned herself to also get a third or more of the independent vote if she had tacked to the center, but she didn't expect to win so she decided to just be herself and run a true-blue left-wing campaign. As a result, you can split the remaining voters 60-40 with Hardy and still come away with the 38 to 40 percent of the statewide total you need to win the election in a three-way contest. That's sort of the worst-case scenario, in my view. I think you actually will beat Hardy two or three to one among Republicans and independents, and I bet you can hold Meade under 33 percent with the right appeal to bipartisan unity in a crisis. Bottom line, you'll top 45 percent, maybe even 50, and win easily."

I looked at Mitch, who had not spoken. His wide-eyed visage and exaggerated nod conveyed emphatic agreement with Chad's assessment.

"That analysis might be accurate in a race where all three candidates are on the ballot, but isn't it hard to get people to write in a name?" I asked.

"It will certainly slow things down—that's for sure," said Chad. "Don't expect the returns to come in right after the polls close. But this is not your typical election where hardly anyone is paying attention. Everyone is tuned in to this bizarre situation. I expect the turnout will be huge, especially with the right appeal on TV. When you announce your candidacy, everyone in Virginia and half the country will be watching. Heck, they'll probably cover it live in Bangalore and Berlin. There won't be a walking, thinking person in Virginia who doesn't know about it. So I don't worry about our ability to motivate folks to cast the write-ins."

"Okay, you mentioned a televised address—that brings up another issue," I said. "Wouldn't I need to spend some time explaining my role in Bart's death … you know, how I confronted him and all that's flowed from that? I mean, it seems like that's relevant. And if I do that, doesn't it then get me into the whole business about Bart's conflict with the Governor and his organized crime connections, their complicity in the boat explosion, and all that? I don't know whether I can even talk about those things while the investigation is pending, but assuming I can, don't I have some obligation to walk people through it all?"

Chad and Abby had responded eagerly to the other questions, but on this one all three sat back, looking at each other. It was Mitch who finally spoke up.

"We've talked about it," he said. "There's neither a need nor a practical ability to get into all that before the election. The fact is, we don't know the facts. The investigations are ongoing and need time to work. The circumstances and cause of Governor Nevers' death are still in doubt, as you well know. In particular, it's unclear exactly what role Bart played personally. I know what you suspect, but he never admitted anything to you—not outright. You could do grave injustice by speaking out before the facts are known, and it would look reckless. And, yes, you're exactly right: You can't explain the strange events of Halloween evening without opening up the whole subject of Nevers' death and your suspicion about Bart's role in it. So you just have to let that lie where it is, and wait for the investigators to present their findings in due course."

"It might be different if you had done something wrong," added Abby. "I mean, if there were something about your role in the Bart thing, you know, his death and all, that could put you in a bad light in the minds of some people, then I could see how you might feel obligated to put it out there before the election. But the fact is, you're going to be regarded as a hero in this whole sordid business, once it all comes out. Bart was deceiving the whole state, and you are the one who forced his hand."

"I'm not so sure people will see it that way," I said. "And the problem is, if they *don't* end up seeing it that way, they won't have a chance to take it into account when they vote. It will all come out after I am safely elected—assuming, of course, that you geniuses have the political calculation right."

"Yeah, well, there's a lot about this whole situation that is far from perfect," said Chad. "We're not talking about the ideal here. People are dead, after all—"

"I get that, Chad. I get briefings, you know."

"Well, yeah, I know you do," Chad continued. "And Mitch has summed up the situation here well. There's no way that you can go on TV in the timeframe we are dealing with—which is, like, *immediate*—and ask for support for governor, and then spend 20 or 30 minutes regaling the people of Virginia with tales of Bart and his buds in the mob and how they took out a governor on a boat one afternoon…."

"There's a bigger point here you need to consider," said Mitch. "When this story does come out—you know, in a proper, factual way—it is going to be a real punch to the gut of the people of Virginia. It's going to be in the headlines for months, even years, and there is no telling what's going to come out about Bart and his crew and their exploits, whether in D.C. or down here. Plus, who knows where the tentacles of this Nevers assassination are going to reach. There's just a whole lot of hard stuff that has to take place before this is behind us."

I wasn't sure where he was going with this, and I made that obvious.

"What I'm saying is that the bigger question—the more important question—is not whether to be straight with Virginians *before* the election. It's about what kind of leadership the Commonwealth will have *after* the election, when the people will have to endure the torture of all the revelations, trials, investigations, and whatever else follows. They are going to need a steady hand at the helm."

I sat back, took several deep breaths, and finally relented—partly. "Okay, you guys obviously have thought this through carefully. Take a shot at the speech and let me have a look at it."

"Does that mean we are a go?" Chad asked.

"It means, 'Take a shot at the speech and let me have a look at it,'" I replied.

"We need to ask for television time if we are going to do this," Abby said.

"Seriously?" I rejoined. "You just told me they are waiting with bated breath for this speech in Bangalore and Berlin. Is there really a question of getting television time?"

"There's not a question about it being covered," Abby elaborated, "but there are extensive preparations to be made if we want it done right. And once we start making those arrangements, it's going to get around that you are planning a major speech. No way to avoid that. And you don't want to have to backtrack once the word is out there."

"When do you want to do it ... the speech, I mean—when should I do the speech?"

"We need a little lead time to hype it, build some anticipation—but not much," replied Chad. It clearly was not the first time that he, and presumably Abby, had considered the issue. "It ought to be an address from the Governor's office at 7 o'clock tomorrow night. That's the optimal time and location," he said.

"You both agree with that?" I turned to Abby and Mitch. They nodded affirmatively.

"Okay, you'll have my answer in an hour, two at most," I said, rising. "Listen, guys, I do appreciate it."

After they left, I sat back down and rested for a few moments, noticing for the first time that the governor's high-backed swivel chair fit me quite well. I stood again and considered the men whose backs had pressed against it, wearing down the now-faded gold seal of Virginia that was impressed on the blue-dyed leather. No one had worn it down more than Bart, I mused. If I became governor by vote of the people, I would have that chair redone so the seal was bright again.

I gazed southward toward the river and the prominent bend that inspired early English reveries of home and gave Richmond its name. It was the river where America had begun, and it had carried on its noble business year in and year out without fanfare for four centuries, asking only that its contemporary custodians—its human stewards—do the right thing. Most of them did ... most of the time. But the exceptions could really wreak havoc.

I headed out through Abby's office and down the stairs to the east entrance of the Capitol. The mansion was just a two-minute walk away, and Martha would be there, supervising the transition.

"MY FELLOW VIRGINIANS"

> *Once to every man and nation comes the moment to decide, in the strife of truth with falsehood, for the good or evil side; some great cause, some great decision, off'ring each the bloom or blight, and the choice goes by forever 'twixt that darkness and that light.*

These lyrics—drawn from James Russell Lowell's anti-slavery poem, *The Present Crisis*, and familiar to me from our church hymnbook back in Orange—had always been a source of worry. It was not the verity that moments of decision, choices between right and wrong, would come, but the danger that I would fail to recognize them when they arrived. The power to rationalize is great; ambiguity's seduction is strong. I lived in fear that "some great cause or great decision" would get past me, that the chance to choose would "[go] by forever," and I would be left to grovel in the pallid gray groaning of regret 'twixt that darkness and that light.

I had committed to give the speech. Now I had to choose the words. And therein lay my great decision.

Contrary to Chad's suggestion, I would not deliver the speech from the governor's office. It somehow seemed presumptuous, and partisans might justifiably object to my politicizing the place. Instead, I chose the Capitol Rotunda, in front of the Houdon statue. It was there that Governor Nevers had lain in repose, his last official act as a servant of the Commonwealth. It seemed a fitting place to pick up the fallen leader's standard and ask the people of Virginia for their trust.

All day Friday the excitement and tension built. It was as if some great saga, an epic made for reality TV, was approaching its climax. Cable news networks hawked the story constantly, reprising the preceding days' saucy developments, interviewing political pundits and legal experts, and venturing wise predictions about the key players' next moves, especially mine. The setting—America's historic birthplace, now a competitive political hotbed—was nearly perfect. The Old Dominion's political establishment faced an extraordinary quandary born of astounding events, and everyone was waiting to see how they—which was "we"—resolved it. Yet, the actual events were far more scandalous even than the viewers, and voters, knew.

I spent a good part of the morning and early afternoon in seclusion, working on the speech. The draft supplied by Abby and Chad was useful, but the words had to be mine.

At the four-hour mark, Miguel arrived as requested, and my assistant placed the scheduled call to Attorney General Cyrus in Washington. There was still time to change the speech if either AG objected to my remarks, but they did not.

With three hours to go, I went over to the mansion to clean up, clear my head, and confer one last time with Martha.

With two hours to go, I met with Mitch, Chad, and Abby in the old governor's office near the mansion entrance. I thanked them for their friendship and their advice, and shared with them the content of my final draft of the speech.

With 90 minutes to go, I went upstairs and prayed, asking mainly for wisdom and courage. It was not the first such prayer that day, nor would it be the last. But in that solitary moment of surrender I opened myself a final time to the possibility that I was bent on pursuing my will, not God's. Even at that late hour, if a change of course was needed, I was prepared to make it.

With 60 minutes to go, I went on auto-pilot as the handlers took over. Make-up was applied. The sound was tested. People buzzed about as all was readied. Like an out-of-body experience, my mind ranged elsewhere … to Orange, with my parents … to Mount Hope Bay, with my granddaddy … to Hampden-Sydney, with Dr. S. D. … to Hollywood Cemetery, with Governor Nevers … to Good Shepherd Church, with Miguel and his gifted messenger … to the Governor's Office, with Mitch, Abby, and Chad … to the mansion, with Martha. I felt their warm encouragement but could not hear their words—only these: *And, lo, I am with you always, even unto the end of the age.*

"My fellow Virginians, good evening…."

The words moved on the teleprompter—the first worry averted—as I alternated awkwardly between the phrases running on the screen in front of me and the printed lines on the lectern below. Soon I found that the words were flowing mainly from my memory, and I relaxed. Having Martha at my side brought additional assurance.

"The events of recent days have reminded us that nothing is certain in this life—nothing, that is, except the 'eternal rules of order and right, which Heaven itself has ordained,' to quote the Father of our Country, the gentle giant who looks over our shoulder and counsels us even today."

I cocked my head ever so slightly, drawing attention to the Washington statute behind me.

The greatest of these "eternal rules" is the rule of love. To love God with all our heart, soul, mind, and strength. To love our neighbors as we love ourselves. To do unto others as we would have them do unto us.

We teach our children this Golden Rule, but too seldom do we manage to live by it ourselves. And, sometimes, when our political leaders break this rule, great harm comes to many innocent people.

So it has come to pass in this Virginia that we love.

In recent days, we have been saddened again by loss and thrust into uncharted political waters. I am grateful for the wise counsel and bipartisan support I have received as we have navigated these troubled times together. I am especially grateful for the words of encouragement so many of you have provided in your emails, cards, and calls.

In difficult moments like this, it is natural to want to quickly turn the page. Tuesday's election presents such an opportunity. And it is tempting to stand before you tonight and offer myself as the perfect page-turner.

Yet, there are other "eternal rules"—the rule of truth, and the rule of justice, and, in this free land, the rule that the people govern.

I deeply respect those who say it is counter-productive to tell the truth too soon … that justice cannot be served until all the facts are known … and that the people can govern best without the cloud of confusion created by a half-complete story.

For me, this is simply not an option.

And so, tonight, I want to share with you what I know about the death of Governor Bell. And, with an even heavier heart, I want to reveal what I have learned about the death of Governor Nevers. Because the truth is this: The "eternal rule"—the Golden Rule—has been viciously violated in the pursuit of power here in Virginia.

That such a thing could happen in this, the cradle of American liberty, will be a source of great shock and sorrow.

It will be a burden for Virginia to bear. Yet, it will be no greater burden for us as a free people than the burden each of us bears every day under the weight of a sinful nature.

The truth will hurt. But, ultimately, the truth will set us free....

I went through all of it, summarizing where I could, giving details where I must: the bitter conflict between Governor Nevers and Lieutenant Governor Bell ... the threats and the permanent breach ... the uncertain character of Bart's past conduct, and his certain tie to organized crime ... the suspicious circumstances of the Governor's death and the reason to suspect foul play ... the research and revelations by Gabe and ensuing disclosure to federal authorities ... my effort to provoke an admission by Bart and our encounter at the Jefferson ... the full scope of the investigation that I had launched even before Bart's death and the truth that there remained more unanswered questions than answers.

I laid it all out factually. It was not in the manner of an impassioned closing summation like you would make to a jury, nor was it like Gabe channeling Joe Friday at the other extreme. I simply tried to convey at once, in word and tone, an overriding sense of obligation, a deep personal sadness, and an abiding confidence in the judgment of the people, armed with the truth.

"On Tuesday," I said, turning finally to the political portion of the speech,

we will go the polls to choose our statewide leaders and members of the House of Delegates. We are inclined to see this as a time of great testing and controversy in the life of our democracy, and indeed it is. The eyes of the world are upon us, and, to be honest about it, we are pretty embarrassed by what they see. This is not the kind of attention we seek.

But I urge you to reflect this evening on our House of Delegates, the oldest continuous representative assembly on the planet, the place where representative government in America began, and consider all the challenges that Virginia has faced since that body's modest beginnings nearly four centuries ago.

Through faith in God, faith in the principles of freedom and justice, faith in ourselves and in each other, we have overcome every adversity.

Through that faith, our forebears overcame fear, famine, dispossession, and oppression to found a new community in the Chesapeake estuary, giving birth to a great nation.

Through that faith, ordinary men and women pledged their lives, fortunes, and sacred honor to the cause of freedom. Their lives and fortunes many surrendered, but never their honor.

Through that faith, a free nation was founded and a great civil struggle soon ensued over its true meaning. Many more gave their lives and fortunes here on the bloody ground of Virginia, each side claiming its cause was just. Yet, God had a plan, and he gave the victory and the verdict to the fundamental principle of equal justice under law.

Through that faith, we turned from a century in which the very survival of the American nation was in doubt to an American century where the freedom of billions in other lands was in our hands.

And then we crossed the threshold into a new century and were attacked here on American soil, on Virginia's soil. Once again, our sons and daughters answered their nation's call, emptying themselves in another epic struggle to turn back the tide of despotism and save liberty.

Through our faith in each other, in our ideals, and in the Providence that guided our forebears, we have emerged from the deepest depths of poverty—from an awful reconstruction and great depression—to become an economic powerhouse for the nation.

We have emerged from the evils of Jim Crow and segregation to become one of America's most diverse and caring communities.

We have emerged from the despair of school closings and defeatism to create a hope-filled partnership for educational excellence, choice, and opportunity for all.

When we consider all the dangers, toils, and snares through which we've already come, who among us can lack faith that an amazing grace will lead us home?

Let no one watching tonight doubt us. For out of these latest trials will come a stronger Virginia—a Virginia more mindful of its moral mission, more determined to be a shining city on a hill for a nation that is a beacon for the world.

We come, then, to the decision you will make in the important election that is now just four days away.

Until recently, I was honored to serve as your attorney general. Now, as a result of tragic events, I have the responsibility of serving as your governor. And it falls to me to answer the call and question of so many: *What should we do on Tuesday?*

I cannot answer this question, but I can offer an observation.

Elections are usually about defining the *differences*: differences of party and philosophy ... differences of promises and platforms ... differences of economic, regional, and other interests.

But, every once in a while, an election is not about what divides us, but what unites us.

There is one personal and political attribute that transcends all our differences. It is integrity. It is one of those "eternal rules of order and right that Heaven itself has ordained." And whenever you're in doubt about how to vote, if you will ask yourself whether one candidate is markedly superior according to that standard, you will rarely regret your decision.

The two parties have chosen. The names are on the ballot. As always, a campaign has occurred, and unpredictable events have intervened. Now the choice is in your capable hands, and you must decide.

May God bless us all as we exercise this sacred freedom he has entrusted to us.

Good-night.

I hugged Martha, and accepted compliments from a few perplexed onlookers before making my hasty exit from the Rotunda. As luck would have it, one of the first people I encountered on the stairwell outside the Senate chamber was an understandably down-in-the-dumps Hardy Barnhard.

"Well, that was some speech," he said. "I expected you to throw me under the bus, but not you, me, and the whole Republican Party!"

"Go home, Hardy. Just go home and get some rest," I said with as much sympathy as I could muster. "And then find a way to make an honest living. There's something out there for you, and politics just isn't it."

What Would Nevers Do?

I had not come to my decision quickly or easily. In fact, for most of the time I had been headed in the opposite direction, or so I thought.

On Thursday evening, I had lain awake in bed for hours, wrestling with it. My friends' logic and passion were irresistible, and I did not want to disappoint them. More even than not disappointing them, I did not want to disappoint a determined destiny by conjuring up strained excuses for not running. The interests of the state, the party, the causes I cared about, and the kids—it is always about the kids—would be best served by my running and winning. If all that good would come from it, then I probably just needed to "man-up," as good old Senator Wise had so indelicately put it a few days earlier. If this was my moment, like Esther's, I dared not miss the opportunity.

Yet, I just never could get there. I had this nagging feeling that I was less like the Bible's Esther and more like Hugo's Valjean. The balance of equities leaned heavily in one direction. To the extent I could foresee, far greater good would come from choosing option A than option B. Option B really had only one thing going for it. And that one thing was the code of personal integrity rooted in my faith.

I recalled the young preacher's message at Good Shepherd a few months— it seemed like a lifetime—earlier. *Danny McGuire, what's your "one thing"?*

Martha had settled the matter, unknowingly, when she rolled over in exasperation in the wee hours of the morning. "For God's sake, Danny, just figure out what the most honest thing is, and do *that*. And go to sleep! You aren't gonna be able to keep your head up long enough to give the silly speech if you don't get some rest. And I can't sleep on a trampoline!"

473

I could tell she was really tired because that trampoline line is a standard one in our household, where tossing and turning are commonplace. The actual line is, "If had wanted to sleep on a trampoline, I would have joined the circus." I had started to correct her but thought the better of it.

Then what she said had registered. As with Valjean—*24601!*—truth broke through in all its liberating simplicity, and my course was clear.

The decision made, I actually had gotten some sleep for a couple of hours after that. I had barely finished showering and dressing when a call came in from Miguel.

"Good morning, Mr. Attorney General," I had said brightly, trying to convince myself that I had not been run over by a freight train. "What's up?"

"Just calling to offer my help on your speech," he had said. "Despite my lofty new duties, I remain your humble and obedient speechwriting servant if you need me."

"That's very thoughtful of you. But I've got this one."

"Okay, well, just call me if you change your mind."

"Understood and appreciated," I had said. "But, hey, don't you want to know what I've decided?"

"No, not really. I know you'll do the right thing."

"Yeah, but what's the right thing—to be or not to be, that is the question."

"Uh-huh," he had said, followed by a click.

Plans fail for lack of counsel, but with many advisors they succeed. At first blush, it might seem like I defied that proverbial wisdom in deciding to tell all instead of staying mum and announcing my candidacy for governor later that evening. My three trusted friends and knowledgeable political advisors had given me their convincing counsel. My peculiar new advisor, Miguel, had withheld his opinion, and Martha's nocturnal exhortation had given no indication of being a considered judgment. But not one person whose advice I valued had urged against my running, and all those who offered counsel had said to do it. In the end, though, I had to listen to my own heart and head, and both reflected the input of many valued advisors and lessons over the years. Chief among them, speaking to me insistently from beyond the grave, was Governor Nevers, whose own principled act of self-denial had set all these awful events in motion.

I had broken the news to Abby, Mitch, and Chad during the afternoon, and all three, of course, had been surprised and displeased. Chad and Mitch had accepted the decision without dissent, understanding that it was grounded in principle: a moral precept, pleasing Mitch; a principle of fair dealing, satisfying Chad. They also had known dissent was futile. Abby alone had endeavored to relitigate the matter, and she had undertaken at great length to review all the good works that I was selfishly thwarting, making me feel as bad as she possibly could.

Finally, I had cut her off mid-harangue and pulled her aside.

"No, Abigail, no! You are wrong, and you've been wrong for a long time; I just never had the courage to tell you!"

I had caught myself after that outburst, pausing, sighing deeply, buying time. But it was too late. I was in it now and had to explain.

> Abby ... dear, moderate, well-meaning Abby ... how can I say this? No one has a better heart than you. You have a passion for helping people born of a love that is as instinctive and natural for you as drawing a breath. You're the model of a servant's heart. But, Abby, you think that the good you do is enough, and there's so much more! There is integrity, and there are principles, and above and beyond them—animating them—there is *faith*. And where there's faith there's grace—a saving grace, yes, for the world to come, but also a living grace for the here-and-now. It's the armor you put on when you realize it's humanly impossible to do all the good the world needs and, what's more, there's evil in the world that good deeds alone cannot overcome. Good works can accomplish much—they truly can change the world—but the one thing they cannot change is our separation from God. We only worsen that separation when we think we can rely on our own devices....

She was looking at me, even more bewildered than hurt, searching for what secret fault had been discovered, what indictment had suddenly been unsealed—and why. I hated the fact that this was a monologue, and a sermonizing one at that. Yet, I had no choice but to press on:

> There is modesty in serving others—no question about it. But there is arrogance—*hubris*—in believing we can do enough good to work our way to salvation, and there is even

greater hubris in believing that salvation doesn't really matter—that we're the greatest power in the universe and all that really counts is how we live our lives. The former denies a hope greater than our reach, and the latter denies the very existence of hope itself.

Look, here's what I believe. Our calling is freedom—freedom from our natural flaws, and freedom from the evil that stalks the world. We attain that freedom through God's counsel, grace, and love. And having obtained it we use it, not as a license for self-indulgence, but as an opportunity to express our love by serving others. We proceed from freedom to faith and from faith to action ... to serving a good purpose. But you cannot shortcut it, Abby. Skip the choosing, skip the grace that guides us to the good choice, and the service, no matter how well motivated, becomes a hollow gesture, a vain pursuit. And it leaves us not only empty but vulnerable. When we think we can rely on our inner strength and good heart, we leave ourselves exposed to the self-delusion and self-justification that are the ruin of so many good people. I have seen that evil, Abby, and I am terrified by it!

We had sat in silence, then, for a couple of moments that seemed like an eternity. She had said nothing, and I could think of no better way to express it.

"I am so, so sorry to disappoint you, Abby—to let you down like this," I had said finally. "I know there are great things we could do together if we had the governorship for four years. But you have to understand why I can't do it. I can't deny people the truth I would insist on for myself. I can't accept the notion that the ends justify the means. I can't deceive myself into thinking it's okay to exploit this situation and take advantage of people when they are so vulnerable. *I can't.* It's not who I am. You have to see that. I *need* you to see that. Not just for my good, Abby, but also for yours—*I need you to see that.*"

Now I was the one doing the pleading.

"One day, I guess, maybe, I'll see it," she had said calmly, sadly, in her eventual reply. "Right now, all I see is a total and utter *waste*. You insist on viewing everything as a gift from God. Well, he's given you a golden opportunity, and you are just throwing it away."

POST MORTEMS

There were two ways to look at the outcome of the election. From one perspective, Dorothy Meade had captured the governorship by overcoming not only a deficit of more than 20 points in the polls but deeply entrenched, if craftily concealed, attitudes of racial bigotry. This feat, matched by only two other gubernatorial candidates in the nation's history, made her an historic— and, to some, a heroic—figure. The other view was that she only managed to defeat a *dead guy* by about an eight-point margin, a less-than-stellar showing that had far less to do with her race than her position well to the left of the Virginia electorate. From this perspective, the achievement was nothing to brag about, and the sobriquet "accidental governor" seemed a perfect fit.

Pundits and commentators twisted themselves around the axle trying to decipher the results. Many found it odd that Governor-elect Meade's 54 percent of the vote against her expired foe was virtually the same as Speaker Percival's share of the tally for lieutenant governor against Hardy Barnhard. But those puzzled by this coincidence had divergent impressions of what should have happened. Some thought Meade should have run much stronger against an opponent who was both discredited and deceased. Others were surprised that she had amassed a statewide vote share as large as that rolled up by her more mainstream, moderate, and popular running mate, Si Percival. It seemed pretty obvious to me that voters simply had cut through the fog and recognized Hardy Barnhard as the Republican alternative in both contests. And having so diagnosed it, Democrats, independents, and more than a few Republicans proceeded to punish the GOP severely for fielding such an unqualified numbnut—not to mention a lackey of the now-reviled Bart Bell—for Virginia's most prized government positions.

Some Republican partisans—the die-hard Bell-Barnhard-Bondurant crowd mainly—tried to blame me for the whole election debacle. My "Washington statue speech," as it quickly became known, was a "tacit endorsement of Meade" and a "signal to cross party lines," they alleged. Even the House defeats—Republicans not only failed to capture the hoped-for House majority, but actually suffered a net loss of five seats—were my fault, according to this chorus of critics. No one denied that the party's sudden collapse was driven by voter disgust at the contemptible actions of the deceased Republican nominee for governor, but I had disclosed those actions—"unilaterally, unnecessarily, and recklessly"—

just before the voting. Moreover, my critics alleged, I had purposely "thrown the election to Meade" at the end of my speech by urging voters to "focus on factors other than party, policies, race, gender, etc."

I did not feel the need to answer a lot of that nonsense. The fact that I was the only Republican running statewide in 2005 to actually *win* his election—I was reelected attorney general by just 8,651 votes out of two-and-a-half million cast—spared me criticism from most quarters that counted. My standard public response to the bashing by the Bondurant crowd was, "If they want to fault me for telling people the truth and telling them that truthfulness matters when you vote, I plead guilty." I tried not to kick Hardy while he was down, but I did remind reporters that all I had really said in the speech was that integrity matters. "If someone wants to say that was code for, 'Don't vote for Barnhard,' then so be it."

Of course, I will not insult anyone's intelligence by suggesting that I did not choose my concluding words in the Washington statue speech very carefully, or that I was indifferent to the outcome of the contest. The truth was this: I did not agree with Dorothy Meade on a single major public policy issue that I could think of, and I feared the damage she would do policy-wise as governor. But I respected her as a person—her intellect, her intentions, her *integrity*—and I was fairly confident that she would bring dignity back to the governorship and serve honorably. I had no such confidence in Hardy. If that sounds vaguely reminiscent of Hamilton's calculus when choosing between Jefferson and Burr in the deadlocked 1800 election, I would not dispute the comparison.

It is pretty apparent in retrospect that Hardy Barnhard was going to lose regardless of what I said in the speech. We Republicans were the ones in charge, and the voters' disgust at the mess we had made of things was entirely predictable even if, in reality, Bart and his sleazy friends were the sole culprits. Given the voters' reaction, I could not have gotten Hardy elected even if I had spent the entire Washington statue speech singing his praises. As it was, I barely resisted the undertow enough to get myself reelected as AG. But I said what I said in the closing section of that speech for the same reason I said what I said in the rest of the speech—because it was the most honest thing.

The day after the election, I stopped by to thank folks at the campaign headquarters on Grace Street in downtown Richmond. I made some brief remarks and then spoke with each of the staff members and volunteers individually. As I was leaving, I paused to slip on my jacket before heading back into the cold, gray November dampness and overheard two young people talking just around the corner. They were disappointed volunteers, evidently students from VCU or UR, and their exchange was probably the most thoughtful post mortem of all.

"So this is the way the world ends ... not with a bang but with a whimper?"

"It's not the end of the world. It's not even the end of politics."

"It sure feels like the end."

"It might feel less like the end if you quoted some of Eliot's more *positive* stuff ... you know, later, after he gave up atheism."

"Oh, so you think he was still an atheist when he wrote about 'eyes I dare not meet in dreams'?"

"I think he was struggling then ... still searching."

"Yeah?"

"Yeah."

"And that's not *positive?*"

PART THREE

PURPOSE

2006~2007

CHAPTER NINE

DEN

"That morning coat fits you well, Danny," the congenial Lieutenant Governor-elect said as we milled about in the Capitol's "Old Senate Chamber" before descending the steps of the South Portico to start the ceremony. It seemed like characteristically benign banter until the needle appeared. "Those 8,000 odd voters who gave you the opportunity to wear it—I hope you gave each of them a personal invitation to come see you sworn in."

"You mean the folks who supplied my landslide victory margin?" I said, buying a moment to craft an artful rejoinder. "I don't think there's anything 'odd' about them, but, yes, I hope they're here so they can see history being made."

Percival glanced over toward the shapely figure in the dark business suit who had just received the keys to the governor's mansion from me in the traditional exchange. Chatting amiably in front of the massive rendering of the battle scene at Yorktown's famous Redoubt Number 10, she looked great and not the least bit "accidental."

"Yes, it's definitely one for the history books: the first governor not to wear a morning coat to the inauguration," he said with a smile, notably of the forced variety.

"Oh, no, Mr. Speaker, I wasn't referring to the inauguration of our first *female* governor," I said with an impish grin. "I was referring to the fact that this is the first inaugural ceremony that's mainly about *demotions*. You know,

I'm the governor, being busted back down to AG, and you're the speaker, being demoted to ...."

"Touché, my friend, touché," he said, barring me from completing the all-too-true observation and diverting me with one of his friendly yet condescending pats on the shoulder.

It was indeed an odd inaugural situation, and no odder for anyone than Percival, the man who for years had been the real power in Richmond and acknowledged leader of the "governing wing" of Virginia's Democratic Party. With the advantage of hindsight, all could see that the cautious patrician had set his sights too low, passing up a seemingly worthless Democratic gubernatorial nomination for what looked like four easy years in the on-deck circle and then his own turn at the plate as his party's consensus gubernatorial nominee in 2009. Suddenly, he was in the shadow of a new Democratic governor who had become an instant sensation and who presumably had designs of her own on the party's nod four years hence. His new post resembled an appendix—irrelevant except for the prospect of rupture—but that prospect was not at all remote. From the moment the election tally was complete on November 8 and their victories were reported, the upstart Meade and the elder statesman Percival were cast as rivals for Democratic affections and nominations down the road. Neither had done anything since election night to dispel that notion, and the tension between their respective camps already was palpable.

On this day, though, there was just one star in Capitol Square, and it was the Commonwealth's surprising new chief executive. She did not garner quite the attention lavished on the nation's first elected African-American governor, who had taken office to international acclaim on the same site two decades earlier, but she nevertheless was a bona fide barrier-breaker and celebrity. The nearly euphoric editors of the liberal *Washington Daily Press* dubbed her the "1-2-3 governor," noting that she was the first woman to hold Virginia's highest office, only the second African American to do so, and just the third African American to be elected governor in the entire United States. "Even more important," they gushed, she was "the embodiment of everything one could hope for in an enlightened political leader." The fawning treatment was too much to bear for the conservative editorialists at *The Richmond Herald*. They urged readers to remember that their newly elected governor was still "a disagreeable feminist far left of the Virginia mainstream" who had reached the governorship "only through the intervention of heretofore unimaginable acts of political violence and her deft theft of a nomination rightfully belonging to someone else." That, they quipped, made Meade "first in gore, first in fleece, and first to throw darts at her countrymen."

The Great Tragedy had come and gone quickly, and the bipartisan good-will had proven just as fleeting. With a polarizing new executive behind the wheel, the state's political insiders knew they were in for a rough ride, and the usual antagonists wasted no time laying on the horn. Ironically, it was the most conservative politician of prominence in the Commonwealth who came to the new governor's aid—and who enlisted mine.

Though they were literally poles apart politically, Mitch Jackson and Dorothy Meade liked each other ... a lot, as I would eventually discover. Shortly before Thanksgiving, Mitch called me with an idea, actually an invitation of sorts. "Sometime soon I'd like to have both you and Dorothy over to my place for drinks and dinner," he ventured. "Completely private and off the record. I think you'll find that maybe you two can do some productive business together."

"Yeah? Like on what?" I probed.

"I don't know for sure. But I think she's going to leave the school choice stuff alone and give it a chance to work, for one thing. She probably doesn't have the votes to do anything about it anyway, but a lot of her party folks want her to put on the brakes administratively. She told me she wasn't inclined to do so because, 'now that it's the law, we ought to see if it can actually do some good, especially in the cities.'"

"She said that?"

"Yeah, and I think she's serious." Mitch replied. "Once you get her out of the political circus, she's actually interested in figuring out what will work."

"Well, she hides that pretty doggone well, Preacher. I don't think I've ever seen her when she wasn't pandering totally to her base. She plays the civil rights card whenever it suits her purposes—race or gender, depending on whom she wants to manipulate or intimidate at the moment—and that tactic gets old fast."

"Hey, you don't have to tell me. I'm the original 'Uncle Tom,' remember? No one has taken more grief from her than I have. I'm just saying...."

"Well, you know me: I'll break bread with anyone. And I don't have anything against her—I made that clear enough back during the election. We just never had any kind of practical working relationship during my time handling the legislature for Nevers. I always assumed she didn't have much use for Republicans—especially white, male, conservative Republicans."

"I can see how you might feel that way."

"Yeah, and then there was that less-than-gracious response after the election when a reporter asked whether my Washington statue speech helped her win," I added, getting to the heart of what riled me.

"I missed that," Mitch said mischievously. "Did she say something unkind?"

"I believe her exact comment was, 'Danny McGuire got 100,000 fewer votes than I got on election day. He was so beat up he barely pulled himself in. If anything, he saved his own sorry bacon by saying good things about me....'"

"And your objection to that was...?"

"Oh, no objection here—it was just great. I mean, if she wants to show zero class and gratuitously poke people in the eye after they say good things about her, well, that's her call. Just an odd way to build bridges as a new governor, that's all.... I mean, if you want to be taken seriously as the governor of a state, especially when people think your election was the most random event ever, then maybe you want to try to work with folks and make some friends. But, hey, what do I know?"

"Okay, now we're getting down to it," said Mitch. "So, look, this is my thinking. You need to get that kind of stuff out of your system. She needs to get the chip off her shoulder about being the 'accidental governor.' At a minimum, you guys need some kind of productive working relationship as attorney and client, right? You also can probably help each other with the Assembly on some issues. So let's sit down with a bottle of bourbon—or a bottle of Burgundy; she doesn't like bourbon—grill some steaks and work on this some."

Like everyone who spends any time in Charlottesville, Mitch had imbibed deeply at the Jeffersonian well, and this proposal struck me as a kind of lame effort to mimic the Sage's famous dinner parlay as secretary of state. I could play Madison well enough, but I was pretty sure Meade was no Hamilton. Mitch said she jumped at the dinner invitation, a claim I doubted. But the bottom line was we sat down together in early December; the room where it happened was in Mitch's apartment on Capitol Hill. It was the first meaningful encounter since our obligatory meeting of outgoing and incoming governors right after the election. We followed it up with two other confidential dinner sessions before Christmas.

By the time the new year arrived, it was clear what each of us wanted out of the rapprochement, and it seemed well worth the effort. Her overarching desire was for *legitimization*: She was eager for everything from helpful hints on how to wield the levers of power as governor—a subject I knew a lot about—to public expressions of regard or at least respect that would reinforce her position and authority. By contrast, I wanted help on just one thing: my comprehensive anti-drug initiative. It had been forcibly shelved due to Bart's machinations, and now I planned to drive it forward. What better time to do so than straight out of the shoot in the 2006 legislative session, fresh on the heels of Bart's overdose and the revelations about his drug-infused lifestyle? The prospects for passage in these circumstances seemed relatively good, but it would not happen without some Democratic votes, and that was where Governor Meade was in a position to help.

The collaboration was signaled publicly for the first time in the new governor's first address to the General Assembly, which followed two days after the mid-January inaugural festivities. The speech repeatedly invoked a spirit of bipartisan cooperation, but few tangible examples or credible prospects were mentioned until she turned to the subject of illegal drugs. In what was clearly the speech's most passionate passage, she outlined a major initiative—one that everyone immediately recognized as the centerpiece of her policy agenda as governor. It stunned political observers in Capitol Square and beyond who had expected the controversial politico to wax eloquently on her favorite ideological causes but offer nothing with any realistic chance of winning approval from the hostile Percival partisans and GOP hardliners in the legislature. Yet, here she was, suddenly behaving like a serious executive who wanted to accomplish something—a civil libertarian turned anti-drug crusader, no less.

"Let us resolve, here and now, to join forces in an all-out fight against drug abuse and drug-related crime," the pertinent section of her speech read.

> It is not lost on me that I am standing here this evening because we have been failing in this fight. We lost one revered governor to a criminal enterprise that thrives by poisoning our fellow citizens, and we saw the life of another warped and ultimately destroyed by this plague.
>
> Worst of all, it happened while we were watching, yet we knew nothing of it until it was too late. And that is tragically

true of far too many individuals, families, and communities ravaged by drug addiction.

For our fellow citizens who are the current and future victims of this epidemic … for our young people whose hope and promise are at risk … for the peace of our neighborhoods, the safety of our schools, and the health of our society … it's time to say, "Enough is enough! We are better than this, and we have a better way!"

The applause line worked as legislators from both parties signaled their approval.

Since the November election, Attorney General McGuire and I and our teams have collaborated on the development of a comprehensive anti-drug plan that carefully balances treatment and enforcement—a plan that is caring, fair, and smart.

First, it includes drug prevention and addiction recovery initiatives that draw on the resources and expertise of the public and private sectors, including both faith-based and secular organizations.

Earlier this month, I visited with a mother and father whose teenage son died of an overdose only days after coming home from a rehabilitation center. They had mortgaged that home to pay for the help their son needed only to learn much later that the program's success rate was less than 5 percent. The reality of the treatment their son received did not come close to matching the hype.

Why doesn't a reliable, accessible resource exist to help parents and families identify the best services for their loved ones who are battling addiction? We rate hotels and restaurants—can't we rate facilities that claim to save lives? At my request, the leaders of the VCU Health System and the UVA Medical Center will convene an expert panel to develop such a rating system for both public and private rehab centers in the Commonwealth, and our administration will reach out to federal and other state officials to encourage development of such a resource nationally.

Second, our plan includes renewed emphasis on anti-drug education in the earliest grades, over the airwaves, and online.

Young and old, but especially our tech-savvy, fitness oriented young people, need to understand that their brain is the hard drive that controls their intellect and memory, their ability to make decisions, indeed all their bodily functions. Taking drugs is like taking a nail file to that hard drive and making a giant gouge that never can be repaired. From kindergarten through college, in workplaces, gyms, houses of worship, and, most important, at family dinner tables, let us stress to the next generation that health and fitness begin with the brain, and that means staying off drugs.

Third is law enforcement. Our plan increases resources for law enforcement agencies, especially in the hardest hit communities and in and around our schools. And it includes dramatically increased statutory penalties for drug traffickers and repeat drug abusers.

We will keep the heat on the dealers who peddle this poison on the streets, but we need a broader strategy on both the supply and demand sides. So, working closely with our federal colleagues, we will be deploying significantly increased assets against the criminal enterprises that supply the street dealers. And we will be getting serious with drug *users* as well—not through more incarceration but through more accountability. No more revolving-door justice without meaningful intervention. If you support our plan, participation in treatment programs will be mandatory, and all drug users who have gone through the judicial system will be subject to random drug-testing for at least a three-year period.

The Governor outlined several other planks in our platform, and then closed with an effective final pitch:

I commend the Attorney General for taking on this cause soon after he took office in 2003. I know he agrees that, working together, we have made this latest plan even stronger, better, and fairer.

Now is the time to act: in this session ... *without delay*. We have the studies, and we have the strategies. We know the sorrows, and we know the solutions. Now we need to do what my grandmother told me a long time ago when she changed my life. She said, "Why Miss Dorothy, if you feel so strong about what's wrong with the world, why don't get up off those darlin' little hindparts of yours and go out and do somethin' about it?"

My friends and colleagues, I say this with all due respect: When it comes to drugs, we've done enough talking. Now we all gotta get up off our darlin' little hindparts and do somethin' about it!

You will have the bill on your desks by this Friday. Please adjust and refine it as necessary, and pass it by February 10th. Some of you will recognize that date; it would have been the 60th birthday of Governor Ned Nevers. Attorney General McGuire and I can think of no better way to honor his memory than to make this crucial commitment to the health, safety, and wellbeing of the people of this Commonwealth he loved so much.

The message was trademark Meade, stating the case on its merits in the manner of a trial lawyer and then bringing it down to a personal level—here, through her grandmother's earthy exhortation—with colorful language that supplied great TV footage and nearly as good copy for the papers. Although in the past her bombast often had obscured her talents, she was an unusually gifted communicator with a dignified bearing and a neighborly knack for connecting. When she shifted her goal from provocation and denunciation to conciliation and inspiration, the striking combination of looks, brains, and elocution made her a force of nature.

I had reviewed the drug initiative portion of the speech at her request and offered only modest refinements. Understanding that inertia is the chief threat to most initiatives, my main contribution had been to insert the deadline for legislative action tied to Nevers' birthday. The result was a reasonably well-crafted speech, but I had no idea how powerful the reaction and how far-reaching the impact would be. It immediately seemed to transform the new governor from "Her Accidency" into "Her Excellency"—from an object of curiosity to an aegis of initiative. Almost overnight she morphed from a politician whose ideas and motives were doubted into a serious chief executive credited with providing deft, bipartisan leadership. The country was still attuned to the Virginia political drama, and she was now the protagonist, so her words had national reach.

There was mutual benefit in our early and unexpected collaboration. More through the anti-drug initiative itself than any personal counsel I provided, my actions had helped Dorothy Meade achieve legitimacy—indeed, much more than mere legitimacy—faster and more thoroughly than either of us could have imagined. But she had done something indispensable for me, too. She had supplied a crucial catalyst for my foremost legislative goal as attorney general, one on which I had been completely stymied since taking office. I did not mind letting her grab the headlines and take the lion's share of credit if that is what it took to get the thing done. Besides, the package bore her unmistakable imprint: its greater emphasis on pre-trial diversion, treatment, and testing made it a better bill than we had developed on our own.

To the untrained eye, this bipartisan cooperation and policy progress must have appeared as unadulterated good news. How could anyone not feel great about this improbable coming-together across party lines to tackle an especially intractable and pressing public problem? Everyone involved was a winner—right?

Well, in fact ... *no*.

In all three key camps—Meade's, Percival's, and mine—the political operatives were coming unglued over it ... for different reasons. Their reactions were intense, but I was unaware.

It should have been no surprise that my collaboration with Governor Meade would infuriate my old partner in legislative conniving, Si Percival. He had a direct political interest in Meade's failure, and the last thing he and his strategists thought they had to worry about was her getting any help from the Republican side. Yet, here I was, providing aid and comfort to their foe. For that reason, among others, I had made several attempts to secure a seat at the table for Percival on the anti-drug initiative. But Meade was too savvy and Percival was too haughty for that to happen, so from the outset of the new administration my previously productive relationship with the former speaker was on the rocks. This was less true, ironically, for the people who were working for us. Richmond is a small town, and I soon got wind that some of my political folks and Si's were drowning their sorrows together at the local watering holes, airing their shared chagrin that the futures of their respective bosses were being imperiled by this altogether unwelcome outbreak of statesmanship and the resulting uplift it likely would give to the new governor's poll numbers.

Like Percival's, my guys had a point. It was entirely possible, even probable, that this collaboration would benefit Meade the most and thus prove to be a net political negative for the GOP and for me. In another time and situation, those political considerations might well have driven my decision. But, on this one, I simply concluded that my higher purpose lay in advancing the fight against illegal drugs cooperatively with Governor Meade rather than in maximizing my party's chance of defeating her reelection. It was an opportunity to gain policy ground mostly on my terms—on *conservative*, *Republican* terms—and to advance the cause that, with the lone exception of school choice, had been my greatest pursuit in politics. If the effort succeeded, it would be well worth the partisan price.

My logic was sound, and I did not even regard it as an especially close call. But it was immediately apparent to everyone that this kind of thinking put me way out of step with some in my party's base, especially the operatives and activists who ran the show behind the scenes. The anti-drug package passed easily—the intense public support assured it—but that success did nothing to diminish the partisan fury over my consorting with the enemy.

I should have seen the consequences coming.

Stoked by passionate, often angry voices that filled the airwaves from both sides, the political environment in America had become increasingly polarized for at least a decade, making any talk of compromise akin to heresy. Political commentators, whose hand-wringing critiques of the phenomenon had become almost as annoying as the phenomenon itself, found no shortage of people and conditions to blame for the new level of toxicity: the rise of talk radio, cable TV, and partisan media; the advent of vitriolic blog posts and anonymous online attacks; the emergence of well-funded single-issue and ideological advocacy groups on the Right and Left; technology-enabled hyper-gerrymandering that produced partisan balkanization in districts and so in legislatures; declining journalistic resources and corresponding erosion of media quality and objectivity; grassroots anger over government gridlock and economic stagnation; and on and on.

Underlying it all was an unmistakable coarsening of the American political culture that, seemingly overnight, somehow had made it acceptable to hurl epithets, assail motives, and rationalize even the most scurrilous attacks on the basis of means-justifying higher ends. Adverse actors on the Manichean political stage were regarded as malign embodiments of a sinister force, to be destroyed rather than persuaded. This phenomenon I attributed mainly to the unprincipled behavior of brash figures at both ends of the political spectrum who advanced themselves by playing on fears, stoking feelings of anger and victimization, and cheapening the discourse with ugly rhetoric. Leadership matters. People respond. And so an appeal to the "better angels of our nature" is calculated to produce a wholesome response; a brute pitch to the darker side typically will prompt the opposite reaction. If the march of totalitarianism across the supposedly sophisticated 20th-century landscape should have taught us anything, it was that lesson.

For a time, Virginia had seemed immune to the growing polarization and acidity that typified national political affairs. The tragic losses of two governors in succession had tempered partisan passions, or at least had masked them. Now, however, the uniquely inflammatory persona of Dorothy Meade was added to the highly combustible partisan kindling, and the flame was instantaneous. Hers long had been among the most strident voices raised in the Commonwealth's corridors of power, and the recent campaign, which she had waged more to make a statement than to gain an office, had done little to soften her image. Her unexpectedly moderate turn as governor, which I took at face value because of our post-election discussions, was seen by the party activists on my side as a transparent political ploy. And I was seen as a fool for falling for it and letting myself be used.

I certainly understood and respected the case for a more partisan course than the one I had chosen. Indeed, the historical analogy that came to mind during this time counseled the more partisan option. Madison had faced a similar decision in 1796 when called upon to advise his friend and ally Jefferson on whether to assume a proffered role in the "Federalist" administration of newly elected President John Adams. Under the constitutional provisions then operative, Jefferson's second-place finish in the Electoral College balloting made him the vice president, and Adams sought to form a unity government in the wake of Washington's contentious second term by inviting Jefferson into his inner councils as a partner. Jefferson was inclined to do it, but Madison, focusing on the longer-term implications, persuaded him to decline. It was a pivotal decision because it enabled Jefferson instead to assume the role of opposition leader, setting the stage for the emergence of his "Republican" party and its quarter-century of presidential rule under Virginians Jefferson, Madison, and Monroe after the revolutionary election of 1800.

Had Madison been wrong to counsel such a self-serving partisan course at the expense of the national interest? Or, had the man now rightly regarded as the father of political parties in America served the national interest by helping to expose the electorate to sharply contrasting visions of their country's future, enabling a decisive choice at the polls? It was an interesting question, and one whose difficulty attested that there is no single answer applicable to all such situations. Partisanship-versus-bipartisanship, principle-versus-practicality, fighting-versus-compromising—all are manifestations of the tension that inheres in politics and in all walks of life: the Man of Idea and the Man of Fact, simultaneously needing each other, defying each other, seeking to become each other, seeking to destroy each other.

Such ruminations were interesting, but my time during the Meade administration would have been better spent assessing the political minefield in which I was then meandering obliviously. I should have foreseen that my allies and Si Percival's would react negatively to any collaboration that enhanced Governor Meade's political standing. But my even bigger error was in failing to appreciate the hostility that I was simultaneously engendering within Meade's own envious inner circle. Nothing in her aides' experience had prepared them to execute a successful governorship and run a complicated state. The same, of course, could be said of most everyone who gains the office—indeed, it is hard to imagine a team less prepared than those of us who arrived with Nevers in 1998—but the unexpected win made Meade's crew especially insecure. I should have been perceptive enough to recognize that reality, but I was incredibly busy and just assumed that my suggestions, many of which proved hugely helpful to Meade, would be appreciated by her aides. In actuality, as I can now see, the opposite was happening. The more our relationship thawed and the Governor came to rely on my advice, the more her coterie of confidants became unsure of their own status and deeply resentful of my influence.

I compounded my miscalculation by failing to put myself in their shoes when it came to the politics of the situation. From the perspective of Meade's political advisors, Percival was not the chief threat to her reelection as governor—*I* was. The political chattering class seemed fascinated by the Meade-Percival rivalry and looming showdown, and the topic preoccupied pundits and journalists. But from the Meade camp's perspective, that was little more than a distraction. Si Percival and some of his Democratic establishment friends might entertain some notion of replacing Meade at the top in 2009, but the Governor's hard-nosed allies knew it would not happen. Democratic Party elders were capable of doing some really dumb things, as her team saw it, but they were not stupid or suicidal enough to alienate the party's vital African-American base by denying re-nomination to an incumbent black governor. The far more plausible threat—even with the GOP brand currently in tatters thanks to Bart Bell—was from the Republican side. And that meant it was from me.

All this would have been discernible if I had been in a discerning mindset. But with Bart's menace gone, my guard was down. I was working across party lines to get things done, transcending divisions and even politics itself, and feeling very good about it. But you never really transcend politics, and I was too experienced by now to indulge such a foolish illusion. It was a rookie kind of mistake, and this time there was no timely call from Mitch reminding me to watch my flank.

LIFE AS A PUNCHING BAG

Not since passage of Governor Nevers' education reform package after nearly three years of cajoling and combat had I felt exhilaration comparable to what I experienced on the day that Governor Meade, with me standing at her shoulder, signed our sweeping anti-drug initiative into law. We were on the South Portico again, less than three months since we took the oath of office on the steps below. The cheering crowds were gone, but now we were surrounded by an eclectic group of earnest Virginians—police officers and other law enforcement agents, prosecutors, doctors and nurses, social workers, clergy, recovering addicts, crime victims, and many others. Besides the Governor and me, only one other person addressed the group—Sally Nevers. When she approached the lectern with one of Bart's sisters on each arm, there were few dry eyes to be found. It was a supreme moment of reconciliation and healing: Virginians turning their great tragedy into greater triumph and setting in motion events that would save the lives of thousands.

For me, it was the happiest sad moment I would experience—the high point of my time in politics.

The low point (or, to be more specific, the events that would produce the low point) followed rapidly thereafter. It began with a call from Miguel three days later that began, "General, we have some trouble here." His steadiness in times of crisis made my chief deputy the master of understatement.

The initial shock came from the Governor's Office. A statement issued by the thirtysomething progressive activist who recently had been named "Counsel to the Governor" carried the blockbuster announcement that Governor Meade had appointed an independent counsel—the statement dubbed him "Special Prosecutor"—to lead the investigation into the Nevers and Bell deaths. That was a bit disconcerting in itself, but three aspects of the statement especially alarmed Miguel and hit me like a cornerback and safety converging on me at maximum velocity.

First, there was the identity of the new Special Prosecutor—Harry Snyder, the Commonwealth's attorney in Alexandria. Harry and I had crossed swords over several matters since I first became AG, including his leaked investigations of a Republican councilman and then a state legislator. Snyder's partisan motivation was obvious in both cases, and in both he lacked jurisdiction as well as credible evidence. But the legal niceties were beside the point—he had accomplished the sullying of their political reputations by his public posturing. Lauded by his young acolyte on the Third Floor as someone who would "do the right thing in matters of public trust," Harry Snyder was universally regarded in serious legal circles as just the opposite. He was a shameless—and, therefore, quite dangerous—political hack.

The second body blow came with these ominous words, which were included within the new investigator's lengthy charge: "The Special Prosecutor also shall examine the actions of senior state officials, including Bartholomew Bell and Daniel McGuire, that may have caused or contributed to the untimely death of either governor and/or impeded the investigations of the same, ... and shall coordinate the ongoing law enforcement investigations into such matters."

Only one of the named "senior state officials" was still alive, so there was no mistaking the primary target.

Finally, there was the determination by the Governor's legal counsel that not only Miguel and I, but the entire Office of the Attorney General, had a conflict of interest arising from "Mr. McGuire's and his staff's apparent involvement in the matters at issue, including activities that may have impeded the investigation of Governor Nevers' death and/or contributed to Governor Bell's death." This finding actually did not affect my involvement or Miguel's— we already had recused ourselves from any role in the investigation—but it had the effect of barring all of the state's capable lawyers from providing legal advice to Snyder or to the blue ribbon investigatory commission that I had established right after Bart's collapse. Instead, both the inquest by that commission and the Special Prosecutor's investigation would be staffed exclusively by the partisan legal team that Snyder would assemble.

When I saw the reference to my blue ribbon commission, I wondered whether that might be the next shoe to drop, and it took less than 24 hours for my suspicions to be validated. Just days before completing the 2006 regular session, the General Assembly's Democratic leaders pushed through emergency legislation creating a new "Special Commission of Inquiry Concerning the Deaths of Governors Edward K. Nevers and Bartholomew Bell." The bill extinguished all other state and local investigations except the Special Prosecutor's. The commissioners I had appointed, including two former governors and numerous other highly respected former leaders in both parties, were politely thanked, excused, and directed to transfer all relevant information to the new legislative panel. This "was necessitated," the Democratic leaders somberly explained in a joint statement, "by the unfortunate fact that the commission established by former Governor McGuire was tainted from its inception by the involvement of the appointing authority in the very matters under scrutiny."

The Democrats suddenly were circling like sharks. Meade and Percival partisans in both branches were maneuvering, obviously in close coordination despite their differences, to make my conduct the central issue in the probes and to stack them against me. Governor Meade's role remained murky; she professed regret about it to Mitch, but those sentiments did not keep her from supporting her counsel's aggressive actions or signing the partisan legislation.

"I did not initiate any of these actions, and I take no joy in them," she insisted plausibly to Mitch, "but look at my position. I made a vow to the people of Virginia that I would ensure an exhaustive investigation led by independent legal and law enforcement professionals. Every one of the legal advisors on my team and all of the others I consulted were unanimous that we had to proceed this way."

"Besides," she added, according to Mitch's account, "if Danny's position is sound he will come out of this just fine."

"That last comment shows she is either naïve or disingenuous," I responded to Mitch, "and Dorothy is not naïve."

"No, she's not," my friend conceded. "But there's another possible explanation. She was so focused for the last two months on running up the score on the anti-drug thing that she didn't pay any attention to what the manipulative gang around her was doing on the investigation. By the time she tuned in, it was a fait accompli."

"I know she's your friend, Mitch," I said, "but that's an awfully charitable interpretation."

It was tempting to cry "Partisanship!" in response to these hostile Democratic moves and the irresponsible rhetoric that accompanied them. But in truth the situation on the Republican side was not much better. I discovered that the erosion of my support there—after the one-two punch of my Washington statue speech and the anti-drug collaboration with Dorothy—had been severe. I could understand why voting against a new investigative commission was a hard political vote to cast, but the legislation had given the new panel a one-sided directive that, like the Special Prosecutor's charge, put me directly in the cross-hairs. Yet, when it came time to vote on the version of the legislation jammed through by the Democratic leadership, only 20 GOP lawmakers in both chambers went up on the board with red lights. A handful of others abstained. I lost all of the hardcore folks aligned with Bondurant and Barnhard, of course, but the shocker was how many of the others also defected, including most of those who had come to my office and implored me to run for governor barely four months earlier.

In less than a fortnight, the political and legal walls had rapidly closed in on me. But the most ominous development came last—from the feds. To most observers, it seemed like the federal officials were just piling on, but I recognized their actions as the most lethal threat. A spokesman for Attorney General Cyrus commented that the federal investigation into "the Virginia matters" was moving to a new phase, "focusing not only on the crimes that may have resulted in the deaths of either or both Virginia governors but the possible obstruction of justice that may have occurred in the course of the investigations into those deaths." The official declined to confirm or deny reports that information already was being presented to a grand jury. Then, in an obviously calculated leak, an unnamed source "knowledgeable about Justice Department matters" told the *Washington Daily Press* that "Attorney General McGuire was aware of the pending federal investigation at the time he made the provocative disclosures to Governor Bell that compromised the probe and set in motion the events resulting in Bell's death." "In fact," the source added, "by that time McGuire already had met personally with senior DOJ officials regarding the crime and ongoing investigation." The anonymous sniping was outrageous—the most unprofessional behavior imaginable—yet there it was. I somehow resisted the temptation to ring up my old classmate, Rick Angelotti, in Hartford and tell him that his stories about the saintly and fair-minded Attorney General Cyrus were, to say the least, apocryphal.

What followed next was a full-blown media blitz executed by my political enemies, who seemed to come out from under every rock. Their strategy worked incredibly well. A classic feeding frenzy developed, with every news outlet in the state and many beyond vying for the most scintillating angle, the most salacious disclosure, the most damning take on even mundane events. It all came too fast and furiously for me to respond even if I had been of a mind to do so. The stories often directly contradicted one another, but they all had a common denominator: the stunning revelation that the real villain in Virginia's sordid saga had been Danny McGuire.

One group of stories pushed the narrative that I had run interference for Bart, protecting him legally and otherwise for my own political gain. By one angry editorialist's reckoning, I was "the willful enabler, the loyal ticket mate who was out campaigning with Bart Bell when I should have been investigating and prosecuting him." Another said I had "taken a pass on the constitutionality of the Barnhard appointment as lieutenant governor when I knew it was illegal and had a duty to say so." I had "failed to authorize a Virginia State Police investigation of Bell's involvement in the Nevers murder even though I was the only statewide official (except Bell) who had the statutory authority to do so." I had "repeatedly turned a blind eye to Bell's drug use and raucous consorting with organized crime figures." And, in the ultimate breach of duty, I had "alerted Bell to the ongoing investigations so he could safely evade them through the election." There was much, much more, but you get the gist.

I was being skewered for covering up for Bell by one set of attack dogs while, at the very same time, another pack was portraying me as his heartless tormenter and executioner. The latter group tended to cast Bart as a hapless victim, a generally well-meaning dupe of criminals, drug peddlers, and "political manipulators like Danny McGuire and his friends." In this narrative I had "shown [my] true colors by floating [my] name for governor while the state's chief executive was lying unconscious barely a stone's throw away." I had "turned my back again and again on a friend who had taken me under his wing since college." And in my final act of merciless treachery toward the tragic hero, I had "driven him to kill himself"—or, worse still, "had driven an overwrought State Police officer to do away with him in a vigilante-style act of vengeance."

That last one was especially upsetting because of its impact on what remained of Trooper Jamie Willis' already tattered reputation. Other than some unexplained bruises on Bart's arms and torso, there never was a scintilla of evidence to refute Willis' version of events. Every investigation would end with a finding that Bart's death had been a suicide. But that did not keep conspiracy theorists from supposing that I had put the impressionable young trooper up to the awful deed. Amazingly, much of that sensational nonsense found its way into print and online chatter.

My reaction to this sudden avalanche of crazy allegations and coordinated attacks, I can now see, was completely inept. Contrary to advice from my most trusted friends and advisors, I hunkered down for weeks as the thing spiraled out of control. Only belatedly did it finally occur to me how thoroughly isolated I had become politically. It all happened with such breathtaking speed that not only did I fail to see it coming; I did not believe anyone possibly could be taking it seriously. Much of it (about 90 percent, I'd say) was stuff that I knew was patently false. I indulged the assumption that there was some reservoir of credibility on my part—and of goodwill on the people's part—that would insulate me from any serious political and personal damage. But that was a foolish assumption, and I knew better. I had known better, in fact, since I was a little kid, watching helplessly as that Young Upstart and his crazy claims tricked the fickle voters into tossing my beloved Grandpappy aside like roadkill. Now I was letting my old nemesis, politics, do the same grievous thing to me and, worst of all, to my own family.

The impact of politics on family members can be harsh in the best of times; few people understand the enormous sacrifices that political families make. But it is hard to imagine anything tougher on a spouse and young children than what our crew endured during that disastrous spring and through the rest of 2006. As the wave of negative publicity built, Martha's distress drove her to a state of physical and emotional exhaustion. We both gamely tried to disguise our anxiety for the good of our kids, especially our alert little fourth-grader, Meg, who was aware enough of events to be traumatized. But even very young children know their parents well enough to see through brave faces that mask despair. The taunting Meg endured from classmates was as inevitable as it was infuriating, and I blamed myself for it. How in the world, when politics had ruined things for me as a child, could I been so oblivious, so stupid, so *selfish* as to let the same thing happen to my own little ones?

We tried to shield them by decamping to Rhode Island for an extended summer vacation once the school year ended. I had been back to Bristol and the surrounding environs maybe a dozen times in the two decades since my parents died, usually for the funeral of an aunt or uncle or some other occasion giving rise to a family obligation. Some, like my cousin Janie's lavish wedding at Castle Hill in Newport or the ordination mass in Providence for her brother Paddy, had been memorable. But most just had been painful because of the overwhelming sense of loss. In a singular display of mercy, Granddaddy and Granny McGuire had been spared the grief of losing their beloved youngest son, the elderly pair having predeceased my father by two and three years, respectively. So, despite the treasure trove of happy childhood memories, there had been little to draw me back as an adult. Now, however, it was a different story. We had young children who needed to know their cousins, learn about their heritage, and experience something of the Ocean State enchantments that had so enthralled me as a boy.

Martha and the kids loved it the first time we spent a week at Little Compton, and we had been back twice since then, staying with relatives in Bristol and Barrington. When I broached the idea of the family spending the heart of the summer there during the investigation, Martha was almost euphoric. It required me to come back and forth a lot, and that meant a day of driving each way because we could not afford the air travel. But it was worth it just to have everyone out of harm's way.

It was, in truth, a vital escape for me, too. Trekking to visit relatives along the Sakonnet River and East Bay, our little ones marveled at the strange stone walls, just as I had as a youngster. They frolicked on the same rocky Briggs Beach near Sakonnet Point, and they sat for hours mesmerized by the Fourth of July parade, responding with oohs and aahs later when the fireworks burst over Bristol Harbor, just as I had. We even went on a bicycle excursion reminiscent of the grand adventures of my youth. Martha and I had trailers rigged on our bikes for Jon and Marty, and Meg's pedaling easily kept pace as we may our way along the bay from Bristol to Barrington, thanks to conversion of the old Providence, Warren and Bristol Railroad into a friendly new bicycle path. And so on our funny-talking, stopping-and-starting *McGuires of Virginia* caravan would go, the kids dazzled by the serious cyclists and fast-weaving rollerbladers, the frozen lemonade, and all the other fun distractions, Martha fretting over them happily, and me stealing moments to gaze across the water, take in the beauty, and ponder the history.

There were vistas, like the one near my cousins' home on Mathewson Road at the confluence of the Barrington and Warren Rivers, that struck me as perhaps the most fascinating I had ever seen. Because I was curious about the history and looked into it, I appreciated the connections. I knew that General Rochambeau had marched his French army through here en route to Virginia and his rendezvous with destiny at Yorktown. I knew that the yacht club across the river on Tyler Point—responsible for many of the anchored sailboats that animated the picturesque scene—occupied the site of an early trading post where the Plymouth colonists and native Wampanoags met and bargained, much as the Jamestown men and Powhatans did down my way. I even knew that one "Master John Hampden" of London had visited here with Edward Winslow in 1623, aiding the ailing Wampanoag chief, Massasoit, and apparently impressing succeeding generations enough to have the land between the two rivers named "Hampden Meadows" in his honor. Historians debated whether this John Hampden was the same Englishman who went on to serve in Parliament, whose stand against the Crown helped launch the English Civil War, and in whose memory my collegiate alma mater had been named at the start of our own Revolution. But I had little doubt they were one and the same.

In running away, I had run home—which proved to be a very good thing. I renewed my spiritual connection to the place; Martha adopted it as her personal refuge; and, by bringing our "little Virginia rebels," as their northern cousins affectionately called them, we made it their home away from home and linked them forever to people and places, ideas and deeds that mattered. It was one of the rare rays of sunshine that managed to poke through the thick blanket of relentless gloom that characterized the months of investigations.

Away from the chaos, I was still desperate for a way to reassure my fretful daughter, and the inspiration came during a morning walk there by the Barrington River. Appreciating the renewal that had accompanied return to these roots, I scribbled out a poem after the walk and left it under Meg's pillow that evening. I titled it "Beyond":

> *There's sun beyond the rain;*
> *There's comfort beyond the pain;*
> *There's sky beyond the cloud;*
> *There's truth beyond the crowd;*
> *There are smiles beyond the tears;*
> *There are hopes beyond the fears;*
> *There is freedom beyond the trial;*
> *And there's evil, for a while.*
> *But there's a hand up when we fall,*
> *And there is God beyond it all.*

The poem is framed now and hangs on the wall beside Meg's bed. It will be with her for the rest of her life. And though I could not imagine it at the time, I am sure now that her life will be very different—and, in some untraceable ways, better—because of those awful times.

The weeks lengthened into months, and the pace of disclosures slowed as the investigations proceeded. The torrent of bad news evolved into a torturous *drip, drip, drip* as reporters searched for any remaining scoop of unearthed dirt and investigators obliged with selective leaks. As I surveyed the landscape, it appeared as barren a wasteland as I could imagine—a hopeless expanse of humiliation and defeat. I knew the insidious effects of self-pity, but I could not keep myself from asking: *What did I do to deserve this?*

For as long as I could remember, all my energies had been directed toward proper purposes, at least to the extent I understood them. I had wandered and wrestled, been tempted and tested, and had often disappointed myself and others. But I had tried to do the right things, and I had brought those good intentions with me when I finally had entered the political arena. Once in that arena, I had discovered good and tried to aid it ... looked evil in the face and defied it ... discovered the thicket of ambiguity and resisted the temptation to hide in it. I knew the subtle seductions of politics, the ways the political business can take a person and his principles and silently shred them before he even realizes it. I was alert to the dangers, so I had *drawn the line*. Why, then, had I been brought to such a point of humiliation? Why would Martha and the kids be forced to endure such pain on my account? Why would all my unfinished business—all my outstanding opportunities to help and contribute—now be wasted? Why had I made it through so many struggles and trials, so many ups and downs, only to exit in this useless way? *Why would a life that I had tried so hard to live well end up so badly?*

No answers came, and a dark cloud of depression began to descend. All the wishful thinking in the world, all the encouragement, prayer, dreams, inner peace, stiff upper lips, unconditional love of family members, empathy of close friends, and whatever else you might throw at it were not going to change the fact that I was in a desolate spot. My alleged misdeeds had been splashed across the newspapers and television screens around the state and across the nation, and I now labored in the public eye under a huge, ugly blot. Behind every visage that I encountered, from friend and foe alike, I imagined a mix of pity and judgment. I almost wished that one of them would simply blurt out what they all must have been thinking: "Man, you really screwed the pooch!"

We had experienced it all—cameras on the lawn, people trampling our shrubs and going through our trash, Martha and the kids being stalked as they tried to go about their lives—the whole sorry nine yards. But at least that had been preoccupying while it was infuriating. Now, the investigations were dragging on impenetrably and without resolution. I imagined the grand jurors secretly imbibing whatever it was the prosecutors were dispensing to them. And my daily tasks as attorney general became a joyless, pointless grind. The anger and self-pity gradually began to give way, making space for a deeper, more dangerous plunge ... into shame.

I soon started to work from home so I did not have to face my staff and the endless, awkward parade of long faces offering sympathy, needing reassurance, and requiring the same soldering-on-bravely, doing-just-fine-thanks-for-asking phoniness that I had to display in that awful gymnasium of death a quarter century earlier. I told myself that was the reason for my staying home, but it was not the real reason. The real reason was that I was ashamed.

You listen to the drumbeat long enough and soon you begin to believe what they are saying about you. Your head and heart may tell you they are wrong, but the doubts creep in, and they grow. How can you be right when it requires so many other people to be wrong? At some point you begin to yield to the collective wisdom. You begin to believe you are getting what you deserve.

That is especially true when, as in my case, you really do deserve much of what you are getting.

It had become increasingly apparent as the tumultuous spring gave way to the oppressive summer and early autumn that something I had assumed absolutely—something that I had come to believe with every fiber of my being—was not being borne out by the various investigations. With each passing update and briefing, each news leak and bit of intelligence that came my way, each media exposé and investigative report, the key thing remained elusive: *There was no evidence of Bart's actual complicity in the Nevers assassination.*

I kept waiting for the smoking gun, the secret cache, the inevitable revelations that had to come. The circumstantial evidence had been overwhelming: Bart had motive, and he had opportunity. He had powerful ambitions that Ned Nevers had been determined to thwart. He had underworld friends who had big plans for the big score at False Cape and wanted him at the helm. He had crucial access to how things worked on the inside, information essential for pulling off the murder of a governor without leaving fingerprints. And if ever someone's post-crime conduct evidenced a guilty mind, it was Bart's. He had affected grief and loyalty to the deceased governor while ruthlessly sacking everyone and everything who had anything to do with Ned Nevers. He could not stand the thought of his victim and the good things for which he had labored so long; he hated every moment when he had to feign affection and sing his praises. The ghost of Ned Nevers haunted him to the very end, demanding justice. Only one more stone needed to be turned, I was certain, and the truth about Bart's pure malevolence would be confirmed. Then all would receive the truth, and I, my vindication.

Except there were no more stones.

Sometime during that stifling summer it finally sank in that I had been wrong. The state and federal probes proved beyond doubt that Bart's underworld cohorts, or some recklessly adventurous subset of them, had killed Nevers to put their puppet in power, with money as their motive. But the evidence of Bart's active participation or at least his advance knowledge—the evil deeds I had ascribed to him without the slightest hesitation—failed to materialize. Finally, I got it: *There was not going to be any proof of Bart's complicity in the murder itself because he had not been complicit.* And with that realization, whatever remained of the rickety steps beneath me gave way and sent me plummeting into the abyss.

Bart was not a killer after all—*but I was.*

I had taken matters into my own hands. My actions had led to Bart's death just as surely as if I had bound and gagged him and sent him off on that ill-fated voyage with the Governor. It was what many people had been saying in the newspapers and over the airwaves for months now, but I had turned a deaf ear because I was sure that Bart was guilty ... and evil, too—purely, completely evil.

What an arrogant fool I had been! The analogy that came to mind now was not historical but biblical: Bart was King Saul, and I should have been David. Despite all of Saul's offenses and assaults, David had been faithful, leaving it to God to execute his own perfect justice in his own perfect time. But not I. I had appointed myself king and executioner, and had handed down the most unjust of sentences. I had gotten so caught up in the conflict that I was blinded by the righteousness of my own cause, and I became the instrument of—*no, the willing practitioner of*—the very evil I thought I was combatting.

I had played God, the most venal of all sins.

Even with all that Bart had done wrong—and the evidence left little doubt that he had conspired to cover up the murder—he had not taken a life, and he had not deserved to die. For all I knew, he even had felt remorse. His descent into addiction and desperation may even have been a product of his guilt, an essential hitting-bottom that was a prerequisite for his eventual redemption. But the world would never know whether Bart Bell could have overcome his demons. It would never see the effects of a loving God's forgiveness in his life because *I had ended that life.*

I cannot adequately describe here, now, how deeply tormented I was during this time. My faith had been shattered. I never seriously considered ending my own life because my core beliefs and my devotion to Martha and my children would not permit that means of escape. But I was done—done with politics and done with endeavor in any form. I would resign my office, plead guilty to whatever they saw fit to charge me, and then go away, far away, to await the inevitable judgment that my awful acts deserved. Mine was an abject form of affliction, the all-enveloping, sick, suffocating sense of wasted gifts and a wasted life, out of which could only come death....

Unless, of course, it was finally sufficient to force a full surrender, leading to redemption and life.

"It's Not All About You"

It was a rainy day, creating the perfect mood for another meeting with my lawyer. He had insisted on taking a leave of absence from the AG's office to represent me, and, while I appreciated the gesture, I was tired of these go-arounds. I saw no point in reexamining yet again what I knew was a personal, political, and legal dead-end.

This time, however, Miguel did not just enter the room in the manner of his previous visits. He swept in and filled the space with youthful effervescence and intellectual fervor, radiating a degree of energy I had not seen before—from him or, for that matter, from anyone. He was girded and ready for battle. His visage conveyed both intensity and urgency, yet there was a transcendent confidence that imparted a measure of peace.

For the first time in this ordeal, I actually would *receive* his counsel.

"I want you to lay aside all your presumptions about this situation and stop wallowing in guilt and self-pity," he began, obviously determined to provoke. "You want to be a martyr? Fine—be one. *Do it.* But don't imagine that you are doing anything noble. *Suicide is not noble.*"

"Now wait a minute, Miguel...," I interrupted, aroused by the affront and eager to offer a rebuttal.

"No, *you* wait, and listen for a change," he countered, clenching his jaw. "By God, if it is the last conversation we ever have, I am going to say what I think, and you are going to listen to me. If you want to fire me at the end of this discussion, I will give you that opportunity. I'll even welcome it. But between now and then, General, I want you to just sit there, be quiet, and listen."

I was so surprised by the young man's boldness that I shrank back in my chair like a lamb cowering before a lion.

"I want to begin with a video clip," he said, throttling back on the intensity and signaling that I was in for an extended counseling session. "Movies are the modern era's parables, as you have often said, so here is a Best Picture winner from back when you were a kid—*A Man for All Seasons*. You know the story: Sir Thomas More at odds with Henry VIII over his unwillingness to approve the King's divorce, facing a charge of treason if he will not take an oath of supremacy that subordinates papal authority to the Word of God—forced to choose between fidelity to God or to the King...."

I knew the story and the movie, but I had no clue where Miguel was headed. The VCR was cued to the portion of the movie he wanted me to view. Once he depressed the "play" button, I recognized it as a brief but intense exchange between Sir Thomas and his daughter Margaret regarding the oath they would be pressed to take.

> Sir Thomas: "What is the wording [of the oath]? It may be possible to take it. Yes, and if it can be taken, you must take it, too."
>
> Margaret: "No!"
>
> Sir Thomas: "Listen, Meg. God made the angels to show him splendor, as he made the animals for innocence and plants for their simplicity. But man he made to serve him wittily in the tangle of his mind. If he suffers us to come to such a case that there is no escaping, then we may stand to our tackle as best we can. And, yes, Meg, then we can clamor like champions, if we have the spittle for it. But it's God's part, not our own, to bring ourselves to such a pass. Our natural business lies in escaping. If I can take this oath, I will."

Miguel tapped the "stop" button and looked back over at me. "Did you catch that, General? 'God made man to serve him wittily in the tangle of his mind.... Our natural business lies in escaping.'"

"Yes, I caught it," I acknowledged, pondering its import.

"Now, I know what you are thinking, General. You are thinking there is a problem here ... a *contradiction*. We tell ourselves the noble thing is to stand on principle and, as Sir Thomas puts it, 'clamor like champions.' But here Sir Thomas is saying our proper course is not to clamor like champions but to escape if it is possible without doing violence to our principles. 'Our natural business lies in escaping'—that doesn't sound very noble, does it?"

"No, it doesn't."

"It seems contradictory," Miguel continued. "But, then, so do a great many things. If we conform to the world's premises and prejudices, we will routinely encounter a conventional wisdom that is at odds with the true state of things. Indeed, even the simplest truths can create great conundrums for the world's most complicated minds. Our 'natural business,' as Sir Thomas puts it, is to strip away those layers of complication and seek the essence … the way out."

I was being lectured to, but somehow I welcomed it.

"In this seeking, we have real limitations. Our knowledge is imperfect and our understanding is imperfect; we see only through a mirror dimly. Yet, we must press on in search of the truth—deploying our reason, consulting our conscience, using the tools God has given us. And when this happens, when we gain insight into the truth of things, we should not be surprised to find that the truth is at odds with the world's accepted wisdom. We should not be surprised to find that the prevailing culture has turned truth on its head. Indeed, we probably should just expect that whenever we get close to the essential reality of things, the common sense of things, the simple truth of things, it is probably going to look like a … *contradiction*."

A presumption of contrariness? This was an interesting proposition.

"You are a student of history, General, so let me go there to illustrate this point."

My counselor knew me well.

"Let's take some of the great foreign policy decisions of the 20th century. How many people initially thought the way to avoid World War II was through appeasing the Nazis rather than confronting them? Or that the way to end the Cold War's threat of nuclear annihilation was through a nuclear freeze instead of a nuclear build-up? Those propositions were not illogical—at least, to a great many people they did not seem illogical. They were advanced forcefully by large numbers of well-meaning folks. But they were completely wrong, and in the case of World War II, the error permitted an unthinkable human holocaust and a raging war over much of the planet. In the case of the Cold War, we can pretty well guess what would have happened if we had followed the siren's song of unilateral disarmament instead of the forceful deterrence strategy of presidents from Truman to Reagan."

"Yet, many people saw Reagan's 'peace through strength' mantra as a glaring contradiction—and *still do*."

"Or, take economics. How many people routinely denigrate the free-market system as a catalyst for selfishness and greed? Yet, that system has yielded abundance and met human needs globally on a scale never experienced in the history of mankind. It seems profoundly contradictory that a system predicated on the pursuit of self-interest could yield so much good for so many. And, yet, it absolutely has done so, even with all its imperfections and inequities."

"We see the apparent contradiction, too, on a personal level. Study after study shows that supposedly hard-hearted conservatives give far more to charities each year than soft-hearted liberals, and this is true even when you control for differences in income. It seems *contradictory* to us that the people who generally have the less benevolent view of government's role in helping others turn out to be more philanthropic, on the whole, than those who have a more liberal view. Yet, it's the fact."

"Or, take the relationship between church and state. Many wise people thought that if we separated church and state in America—if we denied the church the benefit of governmental endorsement and encouragement—then the result would be a decline of religious practice and a loss of national virtue. Many still think that, and it seems like a logical expectation, yet the opposite has happened in this country. Faith has flourished in freedom, and for many people that still seems like a contradiction."

"Indeed, the interplay of religion and politics continues to be an especially rich source of contradictions. When moralizing ministers take to the public square seeking to enact their preferences into law, they tend to chase people, even good religious people, away in droves. You see this in the negative reaction of younger and suburban voters to the intolerant-sounding religious right, don't you? And on the other side of the spectrum you see it in the exodus of many church-going folks from the mainline denominations where very liberal political activists control the hierarchy and justify almost any self-pursuit in the name of tolerance. They're the same activists who take to the church pulpit or rally platform and preach that the way to heed Jesus's command to care for those in need is to pass a law making someone else pay for it."

"Yet, despite the disdain that such attempts to mix religion and politics routinely produce, there is the inescapable historical fact that all of the great civil reforms have tended to follow appeals to religious conviction and conscience. The most notable is the abolition of slavery. And, in our time, just think of Dr. King—*Reverend* Martin Luther King Jr.—and the civil rights movement. Would we insist on not mixing religion and politics if it meant the civil rights movement would not have happened, or would have run its course and failed?"

"The role of religion in the public square is a subject full of contradictions. But that's probably because of the seeming contradictions in faith itself. We look joyfully at the rainbow because we see God's promise of sunshine after the flood. But when we look closer, we see that God didn't promise the sun would shine only on the just and good. He promised it would shine on everyone, including the unjust and even the evil. And that seems like a contradiction."

"The fact is, General, we will invariably see contradictions in all sorts of places if we overlook the fallen nature of man and the miracle of God's mercy. Without that frame, we see only a contradiction when a parent shows love to a child by dispensing discipline ... or when an ambitious person sacrifices what he holds most dear for a friend. It seems contradictory when evil flourishes in a world where God is sovereign and when the Sovereign who established justice dispenses mercy instead. It seems contradictory that the God who gave us the law frees us from its consequences through his grace."

"It all comes back to the same confounding question of why we are here and why we have freedom to choose our way. If God wants to promote goodness, why did his creation end up with a nature that isn't always good ... and with the freedom to act on it? It seems like this whole earthly business is a *contradiction*."

"Reinhold Niebuhr found these contradictions—he called them 'incongruities'—to be pervasive, and listen to what he said about them in *The Irony of American History*:

> There are no simple congruities in life or history. The cult of happiness erroneously assumes them. It is possible to soften the incongruities of life endlessly by the scientific conquest of nature's caprices, and the social and political triumph over historic injustice. But all such strategies cannot finally overcome the fragmentary character of human existence. The final wisdom of life requires, not the annulment of incongruity but the achievement of serenity within and above it.
>
> Nothing that is worth doing can be achieved in our lifetime; therefore we must be saved by hope. Nothing which is true or beautiful or good makes complete sense in any

immediate context of history; therefore we must be saved by
faith. Nothing we do, however virtuous, can be accomplished
alone; therefore we are saved by love. No virtuous act is quite
as virtuous from the standpoint of our friend or foe as it is
from our standpoint. Therefore we must be saved by the final
form of love which is forgiveness.

"And, of course, for people who share our faith, this final imperative of
forgiveness has produced the most glaring contradiction of all: that the most
powerful man ever to walk the planet—God Incarnate—would humble himself
even to the point of a humiliating death on a tree."

"It is an interesting question, isn't it: why this all-knowing and all-powerful
God wraps his truth in mystery and contradictions … why he speaks in parables instead of plain English … why he plays the poet instead of the professor.
If he knows all, why doesn't he just tell all? The presence of mystery itself
seems contradictory. *But is it?*"

"'Let us imagine two prisoners, in neighboring cells, who communicate
by means of taps on a wall,' wrote Simone Weil. 'The wall is what separates
them, but it is also what enables them to communicate. It is the same with us
and God. Every separation represents a bond.'"

"Jesus would often say, 'He who has ears to hear, let him hear'—meaning
that God has given us the means to hear, but the choice to do it is up to us.
Your man Locke wrote, 'God himself will not save men against their wills.' Instead of decreeing our course, duplicating his own perfection, God separated
himself from us, creating a human condition of choices and inquiry and discovery. He sent us on a treasure hunt, but the object is not some hidden chest
of earthly delights, as the world's wisdom claims. The prize is the searching
for—and finding—our way back to him."

"As we empty ourselves in this pursuit, we are filled more and more with
his Truth."

"Your pal Longfellow was right: 'Things are not what they seem.' So we
need to search for the truer meaning, the truer relationship, of things."

"*Are you willing to open your mind to the possibility, General, that this may apply
even to you?*"

The not-so-faint trace of sarcasm in that "*even to you*" part was a bit much,
but I chose to ignore it and merely nodded my assent.

Upon my submission, Miguel approached an easel with a large blank pad and wrote four words in all capital letters. On the upper left side, he wrote the word "JUSTICE." Below it, in the lower left corner, he wrote the word "FREEDOM." In the upper right space, he wrote "ENTERPRISE." And in the lower right, he wrote "CHARITY." Then he lined through "CHARITY" and replaced it with "MERCY."

He then drew an arrow from "JUSTICE" rightward to "ENTERPRISE" and another arrow down the left side from "JUSTICE" to "FREEDOM." Then, rightward again, across the bottom from "FREEDOM" to "CHAR-ITY/MERCY," and on the right side down from "ENTERPRISE" to "CHAR-ITY/MERCY." A rectangle thus formed, he inserted the words *integrity* and *humility* in the center.

Miguel paused as I studied the chart, clueless as to its meaning.

"This chart," he finally said, "depicts the human experience when good overcomes evil. I can draw you a different diagram for the situation where evil overcomes good, but since that scenario loses in the long run, I would like to focus on this one."

I was still studying it and still puzzled.

"You have spent your whole life learning the lessons that are shown on this chart," he observed.

"Oh, I have, have I?" I said, smirking at the young man's presumption. He did not offer even a faint smile in return.

"Yes, you have," he said. "A lot of time and effort has been put into the education process."

"By whom?" I asked.

"If you don't know, I am not going to tell you," he said, now the one with the smirk.

"Whatever," I muttered.

He pointed to the top arrow connecting "JUSTICE" and "ENTERPRISE."

"You learned a long time back that justice—as in a code of rules ensuring fair play—is the precondition for enterprise or commerce, meaning the process by which people create and exchange things of value. Is that right?"

"Yes," I readily conceded, recalling the lengthy and often tedious discussions with Chad on the subject over the years.

His hand now traced the arrow downward from "JUSTICE" to "FREE-DOM."

513

"And you learned that justice is the precondition for freedom. Liberty and justice are both natural rights, but without a system of *ordered* liberty—meaning fair rules that restrain men from imposing their will unjustly on others—there is no freedom as a practical matter. Do you agree with that?"

"I agree that it is *part* of the equation," I said, intrigued at where this philosophical discourse was heading. "But I think I would have said that Freedom and Justice are interdependent conditions, and I would have an arrow running both ways."

"Yes, they are interrelated, but that's not the point," Miguel answered professorially. "They are both natural rights, but they are not both natural consequences. Freedom, like faith, is an antecedent condition to all that is depicted on this chart. But freedom, as a matter of actual practice rather than abstract right, is a *consequence* of justice embodied in the rule of law. The law—meaning the rules, just or unjust—may derive from legislative enactment, judicial decree, monarchical dispensation, or a despot's fiat. The rules don't necessarily arise from a condition of freedom. On the other hand, freedom does depend on having the rules, and not just any rules—*just* rules, rooted in virtue, producing a sense of fairness. If we have Freedom, as in real freedom of action, then it must have been preceded by Justice, and it can only be maintained so long as there is Justice."

The visage that now entered my mind was not Chad's, but Mitch's. Mitch had been beating the drum about virtue and values underlying everything worthwhile in politics—about Justice being the transcendent value—for as long as I could remember. I never acknowledged he was right, but I also never succeeded in answering his main point, which was that without justice rooted in morality, liberty would be nothing more than license, and license would be the ruin of the world.

"Okay, I will accept that, Professor. But before you go on, let me ask you why you don't also have an arrow running diagonally from 'FREEDOM' up to 'ENTERPRISE.' Don't we need freedom for enterprise?" I asked.

"That is a digression, but I will answer you," he said patiently. "You need an arrow there if you are talking about *Free Enterprise*," he answered. "And that's certainly the American way; it is also the most efficient way; and it's the way calculated to produce the most happiness for, and the most benefit to, the greatest number. The more freedom there is, the more beneficial enterprise, efficient commerce, and fruitful exchange there will be. In addition, commercial freedom tends to thrive with other individual and civil liberties, whereas authoritarianism naturally tends to expand its power until it commands not merely our use of property but every other facet of our lives. So you are quite right that freedom and enterprise are connected; indeed, in a free-enterprise system they're indistinguishable. But even the most ardent champion of the free market would not claim that way is the only way. Enterprise—meaning people pursuing their own interests by creating and exchanging with others— can occur with more or less freedom. Just look at China. But enterprise cannot occur at all without justice. If there are no just laws to govern people's commerce and enforce their bargains, men will be slaves to command or caprice, at best subsisting and at worst toiling for others in a condition where might makes right."

He paused as if to see whether I was satisfied with his response.

"Okay, I want to think about that some more, but go on with your show. I am eager to know where you're headed here with my life's story."

"I didn't say it was your life's story—your life's story is still being written. I said these are your life's lessons so far, or at least some of them."

"I stand corrected. Please go on," I nodded.

"Well, here is where it comes to a point, and the point is charity." He pointed to the lower righthand corner of his chart. "In various translations of the Bible—or you can consult a thesaurus or dictionary, for that matter—the words 'charity' and 'love' are used interchangeably. So, too, are 'charity' and 'mercy' and 'kindness.' But the concept is simply one of caring enough, forgiving enough, *loving* enough, to sacrifice something to *help others*. Charity and mercy and love in this sense are one and the same, and they are both cause and condition: a situation in which one is moved to come to the aid of his fellow man."

"… or woman," I interjected, somewhat facetiously, thinking of Abby.

"Yes, a situation in which one is moved to come to the aid of his-or-her fellow man and/or fellow woman," said Miguel. "I was assuming we could skip the politically correct possessive pronouns and conjunctive and disjunctive objects here in the privacy of this room, since we are giving neither a campaign speech nor a jury summation. But I stand corrected."

Abby had come to mind, not only because of her professional admonitions to invoke the feminine whenever possible in speeches and interviews, but because she inevitably had been front and center among my three friends when the focus shifted away from Chad's realm of self-interested enterprise and Mitch's domain of righteous justice to the warmer and gentler venues of mercy and charity.

"The arrow runs from 'ENTERPRISE' to 'CHARITY,'" Miguel resumed, "for the obvious reason that one needs to create or at least possess some asset, some talent or other form of wealth, something of value, before he—*or she*—can surrender it to others."

Yes, that was obvious.

"The relationship between 'FREEDOM' and 'CHARITY' is equally obvious," he said, moving to the horizontal arrow that ran from left to right across the bottom. "Charity is not charity unless it is freely, as in voluntarily, given. But even more fundamentally than that, faith is not faith unless it is a free act of conscience, and grace is not grace unless the gift is freely given. Freedom of thought and action are the essential preconditions for acts of charity. For we know what charity in its purest sense is, don't we? It is faith expressing itself through love."

Still puzzled generally, I nevertheless nodded my concurrence with that fundamental proposition.

"Now, although these relationships between enterprise and charity on the one hand, and between freedom and charity on the other, are self-evident, they are also quite complicated and often appear contradictory. The questions are familiar. How much abundance does one need to achieve from his enterprise before he is moved to become charitable—or before he *should* be so moved? What's the right amount of stuff to have and the right amount to keep? Which is the greater gift—the vast transfer by the wealthy philanthropist or the widow's mite? And what's the motivation? Yes, it must be an act of free will for the transfer to be charitable rather than confiscatory, but *why* do we exercise that freedom to give? Is it always motivated by faith? Can't it be motivated merely by sympathy, or compassion, or some other biological impulse? Or perhaps by a virtuous mind, rooted solely in reason, even self-interest. But if so, from what in nature do sympathy and compassion and virtue and reason arise? Where do we derive the values that prompt us to part with something we prize and to bestow it on others, whether it is our time and talents, our treasure, or even our life? Do we give because in giving we hope to receive—if not a return gift from the donee or a special place in heaven, then at least the psychic reward for the good deed? Or do we give out of a pure heart, willing to sacrifice for the good of others?"

I was following closely, still wondering what the point was.

"Those are all important questions, and there are many possible answers," Miguel said.

"But the point I want to make, General, is a simpler and more basic one: Down through the years you have learned all the lessons about the individual concepts and relationships depicted by the arrows on this chart. But you've never really stepped back and looked at the chart as a whole—you've never put it all together. You like to use water analogies to describe the flow of things. Well, if water lands anywhere on the plane depicted by this chart, where does it flow? It flows down and to the right, doesn't it? *If you follow the slope depicted by the arrows, everything flows from Justice in the upper left corner to Mercy in the lower right.*"

"And that is life, General. Justice does not exist in some ivory tower, reveling in its own perfection and divorced from man's struggle. Justice has a purpose—at least in the scenario where good overcomes evil—and its ultimate purpose is *charity*. Remember the prophet Micah? 'What does the Lord require of you? To act justly and to love mercy and to walk humbly with your God.' Micah's big three were justice, charity, and humility."

"We have covered justice and mercy, but what about humility? I put the words 'humility' and 'integrity' in the center because if we are honest about our tiny place in this awesome universe, then we have to be humble as we walk with God through this mysterious experience called 'life.' And if we are humble—truly humble—then we will not stand proudly by, exalting justice like some Javert and ignoring its ultimate, ennobling object, which is self-denying charity."

"Why this should be so hard for good people to understand, I do not know. It is right there in black and white: 'For God has bound everyone over to disobedience so that he may have mercy on them all.'"

"So, what does all this have to do with you and your present difficulties?" Miguel asked, posing the question he knew was on my lips.

"Well, here's the bottom line: In refusing to defend yourself, in presuming to act as judge and jury and convict yourself, you are affirming your own personal sense of justice. There's no question about that. But you are denying your fellow man—your fellow men and women—the opportunity to confer upon you the same charity, the same mercy, forgiveness, and love, that you would so willingly extend to another person in the same situation. And you may think that's noble—in fact, I'm sure you think you are being noble—but

517

it's not noble at all. You're not walking humbly with anyone—God or man. In fact, your behavior is the antithesis of humility, because you are too proud to accept charity and too haughty even to allow the possibility that you might actually be in need of the mercy of others. Your natural business lies in escaping, as Sir Thomas said, but in your self-absorbed defeatism you deny others the opportunity to help you escape, and you even presume to deny that opportunity to God. You just want to control it all and decide it all yourself."

"Well, guess what, Attorney General Daniel Madison McGuire. It's not all about you!"

He stopped. And there it was.

The young man had put on an impressive case; his analogies were instructive, and his logic was irrefutable. It had all built to this piercing conclusion. *It's not all about you.*

It is a cliché, but pride really does sneak up on you when you least expect it—when you can hardly even recognize it.

"There is perhaps no one of our natural passions so hard to subdue as pride;" Benjamin Franklin once observed, "disguise it, struggle with it, beat it down, stifle it, mortify it as much as one pleases, it is still alive and will every now and then peep out and show itself.... [E]ven if I could conceive that I had completely overcome it, I would probably be proud of my humility."

Indeed.

I know enough to recognize an airtight case when I see one, and this brazen young lawyer-warrior had supplied positive proof that pride had hijacked me at the very time when I thought I was doing the noble, selfless thing. All I could do in response was surrender.

In earlier times, I had always been the counselor, the one sought out for his sound and sage advice. But now what came to mind was the wisdom of Ecclesiastes: "Better a poor but wise youth than an old but foolish king who no longer knows how to heed a warning." Somewhere along the way I had morphed from the wise youth into the foolish king. And the aegis of that subtle transformation had been pride.

"Okay, you're the boss, counselor," I relented, after a few moments of silence. "We'll do it your way. But I hope I don't lose my head over this ... you know, like Sir Thomas."

"We will see," the youthful-seeming Miguel said with a sparkle in his eye that glimmered like light reflecting off a newly unsheathed sword.

The lesson was concluded, but then Miguel added, almost as if reminiscing, "You know, those eventful days of Sir Thomas More and Henry VIII and William Tyndale—now those were transformative days in ways no one could have imagined. That period of English history supplied the improbable soil in which the seeds of religious liberty sprouted. It's another of those seeming *contradictions* where a divine hand brings good out of man's dubious designs. I think you'll find that 'in the tangle of his mind' Sir Thomas More had a lot of issues, not the least of which was that, between his argument for freedom of conscience in *Utopia* and his well-known martyrdom for conscience years later, he somehow rationalized burning at the stake a lot of his fellow Christians for their own acts of conscience. Meanwhile, his nemesis Tyndale was translating the Bible into accessible English and his carnal friend-turned-foe Henry was undermining papal absolutism—both essential preconditions for the emergence of what we now conceive as civil and religious Liberty."

My gifted counselor was someone special—that was for sure.

"But that's a story for another day," Miguel concluded. "There will be time enough to delve into those contradictions later. For now, let's get working on your case...."

THE LION'S DEN

When the Senate President Pro Tem gaveled the Special Commission of Inquiry (the "Morris Commission," as it inevitably became known) to order on November 20, 2006, I was there to make my case. Instead of apologizing for my actions or admitting error, I let the facts speak for themselves. I did my best to describe the course of events as I had perceived them at the time and the reasoning that had guided my actions at each juncture. The questioning by the panel was brutal and glaringly one-sided, but I generally succeeded in staying on track and sticking to my factual narrative.

While the Morris Commission's investigation proceeded in public, a federal grand jury was convening in the new federal courthouse less than three blocks away. Its actual sessions were conducted in secret, but the fact of its deliberations had become a matter of general public knowledge. The Department of Justice was now on an all-out war footing, determined to avoid blame for—and further congressional probes into—its initial inaction in the wake of the Ned Nevers murder revelations. A second governor had died while the ponderous prosecutors who oversaw things from Washington sat on dispositive information about the real cause of the first chief executive's demise. The best way to shift responsibility for that fiasco apparently was to make me the villain. How my actions could have constituted a willful obstruction of justice remained a puzzle to many legal commentators, but the danger of indictment was nevertheless quite real. Grand jurors take their cues from prosecutors—they will "indict a ham sandwich" at the government's behest, according to Judge Sol Wachtler's overworked cliché—and this Justice Department was plainly out to excuse itself by nailing me.

No one who is the target of an investigation ever agrees to testify before a grand jury—at least, no one with a competent lawyer does so. But every rule has an exception. When I proposed to Miguel that I offer to appear before the grand jury and share my narrative, he surprised me by nodding his concurrence without hesitation.

"Good grief. I can't believe you aren't going to push back!" I exclaimed. "Maybe I need to go find me a real lawyer who knows how these things work."

"If you had not suggested testifying, I would have," Miguel replied coolly.

"I thought you were the one who said suicide is not noble. Going into that shark pool is as close to suicide as anything I can imagine."

"Trust your instincts, General. Remember, things are not what they seem. You want to go and tell your story to these fellow citizens, and I think you should do it. Ninety-nine times out of 100, maybe 999 out of a thousand, that would be a terrible idea. But this is different."

When it was all said and done, I had testified in that oppressively unadorned and dimly lit grand jury room for a total of 15 hours in three different sessions spread out over a span of nearly four months.

In the meantime, the public spectacle that was the Morris Commission "inquiry" had about run its course. The Commission's final scheduled hearing was now only days away, after which the members would deliver their predictably harsh verdict via a set of published "findings." Along with the credible evidence and factual information, a lot of rank speculation, unreliable hearsay evidence, personal attacks on me, and misleading nonsense had been presented to the Commission. Miguel insisted that we—meaning, *he*—be given the opportunity for a rebuttal before the Commission voted. Senator Morris reflexively denied the request, but several of his fellow partisans concluded that the appearance of fairness would be enhanced by letting my counsel have his say.

They undoubtedly assumed that Miguel had little of value to add. And so they leaned on Morris to relent.

It proved to be one of those rare times when the legislative wizards wished they had listened to the haughty old Senator.

Once in the spotlight, Miguel shined brilliantly. He had plenty to say about various particulars, but it was his finale that stopped all in their tracks. I am convinced that his concluding words, and their prominent coverage in the media over several ensuing days, produced a decisive change in the Commission's subsequent findings. And, without any proof, I am equally certain that some federal grand jurors—the ones who soon would confound their overseers by refusing to return an indictment—were violating their instructions and watching, too.

"In closing, I ask you to focus on just one thing—the character of this man—in rendering your judgments in the coming report," Miguel concluded with quiet simplicity.

> Errors are our common lot; we all will err, and err badly. And let us stipulate that when "the roll is called up yonder," as they say, Daniel McGuire's errors will be among the worst to be answered for. You may say of those as you must, and as you will. But I submit that what truly matters is not the work of a man's hands and the good or ill that comes from those labors. It is not even what goes through his head, or takes root in his mind, or resides in his heart. No, all that really matters at the end of the day is his soul, the essential character of his being, what lies at his core—what is made of him and what is left of him when the Good Lord finally sees through to completion the good work he has started. Now, if I am right about this, then you there, sitting in the seat of judgment—you who will render a verdict not only, or even mainly, on the *conduct* of this man, but on his *character*—you have a great weight on your shoulders. Because each of you is a person with an essential character, too, and that character is about to be revealed.

> As you approach this task, I ask you to let your minds run back to an evening just a little over a year ago. The air is

cold outside, and inside hearts are heavy. Your leader and friend is dead. You are standing at the feet of the greatest American who ever lived, Washington, and you will be directly in his gaze—and his judgment. You are in the sacred temple to human freedom that Jefferson built. In front of you are lenses and lights, and through them peer the eyes of the nation and the world, and, most of all, the sad, searching eyes of the people of Virginia who have placed in you their solemn trust. You know they are horrified and grief-stricken. You know they will respond to your leadership. You know they will answer your call. And you must choose what to tell them. It is all, only and entirely, up to you. How many of our politicians—how many of *you*—faced with that moment, would not say this: "Yes, I will be your governor. Follow me, trust me, elect me, and I will lead you through this dark night. We will search together for the answers; we will work together for the good. There will be time enough to understand these things, but this much we know: we are strongest together, you and I. So give me your trust and your votes, and I will see you through these stormy seas; I will see you to the safe harbor you seek. Yes, give me your votes: *You will be my people, and I will be your governor.*"

I do not know if those are the words you would have chosen, and you do not know whether it would have been your course. There is only one person whose decision in that moment of truth we can know for certain—because there is only one person whose integrity and faith have been tested and refined in that awful crucible. Consider that as you place his actions and his motives, his rights and his wrongs, under the penetrating microscope of your own judgment in the days ahead. Because the people of Virginia already have witnessed the essential character of Danny McGuire. What they are now about to see is the essential character of each of you.

ANGELS UNAWARES

After the Commission delivered its generally benign verdict and the grand jury refused to indict me, I went to see Miguel. I went to thank him for saving my family from further pain, for saving my reputation and life's work, and for saving me from the lion's den of the world's arrogance, especially my own. But mainly I went to confess that I had doubted his wisdom every step of the way. His response was to laugh and repeat his familiar "O ye of little faith" line with a sympathetic shake of the head.

We parted soon thereafter, but that night, as I lay awake contemplating the events of the last several days, Miguel's chuckling visage was the last conscious image that moved across my mind before I drifted off to sleep. The custodian placed him there, too, as I came to life on the other side of the night, in the world of dreams. In the haze that doubles for my recollection of the night, my counselor appeared in scene after scene in rapid succession, as if I had been channel surfing and on each channel found the same actor playing a different role. In one scene he was presiding over the inexplicable demise of 185,000 invading warriors who, just the day before, had made the destruction of the shining city seem inevitable. Next he was at the deathbed of a great leader, arguing over who was entitled to take possession of the body and so the legacy. He was there with the cloud-like pillar that separated the recently freed Israelites from the Pharaoh's advancing chariots, and he was there with the commanding general before the walls of a powerfully fortified place came tumbling down. In the most absurd scene of the evening, he thwarted a prophet's corrupt designs by causing the seer's defiant donkey to go on a sit-down strike. And in what must have been his very first flick, he was the knight in shining armor battling with a dragon at the beginning of all trouble, his efforts no less heroic because the fight then was futile.

The rapid-fire snippets made little sense to me, but those images did not unsettle me like the last strange scene I saw in that evening's dream. Instead of Miguel, I myself was in the finale. I was standing beside a great river at the place where civilization began, and I saw what seemed like a vision of Perfection, wonderful and terrible all at once. I was struck dumb with awe and fear, but the vision strengthened me, saying, "Do not be afraid, Daniel. Since the first day that you set your mind to gain understanding and to humble yourself before your God, your words were heard, and I have come in response to them." He told me this essential truth: that there is a great battle beyond our ken between Good and Evil, a battle that will tax even the strongest, most virtuous saints from time to time. In fact, as the vision of Perfect Goodness showed me by the river, there are evil times when only mysterious interventions like Miguel's will provide a means of escape.

I reflected on the implications of the dream in the soft morning light. My life's experiences had taught me that instruments of a larger purpose do arrive in times of need, assuming we are open to the aid. The character of these instruments invariably is unclear to us, as are the source, timing, and purpose. And so we overlay on the events our own preconceptions and prejudices about faith, fate, luck, providence, justice, karma, the stars, tea leaves, goodness, malevolence, randomness, or whatever our creed tells us about cause and effect, and then shrug resignedly at the ultimate inexplicability of the thing. We shrug at the inexplicability but then in the next instant most of us are back to demanding rational certainty as the price of belief.

No human error was ever more grievous than this, the evening's vision had shown me. The greatest obstacle to the efficacy of aid proffered to us is not other powers or principalities, but our own haughty ignorance. We are apt to dismiss all that we cannot comprehend as superstition or fantasy, and to seek refuge in what we count in our time as Reason, not pausing to consider that reality remains real even if we do not at this moment have the capacity to fathom it. Reason told learned men in one era that the world was flat, and in another era it told them that the world was round. But the world actually was round during both eras; it was round even when all man's powers of reason told him it was flat.

We know little about the era in which we live, less about what preceded it, and nothing about what will follow it. It is as likely that we are just past the first instant in time as we are just before the last—as probable that we are at the beginning of the acquisition of knowledge as at the end of it. *How stunningly arrogant we are, then, to assume we live in the precise moment in human history when Truth is wholly confined by our present understanding of what is reasonable.*

In my dream, this earthly Reason had exclaimed, "We are all going to die!"

"Yes," a voice within the vision had answered, "but until then we are all going to live! Has your reason led you into such prideful pessimism that you believe God lacks the energy, will, or wit to work through his created instruments to *renew* things in this world? Instead of such dreadful confidence in your impending demise, why not reason that he who began a good work on this planet will see it through to completion? Why not surmise that, if we are his faithful instruments, we will see his goodness in the land of the living?"

"After all," the voice had instructed, "if Scripture teaches us anything, it is that being exiles does not make us prisoners."

In my dream's final scene along the river, I had mustered the courage to ask the image of Perfect Goodness how long it would be before all things came to pass, and what the outcome of it all would be. I asked because it is what we all want to know, whether we count ourselves optimists or pessimists. In my dream came this answer: "Go your way, Daniel, because the answers are sealed for now.... Go your way until your life's work is done. After that you will rest, and then rise to receive your allotted inheritance."

In the clarifying freshness of the morning the dream's encouraging counsel roughly translated to this for me: "Claw your way out of all self-pity and self-doubt. Get up and go back to work. You cannot change the past, but you can do your best to do what is right from here forward. You purposely do not have all the answers; it is your destiny to grope in darkness for a while. Be at peace knowing that God loves you, and if you just do your own part faithfully—if you seek to do justice, love mercy, and walk humbly with your God—the rest will take care itself in the fullness of time."

CHAPTER TEN

SPEECH

The course of my life would be changed by, of all things, a *speech*. It occurred on April 26, 2007. As I explained at the start of this story, the occasion was the 400th anniversary of the English settlers' arrival in Virginia, at Cape Henry. Mindful that the sojourners had marked the end of their harrowing voyage with an expression of thanks, the commemoration's thoughtful planners had chosen an early-morning prayer service on the Cape as an appropriately modest way to open the 18-day-long "America's 400th Birthday" program. Much grander events graced by VIPs like the American president and British monarch would follow at the several historic capitals within the Chesapeake estuary. But the commemoration would begin here beside the great ocean, and, ironically, I would be its voice.

The controversies that had engulfed Virginia, and that nearly had swamped me, only recently had been allayed. But when she called to request that I take her place in leading the prayer service, Governor Meade made no direct reference to those developments. She said only that I was the right person to "do what needs to be done at this event, which is to trace the things that really matter and their essential connections"—a way of framing the assignment that, as she no doubt intended, presented a compelling challenge for me. I accepted and set to work creating an address—actually a series of reflections—that was part history lesson and part sermon, part soothing benediction and part jarring provocation.

527

Impressive arrangements already had been made by the time I was asked to speak. The service would include the music of, among others, the United States Marine Band (also known as "The President's Own"), a large choir assembled for the occasion from church and civic chorale groups in more than four dozen Virginia communities, Virginia Indian drummers in their ceremonial regalia, and a boys choir from a predominantly African-American academy in nearby Norfolk. Prayers would be offered from various faith traditions. Scripture, poetry, and historic tracts would be read. And now, thanks to Governor Meade's invitation, woven throughout would be my commentary on the relationship between freedom and faith in the course of human events.

In choosing to focus on that often-controversial relationship, I would be tackling the topic that mattered most for the future of American democracy. It was the anvil on which fulfilling lives of service and achievement would be forged in a still vigorous and virtuous republic. For me, it was the *big idea* around which things finally had begun to converge: my pursuit of useful purpose in my life and my hope for the happiness of those I loved ... my passion for Virginia's legacy of liberty and my confidence in the Constitution ... my optimism about the creative genius and generosity of free people and my realism about the palpable evil that seeks to seduce and oppress ... my resolve as a public official to keep faith with the sovereign people who had elected me, and my faith in the goodness of the one true Sovereign who created us all. Here, by the sea, all these courses converged in an opportunity for expression. The struggles of life and the pursuit of wisdom, covenants to keep and choices to make ... all gathering on this shore.

I was first puzzled by the Governor's request, then excited about the opportunity, and ultimately anxious about the responsibility. It was an act of faith that had put me in this position, and only an act of faith would get me through it. Fortunately, my parents had equipped me with the timeless counsel of the great apostle, and now I leaned on it: "Do not worry about anything, but in everything, through prayer and petition, with thanksgiving, present your requests to God. And the peace of God, which surpasses all understanding, will guard your hearts and minds in Christ Jesus."

After a softly patriotic prelude brought balm to my soul as only music can, I acknowledged the dignitaries present, carried out the necessary preliminaries, and began ...

It is fitting that we commence these 400ᵗʰ anniversary observances with a service of prayer and thanksgiving to God, whose blessings guided and sustained our forebears, and whose blessings we seek today for our country, our commonwealth, our friends around the world, and all people who yearn to breathe free.

Our forebears knew who was the Author of their liberty and sustenance, their help in ages past and hope for years to come. And so, first here in Virginia, then later at Plymouth, and eventually all across this land, they went to God in humble prayers of praise and thanksgiving. In the words of one timeless hymn, "They gather[ed] together to ask the Lord's blessing...."

I paused as planned, and on that cue the boys choir began its moving *a capela* rendition of the familiar thanksgiving hymn:

> *We gather together to ask the Lord's blessing;*
> *He chastens and hastens His will to make known;*
> *the wicked oppressing now cease from distressing,*
> *Sing praises to His name, He forgets not His own.*
>
> *Beside us to guide us, our God with us joining,*
> *ordaining, maintaining His kingdom divine;*
> *So from the beginning the fight we were winning:*
> *Thou, Lord, wast at our side, all glory be Thine.*
>
> *We all do extol Thee, Thou Leader triumphant,*
> *and pray that Thou still our Defender wilt be.*
> *Let thy congregation escape tribulation:*
> *Thy name be ever praised! O Lord, make us free!*

The angelic singers repeated those last five words and then fell silent, leaving the hymn's concluding prayer to echo through the stillness of the morning until I resumed:

> *"O Lord, make us free!"*
> With that eternal prayer rising anew with the morning

sun, casting its light of hope across the ages, we gather to-gether on a sacred shore.

"The republic is a dream," wrote Sandberg. "Nothing happens unless first a dream."

And so this morning, we greet the new day by recalling a time when the dream of distant possibilities sent men and women searching, not skyward or inward as now, but across a great ocean to a new world. A time of discovery and adven-ture, promise and peril much like our own, or like any in hu-manity's march "from the swamp to the stars."

And yet we mark a special time and place in that march. For here, four centuries ago, brave travelers first strode ashore in a strange new world, raised the symbol of their faith as they sank to their knees in thankfulness, and planted an idea that became an opportunity, that became an enterprise, that became a community, that became a commonwealth, that became a republic, that became a powerful free nation, that became a great force for good throughout the world.

They were freedom's faithful scouts .... liberty's perse-vering pioneers .... our trailblazers.

We got our start from them. But who are "we"?

We are the descendants of those explorers and the im-migrants who for four centuries have followed them from every part of the world.

We are the heirs of those who came from oppression seeking freedom, or who came in freedom seeking opportu-nity, or who came not of their own choosing at all, but in bondage.

We are the successors not only of those who arrived, but of those who were already here—the faithful stewards of this land before it was an object of envy and encroachment.

We are the heirs of all who struggled here—struggled to survive, struggled to gain freedom, struggled to preserve their culture, struggled to live their faith, struggled to gain a share of what we call the American Dream.

We are the heirs of all those who, over four centuries, struggled and sacrificed to build a free and just society, and who have struggled and sacrificed mightily to advance that freedom and justice in the face of formidable foes at home and abroad.

"E Pluribus Unum"—out of many, one.

Our country's first motto reminds us that just as a great river flows from many tributaries, so is our nation the happy convergence of diverse blessings—people and cultures, aspirations and ideas—that have been bestowed on us down through the centuries.

They have formed a mighty river called "America" that has cut a promising new way across a dark and dangerous landscape.

Here in Virginia, we like to recall the unique part our forebears played in the emergence of this promising new way. At times, we can be really insufferable on the subject. We look back fondly on the early 17th century, when the land called "Virginia" stretched from Cape Fear to the Hudson, from the Chesapeake to the Mississippi, the Great Lakes, and on to the Pacific—literally "from sea to shining sea."

Jefferson spoke for a nation when he called Virginia "the blessed mother of us all."

And so today we welcome you all, sons and daughters of Virginia from whatever place, heirs to an American idea that traces its beginnings here, to this place.

The welcome duly delivered, it was time to commence the program formally with the national anthem. The assembled stood and sang along exuberantly as the Marine Corps Band and choirs collaborated in a spine-tingling rendition.

"Today is the beginning of a fortnight-plus of observances that will culminate on May 13th with ceremonies recalling the 400th anniversary of the Jamestown founding," I continued, as the audience settled back into their seats.

As we mark this milestone, let us do so with enthusiasm and celebration, solemnity and contemplation. But let us take care to remember whom and what we honor.

Yes, we will honor the courageous men and women who arrived here and struggled to survive at Jamestown just around this cape and up the river.

Yes, we will honor the visionary Virginians who played such a vital role in the birth of representative government and the framing of this enduring Republic.

And, yes, we will honor all the citizens and patriots who have given of themselves in the planting and nurturing, the winning and defending, the correcting and refining of our free institutions over these four American centuries.

But above all, let us honor him whom the reverent patriot Patrick Henry described as the "just God who presides over the destinies of nations"—the God from whom the blessing of our freedom and all our blessings flow.

The Virginia Company sent men to this land primarily to bring back wealth, but it gave the first settlers these instructions: "Lastly and chiefly, the way to prosper and achieve good success is to make yourselves all of one mind for the good of your country and your own, and to serve and fear God the giver of all goodness, for every plantation which our heavenly father hath not planted shall be rooted out."

The wisdom of that admonition, older even than these 400 years, resonates still today. For our history teaches that no human idea or achievement we commemorate could have occurred except by divine Providence.

A series of thanksgiving prayers ensued from various faith traditions. The ecumenical moment was inevitably a source of unease for some who confused respect for other faith traditions with infidelity to their own. But, for me, it was a heartening moment, a time when men and women set aside doctrinal differences and even more fundamental disagreements to unite in earnest gratitude and humility before their Creator. The last of the prayers, *The Lord's Prayer*, was sung by the boys choir, and it was so soulful and powerful that I wished it were not my duty to break the silence that followed it. After waiting several moments, I proceeded.

As I reflect on the hardships suffered to plant freedom in this good earth, I am reminded of the trials and triumphs experienced by the prophet Daniel—a hero, saint, statesman, and, yes, a politician.

If you have not studied the life and times of Daniel, a Jewish captive who became a senior official in the government of ancient Babylon, then it is worth your while to do so. Because you will learn timeless lessons and discover that things really have not changed much in the more than two dozen centuries since Daniel's day.

We, like Daniel, are exiles in a foreign land, and sooner or later we will find ourselves in a lion's den.

Daniel was an extraordinarily capable man, a gifted leader. Though of noble birth, he was a humble and caring person who lived a life of integrity rooted in his faith. Ripped from his home and family as a young man, cast into servitude and powerlessness in a far-off land, he did not conform to the dominant culture but engaged intensively within it. In the process he came to wield great power. Yet, even with all his gifts and all the influence he acquired, he found himself cast into the lion's den, requiring the saving intervention of Providence.

Daniel's story is a universal story. He was from Jerusalem, born into the Judean ruling class, brought up in the Jewish faith, and cast into Babylonian politics. I am from a little town called Orange, brought up as a Presbyterian and a Republican (not necessarily in that order), and caught up in the political affairs of Virginia. Each of you has your own origin, identity, faith, creed, and forum. Yet here we and our fellow travelers are, two millennia after Daniel, still engaged in the same great struggles—the external ones over liberty and power, religion and politics, and the internal ones over how to overcome ourselves, set our sights on the loftier things, and step out in faith to love and serve.

Daniel trusted God in these struggles, and God intervened to save him from the lions. So has miracle followed miracle in the 400 years since settlers first came to these shores—and all, we trust, for a good purpose....

Let us pause here, though, to acknowledge a robust debate about this proposition. Some ascribe our survival and success these four centuries not to Providence but to progress—not to the beneficent hand of our Creator but to the fortuitous dispensations of fate.

Fair enough. Then let us canvas the extraordinary chain of events, whether planned or merely propitious, that have conspired to bring us to this important intersection and happy anniversary.

It was about 35 million years ago, the geologists now tell us, when a large mass of rock or ice—they are not sure which—smashed through the earth's atmosphere and landed in the vicinity of present-day Cape Charles, across the mouth of this Bay. Scientists say it displaced more than 1,800 cubic miles of earth, created a massive wave that lapped westward to the Blue Ridge Mountains, and left a crater nearly as deep as the Grand Canyon and twice the size of the State of Rhode Island—the largest such crater in North America.

Most important for our purposes, as the waters receded the massive crater played a vital role later in creating one of the world's richest estuaries, which we know as the Chesapeake Bay and its tributaries—a safe haven teeming with resources that beckoned and nurtured first the Virginia Indians, and then the English settlers, making the planting of a new nation possible.

A most portentous celestial event it was. For it marked this place millions of years in advance as the cradle of a great nation and of democracy's flourishing in the modern world.

But how did those first English settlers manage to arrive here and nestle their hopes in the bosom of the Bay?

John Smith's account tells us that the three small ships were caught up in a "vehement tempest" and lost their bearings for days as they searched in vain for their landing place. "But God, the guider of all good actions," wrote Smith, "forcing them by an extream storme to hul all night, did drive them by his providence to their desired port, beyond all their expectations, for never any of them had seene the coast."

After humbling the travelers, the storm relented. Dawn broke, suddenly and majestically, to reveal this Cape of hope, at the entrance to this Bay of destiny.

It was, to say the least, some great good fortune.

But we would hardly say the same about the conditions at the settlement the English voyagers soon founded.

For some time, commentators have tended to make sport of the Jamestown settlers. Lazy, hapless gentlemen, they were said to be—unable to feed and sustain themselves, meriting the derision of the natives of their day and generations of observers since.

There is a measure of truth in the observation. But recently the borings from cypress trees have revealed vital new information about the settlers' lot. Those who struggled on Jamestown Island had the bad fortune, if you will, to arrive as Virginia was in the grip of one of the worst droughts in eight centuries. In fact, it was one of three droughts of historic dimension that coincided, remarkably, with each of the first three European attempts to colonize this part of the New World, the Jamestown endeavor having been preceded by the failed Spanish settlement on the York River in 1570 and Raleigh's "lost colony" on the Outer Banks in the 1580s.

Yet Jamestown succeeded. And with this new scientific information, a performance that long seemed deserving of disdain suddenly seems rather heroic. For now we know that those Jamestown settlers, possessing much-remarked faults but even more remarkable fortitude, survived amid conditions that would have sorely tested even the most hearty of men. Land in which food would not grow. Freshwater wells invaded by poisonous salt that killed hundreds mysteriously. Hardships that radicalized the English and Indians alike.

One of their number, a soldier named Richard Rich, wrote of their ordeal in "News from Virginia," perhaps the first American poem:

> *Where they upon their labour fall, as men that meane to thrive;*
>
> *Let's pray that heaven may blesse them all, and keep them long alive.*
>
> *Those men that vagrants liv'd with us, have there deserved well;*
>
> *Their governour writes in their praise, as divers letters tel.*
>
> *And to th' adventurers thus he writes, be not dismayed at all,*
>
> *For scandall cannot doe us wrong, God will not let us fall.*
>
> *Let England knowe our willingnesse, for that our worke is goode,*
>
> *Wee hope to plant a Nation, where none before hath stood.*

"We hope to plant a Nation where none before has stood." The words send a chill up the spine these 400 years later.

That the planting at Jamestown took root at all in such hostile conditions, let alone that a great nation flowered from it, will strike many of us as, well … miraculous.

But we should not use the "M" word casually this morning, for we might well wear it out. It comes to mind when we think of the improbable, life-saving forbearance of the great Chief Wahunsonacock, known to history as "Chief Powhatan." And we surely could use it to describe the mysterious interventions of that quaint and curious figure Pocahontas—a free-spirited young girl moved for reasons beyond

536

our ken to help the English and to risk her life in doing so, even to the point of disloyalty to her father the Chief.

Yet, there she is again and again—if not saving the indispensable Captain Smith from club-wielding braves during the settlers' first winter, as Smith and legend tell, then certainly providing help and succor repeatedly amid the drought and famine, and endangering herself to save Smith from Powhatan's certain death sentence a year later.

Even more improbable are the events that followed. John Smith, having issued the unpopular decree that able-bodied men shall work or not eat, was injured in an explosion of suspicious origin and returned to England. Several years later, the evidently ungrateful and undeniably desperate settlers captured Pocahontas and held her hostage. Her father, inexplicably, failed to come to her rescue, leaving her disappointed and disillusioned. During her prolonged captivity, she took to English ways and was baptized. She fell in love with John Rolfe, and they were married. And from this unlikely union emerged peace between the settlers and the natives at a critical time—the famous Peace of Pocahontas—affording a respite from hostilities and hardships that allowed the colony to prosper.

"Brilliant!" our friends in the Mother Country might exclaim.

But let us not race past the pivotal partner Rolfe without also inquiring how he came to be so propitiously on the scene. For it seems he either had a guardian angel or a great deal of luck.

He left England aboard a ship called the *Sea Venture* in the summer of 1609, bound for Jamestown as part of a nine-ship re-supply mission. But barely a week from this cape, by Captain Newport's reckoning, the entire flotilla was scattered asunder by a cataclysmic hurricane. Driven by the raging storm for hundreds of miles over three terrifying days and four nights, the crew and passengers worked desperately around the clock just to keep the ship from filling with water.

Finally, with every man exhausted, nine feet of water in the hold, and all hope lost, Rolfe and his ill-fated shipmates prepared, in the words of William Strachey, to commit their "sinfull soules to God." But at that grim moment of disaster and defeat, the skies suddenly brightened, and Sir George Somers shouted, to the surprise of all aboard, "Land!"

Of all the places in the vast ocean, the violent vagaries of wind and wave had driven Rolfe and his fellows hundreds of miles off course and deposited them safely on the tiny limestone island of Bermuda—a life-saving needle in a colossal Atlantic haystack.

They remained shipwrecked on the remote uninhabited island for ten months, using the salvage from the *Sea Venture* and the native cedar to construct two makeshift vessels—aptly named the *Patience* and the *Deliverance*—and then, undaunted, they made their way on to Virginia.

The stunning story apparently would inspire Shakespeare to write *The Tempest*. And the Virginia Company would start a new colony on the magnificent little island, naming it for a while "Virginiola." But the consequences of these dramatic events for the Jamestown adventure would truly be epic. Without Rolfe's remarkable survival, there might well have been no economic lifeline for the Virginia colony later in the form of tobacco and no pivotal marriage and period of peace.

Having been saved miraculously, or so it seemed to them, Rolfe and his fellow survivors finally arrived at Jamestown only to find the settlement in an extreme state, beset by disease and starvation, with just 60 haggard settlers remaining. They did their best to give aid, but within a short time the settlement's leaders concluded their three-year-old enterprise could not be saved and must be abandoned.

One imagines how Rolfe must have felt. Had God really brought him and his fellows through hurricane and shipwreck, through island exile and a fretful improvised voyage to Jamestown—had he sustained their bodies and their wills through so many moments when death seemed imminent and surrender sensible—only to have them witness the final failure of the noble experiment in Virginia?

So, indeed, it seemed. The scraggly band of survivors packed their few belongings, boarded the available vessels and made their way down river, bound for Newfoundland where they hoped fishing ships might provide passage back to England.

Diseased and defeated, their hopes for a new world dashed, they were heading home.

Yet, once again, Providence or fate intervened. For as the colony's beleaguered remnant sailed down the James, preparing to depart the Chesapeake, the settlers waiting to be picked up at Point Comfort, the present-day site of Fort Monroe in Hampton, spotted a magnificent sight across the waves: three great re-supply ships under the command of Lord De La Warr, the colony's new governor.

Had these agents of mercy arrived a day or even hours later, the vital rendezvous would have been missed, and Rolfe and the other Jamestown survivors likely would have been on their way to England or to some less happy fate. Instead, they returned to Jamestown—and the rest, as we say, is history.

I suspended the narrative at this point for an interlude that included the cherished anthem "America," better known as "My Country, 'Tis of Thee," followed by the national hymn, "God of Our Fathers," and several other familiar pieces. Virginia Indians clad in bright regalia performed a traditional dance paying homage to the "Great Spirit"; a rabbi and priest read the 46th and 121st Psalms, respectively; state legislators read excerpts from the thanksgiving proclamations of Presidents Washington and Lincoln; and the young grocery store clerk who won the "Virginia's 400th Birthday" essay competition read an excerpt from her original work.

"We reflect on the richness of our history, its blessings and its lessons," I resumed after those presentations.

Yet, for all the tragedy and triumph that we can neatly chronicle and count, there is so much more shrouded in mystery and wrapped in irony.

539

"Be alert," the apostle Peter warned the early Christian believers, because evil "prowls around like a roaring lion looking for someone to devour." And indeed it was a lion—a ship named, ironically, the *White Lion*—that arrived unexpectedly at Point Comfort in 1619, bringing the first Africans to Virginia ... by force.

Seized during a Portuguese campaign in West Central Africa, most likely from the province of Ndongo in today's Angola, the captured Africans were bound for sale in a Mexican port when their purveyors were attacked by privateers, who then diverted the human cargo to Virginia for sale or trade.

Thus did a white lion convey to these American shores a great and proud people in the most squalid and contemptible of conditions, setting in motion what soon would rank among the most egregious of evils: institutionalized slavery and systemic discrimination based on race.

Yet, evil holds sway but for a time. At length, a divine Hand would deliver African Americans from this lion's den and begin to bring right even out of this most detestable of wrongs. Over time, "We Shall Overcome" would become not only the resolute anthem of a rising people but the song of renewal for a nation that had failed to "live out the true meaning of its creed." America would don a coat of many colors and strive, devotedly if imperfectly, to provide a hope-filled example of unity amid diversity for a world beset by strife.

Perhaps it is a tragic accident of history—a random dispensation of the vilest fate—that slavery and racial exploitation were unleashed in this land, and that they forced Americans, over four centuries, to overcome unspeakable hardships, to confront debilitating prejudices, to look beyond their superficial differences, and at length to embrace their common humanity.

Had there been no *White Lion* docking at Point Comfort, no sad human cargo arriving shackled and sickened in Boston and Bristol, Charleston and Richmond, there would have been no crucible of civil war in the 19th century and no movement for civil rights in the 20th. Much horrible suffering and injustice would have been averted. And, yet, we are left to wonder: If not for this most detestable of evils, would Americans have affirmed that most fundamental of truths—that all people are created equal and endowed with liberty by their Creator?

Would we ever have awakened to the egregious wrongs done not only to persons of African descent, but to all the ostracized "others" down through our history, including the evils inflicted on the "first Americans," the native peoples, who suffered the dispossession of their land, the destruction of their culture, and even the denial of their identity?

Would the scales ever have fallen from our eyes regarding racial, ethnic, religious, gender, and other forms of bigotry and prejudice?

Not only in spite of, but very possibly because of, our monumental national struggle with slavery and racial discrimination, we have been forced to decide what we believe. The vast majority of Americans, people of goodwill of every race and background, have decided we actually believe the eternal truth recited in Jefferson's declaration and mean at last to live by it. And having so decided we are becoming, for the first time, credible and worthy apostles for the ideal of freedom at a time when the world is becoming free to embrace it.

The exodus from oppression, a project still ongoing, fortified the faith of the freedom seekers, confronted the conscience of the comfortable, and inspired a nation.

A miraculous course of human events?

Deliverance by the divine hand of Providence?

Some of us, judging the improbable journeys on which history has borne the hopes of mankind, will eagerly so affirm. Others will continue to doubt and may even deride. Let us respect them all, including those whose conscience has not yet brought them to such a conviction.

As Madison said in arguing for religious liberty, "Whilst we assert for ourselves a freedom to embrace, to profess and to observe the Religion we believe to be of divine origin, we cannot deny an equal freedom to those whose minds have not yet yielded to the evidence which has convinced us."

A former communist spy and avowed atheist, Whittaker Chambers traced his awakening to the moment when he beheld the magnificent complexity of his baby daughter's ear and pondered the creative ingenuity that must have produced it. The ear had been around all along, with all it evidenced, but even after noticing it he had first turned his own deaf ear to its message.

In similar fashion, today's skeptics may one day gaze upon the matchless beauty and bounty of this land, and find chance to be an insufficient explanation ... or reflect on the remarkable chain of cause and effect that produced the great tree of American liberty from the fragile and flawed planting at Jamestown, and see in it the indispensable hand of a divine gardener.

Those who doubt may yet come to believe, with Dr. Martin Luther King Jr., that "the arc of the moral universe is long, [but] it bends toward justice." And, so believing, they will share the joy that makes us victors in the midst of strife, knowing that God's amazing grace is at work in our struggles as well as our successes.

I sat and watched as members of the large choir moved into position. Assembled uniquely for this occasion and embodying the diversity that is contemporary Virginia's hallmark, they sang the hymn that uniquely belonged in this moment—"Amazing Grace." Written by John Newton, the grateful soul whose remarkable journey had taken him from seafaring slave trader to Anglican priest, the song of redemption inspired in Britain had become an American anthem. Its powerful, poetic strains resounded from the Second Great Awakening to the Civil Rights Movement, and were resonating still.

Highlighting the universality of the proffered grace, the musical planners for this occasion had arranged for additional instruments and voices to join in as each verse was sung. Midway through, a waving motion from the Marine officer conducting The President's Own was all that was needed to secure full participation by the audience. The lyrics were printed in the program, but I noticed that few looked down to read. Instead, they looked upward and outward, their voices rising together in a palpable unity born of the hope they shared.

When it was finished, they sat, and nearly all of them, it seemed, were smiling. I savored the moment with them and then stepped forward again.

Almost a century after Jamestown's founding, nearby Williamsburg came to the fore, and it became not only the capital of colonial governance but a center of revolutionary thought. It was there the Virginians honed their skill at self-government and nurtured an independent spirit—there that George Wythe stood for the rule of law, and Edmund Pendleton stood for the principle of order, and Samuel Davies stood for the right of conscience. It was there, at William and Mary, that William Small inspired Thomas Jefferson, and later scholars schooled Edmund Randolph, John Taylor of Caroline, John Marshall, and James Monroe. The scenes were replicated elsewhere as future patriots received their instruction—Adams at Harvard; Madison and Rush at the College of New Jersey, now Princeton; Hamilton and Jay at King's College, now Columbia; and all the rest—preparing ardently, with neither teachers nor students faintly imagining that the result of their educational enterprise would be the utter transformation of the world.

There converged in the education of these instrumental young people powerful ideas—conservative and revolutionary, secular and sectarian—that would in time forge a distinctly American ethos and give birth to the world's most durable and beneficent republic.

It included the "rights of Englishmen" worked out over several centuries but crystallized in the revolutionary settlement that followed the "glorious" ascension of William of Orange and Mary to the English throne in the late 17th century.

It included the ideas of the great English liberals Locke and Sidney and radical Whigs Trenchant and Gordon—expositors of individual liberty and government by consent.

It included the great intellectual flowering known as the Scottish Enlightenment, the legacies of Hutcheson, Hume, Smith, and Reid carried on the current of Witherspoon's creative conservatism at Princeton—profound ideas about empiricism and common sense, about free minds and free markets.

It included the reformed Christian tradition of Luther and Calvin and Knox, fundamental beliefs about the nature of man and his relationship to God, and the crucial concept of covenant.

It included insights about the architecture of liberty and the division of power handed down from Polybius in Rome and Montesquieu in France.

And it included an understanding of natural law that traced its lineage through Plato and Cicero, Augustine and Aquinas: liberty rooted in virtue, virtue rooted in morality, morality rooted in faith.

We give these varied strands of thought labels today: classical republicanism, covenant theology, evangelical Protestantism, commonsense moral philosophy, liberal republicanism.... They sprang from different wells of inspiration at different places and moments, sometimes in tandem, often in tension, sometimes making easy peace with each other, often arousing passionate dispute. But from them emerged an American synthesis that over time has remade the world.

Two decades ago, as we celebrated the 200th anniversary of the American Constitution, there were frequent and too-casual references to the "miracle at Philadelphia." But "miraculous" and "providential" were the very words that the eyewitnesses to those events, the framers themselves, used to describe their handiwork as they emerged on that mid-September day from a conclave that earlier had supplied little cause for optimism.

Reflecting on the unexpected achievement, Madison himself declared: "It is impossible for the man of pious reflection not to perceive in it, a finger of that Almighty Hand which has been so frequently and signally extended to our relief in the critical stages of the revolution."

It was, he wrote to Jefferson in Paris, "impossible to consider [it] as less than a miracle."

Weeks earlier, no lesser light than Benjamin Franklin, the American embodiment of Enlightenment rationalism, had surprised delegates by suggesting they seek divine aid in their faltering deliberations. "I have lived, Sir, a long time," said Franklin, "and the longer I live, the more convincing proofs I see of this Truth, *that God governs in the Affairs of Men*. And if a Sparrow cannot fall to the Ground without his Notice, is it probable that an Empire can rise without his Aid?"

The truly miraculous thing was the timely convergence of influential ideas, some reflecting the wisdom of the ages and others quite revolutionary. Issuing from great minds foreign and domestic, boldly enunciated in places like Runnymede and Westminster, resounding through the earliest colonial charters and refined in the creative efforts of lawmakers throughout the colonies and fledgling states, these ideas found their way into an intellectual vessel that was both profound and punctual: a collection of ingenious statesmen who came along at perhaps the one moment in human history when inventing a new nation actually was possible.

And not just "new" because it had not existed before. It was the first to be founded on an idea—a nation, as Lincoln would say later, "conceived in liberty and dedicated to the proposition that all men are created equal."

If you listen for these ideas, you can hear them echoing on the winds of time.

They resound from the ancient prophet Jeremiah and the noble Roman Cato, from the martyred patriot Sidney and the dissenting pastor Davies—all converging in the soaring exhortations of Patrick Henry at St. John's Church.

You can hear them in Mason's Declaration of Rights and Jefferson's Declaration of Independence, in Madison's Constitution and Washington's Farewell.

They echo on down through American history. Lincoln at Gettysburg. Roosevelt on the radio. King at the Reflecting Pool. Reagan at the Brandenburg Gate.

And they reverberate around the world today, as new nations are born, new democracies are formed, new markets emerge, new freedomes are won, new constitutions are written.

We may be forgiven for gasping when we consider how thoroughly improbable was this founding convergence, how monumentally consequential it would become, and how stunningly precarious it would remain.

The American adventure is an ever-perilous maneuver between mob and monarch, the Scylla and Charybdis of the age. Yet there is nothing mythical about this mission. On America's safe passage rests the happiness of global billions.

Indeed, this Cape is a hallowed site, not only because of those who strode ashore here four centuries ago, but because of all to which it has borne witness in the centuries since.

It was just up-river from here, at Yorktown, where our independence and freedom were gained despite seemingly overwhelming odds, aided by a French naval blockade that the English failed to break in a pivotal engagement right out there, just off this shore.

Ships have been passing this Cape ever since, carrying mankind's hope for freedom, rushing to liberty's rescue.

In the century just completed—a century that began with naïve confidence in man's sophistication, democracy's destiny, and beguiling utopian schemes—America became the last bulwark against the most lethal oppression ever to stalk the world.

During the darkest days of Hitler's advance, with isolationism holding sway here in America and Britain struggling alone to survive, the indomitable Winston Churchill stood resolutely in the path of history's greatest villain. He declared:

Even though large tracts of Europe and many old and famous States have fallen or may fall into the grip of the Gestapo and all the odious apparatus of Nazi rule, we shall not flag or fail.... [W]e shall fight in France, we shall fight on the seas and oceans.... [W]e shall defend our island, whatever the cost may be.... [W]e shall never surrender. And even if, which I do not for a moment believe, this island or a large part of it were subjugated and starving, then our empire beyond the seas, armed and guarded by the British fleet, would carry on the struggle, *until, in God's good time, the new world, with all its power and might, steps forth to the rescue and the liberation of the old.*

Later that same year, Franklin Roosevelt delivered another of his famous fireside chats. He recalled the depression that had brought America almost to its knees eight years earlier, and called on the American people to "face this new crisis—this new threat to the security of our nation—with the same courage and realism."

"Never before since Jamestown and Plymouth Rock," he declared, "has our American civilization been in such danger as now."

And so a nation that had been down and out economically for a decade became the great arsenal of democracy. And ship after ship passed this Cape, reversing the voyage of the *Susan Constant*, the *Godspeed*, and the *Discovery*—returning the favor to Lafayette, Rochambeau, and DeGrasse ... to Steuben, Pulaski, and Kosciusko—the New World, as Churchill had prayed, stepping forth to the rescue and the liberation of the Old.

Not only arms would sail and steam past here, but soon soldiers and sailors, leaving their families behind, sacrificing limbs and lives, all to preserve their country, their way of life, their freedom ... and ours.

Greater love has no one than this: to lay down one's life for one's friends.

In times of desperation and danger—from a world war against the "odious apparatus" of Nazism, to a long cold war against the "evil empire" of Soviet Communism, to the current struggle against fanaticism, fascism and terror—the stalwart lighthouses on this Cape have stood sentinel, snapping their salutes with bursts of light as brave men and women gave up the safety of these shores and emptied themselves in the epic engagements that turned back tyranny and saved liberty for the world.

We thank God for their sacrifice and success.

Indeed, remarkable is the hubris of any person who would *not* thank God for it.

As General Washington wrote after the pivotal early battles of the Revolution, "The hand of Providence has been so conspicuous in all this, that he must be worse than an infidel that lacks faith, and more than wicked, that has not gratitude...."

I paused the narrative again at this point, as the Marine Corps Band and adult choir commenced a moving rendition of "Eternal Father, Strong to Save." Here by the sea the Navy Hymn took on special poignancy. Written by a grateful survivor of the tempest, it is the hymn played and sung during military burials at sea, at services honoring heroes from the USS *Maine* to the USS *Cole*, at presidential funerals from Roosevelt to Reagan. Mindful of its impact on the former Navy assistant secretary who presided over the American government, Churchill had arranged for it to be sung at the ship-borne worship service during his portentous August 1941 meeting with FDR, the session that yielded the Atlantic Charter. A later generation, the first of the television age, would recall its somber strains accompanying Jackie Kennedy as she clasped her two small children by the hand and climbed the steps of the U.S. Capitol behind the flag-draped coffin of her husband, the 35th president.

The choir sang every verse, and the last, a prayer of gratitude and plea for protection, seemed particularly apt on this occasion:

O Trinity of love and power!
Our family shield in danger's hour;
From rock and tempest, fire and foe,
Protect us wheresoever we go;
Thus evermore shall rise to Thee
Glad hymns of praise from land and sea.

I looked about before resuming the podium and noticed, for the first time that day, that many people—almost all of them, it seemed—were dabbing their eyes. I waited several moments for the rustling to stop and composure to return, then took the story in a new direction.

> We celebrate the heroes who won and preserved our freedom, and we thank the God with whom they now dwell in perfect peace.
>
> Yet, we know goodness lies not only in the heroic but also the ordinary.
>
> It lies not only in going to war but in going to work.
>
> America has been the great font of liberty and opportunity, not only because of the extraordinary valor of those in uniform, but because of the exceptional enterprise of those who have donned overalls, lab coats, business suits, and all the varied garb of the world's most productive economy.
>
> It is not only political rights and national might but also the American economic miracle that has brought hope to a world beset by poverty, ignorance, disease, and despotism.
>
> The Jamestown settlement was, first and foremost, an economic venture—"America's first startup," some have dubbed it. In the four centuries since, we have hewed to this fundamental belief: When the creativity of free people is unleashed within a just system of open commerce, the result is expanding opportunity for all.
>
> This is not only an article of our national faith. It is a proposition we have proven empirically. It is a light we have shined, and are shining still, into the darkness of a mean and impoverished world just as surely as the light of science has

illuminated the night and the light of learning has illuminated the ages.

Yet, this essential truth has been challenged throughout our history and is formidably challenged today.

It is challenged by those who proclaim the virtue of private initiative but undermine it with their public actions: the economic interests that manipulate the public sphere for unjust advantage and the politicians who bury future generations under mountains of public debt.

It is challenged by those who consign economic and environmental issues to a zero-sum contest, diverting us with a cathartic clash of warring worldviews rather than engaging in the essential business of innovation, collaboration, and compromise.

But it is challenged most fundamentally today by the fading of hard-learned lessons and the erosion of four centuries of growing confidence in the capacity of free minds and free markets, free institutions and free people.

The underlying issues are not new ones. The first representative assembly that convened at Jamestown in 1619 was concerned about revenue and debt, and revolution flared in the next century over taxation and representation. From the settlers' earliest overharvest of Atlantic white cedar to the fouling of freshwater streams, economic and environmental considerations have constantly collided. Even the Virginia Company's grand enterprise faltered at first on bad economics. Only after the visionary Sir Edwin Sandys reformed the colony's basic economic approach, introducing widespread private property ownership and rewards for entrepreneurship, did the settlement finally begin to flourish.

Indeed, the challenges are not new, which makes contemporary failures to hear and heed the lessons of experience so troubling. Rising anew, as if their notions had not been thoroughly refuted, are the apostles of collectivism and entitlement, and their more subtle cousins, those who sow resentment and sap initiative through relentless demands for redistribution and regulation cloaked in the beguiling garb of "fairness."

We do seek fairness; it is both the ennobling pursuit of modern society and the siren's song of our time. Its nobility resides in its commitment to help those who cannot help themselves and give everyone a chance. Its danger lies in its propensity to confuse opportunity with guaranty and thereby foster dependency.

Mindful of those divergent possibilities, candor compels us to remind our well-meaning fellow citizens that our hard-won legacy of freedom includes not only the right to speak and worship freely, to engage politically and to be treated equally, but also the right to work and to trade, to invest and to build, to take risks and to reap rewards, to own and to keep, to save prudently and to give liberally—the right, in short, to pursue happiness by the very human enterprise of creating.

For without that freedom to create and without free markets in which to exchange the means and fruits of that creativity, America's economic miracle would never have occurred, and much of the world would remain mired in hopelessness.

Fairness, it turns out, is but a false hope without freedom. And depriving men and women of liberty is the *unfairest* cut of all.

Here I paused, partly for effect and partly to signal another turning point in my narrative. Rather than introducing a musical interlude this time, I called forward young Maria Sanchez, a sixth grade student at Brook Run Middle School in Virginia Beach and one of the winners of the poetry contest that the Hampton Roads school divisions had conducted as part of the commemoration. Entitled "The Tree," her work was a song of America, and its imagery— a sturdy tree nurturing and protecting the birds of the air and the varied creatures beneath its branches—gave a sense of assurance and hope to all.

"Thank you, Maria, for giving us a vivid picture of America through your beautiful verse," I said as the gifted young girl smiled and gracefully resumed her seat.

It is truly amazing to think of all this sturdy American tree has wrought, and of all the history that traces back to its fragile planting here: our legacy of unity amid diversity ... our creation as a nation and emergence as a world leader ... our ideas about ordered liberty ... our engine of economic opportunity.

Some divine Hand or fickle finger of fate not only formed this beautiful place called Virginia, from the mighty hills of the west to these windswept shores, blessing our homeland forever.

That same Hand or finger wrote a history to match the beauty—a history full of extraordinary events that not only changed the course of this country but the history of all mankind.

Indeed, from this soil, at a great turning point in mankind's quest for liberty, came one mere mortal who mattered above all others.

History books cannot capture the elusive Washington. He looms too much larger than life. The embodiment of liberty and virtue, he is our Nation's first and greatest and truly indispensable leader.

Against every impulse of human nature, he declined to be king, and thereby gave us the gift we most cherish as Americans: *He gave us our Republic.*

More even than that, he proved by his example that the man of action and the man of principle can be one and the same.

Yet, even Washington, with all his virtue and vigor, did not work alone.

More than a century and a half after representative government got its rudimentary start at Jamestown, Washington's Republic was enshrined in the United States Constitution. And just as we revere Washington as the Father of our Country, we remember James Madison as the Father of that Constitution.

Of all the collaborations among the founders—Adams' with Jefferson on the cause of independence, Jefferson's with

Madison on the statute for religious freedom, Madison's with Hamilton on *The Federalist*—none, perhaps, was more consequential than the quiet collaboration between Washington and Madison in the period leading to and following the "Miracle at Philadelphia." The two men worked together intimately, and often secretly, as a new plan of government was crafted, popularized, ratified, and implemented.

They were the first "odd couple" of American politics.

The magnificent Washington appears resplendent from our first sight of him, destined from his earliest days to become the quintessential American Hero—our own latter-day Daniel, with character and courage too great to be subdued even by the seemingly indomitable British lions.

Madison, by contrast, appears as a most unlikely candidate for greatness. Diminutive, shy, and disdainful of politics as a young man, he had no political ambition whatsoever. But he became indignant as he watched the clergy of the established Anglican church and the Crown's representatives deny dissenting Baptists, Presbyterians, Quakers, and people of other faiths the right simply to follow the light of their conscience in matters of religious belief and practice.

The cause of religious liberty—the freedom of conscience—more than any other thing propelled Madison into a public life of unparalleled fruitfulness. And it was that same cause that occasioned his greatest contribution to the nation and America's greatest gift to civilization.

Religious liberty has been accurately described as the one truly original idea of the American founding. And its consequences have been—dare we say it?—*miraculous.*

In our country, where freedom from governmental imposition in matters of faith was safeguarded in law, religious belief and practice have flourished.

The Founders, it turns out, were not just freeing people to practice their faith. They were freeing faith itself from centuries of corruption and conflict imposed by men and states in religion's name.

Enlightenment-era sophisticates routinely are credited with the innovation of religious freedom, but a closer look reveals that this bedrock principle of human liberty owes little to the skeptical salons of Paris where the very notion of divine truth was rejected. Rather, religious liberty was primarily the hard-won achievement of generations of honest believers and principled dissenters—ordinary people who were unrelenting seekers after truth, who were willing to suffer for their convictions, and who were resolute in their position that faith, by its very nature an act of conscience, was no fit subject for civil coercion.

In every age, the divine pursuit has moved faithful men and women to examine with due suspicion the religious edifices erected with human hands. My own faith, the Christian faith, is rooted in the transcendent endeavor of a rabbi who refused to yield to the religious mores and authorities of his time. He was executed for that refusal, an event accomplished through the edict of the governor, the arm of the state employing the brute force of political power to enforce the religious orthodoxy of the day.

Not only freedom, but Truth itself, is apt to suffer when religion and politics contrive together to compel conformity.

We Americans so understand the principle of religious liberty because we are children of the Enlightenment and the Great Awakening—people of reason and faith. And we see no contradiction there, because both are divine gifts, and experience has taught us that where people of reason are free to choose, they choose to believe.

That is not to say the choice is an easy one, or that the project is ever finished. *We all struggle.* And since the greatest part of the work is not our own, we will never get there with our reason alone. Years ago, a mentor of mine—indeed, much more than a mentor—counselled me through a short poem he had written on this very subject. His name is Dr. Samuel Davies Thomas, and he titled his work, "Therefore":

We are created in God's image,
So our free minds reflect His glory.
His creation has a purpose,
So we commit our minds to choosing.
His purpose is mystery;
Our choice, its pursuit.
In pursuing, our gifts are our greatest obstacles,
And our obstacles are our greatest gifts,
For fear alone can teach us to trust;
And suffering love is trust's reward.
Saintly wisdom unfolds love's secret:
"It is in giving that we receive;
It is in pardoning that we are pardoned;
and it is in dying to self that we are born to eternal life."
Therefore:
Have faith in reason,
And reason on to faith,
Ever ready for His revelation.
Ever grateful for His grace.

We began the day with a familiar Thanksgiving hymn—actually a prayer—that affirms this freedom of reason and faith: "We gather together to ask the Lord's blessings.... Oh, Lord, make us free!"

The hymn, of course, speaks of a freedom beyond civil liberty. It speaks not only of freedom from the imposition of men, but freedom from the imposition of man's corrupt nature.

This freedom is the message of the Gospel and also of the Constitution. It is the foundation of all the great faiths and codes of law. It is the place where Church and State, kept apart for good reason, still find common ground. Because freedom is the essential premise of both—an unalienable human right that our religious and civil trailblazers alike ascribed to divine origin. A condition we enjoy, a right we possess, not because of the beneficence of some government, but because of the endowment by our Creator.

Our preeminent founding document, the Declaration of Independence, declares this truth to a candid world. How strange it is that today we are admonished not to declare it in a candid classroom.

Jefferson was no champion of traditional religion; indeed, many have regarded him as a heretic. But he saw the Declaration, with its explicit appeals to divine power and justice, as the definitive "expression of the American mind."

Four score and seven years later, at a decisive moment for the American experiment, Lincoln recurred to the Declaration in resolving that "this nation, under God, shall have a new birth of freedom."

Though his skepticism of organized religion at times resembled Jefferson's, Lincoln found his ardent faith in the clarifying convulsion of a horrendous war that he came to believe God had ordained for expurgation of the sin of slavery—a war without which neither the American union nor our founding ideal of freedom would have been sanctified, refined, and preserved.

Many more examples of faith animating freedom could be supplied—so many, in fact, that the matter is beyond earnest dispute—and it comes down to this. If we mean to be true to our history and founding ideals no less than to our Creator, we must teach our young people this essential truth: *Freedom is God's gift to mankind; it is our Republic's trust to keep for the people; and it is America's purpose in the world.*

The boys choir now stepped forward for its final offering of the morning—the familiar, happy verses of "America the Beautiful."

I had often wondered on past occasions how many Americans, as they heard this bright favorite, wished it was their national anthem. It certainly was less likely to be mangled at sporting events. More religious and less martial than "The Star-Spangled Banner," it comes closer to capturing the essence of America—its abundant blessings, grateful spirit, and noble aspirations.

A traditionalist, I had never been among those wishing for another anthem. I loved all the patriotic songs, and each had its place. But, for me, no

rendition of a hymn or anthem ever matched the power of this day's performance by these young, wide-eyed kids from Norfolk. Full of hope and promise,
they sang of a nation they would come to love and serve—a nation, I prayed
silently as I listened, that would continue to nurture each of them in the shade
of its sturdy branches.

One of the hymn's stanzas in particular captured my view of what makes
America unique, and I repeated some of those words as I began my final and
most important reflection of the day. Here was where I meant to offer hope
that our politics could be mended and again serve us well.

"America! America! God mend thine every flaw. Confirm thy soul in self-control, thy liberty in law."

The gift of freedom indeed requires self-control—acts
of faithful stewardship from each of us. And good stewardship begins with an attitude of thankfulness and humility.

Indeed, whatever we may believe religion portends for
individual lives and souls, this much is clear: A wholesome
humility is faith's indispensable contribution to the healthy
functioning of a republican society.

The great lawgiver Moses, ever faithful and grateful, said
this to his people:

Remember how the Lord your God led you all the
way in the wilderness these forty years, to humble
and test you.... He humbled you, causing you to
hunger and then feeding you with manna, which
neither you nor your ancestors had known.... When
you have eaten and are satisfied, praise the Lord
your God for the good land he has given you. Be
careful that you do not forget the Lord your God,
failing to observe his commands.... Otherwise,
when you eat and are satisfied, when you build fine
houses and settle down, and when your herds and
flocks grow large and your silver and gold increase
and all you have is multiplied, then your heart will
become proud and you will forget the Lord your

God, who brought you out of Egypt, out of the land of slavery.... You may say to yourself, "My power and the strength of my hands have produced this wealth for me."

This admonition has a message for people of all faiths and of uncertain faith as we reflect today on a journey, not of 40 years, but of 400. For it is from a spirit of humility and gratitude that comes the character to make good choices and a heart that inspires service.

From the dawn of liberty in ancient Athens, the Greeks understood that freedom's great enemy is hubris—the belief on the part of a man that he has the wisdom, the strength, and the right to rule over other men without divine blessing and human consent. The Greeks also understood that the choice between humility and hubris is a matter of personal decision rooted in morality—a capacity for virtuous self-restraint that our Creator gave us when he set our minds free.

So, too, does our landmark charter of religious liberty, the Virginia Statute for Religious Freedom, ascribe our freedom to divine consent, invoking "the plan of the Holy author of our religion, who being Lord both of body and mind, yet chose not to propagate it by coercions on either, as was in his Almighty power to do...."

This fundamental notion—that we enjoy our essential liberties because of divine forbearance—is a crucial premise for republican harmony and constructive community. For if God, who is sovereign and really does have all the answers, nevertheless leaves it to us to make choices and even to err, shouldn't we, who are not sovereign and don't have all the answers, at least accord our fellow citizens the same respect?

Humility born of trust in God's good purpose is what gives us the wisdom to promote our ideas while respecting the ideas of others.

Humility born of awe at God's unlimited power is what gives us the boldness to proclaim the faith we hold as Truth while acknowledging that a sovereign Hand is great enough to work through the varied faiths of others.

Humility born of gratitude for God's abundant blessings is what gives us the passion to jealously guard our freedom and then freely sacrifice it to be a blessing to others.

The great wonder of our freedom is that a God who could command our thoughts nevertheless created the mind free, and in so doing displayed the very humility he desires from each of us.

It is a humility that, for the believing settlers who arrived here four centuries ago, found expression in a cross they erected with thankful hearts—a cross that recalled an act of humility unsurpassed in all time.

At Montpelier, in my home county of Orange, two stone lions lie peacefully in the garden behind Madison's mansion. The powerful pair seems not so much subdued as harnessed, just as Madison's genius helped conceive and enact a constitutional framework that harnessed human interest and passion and arrayed them against one another to preserve our freedom and impel us toward productive compromise.

Madison understood, as we all must, that human nature is immutable. Man is capable of great good but also great evil, and of everything in between.

So, too, can our politics in this free land be a vehicle for virtuous service and vital contribution, or an instrument of selfish ambition, seduction, and destruction. It has been and ever will be so.

You see, my friends, we are still in the lion's den.

In public life as in private, not every decision, not even most decisions, pose momentous choices between good and evil—though some do.

Not every circumstance requires divine intervention to close the mouth of the lions—though some do.

Not every threat is a mortal one—though some are.

But every day we face decisions that present opportunities to act with integrity, principle, and humility, or to compromise our integrity and surrender principle to pride.

We have the unparalleled gift of free will in a free land. And yet we exist on an earthly plane in which the course of history has already been written by One who knows no limitations of time and space. Thus, in the final analysis, it is less important that our decisions yield success or failure, victory or defeat, than that they be right and good decisions, as God empowers us to understand what is right and good.

"[W]ith firmness in the right, as God gives us to see the right," Lincoln said shortly before his labors ended, we must "strive on to finish the work we are in."

What we ought to commemorate, then, during this day and throughout this anniversary year, is the *great blessing of good decisions*. Decisions—often very difficult choices—made by men and women of free will in circumstances we can hardly imagine, under the watchful gaze of a loving God who has a special purpose for our Commonwealth and Nation.

We commemorate the choice of stout adventurers to sail here and land here—to pray here and stay here—to erect a fortress up river for their safety and to erect a mighty fortress down through the stream of our nation's history to protect our liberty.

We commemorate the diverse decisions of men and women who lived exemplary lives of public and private service. For as my favorite "northern Virginian," Longfellow, put it:

> *Lives of great men all remind us*
> *We can make our lives sublime,*
> *And, departing, leave behind us*
> *Footprints on the sands of time....*

We give thanks for those who left footprints to guide us—for the stern, impassioned stress of pilgrims and pioneers who over four centuries made good decisions in times of comfort and crisis, in sunshine and shadow, on the high mountaintops of their sweetest successes and in the deep valleys of their most desperate trials.

Decisions to take a chance and pursue a dream.

Decisions to make promises and keep them ... to admit wrongs and right them.

Decisions to invest and increase rather than husband and divide—to serve rather than subsist and give rather than take.

Decisions to risk everything for an idea, even to pledge one's very life, fortune, and sacred honor to a just cause.

Why do we recall this history, these choices throughout our history that reflect the "better angels of our nature"? Certainly not to indulge some vain triumphalism or self-satisfied exceptionalism. Nor out of some naively optimistic notion of human perfectibility or democratic inevitability.

Indeed, the opposite should be our purpose.

In spite of our modern minds, we must apprehend the existence of an evil that still stalks the land like a lion. It still has the power to astonish us with brutality and cruelty and the capacity, even propensity, of human beings to oppress and harm other human beings. We do not understand it. And what shocks us most is the realization that this evil is not some alien affliction, a tyrant's or terrorist's malevolence that we can fend off through fortification or force of arms. The truly astonishing thing is that this potential—the potential for good and evil, the presence of good *with* evil—lurks within every human breast.

Yet, in this astonishment lies our hope, because it lifts us from our lethargy. It makes us cry out that things are not as they should be. And it sends us on a search for meaning and purpose. It sends us to the lessons of history, to the examples of people who chose well. And it makes us look within, and beyond, at the faith we hold and the character we bring to bear as we choose. We do not know why God gives us the

561

freedom to choose and, in so empowering us, licenses both the good and evil consequences of our choices. But we know the burden of choosing falls on each of us, and we can choose now to choose well.

There is no problem in America today that is beyond the ken of good people striving to make good choices.

There is no politics so dysfunctional that it cannot be remedied through goodwill rooted in good purpose.

The laments about the contemporary state of our politics are exhaustingly familiar: the erosion of the American center and the rise of extremes; the inability to find common ground and compromise for the common good; the prevalence of self-seeking politicians who put partisan ambition first; the dominance of remote and unaccountable bureaucracies; the virulence of ideological news organs and online outlets that stoke anger and alienation; the easy foothold that falsehood gains through our separation into self-reinforcing enclaves of likeminded opinion and perpetual grievance; the loss of civic knowledge and civic spirit and the collective memory necessary to preserve republican principles and a republican culture; the relentless meanness, pettiness, and coarseness of it all.

What must we do?

I will tell you what I believe. There are four things.

First, we must *renew the American narrative.*

Without a story that enables us to make sense of our lives, that gives us hope amid our struggles and lifts our sights, people see only devils.

Our story—America's story—the stories I have told today and a million others—are the story of a shining city on a hill. That city is not our present reality, but it can be our earnest pursuit. And, here, two things matter most.

First, ours is a city forged, not from identity but from ideals—from timeless principles, the cornerstone of which is Freedom. Our foundational belief that all people are created equal and endowed by their Creator with unalienable rights to life, liberty, and the pursuit of happiness. Our conviction that all persons, of every race, place, gender, and creed deserve the chance to pursue their dreams, to go as far as their God-given talents and their character, hard work, and perseverance will take them.

And, second, our city is a caring community. We stand not only for timeless ideals grounded in Freedom but for authentic relationships rooted in Love. We seek to live by the Golden Rule, to hear and understand others' stories and to help them, not because a government commands it, nor because our reputations compel it, nor because a guilty conscience insists on it. We help others because we are grateful for the ways God has blessed us, and we choose to be a blessing to others: faith expressing itself through love.

These are not hostile ideologies—individualism versus communitarianism. They are essential parts of the balanced American narrative that we must recover. Not self-reliance *or* caring communities, but self-reliance *and* caring communities. Not liberty *or* justice, but liberty *and* justice. Not Freedom *or* Love, but Freedom *and* Love.

"I've spoken of the shining city all my political life," Ronald Reagan said in his farewell address, "but I don't know if I ever quite communicated what I saw when I said it.... In my mind it was a tall, proud city built on rocks stronger than oceans, windswept, God-blessed, and teeming with people of all kinds living in harmony and peace; a city with free ports that hummed with commerce and creativity. And if there had to be city walls, the walls had doors and the doors were open to anyone with the will and the heart to get there. That's how I saw it, and see it still."

Let us see it that way, too, and let us not be embarrassed to say so. For if we declare this creed, if we write it on our hearts and teach it to our young people, if we impart not only civic tactics but civic values, then soon we will find that we are living out this ideal more and more, day by day. And with God's help it will heal our land.

So that is number-one: renew the American narrative.

But, closely related to renewing the narrative is stopping the destruction. We cannot hope to build up if we keep tearing down. So the second thing we must do is *stop tearing down each other, and stop tearing down our country*.

This is a choice that belongs to each of us. We can each re-solve that we will not answer offense with offense; that we will not turn our opponents into enemies; that being shunned or shouted at, we will not seek to win by out-shunning or out-shouting others; that being objects of hate, we will not give hate's corrosive powers an opening to compromise our own core.

Fundamentally, in principle and practice, we must firmly resolve this one thing: that we will not seek to overcome evil with evil, but will seek to overcome evil with good.

That is true in our relationships with each other, and hear me on this: it must also be true of our relationship with our country.

Our founders made no claim that they had framed a per-fect nation. They handed us instead the ever-unfinished busi-ness of forging a "more perfect union."

Sure, they had grievances and gave voice to them—in fact, the Declaration of Independence contains a long litany of them. But they did not wallow in their complaints—they set about putting things right. They were imperfect, as are we all, so there is still more work to do. Yet in that work lies the hope-filled, redemptive part of the American story.

Teaching our country's flaws and failures without teach-ing this striving for renewal is telling only half the story. It is like teaching the culprit's crime but not his repentance, the parents' discipline but not their love, the child's study but not discovery, her struggles but not her hopes.

For too long, our learned elites have been building themselves up by tearing our institutions and ideals down. They have raised smug non-belief to an art form while gen-erating precious little new for us to admire. They have rarely given ... only taken away.

Now, when we can see the effects of this fragmentation in the collapse of our communities and the degeneration of our discourse and the endangerment of our democracy, we all must reckon with the reality. And in this reckoning, it would be a really great thing if those who have long been the biggest beneficiaries of the liberal order—those in the academy, in the media, in business, and in government—would become part of the solution instead of the problem.

Having looked into the abyss that is the antithesis of ordered liberty and principled republicanism—having gotten a glimpse of individualism that tends toward narcissism, and diversity that tends toward relativism, and populism that tends toward authoritarianism—having seen the malignancies of nativism and socialism begin to spread anew—maybe it is time to say that America, land of the free and the home of the brave, is not such a bad idea after all.

Maybe it is time to say that ours is a republic worth keeping, with values worth teaching.

Maybe it is time to say that we have amplified well enough our differences. Now let us celebrate the bright tapestry that has been woven from our wonderfully diverse threads. Let us celebrate the ties of freedom and love that bind us. *E Pluribus Unum*—out of many, one.

This is the challenge of our time for all of our leaders, the duly elected and the self-appointed, on college and corporate campuses, in the fourth estate, in the corridors of power and politics, in whatever positions of influence we may find ourselves. To paraphrase JFK: Ask not what you can criticize about your country; ask what you can do to unify and improve it.

Third, as we renew the American narrative and labor to build up rather than tear down, let us *rediscover the brilliant insights of Madison, and put them to work, as he did, in intensely practical and productive ways.*

If Madison could stare human nature, the most intractable of all problems, in the face and not wring his hands

... if he instead could take the landscape as he found it, roll up his sleeves, and build on it ... then surely we can do better in our time than sit around like lumps lamenting today's dysfunction and division.

If he were here today, I imagine the man from Montpelier would have some very pointed things to say.

I think he would begin by reminding us that we don't have it so bad. At least, there are no bayonets at our bellies, no hangman's noose or firing squad awaiting us for defying the king. So we really have no excuse for sitting around feeling sorry for ourselves.

Second, he'd remind us that human beings are not born with an innate understanding of republican principles and practice. Good citizenship is a learned behavior—the product of education and the cultivation of civic habits, including informed and respectful contention, collaboration, and compromise. If we want to be a virtuous self-governing community that exhibits these habits, we must work at teaching them.

Next, Madison would remind us that the American system is predicated on the competition of ideas, so if you do not agree with the agenda of the political factions on the far Right or far Left, then you should join or form your own faction and engage in the great contest.

Don't be bullied by the decibels and deceits, the self-worship of passion over reason. Use the tools of your times to outsmart and outwork your opponents.

He'd be too modest to cite his own example—outworking and outsmarting the mesmerizing Patrick Henry to win a great victory for the Constitution—but there is a lesson there for us all.

Finally, Madison would challenge each of us to get to work in our personal spheres of influence and opportunity, helping our neighbor and our community flourish in freedom.

Here, after all, was a comfortable young man from the backwoods of Virginia who sensibly could have left the deep thought and hard work to more established figures. Instead, he closeted himself in his little library with all the collected wisdom he could lay his hands on and went about the process of preparing a plan.

Somewhere along the way he gained the insight that good governance is about achieving balance, a healthy tension that not only forestalls excess but fosters reasoned deliberation and productive compromise. He made the pursuit of that balance his life's work, and, in so doing, he offered a prescription for ours.

Madison's particular project was balancing the shifting exigencies and excesses of federal and state power—vital work that continues today. As with any such dynamic arrangement, times change, and so do the demands. There was a time not so long ago, for example, when strong federal power was needed to right the civil wrongs in the states where essential liberties and equal justice were denied.

In our day, the balance of national and local power has tilted heavily in favor of Washington, D.C., and the massive bureaucratic and regulatory state ensconced there, producing a distance and detachment that threaten to undermine personal and community responsibility. Our political discourse suffers, too, because civility and self-restraint arise from personal relationships—from friendships, and caring, engaged communities. And these essential elements of republican life are eroded when decisions are made in remote and unaccountable chambers and when debates occur in angry anonymity over the Internet.

If we mean to restore a vibrant republicanism, we must get engaged in the work that is within our reach. For most of us, that means working for the improvement of our neighborhoods and communities, our workplaces, and the people right around us. And because some of the solutions will be public rather than private, we must insist on the return of government decisions to a level within our productive influence.

The theoretical word for it is "federalism," but the point is simply this: the Madisonian vision of balance today requires that we bring freedom *home*.

So we must renew the American narrative, resolve to build up rather than tear down, and exercise our freedom practically and productively in the manner of Madison. But there is one other thing we must do to keep and renew our Republic.

In *The Irony of American History*, Reinhold Niebuhr wrote these words:

> Nothing that is worth doing can be achieved in our lifetime; therefore we must be saved by hope. Nothing which is true or beautiful or good makes complete sense in any immediate context of history; therefore we must be saved by faith. Nothing we do, however virtuous, can be accomplished alone; therefore we are saved by love. No virtuous act is quite as virtuous from the standpoint of our friend or foe as it is from our standpoint. Therefore we must be saved by the final form of love which is forgiveness.

My friends, no one in America today stands more in need of this loving forgiveness than I do, and no one is more grateful for it than I am.

This forgiveness is why, in the American story—indeed, the human story—Freedom and Love are inseparable.

We cannot live in Freedom without making choices. We cannot make choices without committing errors. We cannot overcome our errors without forgiveness. And we cannot find forgiveness without Love.

This is the astonishing freedom story written by the divine Author.

This is the amazing reconciliation modeled by the divine Mediator.

This is the incredible love poured into every human heart by the divine Spirit.

We will never transcend these truths, no matter how much pride and presumption our modern minds bring to the business of self-government. And, try as we might, we will not keep this Republic if we do not affirm these truths for ourselves, practice them in our dealings with others, and pass them along to those who will follow us.

"Stand at the crossroads, and look," the Lord counseled through the prophet Jeremiah in another age, "ask for the ancient paths, ask where the good way is, and walk in it, and you will find rest for your souls."

This timeless counsel is ours today, on this, the 400th birthday of Virginia and America, as we honor all who found themselves at history's crossroads, who looked for the ancient path, who chose the good way, and by whose wisdom and perseverance, through the grace of God, we have reached this blessed station.

Let those who doubt Providence celebrate the startling coincidences of a phenomenally fortuitous fate.

Let those who fear the future one day find a Hope that overwhelms their pride and pessimism.

For the rest of us, let us humbly pray that these choices of four centuries have been acceptable in God's sight, and that he will make us good stewards of his continued blessings upon Virginia and America:

> That he will give us the wisdom and courage to live lives of faithful integrity in the lion's den of our daily lives;

> That he will inspire and embolden us to reach out in loving service as instruments of his peace in our time and place;

> And that, one day, he will bring us home as good and faithful servants who fought the good fight, finished the race, and kept the faith.

My friends, if this is our prayer, then our anniversary commemoration will not be a hollow boast of human achievement or a nostalgic lament for a paradise lost. It will be a celebration of God's abundant blessings—the collaboration of his grace and our enterprise—and a prayer for his continued protection and counsel in the days to come.

For to this a great cloud of witnesses has testified:

Earthly kingdoms rise and fall,
And rulers come and go;
But our Creator watches o'er them all,
And, from Him, all blessings flow.

Let us then use this profound occasion to honor the Father who has so richly blessed us, and, in so doing, renew the noble spirit of Virginia, "the blessed Mother of us all."

The long speech thus ended, its benediction followed by what seemed a deafening silence, I resumed my seat and reflexively closed my eyes as music once again filled the air. This time it was the exultant strains of Beethoven's "Ode to Joy" and the thanks-filled verses of my favorite hymn.

I was grateful for whatever the speech might accomplish, and relieved to be done with it.

But was I really done with it?

Suddenly, I was not sure it was real or finished. Sandberg was reminding me, "Nothing happens unless first a dream."

CHAPTER ELEVEN

CONVERGENCE

If there is a time when I most want to be alone, it is on the shore just before sunrise. So when the older gentleman renting the cottage next door ambled over beneath his crumpled hat and greeted me with a predawn, "Hey, I saw you out here yesterday; you're Danny McGuire, aren't you?" I managed what charitably could be described as a semi-polite grunt.

The price of fame, I sighed … or infamy.

"I wanted to ask, you know, after all that's happened, whether you still believe the system can work," the man said in a tone that betrayed worry but not resignation.

"The system?" I repeated, concealing my irritation with effort. "I guess it depends on what you mean by 'the system.'"

"It doesn't seem like the way the Founding Fathers constructed it is working anymore," the man said. "It doesn't seem like this country can govern itself. You know, I could cash in my chips any day now, but it's my grandchildren I'm worried about."

Part of me wanted to reply that the topic he was raising was a hugely complicated one and certainly not the kind of thing you jaw about with a complete stranger when you are on the beach trying to partake reverently in the awesome sight that is the sun's first appearance to mark a new day. Instead, I found the other part of me, the empathetic and dutiful part, moving to answer.

571

"I still believe in the possibility that free people can govern themselves well. What I have lost faith in is the inevitability of it. I used to be equal parts Madisonian and Jeffersonian, but I think I am fully Madisonian now, and there are even days now when Hamilton doesn't look so bad to me. But, thankfully, there is Washington, who remains the North Star for us all."

There was enough light to see the man's face now, and he seemed to be studying mine quizzically.

"It's up there somewhere," I said, glancing up at the northern sky where the stars recently had receded into the imagination, bowing to the inevitable arrival of a glaring new presence. "We can't lose faith."

Then the other part of me, the selfish, solitary part, took advantage of the pause in conversation and started moving my feet down the beach.

"Gotta go," I said over my shoulder. "Good to chat with you."

The Imprint of Friends

If you are from Virginia, especially if you are a politician from Virginia, you feel a tad guilty about going to North Carolina on vacation. But you go anyway because Corolla is where you and your friends have always gone, even though getting there is always much harder than it needs to be. Your destination is the northern end of the thin sandbar known as the Outer Banks, only about a dozen miles from the Virginia line and less than a day's walk from that False Cape that had been such a well-kept secret until recently. But to get there you have to plunge into the Tar Heel State, all the way down to the vicinity of Kitty Hawk where a bridge transits the Currituck Sound near its southernmost point. Once on the Outer Banks, you then trek back northward in the manner of a resolute tortoise along perpetually over-populated, two-lane Route 12 until you finally arrive at your destination and exhale deeply.

Virginia visitors love to complain about this inconvenient circuity, as if they themselves were not among the nation's foremost slackers when it comes to timely transportation improvements, but I generally was not among the complainers—for one reason. I liked to look south from that bridge over the Currituck, out across what becomes the Albemarle Sound, and see the hazy outlines of Roanoke Island, the place where the 115 English setters of Sir Walter Raleigh's "Lost Colony" tried to make a go of it two decades before

Jamestown. Crossing the sound en route to this Memorial Day retreat, I had mused about the just-completed "America's 400th Birthday" festivities in Virginia. Had fate been more kind to Raleigh's contingent, my big speech likely would have been delivered near Manteo rather than Cape Henry. But then the commemoration actually would have been 20 years earlier; I would have been in my first job out of law school; and some dude or dudette from North Carolina would have been the speaker instead of me.

Sorry, guys, I said in silent tribute to the lost colonists. *It wasn't your fault they left you down here when you belonged in the bosom of the Chesapeake.*

The just-completed commemorative events had been a colossal success. The visits and pronouncements by the President, Her Majesty the Queen, and assorted other dignitaries had garnered broad national notice. Virginia, it seemed, was back on track, and a new generation of Americans had been reminded that the "Old Dominion" was the place their nation began. The President had grabbed the headlines by using the occasion as the backdrop for a JFK-like declaration about the future of space exploration, committing a new generation to an odyssey of discovery akin to that being commemorated. "M-cubed," the project had been instantly dubbed—a manned mission to Mars within the next three decades.

It had fallen to Governor Meade to articulate the meaning of the commemoration for all Virginians, including those whose ancestors lived on the land before the English settlers came, those whose ancestors arrived in chains (as had some of hers), and those who had come to America over the ensuing four centuries, searching, like the first English settlers, for a new world of freedom and opportunity. It had been a unifying occasion, one that reconnected people with their history and made all Virginians feel part of something special. Here, for certain, Dorothy Meade was no accidental governor. Indeed, she appeared to have been made for the moment, her presence in the Commonwealth's highest office conveying a renewed sense of hope that the founding promise of liberty and justice for all could be fulfilled.

My part in it all had been relatively minor. The successive crises surrounding the Nevers and Bell deaths and my personal legal travails had prevented me from participating in much of the planning leading up to the actual anniversary. But on the shores of Cape Henry I had been afforded the chance to share some fundamental beliefs about the interrelation of freedom, faith, and purpose in politics. Though it had a dream-like quality like many of the events during this time, it had been no dream. The moment had been palpably real—and, as things would turn out, transformational.

I was still basking in that triumph's afterglow as I took my solitary morning walk beside the sea at Corolla. Except for one thing—the impending political discussion with my friends—it would have been a carefree stroll. But as I walked along, I reflected on that trio and how much I had benefited from our friendship.

I thought of Preacher and his moral clarity, his fidelity to the law and the uncompromising demands of justice.

I thought of Abby and her passion for good works—deeds divorced from doctrine, rooted in kindness for kindness's sake.

And I thought of Chad's confidence in the unseen hand that orders the interactions of individuals, his belief in self-executing principles and his trust in salutary outcomes flowing from sensible choices.

They represented three faces of my faith. And each was incomplete without the other.

I reflected on Chad's passion for economic freedom, on Mitch's emphatic social conservatism, and on Abby's persistent centrism and moderation.

They represented three factions of my party. And each was incomplete without the other.

I considered the very different journeys that Mitch's and Chad's and Abby's forebears had traveled and the distinctive heritage that was each's birthright. They embodied the three cultures that first came together at Jamestown—the Indians, the English, and the Africans—forerunners of an ethnically diverse Virginia and America.

They had come from varied places to gather around the live oak of liberty—*Quercus virginiana*—and now they were under it together because each was incomplete without the other.

I considered, too, the historical traditions represented by each of my friends. In my mind's eye, I could see Mitch nodding with approval at the revolutionary fervor and uncompromising entreaties of the adamant Adams up north and the fiery Henry down south. I watched Abby smile attentively at the knee of the philanthropic Franklin in Philadelphia and the idealistic Jefferson at Monticello. And I saw Chad frenetically engaged across the Potomac with the calculating visionaries Hamilton and Madison, the former laying the foundation for global enterprise and the latter erecting an elaborate bulwark to make republicanism a practical reality for mankind.

Each of them was incomplete without the other. And even if somehow they had been conjoined, they would have remained incomplete … without *Washington*.

So are we all incomplete without Washington.

Indeed, Washington was incomplete without Washington. He thought he was an 18th-century Gideon, a soldier in the cause of freedom, but he turned out to be a Daniel, too—a politician and statesman. Not only "first in war," but also "first in peace." And, leaving no heir except a nascent nation, he was, in Henry Lee's enduring words, "first in the hearts of his countrymen."

Washington suffered the familiar fate of heroes—becoming an icon at the expense of his ideas. But his ideas were what mattered. He believed the fate of mankind's quest for freedom hinged on America's republican experiment and that his countrymen would remain free only if they found a way also to remain virtuous. Aided by Madison, Washington gave voice to this conviction in his inaugural address:

> No People can be bound to acknowledge and adore the invisible hand, which conducts the Affairs of men more than the People of the United States. Every step, by which they have advanced to the character of an independent nation, seems to have been distinguished by some token of providential agency. And in the important revolution just accomplished in the system of their United Government, the tranquil deliberations, and voluntary consent of so many distinct communities from which the event has resulted, cannot be compared with the means by which most Governments have been established, without some return of pious gratitude, along with an humble anticipation of the future blessings which the past seem to presage….
>
> I dwell on this prospect with every satisfaction which an ardent love for my Country can inspire: since there is no truth more thoroughly established, than that there exists in the economy and course of nature, an indissoluble union between virtue and happiness, between duty and advantage, between the genuine maxims of an honest and magnanimous policy and the solid rewards of public prosperity and felicity:

Since we ought to be no less persuaded that the propitious smiles of Heaven, can never be expected on a nation that disregards the eternal rules of order and right, which Heaven itself has ordained. And since the preservation of the sacred fire of liberty, and the destiny of the Republican model of Government, are justly considered, as *deeply*, perhaps as *finally* staked, on the experiment entrusted to the hands of the American people.

There it is. And that is why, no matter how many geniuses of the founding generation one might succeed in reassembling under that shady live oak today, no matter how many worthy American successors one might place in the seat of power, no matter how many friends might surround and counsel us, they will always be incomplete without Washington.

I learned this not only from our nation's story but from my own journey and from the example of my friends. They and their dynamic interaction over the years had helped forge my own views on politics, religion, and life itself. I had learned from them, and one of the things I had learned was that each of them was incomplete. They needed each other, and now I realized they needed me.

What was it about my journey that filled their need?

I had begun with disdain for politics. But politics had taken me captive—or, rather, a force beyond my control had taken me captive and exiled me to a world where politics was king. In my captivity, I could have embraced the culture of my captors, done okay for myself, and passed the time in relative ease. But, aided chiefly by the entreaties of my friends, the example of my parents, my fascination with history, and the tenets of my faith, I made a different choice.

I listened and learned and studied and prayed. I saw the good and the evil that men do, and for a time I was ecstatic about the good, and then for another time I was petrified by the evil, and I did not understand either of them very well. So I clung to the lifeline of my faith and principles, rode out the storm, and tried to stay true to what I believed. There, in that palace of power and pride and potential, through no design of my own but certainly by no accident, I was called to serve. I made some awful mistakes and also managed a few successes along the way. But I tried to do what was right.

Strolling on the sands, I pondered how others in my life had accommodated themselves to those contradictory realities of politics—to its wonderful potential as a venue for selfless contribution, and to its awful seductiveness and destructiveness as a palace of selfish ambition.

I thought of one who had youthful promise. There had been a slight glimmer of hope, a vague prospect of worthy endeavor, or at least its illusion. But whatever possibility of good once existed, it had been ruthlessly, relentlessly squeezed out of him, suffocated and snuffed and wrung out of him by politics in all its corruptible majesty and power. There had been no evident event, no raw deal or unearned prize, that had thrown his moral compass out of whack. There was no discernible cause and ill effect, no easy lesson to draw, such as "avoid this" or "resist that" and you, too, can emerge from the crucible with your character and integrity intact. Instead, there had been only a stark, stubborn stain and a deeply disturbing mystery about why it was there.

I thought of another—eventually, a mentor and role model for me—who had gotten off to a shaky start. He had ventured near the precipice, but in time he had found his way, had discovered his core convictions, and by God's grace had been given the conscience and courage to change.

Both of them were dead to this world now. I could see that, in life, they had been like two men passing on adjacent escalators, Bart heading down and Governor Nevers heading up. They were at the same place for a short time and engaged each other. They for a while even seemed to be very much like each other. But they were very different men, destined to go in different directions.

They were two sides of the same political coin. On one side was the possibility of redemption; on the other, self-destruction. Heads you win; tails you lose. And yet it was not chiefly a game of chance—it was mostly a matter of choice.

It was apparent to me now that, although church and state are appropriately protected from each other, and in fact each thrives by virtue of that separation, faith and freedom are inseparable. They are inseparable because a palpable evil still stalks the land, and it will always stalk the land, and only the collaboration of freedom and faith is strong enough to overcome it. Freedom affords man the opportunity to choose. Faith equips him to choose wisely. Each blessing is incomplete without the other—meaning, the world is without hope except when it is the object of God's grace and man's endeavor.

Reflecting on that truth at the water's edge brought to mind my favorite line from President Kennedy's majestic inaugural address, delivered some 17 decades after Washington's. It was not the familiar "Ask not what your country can do for you...," though that was a fine sentiment. Rather, my favorite was JFK's closing exhortation: *"[L]et us go forth to lead the land we love, asking His blessing and His help, but knowing that here on earth God's work must truly be our own."* An elegantly simple statement, I thought, and one that captured the proper relationship between church and state. So decoded, the great national conundrum about politics and religion appeared to be no puzzle at all.

I smiled as I thought of Granddaddy McGuire and how pleased he would be that here I was, 40-plus years later and down South, taking inspiration from America's first Irish Catholic president. That this first Catholic chief executive hailed from the former bastion of intolerance, the Massachusetts Bay colony, was ironic enough. That the dispositive pronouncement on religion and politics had come from a playboy and a Democrat seemed almost comical. Yet, the paths all converge eventually—the Democrats and the Republicans, the Green and the Orange, the Redcoats and the Continentals, the Jeffersonians and the Federalists, the North and the South, the liberals and the conservatives, the creators and the consumers, the self-serving and the self-denying, even the believers and the non-believers. In the end, the thing that unites us all is what Robert Penn Warren called the "awful responsibility of Time." It is the price of freedom: *the burden of choosing.*

My father had told me on a distant river of my youth that God does not write the correct choices across the sky for us or send word by winged messengers, at least not in the ordinary course. But he does equip us for the choices that life presents; he shapes and molds the character from which those choices will issue. And it is our business, our charge, to be serious stewards and diligent participants in that preparation. We will fall short at times, inevitably. But we need to work at getting ourselves ready and knowing where to draw the line, so that when our trial comes, as it surely will—when that moment of truth is before us—we will be able to spot it, recognize it for what it is, meet it head on, and do the right thing.

THE MESSENGER RETURNS

On that solid note, my seaside reflections ended, and I headed back to the cottage, refreshed and focused. My consequential afternoon walk with Chad, Mitch, and Abby was still hours away—in fact, all three apparently were still sleeping, as were Martha and our crew. So I busied myself thumbing through the stack of mail that Martha had retrieved the previous day as we hurried out for the nearly four-hour drive to Corolla. One bulging envelope with an unfamiliar Washington, D.C., return address immediately caught my eye.

Six folded, typewritten pages emerged from the envelope. Scribbled at the top of the first was this barely legible note:

> *Miguel sent me a copy of your 400ᵗʰ birthday speech last week, and I enjoyed it very much. I am sending along something you might find interesting. It is a boiled-down version of what I told my congregation after the last election for president.*

There was no name, but it took only an instant for me to surmise the identity of the sender. It was the same gifted young minister who had visited Miguel's church two years earlier ... the one whose powerful "What's your one thing?" message had afforded me clarity at a crucial moment. Now I was in need of his aid again without knowing it.

In forging my own sensible view of the proper relation between religion and politics, I had defined faith's value largely in terms of its contribution to republican virtue. This was fine as far as it went. But religious liberty and church-state separation had freed the church for something far greater.

"The bitter national election is finally over, and it leaves us with hard questions," the sermon text[2] began.

> *What is the role of Christians in our relationship to the government? How do we understand our political moment? And how do we respond as the community of Jesus Christ?*
>
> *Hear these words from Luke 20, verses 20-26: "Keeping a close watch on [Jesus], they sent spies who pretended to be sincere. They hoped to catch Jesus in something he said so that they might hand him over to the power and the authority of the governor. So the spies questioned him, 'Teacher, we know that you speak and teach what is right, and that you do not show partiality but teach the way of God in accordance with the truth. [So tell us, Teacher:]*

---

[2] Author's note: This text is borrowed, with only minor adaptation, from an actual sermon delivered by Reverend Corey Widmer, senior pastor of Third Church, Richmond, Virginia, on November 13, 2016. The author acknowledges with gratitude Rev. Widmer's permission to use the sermon in this volume.

Is it right for us to pay taxes to Caesar or not?' [Jesus] saw through their duplicity and said to them, 'Show me a denarius. Whose image and inscription are on it?' 'Caesar's,' they replied. He said to them, 'Then, render to Caesar what is Caesar's, and to God what is God's.' They were unable to trap him in what he said there in public. And astonished by his answer, they became silent."

What is going on in this little famous episode?

It says they sent spies. Who is the "they" who sent spies?

The "they" are two groups of Jewish religious leaders, we learn from the Gospel of Mark. The first is the Herodians, who were supporters of the Roman imperial power, and the second are the Pharisees, who were not. These two groups were on opposite sides of the political spectrum, yet they were united around one thing—their hatred of Jesus. And so they came to Jesus, and they posed this hot political question of the day in order to trap him: "Tell us, Teacher, is it right for us to pay taxes to Caesar or not?"

Now, this was a very dangerous question for Jesus to answer because either way he answered—yes or no—he had something pretty serious to lose. If, on the one hand, he said, "Yes, pay your taxes," then he would be seen as siding with the Herodians and a supporter of the Roman occupation, and in doing so he would lose his wide support among the people. But if he were to say, "No, don't pay the taxes," then he would be seen as a political revolutionary, and the leaders could report him as someone inciting sedition against the state and have him arrested and even killed. So, either way, they think, "We've got him!" He will either lose his popularity or he will lose his life, but either way he will lose.

Jesus knows, of course, that it is indeed the Father's plan for him to lose both his popularity and his life, but he knows that now is not the moment. And so he answers with this brilliant answer, an answer so simple that it can be spoken in a single phrase, yet so powerful that it has shaped the theological and political philosophy of the Church for two millennia: "Render to Caesar what is Caesar's, and render to God what is God's." And they fell silent.

What is Jesus saying to us here? I want to look at three simple things that I believe he is calling us to in this passage:

580

First, he is saying that we give to the state our <u>limited allegiance</u>.

Second, we give to God our <u>ultimate adherence</u>.

And, third, we give to the world our <u>generous presence</u>.

So let's look at those things.

First, we give to the state our limited allegiance: Jesus says, "Render to Caesar what is Caesar's."

Now, the fact that Jesus chose to use this word "render" is remarkable ... and brilliant. It literally means "to give what is owed" or "to give back." It is brilliant because it has a double meaning.

First of all, Jesus is clearly instructing his people to give the government our support and our loyalty. He is saying, unequivocally, "Yes, pay your taxes. Participate in the public system. Be engaged."

There were many Jewish communities at the time, especially the Essenes, who because of the Roman occupation encouraged the Jews to move out into the desert and to reject the secular society. And Jesus clearly said, "No—give to Caesar what is his ... pay your taxes ... contribute ... participate."

Regardless of how we feel about the elected leader, we Christians are called to be good citizens, to contribute, to work for the common good of all, and to pray. Regardless of how we voted and whom we preferred, we pray for our president and all of our leaders, that God would give them wisdom, because this is clearly what Jesus calls us to do.

But, on the other hand, Jesus also uses this word "render," which means to give a person what is owed. And what was owed to Caesar by those Christians?

Taxes, yes—but also <u>resistance</u>.

This emperor was a man who claimed to be god. He was in a long line of leaders who claimed to be the choice of the gods: "Therefore, you cannot question us—our authority is absolute."

So, with this simple answer, Jesus essentially births the modern theory of limited government. He says, "No, no, no! No government can be equated with God, and don't you ever dare suggest so. Give Caesar only what he is owed, only his money, but do not give him anything that contravenes your commitment to me and my kingdom."

581

Do you see the brilliance of this?

In a single answer Jesus refuses to give either one of these groups what they wanted, which was for him to take sides in their political debate. He refuses because his agenda and his kingdom cannot be reduced to any simple political program. "My kingdom is not of this world," as he says to Pilate in John 18. Therefore, his kingdom cannot be equated with a party or a platform or an earthly state or kingdom or ruler.

What does this mean for us as followers of Jesus? It means that Christians are called to have an ambiguous relationship with political power.

It has always been this way for Christians. We live in every nation state under heaven. We give our loyalty to those states. But we do not give our ultimate loyalty to any party or platform or earthly nation.

We must never do what Jesus refused to do—to say, "Jesus is for that party or that policy or that person." No. Every political party has things we can affirm, and every political party has things that Christians must resist.

There are no parties that can be called the Christian party. There are no platforms that can be called the Christian platform. There are no nations that can be called a Christian nation because no nation can ever embody the fullness of the kingdom of God.

Even our own nation, which was indeed influenced by Christian ideals and has certain elements that we celebrate and model to the world because they were influenced by Christian principles, is the same nation that enslaved nine million of its own citizens based on a blasphemous theology of human personhood.

So we affirm, yes, and we also resist. We give our loyalty, but it is a limited loyalty. We give our allegiance, but it is a qualified allegiance.

As followers of Jesus, there will be things in the months and years ahead that we can affirm—that uphold life and justice and compassion and dignity. And then there will be things that we must resist—that denigrate life and distort the image of God and neglect justice and mercy, especially for the vulnerable.

That would be the case if any ruler was elected. It will be the case in every election until you die. It is what every Christian community has done in every nation under heaven: We are the loyal opposition.

So we give to the State our limited allegiance—that is the first thing. But, second, we give to God our ultimate adherence.

Jesus's second affirmation is, "Give to God (or render to God) what is God's."

He asks to look at a coin, and he says, "Whose image is on it?"

"Caesar's."

"Okay, give him what is his; give him the money." And, of course, the question he is implying is, "Whose image is on you?"

The answer to that question is, "God's."

Therefore, what do you give to God? Everything—your full, ultimate adherence.

We are familiar with the Apostles' Creed today, which is sort of the Pledge of Allegiance of the Church. It is striking to remember that the earliest creed of the Church is even shorter—just two words, "Kurios Iesous," which is Greek for, "Jesus is Lord."

You know who else called himself "Kurios" when they wrote that creed? Caesar! "Caesar is Lord." He demanded ultimate allegiance and commitment.

In the face of that claim, Christians said, "No!" The Son of God and the incarnate Word of the Father stands against and over all human kingdoms and demands our ultimate allegiance. Jesus and his kingdom is the only one that lasts forever. All of the kingdoms of the world, all that have exalted themselves as the final authority—from Caesar to Herod to Diocletian—all of these kingdoms have toppled and fallen. They are dead, in the grave, assigned a place in the dust of history. And, yet, Jesus reigns, and his kingdom endures forever. Of the increase of his government there shall be no end.

So, what does this mean for us?

Well, I believe it shapes our hopes. Our hope for ourselves and our hope for the world is not in a party or a person or a program or a president, but in Jesus who reigns over all.

From some of the reactions to the election this week that I have witnessed among Christians, it is clear to me that we as a Christian community have put far too much salvation in political power. For many followers of Jesus, politics has become a religion—an idol in which we have invested our hopes.

On one side we have heard language about this being our so-called "last chance to restore America"—a fear-driven panic that has now opened up into a cathartic jubilation, as if the Kingdom of God has come. And on the other side we hear apocalyptic proclamations of doom, declarations of cosmic unraveling, sending us over the brink. But behind both of these reactions is the same shared belief that meaningful change only comes through political power. And that is a lie!

If we put our salvation in a system of politics, our lives will stand or fall on a person of flesh. In fact, history has shown the more power Christians have, the more misguided and conformed to the world we become.

There is also this: Because our ultimate loyalty is to Jesus, it also means that our ultimate relational loyalty is to the people of Jesus, the community of Jesus.

Christians are not a voting bloc. We are a counter-cultural community, one that spans nations and cultures and classes. And because we belong to Jesus, we belong to each other. We are called to identify with each other during this moment more than we identify with anyone else.

Friends, the division in our nation is astonishing! Another election has revealed just how tribalized we are and how unable and unwilling we are to hear one another. And yet the Church is called to be different, friends. Different! We are a community that spans history and nations. We are made up of every kind of person God has made. And we must hear and love one another. We must bear one another's burdens and embody a reconciled community.

And let me just say this, friends: <u>If we feel more at home with people who share our politics than our faith, then we very well may have rendered to Caesar what only belongs to God</u>.

So, as we move forward, let us remember who we are, dear church. We are not first Republicans or Democrats, or progressives or conservatives. We are not even first Americans. We are first the Church, the people of the resurrected King who reigns over all. To him and him alone do we give our ultimate adherence.

So we give to the State our limited allegiance, and we give to God our ultimate adherence. But there is one last thing: We give to the world our generous presence.

One of the most amazing elements of this passage is often overlooked, and that is the fact that Jesus did not have any loose change.

Isn't that kind of funny? Jesus did not even have a coin.

And I think what Luke is doing is portraying this contrast between these two kings. So here is this one king on the coin who is exalted as lord, and here is this other king, this very different kind of king. One king who lives in the palace and another king who lives on the streets. One king who has all the silver and gold and another king who does not even have a nickel. One king who rules through power and force and another king who rules through mercy and suffering love.

Have you ever seen a king like that?

Politicians cannot do anything until they win an election and get power. And when a politician loses or retires or dies, it pretty much is the end of his or her impact. But for Jesus, it is the exact opposite. When Jesus dies, his revolution begins. When Jesus loses, his spirit-filled kingdom people are saved and activated and sent into the world.

All the revolutions in human history have started when people have taken power. But the revolution of Jesus comes when people give their power away.

The kingdom of Jesus never advances through spin, or political maneuvering, or the seizure of power. It always advances through subversive acts of suffering love.

As an example of this, in early Rome, when the plague broke out and began killing many, many people and the streets began to fill with the sick and the dying, the Christians, instead of running away, went into the streets! Can you believe it? They went into the streets to care for the dying, and to help them die with dignity, and to even take on their disease upon themselves.

In that early culture, many girl babies were left to die, and the Christians adopted them and brought them into their own families.

Women and widows in that society were treated as objects to be used, but in the Church they were treated with dignity and cared for.

In a society where the poor were trampled and abused, Christians freely gave their money and their time and their homes.

And let me tell you what happened. In this beautiful, quiet way, as common, everyday, ordinary Christians simply lived for Jesus—giving away their time, giving away their money, giving away their homes, giving away everything—that entire Greco-Roman society changed. And it was not through power; it was through suffering love.

Earthly kingdoms always over-promise, and they always under-deliver. But the kingdom of Jesus takes over ... through the most counter-cultural ways, as His people love their neighbors, and seek the shalom of the city, and care for the weakest members of society, and give their money and their time and their lives away for Jesus, their neighbors, and the world.

My dear brothers and sisters, may we not forget this vision.

It is time for the Church to be the Church.

This has been the call of the Church in every age and every nation and every political environment in history.

We do not need political power to do this work. We only need one thing—Jesus Christ and the Spirit of God that he gives us, even now, in abundance.

"Take heart," he says. "I have overcome the world."

TOGETHER AND APART

It was mid-afternoon now. The sunrise walk and messenger's missive had long since imparted their wisdom. We had enjoyed a busy beach session with the young ones, and playtime recently had yielded to lunch and nap time, prompting Martha and the others to retreat into the cool comfort of our large oceanfront cottage. Mitch, Chad, and Abby had lingered on the beach, eager to engage each other—and me—in their pressing political topic. I was open to discussing it, but not yet. So I let them talk on as we sat in our beach chairs just beyond the waves' reach.

If you are trained as a lawyer, you learn to impose a degree of discipline on the thoughts and ideas that tramp across your brain. You make them line up and then march along, proceeding from some basic principles and premises through a gauntlet of cause/effect, cost/benefit, action/reaction, and so forth, until you arrive at the locus of a reasoned conclusion. This they call a "lawyer's way of thinking."

As an alternative to wandering aimlessly or at least impulsively in loops of sentimental irrationality, mindless bliss, or doleful doubtfulness, this linear and logical approach has much to commend it. But it can also be a form of tyranny, a numbingly efficient imposition on the mind that makes a person so intellectually focused on the rules of the road and the facts on the ground and the science of the locomotion that he or she fails to enjoy the journey and misses all the varied sights—the beauty, gallantry, mystery, virtue, antitheses of virtue, and struggles—that can be observed and encountered along the way. The older I get, the more I relish taking an occasional respite from regimented lawyerly reasoning and letting my mind run—letting thoughts, senses, memories, worries, ideas, and hopes emerge, diverge, and converge in whatever random manner they (and the custodian) choose. Of course, even the mind's seemingly random movement has causes and effects, so there is reason behind the rhyme.

It was an easy thing to let the mind run this day, because the ocean has that effect on you. You cannot sit there next to it very long and not be struck anew by its power and permanence, breadth and beauty, submerged bounty and hidden peril. It always amazes and is ready to send the mind on an adventure. So, as the conversation hummed around me, I relaxed and gazed out across the water toward the horizon to the east, letting my imagination sail free across the gray-brown sea.

Soon three ships appeared on the water, tossed by the waves and storm, their bearings lost, their captains fretting that the Lord of the Sea might have an ill fate in store for them. They pondered the cruel possibility that they had made it this long way only to lose all during the supposedly easy last leg up from the Caribbean to their Chesapeake destination. I smiled, knowing their fate from Smith's account. In a short time, the mysterious forces of nature would complement, not thwart, their human ambitions. Having reminded them of their vulnerability, the fierce storm would subside, the fog would lift, the dawn would break, and the entrance to the Bay would be revealed. It was the object of their odyssey, the result of their well-laid plans and long labors, yet they would finally reach it in a way that would make them shake their heads in awe, perceiving divine protection, even a miracle.

That, I thought, was an apt metaphor for America's odyssey. Indeed, it is how America actually began 400 years ago.

My imagination ran next to a great battle on that same sea. I could see the massive ships of the line lumbering and listing as they maneuvered for advantage and then unleashed lethal broadsides that filled the air with cannon fire and smoke and sent masts flying and sailors plunging into the crystal cold depths. The French fleet of Admiral de Grasse was there just to my north, at the mouth of the Bay, having sailed up from the Caribbean like those first Jamestown settlers a century and three quarters earlier. As with that earlier voyage, de Grasse's would be a turning point in history. His ships prevailed in the Battle of the Capes, and the British fleet was unable to relieve Cornwallis at Yorktown. Surrender followed, and the war for American independence effectively was won.

Next my mind's eye spotted a massive black monolith, though it appeared only as a tiny line, a dash on the horizon, from my vantage point. It was the unmistakable silhouette of a great super-carrier, and I imagined it was CVN-76, the *Ronald Reagan*, sailing south parallel to the Outer Banks en route from Naval Station Norfolk, just down river from Newport News where it had been built, to its new West Coast home—San Diego, the self-proclaimed "Jamestown of the Pacific." Like so many other carriers and great vessels, it left the safe haven of Hampton Roads and exited the mouth of the Bay, bound for a place in history sure to be significant, perhaps even pivotal, in mankind's quest for liberty.

The mysterious chapters yet unwritten, if somehow foreseeable, would surely strike any reasonable observer at once as preposterous. For history already had crafted a story line so bizarre, so full of intricate plots and surprising twists and supremely improbable events that one would have been inclined to fault the author for melodrama were the author not *The Author*.

A string of random seaborne images floated in quick succession across my imaginary ocean. Drake and Newport and Gosnold. Davies sailing to England to raise money for the College of New Jersey, then surviving the treacherous return and emerging from the wintertime tempest to spot this coast. My ancestor

Rolfe and his storm-driven fellows, finding safe haven on Bermuda and then improving their way here on the *Patience* and the *Deliverance*. Blackbeard plundering ships over here; the *Monitor* and the *Merrimac* battling over there; German U-boats and Soviet subs lurking ominously in the depths; Teddy Roosevelt looking on proudly as the Great White Fleet commenced its international cruise from the Jamestown Exposition in 1907, ushering in what would become the American century. Mitch returning from his tour in the Gulf, and thousands upon thousands just like him, separated from their wives and husbands and children and parents and friends, coming and going and coming of age, and all of them serving.

History holds the copyright to a million such stories ... and more.

Patrick Henry once observed that there is no way to judge the future but by the past. This I had come to believe, and so I had come full circle. I dwelled anew on the past, on the 400-year odyssey begun at Jamestown, and on the broader story of man and his Maker. Yet, I did not dwell on it in the same manner as in my youth, when history supplied a means of diversion and an escape from the apprehension of any present duty. Now I looked upon history as a part of me, a clue to my identity—the thing that gazed back when I looked in the mirror. Now I was not a spectator but, as Teddy Roosevelt put it, a man in the arena. And so I looked upon history as a resource, a guide, a means of informing choices so that I might influence, as positively as possible, the future course of events.

And, yet, the great ocean also reminded me where true sovereignty resides. "The sea is not less beautiful in our eyes because we know that ships are sometimes wrecked," wrote Simone Weil. "On the contrary this adds to its beauty. If it altered the movement of its waves to spare a ship it would be a creature gifted with discernment and choice, and not this fluid perfectly obedient to every external pressure. It is this perfect obedience that makes the sea's beauty."

And then my thoughts brought me ashore.

My ruminations were suddenly interrupted when I glanced a short ways up the beach and spied a small child, who could not have been more than four or five, frolicking near the water's edge. Knowing the dangers, I scanned quickly and was relieved to spot his attentive guardian—mother, aunt, sister, or friend—eagle-eyeing every movement from beneath an aquamarine umbrella that fluttered in the breeze nearby.

The little boy, when standing, resembled a stubby, two-tone fire hydrant—the top half was all unclad head and torso; the bottom half, a baggy pair of red swimming trunks that draped to the sand's surface like a long skirt or small tent. Yet, the drapery did not impede his movements. He and his tender faculties were engaged in earnest business of the most playful sort, evading the bubbling, chasing remnants of each encroaching wave by racing fitfully onto higher sand and then, with youthful stealth to rival the sand crabs, bounding down airily behind each retreating wave amid the cascading sand and shells, invading the ocean's coveted space for just a brief but victorious moment before the sea spotted the young interloper and sent another good-natured wave to chase him back onto the beach.

This process repeated itself perhaps 30 times or so while I watched, and it was interrupted only when he would spot a well-worn shell that resembled a sizeable flat rock. Those occasional sightings seemed to divert the boy's attention altogether until he disposed of the distraction by leaning low to his right and, with a familiar side-arm motion, hurling the flat object toward the ocean. The big flat shells, worn rock-like by sand and sea, presented him with an opportunity to do what little boys do, which is imitate their fathers. Skipping rocks being one of those skills that fathers use to impress their offspring, it was apparent from his technique that this youngster had been well schooled in the basic art. Now, though, he was engaged in a bit of frustrating self-instruction about corollary principles—among them, that you cannot skip rocks on waves, and you cannot throw them at the proper angle when the surf is in the way, and, most important, a shell is not a rock and does not know what a rock knows about piercing the wind.

These inconvenient discoveries did not appear the least disconcerting to him. The boy was so obviously and obliviously happy in this solitary form of entertainment that it brought to mind a similar scene, though in vastly different elements. Nature, wrote Robert Frost, had supplied ice-covered birch trees for the amusement of young boys who were too far from town to play baseball and whose only entertainment was what they could do alone. And so a boy would subdue his father's birch trees, one by one, by climbing nimbly to the uppermost branches and then flinging himself out, feet first, and kicking his way joyfully to the ground. The clicking trees, once subdued by boy and ice, would stay bent, bearing testimony to the collaboration of man and nature long after the boy was a man and the man was gone.

"So was I once a swinger of birches. And so I dream of going back to be," Frost had written wistfully.

It was a sentiment to which I could well relate, and I smiled at the image created in my mind's eye as I felt the warm comfort of halcyon days back in Orange.

Not compelled to dribble in this free-flowing mind game, I switched pivot feet and let the newly introduced subject of Frost and his poetry carry me in another direction.

"I shall be telling this with a sigh somewhere ages and ages hence: Two roads diverged in a wood, and I—I took the one less traveled by, and that has made all the difference."

That was perhaps Frost's most memorable image, and I imagined that he had written it with me in mind—me, and others like me. Such remarkable journeys marked by consequential choices along the way.

I retraced some of the points where paths had diverged before me, and recalled Dr. S. D.'s early invocation of Yogi Berra's wisdom. "When you reach a fork in the road, you have to take it"—I understand that now. Perhaps there is a right way to go and a wrong way to go. Or perhaps there are just two ways. Perhaps, like those raindrops that fall in the hills near Virginia Tech, some are meant to follow one path to the sea and others are meant to go a strikingly different route. But each in its own way does what it is called upon to do. It nourishes anew the creation through which it flows; it etches its own mark onto the river bed; it delights in its own distinctive journey; and all along it pays tribute to the Source as it makes its way to the same great sea.

I was, by now, thoroughly invested in this watery metaphor and its encouraging message about unity, diversity, and the varied course of things. And yet it also brought to mind a nagging problem, since the metaphor seemed preoccupied with the perspective of the individual traveler.

Individualism is what I long had been about. It was my personal creed. And when I was taken captive by politics, it had become my political creed as well. Yet, my life to this point had borne little witness to the ethic of individualism as ultimate truth. To the contrary, my journey seemed to make a more powerful case for the concept of community. It was human beings in relationship with one another, in collaboration with one another, in creative tension and competition with one another, who were changing the world. Their relationships were what supplied the common effort, the collaborative genius, the constructive compromise, the caring communities, the trust, civility, and solidarity essential for republican success.

And then I thought about Frost's tuft of flowers, among my favorite of all the pictures he painted with his words. The little clump of flowers by the brook had been spared earlier when the grass was mown, and the joy of seeing them there united the later witness of the scene with the one whose labor had created it. The truth disclosed was universal: "Men work together," Frost had said from the heart, "whether they work together or apart."

The story connecting me to this wonderful little poem had been told first by my grandfather when I was a young boy. Not by my Granddaddy McGuire, as one might have supposed given his affinity for Frost, but by my maternal grandfather, Senator Daniel. The details, including the identities that made this a truly impressive family tale, had been filled in by my mother years after his death. A youthful and (by that day's standards) liberal Massachusetts politician—who would turn out to be Camelot's most eminent prince—had come south in the turbulent fifties and had been presented to a skeptical audience by a stalwart conservative Virginia Democrat—who turned out to be my eminent state senator grandfather. As a cross-cultural encounter, I imagined this political event must have somewhat resembled my parents' nuptials, when Irish Catholic McGuires from New England and Southern Protestant Daniels mixed, mingled, and enjoyed each other's company, celebrating with unexpected ease a union that was awkward even during those relatively recent and enlightened times.

With little or nothing in common politically, the Virginia politician had welcomed his New England guest by invoking Frost's insight from the tuft of flowers. Men had worked together, even though apart, at Plymouth and Jamestown, at Boston and Williamsburg, forging a new nation. Men in the North and in the South had worked together, even though apart, for independence, for religious liberty, for free commerce, for individual opportunity, for national defense. In recent years, the Virginian had noted, they sometimes tended to be far apart politically (though, he wryly observed, at least their 20th century disagreements had not occasioned resort to arms as in the 19th). But no matter how far apart they were on the issues of the day, whenever men of conscience and goodwill chose to pursue high ideals and the betterment of others, they "worked together," my Granddad had said from the heart, "whether they worked together or apart."

The message embedded in this cherished Daniel family moment now struck me as profound, and I wondered why the custodian had not served it up for my reflection a bit sooner. We had been talking up Jamestown's 400th birthday for years and had relished correcting—13 years before a like anniversary could be observed at Plymouth—the myth of New England preeminence and *Mayflower* primacy in the founding of America. It was a myth that surely needed correcting, if only in the interest of truth. Yet, Frost's tuft of flowers reminded me that Jamestown and Plymouth worked together in the planting of our nation, as did Jefferson and Adams in the cause of independence and, later, the emergence of party politics, as did Winthrop and Williams, Henry and Madison in the reconciling of faith and freedom, as did so many throughout our history.

They worked together, even though they were far apart.

It brought to mind again the Bard's wisdom: "[M]any things ... may work contrariously," the Archbishop of Canterbury observed in *Henry V*, "as many arrows, loosed several ways, fly to one mark; as many several ways meet in one town; as many fresh streams run in one salt sea; as many lines close in the dial's centre. So may a thousand actions, once afoot, end in one purpose, and be all well borne without defeat."

So may a thousand influences transform one life.

So may one life transform a thousand others.

It is not only politicians and parties and political ideas and ideologies that find themselves alternately in competition, cooperation, and conflict. The underlying ethics of individualism and community, of independence and relationship, of liberty and order, of idea and fact, are locked in tension and have been throughout our history. It has been, and is still today, a healthy, Madisonian kind of tension, producing a felicitous balance.

Ideas and interests collide like atoms, producing heat and light. It is the energy of democracy, of enterprise, of human endeavor writ large. Free individuals discern their values, make their choices, and undertake their initiatives within a system of reliable and fair rules that are honored by the other individuals who comprise the community. Among those choices, where freedom reigns, are the creative actions we call production and commerce and the self-denying acts of compassion we call charity and service. From this intricate pattern of action, reaction, and interaction—this continuously humming engine of creation and destruction, self-pursuit and self-denial—can come great good for the community and those who comprise it.

Unity is able to gain rather than lose from this freedom-inspired tension. A flipped coin has distinct sides, separate heads and tails, yet they are joined forever in the process of choosing. Capitalism exalts self-interest, but the efficacy of its markets rests on competitive cooperation with others, engendering interdependence. "All politeness is owing to Liberty," wrote Shaftesbury. "We polish one another, and rub off our corners and rough sides by a sort of amicable collision."

All this was so—and important. But Frost's tuft of flowers had marked a portal into something even closer to the essence. While turning the grass after another had mown it, his student had discovered a bond that transcends time and distance, characteristic and creed, competition and choice. He discovered a bond of intertwined cause and effect, just like that stunningly efficient, humming engine, yet united by something grander than causation and efficiency. It was united by *joy*. And if a common joy, born of a common humanity and Creator, could unite the loves and labors of kindred spirits unseen and unknown to one another in the manner of the mower and the turner of the grass, then how much more, how much better, could it unite men and women who actually saw one another, who witnessed each other's struggles and sacrifices and successes and failures, who laughed at each other's follies and felt each other's pain, and who could identify with each other's fears and doubts and hopes and loves ... because they had them, too.

In America, this common joy has found broad, if not universal, expression in certain cherished, self-renewing ideals. It has been manifest in a common love of God, a faith that transcends doctrinal differences even as it depends on those same differences to sift out truth. It has been manifest in a common love of Country, a patriotism that transcends political factions even as it depends on those same factions to refine choices and check excess. And it has been manifest in a common love of Liberty, an idea that transcends individual interests even as it depends on principles of individual worth, dignity, and self-fulfillment to give society its moral compass.

These ruminations by the sea were the kind that encouraged. The reflections triggered by Frost's poem brought home, not only that Americans had worked together and apart for shared ideals, but that I myself had played a small but active part in that grand tradition. I certainly had the scars to show that the process of governing in a competitive political system is often a perilous and painful one. But the payoff in terms of positive results had been enormous.

Yet, there nagged a disturbing loose end, an unresolved residue from my mental meandering: What about those who do not share the underlying ideals

... who do not adhere to the basic principles? What about the Barts of the world for whom the pursuit and exercise of power becomes the end in itself? What about the people and politicians who do not know where to draw the line, or even why a line is needed?

"Power always sincerely, and conscientiously, believes itself right," Adams had written to Jefferson.

> Power always thinks it has a great soul, and vast views, beyond the comprehension of the weak; and that it is doing God service, when it is violating all His laws. Our passions, ambition, avarice, love, resentment, etc., possess so much metaphysical subtlety, and so much overpowering eloquence, that they insinuate themselves into the understanding and the conscience, and convert both to their party....

Gosh, I mused, *after all this time I still don't know what is to be done about that.*

"DREAMER, GO LONG!"

I had tuned out my friends' conversation, the better to enjoy my private sojourn. But now Mitch shattered the reverie.

"Dreamer, go long!" he shouted, suddenly on his feet motioning down the beach with his left hand as he pulled the football back toward his shoulder with his right and planted his prosthetic leg in the sand.

"Oh, no, not now, Preacher," I moaned in a weak and irresolute-sounding protest. "I'm chilling here!"

Even as I said this, I was already beginning to climb out of my beach chair, because I knew what was coming and its irresistible effect. It used to happen a lot on the beach, but that had been a while ago. Now the clouds had lifted, and a semblance of unworried youthful exuberance had returned to our lives.

"It's September 14, 1978, and we're here at Madison County High, where the Fightin' Hornets have time for just one more play with the game on the line. With 45 yards to go, everyone in the stadium knows what's coming—it will be Jackson going downfield to McGuire ...."

The sound of Mitch's mock reporting faded as my bare feet dug deeply into the sand and I hurled my body southward down the beach as fast as my now-brittle limbs could carry me. I had heard enough of Mitch's report to know whether to turn in or out. It was the Madison game, so I turned out and hauled the pass in over my right shoulder. But on that field there had been no sand castle remnants, and I had sprinted unmolested into the end-zone. Here, I tripped over the abandoned ramparts and tumbled onto the hard wet sand, fractured shells, and pea-size particles, head over heels, looking ridiculous to anyone watching, and rising with sand pasted from the top of my head to the tip of my toes.

The ball did not come out, however.

I dove into the surf to wash off the sand, and then Mitch and I resumed passing the football as we made our way down the beach and then back a ways. Currituck Light was occasionally in view between the large cottages lining the dunes, and when it poked through it reminded me of my mom in the stands, peering proudly through the cheering crowd at our heroic antics on the field. She always worried about an injury, and I always told her that was silly. I was indestructible, after all. Oh, well....

Abby and Chad headed our way and went on past us. "C'mon," Abby instructed as she passed by. "We've decided to take a walk."

Since the days of my misspent youth on the beaches of the Outer Banks and Virginia Beach down south and Newport and Little Compton up north, I have made a number of salient observations about walks on the beach and the purposes they serve.

First, there is the solitary morning purpose. You walk alone before the noise and rush of the day, spending time with your hopes or worries, your memories, your ideas ... and, if you believe, your God. You work through things in your mind while the ocean, where life itself began, soothes your soul.

The second reason to walk, proceeding chronologically, is the daytime walk of discovery. You walk with kids, looking for shells, chasing gulls and sandpipers, avoiding the waves, eyes peeled for the telltale dorsals of the porpoises paralleling the beach, the powerful, crashing descent of the pelican after he spots his next meal, and other intriguing sights. These are short walks because of little legs and big distractions, but they are walks full of joy and wonder. Sadly, our kids outgrow them very fast, and most of us realize too late how very magical and unique are these fleeting moments.

The third reason to walk is because you are in love. It is the quiet late-afternoon or evening walk, the sunset or moonlight stroll, when you are there with your sweetheart and bride and lover, whether of one year or 25. She is forever young in your heart—your trusted companion and very best friend. And so you walk at the edge of the great sea, and the sunlight or moonlight showers you, in its own way, but always the same way. And you offer a silent pledge and prayer that your love will last as long as these permanent attendants remain, these faithful friends that Creation has provided to fill your senses and refresh and renew whenever you return to the shore.

And, then, there is the fourth reason to walk—the distinctive one that my friends and I developed over the years of beach-borne reflections to preserve our political secrets: we walked so we could talk and no one could overhear.

The context of the day's discussion gave me every reason to assume this was the fourth kind of walk. The beach was sparsely populated, and there would have been no plausible risk of a breach even if we had remained stationary. But the habit of working out our political stratagems in ambulation was now so well established that the original rationale retained little relevance. Our minds seemed to work better when our bodies were in motion.

Mitch and I continued to pass football, but Abby and Chad were already thick into a discussion of polls and voting blocs, potential rivals and allies, donors, endorsements, messages by region, and so forth. I continued to run patterns and work Preacher's arm because I knew that whenever I stopped, I would be drawn into a full-blown discussion of the topic that, until now, I successfully had avoided.

For Abby, who was now leading a large not-for-profit focused on international child relief, the return to political strategizing had a distinct back-to-the-future quality. Her deep dismay over the political turn of events in 2005 had been the catalyst for a dramatic new personal direction, and the changes had not been merely professional. In the course of her new work she had reconnected with an old acquaintance; they had begun dating almost immediately and soon married. The lucky fella—actually a Talmudic scholar who people variously addressed as "Rabbi, "Professor," or "Doctor" but no one referred to as a "fella"—was now busy beyond the dunes in our happily chaotic beach cottage with the precocious pair of little girls that he and Abby recently had adopted from a Thai orphanage.

How Moshe and Abby had connected was a marvel. She had first encountered him, then a handsome young rabbinical student, on that seemingly darkest of days, when a screaming Senator Nevers had bounced her and my other two friends out of his office and off his payroll. Her impulsive stop thereafter at the synagogue on Seminary Road had been brief and apparently inconsequential, but Moshe had been diligent in following up, and a friendship of sorts ensued. With Abby immediately back at work for Nevers and Moshe consumed by his studies, the acquaintance was destined to lapse, and soon did. Then, 17 years later, they found themselves seated a few chairs apart at a gathering of relief-organization board members—a remarkable coincidence—and the embers ignited. Abby, agreed Martha and I, had never seemed happier.

The same was true of Chad—though, of course, he would never agree that "happiness" was the proper metric by which to assess his life. His consulting business was booming, confirming the wisdom of his decision to diversify after the 2005 campaign. Expanding beyond campaign consulting and political polling, Chad and his new partners now guided a full-service public affairs agency in D.C., Richmond, and several other cities that offered strategic advice and advocacy services to for-profit businesses, university foundations, and various nonprofit groups in addition to the usual stable of political (candidate and PAC) clients. The new business was doing quite well, Chad reported to us, and the best thing was that the arrangement freed up time for him to focus on his real passion: teaching bright young people about the virtues of freedom and reason.

In just a few years, using all the political chits, wealthy contacts, social connections, and salesmanship skills at his disposal, which were formidable, Chad had raised north of $15 million to make his dream a reality. When his current negotiations with James Madison University, our alma mater Hampden-Sydney, and several other colleges were concluded, Chad's new "Virginia Institute for Political Freedom and Reasoned Public Choice"—which he shorthanded as the "Freedom to Reason Institute"—would open its doors on at least one campus, perhaps several. The market principles and empirical approaches already known in some economic circles as the "Virginia School" would be stressed there, and the ideas of Smith, Hayek, Strauss, and others in Chad's pantheon of heroes would be taught, studied, and applied. The project, I knew, eventually would draw Chad into its service full-time. But it was clear he planned to run at least one more political campaign before then.

Abby decided it was time to tackle that topic.

"We want you to run for governor," she said squarely. "We have been working on a plan, and we think it's a winner."

"Your numbers have bounced back strongly since the investigation ended, and now they are almost as high as Nevers' were when he ran in '97," said Chad. "Governor Meade is reasonably popular, too, and it will be a fight for sure. But she still is positioned well to the left of the Virginia mainstream, and people are going to vote for substance rather than symbolism in this election. They want a return to normalcy, and you are the most normal guy around."

"Gee, thanks," I said.

"If you are wondering whether I want to run," interjected Congressman Jackson, feigning offense, "the answer is, 'no.' Despite the drumbeat from across the Commonwealth, I have concluded it's not my time."

"Don't think you can win?" I goaded.

"I would win if I ran," Mitch said with no apparent facetiousness, "but I have set my sights elsewhere."

"Yeah, Mitch is breathing that rarefied Potomac air and thinks the governorship is beneath him," mewed Abby.

"No, Mitch's focus is on federal issues because that's where his work is," opined Chad authoritatively. "There is a real opportunity here for you to become governor," he said to me, "and among other benefits, that will put you in a good position to help Mitch win the Senate seat in a few years."

"Never let it be said that Chad the Consultant doesn't plan ahead and make sure he knows where his next gravy train is coming from," said Abby with a smile.

"No apologies for that here," Chad rejoined. "Electing winners is good for business—and I don't mean just mine."

"Hey, guys, I am really pleased that you all are plotting my future," I said, "but what makes you think I *want* to run for governor?"

"Don't you?"

"Don't you?"

"Don't you?"

All three asked separately, but virtually in unison, thinking an answer might finally be looming to the matter I had kept a mystery even to my close friends.

"Maybe," I answered honestly.

Their expressions made it clear they would not let me off the hook.

"Here's what I want to say to you guys," I began, finally engaging seriously and making the points I had arranged in my mind earlier in the day "First, you know how much I appreciate your confidence in me, and how much weight I give to what you think. If you believe this is the right thing to do and the right time to do it, that matters. Second, I agree there is a lot of unfinished business we need to accomplish—at the right time and in the right way. But here's the third thing: I don't have to be governor. You got that? *I don't have to be governor.* Bart *had* to be governor, and Governor Nevers *had* to be governor—for all the right reasons—and I suspect Dorothy Meade pretty much feels like she *has* to be governor again and win it in her own right, so people will stop referring to her as the "accidental governor." I am not like any of them; I'm just *not.* I'm not a natural-born politician or a man hard-bitten by ambition. And I would only run if I felt it was for a really good cause and that it's the thing I'm really supposed to do. Even if all the numbers add up and it makes sense to run based on all the usual political equations, I still need to decide whether it is the right thing to do, you know, instead of some other better thing, some more family-friendly thing, that I could do to make myself useful...."

"Dreamer," interrupted Mitch, "we aren't going to let you wiggle off the hook that way. We have heard you say that before, and we respect you for it. In fact, we all feel the same way. Plus, you and Martha and the kids have been through a lot already. All of us, really, have been through a lot together—"

"A helluva lot," interjected Chad.

"—and we are not suggesting this lightly. You've shown you're one of the scrappiest politicians in this state, and also one of the most steadfast. Sure, your speeches are a bit dry at times, but you'll keep getting better, and it's not all about giving speeches anyway. You've won the respect and even the admiration of people in this state for doing things right when it would have been easy to do something else. And, as bizarre as it has all been, it didn't happen by accident. You have been through hell and back, and in the process you've established a real bond with the people of Virginia. And now it's time for you to step up and spend some of that hard-earned capital to advance the things we believe in and make life better in this state. I hate to say it again, bro', but this time I'm right: it's your *duty.* And we will help you get it done...."

Silence followed Preacher's speech until I finally broke it.

"Schedule the meetings, then," I instructed. "Let's take a good, hard, critical look at it from all angles, pro and con, good and bad, *like our lives really depend on it* ... because I have a feeling mine does."

Then, after giving them what they wanted, I said "Hit me"—which seemed appropriate on several levels—and took off running due north, back toward Virginia, the wind at my back for the first time that day. And as Mitch's perfect spiral sailed straight over my head and into my outstretched hands, I smiled the satisfied smile of one who has the skill and will to win and finally has figured out how to enjoy the game.

Epilogue

(Five Years Later)

There are a lot of cool things about the Executive Mansion. Not only does it make for a short walk to work (the Capitol is right next door), but when you open the front door, your gaze fixes irresistibly on the imposing equestrian statute of General Washington a couple of football field lengths straight ahead at the west entrance to Capitol Square. And that is a good way to start the day.

Inside the residence are many treasures, and it had fallen to Governor Meade to preside over the museum-like mansion's renovation, ensuring that the work was completed comfortably ahead of the historic home's impending bicentennial in 2013. Also recently finished was the makeover of the Capitol, which had been in equally desperate need of attention. The Commonwealth's executive and legislative leadership had wanted to renovate the Capitol before the state's 400th anniversary observances in 2007, but everyone had been far too preoccupied with tragedies and scandals to undertake the complicated project and endure the corresponding dislocations in that timeframe. Now, calm had been restored, the people's business had resumed, and the rescue of Jefferson's temple had been accomplished. It must have taken all of Houdon's marble to contain Washington's legendary irritability in the meantime, I mused. Yet, the preeminent statesman had maintained his serene visage in the Capitol Rotunda during the worst of his heirs' foibles, attesting that a principled permanence will ever transcend transient vanities.

I had only a minute in the mansion doorway to reflect on the exterior, equestrian Washington before an elderly couple—early-arriving brunch guests—doddered their way around the fountain to the several steps of the front porch. I did not recognize the small-in-stature pair but later discovered they were eminences from Middleburg, major backers of the film project that occasioned the day's festivities. Descending the steps to assist their ascent, I was immediately struck by the man's resemblance to Mr. Magoo, a favorite cartoon character of my youth. He even sounded like Magoo as he sputtered jovially, "Thank you, young man, you're a gentleman and a scholar. The Missus and I love the steps; it's the blasted gravity we have a problem with! Isn't that right, Matilda?"

"Oh, hush up, Norman, and pay attention to where you're going," she rasped good-naturedly. "If you fall and break your behind at the governor's house, I am going to say I don't know you. 'Never met the old fool'—that's what I'll say."

The little man seemed intent on assisting his spunky spouse, or at least being perceived as assisting her, but it soon was apparent that he was the one in greater need of help. His nearsightedness was not obvious until he strode emphatically onto a step where none existed, resulting in a loud thwack of shoe on stone. I was afraid he had fractured his knee or leg in addition to his pride, but he was utterly unfazed and immediately repeated the maneuver. This time he made contact with a place where there actually was a step, and then a second and a few more, until he and the "missus" were finally at the front door.

At that point, a very nice black lady extended her arm to assist the couple. "Welcome to the Executive Mansion," she said.

"Good day," replied Mr. Magoo sprightly. But instead of accepting the woman's outstretched hand, he contorted himself for a few moments until his London Fog was off his back, and then he draped the garment over her arm. "Thank you ever so much," he said as he moved forward, expecting her to recede toward the coat closet and make way for the couple to enter and greet their distinguished hosts.

My eyes instantly met Dorothy's, and we both cracked up. Before either of us could say anything, Mrs. Magoo lit into her husband.

"Land of Goshen, you blind old fool! That's not the maid. That's Governor Meade!" she barked. For a moment I thought she was going to pound Mr. Magoo with her massive pocketbook. Then she obviously had another thought and turned to Dorothy, "Actually, I do have that right, don't I—the title, I mean?"

"Just call me 'Dorothy,'" the smiling presence at the door said warmly, in turn clasping each of their hands in both of hers. "And this is Governor McGuire," she said, pointing back down at me.

Now they were really confused.

"Please just call me 'Danny,'" I said, climbing the steps for a more formal greeting.

"Aaaarch!" Mr. Magoo exclaimed, his screech resembling the chalkboard-scraping sound of a disgruntled great blue heron. "They're making sport of us now, Matilda. He ain't no governor!" He smiled and turned to me, "You're the attorney general, aren't you, sonny? My cousin is a 'McGuire' and he says he's kin to the attorney general. He didn't say a thing about being kin to the governor—and, believe me, he would have been spreading that all over the countryside if it was a fact!"

I was happy to just nod agreeably, but Dorothy apparently felt it necessary to explain. "Mr. McGuire actually was my predecessor as governor. And, once a governor, always a governor. But, you're right—he was the attorney general, too."

"She gives me too much credit, folks. I was governor for about 15 minutes once. And ma'am, you're quite right. This is Governor Meade, our hostess for today's festivities."

Curious about the commotion, Mitch and Martha made their way to the front door from the adjacent ladies' parlor where they had been reminiscing. "Who are these fine folks?" Mitch asked as he slipped his arm around the waist of the former chief executive.

"Well, my goodness. We've been so busy talking about titles we failed to make a proper introduction," said Dorothy. "Folks, this is my husband, Governor Jackson, and this is Governor McGuire's wife, Martha. *And you are?*"

"Totally and utterly confounded," Mr. Magoo immediately chirped. "That's what we are. But it's nothing that a Mimosa and a Bloody Mary won't cure." With that, the bespectacled gentleman brushed past all four of us and ambled toward the ballroom where, he surmised, liquid sustenance would be available.

"I am Matilda Farnsworth, and that lunatic is my husband of 62 years, Norman Farnsworth," Mrs. Magoo intoned pleasantly. "It is so nice of you to invite us. I do fear we are early. The old buzzard can't see his watch any better than those steps out there—or the hand in front of his face, for that matter.

He kept telling me we were late, and it was easier just to come on over from the Jefferson than to sit there and argue with him."

"Well, you're right on time, Mrs. Farnsworth, and we are delighted to have you," the First Lady said. Dorothy then left us chatting amiably and slipped down the hallway to make sure someone was in place behind the linen-draped serving table to attend to the parched Mr. Farnsworth. The scheduled start of the brunch reception was still 20 minutes away, but the ever-ready mansion staff had diagnosed the situation quickly and manned the bar. In a matter of moments, Mr. Farnsworth was happy as a clam and on his way back to his bride of six decades with his Bloody Mary in one hand and a Mimosa for her in the other. I encountered him as I headed toward the refreshments myself.

"Gotta keep the old bat in the booze," he leaned and whispered to me as we passed, making sure it was loud enough for all to overhear. "She's mean as the devil when she's sober."

The guy was a stitch. *This is already better than the usual mansion party*, I said to myself, *and it hasn't even started yet.*

I had been to many events at the historic home whose first occupant, Governor James Barbour, like the current one, hailed from my home county of Orange. But this was only the second time the party was in my honor. Governor Nevers had held a reception for me here following my first swearing-in as attorney general, almost a decade earlier. *And what a decade it had been!*

Virginia typically went through governors fast, a phenomenon that was supposed to have been tempered by repeal of the one-term limit. Yet, in a little more than ten years, the roll of chief executives had swollen by five: Nevers, Bell, McGuire, Meade, and now Jackson. As remarkable as that was, it did not even approach the record. Virginians had seen four chief executives come and go during 1811, the year construction of the mansion began. Still, the recent changes had been dizzying, and you did not have to be Mr. Magoo to find it all a bit confounding. Three of those five recent governors—the three living ones—were present today, and soon several other former chief executives would arrive along with much of the Commonwealth's social, political, and business elite, our trio of kids and members of my extended family, friends and former colleagues, and an impressive coterie of Hollywood celebrities, mogul types, and other moneyed patrons. I knew few of the guests would be as entertaining as the spry little couple from Middleburg, but an invitation to this star-studded event was an unusually prized possession, and it would be a most interesting cast of characters.

I was a little embarrassed to be the object of the attention. It made me realize how much I had enjoyed being out of the public eye during the past couple of years. But Mitch had insisted. It was an honor to be feted at the governor's mansion, and I was glad to be back here. Plus, my kids—two teenagers and a pre-teen with far more pressing concerns than politics—had already seen to it that my ego was held in check. "You have to admit it's insane, Dad," my unfiltered 14-year-old, Marty, had said, "that a star like Jack Jencks would come all the way here just because of *you*."

———————————

When Jack Jencks, the renowned Hollywood actor and producer, called me a month after the 400th anniversary event at Cape Henry and asked to come see me, I thought he must be in search of some obscure background information on Virginia history for an upcoming movie that would be set in the Old Dominion. He had produced award-winning movies and more than one acclaimed mini-series set against the backdrop of historical events, including the founding era, Civil War, World War II, and the civil rights movement, among others. I just assumed another such production was in the works and would be filmed in the Commonwealth, the locus of several of his prior projects. That would have been exciting enough, but what he outlined was something far more ambitious. He had in mind an unprecedented production, one that ultimately would morph into a landmark, ten-part, 18-hour mini-series entitled, *LIBERTY!* The subtitle was more descriptive: *How Freedom Made America and America Remade the World.*

"I watched the video of your Cape Henry speech three times, all the way through," Jencks had said to me when we first met. "I watched some parts of it more than that. And I got to thinking: *No one has told this story.*"

"What story is that?"

"The story of freedom!" he had exclaimed, before letting fly a litany that, with multiple variations, I have heard many times since:

> You know … political, national, and personal freedom … religious freedom … economic freedom … civil liberties … personal privacy … the whole concept of *liberty*. It's the most

powerful, the most successful idea in human history (aside from love, of course). But the story hasn't been told—not on film, not as a holistic story. It hasn't been done! It's an amazing story that holds together, and no one has told it! I mean, take it back to the beginning in ancient Greece, the Roman republic, Florence, England, and on from there ... the colliding worldviews—natural rights versus absolute monarchy. The audacious planting and persevering here in America ... Jamestown and Williamsburg ... Plymouth and Boston ... the first legislature at Jamestown in 1619 ... the town hall meetings in New England ... the tea party at Boston Harbor, the Revolution, the victory at Yorktown ... the Constitution, the *miracle* at Philadelphia ... the frontier and the west. And having gained our freedom as a nation, our wrestling with the contradictions and trying to set a proper example before the world ... our struggle to define what freedom really means and make the promise real for everyone ... from brother against brother in the Civil War to brothers and sisters locking arms for civil rights a century later.... And the advance of self-determination and freedom around the world ... the epic struggles against global tyranny and totalitarianism, against communism and nihilism in the 20th century.... Not just the battle for a free world, but for a free society—the work to secure ordered liberty, you know, a community of shared values, a worthy republic, here at home.... The clash of factions and the tensions between liberty and order, the individual and the community, equality and opportunity....

He had seemed about to stop but barely took a breath before proceeding.

There are so many big ideas and big questions. The idea that freedom doesn't have to be a *centrifugal* force that spins away values and turns liberty into license—that it can be a *centripetal* force, a unifying influence that pulls diverse people together so they can live in harmony and pursue their dreams.... The role of faith—yes your faith and my faith, but also the many faiths—and the great moral questions, including the source and value of morality itself. And those nagging questions posed by modernity and now post-modernity that dampen our optimism about democracy: As the gales of mass freedom and mass communications blow from the extremes, *can the center hold?* The political center? The religious center? Any center that is based on principle rather than passion or convenience? We have made much of the world safe for democracy, but have we left it safe for orthodoxy? Has our liberty set us on a path toward Truth, or has it opened a chasm of confusion and relativism that places Truth even farther beyond our grasp? And what of the material obsessions, the *affluenza* that hobbled ancient Rome and afflicts modern America: Can a free society survive when its people become so comfortable that they have little concern for what came before or what lies beyond—when the great existential questions about man's purpose and life's meaning lose their ages-old fascination. During much of civilization it was injustice and oppression in this life that caused desperate people to seek solace in the next, supplying a source of hope…. So, what remains of hope today—can it survive our righting of wrongs and creation of comforts, or must modern man inevitability forfeit hope in anything greater than his own perfectibility? And if so, how can hope itself survive the orgy of materialism, grievance, indulgence, and violence that daily exposes the utter folly of human perfectibility? Must affluent societies fall and make room for others to rise—or can they self-correct? And if capable of self-correction, what does that process look like, and who or what triggers it? Tough questions, all of them … and they bring us back to the business of freedom, which is *politics*: the very same politics that we know brings out the best and the worst of human nature … endlessly objectionable, frightfully dysfunctional … yet it's all we have. So how do we *preserve* freedom—how do we preserve a condition that is a rare exception in human history? Mankind has spent most of its time dreaming up ways to lord over others—to exert power and control. Freedom reverses all that—it frees us from all that—but it's a fragile flower that requires constant care and cultivation. "A republic, if you can keep it," Ben Franklin said. A "more perfect Union," our Constitution says. It's all one great cause … one grand story. I go to bed thinking about it; I spend the night dreaming about it; and I wake up and start thinking about it some more!

The man's excited, almost ecstatic, and amazingly erudite soliloquy had flabbergasted me. I had sat there nodding, in both agreement and wonder, until he had spent himself.

"And it was your speech … that very *long* speech beside the ocean … that got it all started in my head."

I had been thrilled, of course, to learn that my 400th anniversary reflections had impressed this extraordinarily gifted and influential man, and was delighted to hear about the project he had in mind. What had struck me then was his intensity, his evident passion about what he was planning. But clearly he had not come all the way across the country just to thank me for the inspiration. So why had he come?

Before I could ask, he had answered.

"Now, here's why I'm here today. I want you to be the lead historical consultant on the mini-series. I want you on board helping to write it, vet it, put every bit of it together. You will have a team of historians at your disposal, the best researchers, everything and everyone you need. I want you to be the chief architect and also the quality control officer for the substantive side of the story. I need someone who is a scholar, a student of history, and also an experienced practitioner, a political animal."

"You need Churchill," I had interjected.

"Yes, I do. Unfortunately, I am a half-century and change late for that. But you'll do in a pinch. Look, this will be easy for you. You don't have to move; you can stay here in Virginia. But it will take up all of your time—most of it, anyway. And I want to get started immediately."

He had not gotten all of my time—not until my term as AG expired. But he had gotten a good chunk of it before then and every ounce of my energy thereafter. It had not proven "easy" at all. For nearly three years it had been my all-consuming labor, but it had been a labor of love.

Now the premiere was weeks away, and the Governor and First Lady had an eclectic group of 150 or so coming over to celebrate my contributions to the project. Mitch had envisioned it as a reunion of old friends and other Virginians who had been part of my journey. But when Jencks and the folks in Hollywood found out about it, they had insisted on coming, too. So it had turned into this grand social event that was the talk of Richmond and points beyond.

I was in a fun, hail-fellow-well-met sort of mood, eager to see old friends and not overly introspective. But the thought did cross my mind: *what a bizarre chain of events brought us here!* A limitless list of causes and effects could be identified, but among them one in particular stood out. If not for the tumult and tragedy in Virginia in the months preceding my Cape Henry speech—if not for the untimely deaths of two governors, the investigations, and everything else that had put Virginia *and me* ingloriously in the spotlight—almost no one, including most certainly Jack Jencks, would even have heard about me or my speech. There would have been no inspiration for a *Liberty!* mini-series at all.

Well, Governor Nevers, you and Governor Stark certainly were right, I thought. *"When this conscience business starts, ain't no telling where it'll stop...."*

Willie Stark had said something else that had stuck with me. He said, "A man don't have to be governor." I had said it, too—to my friends on the beach at Corolla a few weeks before I picked up the phone and encountered Jack Jencks at the other end of the line.

When I told those same friends the news about my new project, there was not really much to say. "You remember when I told you guys on the beach that 'I don't have to be governor.' Well, now I know there *is* something I have to do. *I have to help tell this story."*

Once a McGuire for Governor campaign was off the table, it took little time to figure out who should run instead. Ever since going to Congress, Mitch had trained his sights on the United States Senate. But I think he always secretly had wanted to be Governor of Virginia. Now the pathway to the nomination was virtually clear. No one was more popular in the Virginia GOP, especially in the all-important conservative base, than Congressman (and Gulf War hero) Jonathan Mitchell Jackson; he would have little difficulty amassing the endorsements and dollars necessary to dispatch any GOP challengers in the primary. While the general election odds seemed far longer—he presumably would face a popular incumbent governor who had surpassed everyone's expectations and had achieved notable successes—it was definitely worth a shot. An added bonus was that Mitch did not have to give up his congressional seat to run for governor. Because state elections are held in odd-numbered years in Virginia and federal contests take place in even-numbered ones, Mitch had the luxury of running for the state's top office while remaining a congressman.

The other shoe dropped in Charlottesville some months later. That is when the University of Virginia's Board of Visitors announced that Dorothy Meade would become the University's eighth president upon completion of her term as governor in early 2010. Mitch had known it was coming, but no one else had. The news landed like a bombshell, and set off a frenzy of activity in the Democratic Party's high councils. Lieutenant Governor Si Percival promptly signaled his intentions, and for all intents and purposes the matter of the Democratic gubernatorial nomination was quickly settled. There were rumblings of discontent, of course, and Governor Meade insisted on withholding her endorsement until the state Democratic convention had worked its will. But Percival finally had his shot.

The gubernatorial shoot-out between the impassioned young conservative GOP congressman and the seasoned Democratic patrician (Percival would be 73 on inauguration day) scrambled the state's usual political alignments. Mitch had honed his campaign skills during his decade and a half in public life, and he was masterful on the stump. While he remained the passionate conservative champion, he by now had added some finesse to his repertoire that was appreciated in the moderate suburbs. He also bridged some divides that had hampered Republican candidates for decades.

From his first congressional campaign, Mitch relentlessly had cultivated the conservative GOP grassroots, sometimes adopting the populist economic themes that stoked resentment toward the party's well-heeled business allies. Never comfortable with the class-warfare undertones of that approach, Mitch by now also had come to recognize its self-defeating character. The populist tactic might help win a GOP nomination from time to time, but it drove away crucial supporters and donors in general election contests, aiding Democratic moderates like Percival who were acceptable to business interests. Mitch remained firmly and passionately committed to Chad's free-market principles, but instead of vaguely deriding "crony capitalism"—a term as likely to turn hearers against capitalism as cronyism—he had cultivated a positive, Reaganesque message about growing the economy by getting government out of the way and letting entrepreneurs and enterprises do what they do best: compete on a level playing field and, in the process, create jobs, extend the frontiers of knowledge, improve performance, and expand opportunity.

"The chief threat to this positive vision," Mitch had taken to saying, "is not the other members of our Republican family with whom we may have minor quarrels from time to time. It's the Democratic Party's insistence on more government, taxes, and entitlements at the expense of freedom, investment, and opportunity."

Nor was the GOP gulf between grassroots conservatives and business interests the only divide Mitch surmounted. He also seemed to have solved the riddle that had frustrated most right-leaning African-American candidates before him. Instead of playing to racial passions at one extreme or pretending they did not exist at the other, Mitch steered it down the middle. He became the thoughtful truth teller, candidly explaining that the social, educational, and economic problems plaguing the African-American community, especially in urban areas, were chiefly the products of historic wrongs, wrongheaded government fixes, and socioeconomic conditions traceable to both. Republicans were wrong to deny the persisting effects of slavery and systemic discrimination, he argued, while Democrats were wrong to cling to the same misguided and demeaning remedies that had made things worse for decades. All could agree, he said, on the need for a positive, new *empowering path forward*.

Perhaps most important, Mitch—*Preacher*—had started lecturing less and doing more. Determined to have a direct impact on young lives, he had given up the peace and comfort of his Alexandria condo after a couple of years and moved to a Capitol Hill apartment within sight of the drug- and violence-plagued Potomac Gardens housing projects, where he immersed himself in the life of the community. He joined a young congregation there and became a constant presence in the activist church's popular tutoring and mentoring programs. The experiences did not change Mitch's policy views—to the contrary, they powerfully reinforced his commitment to school reform and to market-based strategies for promoting inner-city investment. But they did transform his message from one weighted with strident moral exhortations to an intensely practical one leavened with vivid real-life examples and first-hand experiences.

Mitch's permanent residence remained back in Orange, of course—in the heart of his congressional district. But with a statewide race somewhere in the offing, Chad was constantly pushing Mitch to decamp back across the river. "You can find plenty of *Virginia* kids who could use your help in Arlington or Alexandria, and their parents and neighbors will be able to vote for you," Chad would press. Mitch conceded the point, but his loyalty and affection for the young people he had befriended in the Potomac Gardens community would not permit such a self-serving move. It proved to be one of those all-too-rare instances where doing the right thing also was the politically beneficial thing, because, by the time Mitch ran for governor, word of his serious work in D.C. had gotten around online and otherwise. It earned him mainstream credibility in the African-American community, especially among younger voters who regarded him as an authentic champion of change.

When this youthful support was added to Mitch's already significant appeal in the socially conservative African-American churches, the result in the 2009 gubernatorial balloting was unprecedented. Mitch received nearly half of the African-American vote and won majorities in other minority communities, achieving a level of support unmatched by any other GOP statewide candidate, white or black, in modern Virginia political history.

Percival lost the race as much as Mitch won it, however. Like so many master-legislators who wield the levers of power effortlessly as insiders, he proved to be utterly out of his element on the statewide hustings, among the unpredictable and at times unforgiving masses. To his stultified campaign style, he added several unwise tactical decisions, most notably his failure to embrace the accomplishments of the Meade administration—especially the anti-drug initiative—and his refusal to assail his Republican opponent's hard-right congressional voting record. Mitch's built-in advantages gave him the luxury of keeping to the high road, and Percival needed to bring his dynamic opponent down a peg, especially in the suburbs where moderates might bristle at some of Mitch's more provocative positions on social issues. But by the time Si's frustrated campaign operatives finally persuaded their candidate to fire those shots, the target was out of range. Mitch was only too glad to accept Percival's gift. He coasted in with nearly 55 percent of the vote and carried eight of the state's 11 congressional districts.

I have said before that I thought Mitch saw himself as a kind of latter-day Joshua, leading his wandering people into the promised land at last. But after watching the 2009 campaign, I began to wonder whether the more apt biblical analogy was to those post-exilic heroes, Nehemiah and Zerubbabel. After seven decades, Cyrus, the Persian king, allowed the Jewish exiles to return from Babylonia to Jerusalem and rebuild. He gave them a pass not unlike the one Si Percival had given to Mitch. Zerubbabel led the first wave and focused on restoring the temple; Nehemiah came decades later and spearheaded rebuilding the city's walls. I was unsure which Mitch would more closely resemble, the temple-builder or the wall-builder, but I knew he would erect something important. His election, an event with both religious and political implications, seemed to close one chapter and open a new one.

The wedding took place at Montpelier a few weeks after the election. It was a quiet affair with family members and only a few close friends invited. With considerable effort the groom's father was able to officiate at the service. And I was the best man.

State and national news organizations reported on the union, each using the single photo that was released to the news media: a picture of Dorothy and Mitch pledging themselves to one another in the iconic columned gazebo that was Madison's temple. The local Orange County newspaper captured the essence of the event with understated elegance: "Governor-elect J. Mitchell Jackson and outgoing Governor Dorothy Meade were wed today at Montpelier, the stately, serviceable home of President James Madison and First Lady Dolley Madison. Like the Madisons, the Jacksons are both formidable figures, and their union seems similarly fated to have a profound impact on state and national politics."

Unmentioned by the writer, and notably so, was the evident difference between the couples—what Madison himself once labeled "the mere distinction of colour."

———————

The guests were arriving now, and Martha and I stood with Mitch and Dorothy to greet them as they entered. I talked too long with the ones I knew best, causing a logjam in the entrance hall and a back-up outside.

Mitch finally turned to Martha. "Can't you shut him up?" he asked with a grin.

"Don't blame me," she responded. "You should never have turned him into a politician."

A what? My spirited wife had called me a fair number of things through the years but never, to my recollection, a "politician." Yet, there it was. Indeed, I had been turned into a politician, if only for a spell—and now I was mercifully out. At least I was out in an elective sense. In a larger sense, I was in it for good.

Like my parents and forebears, my friends, and so many others, I had been pulled into politics. I had been captivated first by political ideas, and then by political opportunities, and ultimately by political duties. I had some solid successes to show for it—accomplishments that would make a real difference for people—and I had learned important lessons from the failures. The entire process, seeing the dark side as well as the light, accepting finally my own fallibility and need for forgiveness, had deepened my core convictions. I had come to see myself less as an autonomous individual and more as a participant in meaningful relationships, and now I spent my time thinking more about others and less about myself. Most important, I had become inspired by the whole of creation, not just those who looked or behaved or thought as I did. I wanted politics ... and religion ... to work for all of them.

There had been many contributors to this growth, and I hoped there would be many more, yet I knew nothing had shaped me so much as the friends with whom I had bonded during nearly three decades of political pursuits. They were stunningly different people, a fact the evening's banter had impressed upon me anew, yet it was the authentic relationship with each that had molded me. Like a high-tech printer that produces a singular image with complementary hues from thousands of discrete injections of color, Mitch, Abby, and Chad had painted the picture that stared back at me when I looked in the mirror.

What made this day stand out, however, was my heightened awareness that the opposite also was true.

Mitch had told me to be sure to arrive at least 30 minutes early because he had something he wanted to show me. As Martha and I strolled up to the guard house at the Executive Mansion's front gate, Mitch bounded out the front door and past the fountain toward us, motioning so as to redirect us toward the Capitol some 75 yards away. We strolled briskly in the November air to the east entrance and entered to find Jefferson's temple in a condition—cool, dark, and empty save for the lone Capitol policeman who greeted us—that I had not experienced since I worked there. We approached the stairs, our usual mode of rapid ascent to the Third Floor, but Mitch paused, eyes on Martha, and said, "We're going to my office three flights up, counting the mezzanine. Want to take the elevator?"

"Are you kidding? She's in better shape than either of us," I cracked.

"Yes, but she's in heels, you goofball."

"Yeah, you goofball, I'm in heels," Martha sniped good-naturedly as she turned to push the elevator button that was always right at the foot of the stairs. Instead, she encountered open space.

"Ha, the joke's on you—they got rid of the elevators when they restored the Capitol," I chortled. This, I knew, was untrue, but Martha had not yet taken the tour.

"No, they didn't get rid of them, but they did replace and move them," Mitch answered, motioning just down the hall toward the new lift locations near the Capitol's center.

We arrived in the Governor's conference room a few moments later to discover that the elevators were not the only decidedly new thing in the renovated Capitol. When Mitch turned on the lights my eyes immediately were drawn to the high-back swivel chair at the head of the large mahogany conference table. The leather was now a darker, more elegant blue—Mr. Jefferson would never have called it "royal blue" though that seemed the closest hue—but the thing that caught my eye was the iridescent gold seal of the Commonwealth that shimmered brilliantly on its back.

"Is it the same? I mean, it is the same chair? Or is it a new one?" I asked reflexively and, as I now recall it, almost plaintively.

"The very same one," Mitch responded proudly. "Restored by one O. L. Founder of Galax, Virginia, the original craftsman. By the way, he asked about you. Said he met you and Ned Nevers during one of the Governor's campaigns way back when."

"Yes, it was in '97 when Nevers was running for governor the first time. I have thought about it many times," I responded absently, still transfixed by the sight of the seal. "That seal looks fantastic, Mitch. It is really bright."

"The leather is what amazes me," Martha weighed in. "Where did that come from?"

"Ask your husband," Mitch replied, turning to me. "Abby told me you said the leather to restore this chair could only come from one place. Chad did the leg work on it for me, and that's where we got it."

"No, you don't mean ..."

"Yep, the School of Leather."

I knew he was referring to *Scuola del Cuoio*, the leather-making school behind the Basilica of Santa Croce in Florence, Italy.

"It was not easy to arrange, let me tell you. I had to raise private funds and get people to pull strings over there like you would not believe."

I was struck by this news. It was surprising enough that Abby had paid attention to my ruminations. That Mitch and Chad had gone to the trouble to accomplish such a feat left me speechless.

"Now, you have to tell me why it was so important to have the leather come from that one place," the current Governor of Virginia commanded emphatically. "I get it ... it's a great story—Santa Croce dates back to St. Francis himself, as legend has it. After World War II, the Franciscans there got with the local leather artisans and opened the school. And then, you know, everyone came. Their handiwork ended up on President Eisenhower's desk; the Reagans shopped there; their clientele included Katharine Hepburn and lots of other big celebrities, kings and queens, and all the rest. But none of that would turn *your* head, so what's the big deal? Why did you say the leather to re-do the governor's chair had to come from that place? I have my suspicions but I have been dying to hear your answer."

"Martha and I went to Florence for our honeymoon," I replied, "and while there we discovered that right there in that one church, Santa Croce, are the tombs of Michelangelo, Machiavelli, Galileo, and Dante. I was blown away. Think about it—where else could one find, interred in a single place, such remarkably different proofs of God's creative genius, men whose stories attest to the near-limitless human potential for good and evil in all of life's pursuits, especially politics and religion? And then I discovered that Dante was not buried there in the tomb the Florentines built for him because they had exiled him. Because of politics they had exiled perhaps the greatest of all their sons. And it was while in exile that he wrote his masterpiece, *The Divine Comedy*...."

I was about to explain why this was relevant to the governor's chair in Virginia. But before I could do so Mitch interrupted with his own take.

"... And, for you, that was a portrait of Virginia. Like the Florentines, we are surrounded by incredible monuments to God's creative genius. Like them, our struggles bear witness to man's potential for good or evil—and, more typically, for good *and* evil. Like them, we cannot judge our victories and defeats, for their true significance appears only in the fullness of time. And like Dante, we are all exiles, cast out of the garden and into the lion's den ... striving, persevering ... doing the best we can with what we have, and, through grace, knowing that ours is indeed a divine comedy because all's well that ends well...."

I listened to my friend, who obviously had been giving the whole matter a lot of thought. He was smiling with satisfaction now, as I nodded. "Yes, something like that," I said. "But mainly it was the orphans."

Mitch frowned, thought for a moment, and then smiled again broadly. "Ah, of course—the orphans. The whole reason the Franciscans started the leather school there was so they could teach a trade to the many young boys orphaned by the war."

"Yes, they had reminders of Florentine grandeur and wisdom all around, but that was not going to put food in the mouths of those poor, parentless little boys. So they came up with a plan...."

"Right," said Mitch. "It's great to think great thoughts and celebrate great lives, but what counts is what we do with it in the here and now."

"Not a bad lesson for the Governor of Virginia to be reminded about when he plops into this comfortable leather chair," I said, as I settled smoothly into it myself.

For years I had been thankful for the many crucial ways my trio of confidants had shaped my life. Hearing my deepest convictions echo from Mitch's lips, I now was grateful for the ways mine had shaped theirs.

Our differences were what had enabled us to teach each other and what had made it all so interesting. It brought to mind a favorite quote from C. S. Lewis: "How monotonously alike all the great tyrants and conquerors have been: how gloriously different are the saints."

———————

Seeing Mr. Founder's restored chair on the Third Floor lifted my spirits, one of the many highs during this evening devoted to friendship, reminiscence, and renewal. The pinnacle, however, came a short time into the reception, when Mitch made his comments.

"There are many people of note here tonight—actors and producers, politicians and celebrities, and other wonderful folks—but one stands out," the Governor said after calling the First Lady forward to join in welcoming their guests. "His forebears lived and labored long in my native Orange County, contributing to the cause of liberty in ways untraceable yet undoubted. His own freedom was bought at a great price, as is true of us all. And, using that freedom, he has soared above his circumstances and excelled beyond all expectations to become a person of great achievement and even greater promise."

People were nodding and smiling, looking at me knowingly—and mistakenly. I smiled back because I knew what was coming.

"Please join me in welcoming the lead violinist of the Old Dominion Pops ... a 30-year-old virtuoso performing, fittingly, a piece from Beethoven's "Ode to Joy" ... the pride of Orange County and now Richmond, Virginia ... *Lorenzo Washington.*

The music was exhilarating. Listening to the rapid, resonant strains, I thought of Bonita and imagined her looking on from above, tears of joy streaming down. "That's my baby making that beautiful music," Lorenzo's proud mama was telling the saints.

I thought, too, of the many others whose care and skill had made Lorenzo's odds-defying accomplishments possible. *Santa Croce is not the only place where they care for the orphans*, I mused. And now I was thinking not of Lorenzo's journey but of my own.

———

The way things turned out, the 2009 gubernatorial campaign really had been the family affair that Chad and Abby envisioned during our seaside stroll at Corolla two years earlier. The candidate was different but the supporting cast was the same. Setting aside most of their competing obligations, Chad and Abby had steered the Jackson for Governor campaign flawlessly through the mine-laden political landscape that is hyper-competitive 21st-century Virginia. The victory was Mitch's—of that, there could be no dispute. But the other two had played crucial roles, certainly much greater than my own, and they enjoyed not only the intense gratitude of the popular new chief executive but the personal satisfaction of knowing they had helped right Virginia's course.

I spotted the two of them huddling with Dorothy and Moshe in the front room that once served as the governor's office. They were chatting with evident purpose as other guests buzzed nearby, and I wondered about the object of their latest scheming. Mitch had tried to get all three—Chad, Abby, and

Moshe—to assume senior posts in his administration, but he had struck out thrice. Abby and her husband were too committed to their nonprofit, and Chad was too invested in his consulting firm and nascent "freedom to reason" institute, to shed their private interests in the manner required for full-time public service. Bowing to these realities, Mitch had scored a partial victory by persuading Chad to become the citizen chairman of his new "Blue Ribbon Commission on Higher Education and Economic Competitiveness." Given her new responsibilities in Charlottesville, the panel's work was of particular interest to the First Lady, and I surmised—correctly—that the parlor discussion had something to do with that subject.

Giving Chad the lead on higher education policy in Virginia was like sending the proverbial Nixon to China. Chad's disdain for the academy—at least the part of it that engaged politically, typically on the Left—was well known to, and largely shared by, our friend Governor Jackson. But Mitch and Chad also shared a keen understanding of higher education's crucial role in growing a knowledge-based economy and preparing well-rounded leaders, and they recognized the unique asset that Virginia possessed. The American higher education system was among the country's chief competitive advantages internationally, and the Commonwealth's diverse colleges, universities, and community colleges perennially ranked among the best in America. In recent years, the imperative of a balanced state budget had prompted funding cuts that pushed tuition at the state schools ever higher and threatened quality. As in George Washington's day, the notion that you could keep bleeding the patient—in this case, financially—was folly. Mitch was determined to reverse the cuts, but he wanted the reinvestment matched by wide-ranging reform. Chad's job was to make sure the new dollars were spent in ways that produced *economic* results—for Virginia and, especially, for the graduates.

Higher education was indeed the subject of the parlor huddle, and it would not be long before Virginians would hear about the new scheme that occupied my friends that evening. It would begin as a public-private initiative focused on postsecondary educational opportunities for young people in the hills and hollers of Southwest Virginia, a ground-breaking collaboration between Virginia's higher education institutions, the state's largest corporate citizens, and an array of nonprofits mobilized by Abby and Moshe. Soon the partnership would be broadened to include virtually all of the state's distressed rural and urban areas, and eventually it would serve the whole Commonwealth, promoting internships, fellowships, work-study opportunities, and a host of other connections between classrooms and labs and the knowledge-driven workplaces across Virginia. It gave my old roommate a concrete example to highlight as he traveled across the country raising money for his institute and touting the empowering possibilities of honest inquiry and choices rooted in reason.

It was great to see Chad so engaged, but what really intrigued me that evening in the mansion was Abby. She had been so certain that I should become governor in 2005 and so distraught when I had refused. I was afraid to ask—the memory was too painful to risk a recurrence—but I wondered: could she see now that my great decision had been the right one? Though neither of us could have foreseen it, could she now recognize that her own life had become immensely more fruitful because of what my decision denied her?

One day, perhaps, I will get up the nerve to ask.

———————————

During the several years of arduous work, nothing had posed a greater conundrum for Jack Jencks, and so for me, than the question of how to *end* the mini-series.

One element was a no-brainer. There was, I had pointed out to Jack, a quotation on the final page of Madison's notes at the Philadelphia convention that supplied the perfect benediction. It was an enduring expression of optimism by Ben Franklin that the dutiful Virginia scrivener had preserved for posterity—one that American politicians still routinely invoked even as they occasionally mangled the story:

> Whilst the last members were signing [the Constitution], Doctor Franklin, looking toward the President's Chair, at the back of which a rising sun happened to be painted, observed to a few members near him, that painters had found it difficult to distinguish in their art a rising from a setting sun. I have, said he, often and often in the course of the session, and the vicissitudes of my hopes and fears as to its issue, looked at that behind the President without being able to tell whether it was rising or setting; but now at length I have the happiness to know that is a rising and not a setting Sun.

Optimism indeed was warranted, as it always must be. Yet, the mini-series candidly addressed the conflicts, struggles, challenges, and contradictions that had attended liberty's ebb and flow throughout history and down through the present. Especially against the backdrop of the current fractiousness and dysfunction on the American political scene, an altogether rosy conclusion to the story seemed somehow inapt.

Into the breach strode daughter Meg, now a high school sophomore with a thoroughly predictable passion for American history. She was thriving at Richmond's heralded Maggie Walker School for gifted government and social studies students, a specialized regional "Governor's School" named for the capital city's trailblazing female African-American banker and community leader. Delving into the commentary of Alexis de Tocqueville for a U.S. History class project, Meg ran across a passage in *Democracy in America* that struck her as potentially relevant to what we were addressing in our mini-series. And so it is to Margaret Virginia McGuire—a young woman destined, perhaps, to make her own contribution to Virginia's leadership tradition—that Jack Jencks, his viewers, and her proud father are indebted for the poignant passage around which we built our program's final episode.

"I search my memory in vain and find nothing to excite greater sorrow and pity than what is taking place before our very eyes," wrote Tocqueville of his homeland then, and seemingly of ours today.

> The natural bonds that join opinion to taste and action to belief seem lately to have been broken. The harmony that has been observed throughout history between man's feelings and his ideas has apparently been destroyed, and the laws of moral analogy have seemingly been abolished.
>
> Among us one still encounters zealous Christians who love to draw spiritual nourishment from the verities of the other life. They will no doubt thrill to the cause of human liberty, the source of all moral greatness. Christianity, which made all men equal in the sight of God, will not shrink from seeing all citizens as equal in the eyes of the law. But through a strange concatenation of events, religion has for the time being become enmeshed with the powers that democracy is bent on destroying. Often it spurns the equality it loves and

curses freedom as an enemy instead of taking it by the hand and sanctifying its efforts.

Alongside these religious men I see others who look not to heaven but to earth. Champions of freedom, which they see as the source not only of the noblest virtues but above all of the greatest goods, they sincerely wish to establish its power and secure its benefits for mankind. In my view they should hasten to invoke the aid of religion, for they must know that without morality freedom cannot reign and without faith there is no basis for morality. Yet they have seen religion in the ranks of their adversaries, and for them that is enough: Some attack it, and the rest dare not hasten to its defense.

In centuries past some base and venal souls spoke out in favor of slavery, while others of independent mind and generous heart fought a hopeless battle to preserve human freedom. Nowadays, however, it is common to meet men of noble and proud mien whose opinions directly contradict their tastes, men who vaunt a servile and base condition they have never known themselves. By contrast, others speak of freedom as if they could feel what is sacred and grand in it, and vociferously demand for humanity rights they have always failed to recognize.

I see virtuous, peaceful men whose untainted morals, tranquil habits, comfortable circumstances, and enlightened thinking mark them out as natural leaders. Sincere and ardent patriots, they would make great sacrifices for their country. Yet civilization often finds them among its adversaries. They cannot distinguish its abuses from its benefits, and in their minds the idea of evil is inextricably linked to the idea of the new.

Alongside them I see other men who, in the name of progress, seek to reduce man to a material being. They look for what is useful without concern for what is just; they seek science removed from faith and prosperity apart from virtue. Having styled themselves champions of modern civilization, they have arrogantly placed themselves at its head, usurping a position abandoned by others which they are quite unworthy of occupying themselves....

Has every other century been like this one? Has man always confronted, as he does today, a world in which nothing makes sense? In which virtue is without genius and genius without honor? In which the love of order is indistinguishable from the lust of tyrants? In which the sacred cult of liberty is confounded with contempt for the law? In which conscience casts but an ambiguous light on the actions of men? In which nothing any longer seems forbidden or allowed, honest or shameful, true or false?

Am I to believe that the Creator made man only to allow him to flounder endlessly in a sea of intellectual misery? I do not think so....

The immigrants who settled in America at the beginning of the 17th century somehow separated the democratic principle from all the other principles with which it had to contend in the old societies of Europe and transplanted it alone to the shores of the new world. There it could mature under conditions of liberty and, because it advanced in harmony with mores, develop peacefully within the law....

I did not study America, then, simply to satisfy my curiosity, though that would have been a legitimate thing to do. I was looking for lessons from which we might profit.... I confess that in America I saw more than America. I sought there an image of democracy itself—its inclinations, character, prejudices, and passions. I wanted to become familiar with democracy, if only to find out what we had to hope from it, or to fear.

That was the project, then—for Jencks and me in our mini-series, and for anyone and everyone seeking to better the human condition. It was, at bottom, the *Tocqueville Project*: to become familiar with self-government in practice as well as theory, to confront its contradictions, to master at once the interdependent arts of statecraft and soulcraft, and through that enterprise to advance "the cause of human liberty, the source of all moral greatness."

The very hard work of the last several years, I reflected on this most won-derful of evenings, had been good work indeed.

———————

I was in the oval dining room now, conversing and sampling the delicacies, when Martha emerged from the ballroom crunch, heading my way.

"Danny, c'mon, there is someone in the parlor you will want to see."

"Who is it?" I asked.

"Just c'mon. We didn't think he was coming. You will be thrilled."

I wondered what Hollywood luminary or other notable had found his or her way to my party late in the action, and I very much doubted that I would be "thrilled" by the answer. But I was wrong.

There, slumped in a wheelchair in front of the fireplace, struggling to raise his head as I entered the room, was a sight that caused my spirit to soar. A stroke had debilitated half of his frame; his eyesight was nearly gone; and his pursed lips drew his quivering, wrinkled cheeks down to a possum-like point, as if someone had tried to stretch his once handsome face beyond recognition. But the moist old eyes still glimmered, and his visage brightened unmistakably as I entered.

Completely surprised by his presence, I mumbled, "Oh, my God!" as I moved in, gingerly half-hugging his shoulder and then squatting down to en-gage at eye level.

"Dr. S. D., it is so wonderful of you to come. We had no idea you would make it," I said.

"I wouldn't miss it, son," he creaked, managing a grin. "This is quite a fit-ting honor. The Governor tells me it's gone straight to your head."

I looked at Mitch, who was smiling nearby. "He's one to talk," I said jovially.

"Well, I trust you recall Luke 17:10."

"The humble will be exalted, and the exalted with be humbled?" I replied, hopefully.

"Close—that's in the next chapter, if my memory serves me. Luke 17:10 is where the Master counsels us to reply, 'I am an unworthy servant; I have only done my duty.'"

"Ah—I didn't recall. Well, that's exactly right, isn't it?"

"You've done your duty quite well, Daniel. I'm very proud of you. And you will do a great deal more, I trust."

"I guess I'll just keep sharpening the poet's pencil," I replied.

The comment elicited a bright smile from the elderly saint. "I see some of my musings sank in after all. Who would have imagined! You were so distracted whenever we talked, I always assumed your mind was on the young ladies or the next tee time."

"It was," I replied. "But you kept horning in."

"So I did," he responded through a weak but satisfied sigh. "So I did."

"Your namesake, Samuel Davies, would be proud of you," I said encouragingly, patting the old man gently on his shoulder as I rose to relieve my faltering knees.

"As would yours…," he answered. Pausing thoughtfully, he then added, *"Both of them."*

"Both of them?" I repeated. "Who besides Madison?"

"Why, the prophet Daniel, of course."

"Oh, you mean my mother's maiden name. I don't think I can claim to be named for the 'Daniel' you're talking about."

"Of course, you can—you *must!*" he answered, suddenly summoning his strength and exhibiting passion. "Your mother's family didn't *invent* the name. There is a long and noble tradition behind it. It traces back to a principled leader who set a profound example before mankind. He maintained his faith and his integrity despite all the world threw at him. He was without prejudice—his compassion extended to the Jewish exiles and their pagan captors alike. His ministry echoed for generations, perhaps even inspiring the magi who came to worship the newborn savior centuries later! And we are still learning from him today. That is a *grand* heritage, Daniel, and you must claim it!"

His eyes gazed into mine intensely as he breathed deeply, gathering himself for a final charge. "By God, son, we do need more Madisons these days. But it won't do us any good unless they are Daniels, too!"

With that, the wise old man sagged back in his chair, as I stood in stunned silence.

"Ah—well. Listen to me carrying on," he said. "What does an old preacher know?"

"Thank you, Dr. S. D.," I leaned in to whisper. "Thank you … for everything. You changed my life."

"It was God who changed your life, Daniel," he replied, gazing up through those happily humble eyes. "I just sharpened his pencil a time or two."

Postscript

Sitting in the Governor's small private study in the upstairs living quarters, waiting for Mitch, I reflected on what had been a dream-like evening. All was right with the world.

After seasons of tumult, things now seemed to be going well for everyone—for Martha and our kids, for Lorenzo, for Abby and Moshe and Chad, for Jack Jencks and our team, for the saintly Dr. S. D., and certainly for Dorothy and Mitch. Heck, even my fun new friends, Norman and Matilda, had an evening to remember and presumably now were back at the Jefferson enjoying a nightcap.

It was hard to remember a time when I felt more content.

Mitch finally rushed in, entering from the adjoining master bedroom, and closed the door behind him.

"Hey, thanks for hanging around for a few minutes. I want to run something by you," he said with energy.

"Good or bad?" I asked reflexively.

"Oh, good, for sure … definitely."

"Great," I said, with relief. "For a minute there, I thought you were going to bring me crashing back down to earth after my big evening."

"Somebody will do that for you tomorrow. What I have is a big deal—I got a call from Arnold B. Giles yesterday."

"*The Reverend Doctor* Arnold B. Giles? Called you? About what?"

"He wants me to come to West Palm and meet with him and his advisors to discuss it, but he was pretty direct about what is on his mind."

"And?"

"He wants me to run for president. He said he and his friends have been analyzing, discussing, and praying over it for months, ever since they followed the governor's race here, but they really got focused on it this year as the Republican prospects in the presidential race started to go south."

My eyes must have been open very wide, because Mitch had that "Yeah, I was surprised, too, but it's for real" look.

"Dr. Giles said they've vetted me independently, and unless I've got something to reveal that they haven't run across, he and his friends are prepared to get behind me with the full weight of their resources—which, as you and I both know, are virtually limitless. He says they want to put down a marker very soon."

"Wow! What's the catch?"

"None, as far as I can see. Look, you know me—normally I'd recoil at being beholden to anyone or any group. But you can't run for president without a strong financial base, and when the nation's wealthiest Christian entrepreneur and philanthropist calls and says he wants to back you with his billions, well, I mean, this is a guy of great character and reputation who obviously has the nation's best interests at heart."

"It is remarkable," I answered distractedly, weighing the startling news. It was a possibility that had crossed everyone's mind, I suppose, but a presidential contest had just ended, Mitch had a reelection campaign for governor coming right up, and the next presidential race seemed far off in the distance.

"There's a lot to think about here. Dr. Giles says he and his political advisors want to talk it through with me and my people—that obviously includes you, Danny—but they are of the preliminary opinion that I should bypass running for reelection and instead announce my presidential intentions early next year. They think I should take my message on the road, make it a four-year crusade, do my special thing on the stump, become a primary spokesman for the Republican opposition, and preempt the rest of the field."

"That would be a huge step. It would really throw things into chaos here next year," I pondered aloud.

"Yes, it's an extreme suggestion—the part about not running for reelection as governor, that is. But I see their point. This is a full-time job, and so is running for president."

"Uh-huh."

"So what's your honest reaction, Danny? You don't seem very excited by the news. What downsides do you see?"

"No, I am happy for you—*thrilled*, in fact. But you just hit me with it. I am processing and—"

"The thing that bothers me is the big money," Mitch resumed, "but there is nothing wrong with hitching your wagon to someone if they have good motives, right? I mean, that is what people have to do in this business. The thing is, you don't usually have the chance to team up with someone of unlimited resources who shares your ideas and principles and is in it for all the right reasons. I mean, this is the kind of opportunity that rarely comes to people like us who want to do good work. At least, that's how I've been thinking about it...."

We talked a few minutes longer, and then I stood, turned, and reached up on the bookshelf where I knew a small bottle of Blanton's and two small glasses rested. They were there to lubricate the lobbying process when needed and, I presumed, for special occasions such as this.

As I saluted my smiling friend and we clanked our glasses, an unforgettable image entered my mind. Maybe it was then the custodian offered it up, or maybe it was later, as I drifted off to sleep ... or when I awakened. But there was Mitch, cruising along just fine in his gubernatorial SUV, when a guy in a Lamborghini came alongside, seemingly out of nowhere, and settled in.

And there he stayed, right in Mitch's blind spot, as the scene faded to black.

Author's Note (Part II)

W̲elcome back! Whether you streaked, strolled, or studied your way through the story, I hope you ran across something that will prove useful in your life. Politics, after all, is but a microcosm of life in community. We need good citizens— principled, practical people working to preserve freedom, foster renewal, and extend a helping hand to others—whether the pursuit is through politics and government or some other realm of endeavor.

Given the attention routinely given to negative role models in our culture, including both real and fictional political players, I am grateful for this opportunity to hold up some positive exemplars for readers' reflection. In using the timeless biblical story of Daniel as the framework for this contemporary story, I have sought to bring that inspiring figure's exemplary faith and character to life for today's political practitioners and conscientious citizens. And, since no one grows or serves alone, my story likewise seeks to illumine the positive examples provided by Daniel's faithful friends and the others who shaped his journey.

In thanking those who made this work possible, I must begin with the pastor and friend who first brought Daniel's story to life for me. Among Reverend Thomas W. (Tommy) Nance Jr.'s many gifts, an ability to communicate essential truths in practical and powerfully evocative ways ranks foremost. While pastor at New Hanover Presbyterian Church, he preached a series of vivid, thought-provoking sermons on the Book of Daniel in the early 1990s that planted a seed and triggered a process of research and study, prayer and reflection, soul-searching and imagination that culminated finally in this book. Having participated in politics since childhood, I came to see in Daniel's story a lesson that many politicos—myself no less than any

633

other—desperately need to learn. It is a lesson for the ages, which makes it a lesson for right now.

I am enormously grateful to Larry Sabato and Ken Stroupe of the University of Virginia Center for Politics for embracing the project, supporting and shaping it, and patiently guiding me through to its completion and publication. These two longtime friends—in Larry's case, a mentor since college—easily could have waved off this unconventional undertaking in an unfamiliar genre, thereby saving them, and me, much time and effort. But they saw value in the message—value that only seemed to increase over the intervening years as American politics coarsened and convulsed. So they encouraged me to complete the work and provided crucial help along the way.

An advantage of this book's extended development is the time afforded for personal growth and acquisition of new and clarifying insights. The list of people whose contributions I acknowledge below is quite lengthy for this reason; yet, even so, I know many important influences and influencers will go unlisted. I am grateful for everyone—family members and friends, mentors and colleagues, scholars and practitioners, role models worthy of emulation and those less so—who provided encouragement and shaped my perspective on the subjects addressed in this book over a lifetime.

During the most recent phase of work, no one has had a more profound impact on the telling of this story than Reverend Corey Widmer of Third Church in Richmond, Virginia. Indeed, so important and relevant were two of his sermons to the book's message that I took the unusual step, with his permission, of weaving them into the tale almost verbatim. If you streaked past either, I encourage you to venture back to Chapters 7 and 11 long enough to take them in. You will not be sorry.

While the errors in this work are mine alone, many more were avoided through the careful research of some very sharp interns who assisted under the auspices of the Center for Politics. Leading this list is Hundley Poulson, who devoted a portion of his 2017 summer break while an undergraduate at Princeton to chase down all sorts of crucial facts and references included in the book. More recently, Joel Thomas, Cameron Cox, Adam Kimelman, Aidan Parker, and Charlotte Suka found time during their 2018-2019 studies at U.Va. to help flesh out the Reference Notes on the pages that follow. Mary Brown and Autumn Kurtz at the Center for Politics also played important roles, as did Molly Togna, my indispensable assistant at McGuireWoods Consulting. I am deeply grateful to each of them for their contributions; the book could not have made its way to publication without them.

I enlisted quite a few friends, colleagues, and family members as readers of various versions and portions of this manuscript, and their comments were invaluable. Some studied the whole work and provided feedback; others lent their particular expertise to specific sections; some just answered questions, served as a sounding board, or provided encouragement. I was tempted to ask numerous others to review the work, including some who provided similar assistance on my prior books, but the length of this manuscript and my understanding of their time constraints counseled to the contrary. To the following folks (listed, with their indulgence, by familiar names and sans titles), I express particular appreciation for substantive help on this project: Melinda and Ray Allen; Susan and George Allen; Diane Atkinson; Pete Atkinson; Peter Atkinson; Robert B. Atkinson; Jamin Barbour; Betsy and Jim Beamer; Bob Bluford; David Bovenizer; Mark Bowles; Mark Christie; Nancy and Glenn Clark; Tyler Cowen; Kirk Cox; Richard Cullen; Ben Dendy; Jim Dyke; Cordel Faulk; Terry Fletcher; B. K. Fulton; Anita Garland; Kevin Gentry; Randy Gordon; Mark Greenough; Scott Gregory; Rob Harris; Bob Holsworth; Jim Horn; Bill Howell; Debbie Ireland; Kay James; Tim Kaine; Chris LaCivita; Karen and Boyd Marcus; George Martin; Jonathan Martin; Richard McClintock; Bill Mims; G. C. Morse; Tommy Nance; Paul Nardo; Cathy Noonan; Pat Paschall; Bob Patterson; L. F. Payne; Bob Rayner; Dave Robertson; Fred Rosen; Tom Snow; Todd Stottlemyer; Jackie Stone; Mike Thomas; Anne Whittemore; Doug Wilder; Jay Wilkinson; Dubby Wynne.

Three people—Rick Sharp, Bob Hatcher, and Bobby Ukrop—provided generous early financial support to the Center for Politics in support of this project, and I greatly appreciate their confidence in me as the storyteller.

Contributions of a different kind—mainly, encouragement and forbearance—were provided by my McGuireWoods and McGuireWoods Consulting colleagues during my extended work on this project. I am grateful for those contributions and, even more, for the chance to be part of a wonderful team of consultants, lawyers, and staff who serve clients, the community, and each other every day with integrity, creativity, and compassion.

My varied opportunities for public service also aided the crafting of this story. While I could fill many pages with expressions of gratitude on that score, I especially want to salute the dedicated Virginians with whom I have served in preserving, interpreting, and commemorating our Commonwealth's history and the vital beginning at Jamestown. My parents first brought me to Jamestown Festival Park in 1957, before I was born. Later visits made more of an impression and, beginning with my 1996 appointment by Governor George Allen to the foundation's board of trustees, hopefully had more of an impact. This tale has been enriched by my lifelong connection to the place and its powerful stories, and I hope the passages referencing *those stories will remind readers of our shared responsibility as Jamestown's contemporary stewards.*

My most heartfelt thanks are saved for Diane and our sons Robert and Paul, whose love has filled my life with inexpressible joy and gratitude. Only one acknowledgement is more important. To the extent these pages have succeeded in imparting the timeless lessons of Daniel—or, better yet, in prompting readers to go to the real Book of Daniel to let its message illumine their lives and labors—God gets all the credit.

Francis Bolling Atkinson
July 15, 2019

REFERENCE NOTES

Author's Note (Part I)

x - *"To paraphrase Dickens…"*: The character referenced is Sidney Carton. See Charles Dickens, *A Tale of Two Cities* (Penguin Classics, 2000), p. 325.

x - *"great American political novel"*: Robert Penn Warren, *All the King's Men* (Harcourt Brace Jovanovich, 1981).

x - *"my nonfiction work"*: Frank B. Atkinson, *Virginia in the Vanguard: Political Leadership in the 400-Year-Old Cradle of Democracy, 1981-2006* (Rohman & Littlefield Publishers, Inc., 2006). For the preceding period, see Frank B. Atkinson, *The Dynamic Dominion: Realignment and the Rise of Two-Party Competition in Virginia, 1945-1980*, revised 2nd ed. (Rohman & Littlefield Publishers, Inc., 2006).

Preface

xi - *"Longfellow would weigh in…"*: Henry Wadsworth Longfellow, "A Psalm of Life," in *Henry Wadsworth Longfellow: Poems and Other Writings*, ed. J. D. McClatchy (Library of America, 2000), pp. 3-4.

Prologue

xvi - *"The fault, dear Brutus…"*: William Shakespeare, *Julius Caesar*, act I, scene II, in *The Complete Works of William Shakespeare* (Race Point Publishing, 2014), p. 584.

xvi - *"[N]o free government…"*: George Mason, Virginia Declaration of Rights; Constitution of Virginia, Art.1, §15.

xxvii - *"All streams flow into the sea..."*: Ecclesiastes 1:7, 14 (NIV).

xxvii - *"Frost's west-running brook"*: Robert Frost, "West-Running Brook," in *The Poetry of Robert Frost*, ed. Edward Connery Lathem (Holt, Rinehart and Winston, 1969), pp. 257-60.

xxviii - *"tribute of the current to the source"*: Ibid., p. 260.

xxviii - *"Time, like an ever rolling stream..."*: Isaac Watts, "O God, Our Help in Ages Past," in *Sing Joyfully*, ed. Jack Schrader (Tabernacle Publishing Company, 1989), #67.

xxviii - *"justice rolls down..."*: Amos 5:24 (NIV).

xxviii - *"streams of mercy..."*: Robert Robinson, "Come Thou Fount of Every Blessing," in *Sing Joyfully*, #82.

xxviii - *"streams make glad..."*: Psalms 46:4 (NIV).

Chapter One

7 - *"Football is an arena..."*: Regarding sports as a setting in which people generally are judged on merit, see George Allen, *What Washington Can Learn from the World of Sports* (Regnery Publishing, Inc., 2010), pp. 12-18.

12 - *"Scotty, beam me aboard..."*: The insistent command enabled the fictional Captain James T. Kirk (William Shatner) to disappear in the nick of time through the energizing interventions of chief engineer Montgomery Scott (James Doohan). *Star Trek*, directed by Ralph Senensky (NBC, 1967).

16 - *"You have reached a fork..."*: Yogi Berra with Dave Kaplan, *When You Come to a Fork in the Road, Take It!: Inspiration and Wisdom from One of Baseball's Greatest Heroes* (Hyperion E-Books, 2001).

19 - *"When God closes a door..."*: *The Sound of Music*, directed by Robert Wise (Argyle Enterprises, 1965).

20 - *"life and times of ... Samuel Davies"*: For historical background on Davies, see George William Pilcher, *Samuel Davies: Apostle of Dissent in Colonial Virginia* (University of Tennessee Press, 1971); Dewey Roberts, *Samuel Davies: Apostle to Virginia* (Sola Fide Publications, 2017); Gary B. Nash, *The Unknown American Revolution: The Unruly Birth of Democracy and the Struggle to Create America* (Penguin Books, 2005), pp. 10-11; Bernard Bailyn, *The Ideological Origins of the American Revolution* (The Belknap Press, 1967), pp. 249-61; see also Robert Bluford, Jr., *Living on the Borders of Eternity: The Story of Samuel Davies and the Struggle for Religious Toleration in Colonial Virginia* (Historic Polegreen Press, 2004).

22 - *"greatest orator that ever lived..."*: Jefferson so characterized Henry in correspondence to the latter's biographer, William Wirt. See Sandra M. Gustafson, *Eloquence is Power: Oratory and Performance in Early America* (The University of North Carolina Press, 2000), p. 160.

22 - *"Son of Thunder..."*: See Henry Mayer, *A Son of Thunder: Patrick Henry and the American Republic* (University Press of Virginia, 1991). Regarding the source of Henry's "son of thunder" nickname, see William Meade, *Old Churches, Ministers and Families of Virginia* (Forgotten Books, 2015), vol. 1, pp. 220-21.

22 - *"what an orator should be..."*: Pilcher, *Samuel Davies*, pp. 83-85; see also Nash, *The Unknown American Revolution*, p. 10; Jon Kukla, *Patrick Henry: Champion of Liberty* (Simon & Schuster, 2017), pp. 22-24.

23 - *"Lord, I Want to Be a Christian"*: Concerning the hymn's origin, see Miles Mark Fisher, *Negro Slave Songs in the United States* (Carol Publishing Group, 1990), pp. 29-31; see also Bluford, *Living on the Borders of Eternity*, p. 444.

24 - *"[T]he poor neglected negroes..."*: Samuel Davies, March 1755, quoted in William Henry Foote, *Sketches of Virginia* (Romney, Hampshire Co., Virginia, 1849), vol. 1, p. 285.

24 - *"Give me liberty or give me death!"*: Patrick Henry, St. John's Church, March 23, 1775, quoted in *Virginia Reader: A Treasury of Writings from the First Voyages to the Present*, ed. Francis Coleman Rosenberger (E.P. Dutton & Company, 1948), pp. 275-77 (speech text drawn from William Wirt's *Sketches of the Life and Character of Patrick Henry* (James Webster, 1817)); see Kukla, *Patrick Henry*, pp. 169-70.

35 - *"Gentlemen may cry, Peace, Peace, ..."*: Patrick Henry, St. John's Church, March 23, 1775; see Kukla, *Patrick Henry*, pp. 169-70.

36 - *"Prophets and priests tell lies..."*: See Jeremiah 6:13-14, 8:10-11 (NIV).

37 - *"the better angels of our nature"*: Abraham Lincoln, First Inaugural Address, March 4, 1861, in *Abraham Lincoln: Speeches and Writings, 1859-1865*, ed. Don E. Fehrenbacher (Library of America, 1989), pp. 215-24.

39 - *"I wept as I remembered..."*: See Psalm 137:1 (NIV).

39 - *"Never let your head hang down..."*: Leroy "Satchel" Paige, quoted in Kathryn and Ross Petras, *"Don't Forget to Sing in the Lifeboats"* (Workman Publishing Company, Inc., 2011), p. 3; see *Satchel Paige and Company: Essays on the Kansas City Monarchs, Their Greatest Star and the Negro*

Leagues, ed. Leslie A. Heaphy (McFarland & Company, Inc. Publishers, 2007).

Chapter Two

43 - *"character named 'Pig Pen'"*: Charles M. Schulz, *Peanuts* (United Feature Syndicate, 1950-2000).

44 - *"content of their character..."*: See Martin L. King Jr., "I Have a Dream," Lincoln Memorial, August 28, 1963, quoted in *A Testament of Hope: The Essential Writings and Speeches of Martin Luther King Jr.,* ed. James M. Washington (HarperCollins Publishers, 1986), p. 219.

54 - *"what Dr. King called 'transformed nonconformity'"*: See Martin L. King Jr., "Transformed Nonconformist," in *American Sermons: The Pilgrims to Martin Luther King Jr.,* ed. Michael Warner (Library of America, 1999), pp. 841-48.

61 - *"tantamount to election"*: See Larry J. Sabato, *The Democratic Party Primary in Virginia: Tantamount to Election No Longer* (University Press of Virginia, 1977).

79 - *"Thanks, I needed that"*: The advertisement was for Mennen Skin Bracer.

79 - *"God helps those who help themselves"*: See *Discourses Concerning Government by Algernon Sidney,* ed. Thomas G. West (Liberty Fund, Inc., 1996), p. 210.

80 - *"Irish statesman Edmund Burke"*: See Edmund Burke, Speech to the Electors of Bristol, November 3, 1774, discussed in Jesse Norman, *Edmund Burke: The First Conservative* (Basic Books, 2013), pp. 76-79.

95 - *"'I Love to Laugh' scene..."*: *Mary Poppins,* directed by Robert Stevenson, 1964 (Walt Disney Studios Home Entertainment, 2009).

98 - *"stand for something ... fall for anything"*: While the origin of the often-quoted phrase is not known, Congressional records reflect that Reverend Peter Marshall, then U.S. Senate chaplain, used it in his prayer opening the April 18, 1947 session. See Senate Doc. 80-170, p. 20.

99 - *"a just God who presides..."*: Patrick Henry, St. John's Church, March 23, 1775; see Kukla, *Patrick Henry,* pp. 169-70.

100 - *"God doesn't start a project..."*: See Philippians 1:6 (NIV).

Chapter Three

107 - *"the two 'greatest commandments'..."*: Matthew 22:37-39 (NIV).

108 - *"monstrous injustice of slavery..."*: See Abraham Lincoln, Speech on the

Kansas-Nebraska Act at Peoria, Illinois, October 16, 1854, in *Abraham Lincoln: Speeches and Writings, 1832-1858*, ed. Don E. Fehrenbacher (Library of America, 1974), p. 315. Lincoln also quoted this line from his 1854 speech during the first Lincoln-Douglas debate, Ottawa, Illinois, August 21, 1958. See ibid., p. 510.

110 - *"proposed placing so high a duty..."*: Richard Henry Lee, Address to the Virginia House of Burgesses, in *Virginia Reader*, pp. 248-49.

110 - *"[W]e encourage those poor..."*: Ibid.

110 - *"A lone black visitor ... General's lead"*: See R. David Cox, *The Religious Life of Robert E. Lee* (Wm. B. Eerdmans Publishing, 2017), p. 274.

110 - *"circumventing state law by teaching slaves..."*: See James I. Robertson, Jr., *Stonewall Jackson* (Macmillan Publishing USA, 1997), pp. 167-69.

111 - *"As I would not be a slave..."*: See *Lincoln: Speeches and Writings, 1832-1858*, p. 484.

112 - *"bear one another's burdens"*: Galatians 6:2 (NKJV).

112 - *"charging cavalry, flashing swords..."*: Nahum 3:3 (NIV).

112 - *"Where now is the lion's den?"*: Nahum 2:11 (NIV).

113 - *"May we meet there again..."*: Thomas Jefferson to John Adams, April 11, 1823, in *Thomas Jefferson: Writings*, ed. Merrill D. Peterson (Library of America, 1984), pp. 1466-69.

114 - *"As the Catechism had forecast..."*: Ebenezer Erskine, James Fisher, and Ralph Erskine, *The Westminster Assembly's Shorter Catechism* (William S. Young, 1840), p. 211.

114 - *"Lincoln's second inaugural address..."*: See *Lincoln: Speeches and Writings, 1859-1865*, p. 687.

117 - *"he that will not work shall not eat"*: See James Horn, *A Land As God Made It* (Basic Books, 2005), pp. 127-29; 2 Thessalonians 3:10 (NIV).

117 - *"wall of separation ... wilderness of the world"*: See Edwin Scott Gaustad, *Roger Williams: Lives and Legacies* (The Oxford University Press, 2005), p. 43.

117-118 - *"wall of separation between Church and State"*: Thomas Jefferson to Messrs. Nehemiah Dodge and Others, A Committee of the Danbury Baptist Association, in the State of Connecticut, January 1, 1802, in *Jefferson: Writings*, p. 510.

118 - *"Washington unreservedly identified Greene"*: Regarding Greene as Washington's preferred successor in command, see Ron Chernow, *Washington: A*

Life (Penguin Books, 2011), p. 203; see generally Terry Golway, *Washington's General: Nathanael Greene and the Triumph of the American Revolution* (Henry Holt and Company, 2007).

119 - *"The two states' common cause on independence..."*: Regarding Rhode Island's stance and reputation, see Catherine Drinker Bowen, *Miracle at Philadelphia: The Story of the Constitutional Convention, May to September 1787* (The American Past, Book-of-the-Month Club, Inc., 1986), p. 13; Pauline Maier, *Ratification: The People Debate the Constitution, 1787-1788* (Simon & Schuster, 2010), pp. 223-25.

119 - *"primary slave markets in America..."*: See Lorenzo Johnston Greene, *The Negro in Colonial New England, 1620-1776* (Columbia University Press, 1942), p. 30.

121 - *"Orange County is relatively small now..."*: See Frank S. Walker, *Remembering: A History of Orange County, Virginia* (Orange County Historical Society, 2004), p. 23.

125 - *"Great cases ... make bad law"*: *Northern Securities Co. v. United States*, 193 U.S. 197, 400 (1904) (Holmes, J., dissenting).

126 - *"three-fourths ... owned no slaves"*: See Edward L. Ayers, *In the Presence of Mine Enemies: The Civil War in the Heart of America, 1859-1864* (W. W. Norton & Company, 2004), p. 89.

127 - *"Like his relative, Charles Francis Adams Jr...."*: See Charles Francis Adams, "Lee's Centennial," Address, Lexington, Virginia, January 19, 1907 (Houghton, Mifflin and Company, 1907).

127-128 - *"Dr. Adams read a series of passages..."*: See Nehemiah, Ch. 3 (NIV).

128 - *"fight for ... your homes"*: Nehemiah 4:14 (NIV).

128 - *"Liberty would be safe in a large republic..."*: See James Madison, *The Federalist No. 10*, November 22, 1787, in *James Madison: Writings*, ed. Jack N. Rakove (Library of America, 1999), pp. 160-67.

129 - *"The powers not delegated ... the people"*: U.S. Constitution, Amend. 10.

130 - *"For years ... threatening secession on similar grounds"*: Regarding jurisdictions in the northern states considering secession or nullification, see, e.g., Jay Winik, *April 1865: The Month That Saved America* (Harper Perennial, 2008), p. 373; Eric Foner, *The Fiery Trial: Abraham Lincoln and American Slavery* (W.W. Norton & Company, 2010), p. 134.

132 - *"Of all the checks on democracy..."*: See the review of Sir Erskine May's *Democracy in Europe* (1877) by John Emerich Edward Dahlberg (Lord

Acton) in *Selected Writings of Lord Acton: Essays in the History of Liberty*, ed. J. Rufus Fears (Liberty Classics, 1985), vol. 1, p. 84.

132-133 - *"Tocqueville, that keen French observer..."*: Alexis de Tocqueville, *Democracy in America* (Library of America, 2004), pp. 68, 105.

133 - *"It is one of the happy incidents..."*: *New State Ice Co. v. Liebmann*, 285 U.S. 262, 311 (1932) (Brandeis, J. dissenting).

133 - *"There need be little difficulty..."*: Friedrich A. Hayek, *The Road to Serfdom: Text and Documents*, ed. Bruce Caldwell (University of Chicago Press, 2007), p. 224.

133-134 - *"creative impulses of the private person must flag"*: Ibid., p. 234.

157 - *"end of the beginning"*: See Churchill's November 10, 1942 speech following military success in North Africa, described in William Manchester and Paul Reid, *The Last Lion: Winston Spencer Churchill, Defender of the Realm, 1940-1965* (Little, Brown and Company, 2012), p. 591.

Chapter Four

161 - *"Many things ... well borne without defeat"*: William Shakespeare, *King Henry the Fifth*, act I, scene II, in *The Complete Works of William Shakespeare*, p. 488.

163 - *"Politics makes strange bedfellows"*: Charles Dudley Warner, *My Summer in a Garden* (James R. Osgood & Co., 1871), p. 131.

163 - *To his friend Benjamin Rush..."*: Thomas Jefferson to Benjamin Rush, September 23, 1800, in *Jefferson: Writings*, pp. 1080-82.

163-164 - *"May it be to the world ..."*: Thomas Jefferson to Roger C. Weightman, June 24, 1826, in *Jefferson: Writings*, pp. 1516-17.

164 - *"Fix reason firmly in her seat..."*: Thomas Jefferson to Peter Carr, August 10, 1787, in *Jefferson: Writings*, pp. 900-05.

164 - *"of a sect by myself..."*: Thomas Jefferson to Ezra Stiles Ely, June 25, 1819, in *The Writings of Thomas Jefferson*, ed. Albert Ellery Bergh (Thomas Jefferson Memorial Association, 1907), vol. 15, pp. 202–04.

165 - *"Even Jefferson's famous ... Revolution"*: The phrase was Richard Rumbold's at his 1685 execution. See *The World's Best Orations*, ed. David J. Brewer (Ferd. P. Kaiser Publishing Co., 1923), vol. ix, pp. 3350-51; Joseph J. Ellis, *Passionate Sage: The Character and Legacy of John Adams* (W.W. Norton & Company, 2001), pp. 207-08.

165 - *"wall of separation between Church and State"*: Thomas Jefferson to Danbury Baptists, January 1, 1802, in *Jefferson: Writings*, p. 510; see *Everson v. Bd. of Educ.*, 330 U.S. 1 (1947).

165-166 - *"May we meet there again..."*: Thomas Jefferson to John Adams, April 11, 1823, in *Jefferson: Writings*, pp. 1466-69.

169 - *"A Kiss to Build a Dream On"*: Louis Armstrong, "A Kiss to Build a Dream On" (1951).

173 - *"His oracle, F.A. Hayek..."*: See Friedrich A. Hayek, "The Intellectuals and Socialism," University of Chicago Law Review 16 (Spring 1949), pp. 417-33.

174 - *"My country ... drunk or sober"*: G.K. Chesterton, "A Defence of Patriotism," in *The Man Who Was Chesterton: The Best Essays, Stories, Poems, and Other Writings of G.K. Chesterton*, ed. Raymond T. Bond (Books for Libraries Press, 1970).

183 - *"doing just fine ... a few miles away"*: For an illuminating *nonfictional* discussion of educational disparities in the Richmond metropolitan area and potential remedies, see James Ryan, *Five Miles Away, A World Apart: One City, Two Schools, and the Story of Educational Opportunity in Modern America* (Oxford University Press, 2010).

185 - *"all honor to Jefferson"*: Abraham Lincoln to Henry L. Pierce and others, April 6, 1859, in *Lincoln: Speeches and Writings, 1859-1865*, pp. 18-19.

186 - *"my letter ... in 1808"*: Thomas Jefferson to Rev. Samuel Miller, January 23, 1808, in *Jefferson: Writings*, pp. 1186-87.

186 - *"no matter how lame the preaching"*: For a detailed discussion of the interaction between the two influential Scottish thinkers and their influence on each other, especially Hume's impact on Smith, see Dennis C. Rasmussen, *The Infidel and the Professor: David Hume, Adam Smith, and the Friendship That Shaped Modern Thought* (Princeton University Press, 2017).

187 - *"Even this went too far..."*: See James Madison, "Memorial and Remonstrance Against Religious Assessments," June 20, 1785, in *Madison: Writings*, pp. 29-36.

187 - *"'wall of separation' metaphor"*: Thomas Jefferson to Danbury Baptists, January 1, 1802, in *Jefferson: Writings*, p. 510.

187 - *"dead hand of the past"*: See Thomas Jefferson to James Madison, September 6, 1789, in *Jefferson: Writings*, pp. 959-64; James Madison to Thomas Jefferson, February 4, 1790, in *Madison: Writings*, pp. 473-77.

188 - *"errors we must tolerate..."*: See Thomas Jefferson, First Inaugural Address, March 4, 1801, in *Jefferson: Writings*, p. 493.

191 - *"uprightness of the decision"*: See Thomas Jefferson to Peter Carr, August 10, 1787, in *Jefferson: Writings*, pp. 900-05.

194 - *"I do not meddle with Politicks"*: James Madison to William Bradford, September 25, 1773, quoted in William Lee Miller, *The First Liberty: America's Foundation in Religious Freedom* (Georgetown University Press, 2003), p.75.

194 - *"not as unambitious but as useless"*: See Pericles' Funeral Oration in Thucydides, *History of the Peloponnesian War*, book 2, Ch. 40.

201 - *"no big deal—just a movie"*: See *The Emperor's New Groove*, directed by Mark Dindal (Disney, 2000).

201 - *"Helllooo, Wilbuuurrr..."*: See *Mister Ed*, directed by Arthur D. Lubin (CBS, 1961).

201 - *"A horse is a horse..."*: Ibid.

208 - *"Virginia's 'Red-Letter Year'"*: See generally James Horn, *1619: Jamestown in the Forging of American Democracy* (Basic Books, 2018); Warren M. Billings, *A Little Parliament* (Library of Virginia, 2004).

209-210 - *"What does the Lord require..."*: Micah 6:8 (NIV).

210 - *"Truly, I tell you..."*: Matthew 18:3-4 (NIV).

210 - *"the greatest man in the world"*: See Chernow, *Washington: A Life*, p. 454.

210-211 - *"The great object ... happy Nation"*: George Washington, Circular to State Governments, June 8, 1783, in *George Washington: Writings*, ed. John Rhodehamel (Library of America, 1997), pp. 516-26.

211 - *"Liberty cannot be established..."* Tocqueville, *Democracy in America*, p. 12.

211 - *"the plan of the Holy author..."* The Virginia Statute for Religious Freedom (1786), *in The Virginia Statute for Religious Freedom: Its Evolution and Consequences in American History*, eds. Merrill D. Peterson and Robert C. Vaughan (Cambridge University Press, 1988), p. xvii.

213 - *"When God ... redouble his blows"*: John Calvin, *Commentaries on the Book of the Prophet Daniel* (Calvin Translation Society, 1852), p. 245.

215 - *"As a remarkable example..."*: See Samuel Davies, "Religion and Patriotism: The Constituents of a Good Soldier," August 17, 1755, in *Sermons by the Rev. Samuel Davies, A.M., President of the College of New Jersey* (Presbyterian Board of Publication, 1864), vol. iii, pp. 94-119; see also Foote, *Sketches of Virginia*, vol. 1, p. 284. The sermon was preached in Hanover

County to Captain Overton's independent company of volunteers during the French and Indian War.

215 - *"baneful effects of the spirit of party"*: George Washington, Farewell Address, September 19, 1796, in *Washington: Writings*, pp. 962-77.

215 - *"wretched mischievous spirit of party"*: Samuel Davies, "The Sacred Import of the Christian Name," in *Sermons by the Rev. Samuel Davies*, vol. 1, pp. 341-42; reprinted by Soli Deo Gloria Publications, 1993. Another line in Washington's Farewell Address used the same term ("mischief") to describe the spirit of party, referring to the "common and continual mischiefs of the spirit of party." See *Washington: Writings*, p. 970.

220 - *"sunk into the grave nearly at the same time"*: See Joseph J. Ellis, *Founding Brothers: The Revolutionary Generation* (Alfred A. Knopf, 2000), pp. 220-25; Gordon S. Wood, *Friends Divided* (Penguin Press, 2017), pp. 357-64.

220 - *"North and South poles..."*: Dr. Benjamin Rush to John Adams, October 17, 1809, quoted in Ellis, *Passionate Sage*, p. 210.

220-221 - *"given Hampden-Sydney its name..."*: See John L. Brinkley, *On This Hill: A Narrative History of Hampden-Sydney College 1774-1994* (Hampden-Sydney College, 1994), pp. 5-23. For more on the history of Hampton-Sydney College, visit the College's Esther Thomas Atkinson Museum.

221 - *"enough faith to be an atheist"*: See Norman L. Geisler and Frank Turek, *I Don't Have Enough Faith to Be an Atheist* (Crossway Books, 2004).

222 - *"love of an ever-present Parent"*: See Augustine, *The City of God*, trans. by Marcus Dods (Hendickson Publishers, Inc., 2009), pp. 217-70; Charles Mathewes, "Books That Matter: The City of God," *The Great Courses* (The Teaching Company, 2016).

223 - *"why has Thou forsaken me?"*: Matthew 27:46 (ASV); Psalm 22:1 (ASV).

225 - *"a question I do not dogmatize upon..."*: Benjamin Franklin to Rev. Ezra Stiles, President of Yale College, March 9, 1790.

225 - *"greatest happiness for the greatest number"*: Francis Hutcheson, *An Inquiry into the Origins of our Ideas of Beauty and Virtue, in Two Treatises* (1725), treatise II, sec. 3.8.

227 - *"rejected the Randian agnosticism..."*: See, *e.g.*, Ayn Rand, "Faith and Force: The Destroyers of the Modern World," *Philosophy: Who Needs It* (Signet Books, 1984), pp. 58-76; see generally Ayn Rand, *Atlas Shrugged* (Signet Books, 1996); Whittaker Chambers, "Big Sister is Watching You," *National Review*, December 28, 1957.

227 - *"He was … closer to Adam Smith"*: Adam Smith, *The Theory of Moral Sentiments* (1759), pt. 1, sec. I, Ch. 5.

227 - *"times that try men's souls"*: See Thomas Paine, *The American Crisis*, December 19, 1776.

227 - *"begin the world over again"*: See Thomas Paine, *Common Sense*, in *The American Revolution: Writings from the Pamphlet Debate, 1773-1776*, ed. Gordon S. Wood (Library of America, 2015), pp. 649-704.

228 - *"Aristotle, Cicero, Locke, Sidney, etc."*: Thomas Jefferson to Henry Lee, May 8, 1825, in *Jefferson: Writings*, p. 1501.

231 - *"able to put down those who walk in pride"*: See Daniel 4:37 (NRSV).

232 - *"when this conscience business starts…"* See Warren, *All the King's Men*, p. 58.

Chapter Five

235 - *"This is what the Lord Almighty…"*: Jeremiah 29:4-7 (NIV).

235 - *"renewal of all things"*: See Matthew 19:28 (NIV).

239 - *"Mahone's remarkable body of work…"*: For information on the colorful career of William Mahone, see Peter C. Luebke, "William Mahone (1826 – 1895)," *Encyclopedia Virginia* (Virginia Humanities, July 19, 2016), retrieved from http://www.EncyclopediaVirginia.org/Mahone_William_1826-1895.

240 - *"It might have been all different…"*: Warren, *All the King's Men*, pp. 497, 543.

257 - *"enlightened conscience"*: Edmund Burke, Speech to the Electors of Bristol, November 3, 1774, in Norman, *Edmund Burke*, pp. 76-79.

259 - *"Explanations will be wanting…"*: George Washington to James Madison, October 10, 1787, quoted in Stuart Leibiger, *Founding Friendship: George Washington, James Madison, and the Creation of the American Republic* (University Press of Virginia, 1999), p. 91.

259 - *"the only man in this State…"*: Tobias Lear to James Madison, quoted in Leibiger, *Founding Friendship*, p. 91.

259 - *"I was therefore obliged…"*: James Madison to Eliza House Trist, March 25, 1788, in *Madison: Writings*, p. 353.

260 - *"bill of rights … rest on inferences"*: Thomas Jefferson to James Madison, December 20, 1787, in *Jefferson: Writings*, pp. 914-18.

260 - *"never thought the omission a material defect"*: James Madison to Thomas Jefferson, October 17, 1788, in *Madison: Writings*, pp. 418-23.

260 - "*clearest, and strongest provision…*": James Madison to Thomas Mann Randolph, January 13, 1789, quoted in Robert Allen Rutland, *James Madison: The Founding Father* (University of Missouri Press, 1987), p. 48.

260 - "*parchment barriers*": See James Madison, *The Federalist No. 48*, February 1, 1788, in *Madison: Writings*, pp. 281-85.

265 - "*deepest valley … highest mountain*": See "Transcript of Nixon's Farewell Speech to Cabinet and Staff Members in the Capital," *The New York Times*, August 10, 1974.

265 - "*back turned toward the sun…*" James Taylor, "Fire and Rain," produced by Peter Asher (Warner Bros. Records, 1970).

265 - "*in pieces on the ground*": Ibid.

267 - "*Perseverando*": See Brent Tarter, "Seal of the Commonwealth of Virginia," *Encyclopedia Virginia* (Virginia Humanities, June 20, 2014); retrieved from http://www.EncyclopediaVirginia.org/Seal_of_the_Commonwealth_of_Virginia.

274 - "*a leetle mite of trouble back in town…*": Warren, *All the King's Men*, pp. 181-82.

277 - "*dramatically improve results for students*": For a thoughtful discussion of remedies for educational disparities, including enhanced school choice, in the *nonfictional* central Virginia setting, see Ryan, *Five Miles Away, A World Apart*, pp. 271-304.

278-279 - "*eyes on the prize*": See Juan Williams, *Eyes on the Prize: America's Civil Rights Years, 1954-1965* (Penguin Books, 1987). The title of the book was drawn from a traditional civil rights song ("I know one thing we did right was the day we started to fight. Keep your eyes on the prize, Hold on, Hold on.").

281 - "*get all the electricity out of it*": The author is indebted to the late Virginia Governor John N. Dalton for this anecdote, which is drawn from a similar story he would often share with audiences.

287 - "*offer they can't refuse*": The widely used phrase originated with the fictional Corleone organized crime family depicted in Mario Puzo, *The Godfather* (G.P. Putnam's Son, 1969), and *The Godfather*, directed by Francis Ford Coppola (Paramount Pictures, 1972).

287-288 - "*Johnson's excellent biographer…*" See Robert A. Caro, *Master of the Senate* (Alfred A. Knopf, 2002).

290-291 - "*Congressman Jackson is always talking…*": While the substance of the Meade-Jackson debate is drawn from the author's experience and study of the school choice over many years, the author wishes to acknowledge the television series *Boss*, specifically the third episode in the show's first season, for inspiring the idea of a Meade-Jackson debate over school choice and education policy. See "Swallow," *Boss*, written by Lyn Green and Richard Levine, produced by Farhad Safinia, directed by Mario Van Peebles (Lionsgate Television, distributed by Starz!, November 4, 2011). The show, which starred Kelsey Grammer as fictional Chicago Mayor Tom Kane, also inspired some debate content, notably Meade's disparagement of the role and motivations of for-profit companies, Jackson's invocation of declining American rankings for math and science proficiency, and Jackson's emphasis on what works rather than on ideology.

301 - *"take your questions from the floor"*: A joke frequently told by Senator John W. Warner (R-Virginia) inspired this anecdote.

313 - *"Some chicken ... some neck"*: See Churchill's December 1941 speech to the Canadian Parliament, described in Manchester and Reid, *The Last Lion ... 1940-1965*, pp. 458-59.

313-314 - *"Ambition must be made to counteract ambition..."*: James Madison, *The Federalist No. 51*, February 6, 1788, in *Madison: Writings*, pp. 294-98.

314 - *"as iron sharpens iron..."*: Proverbs 27:17 (NIV).

315 - *"If there be not virtue..."*: James Madison, Speech in the Virginia Ratifying Convention on the Judicial Power, June 20, 1788, in *Madison: Writings*, p. 398.

315 - *"the biblical talents..."*: See Matthew 25:14-30 (NIV).

316 - *"bully pulpit"*: The familiar phrase describing the communications platform provided by the executive office was coined by Theodore Roosevelt. See Doris Kearns Goodwin, *The Bully Pulpit* (Simon & Schuster, 2013), p. xi.

317 - *"no free government ... fundamental principles"*: George Mason, Virginia Declaration of Rights; Constitution of Virginia, Art.1, §15.

319 - *"disputable matters"*: Romans 14:1 (NIV).

320 - *"The false religion of lust..."*: C.S. Lewis, *The Great Divorce* (Harper One, 1973), p. 106.

321 - *"shining city on a hill"*: See Ronald Reagan, Farewell Address to the Nation, January 11, 1989, in *The Quotable Ronald Reagan*, ed. Peter Hannaford (Regnery Publishing, Inc., 1998), p. 278. Reagan added the word "shining" to the "city upon a hill" imagery invoked by Puritan leader John Winthrop

in his famous sermon ("A Model of Christian Charity") just before or during the voyage to Massachusetts aboard the *Arbella*. Winthrop was alluding to Jesus' Sermon on the Mount, Matthew 5:14 (KJV).

322 - *"meet triumph and disaster..."*: Rudyard Kipling, "If-," in *Rudyard Kipling: Complete Verse* (Anchor Books, 1989), p. 578.

324 - *"The beauty about Tiny..."*: Warren, *All the King's Men*, p. 21.

Chapter Six

339 - *"'rejoice' in their sufferings..."*: Romans 5:3-4 (ESV).

341 - *"we ... will get to the promised land"*: Martin L. King Jr., "'I've Been to the Mountaintop," Speech in Memphis, Tennessee, April 3, 1968, in *A Testament of Hope*, p. 286.

343 - *"We will win our freedom..."*: Martin L. King Jr., Letter from Birmingham City Jail, April 16, 1963, in *A Testament of Hope*, p. 301.

343 - *"Love those who are foreigners..."*: Deuteronomy 12:19 (NIV).

343 - *"pilgrim feet ... across the wilderness"*: Katharine L. Bates, "America the Beautiful," in *Sing Joyfully*, #600.

344 - *"I would turn to the Almighty ... 'want to be free'"*: Martin L. King Jr., "I've Been to the Mountaintop," April 3, 1968, in *A Testament of Hope*, pp. 279-80.

346 - *"my country ... every mountain side"*: Samuel F. Smith, "America" ("My Country, 'Tis of Thee"), in *Sing Joyfully*, #602.

347 - *"give us your tired, your poor..."*: See Emma Lazarus, "The New Colossus," inscribed on the Statue of Liberty.

348 - *"I look upon my departure ... thanksgiving and praise"*: Frederick Douglass, *Narrative of the Life of Fredrick Douglass* (1845), Ch. V, in *Frederick Douglass: Autobiographies*, ed. Henry Louis Gates Jr. (Library of America, 1994), pp. 35-36.

349 - *"I am a student of history..."* Warren, *All the King's Men*, p. 310.

354 - *"in season and out of season"*: 2 Timothy 4:2 (NIV).

366 - *"Old soldiers fade away..."*: Douglas MacArthur, Address, Joint Session of Congress, April 19, 1951.

367 - *"I Cannot Tell"*: William Y. Fullerton, "I Cannot Tell," in *The Celebration Hymnal*, ed. Tom Fettke (Word Music/Integrity Music, 1997), #354.

367 - *"Danny Boy"*: Frederic Edward Weatherly, "Danny Boy," quoted in Malachy McCourt, *Danny Boy: The Beloved Irish Ballad* (Running Press, 2002), pp. 12-13.

369 - *"As he went along ... displayed in him"*: John 9:1-3 (NIV).

370 - *"Then there was Fanny Crosby..."*: See Bernard Ruffin, *Fanny Crosby: The Hymn Writer* (Barbour Publishing, Inc., 1995), pp. 12-13.

370 - *"And there was young Jimmy McCrury..."*: See McCourt, *Danny Boy*, pp. 23-26.

370 - *"great son of Virginia named Jim Wheat, Jr...."*: For a biography of Jim Wheat Jr., see Anne Hobson Freeman, *A Hand Well Played: The Life of Jim Wheat, Jr.* (Cadmus Publishing, 1994).

370 - *"Sweet are the uses of adversity..."*: William Shakespeare, *As You Like It*, act II, scene I, in *The Complete Works of William Shakespeare*, p. 617; see Freeman, *A Hand Well Played*, p. 118.

371 - *"recall the story of Gideon"*: See Judges 6:14-40, 7:1-25, 8:22-23 (NIV).

371 - *"They tell us ... the brave"*: Patrick Henry, St. John's Church, March 23, 1775; see Kukla, *Patrick Henry*, pp. 169-70.

371-372 - *"No People ... some token of providential agency"*: George Washington, First Inaugural Address, April 30, 1789, in *Washington: Writings*, pp. 730-34.

372 - *"No, my fair cousin, ... not one man more"*: William Shakespeare, *King Henry the Fifth*, act IV, scene III, in *The Complete Works of William Shakespeare*, p. 507.

372 - *"We few ... band of brothers"*: Ibid., p. 508.

373 - *"'I don't know' is not such a bad answer..."*: The author is indebted to Reverend Jeff Lee, formerly associate pastor of New Hanover Presbyterian Church, whose November 2011 sermon on these passages from John's gospel included the idea that turning to one's neighbors and confessing "I don't know" is a source of relief.

373 - *"Whether he is a sinner, ... I see!"*: John 9:24-25 (NIV).

374 - *"added to the ranks of the faithful"*: John 9:35-38 (NIV).

374 - *"Oh, Danny boy, the pipes, the pipes are calling..."*: Frederic Edward Weatherly, "Danny Boy," quoted in McCourt, *Danny Boy*, pp. 12-13.

374-375 - *"I cannot tell why He, the king of Heaven..."*: Fullerton, "I Cannot Tell," in *The Celebration Hymnal*, #354.

376 - *"persevere in prayer"*: Romans 12:12 (NRSV).

376 - *"living sacrifice"*: Romans 12:1 (NRSV).

376 - *"Do not be conformed to this world..."*: Romans 12:2 (NRSV).

378 - *"far, far better thing"*: Dickens, *A Tale of Two Cities*, p. 390.

378-379 - *"There is nothing more ... shall never die"*: Ibid., p. 325, quoting John 11:25-26.

379 - *"The strong tide, so swift..."*: Ibid., p. 327.

380 - *"like a biblical hall of fame..."*: See Hebrews 11:3-28 (NIV).

380 - *"Therefore ... race marked out for us"*: Hebrews 12:1 (NIV).

382 - *"It is the story of a man ... incomplete"*: Warren, *All the King's Men*, pp. 542-43.

385 - *"Join in the fight ... to be free!"*: Claude-Michel Schönberg, Alain Boublil, Jean-Marc Natel, and Herbert Kretzmer, *Les Misérables*, produced by Cameron Mackintosh; adapted and directed by Trevor Nunn and John Caird (1985) (based on the 1862 novel by Victor Hugo).

385 - *"Give us Barabbas!"*: John 18:40 (NIV).

386 - *"Many of those who sleep ... persevere"*: Daniel 12:2-12 (NRSV).

386 - *"fought the good fight..."*: See 2 Timothy 4:7 (NRSV).

Chapter Seven

395 - *"dream can be a 'mighty Power'..."*: John Adams to Dr. Benjamin Rush, quoted in Joseph J. Ellis, *First Family: Abigail and John* (Alfred A. Knopf, 2010), p. 228.

404 - *"Freedom granted only when it is known..."* Friedrich A. Hayek, *The Constitution of Liberty* (University of Chicago Press, 1960), p. 31.

409 - *"third book of J.R.R. Tolkien's Lord of the Rings series..."* J.R.R. Tolkien, *The Return of the King: Being the Third Part of The Lord of the Rings* (Ballantine Books, 1965).

409 - *"But we have no songs fit for... evil times, lord"*: Ibid., p. 73.

410 - *"what the Book of Ecclesiastes calls 'evil times'"*: Ecclesiastes 9:12 (NIV).

410 - *"He does it a lot..."*: Habakkuk 1:2-4, 13 (NIV).

411 - *"Job asks..."*: See Job 24:1 (NIV).

411 - *"Jeremiah says..."*: Jeremiah 15:18 (NIV).

411 - *"In the Psalms, David says..."*: Psalm 88:13-14 (NIV).

411 - *"Jesus: 'My God...'"*: Matthew 27:46 (NIV).

413 - *"Look at the nations and watch..."*: Habakkuk 1:5 (NIV).

413 - *"I will do something you would not believe..."*: Habakkuk 1:6 (NIV).

413 - *"Oh God! Are you not from everlasting?"*: Habakkuk 1:12 (NIV).

413 - *"The righteous will live by faith"*: Habakkuk 2:3-4 (NIV).

416 - *"Have you considered my servant, Job..."*: Job 1:8-10 (NIV).

416 - *"Though the fig tree does not bud…"*: Habakkuk 3:17 (NIV).

417 - *"Though an army besiege me…"*: Psalm 27:3-4 (NIV).

417 - *"Though there are no grapes on the vine…"*: Habakkuk 3:17-19 (NIV).

419 - *"The creation of man … in His wisdom"*: Warren, *All the King's Men*, p. 544.

419 - *"Everyone who seeks to live…"*: 2 Timothy 3:13 (NIV).

419 - *"guilty people whose own strength is their god"*: Habakkuk 1:11 (NIV).

444 - *"'catch the conscience' of the murderous King…"*: William Shakespeare, *Hamlet, Prince of Denmark*, act II, scene II, in *The Complete Works of William Shakespeare*, p. 687.

445 - *"A Prince, whose character is thus marked…"*: Declaration of Independence (US 1776).

Chapter Eight

462 - *"There really are just two parties…"* See Thomas Jefferson to Henry Lee, August 10, 1824.

462 - *"even though the arc of the moral universe …"* Martin L. King Jr., "Love, Law, and Civil Disobedience," Address to the Fellowship of the Concerned, November 16, 1961, in *A Testament of Hope*, p. 52.

462 - *"Who knows … such a time as this"*: Esther 4:14 (NIV).

467 - *"Once to every … and that light"*: James R. Lowell, "Once to Every Man and Nation," in *Sing Joyfully*, #607.

468 - *"And, lo, I am with you always…"*: Matthew 28:20 (NKJV).

468 - *"eternal rules of order and right…"*: George Washington, First Inaugural Address, April 30, 1789, in *Washington: Writings*, pp. 730-34.

471 - *"an American century…"*: See Henry Luce, "The American Century," *LIFE*, February 17, 1941.

472 - *"dangers, toils, and snares…"*: John Newton, "Amazing Grace!" in *Sing Joyfully*, #299.

473 - *"more like Hugo's Valjean"*: See Schönberg, Boublil, et al., *Les Misérables* (1985).

474 - *"As with Valjean…"*: Ibid.

474 - *"to be or not to be…"*: See William Shakespeare, *Hamlet*, act III, scene I, in *The Complete Works of William Shakespeare*, p. 688.

474 - *"Plans fail for lack of counsel…"*: Proverbs 15:22 (NIV).

479 - *"eyes I dare not meet in dreams"*: T. S. Eliot, "The Hollow Men," in T. S. Eliot, *Selected Poems* (Harcourt, Inc., 1930), pp. 77-80.

Chapter Nine

486 - *"the room where it happened…"*: See Lin-Manuel Miranda, "Hamilton: An American Musical," in Lin-Manuel Miranda and Jeremy McCarter, *Hamilton: The Revolution* (Grand Central Publishing, 2016), pp. 186-90.

493 - *"better angels of our nature"*: Abraham Lincoln, First Inaugural Address, March 4, 1861, in *Lincoln: Speeches and Writings, 1859-1865*, pp. 215-24.

494 - *"after the revolutionary election of 1800"*: See Ellis, *Founding Brothers*, pp. 178-85.

504 - *"screwed the pooch"*: See Tom Wolfe, *The Right Stuff* (Farrar, Straus and Giroux, 1979), pp. 84, 214.

506 - *"perfect justice in his own perfect time"*: See, e.g., 1 Samuel 24:1-15 (NIV).

508 - *"exchange between Sir Thomas and his daughter…"* *A Man for All Seasons*, directed by Fred Zinnemann (Columbia Pictures, 1966).

510 - *"conservatives give far more to charities…"*: For more information on the relationship between political views and philanthropic behavior, see Arthur C. Brooks, *Who Really Cares: The Surprising Truth About Compassionate Conservatism* (Basic Books, 2007).

511-512 - *"There are no simple congruities … forgiveness"*: Reinhold Niebuhr, "The Irony of American History, 1952," *in Reinhold Niebuhr: Major Works on Politics and Religion*, ed. Elisabeth Sifton (Library of America, 2015), p. 510.

512 - *"Let us imagine two prisoners…"*: Simone Weil, "The Necessary and the Good," in *Simone Weil: Essential Writings*, ed. Eric O. Springsted (Orbis Books, 2003), p. 74.

512 - *"Jesus would often say…"*: See, e.g., Mark 4:9 (NIV).

512 - *"God himself will not save men…"*: John Locke, *A Letter Concerning Toleration* (1689), *in John Locke: Political Writings*, ed. David Wootton (Hackett Publishing Company, Inc., 2003), p. 406.

512 - *"Things are not what they seem"*: Longfellow, "A Psalm of Life," in *Longfellow: Poems and Other Writings*, pp. 3-4.

517 - *"What does the Lord require…"*: Micah 6:8 (NIV).

517 - *"For God has bound everyone…"*: Romans 11:32 (NIV).

518 - *"There is … proud of my humility"*: See Walter Isaacson, *Benjamin Franklin: An American Life* (Simon & Schuster, 2003), p. 92.

518 - *"Better a poor but wise youth…"*: Ecclesiastes 4:13 (NIV).

520 - *"indict a ham sandwich"*: Judge Wachtler's observation gained widespread notoriety through the reference in Tom Wolfe, *The Bonfire of the Vanities* (Farrar, Straus and Giroux, 1987), p. 624.

523 - *"my counselor appeared in scene after scene..."*: See 2 Kings 19:35 (NIV); Jude 1:9 (NIV); Exodus 14:19-20, 23:20-23 (NIV); Joshua 5:13-15 (NIV); Numbers 22:21-27 (NIV); Revelation 12:7-9 (NIV).

523-524 - *"Do not be afraid ... in response to them"*: See Daniel 10:12 (NIV).

525 - *"Go your way ... allotted inheritance"*: See Daniel 12:9-13 (NIV).

Chapter Ten

528 - *"Do not worry about anything..."*: Philippians 4:6-7 (CSB).

529 - *"the familiar Thanksgiving hymn..."*: Theodore Baker, "We Gather Together," in *Sing Joyfully*, #597.

530 - *"The republic ... first a dream"*: Carl Sandberg, "Washington Monument By Night," in *The Complete Poems of Carl Sandberg* (Harcourt, Inc., 1970), p. 282.

530 - *"from the swamp to the stars"*: See Ronald Reagan, "A Time for Choosing," Televised Address, October 27, 1964.

531 - *"from sea to shining sea"*: Bates, "America the Beautiful," in *Sing Joyfully*, #600.

531 - *"the blessed mother of us all"*: Thomas Jefferson, "Thoughts on Lotteries," February 1826, in *The Writings of Thomas Jefferson*, vol. 17, p. 462.

532 - *"just God who presides..."*: Patrick Henry, St. John's Church, March 23, 1775; see Kukla, *Patrick Henry*, pp. 169-70.

532 - *"Lastly and chiefly ... shall be rooted out"*: The 1606 instructions by the London Council for Virginia are inscribed on the base of the obelisk dedicated by the United States Government in 1907 on the site of present-day Historic Jamestowne; see Catherine E. Read, *Jamestown* (Arcadia Publishing, 2012), p. 81.

534-535 - *"John Smith's account tells us..."*: See Horn, *A Land As God Made It*, p. 44.

536 - *"plant a Nation, where none before hath stood"*: Richard Rich, "News from Virginia," in *Virginia Reader*, p. 112.

537 - *"save Smith ... a year later"*: The author is indebted to James Horn for his assistance and for his seminal work, *A Land As God Made It*, from which the description of events in early Jamestown here and in the next 13 paragraphs is largely drawn. See Horn, *A Land As God Made It*, pp. 120-23,

127-28, 159-63, 169-70, 177-80, 212-33. For additional information on the Jamestown colony, see Billings, *A Little Parliament*; David A. Price, *Love and Hate in Jamestown* (Alfred A. Knopf, 2003); Helen C. Rountree, *Pocahontas, Powhatan, Opechancanough* (University of Virginia Press, 2005); William M. Kelso, *Jamestown, The Buried Truth* (University of Virginia Press, 2006); Bob Deans, *The River Where America Began: A Journey Along the James* (Rowman & Littlefield Publishers, Inc., 2007).

537-538 - *"Somers shouted ... 'Land!'"*: See Horn, *A Land As God Made It*, p. 159.

538 - *"inspire Shakespeare to write The Tempest"*: See William Shakespeare, *The Tempest*, in *The Complete Works of William Shakespeare*, pp. 1135-59. Regarding the wreck of the *Sea Venture* and its probable inspiration for *The Tempest*, see Kieran Doherty, *Sea Venture* (St. Martin's Press, 2007), pp. 166-68.

539 - *"the cherished anthem 'America'..."*: Smith, "America," in *Sing Joyfully*, #602.

539 - *"the national hymn..."*: Daniel C. Roberts, "God of Our Fathers," in *Sing Joyfully*, #599.

540 - *"Be alert... someone to devour"*: 1 Peter 5:8 (NIV).

540 - *"Seized during a Portuguese campaign..."*: See Horn, *1619*, pp. 88-98.

540 - *"Over time, 'We Shall Overcome'..."*: The gospel song "We Shall Overcome" became the unofficial anthem of the American Civil Rights Movement; it apparently was inspired lyrically by the hymn, "I'll Overcome Someday," by Charles Albert Tindley (1900). See Victor V. Bobetsky, "The Complex Ancestry of 'We Shall Overcome,' *The Choral Journal*, vol. 54, no. 7 (February 2014), pp. 26-36.

540 - *"live out the true meaning of its creed"*: Martin L. King Jr., "I Have a Dream," August 28, 1963, in *A Testament of Hope*, p. 219.

541-542 - *"Whilst we assert for ourselves..."* James Madison, "Memorial and Remonstrance Against Religious Assessments," June 20, 1785, in *Madison: Writings*, pp. 29-36.

542 - *"A former communist spy and avowed atheist..."*: See Whittaker Chambers, *Witness* (Regnery Books, 1952), p. 16.

542 - *"the arc of the moral universe ..."*: Martin L. King Jr., November 16, 1961, in *A Testament of Hope*, p. 52.

542 - *"Assembled uniquely ... 'Amazing Grace'"*: Newton, "Amazing Grace!" in *Sing Joyfully*, #299.

543 - *"forge a distinctly American ethos..."*: See generally Gordon S. Wood, *The Radicalism of the American Revolution* (Alfred A. Knopf, Inc., 1992).

543 - *"crystallized in the revolutionary settlement..."*: See generally Michael Barone, *Our First Revolution* (Crown Publishers, 2007).

544-545 - *"It is impossible for any man of pious reflection..."*: James Madison, *The Federalist No. 37*, in *Madison: Writings*, pp. 194-201.

545 - *"impossible to consider it as less than a miracle"*: James Madison to Thomas Jefferson, October 24, 1787, in *Madison: Writings*, p. 144.

545 - *"I have lived, Sir, a long time..."*: Benjamin Franklin, Motion for Prayers in the Convention, June 28, 1787, in *Benjamin Franklin: Autobiography, Poor Richard, and Later Writings*, ed. J.A. Leo Lemay (Library of America, 1987) (emphasis in original); see Isaacson, *Benjamin Franklin*, pp. 451-52.

545 - *"conceived in liberty ... created equal"*: Abraham Lincoln, Address at Gettysburg, Pennsylvania, November 19, 1863, in *Lincoln: Speeches and Writings, 1859-1865*, p. 536.

547 - *"Even though large tracts ... liberation of the old"*: Winston S. Churchill, Speech in the House of Commons, June 4, 1940, regarding the evacuation of Dunkirk, described in Manchester and Reid, *The Last Lion ... 1940-1965*, p. 86 (emphasis added).

547 - *"face this new crisis..."*: Franklin D. Roosevelt, December 29, 1940 fireside chat, quoted in Jon Meacham, *Franklin and Winston: An Intimate Portrait of an Epic Friendship* (Random House, 2003), pp. 78-79.

547 - *"Never before since Jamestown..."* Ibid.

548 - *"Greater love has no one..."*: John 15:13 (NIV).

548 - *"odious apparatus"*: See Manchester and Reid, *The Last Lion ... 1940-1965*, p. 86.

548 - *"evil empire"*: See Ronald Reagan, Address to the National Association of Evangelicals, March 8, 1983, in *The Quotable Ronald Reagan*, p. 105.

548 - *"The hand of Providence ..."*: George Washington to Thomas Nelson, August 20, 1778, in *Washington: Writings*, pp. 319-21.

548 - *"Churchill had arranged for it to be sung..."*: See Meacham, *Franklin and Winston*, pp. 113-16.

549 - *"O Trinity of love and power..."*: William Whiting and Robert N. Spencer, "Eternal Father, Strong to Save," in *Sing Joyfully*, #459.

550 - *"overharvest of Atlantic white cedar"*: See generally Robert Atkinson, Timothy Morgan, David Brown, and Robert Belcher, "The Role of Historical

Inquiry in the Restoration of Atlantic White Cedar Swamps," in *Proceedings of a Symposium: Restoration and Management of Atlantic White Cedar Swamps*, eds. Robert Atkinson, Robert Belcher, David Brown, and James Perry (Christopher Newport University, 2003), pp. 43-54.

550 - *"Only after the influential Sir Edwin Sandys..."*: See Horn, *1619*, pp. 43-66.

554 - *"Enlightenment-era sophisticates routinely are credited..."*: See generally Michael Farris, *From Tyndale to Madison: How the Death of an English Martyr Led to the American Bill of Rights* (B&H Publishing Group, 2007).

555 - *"We gather together ... make us free"*: Baker, "We Gather Together," in *Sing Joyfully*, #597.

556 - *"expression of the American mind"*: Thomas Jefferson to Henry Lee, May 8, 1825, in *Jefferson: Writings*, p. 1501.

556 - *"new birth of freedom"*: Lincoln, Gettysburg Address, November 19, 1863, in *Lincoln: Speeches and Writings, 1859-1865*, p. 536.

556 - *"America the Beautiful"*: Bates, "America the Beautiful," in *Sing Joyfully*, #600.

556 - *"The Star-Spangled Banner"*: Francis Scott Key, "The Star-Spangled Banner," in *Sing Joyfully*, #601.

557 - *"America ... thy liberty in law"*: Bates, "America the Beautiful," in *Sing Joyfully*, #600.

557-558 - *"Remember how the Lord ... wealth for me"*: Deuteronomy 8:2-3, 10-14, 17 (NIV).

558 - *"the plan of the Holy author..."*: See *The Virginia Statute for Religious Freedom*, p. xvii.

560 - *"strive on to finish the work..."*: Abraham Lincoln, Second Inaugural Address, March 4, 1865, in *Lincoln: Speeches and Writings, 1859-1865*, pp. 686-87.

560 - *"Lives of great men all remind us..."* Longfellow, "A Psalm of Life," in *Longfellow: Poems and Other Writings*, pp. 3-4.

561 - *"better angels of our nature"*: Abraham Lincoln, First Inaugural Address, March 4, 1861, in *Lincoln: Speeches and Writings, 1859-1865*, pp. 215-24.

563 - *"I've spoken of the shining city ... see it still"*: Ronald Reagan, Farewell Address to the Nation, January 11, 1989, in *The Quotable Ronald Reagan*, p. 278.